Leigh Brackett

Shannach–The Last

Farewell to Mars

Books by Leigh Brackett

Science Fiction
Shadow Over Mars (*aka* The Nemesis from Terra)
The Starmen (*aka* The Starmen of Llyrdis; The Galactic Breed)
The Sword of Rhiannon
The Big Jump
The Long Tomorrow
Alpha Centauri or Die!

The Adventures of Eric John Stark:
The Secret of Sinharat / The People of the Talisman
    (*aka* Eric John Stark: Outlaw of Mars)
The Ginger Star
The Hounds of Skaith   } *collected as* The Book of Skaith:
The Reavers of Skaith   }   The Adventures of Eric John Stark
Stark and the Star Kings (w/Edmond Hamilton)

Mystery/Suspense
No Good from a Corpse
Stranger at Home (*as by "George Sanders"*)
An Eye for an Eye
The Tiger Among Us
Silent Partner

Western
Rio Bravo
Follow the Free Wind

Collections
The Coming of the Terrans
The Halfling and Other Stories
The Book of Skaith: The Adventures of Eric John Stark
The Best of Leigh Brackett, *Edmond Hamilton, ed.*
No Good from a Corpse:
    The Pulp Detective Fiction of Leigh Brackett
Martian Quest: The Early Brackett
Sea-Kings of Mars and Otherworldly Stories
Lorelei of the Red Mist: Planetary Romances
Shannach—The Last: Farewell to Mars

as Editor
The Best of Planet Stories #1
The Best of Edmond Hamilton

Shannach–The Last
Farewell to Mars

LEIGH BRACKETT

Introduction by
Anne McCaffrey

HAFFNER PRESS
Royal Oak, Michigan
2011

FIRST EDITION

Published by arrangement with the agent for the author's estate,
Eleanor Wood of the Spectrum Literary Agency

HAFFNER PRESS
5005 Crooks Road Suite 35
Royal Oak, Michigan 48073-1239

info@haffnerpress.com
http://www.haffnerpress.com

ISBN: 978-1-893887-44-2 (Trade Edition)
ISBN: 978-1-893887-45-9 (Limited Edition)

Library of Congress Control Number: 2010923278

Printed in the United States of America

Publisher's Acknowledgments

The publisher wishes to thank the following for their assistance in the preparation of this book:

Gene Bundy and the staff of the Jack Williamson Science Fiction Library at Eastern New Mexico University's Golden Library, for many of the stories and materials in this collection.

Dr. John L. Carr for his biography, *Leigh Brackett: American Writer*, and Gordon Benson, Jr. for his bibliography, *Edmond Hamilton and Leigh Brackett: The Enchantress and the World-Wrecker* (2nd revised ed.).

Eleanor Wood of the Spectrum Literary Agency, literary agent for the Hamilton–Brackett estate.

Mr. and Mrs. Richard C. Jones, formerly of the Mahoning National Bank, for his anecdotes and the tour of downtown Kinsman, Ohio.

Emily W. Love and her staff for their kind hospitality and gracious tour of her Kinsman, Ohio farmhouse.

Don Sutton of Market Square Books in Kinsman, Ohio.

Scott Edwards of Dearly Departed Books in Alliance, Ohio.

Zuma Coffee House (formerly Java Hutt Cafe) in Birmingham, Michigan, Caribou Coffee in Royal Oak, Michigan, and Bailey's Sports Pub & Grille in Troy, Michigan.

Rick Yuille, Bonnie Dee, and Rick Ollerman for proofreading the manuscript.

Laura Brodian Freas and Carol Emshwiller for their kind permissions to make use of Frank Kelly Freas' and Ed Emshwiller's artwork for this volume.

Anne McCaffrey for her introduction.

Contents

INTRODUCTION

Leigh Brackett: Boy, did she have it made, and made a lot of it! Imagine, being the first eye, human or otherwise, to see a brand new world which no other intelligent or perceptive mind had seen; then to continue to remark of its history, and its expansion into history, in all its untouched glory and so many possibilities. Astounding! As it must have been to the initial explorers of the North American Continent . . . a glory that men had to explore and penetrate—but not so many women. Leigh Brackett was one of the first, true explorers of unseeable worlds. And did she revel in it, allowing her own vivid imagination to set scenes and tribulations that were not to be marred by 'science' and 'knowledge'; which became epic adventures on a cosmic scale, her cosmic scale, such as "Stark and the Star Kings" or *The Ginger Star.* Her green-skinned Venusians, her scaly Martians and associations of star kings, battering down through Magellanic clouds or the stony halls of Fomalhaut, and somehow, though we are just beginning to understand the magnitude of our insignificant existence in this galaxy, she was there, writing tourist reports and war bulletins even as brave female reporters relate to us, now, of the scenes of destruction in Cairo and Tripoli.

I've been mildly amused to note the names of some of the other people who've written introductions to Leigh's works—Michael Moorcock, Ray Bradbury, Harlan Ellison: after all, they had actually met and talked to her. So, now, here am I, not having had their advantage, giving a female writer's take on such an illustrious personage. (How I envy them!) Modern writers, meaning those of us alive and working hard, such as Lois Bujold McMasters and Elizabeth Moon, leap to mind more so than myself. But I was asked. And couldn't resist the temptation . . .

Shannach—The Last: Farewell to Mars includes seventeen stories from 1950 through 1974, originally published in the pulp magazines, and showing to this reader, new facets of an unusual writer, still animating her insights into future possibilities and situations: concise, imaginative, poignant vignettes—still peering over the dunes of future sands at life continuing as she watches. Science fact is beginning to catch up with her fiction but she manages to ignore it for a few more instances of absorbing tales.

Leigh Bracket, the writer, would have been an unusual woman for any era and, although I never encountered her . . . or, for that matter, knew way back when, that there were special conventions featuring science fiction writers and artists, I most surely would have liked to meet her. But judging solely by what she wrote, she was a quick-witted personality, with great charisma and courage, capable of shrewd perceptions, witty dialogue and deep insights. I read many of her pulp stories, having belatedly discovered the whole world of s-f and fantasy, and greedily devoured stories co-written with her husband, Edmond Hamilton when they were printed in double-novels form. Haffner Press earns my heartfelt *bravo!* for publishing this collection of Leigh's SF stories.

Clever enough to turn her hand to other formats, Leigh also write marvellous movie scripts, (*Rio Bravo, The Big Sleep* and *The Long Goodbye* to name but a few) and, of course, she wrote the first screenplay for *The Empire Strikes Back.* I wonder what else she would have written had she survived. But, here, at least, are more fascinating yarns by this incredible woman who did go where no man has yet gone!

Anne McCaffrey
Dragonhold-Underhill
Wicklow, Ireland
March 2011

THE TRUANTS

Startling Stories, July 1950

CHAPTER I

PRELUDE TO NIGHTMARE

The farmhouse was tall and white. For eighty-three years it had stood in the green countryside where the shaggy Pennsylvania hills slope down to the meadows of Ohio. It was a wise house and a kindly one. It knew all there was to know of the wheeling seasons, birth and death, human passion, human sorrow.

But now something had come into the night that it did not know. From the starry sky it came, a sound and presence not of the Earth. The house listened and was afraid…

PRELUDE to nightmare. Hugh Sherwin was to remember very clearly, in the days that followed every second of those last calm precious minutes before his familiar world began to fall about him.

He sat in the old farmhouse living room, smoking and drowsily considering the pages of a dairy equipment catalogue. From outside in the warm May night came a chorus of squeals, yelps and amiable growlings where Janie played some complicated game with the dogs.

He remembered that the air was soft, sweet with the smell of the rain that had fallen that afternoon. He remembered the chirping of the crickets. He remembered thinking that summer was on its way at last.

Lucy Sherwin looked up from her sewing. "I swear," she said, "that child grows an inch every day. I can't keep her dresses down to save me."

Sherwin grinned. "Wait another five years. Then you can really start worrying about her clothes."

His pipe had gone out. He lit it again. Janie whooped with laughter out on the lawn. The dogs barked. Lucy went on with her sewing.

Sherwin turned the pages of the catalogue. After a time he realized, without really thinking of it, that the sounds from outside had stopped.

The child, the dogs, the shrilling crickets, all were silent. And it seemed to Sherwin, in the stillness, that he heard a vast strange whisper hissing down the sky.

A gust of wind blew sharp and sudden, tearing at the trees. The frame of the old house quivered. Then it was gone and Lucy said, "It must be going to storm."

Janie's voice lifted up in a sudden cry. "Daddy! *Daddy!* Come quick!"

Sherwin groaned. "Oh, Lord," he said. "What now?" He leaned over and called through the open window. "What do you want?"

"Come here, Daddy!"

Lucy smiled. "Better go, dear. Maybe she's found a snake."

"Well, if she has she can let it go again." But he rose, grumbling, and went out the door, snapping on the yard light.

"Where are you, Janie? What is it?"

He heard her voice from the far side of the yard, where the light did not reach. He started toward her. The dogs came running to him, a brace of lolloping spaniels and a big golden retriever. They panted happily. Sherwin called again.

"Jane!"

She did not answer. He had passed out of the light now but there was part of a moon and presently he saw her, a thin intense child with dark hair and very blue eyes, standing perfectly still and staring toward the west.

She said breathlessly, "It's gone now, down in the woods."

Sherwin followed her intent gaze, across the little creek that ran behind the house and the great white dairy barn, across the wide meadow beyond it, and farther still to the woods.

The thick stand of oak and maple and sycamore covered acres of marshy bottomland too low for pasture. Sherwin had never cleared it. The massed darkness of the trees lay silent and untroubled in the dim moonlight. The crickets had begun to sing again.

"What's gone?" demanded Sherwin. "I don't see anything."

"It came down out of the sky," Janie said. "A big dark thing, like an airplane without any wings. It went down into the woods."

"Nonsense. There haven't been any planes around and if one had crashed in the woods we'd all know it."

"It didn't crash. It just came down. It made a whistling noise." She all but shook him in her excitement. "Come on! Let's go see what it is!"

"Oh, for heaven's sake, Jane! That's ridiculous. You saw a cloud or a big bird. Now forget it."

HE started back to the house. Janie danced in the long grass, almost weeping.

"But I saw it! I saw it!"

Sherwin said carelessly, "Well, it'll keep till tomorrow. Go down and make sure the gate's locked where the new calf is. The cow has been thinking about getting back to the pasture."

He had locked the gate himself but he wanted to get Janie's mind off her vision. She could be very insistent at times.

"All right," she answered sulkily. "But you wait. You'll see!"

She went off toward the pen. Sherwin returned to his catalogue and his comfortable chair.

An hour later he called her to go to bed and she was gone.

He hunted her around the barn and outbuildings, thinking she might have fallen and been hurt, but she was not there. The dogs too were missing.

He stood irresolute and then a thought occurred to him and he looked toward the woods. He saw a tiny gleam of light—a flashlight beam shining through the black fringes of the trees.

Sherwin went down across the creek into the meadow. The dogs met him. They were subdued and restless and when he spoke to them they whined and rubbed against him.

Janie came out from the pitch darkness under the trees. She was walking slowly and by the torchbeam Sherwin saw that her face was rapt and her eyes wide and full of wonder. There was such a queer breathless hush about her, somehow, that he checked his first angry words.

She whispered, "They came out of the ship, all misty and bright. I couldn't see them very well but they had wings, beautiful fiery wings. They looked like angels."

Her gaze turned upon him, not really seeing him. She asked, "Do you think they could be angels truly?"

"I think," said Sherwin, "that you're going to get a thrashing, young lady." He caught her arm and began to march her back across the meadow. "You know perfectly well that you're forbidden to go into the woods after dark!"

She wasn't listening to him. She said, in the same odd distant voice, "Do you think they could be, Daddy?"

"What are you talking about?"

"Them. Could they be angels?"

"Angels!" Sherwin snorted. "I don't know why angels should turn up in our woods and if they did they wouldn't need a ship to fly around in."

"No," said Janie. "No, I guess they wouldn't."

"Angels! If you think you can excuse yourself with a story like that you're mistaken." He quickened the pace. "March along there, Miss Jane! My palm is itching."

"Besides," murmured Janie, "I don't think angels laugh – and they were laughing."

Sherwin said no more. There seemed to be nothing more to say.

He was still baffled at the end of a stormy session in the living room. Jane clung stubbornly to her story, so stubbornly that she was on the verge of hysterics, and no amount of coaxing, reasoning or threatened punishment could shake her. Lucy sent her sobbing off to bed.

4

"I can't understand the child," she said. "I've never seen her like this before."

Sherwin shrugged. "Oh, kids get funny streaks sometimes. She'll forget it."

He had forgotten it himself by morning. He saw Janie go off to school with Richard Allerton, the boy from the neighboring farm. They always walked together, trudging the half mile into the village. Janie was chattering sixteen to the dozen and now and again she whirled about in a sort of dance, holding out her arms like wings.

Toward noon Lucy called him in from the barn. "Miss Harker just phoned," she told him. "She wanted to know if Janie had come home."

Sherwin frowned. "You mean she isn't in school?"

"No—not after recess. Miss Harker said a number of children were missing. Hugh, I'm worried. You don't suppose—?"

"Nonsense. The little devil's playing hooky, that's all." He said angrily, "What's got into the kid all of a sudden, anyway? All that cutting up last night—*hey!*" He turned and looked at the woods.

After a moment he said, "I'll bet that's it, Lucy. I'll bet she's taken her pals down to look at the 'angels.'"

Lucy said anxiously, "I wish you'd go and see."

"That," said Sherwin, "is exactly what I'm going to do—right now!"

THE dogs came with him, chasing each other merrily after imaginary rabbits. But when he reached the edge of the wood they stopped and would come no farther.

He remembered that they had not gone in with Janie the night before and he could not understand what was the matter with them. The woods were full of small game and normally the dogs spent half their time there, hunting by themselves.

He called, whistled and swore but they hung back, whimpering. Finally he gave up and went on alone, shaking his head.

First his child, now his dogs—everything seemed to have gone queer at once.

The day was leaden, heavy with the threat of rain. Under the thick-laced branches of the trees it was almost as dark as though it were night. The air was moist, dank with the smell of the marshes. Sherwin forced his way through the undergrowth. From time to time he shouted Janie's name.

Once, some distance away, he thought he heard a chorus of voices, the shrill laughter of a number of children. But the trees clashed and rustled in the wind so that he could not be sure—and Janie did not answer his call.

Gradually, creeping in some secret way along the channels of his nerves, the realization came to him that he was not alone.

He began to move more slowly, looking about him. He could see nothing and yet his heart pounded and the sweat turned cold on his body. Presently he stopped. The dark woods seemed to close around him, a smothering weight of foliage. He called again once or twice, quite sharply. And then he caught a flicker of motion among the trees.

He thought at first that it was the child, hiding from him, and that he had glimpsed her dress moving. But as he went toward it there was a subtle stirring in the underbrush that was never made by human feet. And as the green fronds were disturbed he saw a muted flash of fire and *something,* large and misty and glowing bright, darted swiftly through the lower branches. The leaves were shaken and there was a sound as of the beating of wings.

He caught only the briefest glimpse of it. He was not sure of anything about it, its shape, size or substance. He knew only that it was not Earthly.

Sherwin opened his mouth but no cry came. Speechless, breathless, he stood for a moment utterly still. Then he turned and bolted.

Chapter II

NIGHTMARE BY DAYLIGHT

SHERWIN had not gone very deep into the woods. Within a few minutes he came plunging out into the open meadow and fetched up in the midst of part of his dairy herd. The cows went lumbering away in alarm and Sherwin stopped, beginning to be ashamed of himself.

He turned to look back. Nothing had followed. The dogs sighted him—he had come out of the trees lower down, toward Allerton's land—and ran to greet him. He patted their rough reassuring bodies with a shaking hand and as his brief panic left him he became angry.

"It was only a trick of light among the trees," he told himself. "A wisp of ground fog, with the sun touching it."

But there was no sun, no fog either.

He had seen something.

He would admit that. His pride forced him to admit it. That he should take to his heels in his own woods…! But his mind, which he had found adequate for forty years of successful living, began to function normally, to reject the impossible thing it had thought such a short time before.

The thing had startled him, the stealthy movement, the sudden glowing flash. That was why he had—imagined. Some great tropical bird, strayed far north, hiding frightened in the unfamiliar woods, rocketing away at his approach. That was what he had seen. That had been Janie's 'angel.' A big, strange bird.

His mind was satisfied. And yet his body trembled still and some inner sense told him that he lied. He ignored it. And he started only slightly when a man's voice hailed him loudly from across the meadow.

He turned to see Allerton approaching. The man was like a large edition of his son, stocky, sunburned, with close-cropped head. Sherwin could see on his face all the signs of a storm gathered and ready to break.

"Saw you down here, Hugh," said Allerton. "Is Rich at your place? The teacher says he's cut school."

Sherwin shook his head. "Jane's up to the same tricks. I'm pretty sure they're in the woods, Sam. Jane found something there last night—"

He hesitated. Somehow his tongue refused to shape any coherent words.

Allerton demanded impatiently, "Just what do you mean, she found something?"

"Oh, you know how kids are. They run a high fever over a new kind of bird. Anyway, I'm sure they're in there. I heard them awhile ago."

"Well," said Allerton, "what are we waiting for? That boy of mine has got some questions to answer!"

He started off immediately. Sherwin fought down a great reluctance to go again into the shadows under the trees and followed.

"Which way?" asked Allerton.

"I don't know," Sherwin said. "I guess we'll just have to call them."

He called. Both men called. There was no answer. There was no sound at all except the wind in the treetops.

Shouting at intervals the names of their children the men went deeper and deeper into the heart of the woods. In spite of himself Sherwin started nervously now and again when the branches were shaken by a sharper gust, letting the gray daylight flicker through. But he saw nothing.

After a long time they splashed through an arm of the swamp and scrambled up onto a ridge covered with a stand of pines. Allerton halted and would go no farther.

"Blast it, Hugh, the kids aren't in here! I'm going back."

But Sherwin was bent forward, listening. "Wait a minute. I thought I heard—"

The tall pines rocked, sighing overhead. And then, through the rustle and murmur of the trees there came a burst of laughter and the cries of children busy with some game.

Sherwin nodded. "I know now where they are. Come on."

He scrambled down the far side of the ridge, heading south and west. There was a knoll of higher ground where some ancient trees had fallen in a winter's storm, carrying the lighter growth with them. The children's voices had come from the direction of the clearing.

He went perhaps a hundred yards and then paused, frowning. He began to work back and forth in the undergrowth, growing more and more perplexed and somehow frightened. The heavy gloom melted away oddly between the trees and his vision seemed blurred.

"I can't find the clearing," he said.

"You've missed it. You took the wrong direction."

"Listen, these are my woods. I know them." He pointed. "The clearing should be ahead there but I can't see it. Look at the tree trunks, Sam. Look how they shimmer."

Allerton grunted. "Just a trick of the light."

Sherwin had begun to shiver. He cried out loudly, "Jane! Janie, answer me!"

HE began to thrash about in the underbrush and as he approached the strangely shimmering trees he was overcome by dizziness and threw his arm across his eyes.

He took a step or two forward blindly. Suddenly almost under his feet there was a crackle and a swish of something moving in haste, a sharp, breathless giggle.

"Hey!" said Allerton. "Hey, that's Rich!"

He plunged forward angrily now, yelling, "Richard! Come here, you!" As he came up beside Sherwin he too was stricken with the queer giddiness. The two men clung to each other a moment and there came a squeal of laughter out of nowhere and the voice of a little girl whispering.

"They look so *funny!*"

Sherwin moved back carefully until he and Allerton were out of the space where the light seemed so oddly distorted. The dizziness left him immediately and he could see clearly again. A sort of desperate calm came over him.

"Jane," he called. "Will you answer me? Where are you?"

He heard her voice – the teasing impish voice of a child having a wonderfully good time.

"Come and find me, Daddy!"

"All right," he said. "I will."

There began an eerie game of hide and seek.

The children were close at hand. The men could hear them plainly, the giggling and muffled whispers of a number of boys and girls, but they were not to be seen or found.

"They're hiding behind the trees in the undergrowth," said Allerton. He was angry now, thoroughly angry and baffled. He planted his feet, refusing to hunt any more. He began to roar at Richard.

"You've got to come out sometime," he shouted, "and the sooner you do, the better it'll be for you." He held up his wristwatch. "I'll give you just two minutes to show up!"

He waited. There was a great whispering somewhere. A small boy's voice said scornfully, "All right, scairdy-cat! Go on."

Richard's voice mumbled something in answer and then Richard himself appeared, oddly as though he had materialized out of the empty space between two maples. He shuffled slowly up to his father.

Allerton grabbed him. "Now, then, young man! What are you up to?"

"Nothing, Pa."

"What's going on here? Who's with you?"

"I don't know. I was just—playing."

"I'll teach you to play games with me," said Allerton and laid on. Richard howled.

Without warning, from out of nowhere, terrifyingly bright and beautiful in the shadowy darkness, two misty shapes of flame came rushing.

Sherwin caught a glimpse of Allerton's face, stark white, his mouth fallen open. Then the men were enveloped in a whirling of fiery wings.

This time there was no doubt. The creatures were not birds. They were not anything Sherwin had ever seen or dreamed of before. They were not of this world.

A chill of absolute horror came over him. He flung up his hands to ward the things away and then the buffeting of the flaring pinions drove him to his knees. The wings were neither flame nor fire but flesh as solid as his own. The brightness was in their substance, a shining of inner light. But even now, close as they were, he could not see the creatures clearly, could not tell exactly the shape of their bodies.

Tiny lightnings stabbed from them at the men. Allerton yelled in mingled pain and panic. He let go of Richard and the boy fled away into the undergrowth. A chorus of frightened cries rose out of the blankness among the trees and Janie's voice screamed, "Don't you hurt my Daddy!"

A last rough thrashing of the wings, a final warning thrust of the queer small lightnings and the things were gone. A great silence descended on the woods, broken only by furtive rustlings where the unseen children crept away. Allerton stared at his hand, which showed a livid burn across the back.

Presently he raised his head. Sherwin had never seen a man so utterly shaken.

"What were they?" he whispered.

SHERWIN drew a deep, unsteady breath. The beating of his heart rocked him where he stood. He tried several times before he could make the words come.

"I don't know. But they want the kids, Sam. Whatever they are they want the kids."

"Richard," said Allerton. "My boy!" He caught Sherwin's arm in a painful grasp. "We've got to stop those things. We've got to get help!"

He went away, crashing like a bull through the underbrush, tearing at the branches that impeded him. Sherwin followed. After what seemed an eternity he saw gray daylight ahead and the open field.

"Sam," he said, "wait a minute. Who are we going to ask for help? Who's going to believe us?"

"I'm going to call the sheriff and he blasted well better believe me!"

"He won't," said Sherwin heavily. "He'll laugh in your face. What are you going to tell him, Sam? Are you going to say you saw angels or devils or things that came out of the sky in a ship you can't find and can't see?"

Allerton's jaw set hard. "I'm going to try anyway. I'm not going to let *Them* get hold of my kid!"

"All right," Sherwin said. "My place is closer. Use my phone."

He ran beside Allerton across the meadow but he was dreadfully afraid and without hope.

Lucy was waiting in the yard. She gave a little scream when she saw their faces and Sherwin said sharply, "Jane's all right. Go ahead and make your call, Sam. I'll wait here."

He put his arm around Lucy. "The kid's perfectly safe this time. But—"

How to say it, even to your own wife? How to tell her, without sounding insane even to yourself?

"Listen, Lucy, there's some kind of—animal in the woods. I don't know what it is yet. Something mighty queer. Janie mustn't go in there again, not for one minute. You've got to help me watch her."

He was still evading her questions when Allerton came out again, red-faced and furious.

"He didn't believe a word of it. He told me to get off the bottle." Something desperate came into Allerton's eyes. He sat down on the steps. "We've got to think, Hugh. We've got to think what we're going to do. If it was fall we could burn the woods."

"But it isn't fall," said Sherwin quietly, "it's spring. The kids are coming now. I'm going to talk to them."

A raggle-taggle of small forms had appeared among the fringe of trees. They dispersed in various directions and Richard and Jane came on alone toward the house. They walked very close together, bent over some object that Jane held in her hands.

"Yes," said Sherwin, "they're the only ones that can help us. Let me handle this. I don't want them frightened off."

The children came on, slowly and reluctantly now that they saw their parents waiting. They had straightened up rather guiltily and stepped apart a little and Sherwin noticed that Janie now held one hand behind her back.

Her face had a peculiar expression. It was as though she looked with pity upon adults, who had got somehow far beneath her—so far that even their laws and punishments could not affect her much. "What have you got there, Jane?" he asked.

"Nothing."

"May I have it, please?"

He held out his hand. She hesitated, her chin set stubbornly, and then she said, "I can't, Daddy. *They* made it for me, for my very special own. It won't even work unless I want it to."

Sherwin felt a chill contraction of the nerves. He held his voice steady.

"Who are They?"

"Why, *Them*," she said, and nodded toward the woods. "I found Them, you know. I was first. That's why They gave me the present." Suddenly she burst out, "Daddy, They didn't mean to frighten you just now. They're sorry They burned Mr. Allerton's hand. They thought he was hurting Richard."

Lucy, whose face had grown quite pale, was on the verge of speaking. Sherwin gave her a stern look and said to the child, "That's all right, Janie. May I see your present?"

Still doubtful, but very proud, she extended her hand. In it was a flat smooth oval of the clearest crystal Sherwin had ever seen.

"Lean over, Daddy. There, like that. Now watch. I'm going to make it work."

She placed her hands in a certain way, holding the crystal between them.

At first he could see nothing but the reflection of the cloudy sky. Then, slowly, the crystal darkened, cleared...

CHAPTER III

TERROR FROM OUTSIDE

THE Ohio farmland vanished, forgotten. Sherwin bent closer over the uncanny thing held in the hands of his child.

He was looking at another world.

Pictured small and far-away in the tiny oval, he glimpsed a city built all of some glassy substance as pure and bright as diamond, half veiled in a misty glory of light.

The high slim towers swam in a sort of lambent haze, catching soft fire from the clouds that trailed their low-hung edges over them, rose and purple and burning gold. Above in the glowing sky two suns poured out muted, many-colored lights as of an eternal sunset.

And through that shining city that was never built for human kind shackled to the land, flame-winged creatures soared—creatures large and small, coming and going between the diamond spires.

As from a remote distance Sherwin heard Janie's voice, wistful and eager. "It's where They live, Daddy, way off in the sky. Isn't it just like fairyland? And look at this!"

The scene shifted as she spoke. Sherwin looked into a nightmare gulf of black and utter emptiness. He seemed to be racing through it at incredible speed, watching the red and green and yellow stars go plunging and streaming past.

"It's what They saw on Their way! Oh, Daddy, isn't it beautiful?"

It was the tone of the child's voice, far more than the unearthly vision in the crystal, that sent the pang of fear like a knife into Sherwin's heart. He reached out and struck the thing from her hands, and when it fell he kicked it away in the long grass. Before she could cry out her anguish he had caught her fast.

"What do They want with you?" he demanded. "Why do They give you things to tempt you? *What do They want with you?*"

"They only want to be friends!" She pulled free of his grasp, her eyes blazing with tears and anger. "Why do you have to be so mean? Why do you have to spoil everything? They haven't hurt anybody. They haven't done a thing wrong. They gave me a better present than anybody *ever* gave me before and now you've gone and broken it!"

She would have hunted for the crystal but Sherwin stopped her. "Go to your room, Jane. Lucy, go with her. Try to get her calmed down."

Looking at his daughter's white rebellious face, Sherwin felt that he had blundered badly. He had roused her antagonism where he wanted to help. But the unhealthy excitement in her voice had frightened him. He had not realized that Their hold on her was already so strong.

With full force the realization of what he had seen in the evil little toy came over him. He was not an imaginative man. He had never before looked up at the sky and shuddered, thinking what lay beyond it. He felt suddenly naked and defenseless, very small before huge unknown powers. Even the green familiar land did not comfort him. *They* were in the woods. And if They could come, then there were no barriers against anything.

He saw Allerton scuffling about in the grass. Presently he found what he was looking for and stamped it methodically to bits under his heavy boots.

"I saw into it too," he said, "over your shoulder. I don't know what kind of devilment it is but it's no fit thing to have around."

Thud, thud, went the great earth-caked boots. Richard was crying.

"They thought pictures into it," he said. "They were going to make me one too." He glared at his father, and at Sherwin. "Janie's right. You just want to be mean."

Allerton finished his task and went to Richard. There was something almost pathetic in his expression.

"Rich," he said, "did They promise you anything else? Did They ask you to do anything?"

Richard shook his head, looking sulky and mulish, and Sherwin could not tell whether or not the boy was holding back.

"Can They talk to you, Rich?" he asked.

"Uh-huh."

"How?"

"I don't know. You can hear Them, sort of, inside your head. They can make you see pictures too, anything They want you to see. Stars and comets and all kinds of funny places with funny-looking people and animals and sometimes no people at all."

His round tear-streaked face was taking on that same remote, rapt look that had upset Sherwin so in Janie. He whispered, "I'd sure like to ride in that ship, right across the sky. I'll bet it goes faster than a jet plane. I'd go to all those places and get a lot of things nobody ever saw before and then I'd—"

He broke off in the middle of a dream. Allerton had caught him by the arm.

"You're not going anywhere but home," he said. "And I'll lock you in, if I have to, to keep you there." His eyes met Sherwin's. "See you later, Hugh."

He took the boy away down the road. Sherwin went into the house. He locked the door behind him and loaded his shotgun and set it by. Then he sat down and put his head in his hands and listened dully to the beating of his own heart and wondered.

LUCY came downstairs. "I gave her some aspirin," she said. "She's sleepy now." She sat on the floor at Sherwin's feet and put her arms around his waist. "Hugh, you've got to tell me what's going on!"

He told her slowly, past caring whether she believed him or not.

"Sam and I both saw Them. I thought They were going to kill us, but They only burned Sam's hand. That's why the kids played truant today, to go to Them. There was a whole bunch there, laughing—"

He did not tell Lucy that somehow They had made the children, Themselves and the clearing invisible. Her face was white enough already.

She did not say much. She rose and stood for a moment with her hands clasped hard together. Then she ran back up the stairs and Sherwin heard the door of Janie's room open and then shut tight.

Toward evening he called Allerton. "I gave Rich a good thrashing," Allerton said. "He's shut in his room and his mother's with him. They'll be all right, Hugh. As long as we watch them the kids will be all right."

His voice did not carry much conviction. Sherwin hung up. He sat in the big chair in the bay window overlooking the woods. He did not turn on the lights. The clouds had broken under the rising wind and the moon threw a pale beam into the high-ceilinged room, touching the ivy wallpaper and the tall white doors. Sherwin waited, as a man waits in dubious refuge, crouched in the chair, trembling from time to time. The silence of the old house was painful in his ears.

He must have dozed, for when suddenly he started up in alarm the moon was gone. And *They* had come out of the woods.

Even through his hatred and his fear Sherwin sensed that They were glad to be free of the confinement of the trees. The wind swept strong across the open meadow and They rose and swooped upon it, a number of Them, their cloudy wings streaking across the rifted stars in wheeling arcs of fire.

He took the shotgun across his knees. His hands were quite steady, but very cold. He watched Them and he could not help thinking, *How beautiful They are!* — and he loathed Them for their beauty because it was luring his child away from him.

His child, Allerton's child — the children of the farms, the village, the other ones who had gone secretly into the woods. What could They want with the human children, these creatures from outside? What dreadful game were They playing, the bright-winged demons with Their hellish toys?

You can hear them talking inside your head. They can make you see pictures too — anything They want you to see.

Suppose They could control the minds of the children? What would you do then? How would you fight it?

Tears came into Sherwin's eyes. He sat with the shotgun in his lap and watched Them frolic with the dark sky and the wind and he waited. But They did not come near the house. Suddenly They darted away, high up, and were gone. He did not see Them again that night.

He debated in the morning whether to send Jane to school at all. Then he thought that she would be better there than cooped up brooding in the house, within sight of the woods. He drove her in himself — a silent, resentful little girl with whom he found it difficult to speak — and passed Allerton's car on the road. Both men were taking the same precautions.

They took the children into the small white schoolhouse and spoke to Miss Harker about keeping a careful eye on them. Then the men went home to their work. The day was oppressive and still with great clouds breeding ominously in the sultry air. Sherwin's uneasiness increased as the hours went by. He called the school twice to make sure Jane was there and he was back again a full hour before the last bell, waiting to take her home.

He sat for a time in the car, growing more and more nervous. The leaves of the trees hung utterly motionless. He was drenched with sweat and the heavy humid air was stifling.

A thunderhead gathered in the west, pushing its boiling crest with terrible swiftness across the sky. He watched it spread and darken to the color of purple ink and then the little ragged wisps of dirty white began to blow underneath its belly and the wind came with sudden violence across the land.

He knew it was going to be a bad one. He left the car and went into the schoolhouse. It was already too dark to see inside the building and the lights came on as he pushed open the door to Janie's classroom. Miss Harker glanced up and then smiled.

"It's going to storm," he said rather inanely. "I thought I'd wait inside."

"Why, of course," she answered and pointed out a chair. He sat down. Miss Harker shook her head, remarking on the blackness of the sky. Two boys were shutting the windows. It was very hot and close. Richard and Janie sat in their places but Sherwin noticed that several seats were empty.

"More truancy?" he asked, trying to be casual.

Miss Harker peered sternly at the class.

"I'm ashamed of them. They've spoiled a perfect record for attendance and they seem to have infected the whole school. There are several missing from other classes today. I'm afraid there's going to be serious trouble unless this stops!"

"Yes," said Sherwin. "Yes, I'm afraid there is."

THE first bolt of lightning streaked hissing out of the gloom with thunder on its heels. The little girls squealed. Rain came in a solid mass and then there was more lightning, coming closer, the great bolts striking down with a snarl and a crack. Thunder shook the sky apart and abruptly the lights went out.

Instantly there was turmoil in the dark room. Miss Harker's voice spoke out strongly. The children quieted somewhat. Sherwin could see them dimly, a confusion of small forms milling about, gathering toward the windows. There was a babble of excited whispering and all at once a smothered but triumphant laugh that he knew came from Janie.

Then a positive fury of whispers out of which he heard the words, "Billy said he'd tell Them we couldn't come!"

Sherwin rose. He looked over the crowding heads out the window. A blue-white flare, a crash that made the walls tremble and then he saw shapes of fire tossing and wheeling in the sky.

They had come into the village under cover of the storm. They were circling the schoolhouse, peering in, and the children knew it and were glad.

"What strange shapes the lightning takes!" said Miss Harker's cheerful voice. "Come away from the windows, children. There's nothing to be afraid of, nothing at all."

She marshalled them to their seats again and Sherwin clung to the window frame, feeling a weakness he could not control, watching the bright wings play among the blazing bolts.

They did not try to enter the school. They moved away as the storm moved, swooping and tumbling along the road and across the fields, overturning hayricks, putting the frightened cows to flight, ripping slates from the roofs of houses and whirling them on the wind. Even Miss Harker watched, fascinated, and he thought surely she must realize what They were.

But she only said in a rather shaken voice, "I never saw lightning behave like *that* before!"

The flashes grew more distant, the thunder lessened and she sighed. "My, I'm glad *that's* over."

She went back to her desk and began to straighten up the ends of the day's schoolwork. Even the rain had stopped when Sherwin took Janie and Richard out to the car and drove them both home. But the sky was still leaden and fuming and all that afternoon and evening distant storms prowled on the horizon and the air was heavy with thunder.

Sherwin watched his daughter. His nerves were drawn unbearably taut as by long tension growing toward a climax. He smoked his pipe incessantly and started at every flicker of far-off lightning.

Shortly after nine, from the village, there came a sound like the final clap of doom and immediately afterward the trees and even the house itself seemed to be pulled toward the source of the sound by a powerful suction of air.

It was all over in a minute or two. Sherwin ran outside but there was nothing to see except a violent boiling of the clouds.

He heard the phone ring and then Lucy cried out, "Hugh, there's been a tornado in the village!"

Sherwin hesitated briefly. Then he returned to the house and locked Janie carefully in her room and gave Lucy instructions about the doors.

"I'll be back as soon as I can," he told her. "I've got to see what's happened."

He was thinking of Them, playing in the heart of the storm.

Before he could get his own car out he heard Allerton sound his horn from the road.

"Tornado, huh?" said Allerton. "What it looked like, all right. I figured they might need help. Climb in."

They had no trouble finding the center of damage. There was a crowd already there and growing larger every second, shouldering, staring, making a perfect explosion of excited talk.

The schoolhouse was gone, lifted clean from the foundations.

Sherwin felt a cold and heavy weight within him. He looked at Allerton and then he began to question the men there.

Nothing else had been touched by the freak tornado—only the schoolhouse and that was not wrecked but gone. Several people had seen what they took to be lightning striking all around the building just before it vanished with the clap of thunder and the violent sucking of air.

Sherwin took Allerton by the arm and drew him aside. He told him what he had seen that afternoon.

"*They* didn't like the school, Sam. It kept the kids away from Them." He stared at the bare foundations, the gaping hole of the cellar. "*They* didn't like it, so it's gone."

A MAN came running up to the crowd. "*Hey!*" he yelled. "*Hey,* my wife just got a call from her sister down by the state line. You know what that wind did? It took the schoolhouse clear down there and sat it on a hill, just as clean as a whistle!"

A chill and desperate strength came to Sherwin. "This has got to be stopped, Sam. The devil alone knows what They're up to but it'll be the kids next. I'm going to try something. Are you with me?"

"All the way."

Sherwin fought his way through the crowd. He got to the center of it and began to yell at the men and women until they turned to look at him. A story had come into his head—a wild one but less wild than the truth and he told it to them.

"Listen, while you're all here together! This doesn't have anything to do with the tornado but it's more important. How many of you have had kids playing hooky out of school?"

A lot of them had and said so.

"I can tell you where they're going," Sherwin said. "Down in my woods. There's somebody hiding out in there. Escaped convicts maybe, or men running from the law. They've got the kids bringing them food, helping them out. That's why they're ducking school. Isn't that so, Sam?"

Allerton took his cue. "It sure is! Why, my boy's locked up in his room right now to keep him out of trouble."

The crowd began to mutter. A woman cried out shrilly. Sherwin raised his voice. There was a deadly earnestness about him that carried more conviction than any mere words.

"I'm afraid for my daughter," he said. "I'm afraid for all our children unless we clean those—those criminals out of the woods! I'm going home and get my gun. Do any of you men want to come with me?"

They roared assent. They forgot the freak wind and the vanished schoolhouse. This was something that threatened them and their homes and families, something they could understand and fight.

"Call the sheriff!" somebody yelled. "Come on, you guys! I'm not going to have my kids murdered."

"We'll use my house as a starting point," Sherwin told them. "Come as soon as you can."

The men of the village and the nearby farms dispersed, calming their women. Sherwin wondered how they would feel when they learned the truth. He wondered if bullets would kill Them. At any rate, it was something to try, a hope.

Allerton drove him home, racing down the dark road. He dropped Sherwin off and went on to his own place to get his rifle. Sherwin ran into the house. He found Lucy sitting in the middle of the living room floor. Her eyes had a dreadful vacant look. He shook her and it was like shaking a corpse.

"Lucy!" he cried. *"Lucy!"* He began to slap her face, not hard, and plead with her.

After a bit she saw him and whispered, "I heard a little noise, just a little noise, and I went upstairs to Janie's room…"

Tears came then. He left her crying and went with great strides up the stairs. The door to Jane's room was open. He passed through it. The room was in perfect order, except that the northwest corner had been sheared clean away, making a narrow doorway into the night.

The child was gone.

Chapter IV

Truant's Reckoning

HE had looked for Janie's body on the ground below her room. He had not found it. He had known it would not be there. He had given Lucy sedatives and talked her into quietness with words of reassurance he did not feel himself.

Now the men from the village were coming. The cars blocked the drive, formed long lines on the road. The men themselves gathered on the lawn, hefting their rifles and their shotguns and their pistols, talking in undertones that held an ugly note, looking toward the black woods.

Some of them were afraid. Sherwin knew they were afraid but they were angry too and they were going. They had a peaceful lawful place to live and they were willing to go into the woods by night with their guns to keep it so.

He came out on the steps and spoke to them. "They've taken my daughter," he said. "They came and took her from the house."

They looked at his face in the glare of the yard light and after their first outraged cry they were silent. Presently one said, "I called my kid but I couldn't find him."

There was more than one father then who remembered that he had not seen his child at home. And now they were all afraid but not for themselves. Sherwin went down the steps. "Let's go."

He was halfway across the little bridge when Allerton came running, crying Sherwin's name. "They took Richard," he said. "My boy is gone."

The men poured out across the meadow, going like an army on the march, running in the long grass—running to where the cloudy moon was lost beneath the branches of the trees.

"Head toward the knoll," cried Sherwin. He told them the direction. "I think that's where They are. And be careful of the swamp."

They went in among the close-set trees, laboring through the undergrowth, the beams of their flashlights leaping in the utter dark. Sherwin knew the woods. He rushed on ahead and Allerton clung close behind him. Neither man spoke. Lightning still danced faintly on the horizon and now and again there was a growl of thunder. The mists were rising from the marsh.

Abruptly Sherwin stopped. From behind him came a yell and then the crash and roar of a falling tree. There was silence then and he shouted and a distant voice answered.

"Tree struck by lightning, right in front of us. No one hurt!"

He could hear them thrashing around as they circled the fallen tree. And then there was a second crash, and another, and still another.

Sherwin said, "It's Them. They're trying to block the way."

Muffled voices swore. The men were trying to scramble out of the trap that had been made for them. Sherwin hurried on, Allerton panting at his side. He could not wait for the men. He could not wait now for anything.

A swoop and a flash of light, an ominous cracking—and ahead a giant maple toppled to the earth, bearing down the younger trees, creating an impassable barrier.

"All right," said Sherwin to an unseen presence. "I know another way."

He turned aside toward the river. In a minute or two he was ankle deep in mud and water, splashing heavily along an arm of the swamp. Reeds and saplings grew thick but there were no trees here to be thrown down against them.

The men went fast, careless of how they trod, and all at once Allerton cried out and fell. He floundered in the muck, trying to rise. Sherwin lifted him up and he would have gone on but he went to his hands and knees again, half fainting.

"I've hurt my ankle. A loose stone—it turned!"

He had lost his rifle. Sherwin got an arm around him and held him up. He was a big man and heavy. It was hard going after that and very slow. Sherwin would have left him but he was afraid that Allerton might faint and drown in the inches of sour water.

The ridge loomed up before them, the tall pines black against a brooding sky. The men staggered out onto hard ground and Sherwin let his burden drop.

"Wait here, Sam. I'm going on alone."

Allerton caught at him. *"Look!"*

Cloudy wings soared above them, swift as streaming fire and one by one the tall pines went lordly down, struck by the lightning They carried in Their hands.

The ridge was blocked.

When the night was still again, and empty, Allerton said, "I guess that does it, Hugh. We're licked."

Sherwin did not answer. He remained motionless, standing like an old man, his shoulders bent, his head sunk forward on his breast.

THE earth began to vibrate underneath his feet. A sound, more felt than heard, went out across the woods—deep, powerful throbbing that entered Sherwin's heart and shook it and brought his head up sharply.

"You hear that, Sam?"

"What is it? Thunder?"

"It's machinery," Sherwin whispered. "Motors, starting up."

Unfamiliar motors, so strong and mighty that they could shake the ground and still be silent. *Their* motors. *Their ship!*

"They're getting ready, Sam. They're going to leave. But what about the kids? Sam—*what about Janie and the kids?"*

He turned and fled back into the swamp, along the ridge and around it, and faced a wide expanse of stinking mud and mist. He started out across it.

The marsh quaked beneath him. Going slowly and by day he would have been afraid, wary of the bog-holes and the sucking sands. He did not think of them now. He could not think of anything but that vast and evil thrumming that filled the air, of what it meant to his child—his child, that might have died already, or might be…

He did not know. That was the worst of it. He did not know.

He took a straight line toward the knoll, slipping, floundering, falling now and again and scrambling up, wet to the skin and foul with ooze, but going on, always going on, and at last there was solid ground under his feet and only a belt of trees between him and the clearing.

They were not looking for him now. They thought he was trapped and helpless, back on the ridge. At least They did not try to stop him. He forced himself to go quietly.

This time he could see the clearing. It crossed his mind that whatever trick They had used before to bend and twist the light-rays around that space so that it could not be seen had depended on some mechanism in the ship, that now They could not spare the power for it.

A dark and monstrous bulk filled more than half the opening. The moon had broken clear, and by its light he could see the metal sheathing of the ship, scored and pitted and worn by unimaginable voyages. The mighty throb of its motors gave it an illusion of life, as though it were anxious to be away again. Sherwin remembered the crystal and the glimpse of streaming Suns and he shuddered, thinking of where this ship had been.

They were hovering around an open hatch in the belly of the ship and the children were there also—Janie, Richard, a half dozen more, grouped beside the doorway.

And Jane was climbing in.

Sherwin screamed. He screamed her name and ran out across the clearing. He dropped his gun. He could not use it anyway for fear of harming the children and this had gone beyond such things as guns. The child turned and looked at him and then *They* came.

They did not harm him. They held him fast and even now, with Their solid strength binding him, he could see Them only as misty shapes with wings of cloudy fire spread against his struggles.

Perhaps the light was different on Their world. Perhaps in the glow of those twin suns They would be as real as he was. But here They were like ghosts, alien phantoms that made him cold with horror.

"Jane!" he cried, "come back! *Come back!"*

Reluctantly she came toward him. "They won't hurt you, Daddy. Don't be scared. Daddy, I want to go with Them. Just for a little while! They'll bring us back. They promised. And I want to go with them—out *there."*

She pointed to where the stars burned clear in the valleys between the clouds.

"I didn't mean to sneak away, Daddy, but I knew you wouldn't let me go and I have to—oh, I *have* to! They came and got me, so I could."

"No," he said. "Oh, *no!"* They were not words so much as a groan of agony. "Listen, Janie, please listen. I'll give you anything you want. I'll buy you a pony, I'll take you clear around the world, I'll do anything."

"But I don't want any of those things, not now."

"Jane," he said, "don't you care anything about your mother and me at all? Do you want to kill us both?"

"I don't see why everybody has to die just because I want to go somewhere!" But she began to cry a little and he shouted to the other children, pleading with them, telling them how their parents felt, trying to make them understand the danger, the enormity of the thing that they were about to do.

Richard looked stubbornly at the ground and said, "We'll never have a chance again. We'll never see those other places out there if we don't go now. I don't care what my father says. I'm going."

One of the little girls said doubtfully, "I'm scared. I think I want to go home."

Some of them began to waver, thinking of the things Sherwin had said. And then Sherwin heard a silent voice speaking within his mind.

He knew that the children could hear it far more clearly than he. Their minds were young and plastic, open wide to all things. But he could hear it well enough.

What are you afraid of? it said. *Come on! There are all sorts of worlds beside this one. We'll show them to you. We'll show you how the stars look, out beyond your sky. We'll teach you how to run the ship. Think of the fun we can have together, all across the galaxy!*

OTHER voices joined in, telling of colored Suns and bright strange planets, of toys and pets and treasures, of adventures unthinkable. Child's talk, couched in the language of children – cunningly wrought to lure them on with promises that set their heads whirling with wonder and delight.

Suppose you do get punished when we bring you back? Are you going to miss it all just because you're afraid of a little punishment?

"That's right," said Janie, turning to the others. "Think what *They're* going to catch when They get home and *They're* not afraid. They didn't let *Their* parents stop them!"

"No sir!" said Richard. "*They* weren't scared."

Slowly, very slowly, Sherwin said, "Their parents? Jane, did you say – *Their parents?*"

"Yes, Daddy. *They* ran away and They've had all kinds of fun and haven't got hurt a bit and They weren't any older than we are. And if They can do it, so can we!"

Parents!

They ran away, and They aren't any older than we...

Sherwin said nothing for a long moment.

At last he whispered, "Do you mean that *They* are children, too?"

"Why, of course," she answered. "I thought you knew."

Sherwin began to laugh. It was not healthy laughter and he made himself stop it at once.

Children!

The fright, the anguish, the pain of the past two days and nights—a whole village in arms, terrified parents combing the woods for the missing, the awful dread of the unknown that had beset him and Allerton!

Children. Children had done all this!

He looked at Them and he could not believe it. "It's a lie," he said. "It's a lie They've told you to lead you on."

Jane said impatiently, "Don't be silly, Daddy. Why would They want to play with us if They were grown up?"

He remembered the winged creatures, large and small, going between the diamond towers of the city he had glimpsed on the world of a distant star.

Large and small, old and young...

Why not?

A race that could build such ships to ply between the Suns, a race that could put thought into crystals and make themselves unseen, that could cause whole buildings to vanish and topple trees at will—would not their young be children still in spite of a vaster knowledge?

He heard Them laugh, soundless gleeful laughter, as though They had played an excellent trick upon him to frighten him so, and he knew that it was true.

Children—these unhuman creatures with all their unholy powers. Truant children, like his own!

A queer sort of anger came to Sherwin then and with it a faint and desperate hope. He straightened up and turned to face the two that held him. He told Them sternly, "Let me go!"

They relaxed their gasp but the others had come closer now and were around him, mingled with the children of Earth.

Sherwin was thinking, *The species doesn't matter, even a lion cub will obey. Maybe—Maybe!*

He spoke to Them. "You're telling our children not to be afraid of punishment. What are your own elders going to say to you when you get back?"

They rustled Their wings and did not answer. "You're being very brave, aren't you? You're just going to go on having fun. Well, I know kids, and I know different. You're afraid. You're afraid to go home!"

Their voices reached him in defiant chorus.

No! We are not afraid!

"Oh, yes, you are. You're scared stiff. You've stolen a ship and run away and there'll be the devil to pay about it and you know it."

He stepped toward Them, forcing himself to be stern and assured, the single adult among a group of children, the angry adult asserting his authority. He hoped They could not read the fear that threatened to choke the words in his throat.

"If I were you," he told Them, "I'd get home and face the music before you make things any worse. The longer you stay away, the harder it'll be for you. And you might as well know right now, nobody's going with you!"

He turned to his own. "Come here to me, Jane. The rest of you, get home as fast as you can make it. Your fathers are coming and you know what you'll get if they catch you here!"

He waited. There was nothing more to do but wait. For a moment no one moved nor spoke. The children hung their heads and looked at each other sidelong and it seemed to Sherwin that the wings of the strangers drooped a little.

Imperceptibly the two groups began to draw apart.

The little girl who had spoken before ran suddenly into the woods, crying. And They commenced to mutter among Themselves.

They were speaking only to each other now and Sherwin could not hear Their thoughts but it seemed that They were quarreling, some hanging back, others arguing with flashing motions of Their wings.

Jane came slowly and stood beside Sherwin. Her eyes were on the earth. She did not raise them.

They began to drift toward the ship. They were not talking now.

They stopped beside the hatchway and looked back. Most of the human children had already melted into the darkness between the trees. Sherwin took Jane's hand and held it. They must have called to her, for she said good-by and They went slowly and gloomily into the ship. The hatchway closed.

Sherwin took his daughter into his arms and carried her away.

Behind him the heavy throbbing deepened and then seemed to rise and fade. Looking upward through a rift in the branches he saw a dark shape sweep out across the stars and vanish, bearing those other children to their homeplace far across the sky.

Janie was crying, her head pressed hard against his shoulder.

A little later he met the other men.

"Whoever was in the woods has gone away," he said. "Everything's all right now and the truants—*all* of them—are going home."

The Citadel of Lost Ages

Thrilling Wonder Stories, December 1950

Chapter I

STRANGE AWAKENING

DARKNESS—nothingness—a void and a voice that spoke to him across the muffled deeps. "Remember! Think, and remember! Who are you?"

It was painful to be thus aroused. And yet he tried to answer and could not. He said, "I don't know."

"Yes, you know. You can remember if you will. *Who are you?*"

The voice continued to torture him, calm and insistent, and in order to quiet it he tried desperately to remember. It seemed that he should know. He had known, once.

"I am…"

A pause, a groping and then, "I am—Fenway."

"Ah!" said the voice. *"Good!* You see, you do know—you can re-member. Now—*where* are you, Fenway? Where?"

Again he answered, "I don't know." The mists were thick and he was growing tired.

But the voice went on. "You are walking, Fenway. There is a street, buildings, people. Where are you going?"

Suddenly he knew. Of course he knew! He must have been asleep or dreaming not to know. He was walking down the Avenue of the Americas. He had just left his office in Rockefeller Center. It was dusk and a thin snow was falling. He could see the immense towers of the city leaping skyward, their ledges rimmed with white, their

31

myriad windows blazing and above them in the smother the blinking lights of the airways.

He said, answering the voice, "I am in New York. It is winter and I am going home."

"Good! Now the year. What year, Fenway?"

"I'm tired," he said. "I want to sleep."

"Tell me the year, Fenway. The *year!*"

He said uncertainly, "The year I was born, the year I married, the year my son was born. The year, this year. I don't... Yes, nineteen hundred and eighty-seven."

He *was* tired. The voice was growing faint, the restful dark increasing.

"Fenway!" It seemed to him that the voice quivered with a terrible excitement. "Fenway, the Citadel! *Do you know of the Citadel?*"

"The Citadel?" Some chord within him stirred to the touch of that word, a chord of fear, of doom and desolation.

"Perhaps it won't happen," he murmured. "Perhaps they're wrong. The Citadel—I can't think about the Citadel. Let me sleep!"

He let himself drift into the enfolding darkness. From far off he heard the voice clamoring his name and another voice that cautioned, "Softly. Don't force him! You know the danger of force."

For a brief instant, blurred and gigantic in the void above him, he thought he saw their faces, bearded, bright and hateful—the faces of torment. He thought he heard the voice say softly in triumph, "One more time. Once more and he will remember!"

Then it was all gone—sight and sound and sense. There was only slumber, the deep deep night of silence and forgetting.

DAYLIGHT—a narrow shaft of it, red and rusty on the stone floor. He lay for a long time looking at the light, not understanding it, not understanding anything. His head was heavy, as though weighted with iron bands.

He was enclosed in a small chamber of stone. It was very still. Except for the single spear of light it was dark. He could not remember having seen this place before. He looked at the light, and wondered, and his wondering was slow and vague.

He wondered who he was and where he was and why.

Once he had known. Once he had had a name and a place and a reason.

They were gone beyond remembering. He felt that this should have frightened him but it did not. He was puzzled and worried but not afraid. Not very much afraid.

He stood up suddenly, trembling, bathed in a chill sweat. Dim broken images whirled across his mind, too formless for grasping, and he cried out, "I can't remember!"

The cry was only a groan. It echoed dully from the stones with a sound like heavy laughter.

He looked down at himself. He saw his feet, shod in rawhide sandals. His legs, brown and long-thighed and muscular, were marked here and there with old scars. A strip of white cloth was wound tight around narrow loins, above that was a flat brown midriff.

He studied his hands. They were strong but they had no meaning for him. He lifted them and felt his face, the hard high ridges of bone, the hollow planes of flesh. He ran his fingers through short-cropped hair and did not know the color of it nor the color of his eyes—nor his name.

It was an evil thing, to be shut in a place of stone without a name. He stood still until the spasm passed.

The narrow shaft of light drew him, three slow unsteady steps. He leaned his face to the slit in the wall and looked out—out and down and far away. And again there came the chill sweat and the trembling, the poignant sense of memory hiding just beyond the threshold of his mind.

A copper Sun hung in the sky and the sky was coppery and thick, streaked with clouds of reddish dust that deepened into crimson where they touched the far-off hills.

He looked at the sky and something said within him, *The sky is wrong.* It did not tell him how.

Below him, at the foot of granite cliffs that seemed to fall forever down from where he stood, there was a city.

It was a great city. There were many buildings, some huge and built of stone, some built of wood, some of clay brick and endless crowding masses of little huts that seemed like lumps of earth itself. It was a bright city, blazing with sullen color under the copper sky.

It was a rich city. He could see the market places, the patterns of the streets and lanes and huddled alleys thronged with men and beasts, the pens and paddocks and the roads that led in and out. The sound of it rose up to him, soft with distance – the speaking of many voices and of much motion.

A large rich busy city – but again the inner something told him, *It is wrong.* And he visioned white towers rearing godlike, thundering with light and sound, roaring with a great voice of wheels and motors and swift wings in the sunset sky.

He visioned them as a man sees a wisp of smoke erased by the wind. And they were gone, without form or meaning, as though they had never been.

He stood where he was, gazing dully at the city and the wide land that spread beyond it, patched with forest and cleared meadows and the roofs of villages. There were streams and three broad roads that led away toward the hills. The roads were hung with dust where men and horses moved.

The shadows did not change. The Sun hung unmoving in the sky. He did not know how long he stood. There was no time. And that too was somehow wrong, that red unstirring Sun in a dusty sky.

From somewhere above him, as though on the roof of whatever place this was, there came the brazen thunder of a gong.

The stone walls shuddered with it. He could hear the echoes rolling out across the land, solemn and fierce, and he thought it must be a great gong indeed, fashioned by giants. When the ringing strokes were ended the world seemed filled with silence.

Below him the city quieted. The voices were stilled, the streets and the market places grew empty. Out on the plain the caravans left the roadways and lay down under the shelter of the trees. The villages were silent. The world slept.

And still the sun had not shifted in its place.

HE began to be afraid again. The city and the plain seemed deathly, too quiet in the unchanging sunlight. He turned from the narrow window place. There was an iron door in one wall, a low thing heavily made. He hammered on it with his fists and shouted. He did this again and again until he was hoarse and his hands were bruised. There was no answer, not the slightest sound from beyond.

He went back to the couch where he had wakened. He saw a water jug on a ledge beside it and an earthen plate with meat and black bread. He was not hungry. He drank from the jug and then sat down and put his head between his hands and set himself to remember, to know. And that was as useless as the pounding.

His eyes fell again on the food and water. They glittered with a sudden realization.

"Someone will come," he whispered. "Sooner or later, someone will come with food. They will know. They will tell me who I am!"

He would *make* them tell him—who he was, where he was and why. He shivered again but now it was not with fear but with hope. He waited, his brown hands curved and sinewy and cruel.

He waited.

The wall and the iron door must have been very thick for he heard nothing until there came to him the sound of a bolt drawn softly. He lay back on the couch as though in heavy sleep. A second bolt, a third. The door swung in.

Light footsteps crossed the stones. Peering through his lashes in the half dark he could see only a blurred small shape that came and bent over him.

He reached up and caught it.

Chapter II

ARIKA

WHATEVER it was he had hold of, it behaved like a small panther. He clamped one hand over its face to keep it from crying out and then he rose and dragged it, struggling, into the red shaft of daylight.

He saw that he had caught a girl.

Her hair was black and her eyes were two dark points of fire looking at him over the rim of his hand. He held her so for a moment, watching the empty doorway, listening. Then he whispered:

"Stop struggling and I'll take my hand away. But if you make a sound I'll kill you!"

She nodded. Cautiously he lifted his hand from her face. He saw a pointed chin, a red mouth drawn into what was almost a snarl—a cat-face, predaceous, startled, capable.

Only for a moment did he see that face. Then it softened and the cat-look was gone, and the hardness, so that he thought he had only imagined them. Her expression now was as sweet and plaintive as the voice that whispered:

"Why do you treat me so? Don't you remember me—Arika?"

"Arika," he repeated slowly. And again, "Arika?" His fingers tightened on her arms. "No, I don't remember you, Arika." He began to shake her, not meaning to, hardly knowing that he did so. "I don't remember you. I don't remember anything. Who am I? Tell me who I am!"

Soft pity welled in the dark eyes. "It was so before. But I thought you would remember me. I came only four nights ago to tell you that your escape was arranged."

She touched him, pleading. "Don't shake me so. I don't know who you are or where you came from or even why you're here. I only know you're human and a captive and—I hate the Numi."

With a part of his mind he heard that and was conscious of a crushing disappointment. But his brow was drawn and he stared at her, saying, "Night? This is *night?*"

"You must have heard the gong."

"Night!" His gaze turned to the shaft of light. Tentatively he formed the word, "darkness."

HE felt the girl quiver. "Don't say that word. It's evil like the Numi. Let me go—we'll talk later when it's safe. Come now, we have a long way to go before the day-gong."

Slowly he released her. The full impact of what she had said about escape reached him. He had a terrible desire to be out of this cage of stone, yet he was afraid somehow of the world he had seen below the window-slit, the world that seemed so strangely wrong.

"Night," he said again.

Sunset, dusk and dark. A man walking in the dusk, going—some-where....

His head swam and for a moment he thought the veil had lifted. He cried out hoarsely, "Fen...my name...Fen!" Then he covered his face with his hands and whispered, "I don't know. I can't remember. It's all gone."

She picked up that syllable and used it. "You will remember—Fenn. But you must come now. I'm only a temple slave. If they catch me..." She finished with a shudder and added, "You'll never have another chance."

She pulled at his hand and he suffered himself to be led through the iron door into a corridor shrouded in utter darkness. In his mind he turned the word Fenn over and over and still he did not know.

Somehow it was worse than being nameless to be called by a name that had no meaning.

The girl Arika guided him surely. The corridor was short, little more than a landing. Then there were steps, cut in the living rock and leading steeply downward.

When they reached the foot of the steps Arika's hand stayed him. "Make no sound," she whispered. "There is danger here."

She moved forward a few cautious steps. Fenn could see nothing in the complete blackness. Then a crack of sombre light appeared and widened slowly and he saw that a block of stone had swung soundlessly on a pivot, revealing an opening large enough for a man to pass through.

Arika made again an intense gesture of silence. She stepped through the doorway and Fenn followed. Behind him the block of stone swung shut and became an indistinguishable part of a massive wall.

Arika gave him a quick bright glance as though seeking acknowl-edgement of her cleverness and he gathered that the stone block, with the passage and cell beyond it, were very secret things that she should not have known existed.

They stood now in a space no more than three feet wide. Behind them was the wall. Before them was a hanging of some heavy black stuff. Overhead both wall and hanging vanished upward into shadow.

The girl beckoned him on, keeping close to the wall lest she should brush against the hangings and disturb them. Fenn copied her every movement with great care. The air was heavy and still and there was a quality in the silence that set his nerves prickling.

The wall curved and curved, it seemed, without end and they crept mouselike in that narrow space behind the black curtain that was as endless as the wall.

Fenn was consumed with a great curiosity as strong as his unease. At last Arika stopped and he brought his mouth close to her ear, pointing to the curtain.

"What is beyond it?" he breathed.

SHE hesitated. Then she smiled, a rather wicked smile. Without touching the hanging she studied it until she found the place where two sections overlapped. Very slowly, very carefully, she drew the edges apart the merest crack so that he might see through.

He looked out into a vault of glimmering darkness. How large it was, how high, he could not tell but it seemed to stretch up and away as high as the sky and as wide as half the Earth. And again painful submerged memories wrenched at him.

He knew that it was all a cheat. The black hangings covered ordinary walls of stone and the upper vault also would be shrouded in the sombre cloth. But the black "sky" burned with points of diamond fire, blazing, magnificent and sown so thick that all the space below was filled with a pale shining, reflected back from peaks and plains of purest white.

Fenn knew that the peaks were only painted on the black cloth and that beneath the white substance underfoot there was only stone. But a shivering of awe and recognition ran through him and a terrible giddiness that made him reel.

Somewhere, sometime before he had seen those fires in the night sky and known a whiteness on the Earth!

Arika's voice whispered in his ear, softer than thought. "This is the Temple of Eternal Night. See them sleeping there, the Numi priests, trying to appease their own dark gods?"

He saw them then and all sense of recognition or kinship vanished. Whatever night or winter he had known, it had no part with this!

On pallets of white fur they slept, row upon row, the ones she had called the Numi priests. And they were not men.

Or were they? Their form was like his own except that the bodies of the Numi had a look of tremendous toughness and strength, more like the bodies of lions than of men. And like lions they were furred. He could see the soft gleaming pelts of them, their long hair and their silken beards. They were beautiful, lying there in their sleeping strength.

Some were light and some were dark and some were reddish and some gray, exactly as color runs in the human hair. And in spite of their strength and their gleaming fur there was nothing beastlike about them. Rather they seemed to Fenn to be above men like himself, as he was above the brutes.

It was their faces, he thought—their cold wise cruel beautiful faces, so full of knowledge and power even in sleep.

A terrible anger swept suddenly over him. He had seen faces like that before. His clouded mind could not remember where but he knew that they were the faces of torment, of pain, of loss.

He lifted up his eyes then to the fireshot vault, the darkness and the glistening hills. He saw the awful savagery of that cunningly wrought landscape, the remote uncaring sky and the white peaks sharp as fangs to rend the flesh—a landscape that hated man.

A revulsion of fear and loathing shook him. He stepped back, turning his face away, and Arika dropped the edges of the curtain. He saw that she was still smiling that strange smile full of secret thoughts.

She turned, her fingers gliding surely over the stones of the wall. Presently another silent door swung open and he followed her onto yet another lightless stairway, going down.

The descent was very long. Arika counted the treads with great care. Several times she guided him over traps, balanced stones that would have triggered death upon him had he stepped on them. Once he thought he heard her drop some soft thing as though deliberately but he did not speak to disturb her counting.

When at last they stood on the level again she laughed a little shakily and said, "The Numi built the temple with human slaves and then took care to kill them all so that the passages should be unknown. But we humans are clever too in our way."

She was proud of herself. Fenn laid a grateful hand on her shoulder. But his mind was on other things.

"Arika," he said, "what are the Numi?"

He could feel her staring at him and when she spoke her tone held incredulity. "Surely you haven't forgotten *them?*"

"But I have," he said. *I have forgotten them and the world and myself. I live now but did I live before? When and where and how did I live before?*

His hand tightened on Arika's shoulder. She seemed to understand and she did not rebuke him. "Numi means in their language New Men," she told him quietly. "They are the race that came from out of the Great Dark to conquer us. And you and I aren't free of them yet."

They came to the end of the short passage. Arika stopped and he heard her draw a deep breath. "Go carefully, Fenn," she whispered. "If we can pass the tomb of the Numi kings we'll be safe."

She opened the third pivoted door of stone.

Fenn stepped after her into a low square chamber lighted by a golden lamp that burned upon a tripod. The dressed blocks of the wall were hung with golden wreaths and inscribed with the names of men. Fenn thought at first this was the tomb Arika had mentioned. Then he looked through an archway that had been hidden from him by the outswung door.

Arika's murmur reached him. "In here are the names of the honored ones, the favorites. *There* is the place of the kings."

Fenn glided forward to peer cautiously around the side of the arch. The space beyond was empty of life, steeped in a drowsing silence and a haze of red-gold light that came softly through hidden openings.

It was a large space. It was grand and strong and somehow insolent in its sheer lack of adornment, as though the Numi needed nothing but themselves. And around its walls of sombre stone were ranked the kings of the New Men, embalmed and dressed in their crimson robes, buried upright in pillars of clear shining crystal, a solemn company too proud to bend their necks even to the Lord of Death.

It seemed to Fenn that the bearded kings looked at him from out their upright crystal coffins and smiled with their handsome mouths, a chill and secret smile.

He heard Arika breathe a deep sigh. "The gods are with us, Fenn. Come on."

He had no desire to linger there. The human-unhuman faces of the dead filled him with a kind of horror. He followed more than halfway to the great arch at the far end when they heard the stamp of hoofs and the jingle of harness outside and then the sound of voices.

They remained poised for a moment, frozen. There were a number of voices. Many feet moved sharply in the dust and the horses stamped and snorted. Fenn glanced at Arika.

Her dark eyes had the fear of death in them but her mouth was set hard. "Back into the alcove, Fenn — and *pray!*"

CHAPTER III

THE TRAP

RIGID and still as the dead kings they stood, pressed back into the corners on either side of the arch. By moving his head a little Fenn could see a part of what went on in the tomb.

They were all Numi who entered. Some of them wore the harness of soldiers and these remained by the outer door. Two came on, a man and a woman, walking slowly along the lines of crystal pillars.

The man was golden-bearded, dressed in black robes frosted with silver. The woman held herself regally, moving with the deliberate pace of age. She was gowned and cloaked in purple and her hair was white. Fenn noted that her face was as smooth as Arika's. It was haughty and sorrowful and her eyes were quite mad.

Neither of them spoke. They came on until Fenn thought surely they were not going to stop short of the alcove. Then the man—Fenn guessed from his robes that he was a priest—inclined his head and drew back, leaving the woman standing alone before the crystal-sheathed body of a tall king, big and black-bearded, with an eagle look about him even in death.

For what seemed an endless time she stood there, her mad eyes studying the face of the dead king. Then she spoke. "You never change, my husband. Why do you not change? Why do you not grow old as I do?"

The king regarded her with a lightless agate gaze and did not answer.

"Well," she said, "no matter. I have much to tell you. There is trouble in your kingdom, trouble, always trouble, and no one will listen to me. The human cattle grow insolent and your son, who does not fill *your* throne, my lord, is soft and will not punish them."

Her voice droned on and on, full of disquiet. An eerie qualm crept over Fenn. It began to seem to him that the dead king had a curious air of listening.

The priest had withdrawn himself beyond Fenn's vision. The soldiers stood motionless by the outer door, bored and heavy-eyed. Fenn looked at Arika. The expression of catlike ferocity he had surprised before in the cell was on her face again—and this time there was no mistaking it. Her hands opened and closed like the flexing of claws and her body was drawn with tension.

Fenn began to sweat.

The Numi queen talked. She told of endless slights and injuries, of the misdeeds and follies of the courts. She was a vain spiteful old woman, mad as a March wind, and she would not have done with talking.

Arika's lips moved. She made no sound but Fenn could read the words as she shaped them.

"Be still, be still! Gods above, make her be still and go! If we don't get into the city before the day-gong we are lost, both of us, and all because she won't shut up!"

Presently she went from prayers to curses and still the old queen talked.

Arika glanced from time to time at Fenn and her eyes were desperate. Fenn himself began to feel the pressure of moments passing. He did not clearly understand the reason but Arika's fury was convincing enough.

Fenn's legs began to ache with standing in one place. The sweat trickled down his breast and back. It came to him that the air was hot and the old queen's unending words filled it like a swarm of bees.

Abruptly she said, "I am tired. And I do not think you listen. I shan't stay any longer. Good night, my lord!"

She turned and moved away in a whispering of purple robes. The priest appeared, hovering discreetly at her elbow. The guard formed ranks.

Fenn glanced at Arika and her eyes warned him to be still. He found time to wonder what sort of girl she was and why she should be taking these risks for him.

The woman, the priest and the guards went out of the tomb.

Fenn's knees grew weak with relief. He remained where he was, listening to the sounds that reached him from outside. At last he sighed.

"They've gone now, Arika. Hear the horses?"

She nodded. "The old sow! I've heard that she comes here often at night to talk to *him*. But why, of all nights – !"

"We're all right now," said Fenn soothingly.

And as he spoke the priest returned alone into the temple.

HE was moving fast, a man who has got rid of a confining duty and is on his way to better things. He reached out and struck one of the crystal pillars so that it rang and all the others picked up the sound and gave it back like the distant chiming of bells. The priest laughed. He strode on, straight for the alcove, and this time there was no hope. He was going up into the temple by the stairway in the rock.

As though they were doing it of themselves Fenn felt his muscles twitch and tighten. He held his breath that there should be no warning sound. Arika's eyes were two black narrow sparks and he saw that one hand had fallen to the girdle of yellow cloth she wore above her waist.

The priest came through the archway, and Fenn made his leap from behind.

He got one arm around the Numi's neck and his thighs locked tight around his loins. He had gauged the strength of the priest by the strength of a strong man and any man would have been borne over forward by the rush and the weight. But Fenn had forgotten that the Numi were not men.

He had not realized that anything living could be so strong. The body under the black robes seemed not of flesh, but of granite and whalebone and steel. Instead of falling as he should have done the priest threw himself backward, crushing Fenn beneath him on the stone floor.

The breath went out of him in a sickening grunt. His skull rang on the stone and for a moment he thought he was done for. From somewhere above him he heard Arika's voice and knew it had a deadly urgency but he could not grasp the words.

He was suddenly aware that he hated this golden-furred creature he had between his hands.

It was a hatred without memory or reason. But it was so red and furious that he found himself growling like a beast, forgetful of everything except that he was going to kill. New strength poured into him and a terrible excitement. He locked his thighs tighter and made of his arm an iron vise to shut off voice and breath and the moving blood. He was no longer conscious of Arika. He had forgotten escape. There was nothing in the world but this straining powerful golden body that he was going to destroy.

They were out of the alcove, thrashing among the crystal pillars where the red-robed kings looked down and watched them. The strength of the Numi priest was a wonderful thing. Fenn thought it was like trying to pinion a storm wind or ride the crest of a flood.

Their lunging bodies rolled and crashed against the ringing pillars. The robes of the Numi wrapped them both and presently there were stains of crimson against the black and silver. Fenn would not relax his grip. He was oblivious to pain. He knew that if he once let go he was lost and he would not let go.

The fingers of the priest clawed at his legs, threatened to tear the living muscle from his arms. He set his teeth in the gold-furred flesh and tasted blood and tightened, tightened, tightened the pressure of his limbs.

"Fenn!"

It was Arika's voice, far off. Arika, calling, touching him, urging. He was getting tired. He could not hold on much longer. Why did she bother him now before the priest was dead?

He turned his head to snarl at her. And he realized then that the Numi was very still in his arms, that there was no slightest movement between his straining thighs.

"Let him go, Fenn. He's dead. He's been dead for minutes. Oh Fenn, wake up and let him go!"

Very slowly, Fenn relaxed. The body of the Numi slipped heavily away from him. He watched it. After awhile he tried to rise. His muscles were palsied with tremors like the muscles of an old man. Dark streams of blood ran from his torn wrists and down his thighs and his bones ached.

Arika helped him. She looked at him now with a kind of awe, mingled with something else that he was too tired to read. Doubt, perhaps, or even fear—a shrewd calculating something he did not like. It occurred to him to wonder again why she was so bent on his escape from the Numi.

The dead priest wore a gown of fine white linen under his robe. Working very swiftly Arika ripped it and gave the worst of Fenn's wounds a hasty binding.

"You'd leave a trail a blind man could follow," she explained. "Now come!"

She led him out of the tomb into the glare of the sullen copper Sun that never moved. A strong wind blew. It smelled of heat and dust and the edges of the world were veiled in crimson.

High above him Fenn could see the half-monolithic temple crowning the cliff. It looked an evil place to be prisoned in. Why had the Numi had him there? What did they want with him?

WHAT did Arika want with him? He was glad to be free of the temple.

He stumbled after Arika down a slope clothed in tall trees that thrashed in the wind. The tomb of the kings was built on a ledge of the cliff itself and almost beneath it the city began. It must still be night for no one was stirring in the streets.

Again that word "night" evoked a sense of wrongness and Fenn glanced at the burning sky and shook his head.

Halfway down the slope Arika stopped and brought forth from its hiding place in a thicket a bundle of cloth. "Here," she said, "wrap this around you. Over your head, Fenn! Keep your face hidden."

He struggled clumsily with the garment—a large shapeless length of cotton much smeared with dust and gray ash. Arika draped her own around her and helped him impatiently with his.

"What are these?" he asked her.

"Mourners' cloaks. Since humans are allowed to visit their burying grounds only at night no one will pay any attention to us if we're seen in the streets." She added wryly, "There are always mourners!"

"But why only at night?"

"Would you have them go by day and waste the time they should be working? The Numi don't keep humans just for pets!"

She led off down the slope again, going almost at a run. Fenn could not keep up with her. A number of times she came back to him and urged him on, snapping at him, cursing him in an agony of worry. Now and again she glanced upward at the temple and as the angle changed Fenn could see the cause of her apprehension—a great gong as tall as several men, glinting dully in the sunlight upon the temple roof.

They entered the city, slowing their pace to a walk. These were the mean quarters, the vast huddle of huts that girdled the magnificence of the palace and the opulent dwellings of the Numi like a muddy sea. Here were refuse and filth and the scuttering feet of rats. Here were twisting lanes and the ancient smells of humanity crowded and unwashed. Fenn snorted in disgust and Arika shot him a smouldering glance from under her ash-smeared hood.

"The air was cleaner in the cell, Fenn, but you'll live to breathe this longer!"

They did not speak again. The crumbling mud-brick houses slept under the dusty wind, their windows covered with bits of cloth or hide. Here and there a child cried and an occasional cur-dog barked. They did not pass anyone in the bewildering tangle of lanes and if anyone saw them there was no sign of it. Arika's face was drawn and anxious and Fenn knew that she held herself from running only by the greatest restraint. She was cursing the old queen under her breath.

Up on the temple roof two black-robed priests appeared, tiny dolls in the distance.

Arika turned into an even narrower way, hardly more than a crack between the walls. Here she risked a faster pace, dragging Fenn without pity.

The distant priests bent and a second later a great hammer swung on counterweights and the day-gong sent its first harsh sonorous stroke echoing over the land.

A low doorway curtained with greasy cloth appeared on Fenn's right. Arika thrust him through it, into a stifling dusk that was blinding after the light.

Something large stirred in the shadows and a man's voice whispered, "All right?"

Arika said, "He killed a priest." And then to Fenn, "Stay here!"

The curtain rose and fell again. Fenn turned, reaching out for her. But the mourner's cloak lay on the earthen floor, and Arika was gone.

Again the large bulk moved, very lightly for its size. The shadow of a man came between Fenn and the curtain. He bent slowly and picked up the fallen cloak and as he straightened Fenn caught a glimpse of his face in the dusty gloom.

It was the face of a Numi.

CHAPTER IV

REMEMBERED DOOM

A KIND of bleak fury came over Fenn. He had had it in the back of his mind that Arika was engineering some treachery but this he had not expected. His two hands reached and encircled a corded throat, and under the vast booming of the gong he said the one word:

"Numi!"

The voice of the man said harshly, "Wait!" The curtain was lifted to admit a single beam of light. Gasping against Fenn's grip the man said, "Look again!"

Fenn looked. Uncertainly his fingers loosened. The man was beardless, his cheeks shaven close to smooth skin. His hair was cropped and his body, naked except for a twist of cloth, showed only a fine down and not the silken fur of the New Men.

And yet in the eyes, the shape of the head, the unmistakable cast of the features...

The man lifted his arms and struck Fenn's hands away. "I'm Malech. I'm Arika's brother."

"Arika's brother? And who is Arika? What does she want with me?" Fenn's hands were still raised, and hungrily curved. "What do *you* want with me, Malech? And why do you look like a Numi, a Numi plucked and stripped?"

"I'm a half blood," Malech said sourly. "So is Arika. I can assure you we have no love for our fathers, who give us their blood and then despise us for it. As for the rest of it, it will have to wait until tonight.

"I'm a slave. I work in the palace gardens. If I don't go there at once I shall be flogged, with ten stripes extra because I'm half the breed of the masters. Arika has the same problems at the temple. Besides, she might draw suspicion by her absence. So..."

He thrust Fenn ahead of him, into another room. It was not large but it was clean. There was a hearth, two box beds filled with straw, a table, three or four rough benches.

"This is the house," said Malech. "All of it. Stay in it. Don't even

48

look out the window. You'll find water, wine and food. Be quiet and trust us if you can. If you can't, after all we've risked to get you free—why, the priests will be delighted to have you back."

He swung on his heel to go, and then paused, turning to look again at Fenn as though he found in him something of special interest.

"So you killed a priest." Malech's eyes, which were lighter than Arika's, almost tawny, gleamed with an evil joy. "With a knife? A strangling cord? How?"

Fenn shook his head slowly. "I had no weapons."

"With your hands? Don't tell me with just your hands!" Malech's smile was the feral grin of a tiger. "May the gods of the humans beam upon you, my friend!"

At the door into the lean-to he said over his shoulder, almost casually, "As half-blood Numi, my sister and I—particularly my sister—share some of the mental peculiarities of our illustrious fathers. It's quite possible, if you do decide to trust us, that we can restore the memory Arika tells me you have lost."

He was gone before the other could speak.

Fenn stood where he was for some time without moving, his gaze fixed upon the doorway. The mighty voice of the gong was stilled and in its place came the numberless tongues of the waking city, jarring, clattering, settling at last to a steady beehive drone, punctuated by the shrill cries of children.

But Fenn was conscious of nothing except those words of Malech's that were still ringing in his ears. "*…we can restore the memory Arika tells me you have lost.*"

He sat down and tried to think but he was very weary. His wounds were stiffening and his body ached beyond endurance. He did not like Malech. He did not trust Arika. He understood nothing—why he had been imprisoned, why he was free. But whatever else happened he did not want to be taken back to the temple. And—if he could remember again, if he could have a name he knew was his own and a past that was longer than yesterday…

If Malech had been a horned demon and Arika his sister Fenn would not have left that place.

He washed his cuts with wine and then drank off a good bit of what remained. He was seized with a desire to go after Malech, to drag him back and force him to do his magic now. He felt he could not wait for night. But he realized that was folly speaking. He lay down in one of the straw-filled beds but he could not sleep.

To remember! To be again a man with a whole mind, a whole life!

What kind of memories would they be? How would he appear to himself after he remembered? What stains would he find upon his hands?

Even evil memories would be better than none, better than this terrible groping into nothingness.

Suppose that Malech lied?

IT was hot and the fumes of the wine were clouding his thoughts. His body wanted rest even if his mind did not. The world began to slip away from him. He thought how strange it was that Arika was half Numi—such a handsome girl for all he did not trust her. Very handsome...

He slept and in his dreams ghostly towers brightened against a dusky sky and the word "night" returned to plague him.

Twice he spoke aloud, saying, "I am Fenway."

Arika woke him. He had not heard the gong that marked off night from day nor had he heard the others return. Yet they must have been there for some time. A pot bubbled fragrantly on the hearth and the cloth was laid for supper. Outside the wind howled in the alleys, filling the air with dust.

He rose, feeling stiff and sore but otherwise normal and ravenously hungry. Yet he hardly thought of food. He was shaken with an eager half-fearful excitement. He told Arika what Malech had said and demanded, "Is that true? Can you do it?"

"Not all at once perhaps—but I can try. You must eat now, Fenn. Otherwise the body will disturb the mind."

That seemed reasonable and he curbed his impatience. He watched the others for awhile in silence, trying to judge them, but there was something about their strange breed that was beyond his grasp.

He demanded abruptly, "Why did you rescue me?"

"As I told you," answered Arika. "You were human and a captive of the Numi. This isn't the first time a human has vanished out of the Numi dungeons—though not, I'll admit, out of the temple. That was a brilliant feat, Fenn. You should appreciate it."

"I'd still like to know why."

"Does there have to be a reason?" asked Malech. "Haven't you ever done anything without a reason except that it was a good thing to do?"

Fenn shot him a hard glance. "You don't have to remind me that I don't know the answer to that. However, I won't quarrel with your motives—not now." He turned to Arika again. "What did the priests want of me? Why was I there?"

She shook her head. "I couldn't find out. RhamSin—he was your special jailor, Fenn—is a very brilliant man. He rules in the temple as the king rules in the palace and there is great rivalry between them.

"Whatever purpose he had with you, it was something of great importance to him, something he wanted to keep secret from the king and even from the other priests. Else you would not have been hidden away in that cell. The Numi are free to use humans in any way they wish, just as we use cattle, so there could be no other reason."

She met Fenn's gaze directly. "Perhaps that's why I rescued you, Fenn. I hate RhamSin. Remember, I've been a temple slave since I was old enough to climb there. Perhaps I wanted simply to cheat him of whatever success he was after just to make him sweat."

An expression of such diabolical hatred crossed her face that Fenn was convinced she had told at least a part of the truth.

Suddenly she smiled. "All that being so—have you wondered why RhamSin hasn't searched the city for you?"

"Perhaps it's easier just to get another human."

"Maybe. But I made sure—partly, of course, to clear myself. Only the priests and the royal family and some of the nobles are supposed to know about those temple passages. So on the stair I dropped a girdle belonging to a man of the royal house—which Malech managed to steal for me. Therefore it will appear to RhamSin that *he* stole you away and took you directly to the palace. So I am safe and you are safe—at least for a while."

"You're a clever girl," said Fenn admiringly. "Very clever indeed." Arika's smile broadened. And Fenn wondered silently, *Just how clever are you, Arika? Too clever to trust?* In one thing he was forced to trust, whether he would or not.

He got up with sudden violence. "I can't wait any longer! Get to work, blast you, do your magic—I can't wait any longer!"

"Softly, Fenn," said Arika. "All right." She pointed to the bed. "Lie down. Let your body relax. You'll have to help me, Fenn. I'm not like the Numi, who can do what they want to with the minds of men and beasts. You'll have to open the way for me, Fenn. Don't fight me. Let your mind be easy."

HE stretched out. He tried to do as she said, to relax his limbs and let his mind go free. Her face hovered above him, white in the shrouded light from the windows. She *was* handsome. Her eyes had strange dark fires in them. Her voice spoke to him softly.

"You'll have to trust me, Fenn, if you want to remember." Malech handed her a drinking cup and she held it to Fenn's lips. "There is a drug in this wine. It will not hurt you. It only makes the way easier and the time shorter. Drink it, Fenn."

He would not drink it. His muscles tensed again and he looked at her with narrow-eyed suspicion, almost ready to strike her aside and run. But she only took the cup away and said, "It's up to you. Your memory is your loss, not mine."

After a minute he said, "Give me the cup."

He drank it. Again he lay still, listening to her voice, and now it was easier to relax. Gradually he lost all sense of time. Arika's eyes were huge and dark and full of little dancing lights. They drew him. They compelled him. Soft folds of colorless mist slowly blotted out the face of Malech in the background, the mud-brick walls, the roof, Arika herself—all except her eyes.

Just at the last he felt the power that lay behind them but it was too late. They willed him into the final darkness and he could not but go.

Deep, deep, timeless dark.

A voice…

Under the prodding of that voice he roused a bit as though from slumber. Another voice had spoken once, asking, asking—but this time it was easier to answer.

"My name is Fenway," he told the voice. "I am in New York."

Yes, it was much easier to answer. He told about Times Square on a summer night, the blaze of light and the crowd. He told about Central Park in the morning after rain.

"And pretty soon it will all be gone," he said. "All the buildings and the subways and the people—gone, erased, forgotten."

He laughed. "They're working on the Citadel. They're burying it deep in the rock above the Palisades. It's almost finished—and for what? What good is a citadel without men?"

He laughed again, dreadful laughter. "'Repent ye, for the end is at hand!' I repent me that I had a son. I repent me, I repent me that I begot him just for death!"

"Fenway—*Fenway!*" The voice shook him, brought him to himself. "You must remember—yourself, New York, the Palisades. Draw it, Fenway. Draw the size and shape of New York, of the Palisades, so that when you wake you will remember."

Dully under the urging of the voice be began to draw. Whether he had pencil and paper he neither knew nor cared. He drew as one does in a dream, the familiar outlines, and as he did so he was filled with sadness and a sense of loss and he began to weep.

"I will not draw," he said. "What good is drawing on the evening of Destruction?"

The voice called to him. It called again and again and he fled away from it. He was running beside the wide gray river. Night was closing down and from the darkling water the mist rose thick and cold, clinging round him, drowning out the world that was so soon to die.

CHAPTER V

SECRET OF AGES

THERE was a drawing, done with charcoal on a slab of wood. It was lopsided and clumsy and unfinished, showing a long, narrow little island between two rivers near the sea.

Fenn stared at it. His hands trembled. Arika said softly, "You told me its name was New York. Do you remember?"

"I—I don't know." His mouth was dry and it was difficult to talk. "My head feels queer. It's full of smoke. Sometimes I see things and then they're gone again."

He looked up, almost pleadingly, from Arika to Malech and back again. "Where is this place I called New York?"

Malech shook his head. "I never heard of it."

There was an odd tone to his voice. Arika rose and removed two bricks from the wall above the bed. From the cavity behind them she drew a bundle of parchment scrolls. Even in his distress Fenn could see that she was laboring under some great excitement. She spread the scrolls beside him on the bed.

"When the Numi came out of the Great Dark and into the human part of the world they made pictures of the lands they passed through. I stole these from the temple long ago. Let us see if the pictures of the Numi show your island."

Fenn studied the maps. Strange maps of a strange Earth. The Numi must have traveled far. The names and inscriptions were in a tongue he did not know but Arika pointed out desert and jungle and mountains, forest land and sea, and there was nothing that resembled the island he had drawn while in that uncanny sleep.

"No," he said. "It isn't here."

A quick glance passed between Arika and Malech. She unrolled another scroll, the last.

"This," she said, "is the birthplace of the Numi. You remember the Hall of Eternal Night in the temple, Fenn? All their birthland is like

54

that, I have heard, white and cruel and very cold. It is what humans call the Great Dark."

"I don't understand," said Fenn. "What is the Great Dark?"

"The other side of the world," she answered. "Its face is turned always away from the Sun, toward the black gods of night that men say spawned the Numi."

Fenn concentrated on that last map. Endless areas of whiteness, broken here and there by the dim outlines of continents. In imagination, remembering that hall that he had glimpsed, he could see the jagged mountains rearing under a black sky shot with fire and at their feet the wrinkled ice of oceans.

It was Malech's quick eye that saw it first. "Here!" he said. "Look here, see it!" He traced with his strong finger. "Away from the Sun, beyond even the Shadow, well into the Great Dark itself. Here is the edge of the sea and here–two rivers and an island!"

He laughed, a short harsh burst of merriment, and then was still.

Arika whispered, "This is a thing of wonder. It is a miracle from the gods."

And Fenn said, as he seemed always to be saying, "I don't understand."

"Nor do I! Listen to me, Fenn–listen carefully and try to remember." Her hand had caught his now, gripping it almost cruelly, as though she would grip his mind that way.

"I tried to call your memory back. I gave you the drug to throw down all your conscious barriers and I tried to draw aside the bars that keep your memory prisoned. I called to you and you answered, naming yourself Fenway, and you talked quite readily.

"But the things you spoke of were not of this world you stand in now! You told of great buildings and of things that roared in the sky and in the streets and under the earth. You told of day and night, of the things we have never seen–the moon, the stars, dawn, sunset."

Her fingers tightened until her nails brought blood. *"Fenn, your memories were of the world that was before the coming of the dark star–the world before Destruction!"*

He was glad of her hand holding him. Because suddenly the solid earth dissolved beneath him and he was falling, spinning, crying through a reeling vortex.

He whispered, "I remember, I remember."

He put his face between his hands. He shivered, a shallow rippling of the flesh, and presently the palms of his hands were wet with a salty moisture.

I remember.

But did he? He still had no full memory of a past life. He had only flashes of a life, disjointed, infinitely strange—painful and yet somehow distant, somehow not of his flesh.

He asked hoarsely, "If I remember that far past, does that mean that I *belong* to that past? That RhamSin somehow dragged me out of it?"

Arika shook her head. "It seems impossible. And yet the powers of the Numi priests are great."

Malech interrupted, asking him passionately, "Where are the Palisades?"

Fenn was too numbed with horror to answer. He felt suspended over an abyss that yawned between two worlds, himself a stranger to them both.

Malech's hands rose in a fierce aborted gesture and Arika warned him back. She said in the compelling voice that Fenn had answered in his dream, "Fenn, show me the Palisades."

Without thought or volition, he placed a finger on the charcoal map.

MALECH'S eyes suddenly blazed. He said in an exultant whisper, "It was what RhamSin was trying to get from him—the secret of the Citadel's location. And now we have it. In Fenn we have it!"

Fenn had begun to talk. It was like a dead man slowly speaking.

"The dark star," he said to no one. "They looked at it through their telescopes. They watched it rushing closer and they told us that the world as we knew it would die. A dark star, coming out of space to kill the world."

Arika whispered, "Do you remember the Destruction?"

"No. It was not to be—not just yet. The dark star would pass the

Sun. They had it charted, they knew what it would do. It would take away some of the planets, the outer ones, and go on—and the worlds that were left would be torn and changed."

He added slowly, "There was a terrible fear on the world. Not for ourselves but for our children. Sometimes we would not believe it could happen. We looked at the great cities and the mountains and the green land. We looked at the sea and we did not believe it could ever change."

"But it did," Arika said somberly. "Legend tells how it did—how when the dark star passed all Earth was rent and shaken and its spinning slowed, so there was no more day and night. How the cities were thrown down and the mountains moved and the seas ran wild and millions died."

"They knew what was coming," said Fenn in his dead strange voice. "It was why they built the Citadel, to preserve man's knowledge and power for those who might survive."

Malech was shaken with bitter mirth. "And the Numi have hunted for that legended Citadel without dreaming that it lay in the Great Dark from which they came! They mapped this place New York and didn't know the Citadel was there! And now, with Fenn's help, *we* shall find it!"

Fenn looked at him and at Arika with hopeless eyes. "What difference does it make to me who wins the Citadel? The only world I can remember perished—how many thousand years ago?"

Arika's face flashed and she took his hands warmly, strongly, into hers. "Fenn, don't you realize what you can do? You are human—all human. You've seen a little of how humans live in this world—slaves of the Numi here in the cities or as outlaw tribes in the wilds. That has gone on since the Numi first came out of the darkness that bred them.

"But you can change all that, Fenn. You can free us from the Numi. You can make the world as it was before the Destruction—a good world for men to live in. *You can give men back all their lost knowledge!*"

"Or would you prefer," Malech said, "to give the Citadel to the

Numi so that with the knowledge in it they can rivet fetters on us forever?"

A blaze of anger leaped up in Fenn's mind. "No! Men built the Citadel, men like us—*for* men like us!"

He was remembering again the tragic last hope of that doomed world, the hope centered in the Citadel that was to be man's answer to the coming night.

"Then help us find it, that its secrets may belong to man!" Arika pressed. "We can get you out of the city and the outlaw humans out in the wilds will aid us in *this* quest. Will you lead the way?"

Fenn felt iron resolution hardening swiftly in his mind, a resolve born as much of bitter hatred of the Numi as of loyalty to his own kind.

He said between his teeth, "I will lead you. And if the Citadel has power in it—it will be used to destroy the Numi or to drive them back into their darkness."

He added eagerly, "And it may be that there at the Citadel, at the place New York that I remember so strangely, I shall remember *all* my past!"

Malech was on his feet, his face flaring with excitement. "I'll begin preparations at once! We'll need to have horses ready and slip out of the city tomorrow 'night!' "

He swung aside the curtain to leave. As he did so, with startling suddenness, a man stumbled in from outside. He came as though the howling wind had brought him—a quite human man, with the marks of the lash on his back.

"Temple soldiers are searching the quarters!" he cried and then he caught sight of Fenn. His eyes widened and his mouth became an open oblong in his seamy face. He started to speak.

Malech stepped between them, reaching one hand to the small man's shoulder, turning him around as he demanded, "Which way are they coming?"

"From the tomb of the kings, ransacking every house. We're spreading the word."

The edge of Malech's free hand took him in a slicing blow under the ear. The little man folded quietly over his own middle and Malech shoved him behind a water cask in the lean-to.

Fenn crossed the room. He gripped Malech by the shoulders. "That man knew me," he said harshly. "Why would you not let him speak?"

"Don't be a fool," snapped Malech. "He saw a stranger and was surprised. He would have sold you to the Numi for a sack of corn."

Arika's face was white with fury and despair. "RhamSin was too cunning to be completely deceived by my trick! If we had had but one day more...."

FENN'S hard new determination would not let him share their despair. He said, "We are going to find the Citadel! Since we can't wait until tomorrow night we go now."

"But horses—" Malech objected.

Fenn cut him short. "I saw paddocks of horses near the gates. We can steal mounts. Quickly!"

Arika gave him a startled glance as though revising her estimate of him. But she caught fire from his resolution. "He is right, Malech—we must risk it now!"

She brought forth the mourner's cloaks for them. While Malech was hastily improvising one for himself from a length of cotton smeared on the hearth, Arika rolled the map-scrolls and tied them in her girdle.

Fenn led the way out. The narrow valley was deserted but in the distance they saw furtive figures runing from house to house with the warning. The parching wind enveloped them in clouds of dust and the Sun burned red and evil in an ochre sky.

"Which gate?" snapped Fenn.

"This way," said Malech. "The Desert Gate."

The driven dust made everything obscure as they went swiftly, their heads down. Temple and cliffs were veiled by the blowing haze. Fenn could see no soldiers yet.

They skirted the edge of a market square, deserted except for a few folk sleeping huddled in the stalls. Beyond the market were the great stock pens and the quartering places of the caravans lying inside the Desert Gate.

Next to the wall of the caravan building was the fenced horse-paddock. There were at least fifty horses in it, shaggy creatures patiently standing with their heads away from the wind-driven dust. There were also a half dozen saddled horses, powerful sleek animals, tethered separately.

"There are our mounts, waiting for us," Fenn said.

"They're Numi horses!" Malech warned. "They don't like human riders and you'll have trouble...."

"Don't worry—I'll manage," Fenn snapped. "But first I want a look at the gate."

From around the corner of the paddock fence he peered. He saw the road, hollowed deep by the wind, and the posts that marked the gateway and beyond them the way that led over the hills to the desert and freedom.

A dozen Numi soldiers guarded the gate and their big, sleek steeds were picketed within the gateway.

"We can't ride through them!" Malech said. "It's hopeless!"

Fenn's eyes had begun to gleam with an unholy light. He said to Arika, "Give me your dagger—and then you two mount and hold a horse ready for me."

Arika stared, then gave him the weapon. She and Malech slipped back to the corner of the paddock where the saddled Numi horses were tethered.

Fenn sprang to the bars of the paddock gate. He took them down silently. Then he went through the shaggy horses to the rear of the paddock.

He suddenly drew the dagger point in a long shallow scratch down the quarter of the nearest horse. The animal recoiled with a whinnying scream of pain and terror.

Fenn scratched another horse. It too screamed. The shaggy herd began to mill frightenedly, seared by the outcries and the smell of blood.

Fenn suddenly cried out, a long shrill howl with an eerie wolf note in it, and leaped forward at the herd with his reddened dagger upraised. Instantly, the whole herd bolted out of the paddock.

There was only one way for them to go. They poured out with a great thundering of hoofs and an explosion of dust—fifty horses, stampeding in panic toward the Desert Gate.

The Numi had no chance against that onslaught. It came too suddenly even to give them time to run. The wild-eyed herd crashed over them, broke their picket-line, carried their own steeds out with them.

And close on the heels of that stampede, so close that they were almost a part of it, came Fenn and Malech and Arika.

Fenn had been fighting the Numi horse since the instant he had leapt on its back and only the fact that it too was panicky kept it from setting itself to throw him.

"Swords!" he yelled to Malech. "Get *swords!"*

Ahead of them in the gate sprawled the broken furry bodies of the Numi soldiers caught by the stampede. They would need the weapons that lay there but Fenn dared not check his own steed now.

Malech heard him and with catlike deftness pulled up his steed long enough to reach down for two of the Numi blades.

"Soldiers come!" warned Arika's cry.

A half-dozen Numi were running out from the horse-paddock, after them. Fenn laughed, as he caught the sword Malech tossed him and gave his bolting steed its head.

"We have their horses—let them catch us!"

They went full gallop down the road. The forefront of the stampede had gone on to wear itself out among the villages.

The road climbed to a low pass through the hills. Beyond the pass lay desolation—of copper Sun and coppery sky and under them the rusty barren earth.

"It is far to the Great Dark—and RhamSin will follow!" Arika warned. "He will follow to the world's end for the Citadel!"

Chapter VI

THE QUEST OF YESTERDAY

THEY had left the caravan track and struck out across the open desert. They had no guide but the gossip of the drovers that Malech had heard in the market place.

"Where or how far the place of the outlaw tribesmen may be I don't know," he told Fenn. "But it lies in this direction, away from the Sun." He pointed to his shadow stretching out before him.

Fenn asked, "How do you know these men will help us?"

"They have all suffered from the Numi. Every living human has in one way or another. And to find the Citadel—they'll help!"

Fenn looked at the barren earth and said, "We had better find them soon."

They went on, keeping their shadows always before them, pushing the horses as hard as they dared.

Fenn rode silently, withdrawn in his own thoughts. He had had it out with the Numi horse and won his battle and after that brief violence his mind had turned again to himself. He thought of the things that had been said between himself and Arika and Malech and the decision that he had made so swiftly and with such conviction.

His mood was not one of doubt or hesitation. It was only a hardening and clarifying of what was in his mind. In the city he had felt confused and driven, tortured by the blankness of his memory, raging against a world he could not understand. Here, where he was free of walls and houses, he could think again.

He still did not know who he was or where he came from or how. He had a feeling that when he reached New York he would remember. But even if he did not he remembered other things—the world that was before the dark star and the Numi, the pride and the courage of the men who had built the Citadel so that knowledge might not perish from the Earth.

It holds all the past of man, they said, and it will hold the future. The Citadel will stand forever, man's challenge to the coming night.

Men had built it and it should be given back to man. A deep anger rose in Fenn against RhamSin, who had tried to steal knowledge that did not belong to him—human knowledge to use against humankind! Fenn's hatred of the Numi was a towering thing and it stood large over everything else—larger even than his passionate desire to know himself.

He looked. He looked ahead across the desert, and he thought, *Once this earth was green and men lived upon it and were free. It shall be so again!*

He smiled at Arika and urged his horse a little faster, impatient of every step that lay between him and his goal.

Here there was no temple gong to tell them day and night. The angry Sun burned forever in the sky. The fierce wind lashed them and the dust-clouds rolled in red and ochre across the land and there was no time. They hungered and they thirsted and now and again they stopped to rest the horses and to sleep.

They had slept twice when Fenn looked back and saw atop a distant rise a plume of dust that was not made by any wind.

He said, "RhamSin."

Malech nodded. "They will have spare horses, food and water. They will push hard and the Numi are stronger than men."

Fenn smiled, an ugly smile. He began to lead by devious ways, covering and confusing the track, going on bare rock or on loose earth where the wind would blow away the prints of the horses' hoofs. And for a time they lost the distant plume of dust.

But Malech said, "They know our direction. They will follow without a track. And remember, RhamSin is a Numi and a priest. He may be able to touch our minds with his enough to guide him."

Fenn's mouth hardened. He said nothing and they went on across the bitter land. Hunger became a gnawing pain and then a weakness and an agony but it was forgotten in the pangs of thirst. The splendid horses began to falter. Arika rode bowed and silent and the men were not much better.

At rare intervals Fenn would stop and dig, wherever there was a shadow of green life in some sunken spot or the hollow of a dead watercourse. Sometimes a few drops of muddy water welled up to keep them alive.

They stopped for the third time to rest. Fenn did not sleep. He sat looking over the desert with red-rimmed eyes, thinking of the Citadel and feeling an iron determination not to die.

The plume of dust showed itself again on the horizon. He cursed it and rose to wake the others.

They started on again. The wind blew, never ceasing, and all at once Fenn's horse lifted his head and snorted, pulling against the rein. The others snuffed the wind and they too began to go aside from the straight line they followed. A kind of madness seemed to have come over them. Their dragging pace quickened to a shambling gallop.

"They smell water," Fenn said. "Let them go."

A RAW scarp of rock lifted from the desert. The ground sloped downward to form a ragged basin at its foot. Fenn saw that a sullen river ran from a cleft in the scarp and spread into a great marsh before the thirsty desert drank it up. He set his heart on that vivid patch of green that seemed so far away and would not come closer.

Then he saw the men riding toward them—leathery sun-bitten men, well mounted and riding fast, carrying long spears that glinted red in the angry daylight.

There were half a dozen of them. They swept up and ringed the three fugitives round and made them stand, holding the plunging horses. They looked at Fenn and Arika and Malech and when they saw Malech their lips drew back as though they were wolves about to tear their prey.

One said, harshly, *"Numi!"*

"Half-blood—slave." Malech's voice was a croaking whisper. He turned to let them see the old scars of the lash across his back and Fenn tried to crowd between him and the hungry spears.

"They saved my life," he said. He too was almost mute with thirst. "They saved me from the temple." Then, angrily, "Let us drink!"

They studied Fenn a long time without answering. Their hesitation alarmed him and he knew that Malech was the cause of it—Malech, who looked so much like the hated creature that had fathered him. The green marsh tortured Fenn with the promise of water. He looked at Arika's drawn face and the suffering horses and he became so furious that he lost all caution.

He reached out to the man who was holding his horse and caught him by his long hair and pulled him out of the saddle, shouting as loud as he could out of his swollen throat, "If we die, no one will ever find the Citadel! I know where it is. Do you hear that? *I know!*"

Arika whispered, "The Numi priests are hunting us to get the secret. We ask protection." She managed the ghost of a laugh. "What are you afraid of? We are only three."

The cold suspicion did not leave the face of the outlaws but Fenn saw that they were uncertain now. The leader said, "No one knows that secret."

Fenn met his hard gaze fairly. "All right. Kill us. Let the Numi rule forever over slaves and outlaws. You haven't the courage to be free."

The leader looked again at Malech, saying, "You travel in bad company for an honest human. But I'll let Lannar decide this one. Give me your swords." When he had them he reined his horse around. "Come on."

They started on again toward the marsh. It spread for several miles along the base of the scarp, wide, lush, dotted with islands of higher ground on which there were trees and thick scrub. It was beautiful, green, soft and moist under the red haze of the desert.

They were allowed to stop beside a shallow pool, to drink and wallow in brackish water that tasted to Fenn like the wine of heaven. Then they were made to mount again.

"Keep your horses exactly in line," said the outlaw. "One slip and you'll never be found again."

He began to thread an invisible path through mud and quaking bog and green water. Here and there submerged bridges had been laid, narrow things of slippery planks that could be taken up, Fenn guessed, to make the marsh impassable.

At first he saw no sign of any dwelling places. Then as they got deeper and deeper into the marsh he saw there were huts of mud and wattle under the trees of the larger hammocks. Men and women watched the strangers pass and naked children splashed out through the mud to shout at them.

They came onto dry ground again, on a long narrow island close under the scarp. A man stood waiting for them. There were others behind him but Fenn saw only the one, a lean dark laughing man who looked all fire and acid and steel, controlled and shaped by a keen intelligence.

Fenn knew that this must be Lannar. He began to hope again. The man who had brought them in from the desert dismounted and began to speak. While he talked Lannar's gaze moved slowly over the three.

The man finished, pointing to Fenn, *"He* says he knows the secret of the Citadel."

Imperceptibly the muscles of Lannar's face tightened until the lines of it were hard as iron. He looked up at Fenn, a gaunt parched man sitting a jaded horse and waiting now with a strange sort of patience.

"Is that true?" asked Lannar.

"It is true."

A muscle began to twitch in Lannar's cheek. "Dismount. I want to talk to you." His gesture included all three. He turned away toward a large hut, first giving a rapid order or two that Fenn could not hear.

FENN and the others got stiffly down and followed him. The men who had been with Lannar stared at them with a mixture of hostility and wolfish eagerness as they went with the three into Lannar's house.

The shadowy interior was furnished with a haphazard richness. Bright silks, rugs and furs and bits of ornate furniture and dishes of crystal and gold—the loot of the caravans that went between the Numi cities, consorting oddly with the mud walls and floor of beaten earth.

Women came from somewhere in the back, bringing bread and dried meat, water and wine. Fenn and the others ate and drank voraciously. The portions seemed very small.

"You can have more later," Lannar said. "Too much now will make you sick." He leaned forward, his wiry body poised and unrelaxed in a gilded chair. "Now! What is this about the Citadel?"

Fenn told him, speaking without haste. Lannar listened. His eyes glowed with a still hot light. The men in the shadows listened too. Fenn could hear their breathing, tense and short. From time to time Arika spoke and Malech. At last the scroll was spread out at Lannar's feet, showing the island that was lost in the Great Dark.

"There is the Citadel," Fenn said and was silent.

Lannar voiced a harsh sigh. He rose and began to move back and forth, a catlike man suddenly drunk with hope but suspicious none the less, too old and hard to take anything for granted.

Abruptly he took Fenn's head by the hair and bent it back, studying his face with those hot shrewd eyes that saw everything.

"You tell the truth," said Lannar. "But perhaps it is a truth these Numi spawn have put into your head, so that you believe it."

"It is the truth," said Fenn steadily.

"Memories – *dreams!*" said Lannar, and let him go. "You cannot prove these things. There is no bone and flesh in them for a man to get his hands on."

Arika said, "I can open his mind again. Then you can hear him speaking of the past he knows."

He glanced at her half contemptuously. "I know the tricks of the Numi, the things they can do with a man's mind. I would hear words but they would not prove themselves."

Malech asked quietly, "What have we to gain by such a deception?"

"I don't know. I cannot see a gain now but there may be one that is hidden from me." He faced the half-blood, saying with a vicious softness, "I learned so long ago, with so much blood and pain, never to trust a Numi!"

"Numi!" whispered Malech. *"Numi!"* He got up. He was a big man. He towered over Lannar. His eyes blazed with such a passion of fury that it seemed he would take the smaller man between his hands and tear him to bits. He laughed.

"Numi. That's funny, Lannar. You don't know the humor of it. All my life I have lived with that joke. The Numi spit upon me because I'm human and the humans want to kill me because I'm Numi."

He glanced at Arika with a flash of sheer hatred that startled Fenn. "My sister is more fortunate. She *looks* human." He turned again to Lannar, who had not moved or even raised his hands. Malech seemed to sense contempt in that very lack of fear. He laughed again, a short harsh ugly sound.

"If I stood over you, full-furred and bearded and wearing the trappings of a Numi, it would be different, Lannar. Oh, yes! But I am naked and shorn and therefore nothing." He sat down again abruptly, hunched sullenly over his knees. "Try your courage on RhamSin, Lannar. See if you can face *him* down!"

Lannar said, "RhamSin?" From the tone of his voice it was obvious that he held that name in great respect. Fenn rose.

"Yes," he said. "RhamSin. I have told you all the story, and it's a true one. RhamSin will prove it to you. He has followed me from the city to get the secret back."

He paused to let that sink in. And Lannar said to himself, "He would not do that for any ordinary captive nor for any slave."

He began to pace again, more slowly. Fenn moved to stand before him. "Give us the things we need, Lannar, and we'll go on alone."

"No," said Lannar. He was silent for a time, looking up into Fenn's gaunt face, his gaze narrowed and withdrawn. Then he murmured, "He has the stamp of the deserts on him, the same as I." He laughed. "No, Fenn—we'll go together. After all I gamble my life against every caravan I plunder—and even the chance of finding the Citadel is worth the risk. There are others here who will think so too."

Arika leaped up. She looked at Lannar but it seemed she could not speak. Her eyes were very bright and Fenn saw that there were tears in them. She turned suddenly and put her arms around him.

"The gods are with you, Fenn," she whispered.

He found that he had caught her to him almost without knowing it. Over her shoulder he said fiercely to Lannar, "We will find it!"

From outside came the heavy splashing of a horse through mud and water and a man's voice crying, "Lannar! *Lannar!* The Numi come!"

Chapter VII

THE GREAT DARK

THE harsh braying of horns spread the alarm across the swamp. Two or three more riders came in from the desert, the last of the patrols. The bridges were taken up. From among the trees of the island Fenn watched the company of the Numi come down to the edge of the green water and stop. Lannar laughed with savage humor.

"They have done this for generations, trying to wipe us out. But they can't pass the swamp." He pointed among the hammocks. "See how our bowmen are placed? Even if, by treachery or miracle, the Numi were able to come in our arrows would kill them on the path. So they come and threaten us and offer bribes and go away again when their food runs out."

His brows drew down. "All in the black and silver of the temple, eh? It seems you were not lying, Fenn!"

He turned aside, talking with rapid urgency to his chieftains. Fenn remained, watching the Numi. They were too far away to distinguish details. But there was one commanding figure robed in black and riding a black horse, and Fenn shivered.

Arika was close beside him. Her face was worried.

A captain of the Numi began to speak, using a trumpet of bark that magnified his voice. In the name of RhamSin, he offered pardon, power, and reward for the return of a runaway slave who had murdered a priest.

There was no answer from the marsh. He repeated the offer three times and still there was no answer.

The distant figure that was RhamSin reached out and took the speaking tube.

The voice of RhamSin spoke, carrying clear across the silent marsh.

"Fenway! There is no escape from me. I brought forth your mind and it belongs to me. When the time comes I will call—and you will obey!"

That voice seared into Fenn's brain like fire. He had heard it before, commanding, torturing. He had heard it and obeyed.

RhamSin wheeled his horse and galloped away and his men turned to follow.

Fear rose up and caught Fenn by the throat. He tried to shout defiance after the Numi priest but the words would not come. The hot Sun burned him but he was cold and his face was damp with a clammy sweat.

"He lies, Fenn. He lies!" cried Arika but Fenn shook his head.

He muttered, "I am not sure that RhamSin lies."

He turned to Lannar and his eyes had a strange look. "How long will it take to be ready?"

"My men are already gathering horses and supplies." Lannar gave him a sidelong glance that seemed to penetrate him like a sword-thrust but he did not mention RhamSin's words. He nodded toward the retreating Numi.

"They have drawn off so that we may feel free to go where we will. But they will watch and follow. However, we have a back door—a way up the scarp, hacked out long ago in case of need. The Numi will have to go many miles around to get up onto the plateau, so we'll have that much start of them."

He smiled, a nervous, vulpine baring of the teeth and Fenn knew that Lannar, too, was eager to be moving.

"I can't spare many men," he said. "But a light force moves faster and is easier to feed. But in the end we'll need help. The Numi are twice our number and better armed. So I have ordered messengers to go among the other outlaw tribes, asking them to follow."

He paused, and added, "This is all madness, Fenn. We can't live long in the Great Dark without warmth or sight of the Sun. But the Numi will be on their own ground. Even though RhamSin's generation may never have seen the homeland, it is the place that bred them as they are."

He shrugged. "Well, we shall see what madmen can do! And now you had better sleep while you can."

In Lannar's house Fenn slept—a nervous slumber plagued with ugly dreams. He was glad when the time came to mount and go. Malech was of the party. No one had suggested otherwise. But he rode a little apart with a proud sullen look, speaking to no one, and Fenn saw that Lannar kept a close eye upon him.

They scrambled up the steep trail to the plateau, twenty men armed with sword and bow and axe, and from every island in the swamp the eyes of men and women watched in fear and hope and wonder.

At the crest of the scarp, Fenn looked back across the vast emptiness of the desert, a wind-torn desolation under a copper sky. He had survived it and now it seemed familiar to him. He felt almost a sadness at leaving it to go into the trackless dark that was forbidden to humankind.

He saw the dusty plume that marked the march of the Numi following the scarp, knew that they had already begun the chase.

Ahead, the plateau stretched to the short horizon. The rusty clouds seemed lower here, scudding close over the earth. Stiff grasses bent before the wind. They had climbed a long way up from the desert and it seemed to Fenn that the wind had an edge to it, a memory of cold.

They formed their ranks for the long trail, twenty men and forty horses, heading outward toward the Shadow and the Great Dark.

It was a strange and timeless journey. For some distance the way was known to Lannar. There was game on the plateau and good forage at certain times of the year and the men of the marshes made use of both. But they were soon beyond those limits, plodding across an endless dreary upland of tumbled hills. The shadows grew longer and the Sun sank lower and lower at their backs and the teeth of the whistling wind grew sharper.

The country was too rough to let them see far along their backtrail. But they would spot from time to time the distant smoke of cooking fires and Fenn thought that they drew always closer.

The desert horses were small but tough and enduring and more used to short rations and hard work than the Numi beasts. Fenn loved the rough ill-tempered little brutes and that gave them this one advantage over the Numi.

"Wait though," said Lannar. "Wait until we are all on foot."

The wind boomed ever stronger and colder and there were bursting storms of rain and then, at one sleep period, Fenn roused to find the whole earth mantled with a chill whiteness. From that time on the men grew more morose and silent and he knew that they were afraid.

He was beginning to be afraid himself.

ARIKA clung close to him. She seemed very strong for her slight body, riding as long as the men and never complaining. When they slept, huddled together around the fires, it seemed natural that she should be near Fenn. They did not talk much—no one did. They rode and ate their meagre rations and slept and were too weary for anything else.

Malech kept always apart. He seemed to have taken a dislike even to his sister, who was tolerated if not welcomed by the humans. His beard had grown and his hair was longer. He was wrapped in fur and leather like the others and with his body covered it was impossible to tell him now from a true Numi. He did not seem to need the warmth of the fire and he slept alone with an air of contemptuous strength.

And as Malech grew more like a Numi the tribesmen's distrust and hatred of him deepened. But Malech's strength and unhuman endurance helped enormously in the tight places of the trail. That held their aversion to him in check.

One of the horses died. They flayed him and dried the meat.

"They will all die," said Lannar grimly. "They will give us hides and food for the rest of our journey." He was a desert man and did not like to watch the death of horses.

The Sun became a red ember on the horizon behind them. They went down into a valley filled with snow and darkness and when they reached the other side the Sun was gone beyond the higher hills. Arika whispered, "This is what men call the Shadow."

There was still light in the sky. The land began to slope gradually downward, flattening out. Here there were no trees, nor even the stunted scrub that had grown to the edge of the Shadow. The wind-swept rocks were covered with wrinkled lichens and the frozen earth was always white.

One by one the horses died. The frozen meat was hidden by the way so that there should be food for the return march—if there was to be one. The men suffered from the cold. They were used to the dry heat of the deserts. Three of them sickened and died and one was killed by a fall.

The Shadow deepened imperceptibly into night. The rolling rusty clouds of the dayside had become the grayer clouds of storm and fog. The men toiled through dimming mist and falling snow that turned at last to utter darkness.

Lannar turned a lined and haggard face to Fenn. "Madmen!" he muttered. And that was all.

They passed through the belt of storm. There came a time when the lower air was clear and a shifting wind began to tear away the clouds from the sky.

The pace of the men slowed, then halted altogether. They watched, caught in a stasis of awe and fear too deep for utterance. Fenn saw that there was a pallid eerie radiance somewhere behind the driving clouds. Arika's hand crept into his and clung there. But Malech stood apart, his head lifted, his shining eyes fixed upon the sky.

A rift, a great ragged valley sown with stars. It widened, and the clouds were swept away, and the sky crashed down upon the waiting men, children of eternal day who had never seen the night.

They stared into the black depths of space, burning with a million points of icy fire. And the demoniac face of the Moon stared back at them, pocked with great shadows, immense and leering, with a look of death upon it.

Someone voiced a thin, wavering scream. A man turned and began to run along the backtrail, floundering, falling, clawing his way back toward the light he had left forever.

Panic took hold of the men. Some of them fell down and covered their heads. Some stood still, their hands plucking at sword and axe, all sense gone out of them. And Malech laughed. He leaped up on a hummock of ice, standing tall above them in the cold night so that his head seemed crowned with blazing stars, "What are you afraid of? You fools! It's the moon and stars. Your fathers knew them and they were not afraid!"

The scorn and the strength that were in him roused the anger of the men, giving their fear an outlet. They rushed toward him and Malech would have died there in the midst of his laughter if Fenn and Lannar together had not turned them back.

"It's true!" Fenn cried. "I have seen them. I have seen the night as it was before the Destruction. There is nothing to fear."

But he was as terrified as they.

Fenn and Lannar and the bearded Malech, who had shed every trace of humanity, beat the men into line again and got them moving, fifteen of the twenty who had started, alone in the Great Dark. Tiny motes of life, creeping painfully across the dead white desolation under the savage stars. The cold Moon watched them and something of its light of madness came into their eyes and did not go away.

Fifteen—twelve of these lived to see the riven ice of the ocean, a glittering chaos flung out across the world. Malech looked toward the east, where the Moon was rising.

Fenn heard him say, "From beyond the ocean, from the heartland of the Great Dark—that is where we came from, the New Men who conquered the earth!"

Following the tattered map they turned northward along the coast. They were scarecrows now, half starved, half frozen, forgetting that they had ever lived another life under a warm Sun—almost forgetting why they had left that life behind them.

Nine of them lived to see an island between two frozen rivers near the frozen sea and on that island the skeletal towers of a city buried in the ice.

Nine of them lived to see New York.

CHAPTER VIII

74

The Citadel of Lost Ages

FENN stood alone with Arika on the high cliff above the river. The others waited at a distance and their waiting was a cruel thing. Their faces made him feel afraid.

Then he forgot them. He looked out across the white river, across white snow and reaches of gleaming ice to the island city lying silent under the stars and the black sky.

There was no light in that city now but the cold shining of the Moon. No voice spoke there but the voice of the wind. Yet even in death the grandeur was not gone from it. The shattered towers stood up proudly from the ice that shrouded them, the massive bulk and size were not lessened. New York was not a city. It was a dream of titans and the destruction of half a world had not effaced it.

A feeling of pride and sorrow came over Fenn, mixed with a despair so deep that he could not bear it. Memories crowded in on him, fleeting pictures of another time, half seen but poignant with regret and longing.

He whispered, "Once it lived!" And the tears ran down his cheeks and froze in glittering drops.

Arika said, "Remember, Fenn. Remember those days when the city lived. Remember this place and the building of the Citadel."

Her face came before him, pale in its dark frame of fur. Her eyes were huge, filled with the frosty moonlight, compelling, inescapable.

"Here you can remember, Fenn-way. Here is your past. Look at the city. *Remember!*"

Her eyes probed deep into his brain and her voice spoke, ringing down dark hidden corridors. Fenn looked past her at the city. His face changed slowly. He was no longer Fenn. He was another man, seeing another world.

He had come to see the Citadel. Everyone came. It was the ninth wonder, the greatest work of mankind. It drew them with an ugly fascination. It was the symbol of death but a death that would not come in their time and so they could find in it excitement and a gratifying pride.

There were lights on the Palisades. There were crowds, children shouting in the summer night, vendors, music. Across the Hudson loomed the immense and blazing bulk of New York, thrusting giant shoulders against the sky.

He began to walk. And as he walked he thought he saw also a phantom landscape, a place of ice and desolation, with the wreck of a city lifting broken girders through the snow.

He had come to see the Citadel. Floodlights, many people, many voices, guards in uniform, a man talking through a loudspeaker.

"Sunk a half mile deep in solid rock—area larger than the Empire State Building—lined and reinforced with steel—earthquake-proof, floodproof—heat and air supplied by sealed atomic generators with an efficiency period of five thousand years…"

There wasn't much to see on the surface. Only the great uplifted valve of the door, a core of rustproof alloy many feet thick that fitted into a seat of similar metal sunk into the rock.

The voice of the loudspeaker talked on, explaining that valve, the compressed-air mechanism that would outwear time, the system of levers that would open the door again after it was sealed—after the Destruction.

A system that needed no tool but the human hand and the intelligence to use it. An intelligence capable of operating that door would be on a level high enough to profit by the things that were behind it.

The crowd moved on toward the entrance to go down into the Citadel. He moved with them. The doorway was before him. But he could not reach it. There was a barrier between him and the door, something cold and hard and shining.

He thought he must have fainted then. It was all very strange. He heard the sound of axes and sometimes everything was dark and unsteady and sometimes there were glimpses of things flowing like smoke across his vision. He was frightened. He thought he must be very ill.

Voices—shouting, laughing, sobbing, praying. The voices of crazy men. The axes and the chopping sounds had stopped.

Another voice, saying clearly, "Fenn-way, open the door!"

He could see it, then. It was closed. It had never been closed before. The round metal gleamed at the bottom of a ragged pit, hacked out of ice.

Ice? But it was summer!

He slid down into the pit. The levers were countersunk, sealed against freezing. But they were frozen. He put all his strength into it and one by one they moved, stiff, protesting. He heard the shrill hissing of compressed air...

The great valve swung slowly upward.

He saw light in the opening below it. Warm air touched his face. And then the world blanked out.

When his mind cleared again he found himself lying on a metal floor. Someone had taken off his furs. It was warm, blessedly warm – almost hot, after the gelid cold. Above him he could see a web of girders mighty enough to hold a mountain. There was light.

Arika bent over him. Her eyes shone with a feral joy. "You've done it, Fenn," she whispered. "We're in the Citadel!"

His heart began to pound. He sat up, remembering that he had dreamed. Lannar was standing near him. He had been weeping, the hard man of the desert.

"I would have killed you," he said. "If you had failed I would have broken you in my hands."

HE reached out to Fenn and Fenn nodded. "I knew that." He took Lannar's hand and rose and the men crowded around him. They blazed now. They knew what they had done and it was a great thing. They were proud. But they looked at Fenn with an awe that was close to veneration.

Lannar said, "I have set guards at the door. The stair that leads down is narrow, and if the Numi come, they must do it one at a time." He frowned uneasily. "Is there no other entrance?"

"None."

"I don't like a place with only one door," said Lannar.

Fenn laughed. "We have the Citadel. Let us not worry about doors!" He caught Arika to him. He was wild with elation. He looked at the long still corridors that rayed away from the central place where they stood. He thought of the many levels below this one, and of all the knowledge and the strength that waited there, to build the world again. Tears stung his own eyes, and there was no room in him now for fear.

He started to walk, and the others came with him. Like men in a dream they went through the silent halls of the Citadel that had waited twelve hundred years for their coming.

Twelve hundred years ago they had sealed this place, those men of the past who had known they were doomed. This was their gift—their last great offering to the future.

Fenn's mind wavered uncertainly between that time and this. Sometimes he was Fenn-way, going with a guided group through the myriad rooms. Sometimes he was Fenn, holding a half-Numi girl in the hollow of his arm, walking with the naked riders of the desert. Sometimes he understood fully all that he saw and again only native intelligence enabled him to guess at the nature and uses of the complex things about him.

But whether he was Fenn or Fenn-way the sense of awe did not leave him. It grew and deepened with every step he took. And with the awe came pride—not for himself but for the blood that was in him, and Lannar and every son of man. He felt the heavy obligation they owed to those long-dead builders of the Citadel. He felt the challenge that was inherent in their gift.

Knowledge is a two-edged sword, they seemed to say. *We gave ourselves deep wounds. How will you use knowledge, you men of the future? To build or to destroy?*

They had done their work well, the builders of the Citadel. There were books, countless microfilm volumes stored in countless rooms. There were objects, from the first crude axe of stone to a tiny complex model of a cyclotron. There were a million working models of every conceivable type of machine. There were films.

Whole levels had been devoted to chemistry and physics, to engineering and agriculture, to medicine, to every science man had learned to help him live. The art and the music and the thought of a world were stored there too and the records of man's history and his hopes and dreams and follies. Only one thing had been left out.

There were no weapons.

Thinking of the Numi they searched for weapons, for strong implements of war to use against RhamSin and the conquerors they would have to fight after him. And there was nothing.

Frowning, groping for memory, Fenn said slowly, "I think—they said that in all the Citadel there would be no instrument of death."

Lannar's hand tightened on his bow. He laughed, a bitter sound. "That was noble. But they reckoned without the Numi!"

A shadow of dread began to grow in all their minds. Fenn saw how carefully the incredible multitudes of books and models and diagrams had been arranged so that one could grasp the simple things first and use them as steps to climb on. Some knowledge still lived in the world. If nothing had survived but man's own vigor and intelligence the treasures of the Citadel could still have been used, so magnificently had every step been planned.

They did not see more than a hundredth part of that colossal monument to the faith and courage of man. Their own faith and courage had brought them half across a world to find it. They were tired and they had an enemy at their backs. Dazed, stricken with awe and wonder, they returned to the central hall.

The guards at the stairway had seen nothing.

"They will come," said Malech. He walked over to a globe of the world as tall as two men that occupied the center of the hall. Idly he set it spinning, watching the play of light and shadow on the countries and the seas. He had shed his wrappings and Fenn saw that the light down on his body had grown thicker. It was as though the intense cold had brought out the last of the latent Numi characteristics in Malech.

Fenn went to him. He asked a question he had asked before. "Malech—what are the Numi?"

Malech's large hand stopped the globe from spinning. His fingers rested on a land that had once been called Europe.

"Here," he said. "When the Earth's spinning slowed, all this side of it turned its face forever away from the Sun and was trapped in the Great Dark. The air here did not freeze, for there was still warmth from Earth's heart. But all else here froze and died.

"All except a very few men and women—a few strong enough

to survive. These few survivors gathered together and found ways to live. They adapted themselves to the dark and cold, even growing furred against it and their minds sharpened by necessity."

Malech smiled and spun the globe again. "They were the New Men—the Numi. But they were men still and they remembered the Sun! And they came at last to take their place under it!"

Lannar had come soft-footed up behind them. "So they did," he said. "And where is *your* place, Malech? With the Numi or with us?"

Malech turned slowly. Fenn thought of another time they two had faced each other and now Malech towered over the smaller man, arrogant—and strong. The journey had not told on him too much.

"I made my decision long ago," he said to Lannar.

"Tell me, Malech."

But the tall man laughed and did not answer. He stood there looking down at Lannar and the globe spun round and round behind him. The hand of the desert man dropped to his sword.

Fenn had gripped his own blade. And then there came the swift sharp twang of a bowstring, and a cry and a man pitched head first down the stairs.

He was a Numi, wearing the black and silver of RhamSin.

CHAPTER IX

THE COURAGE OF FENN

ANOTHER soldier of the temple died on the stairway, and a third retreated with an arrow through his thigh. Then there was silence. Fenn sprang to the foot of the narrow well.

"Come down!" he shouted. He cursed the Numi and bade them come and die. Above in the outer darkness, the voice of RhamSin spoke.

"When it is time we'll come!" He laughed. "What will you do with the Citadel now that you have it?"

"Keep it for mankind!" cried Fenn defiantly, and again RhamSin laughed.

"Mankind," he said, "is a long way off."

He seemed to withdraw and Fenn heard the Numi making camp in a circle around the doorway.

Lannar plucked with hard fingers at his bowstring, making it thrum like the string of a harp. He looked angrily around the great hall, including by inference the whole Citadel.

"In all this place, not a weapon. Nothing!" He had counted on the strength of the Citadel. Fenn realized that they all had.

Lannar continued bleakly, "They can't get in, we can't get out. They have food and snow to make water. We have a little food. They're cold and we're warm and the toughest hide will hold out the longest. I only hope the tribesmen don't linger on the way."

"If," said Fenn, "they had faith enough to come at all."

He turned from the mocking stair, desperately searching his mind and the fragments of memory for something, anything, that could be used to help them. And he saw something huddled on the floor near the great globe of the world.

It was Arika.

She stirred in his arms as he lifted her and whispered, "Malech. I tried to stop him." There was a reddening welt on her temple where an iron fist had struck her.

Savagely angry Fenn looked around at the knot of men by the stair, at the huge empty hall.

Malech had disappeared.

A twang and hiss from somewhere up above and the man next to Lannar fell with an arrow through his body. Fenn thought that Lannar would have died then except that he was sheltered by the stair.

Malech's voice cried, "Clear the stair, you human dogs! Stand away!"

The men scattered then, wildly, taking cover where they could behind the pillars that upheld the girders of the roof, and as they went a second shaft took one tribesman through the leg. A cat-squall of sheer animal rage came from Lannar and Fenn dragged the still-dazed Arika close under the bulge of the globe.

He unslung his bow and set an arrow to the string and then he peered into the cold upper light of the hall, following the sound of Malech's voice.

Some distance from the narrow well of the stair, a steel ladder climbed the wall to a small blind gallery set high among the sockets of the girders. Fenn guessed that behind that gallery was the chamber of the valve mechanism. The gallery itself was little more than a platform but it was large enough for Malech.

He glimpsed the dark bulk of Malech's body, half hidden in the shadows of the niche. He raised his bow, then let it drop. He could not hope to hit him at that angle.

He called to Lannar, and Lannar and his men answered with a flight of arrows that rattled against the corners and the railing of the gallery.

Malech shouted, "Shoot away!"

He sounded as though he were enjoying himself. He had everything on his side, the light, the angle, the elevation. He covered the whole area around the stairway. He could keep it clear so that the next time the Numi could come down without too much interference.

He said as much, and Lannar cursed him for a traitor.

Malech answered, "I was born to be one. The only choice I had was to betray—my mother or my father." He laughed. "Arika decided for the mother's blood and cast her lot with you humans. She told me on the trail and I knew it was because she loves Fenn.

"So, since she had ruined our plans, I too made my choice on the trail. I knew which blood was strongest in *me*. I left a message, scrawled in charcoal on a strip of hide. RhamSin was sure to find it. Let the humans do the work, I told him. What matter? They are weak, and they will be weaker. I promised him the Citadel."

"What was your price?" asked Lannar bitterly. "What was the price of the human world?"

"To let it be forgotten that my blood is tainted! To be accepted for what I am—a Numi!"

Again his humming bow sent a shaft through the breast of a man who exposed himself to shoot.

FENN reached up and set the world globe to whirling. Arika caught his arm but he flung her hand aside. He went low and fast, belly down, keeping the globe between him and the gallery.

Malech called his name. "Will you die now, Fenn-way? *Fenn-way!* All that talk about time and the past and how the Citadel belonged to men. Listen to me, man without a memory! Do you know who found the Citadel? Not men, who had lost it! No. The Numi found it. Numi wisdom, Numi science! You were only the little tool in the hands of RhamSin."

He paused. Fenn had gained the far wall. He crouched behind a pillar, measuring the distance to the next. Malech said, "Don't bother, Fenn. Come here, where you want to be. I won't harm you."

Fenn did not move. Lannar shouted, *"Don't!"*

"Why not?" asked Malech. "It's his only chance. I will have killed him by the third pillar, if he works his way around."

Under the spinning globe Arika crouched and looked at Fenn with eyes that hurt him, full of fear and sorrow and none of it for herself.

Fenn stepped out from behind the pillar. He began to walk toward the gallery, across the wide still hall. He held his bow slack, the arrow nocked point down. Malech kept back in the angle and the shadows. He did not show himself.

He talked. "You told me once that you wanted to remember. Very well, you shall. Why do you stop, Fenn? Are you afraid to remember?"

Sweat glistened on Fenn's drawn face, on his naked breast. The muscles of his arms stood out like ropes.

"Or," asked Malech softly, "are you afraid to have the others know the truth? They're watching you, their great god Fenn-way, who led them to the Citadel. Don't you want them to know the truth about you, about humanity?"

Fenn started on again. He said, "I am not afraid." And it was a lie.

"Then I'll tell you the real story of the finding of the Citadel. You had lost it, you humans, and it would have been lost forever if it had not been for RhamSin. He took a rebel tribesman off the desert—another such as Lannar there, captured in a raid—and used his science on him, so carefully, so patiently, making the little mind of the captive a mirror of the past."

He laughed softly. "Are you faltering again? You don't like to hear this, do you? You're so proud of your achievement!"

The bowstring burned Fenn's fingers. His heart was pounding. Somewhere in him was a sickness that grew and grew. He went on toward the gallery. Malech's voice continued relentlessly, like the biting of salt in a raw wound.

"Arika knew. She watched. She watched RhamSin blot out the memories of this tribesman's own life, closing the channels of his own remembrances. That opened the way. RhamSin probed back then into memories that were *not* the tribesman's own—the memories of his fathers who had lived before him, ancestral memories, the inherited books of knowledge we do not know we possess but which are there, buried deep in the secret parts of the brain.

"Arika waited. And just before this raw sun-bitten rat of the deserts, under the power of RhamSin's mind, was about to speak with the voice of his long-dead ancestors, telling the secrets of the Citadel, she stole him away from the temple. And why? You wondered about that, Fenn. I will tell you. *So that the Numi powers that she and I possess might gain that secret for ourselves to sell to the highest bidder!*"

Fenn had stopped entirely. He stared up at Malech. Malech's bow was ready with an arrow aimed at his heart and his own arrow was on the string. But Fenn was not concerned with killing in this moment. His mind was lost in a dark turmoil.

It seemed that he could remember dimly the agony of that probing into his mind. RhamSin's voice, forbidding, commanding, opening hidden doors…

Ancestral memory—the Fenn-way of the past had known that term. There was a word to go with it—hypnosis.

Malech cried, "Look at your hero, you humans! We were only slaves and half-breeds, my sister and I—but he was a tool in our hands! Now tell me who has the best right to the Citadel?"

A cold bleak anger took possession of Fenn. It drove away all thought and emotion, all concern with himself. He began to raise his bow.

"It's too late, Fenn," said Malech, laughing. His own shaft pointed unwaveringly at Fenn's heart, ready to fly. "Too late—your masters are already here!"

IT was true. From the corner of his eye Fenn saw the Numi soldiers coming one by one, swiftly down the narrow stair. Lannar and what men he had left had fallen back. Their arrows killed a few but they could not stop the Numi rush. Their only hope had been to hold the stair and Malech had prevented that.

Malech!

Fenn's eyes glittered with a hard malevolence. He dropped to one knee to let fly his arrow, knowing that Malech would instantly shoot.

He expected instant death. But in that second a black shaft suddenly stood out from Malech's breast. The bow of the half breed fell from his hands unused. He stood for a moment with the long arrow in him, staring over Fenn's head with a look of shocked incredulity.

Fenn heard the voice of RhamSin speak to Malech. "The man's mind can still be useful to me. And *your* usefulness is done."

MALECH went down on his knees. And Fenn laughed.

Two long strides took him to the ladder. He went up it with a bound and crouched behind the railing. Malech looked at him, still with that hurt unbelief.

He was quite dead. Fenn began to shoot into the ranks of the Numi around the stair.

He shouted, "Lannar! Up here!"

They made a bolt for it, Lannar and his men and Arika. From his vantage point Fenn gave them what cover he could. Lannar, Arika, and three men made it. Lannar and two others were wounded.

They were crowded on the gallery. Fenn shoved the body of Malech down the ladder and there was room enough for them to crouch together behind the railing.

"What use?" asked Lannar grimly. "We have shot away our arrows.

"Because," Fenn said with a queer desperate hope in his voice, "there may still be a weapon here! One that I can't quite remember."

He was looking down into the hall at the Numi who were gathering there, at the globe of cold light that hung above them.

Cold light? What was it that he could not remember? He looked at the globe and the web of girders close above his head and his brows knit in a cruel effort.

The last of the Numi came down the stairs. RhamSin said, "Will you come down peaceably or must we come up after you?"

"Come if you will," snarled Lannar. "We still have our swords."

Fenn turned to Arika. His fingers bit into her flesh. He whispered, "Help me to remember! The Citadel—the guide that took us through—something he said…"

RhamSin's voice rang in her ears like the voice of doom. "I told you once that I would call you and you would come. I call you now. And I warn you—your usefulness will not save your life if you anger me too far."

Arika said, "Don't listen, Fenn! Remember!"

Her eyes burned deep into his. The voice of RhamSin called and Fenn felt a terrible compulsion to obey. But there was an iron fury in him and he would not yield.

The Citadel, the crowd, the guide, talking— *Cold light. Radioactive dust suspended in an inert liquid. Deadly compound, harnessed for the peaceful use of man. Bulbs of plastic that screened out harmful rays—absolutely safe—will give light almost forever.—*

"Stay here," said Fenn to the others very softly. "Keep down. Don't move or lean out to look!"

He leaped up and caught the girder overhead, swinging himself upon it. Balancing precariously on that narrow bridge of steel he began to run.

RhamSin shouted.

Arrows began to fly around Fenn—black arrows with barbed tips. But he was a hard mark to hit, running high among the interlacing shadows of the girders. And he had not far to go.

Below him he could see the Numi, their angry faces looking up, tall proud lords of conquest in a citadel of peace. He flung himself down across the girder. Here were bolted the chains that held the globe of radioactive light.

He took his sword, a good keen blade of tempered Numi steel. With every ounce of strength and madness that was in him he struck downward at a single chain.

It parted, helped by the weight of the massive bracket it upheld. And Fenn found it in his heart to laugh a little bitterly. Even in a citadel of peace the ingenious mind of man could find a means of killing!

The globe of light fell with the snapping of the chain. Out of the round bracket that swung now by one edge it fell—down, down, to smash upon the metal floor below.

Fenn hugged the girder. There was a crash and a burst of vicious light, a hissing, snarling explosion, and then…

He thought that even Numi did not deserve to die that way, in such corrosive agony of the body, in such shocked terror of the mind.

He waited until the last one had stopped screaming. He did not look again at the seared scored twisted bodies. He worked his way back along the girder and this time he did not run. He was sick and shaken and full of a sense of guilt.

ARIKA and Lannar helped him back down onto the gallery. They too looked sick and pale from what they had seen on the floor below. "They are all dead," whispered Arika. "But how—"

Fenn said heavily, "The men of the far past built this Citadel to be a light in the darkness, a light of hope and peace and knowledge. And now war and death have come into it. And my hands are red."

"You were forced to do it, Fenn!"

He knew that she was right. And men would be forced to war against the Numi, and the knowledge of the Citadel would free them from that alien yoke. But after that…

He spoke and his whisper was not for those beside him but for men dead twelve hundred years, the men who had bequeathed them this heritage of the ages. "After that," he whispered, "we will learn to build and not destroy. I will redeem my guilt, men of the past."

The Woman from Altair

Startling Stories, July 1951

Chapter I

AHRIAN

WHAT A GREAT DAY it was for everybody, when David came
home from deep space. It was a day that will remain for a long while
on the calendar of the McQuarrie family, marked heavily in red.

We had driven down to the spaceport to meet him—myself, and
Bet, who was David's and my sister, just out of college, and David's
fiancée, a Miss Lewisham. The Miss Lewisham had family but no
money, and David had both, and that was as far as it went. She was
one of these handsome, shallow-eyed babes as perfectly machined as
a chunk of bakelite, and just as human. Bet thought she was terrific.
She had spent hours getting herself up to be as like her as possible,
but it was all in vain. Bet's hair still behaved like hair, and blew.

The spaceport was swarming. Interplanetary flight had long ago
ceased to be a thing of breathless wonder to the populace, but star-
ships were still new and rare, and the men who flew them were still
heroic. Word had gone out that the *Anson McQuarrie* was due in from
somewhere beyond the Pleiades, and there were thousands of people
backed up behind the barricades. I remember that there were flags,
and somebody had prepared a speech.

"Isn't it wonderful!" said Bet, around a lump in her throat. "And
all for David."

"There are some other men on that ship, too," I said.

"Oh, you always have to be so nasty," she snapped. "David's the captain, and the owner, too. And he deserves the reception."

"Uh huh," I said, "and what's more, David himself would be the last to disagree with you."

Officials were opening a way for us, and I shoved Bet along it with the Miss Lewisham, who headed like a homing duck for the TV cameras. At about that moment a feminine voice hailed us, and Bet whirled around, crying out, "Marthe!"

An extremely attractive young woman detached herself from a group of obvious reporters and joined us.

"I'm going to be quite shameless," she announced, "and presume on an old school friendship."

I liked the way she grinned and practically dared me to throw her out of the family circle. I should have done so, but didn't because of that cheeky grin, and that's how Marthe Walters came to be mixed up in this mess. I wished so desperately afterward that I had pushed her face in. But how is one to know?

Bet was offering explanations. "Marthe was a senior when I was a freshman, Rafe. Remember? That was when I was going to be a journalist." She rushed through the introductions, and memory clicked.

"Oh, yes," I said. "You're the Marthe Walters who does those profile sketches for *Public.*"

"It's honest work, but it's a living."

"You've come to the right place. My brother has the devil and all of a profile."

SHE cocked her head on one side and gave me a peculiarly intelligent look. "Yours isn't so bad. And come to think of it, I've never heard of you."

"I'm the forgotten McQuarrie," I said. "The one who didn't go to space."

All this time we were being assisted onward to the place that had been reserved for the family. Bet was burbling, the Miss Lewisham was being statuesque and proud, and this bright-eyed intruder, Marthe, was thinking questions and trying to devise a politic way of asking them.

"You're David's older brother?"

"Ancient."

"And you're a McQuarrie, and you didn't go to space." She shook her head. "That's like being a fish, and refusing to swim."

"It's not Rafe's fault," said Bet, with that touch of womanly pity she could get in her voice sometimes. "How soon will he land, Rafe? I just can't wait!"

I was trying to figure out what color Marthe's eyes were. I got them pegged for blue, and then there was some change in the light or something, and they were green as sea-water.

"Surely," she said, "you didn't wash out."

"No, it was noisier than that. I crashed. It was a light plane, but it came down heavy."

"He was on his way to the spaceport from the Academy," said Bet sadly. "He had his papers and everything, and was going out on his first voyage as a junior officer. The disappointment nearly killed Father, Rafe being the oldest son and everything. But then, he still had David."

"I see," said Marthe. She smiled at me, and this time it wasn't cheeky, but the sort of smile a man would like to see more of. "I'm sorry. I thought that walking stick was pure swank."

"It is," I told her, and laughed. "I think that's what really disgusts the family—I'm healthy as a horse. I only carry the thing to remind them that I'm supposed to be frail."

They were in radio communication with the *Anson McQuarrie*. The reports of position kept coming in, and an amplifier blatted them out. Men ran around looking harried, a million voices chattered, necks craned, the tension built up. The towers of Manhattan glittered mightily in the distance. Marthe and I talked. I think we talked about her.

A great roar went up. Bet screamed in my ear. There was a perfect frenzy of sound for a few moments, and then there was silence, and in it the sky split open like tearing silk. A speck of silver came whistling down the cleft, growing rapidly, becoming a huge graceful creature with tarnished flanks and star-dust on her nose, and pride in every rivet. Oh, she was beautiful, and she settled light as a moonbeam on the landing field that had been cleared of any lesser craft. The *Anson McQuarrie* was home.

I noticed then that Marthe had not been watching the ship at all. She was watching me.

"You," she said, "are a rather puzzling person."

"Does that bother you?"

"I don't like a book that has the whole story on the first page."

"Good," I said. "Then you won't like David. Come along. And oh, yes, any time you want to catch up on your reading—"

"There he is!" shrieked Bet. "There's David!"

The barricades were keeping back the crowds, and officials were forming a second line of defense against the mob of reporters. We, the family, were allowed to be first with our greetings. The under-hatch had opened in that vast keel, the platform was run out, and a tall figure in absolutely impeccable uniform had emerged onto it. Bands played, thousands cheered, the TV cameras rolled, and David lifted his hand and smiled. A handsome beggar, my brother, with all the best points of the McQuarrie stock. I think he was a little annoyed when Bet flung herself up the steps and onto his neck. She mussed his collar badly.

I waved. The Miss Lewisham mounted to the platform, showing her splendid legs. She held out her arms graciously, prepared to grant David the dignified kiss due a hero from his future wife. But David gave her a horrified look as though he had forgotten all about her, and his face turned six different shades of red.

He recovered magnificently. He caught those outstretched hands and shook them warmly, at the same time getting her off to one side so smoothly that she hardly realized it. Before she could say anything, he had spoken, to the world at large, with boyish pride.

"I have seen," he said, "many strange and precious things on the worlds of other stars. And I have brought back with me the most wonderful of them all. I want you to welcome her to Earth."

Here he turned to someone who had been waiting inside the hatch, and handed her out.

I DON'T think that any of us, least of all the Miss Lewisham, caught on for a moment. We were too busy, like everybody else, staring at the little creature who was clinging to David's hand.

She seemed incredibly small and fragile to be a grown woman, and yet that is what she was, and no mistake about it. She wore a very quaint drapery of some gossamer stuff that shimmered in the sunlight, and the lovely shape of her beneath it was something to wonder at. Her skin was perfectly white and beautiful, like fine porcelain, and her little face was pointed and fey-looking, with eyebrows that swept up toward her temples like two delicate feathers. Her hair was the color of amethysts. There was a great deal of it, piled high on her head in an intricate coiffure, and the lights in it were marvelous, as though every conceivable shade of that jewel had been melted and spun together and made alive. Her eyes, slanting under those sweeping brows, were the same color, but deeper, a true purple. They looked out in great bewilderment upon this noisy alien world.

"She is from Altair," said David. "Her name is Ahrian. She is my wife."

The reactions to that last simple statement were violent and more than a little confused. Sometime before the shouting died, and while Bet was still staring like an absolute idiot at her unexpected sister-in-law, the Miss Lewisham departed, with every hair still perfectly in place. Where her temper was, I don't know. The reporters stampeded, and no one and nothing could hold them back. The TV men were in transports when David kissed his little bride from Altair. I looked down at Marthe.

"I suppose," I said, "it wouldn't be any good asking you to go away now."

She said it wouldn't be. She was shivering slightly, like a wolf that has found a fat lamb asleep under its nose. "A woman from Altair," she whispered. "This isn't a story, it's a sensation."

"It's certainly a surprise for the family!"

"Poor little thing, she looks scared to death. Whatever you feel, don't take it out on her." Marthe glanced up at me, as though a sudden thought had occurred to her. "By the way," she asked, "is your brother quite right in the head?"

"I'm beginning to wonder," I said.

Up on the platform, the focus of the excitement, the new Mrs. David McQuarrie trembled against her husband and stared with those purple enigmatic eyes at the alien hosts of a world that was not her own.

CHAPTER II

STRANGER ON EARTH

GRIMLY WE SET OFF on the ride home. I had managed to get Bet on one side and threaten her with bodily injury if she didn't keep her mouth shut. David himself, what with the exultation of homecoming and the sensation he had created with his dramatic announcement of marriage, was flying too high to notice any of us too much. He held Ahrian in the circle of his arm as if she had been a child, and talked to her, and soothed her, and pointed out this and that interesting thing along the road.

As she looked at the houses and trees, the hills and valleys, the sun and the sky, I couldn't help being sorry for her. In my younger days I had gone, as supercargo in my father's ships, to Venus and Mars and beyond the Belt to Jupiter. I knew what it was like to walk on alien soil. And she was so far away from home that even her familiar sun was gone.

She glanced at us now and then, with a kind of shy terror. Bet sulked and glowered, but I managed a smile, and Marthe patted Ahrian's hand. David had taught her English. She spoke it well, but with a curious rippling accent that made it sound like a foreign tongue.

Her voice was soft and low and very sweet. She did not talk much. Neither did we.

David barely noticed that we had a stranger with us. I had said vaguely that Marthe was a friend of mine, and he had nodded and forgot her. I was rather glad to have her along. There are times when families should not be alone together.

The McQuarrie place is built on top of a rise. The house is large, and was originally built almost two centuries ago, when old Anson

McQuarrie founded the family fortune with a fleet of ore carriers for the Lunar mines. There are old trees around it, and a thousand acres of land, and it is one of those places that exude from every pore a discreet odor of money.

Ahrian looked at it and said dutifully, "It is very beautiful."

"Not quite the sort of place she's used to," David remarked to us. "But she'll love it."

I wondered if she would.

We all piled out of the car, and Marthe hesitated. She had been so completely absorbed in studying Ahrian that I doubt if she had thought of her own position at all. Now the sight of our rather hulking house seemed to daunt her.

"I think maybe I better go back now," she said. "I've imposed enough, and I've got a lot to go on. I'd like to really interview them both, but this is hardly the time for it."

"Oh, no," I told her emphatically. "You're staying. Bet's got to have somebody to yak to, and it isn't going to be me. You're her old school chum, remember?"

MARTHE took a good look at Bet's furious countenance and muttered, "I have a feeling I'm going to hold this against you, Mr. Mc-Quarrie."

She was so right. Except that I held it against myself, the other way round.

Suddenly Ahrian, who was a little distance up the walk with David, let out a quivering scream. David began to yell angrily for me. I went on to see what was the matter.

"It's only Buck," I said.

"Well, get him out of here. He's frightening Ahrian."

"She might as well get used to him now," I said, and took Buck by the collar. He was a very large dog, and one of the best I ever had. He didn't like Ahrian. I could feel him shiver, and the hair on his back bristled under my hand.

David was going to get ugly about it, and then Ahrian said, "It is that I have not before seen such a creature. It means no harm. Only it is uneasy."

She began to talk to Buck, in her own soft liquid tongue. Gradually his muscles stilled and the hackles flattened and the ears relaxed. His eyes had a puzzled look. Presently he stalked forward and laid his head in her hands.

Ahrian laughed. "You see? We are friends."

I looked at the dog. There was no joy in him. Ahrian took her small white hands from his head. Abruptly he turned and went away, running fast.

Ahrian said softly, "I have very much to learn."

"Just the same," said David, glaring at me, "you be careful with your confounded livestock." He swept Ahrian on up the walk. The door had been opened. David did the inevitable thing. He picked Ahrian up in his arms and bore her with a courtly flourish across the threshold.

"All I've got to say is," Bet snarled, "I hope they can't—I mean, I just couldn't bear it to have a little nephew with lavender hair!"

She stamped on into the house. I took Marthe firmly by the arm. "Bet can fix you up with suitable garments."

"What for?"

"We are having a dinner tonight, in David's honor. Formal, of course. There will be many people."

"How delightful," she said, and groaning, followed Bet.

That dinner may not have been delightful, but it certainly was not dull. The drawing rooms teemed with what Daisy Ashford would have referred to as costly people, all quite ill at ease. Ahrian, sitting at the table in the place that was to have been the Miss Lewisham's, was a little figure fashioned in some Dresden of Fairyland, dressed in a matchless tissue of pale gold and crowned with that incredibly beautiful hair.

The women didn't know how to deal with her, and the men were fascinated, and all in all it was not a successful social occasion. Late in the evening David made her sing. She had a curious stringed instrument from which she drew soft wandering music, and she sang songs of her own world that were sweet and very strange. Some of them didn't have any words. They told of the things that lie hid beyond mountains, and of the secrets oceans know, and of the long, still thoughts of deserts. But they were not the mountains or the deserts or the seas of Earth. Toward the end there came into her eyes two great crystal tears.

Soon after that I noticed that she had disappeared. David was holding the center of the stage with some thrilling recital of events beyond the stars, and it seemed to be up to me to look for her.

I found her at last, standing disconsolate on the steps that led down from the terrace into the garden. There were many shadows in it, and the shrubs rustled in the wind, so that it must have seemed a frightening place to her. There were clouds, I remember, veiling the sky.

She turned and looked at me. "Why did you come to me?"

"I thought perhaps you might be lonely."

"There is David," she answered. "Why might I be lonely?"

I could not see her face, except as a small blurred whiteness in the gloom. "Yes," I said, "you have David. But it's still possible to be sad."

She said, "I will not be sad." I could read nothing in the tone of her voice, either.

"Ahrian, you must try to understand us. We were upset today, because we hadn't expected you, and—well—" I tried, rather lamely, to explain how things had stood. "It wasn't anything personal. You're part of the family now, and we'll do all we can to make you welcome."

"The little one—she is full of anger."

"She's just a kid. Give her time. A month from now she'll be wanting to dye her hair to match yours." I held out my hand. "We have a custom here of clasping hands as a token of friendship. Will you take mine, Ahrian?"

SHE hesitated, a long, long moment. Then she said gravely, as if it were something I must remember, "I do not hate you, Rafe." She put her hand in mine, a fleeting touch as light and chill as the falling of a snowflake. Then she shivered. "It is cold on your world when the darkness comes."

"Is it always warm on yours?" We started toward the house, and looking down at her beside me, I thought I could understand why David had not been able to let her go.

She answered softly, "Yes, it is warm, and the moons are like bright lamps in the sky. The spires and the rooftops glisten, and there are dark leaves that shake out perfume—"

She broke off, too quickly, and said no more.

"You must love David very deeply to have come all this long way home with him."

"Love is indeed a great force," she murmured.

We went inside, and David claimed her again.

For several days I did not see much of Ahrian. I handle the financial end of the McQuarrie business, not because I like it but because I have to do something to justify the money I spend. David had brought back an invaluable cargo, some of it from worlds that, like Ahrian's, had never been touched before. I think we cleared around a million dollars on it, over and above the cost of the voyage.

I was so busy that I hardly had time to see Marthe. Strange, how important it had become to see Marthe, so quickly and without anything being said about it. She had left our house, of course, in high spirits over the inside stuff she had got for her articles. I had said, "When will I see you again?" And she had answered, "Any time." That's how it was—any time we could possibly make it.

One night, when by chance the family were all together at dinner, Ahrian said shyly, "David, I have been thinking—"

Instantly he was all attention. He really did seem to adore her. I will admit that I had a few sneaking suspicions, or perhaps it was only a puzzled wonder, since David so far in his life had had only three loves—star-ships, himself, and the McQuarrie name, in that order. But his manner with Ahrian appeared to show that he had found the fourth.

"In my home," said Ahrian, "I had a small place that was my own, in which I found much pleasure in fashioning little gifts for those I loved. Only a very small place, David—might I have one here?"

David smiled at her and said that she might have anything there was on Earth or the other planets, except the ugly clothes that might be all right for Earthlings but were not for her. Ahrian smiled back, asking, still with that shy hesitance, for some gem stones of small value, and some fine wires of platinum and gold.

"Diamonds," said David. "Emeralds. All you like."

"No. I will have the crystal and the zircon. Uncut, please. I wish to shape them myself."

"With those tiny hands? Very well, darling. I'll have them here tomorrow."

Ahrian thanked him gravely and glanced across at me. "I am learning very quickly, Rafe. I have seen all your horses. They are a wonder to me, so large and beautiful."

"If you like," I said, "I could teach you to ride."

"Perhaps on that very little one?"

I laughed and explained to her why a three-week foal was not suitable for that. David said fiercely that he was not going to have Ahrian trampled to death by one of my lubberly beasts, and forbade anything of the sort.

After dinner I got Bet alone and asked her how she was making out with Ahrian.

"Oh, I suppose it isn't her fault, but she gives me the creeps, Rafe! She goes drifting around the place like a funny little shadow, and sometimes the way she looks at you... I get the feeling she's studying me—way deep inside, I mean. I don't like it—and I don't like her!"

"Well, try to be as nice as you can. The poor little critter must be having a hard enough time of it. Remember we're as alien to her as she is to us."

"She wanted to come," said Bet, without pity. I left her, and went off to keep a date with Marthe....

CHAPTER III

GIFTS OF—LOVE

DAVID FIXED up a wonderful workshop for Ahrian, where she could make pretty trinkets to her heart's content. She would remain there for hours, humming softly to herself, letting no one, not even David, in to see what she was doing. She worked for weeks, and then one evening she came in to dinner with the pleased air of a child who has done a nice thing. I saw that she was carrying some light burden in a fold of her gown.

She was wearing a kind of tiara that went very well with her masses of amethystine hair and her curious little face. It was a delicate thing, exquisitely wrought of mingled wires of platinum and gold woven into a strange design of flowers and set with a flawless crystal that she had cut herself in a way that I had never seen a crystal cut before.

She strewed her small burden glittering on the tablecloth. "See! I have made a gift for everyone. You must wear them, or I shall be so unhappy!"

They were beautiful. For David and me she had made rings—for, as she said, we did not wear jewels as the men of her world did, and so she had had to be content with rings. For Bet there was a necklace, of a sort that no girl could resist if the Devil himself had given it to her.

There was a chorus of astonished comment. David told Ahrian that she could make a fortune for herself if she would make and sell these things to the world. Ahrian shook her head.

"No. These are gifts and must be fashioned with a meaning from the heart. Otherwise I could not make them."

The stones were all most curiously cut.

It was exactly eight days after that giving of gifts that the thing happened.

David was away on some business in the city. Marthe was spending the weekend—Ahrian seemed an odd kind of chaperone, but we thought she would serve—and we had been taking a stroll in a wood that there is north of the house.

All of a sudden we heard the sound of someone screaming.

We started to run back toward the house. A scream has no identity, but somehow I knew this one came from Bet. Marthe got some distance ahead of me, and then she began to scream, too. There were other sounds mixed with the screaming. I made all the speed I could. Where the wood ended, there was a wide stretch of turf, with the house way at the back of it and here and there apple trees that were part of an old orchard.

Bet had got herself up into one of these old thorny veterans. Her clothes were torn and there were dabbles of blood on her face and dress. Her cries had ceased to have any meaning. In a minute she was going to faint.

MY BIG DOG Buck was under the tree. He leaped and sprang, and his teeth flashed like knives in the sunlight, snapping shut no more than a short inch beneath the limb Bet huddled on. He moaned as he leaped, a strange and dreadful sound as though he were being tortured and were pleading for release.

I shouted his name. He turned his head, gave me one pitiful look, and then he went back to trying to kill my sister. I was carrying the heavy blackthorn stick I used when I walked in the country. I hit him with the knob of it. Poor Buck! He was dead in a minute or two, as quick as I could make it, and he never tried to defend himself. I caught Bet as she tumbled out of the apple tree, and Marthe and I between us got her to the house.

Ahrian was there. She gave a little cry of horror and bent her head, and I remember the flash of crystal on her forehead in the dim hall. Servants came and took Bet. Marthe ran off somewhere to be sick, and I called town for David and a doctor.

For a while I was busy with brandy and restoratives. Presently Bet came around, more terrified than hurt. Her scratches had come mostly from climbing into the tree. She said she had been looking for Marthe and me, when suddenly Buck had appeared out of nowhere and, for no reason at all, tried to tear her throat out.

"I never did him any harm," she whimpered. "I like him, and he liked me. He must have gone mad."

I was glad when the doctor came and put her under for a while. Buck was taken away for autopsy. He was not rabid, nor was there a sign of any other disease. I had that stick burned up. I couldn't forget the way Buck had moaned, the way he had looked at me before he died. David had some bitter words to say, and I nearly hit him, which was unfair under the circumstances.

Anyway, the dog was dead, and Bet was all right. In time everybody's nerves calmed down, and even Bet got tired of talking about it. David had a birthday coming up. Ahrian made great preparations, asking us all incessant questions about how things should be done according to our customs, and adding a few of her own.

David liked lavishness, so there was another big dinner and a lot of people. Ahrian had gained confidence, and everybody had had time to gossip themselves out about her by now. It was a much more successful occasion than the first. Even some of the women decided not to hate her.

Marthe and I retired into the library for a little quiet love-making. Between times we discussed getting married. Through the closed doors we heard Ahrian singing for a while, not the longing heartsick things she had sung before, but something gay and wicked. When she stopped, there was only the usual buzz and chatter of people.

Some time went by, I don't know how much. Without any warning a terrible racket arose of horses squealing, and of yelling, and I remember thinking that the barns must be on fire.

I got outside in a hurry. The guests were beginning to pour out onto the veranda and peer curiously into the darkness to see what the trouble was. Among them, I noticed Ahrian with a cloak around her.

The stables and the big open paddocks are some distance from the house. Halfway there I saw Jamieson, my head groom, running toward me.

"It's Miss Bet," he gasped, white-faced and shaking. "Hurry!"

I hurried, but there was a cold, sick feeling in me that told me hurrying was no use.

There was an old brood mare, gentle as a kitten, long past her usefulness and pensioned off. She was Bet's especial pet, and old Hazel would muster up a stiff-legged canter from wherever she was to come and snuffle over her for sugar-lumps.

All the big floodlights were on. There was a confusion of men and horses and noise. Old Hazel was pressed up against the paddock fence, her coat dark with sweat, trembling in every muscle. There was blood on her legs. Bet was dead. In her long white party dress and her silver sandals she had come all the way down there and gone into the paddock, and the old mare had trampled her. It didn't make any sense at all. I kneeled there beside her in the dirt, and the necklace of zircons that Ahrian had given her glittered among the splashes of blood.

The men had got ropes on the mare now, and she began to thrash and scream like a crazy thing. Somebody handed me a gun, and I used it, all the time knowing that the poor old beast had no more killing in her than Buck had had.

It made no kind of sense. But Bet was dead.

It was a fine ending to a gay evening.

You know how it is with a kid sister. Sometimes she's a pest, and sometimes she's ridiculous, and she always talks too much, but even so – And it was such an ugly way to die.

David was going down and shoot every horse in the place. When I stopped him, he turned on me. There was a bad scene. They were my animals. One had tried, and one had succeeded, and that made me practically a murderer. I let it go, because he was hard hit, and so was I. But from then on there was a wall between me and my brother, and the hate he had against me over Bet's death seemed to grow day by day. I couldn't understand why. It seemed almost insane, but whatever shortcomings David had, insanity was not one of them.

We buried Bet, and no one wept more bitterly than Ahrian. She was David's loving comforter, and for the first time I was genuinely glad she was there.

CHAPTER IV

STAR DREAMS

ON THE NIGHT after the funeral I began to dream.

At first the dreams were brief and vague. But they got longer and clearer, until my days became nightmares and my nights an unbearable hell. Sleep became a torture. I dreamed of space.

The McQuarries are spacemen. From old Anson down the sons have flown the ships, and the daughters have married men who could fly ships, and the McQuarrie flag has been carried a long, long way. As far as I know, we never did anything more sinful than to get there first, but the McQuarrie ships have gained and held the richest cream of the trade between the worlds, and now they are breaking the trails between the stars.

I was a McQuarrie, and the oldest son to boot, and I had to go to space. That was a thing as inevitable as sunrise, and as little questioned. I went.

Now I dreamed of space. I was caught in it, quite alone, between the blackness and the blaze, with nothing above or below or around me but the cruel bright eyes of far-off suns to note my fall. I fell, through the millions of silent miles, turning over and over, voiceless, helpless, and when I had done falling the stars looked just the same, and it seemed I had not moved. I knew that I was going to fall forever and never be allowed to die, and at the end of forever the stars would not have changed.

They were ghastly dreams. Opiates only made them worse. I spent whole days riding, until both my horse and I were weary enough to drop, so that I might sleep. It was no good. I tried drinking, and that was no help either.

There was guilt in those dreams. One part of them recurred over and over—myself, knowing about the unending doom that waited for me out there beyond the sky, and running away from it, running like a hunted hare. Everywhere I turned, there was my father with his arms stretched wide, barring the way. His face was turned from me, and my fear lest he should suddenly see me and know the truth was as great in a different way as my fear of space. So I would creep away, but in the end there was no escape, and I was falling, falling down the timeless universe.

I didn't see Marthe. I didn't have the heart to see anybody. I began to think of death. It seemed preferable to a padded cell.

David relented enough to be worried. Ahrian hovered over me sweetly. I didn't tell them anything, of course, except that I was having trouble sleeping.

Then, curiously enough, Ahrian got mixed up in my nightmares. Not Ahrian herself, but her world, the world of Altair she had left for David.

THAT was strange, because she had spoken very little about her world. She had, in fact, refused to talk about it. David had not discussed it either, except from the standpoint of trade. Yet here I was, seeing it in detail, in sudden bright flashes that came without reason in the midst of my horrible plunging through space. I could see every leaf and flower, each single turret of a pale and gleaming city of which I knew the streets as well as I knew my own woods. I saw in detail the quaint shapes of the roof-tops with the carving on them, and the wide plain of some feathery grass, the color of blue smoke, that sloped away toward an opalescent sea. I knew the separate colors of the several moons, and the particular perfume that came on the wind at the sinking of Altair.

This was so extremely odd that I mentioned it to Ahrian, not, of course, telling her that I had had other dreams as well. She gave a little start and said, "How strange!"

I went on to tell her some of the details, and suddenly she laughed and said, "But it is not so very strange, after all. I have told you all those things."

"When?" I said.

"Some few nights ago. You had had a number of drinks, Rafe, and perhaps you do not remember. I talked to you, thinking that it might help you to sleep, and it was of my own world that I talked."

That seemed as good an explanation as any; in fact, the only one. So I let it drop, and after that I dreamed no more of Ahrian's world.

I felt wretched about Marthe, but this wasn't a thing you dragged someone else into, especially someone you cared about. I put her off, and fought, not very gallantly, a fight I knew I was losing. I began to have blank periods during my waking hours. Once I found my horse on the edge of a cliff, with the dirt already sliding from under him. Another time I was looking at the sharp blade of my big pocket knife that had drawn a tentative line of red across my wrist.

I stopped riding. I stopped driving my car. I locked up all my guns and made Jamieson hide the key. I knew I ought to die, but I wasn't quite ready, not quite....

Marthe came one day, unannounced and uninvited. She came into the house and found me, and politely shut the door in everyone's face. Then she came and stood in front of me.

"I want the truth, Rafe. What's gone wrong?"

I said something about not having felt well, assured her I was all right, thanked her for coming, and tried to put her out. She wouldn't be put.

"Look at me, Rafe. Is it because you don't love me?" She made me look at her, and presently she smiled and said, "I didn't think so."

I caught hold of her, then. After a while she whispered, "There's something evil in this house. I felt it when I came in the door. Something wicked!"

"Nonsense," I told her.

She clung to it, though, and cried a little, and swore at me because I had worried her. Then she stepped back and said flatly:

"You look like the devil. What is it, Rafe?"

"I don't quite know." Suddenly, perhaps because of what she had said, I wanted to be out of that house. Irrational? But I wasn't being rational then. "Let's take a walk. Maybe the air will clear my head."

We didn't go far. The last few weeks had worn me down badly, and every crack and jar I had in my frame was plaguing me. By the time we made it to a grassy knoll well away from the house and sat down, Marthe was looking genuinely frightened.

I hadn't meant to tell her anything. I had determined not to tell her. And, of course, I did tell her. I don't know what she made of it, because it wasn't very coherent, the dream part, but she got quite white and flung her arms around me.

"You need a psychiatrist," she said, "and a good doctor."

"I've had a doctor. And a psychiatrist isn't any good unless you're hiding something from yourself. I'm not."

"But there must be some reason for the dreams."

"It isn't any buried guilt. Listen, Marthe, I'll tell you something, and that will make two people in the world who know it. Maybe you won't think much of me after you hear it, but I'd have to tell you sometime and it better be now. That time my plane crashed, on the way to the spaceport. I crashed it myself. Deliberately, intentionally crashed it."

HER eyes widened. Before she could say anything, I rushed on.

"I never wanted to go to space. When I was a little kid, and my father would talk to me about it, I didnt want to go. I liked Earth. I liked dogs and horses and prowling in the woods. Above all, I resented being forced into a set mold that didn't fit me, just because generations of McQuarries had been poured into that mold. My father and I had some bitter words over that, when I was little.

"When I got older I still felt that way, but I'd discovered it wasn't any use to fight. Besides, I liked my father. You know how some men are–pride, family tradition, all that business. Space was his life. It meant more to him to have me be a spaceman than it did to me not to be one. So I went. I didn't like it. I hated it, as a matter of fact. But I kept my mouth shut. Then, coming back from Mars on that first voyage, we lost a man.

"He'd gone outside the hull to repair something, and his magnetic grapples didn't hold, and he drifted off. I saw him through the port, growing smaller and smaller as we left him behind, until he disappeared. You know how fast a spaceship moves at full acceleration? Even by the time we got the boats out it was too late. He's still there. He'll always be there.

"After that, I had a horror of space, the way some people used to have for the sea. It wasn't that I was afraid of getting killed, it was the emptiness, the dark and the cold and the silence, and the *waiting*. I hate being cooped in, and the ship was like an iron coffin. I tried to fight it. I made two more voyages, and I was sick for months after the second one. I didn't tell anybody why. Finally I went up to the Academy to get my ticket, and my father was proud and happy. Blast people's pride and their ideas that their children have to love just what they do! He gave me a berth on his flagship.

"I couldn't tell him the truth, and I couldn't go. I didn't have any right to–to ask men to depend on me and then maybe– So I crashed my plane. If I died, I wanted to do it decently and alone. If I didn't, I figured I'd get smashed up enough so that I couldn't pass a space-physical, and that would be that, with everybody's honor still intact. I guess God was on my side. Anyway, I judged the impact just right. After that, David carried the torch, and my father died happy."

We didn't talk for a while. I sat turning round and round on my finger the ring that Ahrian had given me. Presently Marthe said, "That explains it."

"What?"

"The look I saw in your face when David's ship came in. No regret, no envy. You didn't want to be where he was. But you were as proud of him as Bet was."

"He likes to strut a bit," I said, "but the son-of-a-gun is just as good as he thinks he is. Maybe better. I've talked to his men.... Well, what about me?"

She said some things that did me more good than any psychiatry, and for the first time in weeks I began to think perhaps there was some hope in the world. We made up a little for all the time we had lost, and then Marthe became thoughtful again.

"Rafe, you started once to say something about Ahrian. Where does she come into this?"

"Nowhere, really." I told her about seeming to see Ahrian's world. "Turned out she'd described it to me, and imagination did the rest."

"I wonder."

She sat still and intent, and then she questioned me about those particular dreams, what Ahrian had said, what I had said, what I remembered. Finally I demanded to know what she was getting at.

"Has it ever occurred to you, Rafe, that all this trouble has come onto you since Ahrian came? All the tragic things there are no real explanations for—Buck, and the old mare, and Bet going down into the paddock in her white formal, a thing no woman in her right mind would do, and at that hour of the night! And now these nightmares that are driving you to—to— Oh, you didn't tell me that part of it, but I can see it in your face! It's all wrong, Rafe. It's all without reason."

"But what on earth could Ahrian have to do with it? That's just wild talk, Marthe."

"Is it? How do we know what the people of her world can do, what powers they may have?"

"But she loves David! Why would she want to destroy his family?"

"How do you know she loves him? Did she ever tell you so?"

"Yes." Then Ahrian's words came back to me, and I corrected myself. "No, come to think of it. She only said love was a great force. Hang it all, though, she came with him, didn't she? All the way to Earth."

FOR some reason, this talk was disturbing me deeply. It oppressed me, in that open empty place, and gave me a sense that someone was listening and that Marthe had better not say any more—for her own sake.

"That's all nonsense," I said roughly. "People can't send dreams on each other, or make people do things, or—or kill by remote control."

"People like us—no. But Ahrian isn't—people. I'm afraid of her, Rafe. She's strange, inside. Bet said the same thing."

"Woman talk."

"Maybe. Or maybe sometimes we're nearer the truth than men because we aren't ashamed to rely on the instincts God gave us. She's evil. She's filled the house with death."

Marthe shivered as though a cold wind had struck her, and suddenly she reached out and tore Ahrian's ring off my finger and threw it far away into the deep grass.

"I don't want anything of her about you. Nothing!"

Then it was my turn to shiver. Because the minute that ring was gone, so were the oppression and the vague fear, and my screwed-up nerves began to slacken off again.

Still I would not believe. I knew the power of suggestion, and considering the state I was in, none of my reactions would be worth a plugged nickel anyway.

"I still say this is all nonsense, Marthe. Ahrian's never shown the slightest sign of having any special 'power.' She's never been anything but sweet and friendly, and she follows David around like a spaniel. And there just isn't the shadow of a motive."

"I know how we can find out."

I stared at her. "How?"

"Those dreams you had of Ahrian's world. She couldn't have described all the details to you, and you couldn't have imagined all the rest of them exactly right. Someone who had been there would know. If the dreams were wrong, then Ahrian told the truth and they were nothing worse than dreams. But if they were right—*all* right—then they weren't dreams but memories from Ahrian's own mind, mixed in with the awful things she was sending to torture you."

I remembered that I hadn't had a single glimpse of that world since I mentioned it to Ahrian, which seemed an odd coincidence.

"Even so, how could she know how I felt about space? How could she— Oh, all right. We'll go ask David."

"No, not David! Not anyone who has anything to do with her. Besides, if she has some deep reason to hate David, *he* wouldn't be likely to tell us, would he?"

"So that's it. Don't you think maybe your reporter's mind is running away with you?"

"I'm trying to save your neck, you stubborn fool!" she snarled, between rage and tears.

I got up. "Come on, then. There's Griffith—he's observer on the *Anson McQuarrie,* and I know him fairly well." It occurred to me suddenly that Griffith hadn't been around since the night of the *Anson McQuarrie's* landing, and I wondered why, since he had always been a good friend of David's. For some reason, that unimportant fact made me as curious as a woman to know why.

Marthe's car was in the drive. Ahrian called to us from the terrace, looking very lovely with her filmy skirts blowing around her and her hair full of those incredible purple gleamings in the sunlight. Marthe said she was going to take me for a drive, and Ahrian said it would do me good. They both smiled, and we drove away.

"Does she always wear that tiara?" asked Marthe.

"I don't know. She wears it a lot. Why?"

"It's extremely bad taste in the daytime."

"Part of her native costume, I reckon."

"She didn't have it when she came."

"No, she made it— Oh, who cares!" I yawned and went to sleep. I slept like a baby and never dreamed of anything. I was still asleep when Marthe stopped at the address in the city I had given her and only woke when she shook me half out of the car.

CHAPTER V

ABOUT ALTAIR

GRIFFITH WAS HOME. Spacemen are usually home between
voyages, with their shoes off and their feet up, getting acquainted
with their wives and kids. He seemed glad to see me, but not too
glad. He asked how everything was, and I said, "Fine," and he said
he'd been meaning to come up but he'd been too busy, and we both
knew that neither statement was true. Then he said awkwardly that
he was sorry about Bet, and I thanked him. When he couldn't think
of any more ways to stall, he asked me what he could do for me.

"Well," I said, "my fiancée is wild to see the pictures you shot on
the last voyage. New worlds, and all that." I explained to him who
she was. "She's thinking of doing an article—how a special observer
works, how the records are turned over to the government and the
scientific bodies, and so on. I thought, as a special favor, you might be
willing to show her the reels."

"Oh," he said, almost with a sigh of relief. "Sure, I'll be glad to."

He took us off to a small building at the rear of the house, where
he had his photo lab and a projection room. He found the reels he
wanted while chattering about some fine astronomical stuff that he'd
been given an award for. Marthe asked him all the questions she
could think of about his work, taking notes in a business-like way.
The projector began to hum. We watched.

The reels were magnificent. Griffith knew his job. Interstellar
space came alive before us. Nebulae, clusters, unknown Suns, glittering star streams, swept across the tridimensional screen in perfect
reproduction of color.

We watched strange solar systems plunge toward us, and then the
slow unveiling of individual planets as the *Anson McQuarrie* sank toward them. Some were dead and barren, some furiously alive, and
some were peopled, not always by anything approaching the human.
Each had its spectrum analysis and an exhaustive list of what ores

and minerals might be found there, also atmosphere content, gravity, types and aspects of native flora and fauna.

In the fascination of watching, I almost forgot what I came for. Then—

It was there. The world, the country of my dream—Ahrian's world. Each leaf and flower and blade of grass, each shading of color, the gleaming city with the curious roofs, the plain that swept toward the opalescent sea.

I felt very sick and strange. I'm not sure what happened after that, but presently I was back in Griffith's house and Marthe was feeding me brandy. I asked for more, and when I stopped shaking I turned to Griffith, who was much upset.

"That was the second world of Altair," I said. "The home world of my brother's wife."

"Yes," said Griffith.

"What happened there?" I got up and went close to him, and he stepped back a little. "What happened between my brother and Ahrian?"

"You better ask David," he muttered and tried to turn away. I caught him.

"Tell me," I said. "Bet's already dead, so it's too late for her. But there's David—and me. For God's sake, Griff, you used to be his friend!"

"Yes," said Griffith slowly, "I used to be. I told him not to do what he did, but you know David." He made an angry, indecisive gesture, and then he looked at me. "She's such a little thing. How did she— I mean—"

"Never mind. Just tell me what David did to her. She didn't come with him of her own free will, did she?"

"No. Oh, he tried to make out that she did, but everybody knew better. To this day I don't know exactly what the deal was, but her people needed something, a particular chemical or drug, I think, and they must have needed it badly. The ship, of course, was heavily stocked with all sorts of chemicals and medical supplies—you know how useful David has found them before in establishing good relations with other races.

"If it isn't their kids, it's their cattle, or a crop blight, or polluted water, and they're always grateful when you can fix things up, especially the primitives. Well, Ahrian's people are far from primitive, but I guess they'd run out of the source for whatever it was. David was mighty secretive about the whole thing."

He hesitated, and I prodded him. "What you're trying to say is that David gave them the chemicals or drugs they needed in exchange for Ahrian. Bought her, in fact."

Griffith nodded. He seemed to feel a personal sense of shame about it, as though the act of service under David had made him a party to the crime.

"Blackmailed her would be closer to the truth," he said. "The ugliest part of it was that Ahrian was already pledged... At least, that's what I heard. Anyway, no, she didn't come of her own free will."

I THINK, if I had had David's neck between my hands then, I would have broken it. How evil a mess could a man make? And where were you going to put justice?

Marthe said to Griffith, "Did her people have any unusual abilities? It's very important, Mr. Griffith."

"Their culture is very complex, and we weren't there long enough to study it in detail. Also, there was the language barrier. But I'm pretty sure they're telepaths—many races are, you know—though to what extent I couldn't say."

"Telepaths," said Marthe softly, and looked at me. "Mr. Griffith, do the women there wear a sort of tiara, shaped like—" She described Ahrian's headgear minutely, including the oddly cut crystal. "Habitually, I mean."

He stared at her as though he thought it was just like a woman to worry about fashions at a time like this. "Honestly, Miss Walters, I didn't notice. Both sexes go in for jewelry, and nearly all of them make it themselves, and nobody could keep track—" He halted, apparently struck by a sudden memory. "I did see a marriage ceremony, though, where little crowns like that were used as we use rings. The man and woman exchanged them, and as near as I could figure the words the rite was called something like the One-Making."

"Thank you," said Marthe. "Thank you very much. Now I think I'd better get Rafe home."

I said something to Griffith, I'm not sure what, but he shook hands with me and seemed relieved. I sat in the car, thinking, and Marthe drove, not back toward the house, but to her apartment. She told me she'd be back in a minute and went off, taking the keys with her. I sat thinking, and my thoughts were not good. Marthe returned, carrying a small suitcase.

"What's that for?" I demanded.

"I'm staying with you."

"The devil you are!"

She faced me, with a look as level as a steel blade and just as unyielding. "You mean more to me than propriety, or my good name, or even my own skin. Is that clear? I am staying with you until this business is finished."

I roared at her. I pleaded with her. I explained that if Ahrian were out for me, she would be out for Marthe too, if she got in the way. I told her she'd only make it harder for me, worrying about her.

All the time I was roaring, pleading, and explaining, Marthe was driving out of town, immovable, maddening, and wonderful. Finally I gave up. I couldn't throw her out of the car. Even if I had, it wouldn't have prevented her coming.

She spoke at last. "Of course, you know there's a simple solution to all this—simple, logical, and safe."

"What?"

"Go away out of Ahrian's reach, and let David take his own consequences."

"He deserves it," I said savagely.

"But you won't go away."

"How can I, Marthe?" And I began to yell at her all over again because *she* wouldn't go.

"All right, that's settled. Now let's start thinking. Obviously, we can't go to the police."

"Hardly." It was frightening to consider what a hard-boiled cop would make out of a woman who had lavender hair and performed witchcraft. "You believe that tiara Ahrian wears has something to do with her—well, her power over other people's minds?"

"Possibly. I don't know. That's just it, Rafe—we don't *know*, and so we have to be suspicious of everything."

I remembered the unexplainable sensation I had had when Marthe threw that ring away. Could it have been a contact, a sort of focal point to concentrate the energy of her thought-waves which were, perhaps, amplified and controlled by the aid of that mesh of gold and platinum wires and that strangely faceted crystal? I remembered also the necklace of zircons that glittered on Bet's throat, the night she died.

These gifts must be fashioned with a meaning from the heart...

"I don't know what we're going to do, Rafe. Do you?"

"Face them with it, I suppose. Face them both. Drag it out in the open, anyway."

Marthe sighed, and we drove on in gloomy silence.

Chapter VI

THE LAST MAGIC

IT WAS DARK when we reached the house. Ahrian welcomed us with little cries of delight.

"I am so happy you have brought Marthe back with you. It has been too long since we have seen her."

"She's staying for a while," I said.

"How very nice. Since the little one is gone, I am lonely with no woman to talk to. Come, I will see that all is well in the room of guests."

"Where's David?" I asked.

"Oh, he has gone into the city and will not be back tonight. And my heart is sad, for I think that he has gone to talk of another voyage."

She took Marthe away. I followed, on the pretext of making sure that Marthe had everything she needed, and stayed until the arrival of the maid. Then I went and changed for dinner, cursing David.

I got a word alone with Marthe before we went down. "We'd better wait," I said. "I want to tackle them together. It's the only way I know to put David on his guard."

"Has he mentioned another voyage to you?" Marthe wanted to know.

I shook my head. "But then, he seldom mentions anything to me any more."

"Ahrian's doing."

There didn't seem to be any doubt about that. David and I had never exactly loved one another, but there had certainly never been any real ill feeling between us, either. Since Bet's death, all that had been changed.

Ahrian put herself out to be nice to Marthe. If we hadn't known what we knew, it would have been a delightful evening. Instead, it was rather horrible. All the time I was remembering how I had felt out there on the hill and wondering how much Ahrian knew, or suspected, and what she might be going to do about it.

All at once she cried out, "Oh Rafe, you have lost your ring!"

I told her some reasonably plausible lie. "I'm awfully sorry, Ahrian. You must make me another some time."

She smiled. "There will be no need for that. Wait." She ran off. Marthe and I looked at each other, not daring to speak. Presently Ahrian came back, presumably from her work room, carrying a cushion made of silk.

"See? I have made these for you both—a betrothal gift."

On the cushion were two rings, identical in design, one large, one small. The zircons made a pale glittering, like two wicked eyes that watched us.

"Will you not exchange them now? I should be so happy!"

Marthe was going to say something violent. I gave her a look that shut her up and thanked Ahrian profusely. It was one of those things. If she knew we suspected her and her gifts, that was that. But if she didn't know, I didn't want her to find out just yet.

"But," I said, "they are too beautiful for mere gifts. We'll save them for the wedding, Ahrian. We were planning on a double ring ceremony anyway, and these will be perfect. Won't they, Marthe?"

"Oh, yes," she said.

AHRIAN beamed like a happy child, and murmured that her little trinkets weren't worthy of such an honor, and in that moment I began to doubt the whole crazy story again. No one could look so guileless and innocent and sweet as Ahrian did, and be guilty of the things we thought she was.

Marthe must have seen me wavering, because she said, "Rafe, darling, put them away where they'll be quite safe. I wouldn't want anything to happen to them before the wedding."

I took them up to my room and hid them in the farthest back corner of a bureau drawer under a pile of shirts. While I was up there alone, the most awful temptation came over me to put the big one on my finger—just to look at it, to admire the sparkle of the queerly cut stone and the wonderful filigree work of the band. What harm could there be in a ring?

I guess it was the very strength of that compulsion that saved me. I got scared. I slammed the drawer shut, locked it, and threw the key out the window. Then I turned around to find Marthe standing in the doorway.

"I wouldn't have let you put it on," she whispered. "But you see, Rafe? You see how right we were!"

I began to shake a bit. We started downstairs again, and Marthe said in my ear, "She knows. I'm sure she knows."

I agreed with her, and I was afraid. It shamed me to be afraid of such a frail little creature, but I was.

Marthe and I were both relieved when it came time to go to bed. It freed us from the weird necessity of making conversation with Ahrian. I had no intention of sleeping, but it was good to be away from her. Marthe's room was down the hall from mine, farther than I liked but plenty close enough to hear her if she called me.

I told her to leave the door open and yell like the devil if anything—anything at all—seemed wrong to her. I left mine open, too, and sat down in a chair where I could see the lighted hall. I wished

I had a gun, but I didn't dare leave Marthe for all the time it would take to rouse out Jamieson and get the key. I picked out the heaviest stick I had and kept it in my hand.

The house was quiet, and nothing happened. The huge relic of a clock that stood on the stair landing chimed peacefully every fifteen minutes, and every hour it counted off the strokes in a deep, soft voice. I think the last time I heard it was half-past two. I didn't mean to sleep. I had purposely drunk nothing but black coffee all evening. But I had been so long without sleep!

I remember getting up and walking down the hall to Marthe's door and glancing in at her, curled up in the big bed. After that things got dim. I don't believe that I slept very deeply, or very long, but it was enough. I dreamed with a terrible vividness of Marthe. She was standing in the garden, wrapped in a plaid bathrobe, and she was in danger, very great danger, and she needed me.

Starting up out of the chair, I listened for a moment. The house was silent, except for the clock ticking gently to itself on the landing. I ran down the hall and into Marthe's room. At first I thought she was still there, and then I saw that the shape in the bed was only a mockery of tumbled blankets. I called her. There was no answer. Calling, I ran down through the house, and there was no answer at all until I came out on the terrace above the shadowy garden. Then I heard her say my name.

She was standing in a patch of moonlight with the plaid robe wrapped around her, and her face was white as death. In a minute I had my arms around her and she was sobbing, asking if I were safe.

"I must have been dreaming, Rafe, but I thought you were some-where out here, hurt, maybe dying."

She was in a terrible fright, and so was I. Because I knew who had sent those dreams—easy dreams to send, without any aids to te-lepathy, since with each of us the thought of danger to the other was right on top of our minds, conscious and screaming.

I wanted out of that garden.

WE WENT up the steps together and onto the wide terrace, in that clear, white, damnable moonlight. From the long doors that opened into the library David stepped and barred our way. He held a heavy double-barreled shotgun, and at that range he couldn't miss.

David.

He hadn't gone to town. He had been in his room all this time – waiting. His eyes were wide open, empty and bright, reflecting the cold fire of the moon.

Ahrian was with him.

I made some futile gesture of getting Marthe behind me, and I cried out, "David!" He turned his head a very little, like a man who hears a sound far off, and his brow puckered, but he did not speak.

Ahrian said softly, "I am sorry that it must be so, Rafe and Marthe. You are blameless, and you have been kind. If only Marthe had not sensed what was within me… But now it must be finished here, to-night."

"Ahrian," I said, and the twin black barrels of the shotgun watched me, and the stone of David's ring sparkled against the stock. "David did a wicked thing. We know about it – but does it give you the right to kill us all? Bet, and Marthe…"

"I made a promise to my gods," she whispered. "I had a mother and father, a brother, a sister – and more than all of them, though I loved them dearly, there was one who would have been my other self."

"I'll take you back," I said. "I'll send a ship out to Altair – only let Marthe go!"

"Could I go back as I am, as he has made me? Could I find my life again, with the blood that is already on me? No. I will take from David everything that he loves, even space itself, and in the end I will tell him how and why. Then – I will die."

"All right. All right, Ahrian. But why Marthe? She can't stop you. If David kills me, that's enough. He'll be tried for murder, the whole story will come out, and that will be the end of him whether he's convicted or not."

Ahrian smiled, a tender thing of ineffable sadness. "Marthe is speaking within herself, words that you should hear. Her body wishes much to live, but her heart says, 'Not without him,' and her heart is stronger. No, Rafe. If she lives, she will slip David out of the cage I have built for him. Now let us stop torturing each other!"

Her face contracted in a spasm of pain. She turned her head toward the motionless effigy of a man who stood beside her, and I saw the gun go up, and I knew this was the finish.

I shouted his name once more, pure reflex, and shoved Marthe aside as far as I could. David was twenty-five or thirty feet away. I bent over and began to run toward him. I didn't know why. It was hopeless, but it was all I could think of to do. The distance looked like thirty miles—and then I heard him moan. He was moaning the way old Buck had moaned that day, and his head was pulled back as though he were straining away from something. I knew he didn't *want* to kill me, even then.

Ahrian whispered. The crystal glowed in the moonlight, and there was in her face a magnificent and awful strength. David gave a low wail of agony. The cords stood out on the backs of his hands. The eyes of the woman from Altair blazed like purple stars. The gunstock settled into place, and David's finger curled in on the trigger.

Someone sped by me, off to one side and going like the wind. Someone in a plaid robe, headed not for David, but for Ahrian.

There was a scream, I don't know whose. Maybe mine. The gun let off, both barrels, right above my shoulder, and the hot metal seared my hand where I shoved the thing up at the last second so that it hit nothing but the tree tops. David groaned and let it drop, and so did I. I reeled around, and there was Marthe leaning over the stone balustrade, shivering, sobbing, triumphant, holding in one hand the crystal tiara.

I CARRIED Ahrian into the house. Her body, light and frail as a bird's, was broken. It was a long fall into the garden, and she had hit hard. Her hair had come loose and hung over my arm in a long thick pall, dark purple in the moonlight.

I laid her on the couch, as gently as I could. She looked up at me and said quite clearly, "The beasts I could force against their will. The human mind is stronger. With all my skill and care—a little too strong."

She was still a while, and then she whispered, "I am sad, Rafe, that I must die so far away from home."

That was all.

The shot had roused the servants, who began to straggle in from the far wing of the house. I told them that David thought he had heard prowlers and fired at them, and in the excitement Ahrian had fallen from the terrace. They believed it. Why not? David was still sitting out there, doubled up on the cold stone, looking at nothing. Somehow I couldn't speak to him, or touch him. I sent the servants to get him in, and told them to call the people who had to be called. Then I took Marthe up to her room.

"It'll be all right," I told her. "It was an accident. Let me tell the story. You won't even be named."

"I don't care," she said, in a strange harsh voice. "All I care about is you, and you're alive and safe." She put her arms around me, a fierce and painful grip. "I'm sorry I killed her, I didn't mean to, but I'd do it again, Rafe, I'd do it again—she wanted to kill you!" She caught her breath, still clinging to me, and then she began to cry. "You fool, oh you fool, rushing David like that to make him fire at you instead of me." She said some more things, and then her voice got faint. I put her on the bed and made her take a sedative, and presently she was asleep.

I left the maid with her, and went downstairs. There were things I had to say to David.

That was how the McQuarrie tradition came to an end after two hundred years. Even the house is gone, for none of us could bear it any longer. David will never go to space again.

I'm glad. What did it gain the McQuarries? What has it ever gained men? Have men ever brought back more happiness from the stars? Will they ever?

Well, it's too late now to wonder about that. It's been too late, ever since the first skin clad barbarian stared up at the moon and lusted for it. If Marthe and I have sons, I am afraid that McQuarries will go to space again.

THE SHADOWS

Startling Stories, February 1952

FOR COUNTLESS numbers of its years there had been no sight or sound or sense of man upon the world of the little blue star. But now, without warning, a remembered thing had come suddenly into the air again—a quiver, a subtle throbbing that meant only one kind of life. The Shadows felt it, the Shadows that had waited so long and patiently. They began to stir among the ruined walls. They rose and shook themselves, and a soundless whisper ran among them, a hungry whisper, wild and eager. "Man! Man! Man has come again!"

THE GALACTIC SURVEY ship lay in an expanse of level plain, ringed on one side by low mountains and on the other by a curving belt of forest. A river ran across the plain and there was much grass. But nothing cropped it, and there were no tracks in the mud of the river bank to show that anything had.

Hubbard sniffed the warm air and dug his feet into the soil, which was rich and dark. He grinned broadly. "This is something like it," he said. "A pretty world. Real pretty."

He was a young man. His field was anthropology, and this was his first voyage out. For him, the stars still shone brightly. Barrier looked at him between envy and sadness. He said nothing. His gaze roving off across the plain and the forest, studied the sky—a suspicious, sombre gaze. He was old enough to be Hubbard's father and he felt every year of it, pressed down and running over.

"Of course, the colors are all wrong," said Hubbard, "but that's nothing. After they'd lived with a blue sun for a while people would think it was the only kind to have."

Barrier grunted. "What people?"

"Why, the colonists, the people that will live here some day!" Hubbard laughed suddenly. "What's the matter with you? Here at last we've found a beautiful world, and you're as glum as though it were a hunk of dead rock."

"I guess," said Barrier slowly, "that I've seen too many hunks of dead rock, and too many beautiful worlds that—"

He broke off. This was no time to talk. In fact, it was not his place to talk at all. If he didn't like what he was doing any more he could go home to Earth and stay there, and leave the stars to the young men who had not yet lost their faith.

The mountains, the plain, and the forest were very still in the bright blue morning. Barrier could feel the stillness. No wing cut the sweet air, no paw rustled the tangled grass, no voice spoke from among the curious trees. He moved restlessly where he stood, looking rather like an old hound that scents danger where there should be game. That was Barrier's job, his science, the oldest science of mankind—to venture into strange country and feel the invisible, sense the unknown and survive. He was head of the Ground Exploration team, and an expert on exploring. He had been at it all his life. Too long.

Hubbard said, "I wish Kendall would come back. I want to get started."

"What do you think you're going to find?"

"How do I know? That's the fun of it. But on a world like this there's bound to be life of some kind."

"Human life?"

"Why not?"

Again Barrier grunted, and again he said nothing.

They waited. Other men were scattered about the plain and the river bank, taking samples of soil, rock, water, and vegetation. They stayed close to the ship, and all were armed. The technical staff, after checking solar radiation, atmospheric content, temperature, gravitation, and the million and one other things that go to make a world habitable or otherwise for Earthmen, had rated this planet Earth-Type A, and in obedience to Survey ruling the ship had landed to determine surface conditions. So far, they had all been favorable. So far.

Barrier fidgeted, and listened to the silence.

PRESENTLY a speck appeared far off in the sky. It gave off a thin droning, coming closer, and developed into a small 'copter which settled down beside the ship, a gnat alighting beside a whale. Kendall and his observer and cameraman got out.

Barrier went up to him. "What did you find?"

"More of the same," said Kendall, "and nothing in it. Except—" He hesitated.

"Except what?"

"Over there beyond the forest. I thought it might be the ruins of a city."

"There!" cried Hubbard. "You see?"

Kendall shrugged. "The boys said no, it was just a bunch of rocks grown over with the woods. I don't know. You can decide for yourselves when you see the pictures."

The men who were out on the plain and the river bank had come running up. They were all young men, like Hubbard. Only the Captain, the chief of Technical, a couple of research scientists and Barrier were old. There was an uproar of voices, all talking at once. The Survey ship had made few landings, and it had been a long time since the last one. They were like youngsters let out of confinement, bursting with excitement and pride at what they had found.

Barrier went with them into the ship, into the main salon. There was a brief wait while the film, which had been developed automatically on exposure, was fed into the projector. The lights were cut. The small screen came to life.

They all watched, with intense interest. The panorama unfolded in natural color, like and yet unlike Earth. On closer inspection, the forest trees were not trees at all, but monstrous flowers with stems as thick as trunks, bearing clusters of brilliant and improbable blooms. Barrier caught a glimpse of something that might have been a butterfly or a drifting petal, but other than that, nothing moved.

He asked, "Were there any signs of animal life?"

Kendall shook his head. "No."

Impatiently, Hubbard said, "The 'copter probably frightened it away."

"Frightened things run," said Barrier. "There's nothing running."

Hubbard swore under his breath, and Barrier smiled. It had become a personal necessity for Hubbard to discover life here, and no wonder. He had had very little chance to practice his anthropology, and the voyage was almost over. His insistence on animals arose from the fact that without them there were not likely to be men.

"There," said Kendall, and held up his hand. The film was stopped, on a frame showing an area of tree-flowers and clambering vines rather more open than the forest proper. Humps and ridges of stone showed here and there among the tangled growths.

"You see what I mean," said Kendall, and gestured again. The film rolled, repeating the long low swings the 'copter had made across the area. "I got as close as I could, and I still couldn't figure it."

"It sure looks like a city," said Hubbard. He was quivering with excitement. "Look there. See how regular those lines are, like streets, with houses fallen down on either side."

Two other voices spoke up. Aiken, the expert on planetary archaeology, admitted cautiously that it might be a city. Caffrey, the geologist, said that it might just as well be a natural rock formation.

"What do you think, Barrier?" asked Captain Verlaine.

"Can't tell from the picture, sir. I'd have to examine the stones."

"Well," said Verlaine, "that seems to settle it. Make that area your first objective. Don't you agree, Cristofek?"

Cristofek, who was Chief of Technical, nodded emphatically. "And Barrier, in case it does turn out to be a ruin, make every effort to discover what sort of inhabitants it had and, above all, what happened to them."

Barrier stood up. "All right," he said. "Let's be on our way."

The seven men of his team joined him—all, like Hubbard, specialists, young men picked for physical condition and trained in the use of arms. Aiken and Caffrey were among them, also a lad named Morris who was in charge of the walkie-talkie. Barrier consulted Kendall about bearings, and then went with the others to get his gear. Within a quarter of an hour they were marching off across the plain.

BARRIER felt a twinge of nostalgia so strong as to be a physical pain – nostalgia for the days when he had been green and eager like the rest, leaving the ship, which he hated, for the uncrossed horizons of new worlds, full of a shivering fascination, full of hope. The hope had been the first to go, and then the fascination.

Now, looking at the bright landscape, beautiful in spite of its unearthly tints, he found himself thinking that he would like to be in a certain bar he remembered in Los Angeles, not worrying about anything, not pondering meanings and significances and the shapes of alien leaves, forgetting completely the dark conviction that had grown in him over the years.

Schmidt, the entomologist, was chattering with Gordon, whose field was zoology, about worms and insect forms, of which many had been found. Hubbard speculated with Aiken on The City. They already called it that. The high grasses swished against their boots. The wind blew softly and the sun was warm. But apart from the eight invading humans there was nothing sentient to enjoy these blessings. Barrier disliked the empty silence. It was unnatural in such a lush and joyous setting.

His eyes roved constantly, gray eyes set in a face the color of old leather and surrounded by the complex wrinkles that come from squinting against numberless foreign suns. For a long time they saw nothing. And then, more and more, they narrowed and watched a certain sector to their left.

Barrier lifted his hand, and the little column stopped.

"Over there," he said. "Do you see those shadows?"

They all stared.

Hubbard laughed. "Cloud shadows."

"There are no clouds."

"Well, then, it's the wind making ripples in the grass." He glanced sidelong at Barrier. "What's the difference what makes them? They're only shadows!"

Barrier said heavily, speaking to them all, "Will you please try to remember that you are not on Earth? In a strange world anything, a shadow, a blade of grass, may be alive and deadly."

Their faces regarded him, intelligent, uncomprehending, trying not to show that they thought he was being a trifle ridiculous. He knew that they now felt hardened veterans of the star-worlds, with the vast experience of their four or five landings behind them, and all on planets that had had only normally dangerous life-forms. He could not make them understand the things he had seen, the inimical stealthy things that hated man.

He motioned them on again. They had already forgotten the shadows, but he had not. There seemed to be a number of them—how do you count shadows? Smallish clots of darkness they were that flitted along some distance away, losing themselves in the waving grass, difficult to see in the brilliant sunshine, but unmistakably there. They seemed to be running parallel with the men. They looked like perfectly normal shadows and Barrier would not have given them a second thought—except that in his experience a shadow must be thrown by something, and here there was nothing, not even so much as a patch of cloud or a bird's wing.

They marched on across the beautiful, empty, silent plain. And then, again, Barrier called a halt.

They had come to the edge of a stream that ran down toward the river, cutting itself a cleft in the soil of the plain. Caffrey immediately scrambled down the steep bank and began to study the layers of silt and sand and clay. Gordon followed him, casting back and forth along the edge of the water. He became vastly excited when he discovered a hideous small creature that resembled a purple prawn. Something else, that might have been a snake or an eel, went off with a ropy slither between the wet rocks.

Hubbard danced up and down. "I told you there was life here!"

Barrier said gently, "I never denied it."

He glanced upstream. The shadows were bunched together, hovering over the cleft. They had not come any closer, but they were watching. He could not see with his eyes that they were watching, for they were only featureless blobs of gloom. But he felt it, in every nerve, in every pore of his prickling skin. There was something ugly about being watched by shadows.

ABRUPTLY, Caffrey began to dig like a terrier in the soft ground midway up the bank. Presently he held up an object like a blackened, broken stick that was knobbed at one end. He handed it to Gordon, who voiced a sharp exclamation and cried out for Barrier.

"It's a bone," said Gordon. "The leg bone of a large deer, I should say, or a small horse. You know what I mean, the equivalents thereof."

Hubbard was quite beside himself. "Vertebrate life! That proves that evolution here has followed practically the same path it did on Earth." He looked around, as though he expected to see a man materialize from among the rocks.

Barrier said to Gordon, "How old is that bone?"

Gordon shook his head. "It's been in the ground a long time. How long would you say, Caffrey?"

Caffrey squinted at the bank. "Judging from its depth under the present topsoil, I should guess five or six hundred years, maybe more. That's only a guess, of course. There are so many factors I haven't any data for."

"In other words," said Barrier, "a long time." He frowned at the ancient bone, and then at the deserted landscape around him.

Morris sent word of their find back to the ship. They marched on.

The shadows followed.

There were several miles of the flat grassland now between them and the ship. It lay glinting dully in the blue light, Leviathan at rest. The outposts of the forest, solitary clumps and little clustered groves of the giant flowers and equally lofty ferns, sprang up around the men, gradually screening off both the plain and the sky, until they walked in a warm blue gloom shot through with the brilliant spectral colors of the blooms.

At first they went slowly, on the watch for dangerous plant-forms. Apparently there were none. Hansen, the botanist, chanted aloud with wonder at every step. Schmidt was entranced by huge butterflies and numerous insects that crept and flew and made tiny buzzings. Gordon and Hubbard peered eagerly, but there was nothing for them to see.

Barrier walked ahead, going with a lanky noiseless stride like an Indian. His eyes were anxious, and his nerves on edge.

It was very lovely in the forest, with the blooms of many colors nodding overhead. Barrier thought of a garden at the bottom of the sea. The glades were full of blueness like still water. There began to be wisps of mist along the ground.

He thought for a time that they had lost the shadows. Then he saw them again, low down, slipping along between the rough, pale flower-trunks. They had changed their formation. They were all around the men now, in a circle. They had come closer. Much closer.

Barrier made the men bunch up. He pointed out the shadows to them, and this time they were less inclined to shrug them off.

"Better let me talk to the ship," he said, and Morris clicked the switch on the walkie-talkie. He did that several times, repeating the call letters, and then he shook his head.

"Sorry," he said nervously, "I'm blanked out. There's some electrical disturbance, very strong…"

Barrier glanced at the shadows. Creatures of force? They must be, since they were not solid matter. Electronic discharge from their bodies might well disrupt the small transmitter.

He considered turning back. They were now about equidistant from the ship and the area of the possible ruins, and if the shadows had anything evil in mind, turning back could not stop them. The ship was well out of reach. Besides, he had his orders, and if these shadows were a native life-form, it was his duty to find out about them.

They had made no hostile move as yet. Hostile or not, could shadows hurt men? And if so, how did you fight them?

The ground mists were thickening. They must be approaching swampy ground, although he had not noticed any on Kendall's films. Tenuous wreaths and veils hung in the blue glades, each separate droplet glittering with diamond fires in the filtered sunlight. The breeze rippled them to and fro very prettily. They were not fever mists. Barrier forgot them, returning his watchful attention to the shadows.

Within the past few minutes they had drawn their circle in until they were only a few feet away from the men. They glided round and round, utterly silent, in a kind of nervous dance. The men were all watching them now. Hubbard spoke to Barrier, and his voice had an edge of fright.

"What are they? What do they want?"

"They're only shadows," said Barrier irritably. "What does it matter what they want?" Then he called out to the others, "Keep together. If things get rough we'll turn back. But no matter what happens, don't bolt. If you do, there won't be any way to help you."

THEY WENT on, treading on each other's heels, staring around them. The shadows wove and bounded. Quite suddenly, Schmidt screamed. His gun went off with a snarling hiss. It flared again and again into a clot of darkness, which did not flinch.

"It touched me," Schmidt shuddered. "It touched me!"

He began to run, not very far, because there was no space within the ring of shadows to run in. Barrier caught him by the arm.

"Shut up," he snarled. "Shut up!"

Schmidt stood shivering. "It was cold. Cold as death."

"You're not dead, are you?"

"No."

"You're not hurt?"

"I – No."

"Then shut up." Barrier glared at Schmidt, at the others. "The next one of you that panics, I'll knock him flat."

He was afraid himself. Miserably afraid. But he said, "They haven't hurt us yet. Maybe they can't. Anyway, let's wait a while before we blow our tops."

The young men swallowed and straightened their faces out into stiff lines and tried hard not to see the shadows. Schmidt twitched as he walked. Barrier wished there was a sound in the forest. A squeak, a grunt, a roar that meant something warm-blooded and alive. There wasn't. Even their own footfalls were deadened on the soft ground.

The mists thickened, sparkling, bright. The alien sun was blotted out. The shadows skulked and clung. Sweat poured down the cheeks of the men, stained their drill jackets. Hubbard said, licking his lips, "How much farther?"

"Another mile or two."

Barrier wished the mists were not there. They made him feel shut in and suffocated. He worried about bogs. The blue daylight was maddening. He thought of the honest yellow glare of Sol and wondered what madness it was that sent men out to the ends of the galaxy seeking other suns.

He stumbled suddenly, and looked down. At first he thought the obstacle was a rounded stone half buried in the mold of fallen petals. And then he knew it wasn't. He stooped and lifted it up and held it out to Hubbard.

"You wanted man," he said.

Hubbard rubbed his palms up and down along his thighs. He stared at the thing in Barrier's hands, and the others stared over their shoulders, and the thing grinned at them with a single gaping line of teeth.

Hubbard reached out and took it.

"It's very old," he said. "As old as that." He pointed to Gordon's trophy.

Schmidt said in a curiously shrill voice, "There were men here once, and animals. Now there aren't any. They're all dead, and I know what killed them." He stared hard at the shadows.

Barrier swore. "That's fine talk from a scientist. I thought you people were trained not to jump to conclusions."

Hubbard muttered, "Barrier is right." He looked at the skull and repressed a shiver. "Come on, I want to see those ruins."

They went on, so close together that their shoulders rubbed. The mists grew denser and brighter and heavier. The men sweated, ignoring the shadows, desperately ignoring them.

Without any warning, the shadows sprang.

There was a moment's terrible screaming from the men, and then there was silence, and after that a few stifled, horrid sounds. The skull fell from Hubbard's grasp and rolled away, grinning a wise grin as it went. Barrier swayed where he stood, clawing blindly with his hands at his own flesh.

He could see the others. Through a veil of shadowy gloom he could see them, dimly, and the gloom was behind his eyes and not before them. Some of the men had tried to run, and the shadows had caught them as they ran. Two of them kicked and grovelled on the ground. Their outlines were indistinct, blurred over. Their eyes were crazy. So were Barrier's.

The shocking swiftness of that leap, the noiselessness, the awful cold that poured in suddenly upon the flesh—the loathsome sense of an intruder grasping at mind and body, taking them over *from within*....

It was inside him. The shadow was inside him. Its icy substance interpenetrated his warm and living flesh, its alien and unreadable intelligence was clinging tight against his own, and it was shaking him, driving him, and he was going to die....

They're dead, all the men and animals, and I know what killed them—Schmidt was gone, plunging off into the mist, taking with him the terrible invader in his flesh. There were still shadows, a lot of them, running loose, for there had not been enough men. Some of these went after Schmidt.

Barrier forgot his orders, his command, his pride. Blind black terror overwhelmed him and he ran. He wanted to outrun the thing that held him, to shake it free and lose it utterly, and go on running right off this filthy blue-lit world. But he couldn't. It was part of him. He would not lose it till he died.

He ran, through the silent forest, where the nodding blossoms were shrouded thick in mist and the flower-trunks were hidden, and there was nothing but himself and the nightmare that dwelt in his flesh, and a darkness in the air around him.

Several times he fell, but something forced him up and on again. He had lost all track of the other men. He had almost forgotten them. Once, far off, he heard a shriek and knew that someone was dying, but he did not care. His mind was lost inside the shadow.

He was only distantly aware that suddenly the mists were gone and he was staggering over ground that had once been cleared but now was overgrown, though not so thickly as the forest. He stumbled among stones, reeled and scrambled around great hummocks from which peeped shattered cornices, and crossed an open space where his feet brought forth a sound of dry sticks cracking. He looked down and saw that the sticks were human bones.

He sobbed and turned his head to see the little group of shadows that hovered at his heels.

"Are you waiting your turn?" he yelled at them, or tried to yell, and made only a hoarse whispering. His face, so strangely blurred and dimmed, twisted into an insensate mask of rage. He bent and picked up the old bare bones from around his feet and threw them at the shadows, and cursed, and sobbed, and then he ran again, five paces, ten, across the crackling open space, and there was a hummock too high to climb and too wide to go around. He butted himself against it, into a knee of stone that thrust out between the creepers, and then he fell. His body jerked convulsively, and was still....

HE WAS looking at a moon. It was a red moon, small but very close. There were mountains on it, and gouged-out hollows. His mind made idle pictures of them, a face, a crouching rabbit. There were stars. He did not recognize them. Presently another moon came up, a larger one, and pallid green. He tired of making pictures on the moons.

Someone was moaning, close at hand.

Mildly curious, Barrier turned his head. He saw a man, lying curled up with his knees against his chest and his arms clasped over his head. He seemed to know the man. He studied the partly visible face. Of course he knew him, it was young Hubbard, who had been looking for men....

Barrier sprang up. Cold sweat burst out on him and his body trembled, standing rigid in the moonlight. He searched inside himself as a man will search for a remembered pain, sick and praying not to find it.

It was gone. The shadow was gone. He clutched at Hubbard, and saw that the unholy dimness had left his features. He shook Hubbard and shouted at him, and then he saw that there were other men huddled on the ground, two, three, four of them. He ran from one to the other, and they looked up at him with empty, frightened eyes. Schmidt was not among them, nor Morris.

Six. Six living out of eight. And the shadows had gone away out of their flesh.

For one short second he was hopeful. Then he looked out across the open space where the bones were and saw the company of dark and restless blots that moved among the spiky ribs and tumbled, careless limbs. He almost laughed that he had considered hope.

He returned to Hubbard. "How did you get here?" he asked, and slapped the young man's face until he answered.

"I don't know. I—just ran." Hubbard gave a racking shiver. "Oh God, Barrier, that thing inside me just like smoke blows through a bush, and *cold....*"

Barrier slapped him again. "Where're Schmidt and Morris?"

"I don't know."

Barrier set about getting the others on their feet. None of them knew precisely how they had gotten there. None of them knew what had happened to Morris, but Aiken said:

"I saw Schmidt. I was running and I passed by Schmidt lying on the ground, at least I think it was Schmidt, it had his specimen case still strapped around it, and it was dead. Oh yes, there wasn't any doubt at all about its being dead."

He turned away suddenly and tried hard to be sick.

Barrier said slowly, "So they finished off two of us, and brought the rest of us here. I suppose they want to complete the job at their leisure. So here we are. We can't communicate with the ship, and they won't send Kendall out to look for us before morning. And if we're still alive by then, and Kendall does happen to find us, and lands—what do you think *they'll* do about it?"

He glanced toward the shadows.

Nobody answered.

"I wonder," said Barrier at last, "if fire would keep them off."

The others stared at him. Then they scurried about, gathering dead creepers, dry grass, anything that would burn. They made fires, a ring of them across the mouth of the cul-de-sac where they were caught. They waited, breathless with hope.

The shadows crept up toward the flames. Then, as though delighted with them, they began to flit back and forth around the fires, frolicking over and through them, almost, it seemed, playing tag among the columns of smoke.

Hubbard wept.

Mist was crawling up out of the forest. The small red moon was sinking, and the larger pale green one shed a ghastly light. The fires burned low and the shadows danced around them.

"They look real cute there, don't they?" said Barrier viciously. "Having fun."

The flames died down, became beds of embers. Some of the shadows began to make tentative small rushes toward Barrier and the five who were left of his team.

Caffrey whispered, "I guess they're coming for us." He still had a withered blossom stuck in his buttonhole.

The shadows darted nervously, toward the men and then back to the glowing red embers. Beyond them tenuous arms of mist advanced and coiled between the ruins. They began to obscure the remaining moon, and as the light faded the shadows moved more swiftly, with a greater eagerness.

Aiken had been rooting among the creepers that shrouded the hummock. Suddenly he bleated, "There's a passage here, a doorway. Maybe we could get inside and—and barricade it."

"Against shadows?" said Barrier, and laughed.

"It's better than nothing," Hubbard said. "Anything's better than just sitting here."

HE SCRAMBLED toward Aiken, who had disappeared, and the others followed. All at once, Barrier began to laugh. They stared at him, their faces round and startled. Barrier shouted at them, laughing.

"You still don't get it, do you? You still think you can run and hide, and put up little defences, and win out somehow in the end because you're men and man always wins out. You haven't learned yet, have you?"

"Learned what?" asked Hubbard, in a low, queer voice.

Barrier studied the shadows. "Why should I tell you, though? It took me half a lifetime and a lot of worlds to learn the truth. Why shouldn't I keep it to myself, and let you die happy?"

Abruptly, Hubbard sprang at him. He was like an enraged child, boiling with a confused fury of which the greater part was the fear of death. Barrier caught his wrists.

"You dirty yellow-belly," Hubbard squealed. "You're supposed to be our leader, you're supposed to show us what to do, and what do you do? You give up." He called Barrier a number of evil names. "The great explorer, the big brave leader, hell! You're just an old man with all the guts run out of you. You should have gone back to Earth and let somebody that could fight take over."

Barrier thrust him away, quite hard but without anger.

"All right," he said, "I'll let you in on it. Earth was a soft planet. Oh, she tried to put her foot down—ice ages, volcanoes, plagues, floods, droughts, and famines—but it was too late, and it wasn't enough, and now we've got the upper hand of her. But the other worlds are tougher. Sooner or later, they find a way....

"We aren't welcome in the universe. I don't know why. Maybe it's because we aren't content to be the animals we are, but must always be pretending that we're something else, prying about and upsetting things, grasping after stars, making trouble and screaming because it hurts. I don't know. I only know that we're hated. Everywhere I've been, wherever there was a man, they'd been gotten rid of somehow."

He glanced up at the alien stars, dimming now with the mist that rolled across them.

"They hate us," he said softly. "Their children hate us. Everywhere we have enemies, but never any friends."

Then he sighed. "You're right, Hubbard. I am an old man, with the guts worn out of me. You run on in and hide, now, and I wish you luck. Me, I don't like holes."

The shadows were hard upon him now. One brushed against him, and its touch was cold, cold as the bones that lay in the open space. Swiftly, so swiftly that none of the men could stop him, Barrier whirled and leaped through them, running like a deer.

He took them by surprise, the small dark blots that hung so close to him. He got past them, trampling on the brittle bones. And then the shadows followed, spreading out fanwise behind him, with three or four racing on to catch him.

He was some distance ahead of them. He heard Hubbard's voice shrieking after him, but not the words it said. He put out every ounce of strength that was in him, rushing between the heaped-up ruins, into the arms of mist that reached along the ground.

The shadows were closing in. But it was the mist that sprang.

It rolled around and wrapped him in, and where it touched his flesh he knew that the glittering droplets were not drops of mist at all but tiny flecks of life, separate, sentient, gathered together in formidable colonies of cloud. And he knew two other things, in that second when it was too late for knowledge—that the mist had not touched him nor the others in the forest, and that it had moved into the ruined city after them, against the wind.

Tiny flecks of life, glittering like powdered gems. And they hated man with a curious, inherited enmity.

There was a numbing agony in Barrier, an ecstasy of curious anguish that made his body twitch and dance. His throat convulsed, but no sound came out of it, and his eyes were filled with motes of fire. He tried to run again, and could not, and somewhere far away in another world, Hubbard was still shouting.

The shadows came. A broken thought went tumbling into the stricken emptiness of his mind—*They work together, damn them, and they both hate man.* Then there was the horrid cold, the alien presence sweeping through him, and this was death....

The mists drew back. The tearing anguish left him, and the chill darkness that possessed him was somehow healing to his seared nerves. It was like being shocked with icy water, so that suddenly he could see and think again, even through the gloomy veil that dimmed his sight and mind.

The shadows leaped and swirled around him, and where they

leaped the mists that were not mists at all drew back, sullen and reluctant, but coiling all the same upon themselves. And the shadow-thing that was inside of Barrier made him turn and go back toward the ruins, not fast this time, but slowly because he had been hurt, giving Barrier, in some unfathomable way, of its own strength.

The others came behind, a rear guard, dodging, weaving, pouncing on the stealthy tentacles of mist that sought to reach around them to the men who stood gaping by the great hummock. Here and there a glistening cloud engulfed a single shadow, and suddenly it was not.

Barrier's face, obscured by the dim aura, took on a strange expression.

He sat down at Hubbard's feet and the shadow left him, and they were as they had been before, the men, the shadows, the little beds of ash still glowing, and the wavering mist beyond.

Hubbard swore meaningless oaths meant to conceal his shame. "Were you crazy, Barrier? Did you think you could draw them all away from us?"

Aiken said, "He was trying to get away, to get a warning to the ship so maybe they could save us." He bent over. "Barrier, listen. Barrier...."

He paid them no attention. He was watching the shadows that hovered between them and the mist. A few of them were darting as they had before, from the burned-out fires to the men and back again.

"They want us to put on more fuel," he said slowly. "The fires help them keep the mist away." He turned abruptly to the others. "They saved me, did you see that? They came after me, and one protected me with its own body, and some of them died." He was shaking a little. "We were wrong about them. They were trying to help us in the forest. They followed us like—"

A word hovered on his tongue and he considered it, thinking of his boyhood and a small soiled terrier who had eaten his boots and loved him and once had interposed his body between Barrier and a fearsome hissing thing. It had only been a gopher snake, but the idea was the same.

"I think," he said, "that those shadows were the dogs, the protectors, of the men who lived here once. Different from our own, but trained to hunt down and turn aside enemies from their men. It was the mist that killed Schmidt and Morris, of course. We didn't keep together, and the shadows couldn't save us all."

The men stared at the shadows. It was hard to change their minds now, but they could not deny what they had seen. Their faces softened, just a little, losing some of the hard fear. Then Hubbard said:

"But what about *them?*" and he pointed at the bones.

Barrier shook his head. "Whatever killed them, it wasn't the shadows." His voice had an odd far-away note. His mind was very busy with something, taking it apart and studying the pieces intently and then putting it back together a different way. At last he smiled a little and went toward the shadows. He began to talk to them, putting out his hands, and they clustered around him, bounding up playfully.

"They must have been lonesome all this time," he said, "guarding their masters' bones."

Aiken said, "Down there in that passage—it's built of solid rock and hasn't crumbled a bit—there are some symbols cut in the wall. I haven't really looked at them, but—well, it seems as though all the people in the city gathered here to die at once, and it could be that they left a message or two in the strongest places."

"Let's look," said Hubbard.

They went down through the opening Aiken had found, all except Barrier, who was still playing with the shadow-dogs, and smiling. He was only mildly interested when they came back, Aiken and Hubbard both flushed and joyous.

"Those symbols," said Aiken. "They're pictographs, so simple and clear that anyone could read them. They must have hoped, those people, that someone would come along sooner or later. Anyway, they told what happened to them, or rather, what was going to happen. The planet had already entered the edges of a cloud that was death for lung breathers. That's why the animals died too, and only the lungless creatures lived. And Barrier...."

"Yes?"

"They mentioned the dogs. They drew quite clear pictures of them at work, so that strangers would know."

Barrier nodded. He looked at the dark blots romping about his feet. "They've waited all this time. Well, they can wait a little longer."

Then he straightened up, still with that odd, wry smile.

"Seems like I spoke too soon," he said. "Maybe there's enough worth in us that here and there some little world will give us another chance. Anyway, it's nice to know there's one place where we have some friends."

They heaped fuel on the fires, and the shadows danced. Barrier watched them, looking somehow younger, like a man who has rediscovered hope.

The Last Days of Shandakor

Startling Stories, April 1954

I

HE CAME alone into the wine-shop, wrapped in a dark red cloak, with the cowl drawn over his head. He stood for a moment by the doorway and one of the slim dark predatory women who live in those places went to him, with a silvery chiming from the little bells that were almost all she wore.

I saw her smile up at him. And then, suddenly, the smile became fixed and something happened to her eyes. She was no longer look-ing at the cloaked man but through him. In the oddest fashion – it was as though he had become invisible.

She went by him. Whether she passed some word along or not I couldn't tell but an empty space widened around the stranger. And no one looked at him. They did not avoid looking at him. They sim-ply refused to see him.

He began to walk slowly across the crowded room. He was very tall and he moved with a fluid, powerful grace that was beautiful to watch. People drifted out of his way, not seeming to, but doing it. The air was thick with nameless smells, shrill with the laughter of women.

Two tall barbarians, far gone in wine, were carrying on some in-tertribal feud and the yelling crowd had made room for them to fight. There was a silver pipe and a drum and a double-banked harp mak-ing old wild music. Lithe brown bodies leaped and whirled through the laughter and the shouting and the smoke.

The stranger walked through all this, alone, untouched, unseen.

He passed close to where I sat. Perhaps because I, of all the people in that place, not only saw him but stared at him, he gave me a glance of black eyes from under the shadow of his cowl – eyes like blown coals, bright with suffering and rage.

I caught only a glimpse of his muffled face. The merest glimpse – but that was enough. *Why did he have to show his face to me in that wine-shop in Barrakesh?*

He passed on. There was no space in the shadowy corner where he went but space was made, a circle of it, a moat between the stranger and the crowd. He sat down. I saw him lay a coin on the outer edge of the table. Presently a serving wench came up, picked up the coin and set down a cup of wine. But it was as if she waited on an empty table.

I turned to Kardak, my head drover, a Shunni with massive shoulders and uncut hair braided in an intricate tribal knot. "What's all that about?" I asked.

Kardak shrugged. "Who knows?" He started to rise. "Come, JonRoss. It is time we got back to the serai."

"We're not leaving for hours yet. And don't lie to me, I've been on Mars a long time. What is that man? Where does he come from?"

Barrakesh is the gateway between north and south. Long ago, when there were oceans in equatorial and southern Mars, when Valkis and Jekkara were proud seats of empire and not thieves' dens, here on the edge of the northern Drylands the great caravans had come and gone to Barrakesh for a thousand thousand years. It is a place of strangers.

In the time-eaten streets of rock you see tall Keshi hillmen, nomads from the high plains of Upper Shun, lean dark men from the south who barter away the loot of forgotten tombs and temples, cosmopolitan sophisticates up from Kahora and the trade cities, where there are spaceports and all the appurtenances of modern civilization.

The red-cloaked stranger was none of these.

A GLIMPSE of a face – I am a planetary anthropologist. I was supposed to be charting Martian ethnology and I was doing it on a fellowship grant I had wangled from a Terran university too ignorant to know that the vastness of Martian history makes such a project hopeless.

I was in Barrakesh, gathering an outfit preparatory to a year's study of the tribes of Upper Shun. And suddenly there had passed close by me a man with golden skin and un-Martian black eyes and a facial structure that belonged to no race I knew. I have seen the carven faces of fauns that were a little like it.

Kardak said again, "It is time to go, JonRoss!"

I looked at the stranger, drinking his wine in silence and alone. "Very well, *I'll* ask him."

Kardak sighed. "Earthmen," he said, "are not given much to wisdom." He turned and left me.

I crossed the room and stood beside the stranger. In the old courteous High Martian they speak in all the Low-Canal towns I asked permission to sit.

Those raging, suffering eyes met mine. There was hatred in them, and scorn, and shame. "What breed of human are you?"

"I am an Earthman."

He said the name over as though he had heard it before and was trying to remember. "Earthman. Then it is as the winds have said, blowing across the desert—that Mars is dead and men from other worlds defile her dust." He looked out over the wine-shop and all the people who would not admit his presence. "Change," he whispered. "Death and change and the passing away of things."

The muscles of his face drew tight. He drank and I could see now that he had been drinking for a long time, for days, perhaps for weeks. There was a quiet madness on him.

"Why do the people shun you?"

"Only a man of Earth would need to ask," he said and made a sound of laughter, very dry and bitter.

I was thinking, *A new race, an unknown race!* I was thinking of the fame that sometimes comes to men who discover a new thing, and of a Chair I might sit in at the University if I added one bright unheard-of piece of the shadowy mosaic of Martian history. I had had my share of wine and a bit more. That Chair looked a mile high and made of gold.

The stranger said softly, "I go from place to place in this wallow of Barrakesh and everywhere it is the same. I have ceased to be." His white teeth glittered for an instant in the shadow of the cowl. "They were wiser than I, my people. When Shandakor is dead, we are dead also, whether our bodies live or not."

"Shandakor?" I said. It had a sound of distant bells.

"How should an Earthman know? Yes, Shandakor! Ask of the men of Kesh and the men of Shun! Ask the kings of Mekh, who are half around the world! Ask of all the men of Mars—they have not forgotten Shandakor! But they will not tell you. It is a bitter shame to them, the memory and the name."

He stared out across the turbulent throng that filled the room and flowed over to the noisy street outside. "And I am here among them—lost."

"Shandakor is dead?"

"Dying. There were three of us who did not want to die. We came south across the desert—one turned back, one perished in the sand, I am here in Barrakesh." The metal of the wine-cup bent between his hands.

I said, "And you regret your coming."

"I should have stayed and died with Shandakor. I know that now. But I cannot go back."

"Why not?" *I was thinking how the name John Ross would look, inscribed in golden letters on the scroll of the discoverers.*

"The desert is wide, Earthman. Too wide for one alone."

And I said, "I have a caravan. I am going north tonight."

A light came into his eyes, so strange and deadly that I was afraid. "No," he whispered. *"No!"*

I sat in silence, looking out across the crowd that had forgotten me as well, because I sat with the stranger. *A new race, an unknown city. And I was drunk.*

After a long while the stranger asked me, "What does an Earthman want in Shandakor?"

I told him. He laughed. "You study men," he said and laughed again, so that the red cloak rippled.

"If you want to go back I'll take you. If you don't, tell me where the city lies and I'll find it. Your race, your city, should have their place in history."

He said nothing but the wine had made me very shrewd and I could guess at what was going on in the stranger's mind. I got up.

"Consider it," I told him. "You can find me at the serai by the northern gate until the lesser moon is up. Then I'll be gone."

"Wait." His fingers fastened on my wrist. They hurt. I looked into his face and I did not like what I saw there. But, as Kardak had mentioned, I was not given much to wisdom.

The stranger said, "Your men will not go beyond the Wells of Karthedon."

"Then we'll go without them."

A long, long silence. Then he said, "So be it."

I knew what he was thinking as plainly as though he had spoken the words. He was thinking that I was only an Earthman and that he would kill me when we came in sight of Shandakor.

II

THE CARAVAN TRACKS branch off at the Wells of Karthedon. One goes westward into Shun and one goes north through the passes of Outer Kesh. But there is a third one, more ancient than the others. It goes toward the east and it is never used. The deep rock wells are dry and the stone-built shelters have vanished under the rolling dunes. It is not until the track begins to climb the mountains that there are even memories.

Kardak refused politely to go beyond the Wells. He would wait for me, he said, a certain length of time, and if I came back we would go on into Shun. If I didn't—well, his full pay was left in charge of the local headman. He would collect it and go home. He had not liked having the stranger with us. He had doubled his price.

In all that long march up from Barrakesh I had not been able to get a word out of Kardak or the men concerning Shandakor. The stranger had not spoken either. He had told me his name—Corin—and nothing more. Cloaked and cowled he rode alone and brooded. His private devils were still with him and he had a new one now—impatience. He would have ridden us all to death if I had let him.

So Corin and I went east alone from Karthedon, with two led animals and all the water we could carry. And now I could not hold him back.

"There is no time to stop," he said. "The days are running out. There is no time!"

When we reached the mountains we had only three animals left and when we crossed the first ridge we were afoot and leading the one remaining beast which carried the dwindling water skins.

We were following a road now. Partly hewn and partly worn it led up and over the mountains, those naked leaning mountains that were full of silence and peopled only with the shapes of red rock that the wind had carved.

"Armies used to come this way," said Corin. "Kings and caravans and beggars and human slaves, singers and dancing girls and the embassies of princes. This was the road to Shandakor."

And we went along it at a madman's pace.

The beast fell in a slide of rock and broke its neck and we carried the last water skin between us. It was not a heavy burden. It grew lighter and then was almost gone.

One afternoon, long before sunset, Corin said abruptly, "We will stop here."

The road went steeply up before us. There was nothing to be seen or heard. Corin sat down in the drifted dust. I crouched down too, a little distance from him. I watched him. His face was hidden and he did not speak.

The shadows thickened in that deep and narrow way. Overhead the strip of sky flared saffron and then red—and then the bright cruel stars came out. The wind worked at its cutting and polishing of stone, muttering to itself, an old and senile wind full of dissatisfaction and complaint. There was the dry faint click of falling pebbles.

The gun felt cold in my hand, covered with my cloak. I did not want to use it. But I did not want to die here on this silent pathway of vanished armies and caravans and kings.

A shaft of greenish moonlight crept down between the walls. Corin stood up.

"Twice now I have followed lies. Here I am met at last by truth."

I said, "I don't understand you."

"I thought I could escape the destruction. That was a lie. Then I thought I could return to share it. That too was a lie. Now I see the truth. Shandakor is dying. I fled from that dying, which is the end of the city and the end of my race. The shame of flight is on me and I can never go back."

"What will you do?"

"I will die here."

"And I?"

"Did you think," asked Corin softly, "that I would bring an alien creature in to watch the end of Shandakor?"

I MOVED first. I didn't know what weapons he might have, hidden under that dark red cloak. I threw myself over on the dusty rock. Something went past my head with a hiss and a rattle and a flame of light and then I cut the legs from under him and he fell down forward and I got on top of him, very fast.

He had vitality. I had to hit his head twice against the rock before I could take out of his hands the vicious little instrument of metal rods. I threw it far away. I could not feel any other weapons on him except a knife and I took that, too. Then I got up.

I said, "I will carry you to Shandakor."

He lay still, draped in the tumbled folds of his cloak. His breath made a harsh sighing in his throat. "So be it." And then he asked for water.

I went to where the skin lay and picked it up, thinking that there was perhaps a cupful left. I didn't hear him move. What he did was done very silently with a sharp-edged ornament. I brought him the water and it was already over. I tried to lift him up. His eyes looked at me with a curiously brilliant look. Then he whispered three words, in a language I didn't know, and died. I let him down again.

His blood had poured out across the dust. And even in the moon-light I could see that it was not the color of human blood.

I crouched there for a long while, overcome with a strange sick-ness. Then I reached out and pushed that red cowl back to bare his head. It was a beautiful head. I had never seen it. If I had, I would not have gone alone with Corin into the mountains. I would have understood many things if I had seen it and not for fame nor money would I have gone to Shandakor.

His skull was narrow and arched and the shaping of the bones was very fine. On that skull was a covering of short curling fibres that had an almost metallic luster in the moonlight, silvery and bright. They stirred under my hand, soft silken wires responding of them-selves to an alien touch. And even as I took my hand away the luster faded from them and the texture changed.

When I touched them again they did not stir. Corin's ears were pointed and there were silvery tufts on the tips of them. On them and on his forearms and his breast were the faint, faint memories of scales, a powdering of shining dust across the golden skin. I looked at his teeth and they were not human either.

I knew now why Corin had laughed when I told him that I stud-ied men.

It was very still. I could hear the falling of pebbles and the little stones that rolled all lonely down the cliffs and the shift and whisper of dust in the settling cracks. The Wells of Karthedon were far away. Too far by several lifetimes for one man on foot with a cup of water.

I looked at the road that went steep and narrow on ahead. I looked at Corin. The wind was cold and the shaft of moonlight was growing thin. I did not want to stay alone in the dark with Corin.

I rose and went on along the road that led to Shandakor.

It was a long climb but not a long way. The road came out be-tween two pinnacles of rock. Below that gateway, far below in the light of the little low moons that pass so swiftly over Mars, there was a mountain valley.

Once around that valley there were great peaks crowned with snow and crags of black and crimson where the flying lizards nested, the hawk-lizards with the red eyes. Below the crags there were for-

ests, purple and green and gold, and a black tarn deep on the valley
floor. But when I saw it it was dead. The peaks had fallen away and
the forests were gone and the tarn was only a pit in the naked rock.

In the midst of that desolation stood a fortress city.

There were lights in it, soft lights of many colors. The outer walls
stood up, black and massive, a barrier against the creeping dust, and
within them was an island of life. The high towers were not ruined.
The lights burned among them and there was movement in the
streets.

A LIVING city—and Corin had said that Shandakor was almost
dead.

A rich and living city. I did not understand. But I knew one thing.
Those who moved along the distant streets of Shandakor were not
human.

I stood shivering in that windy pass. The bright towers of the city
beckoned and there was something unnatural about all light life in
the deathly valley. And then I thought that human or not the people
of Shandakor might sell me water and a beast to carry it and I could
get away out of these mountains, back to the Wells.

The road broadened, winding down the slope. I walked in the
middle of it, not expecting anything. And suddenly two men came
out of nowhere and barred the way.

I yelled. I jumped backward with my heart pounding and the
sweat pouring off me. I saw their broadswords glitter in the moonlight. And they laughed.

They were human. One was a tall red barbarian from Mekh, which
lay to the east half around Mars. The other was a leaner browner man
from Taarak, which was farther still. I was scared and angry and astonished and I asked a foolish question.

"What are you doing *here?*"

"We wait," said the man of Taarak. He made a circle with his arm
to take in all the darkling slopes around the valley. "From Kesh and
Shun, from all the countries of the Norlands and the Marches men
have come, to wait. And you?"

"I'm lost," I said. "I'm an Earthman and I have no quarrel with anyone." I was still shaking but now it was with relief. I would not have to go to Shandakor. If there was a barbarian army gathered here it must have supplies and I could deal with them.

I told them what I needed. "I can pay for them, pay well."

They looked at each other.

"Very well. Come and you can bargain with the chief."

They fell in on either side of me. We walked three paces and then I was on my face in the dirt and they were all over me like two great wildcats. When they were finished they had everything I owned except the few articles of clothing for which they had no use. I got up again, wiping the blood from my mouth.

"For an outlander," said the man of Mekh, "you fight well." He chinked my money-bag up and down in his palm, feeling the weight of it, and then he handed me the leather bottle that hung at his side. "Drink," he told me. "That much I can't deny you. But our water must be carried a long way across these mountains and we have none to waste on Earthmen."

I was not proud. I emptied his bottle for him. And the man of Ta-arak said, smiling, "Go on to Shandakor. Perhaps they will give you water."

"But you've taken all my money!"

"They are rich in Shandakor. They don't need money. Go ask them for water."

They stood there, laughing at some secret joke of their own, and I did not like the sound of it. I could have killed them both and danced on their bodies but they had left me nothing but my bare hands to fight with. So presently I turned and went on and left them grinning in the dark behind me.

The road led down and out across the plain. I could feel eyes watching me, the eyes of the sentinels on the rounding slopes, piercing the dim moonlight. The walls of the city began to rise higher and higher. They hid everything but the top of one tall tower that had a queer squat globe on top of it. Rods of crystal projected from the globe. It revolved slowly and the rods sparkled with a sort of white fire that was just on the edge of seeing.

A causeway lifted toward the Western Gate. I mounted it, going very slowly, not wanting to go at all. And now I could see that the gate was open. *Open* — and this was a city under siege!

I stood still for some time, trying to puzzle out what meaning this might have — an army that did not attack and a city with open gates. I could not find a meaning. There were soldiers on the walls but they were lounging at their ease under the bright banners. Beyond the gate many people moved about but they were intent on their own affairs. I could not hear their voices.

I crept closer, closer still. Nothing happened. The sentries did not challenge me and no one spoke.

You know how necessity can force a man against his judgment and against his will?

I entered Shandakor.

III

THERE was an open space beyond the gate, a square large enough to hold an army. Around its edges were the stalls of merchants. Their canopies were of rich woven stuffs and the wares they sold were such things as have not been seen on Mars for more centuries than men can remember.

There were fruits and rare furs, the long-lost dyes that never fade, furnishings carved from vanished woods. There were spices and wines and exquisite cloths. In one place a merchant from the far south offered a ceremonial rug woven from the long bright hair of virgins. And it was new.

These merchants were all human. The nationalities of some of them I knew. Others I could guess at from traditional accounts. Some were utterly unknown.

Of the throngs that moved about among the stalls, quite a number were human also. There were merchant princes come to barter and there were companies of slaves on their way to the auction block. But the others...

I stayed where I was, pressed into a shadowy corner by the gate, and the chill that was on me was not all from the night wind.

The golden-skinned silver-crested lords of Shandakor I knew well enough from Corin. I say lords because that is how they bore themselves, walking proudly in their own place, attended by human slaves. And the humans who were not slaves made way for them and were most deferential as though they knew that they were greatly favored to be allowed inside the city at all. The women of Shandakor were very beautiful, slim golden sprites with their bright eyes and pointed ears.

And there were others. Slender creatures with great wings, some who were lithe and furred, some who were hairless and ugly and moved with a sinuous gliding, some so strangely shaped and colored that I could not even guess at their possible evolution.

The lost races of Mars. The ancient races, of whose pride and power nothing was left but the half-forgotten tales of old men in the farthest corners of the planet. Even I, who had made the anthropological history of Mars my business, had never heard of them except as the distorted shapes of legend, as satyrs and giants used to be known on Earth.

Yet here they were in gorgeous trappings, served by naked humans whose fetters were made of precious metals. And before them too the merchants drew aside and bowed.

The lights burned, many-colored—not the torches and cressets of the Mars I knew but cool radiances that fell from crystal globes. The walls of the buildings that rose around the market place were faced with rare veined marbles and the fluted towers that crowned them were inlaid with turquoise and cinnabar, with amber and jade and the wonderful corals of the southern oceans.

The splendid robes and the naked bodies moved in a swirling pattern about the square. There was buying and selling and I could see the mouths of the people open and shut. The mouths of the women laughed. But in all that crowded place there was no sound. No voice, no scuff of sandal, no chink of mail. There was only silence, the utter stillness of deserted places.

I began to understand why there was no need to shut the gates. No superstitious barbarian would venture himself into a city peopled by living phantoms.

And I—I was civilized. I was, in my non-mechanical way, a scientist. And had I not been trapped by my need for water and supplies I would have run away right out of the valley. But I had no place to run to and so I stayed and sweated and gagged on the acrid taste of fear.

WHAT were these creatures that made no sound? Ghosts—images—dreams? The human and the non-human, the ancient, the proud, the lost and forgotten who were so insanely present—did they have some subtle form of life I knew nothing about? Could they see me as I saw them? Did they have thought and volition of their own?

It was the solidity of them, the intense and perfectly prosaic business in which they were engaged. Ghosts do not barter. They do not hang jeweled necklets upon their women nor argue about the price of a studded harness.

The solidity and the silence—that was the worst of it. If there had been one small living sound...

A dying city, Corin had said. *The days are running out.* What if they had run out? What if I were here in this massive pile of stone with all its countless rooms and streets and galleries and hidden ways, alone with the lights and the soundless phantoms?

Pure terror is a nasty thing. I had it then.

I began to move, very cautiously, along the wall. I wanted to get away from that market place. One of the hairless gliding non-humans was bartering for a female slave. The girl was shrieking. I could see every drawn muscle in her face, the spasmodic working of her throat. Not the faintest sound came out.

I found a street that paralleled the wall. I went along it, catching glimpses of people—human people—inside the lighted buildings. Now and then men passed me and I hid from them. There was still no sound. I was careful how I set my feet. Somehow I had the idea that if I made a noise something terrible would happen.

A group of merchants came toward me. I stepped back into an archway and suddenly from behind me there came three spangled women of the serais. I was caught.

I did not want those silent laughing women to touch me. I leaped back toward the street and the merchants paused, turning their heads. I thought that they had seen me. I hesitated and the women came on. Their painted eyes shone and their red lips glistened. The ornaments on their bodies flashed. They walked straight into me.

I made noise then, all I had in my lungs. And the women passed through me. They spoke to the merchants and the merchants laughed. They went off together down the street. They hadn't seen me. They hadn't heard me. And when I got in their way I was no more than a shadow. They passed through me.

I sat down on the stones of the street and tried to think. I sat for a long time. Men and women walked through me as through the empty air. I sought to remember any sudden pain, as of an arrow in the back that might have killed me between two seconds, so that I hadn't known about it. It seemed more likely that I should be the ghost than the other way around.

I couldn't remember. My body felt solid to my hands as did the stones I sat on. They were cold and finally the cold got me up and sent me on again. There was no reason to hide any more. I walked down the middle of the street and I got used to not turning aside.

I came to another wall, running at right angles back into the city. I followed that and it curved around gradually until I found myself back at the market place, at the inner end of it. There was a gateway, with the main part of the city beyond it, and the wall continued. The non-humans passed back and forth through the gate but no human did except the slaves. I realized then that all this section was a ghetto for the humans who came to Shandakor with the caravans.

I remembered how Corin had felt about me. And I wondered—granted that I were still alive and that some of the people of Shandakor were still on the same plane as myself—how they would feel about me if I trespassed in their city.

There was a fountain in the market place. The water sprang up sparkling in the colored light and filled a wide basin of carved stone. Men and women were drinking from it. I went to the fountain but when I put my hands in it all I felt was a dry basin filled with dust. I lifted my hands and let the dust trickle from them. I could see it clearly. But I saw the water too. A child leaned over and splashed it and it wetted the garments of the people. They struck the child and he cried and there was no sound.

I went on through the gate that was forbidden to the human race.

The avenues were wide. There were trees and flowers, wide parks and garden villas, great buildings as graceful as they were tall. A wise proud city, ancient in culture but not decayed, as beautiful as Athens but rich and strange, with a touch of the alien in every line of it. Can you think what it was like to walk in that city, among the silent throngs that were not human – to see the glory of it, that was not human either?

The towers of jade and cinnabar, the golden minarets, the lights and the colored silks, the enjoyment and the strength. And the people of Shandakor! No matter how far their souls have gone they will never forgive me.

How long I wandered I don't know. I had almost lost my fear in wonder at what I saw. And then, all at once in that deathly stillness, I heard a sound – the quick, soft scuffing of sandaled feet.

IV

I STOPPED where I was, in the middle of a plaza. The tall silver-crested ones drank wine under canopies of dusky blooms and in the center a score of winged girls as lovely as swans danced a slow strange measure that was more like flight than dancing. I looked all around. There were many people. How could you tell which one had made a noise?

Silence.

I turned and ran across the marble paving. I ran hard and then suddenly I stopped again, listening. *Scuff-scuff*—no more than a whisper, very light and swift. I spun around but it was gone. The soundless people walked and the dancers wove and shifted, spreading their white wings.

Someone was watching me. Some one of those indifferent shadow was not a shadow.

I went on. Wide streets led off from the plaza. I took one of them.

I tried the trick of shifting pace and two or three times I caught the echo of other steps than mine. Once I knew it was deliberate. Whoever followed me slipped silently among the noiseless crowd, blending with them, protected by them, only making a show of footsteps now and then to goad me.

I spoke to that mocking presence. I talked to it and listened to my own voice ringing hollow from the walls. The groups of people ebbed and flowed around me and there was no answer.

I tried making sudden leaps here and there among the passers-by with my arms outspread. But all I caught was empty air. I wanted a place to hide and there was none.

The street was long. I went its length and the someone followed me. There were many buildings, all lighted and populous and deathly still. I thought of trying to hide in the buildings but I could not bear to be closed in between walls with those people who were not people.

I came into a great circle, where a number of avenues met around the very tall tower I had seen with the revolving globe on top of it. I hesitated, not knowing which way to go. Someone was sobbing and I realized that it was myself, laboring to breathe. Sweat ran into the corners of my mouth and it was cold, and bitter.

A pebble dropped at my feet with a brittle *click*.

I bolted out across the square. Four or five times, without reason, like a rabbit caught in the open, I changed course and fetched up with my back against an ornamental pillar. From somewhere there came a sound of laughter.

I began to yell. I don't know what I said. Finally I stopped and there was only the silence and the passing throngs, who did not see nor hear me. And now it seemed to me that the silence was full of whispers just below the threshold of hearing.

A second pebble clattered off the pillar above my head. Another stung my body. I sprang away from the pillar. There was laughter and I ran.

There were infinities of streets, all glowing with color. There were many faces, strange faces, and robes blown out on a night wind, litters with scarlet curtains and beautiful cars like chariots drawn by beasts. They flowed past me like smoke, without sound, without substance, and the laughter pursued me, and I ran.

Four men of Shandakor came toward me. I plunged through them *but their bodies opposed mine, their hands caught me and I could see their eyes, their black shining eyes, looking at me....*

I struggled briefly and then it was suddenly very dark.

The darkness caught me up and took me somewhere. Voices talked far away. One of them was a light young shiny sort of voice. It matched the laughter that had haunted me down the streets. I hated it.

I hated it so much that I fought to get free of the black river that was carrying me. There was a vertiginous whirling of light and sound and stubborn shadow and then things steadied down and I was ashamed of myself for having passed out.

I was in a room. It was fairly large, very beautiful, very old, the first place I had seen in Shandakor that showed real age — Martian age, that runs back before history had begun on Earth. The floor, of some magnificent somber stone the color of a moonless night, and the pale slim pillars that upheld the arching roof all showed the hollowings and smoothnesses of centuries. The wall paintings had dimmed and softened and the rugs that burned in pools of color on that dusky floor were worn as thin as silk.

There were men and women in that room, the alien folk of Shandakor. But these breathed and spoke and were alive. One of them, a girl-child with slender thighs and little pointed breasts, leaned against a pillar close beside me. Her black eyes watched me, full of dancing lights. When she saw that I was awake again she smiled and flicked a pebble at my feet.

I got up. I wanted to get that golden body between my hands and make it scream. And she said in High Martian, "Are you a human? I have never seen one before close to."

A MAN in a dark robe said, "Be still, Duani." He came and stood before me. He did not seem to be armed but others were and I remembered Corin's little weapon. I got hold of myself and did none of the things I wanted to do.

"What are you doing here?" asked the man in the dark robe.

I told him about myself and Corin, omitting only the fight that he and I had had before be died, and I told him how the hillmen had robbed me.

"They sent me here," I finished, "to ask for water."

Someone made a harsh humorless sound. The man before me said, "They were in a jesting mood."

"Surely you can spare some water and a beast!"

"Our beasts were slaughtered long ago. And as for water…" He paused, then asked bitterly, "Don't you understand? We are dying here of thirst!"

I looked at him and at the she-imp called Duani and the others. "You don't show any signs of it," I said.

"You saw how the human tribes have gathered like wolves upon the hills. What do you think they wait for? A year ago they found and cut the buried aqueduct that brought water into Shandakor from the polar cap. All they needed then was patience. And their time is very near. The store we had in the cisterns is almost gone."

A certain anger at their submissiveness made me say, "Why do you stay here and die like mice bottled up in a jar? You could have fought your way out. I've seen your weapons."

"Our weapons are old and we are very few. And suppose that some of us did survive—tell me again, Earthman, how did Corin fare in the world of men?" He shook his head. "Once we were great and Shandakor was mighty. The human tribes of half a world paid tribute to us. We are only the last poor shadow of our race but we will not beg from men!"

"Besides," said Duani softly, "where else could we live but in Shandakor?"

"What about the others?" I asked. "The silent ones."

"They are the past," said the dark-robed man and his voice rang like a distant flare of trumpets.

Still I did not understand. I did not understand at all. But before I could ask more questions a man came up and said, "Rhul, he will have to die."

The tufted tips of Duani's ears quivered and her crest of silver curls came almost erect.

"No, Rhul!" she cried. "At least not right away."

There was a clamor from the others, chiefly in a rapid angular speech that must have predated all the syllables of men. And the one who had spoken before to Rhul repeated, "He will have to die! He has no place here. And we can't spare water."

"I'll share mine with him," said Duani, "for a while."

I didn't want any favors from her and said so. "I came here after supplies. You haven't any, so I'll go away again. It's as simple as that." I couldn't buy from the barbarians, but I might make shift to steal.

Rhul shook his head. "I'm afraid not. We are only a handful. For years our single defense has been the living ghosts of our past who walk the streets, the shadows who man the walls. The barbarians believe in enchantments. If you were to enter Shandakor and leave it again alive the barbarians would know that the enchantment cannot kill. They would not wait any longer."

Angrily, because I was afraid, I said, "I can't see what difference that would make. You're going to die in a short while anyway."

"But in our own way, Earthman, and in our own time. Perhaps, being human, you can't understand that. It is a question of pride. The oldest race of Mars will end well, as it began."

He turned away with a small nod of the head that said *kill him*—as easily as that. And I saw the ugly little weapons rise.

V

THERE WAS a split second then that seemed like a year. I thought of many things but none of them were any good. It was a devil of a place to die without even a human hand to help me under. And then Duani flung her arms around me.

"You're all so full of dying and big thoughts!" she yelled at them. "And you're all paired off or so old you can't do anything but think! What about *me?* I don't have anyone to talk to and I'm sick of wandering alone, thinking how I'm going to die! Let me have him just for a little while? I told you I'd share my water."

On Earth a child might talk that way about a stray dog. And it is written in an old Book that a live dog is better than a dead lion. I hoped they would let her keep me.

They did. Rhul looked at Duani with a sort of weary compassion and lifted his hand. "Wait," he said to the men with the weapons. "I have thought how this human may be useful to us. We have so little time left now that it is a pity to waste any of it, yet much of it must be used up in tending the machine. He could do that labor—and a man can keep alive on very little water."

The others thought that over. Some of them dissented violently, not so much on the grounds of water as that it was unthinkable that a human should intrude on the last days of Shandakor. Corin had said the same thing. But Rhul was an old man. The tufts of his pointed ears were colorless as glass and his face was graven deep with years and wisdom had distilled in him its bitter brew.

"A human of our own world, yes. But this man is of Earth and the men of Earth will come to be the new rulers of Mars as we were the old. And Mars will love them no better than she did us because they are as alien as we. So it is not unfitting that he should see us out."

They had to be content with that. I think they were already so close to the end that they did not really care. By ones and twos they left as though already they had wasted too much time away from the wonders that there were in the streets outside. Some of the men still held the weapons on me and others went and brought precious chains such as the human slaves had worn—shackles, so that I should not escape. They put them on me and Duani laughed.

"Come," said Rhul, "and I will show you the machine."

He led me from the room and up a winding stair. There were tall embrasures and looking through them I discovered that we were in the base of the very high tower with the globe. They must have carried me back to it after Duani had chased me with her laughter and her pebbles. I looked out over the glowing streets, so full of splendor and of silence, and asked Rhul why there were no ghosts inside the tower.

"You have seen the globe with the crystal rods?"

"Yes."

"We are under the shadow of its core. There had to be some retreat for us into reality. Otherwise we would lose the meaning of the dream."

The winding stair went up and up. The chain between my ankles clattered musically. Several times I tripped on it and fell.

"Never mind," Duani said. "You'll grow used to it."

We came at last into a circular room high in the tower. And I stopped and stared.

MOST of the space in that room was occupied by a web of metal girders that supported a great gleaming shaft. The shaft disappeared upward through the roof. It was not tall but very massive, revolving slowly and quietly. There were traps, presumably for access to the offset shaft and the cogs that turned it. A ladder led to a trap in the roof.

All the visible metal was sound with only a little surface corrosion. What the alloy was I don't know and when I asked Rhul he only smiled rather sadly. "Knowledge is found," he said, "only to be lost again. Even we of Shandakor forget."

Every bit of that enormous structure had been shaped and polished and fitted into place by hand. Nearly all the Martian peoples work in metal. They seem to have a genius for it and while they are not and apparently never have been mechanical, as some of our races are on Earth, they find many uses for metal that we have never thought of.

But this before me was certainly the high point of the metalworkers' craft. When I saw what was down below, the beautifully simple power plant and the rotary drive set-up with fewer moving parts than I would have thought possible, I was even more respectful. "How old is it?" I asked and again Rhul shook his head.

"Several thousand years ago there is a record of the yearly Hosting of the Shadows and it was not the first." He motioned me to follow him up the ladder, bidding Duani sternly to remain where she was. She came anyway.

There was a railed platform open to the universe and directly above it swung the mighty globe with its crystal rods that gleamed so strangely. Shandakor lay beneath us, a tapestry of many colors, bright and still, and out along the dark sides of the valley the tribesmen waited for the light to die.

"When there is no one left to tend the machine it will stop in time and then the men who have hated us so long will take what they want of Shandakor. Only fear has kept them out this long. The riches of half a world flowed through these streets and much of it remained."

He looked up at the globe. "Yes," he said, "we had knowledge. More, I think, than any other race of Mars."

"But you wouldn't share it with the humans."

Rhul smiled. "Would you give little children weapons to destroy you? We gave men better ploughshares and brighter ornaments and if they invented a machine we did not take it from them. But we did not tempt and burden them with knowledge that was not their own. They were content to make war with sword and spear and so they had more pleasure and less killing and the world was not torn apart."

"And you—how did you make war?"

"We defended our city. The human tribes had nothing that we coveted, so there was no reason to fight them except in self-defense. When we did we won." He paused. "The other non-human races were more stupid or less fortunate. They perished long ago."

HE TURNED again to his explanations of the machine. "It draws its power directly from the sun. Some of the solar energy is converted and stored within the globe to serve as the light-source. Some is sent down to turn the shaft."

"What if it should stop," Duani said, "while we're still alive?" She shivered, looking out over the beautiful streets.

"It won't—not if the Earthman wishes to live."

"What would I have to gain by stopping it?" I demanded.

"Nothing. And that," said Rhul, "is why I trust you. As long as the globe turns you are safe from the barbarians. After we are gone you will have the pick of the loot of Shandakor."

How I was going to get away with it afterward he did not tell me.

He motioned me down the ladder again but I asked him, "What *is* the globe, Rhul? How does it make the—the Shadows?"

He frowned. "I can only tell you what has become, I'm afraid, mere traditional knowledge. Our wise men studied deeply into the properties of light. They learned that light has a definite effect upon solid matter and they believed, because of that effect, that stone and metal and crystalline things retain a 'memory' of all that they have 'seen.' Why this should be I do not know."

I didn't try to explain to him the quantum theory and the photo-electric effect nor the various experiments of Einstein and Millikan and the men who followed them. I didn't know them well enough myself and the old High Martian is deficient in such terminology.

I only said, "The wise men of my world also know that the impact of light tears away tiny particles from the substance it strikes."

I was beginning to get a glimmering of the truth. Light-patterns 'cut' in the electrons of metal and stone—sound-patterns cut in un-likely-looking mediums of plastic, each needing only the proper 'needle' to recreate the recorded melody or the recorded picture.

"They constructed the globe," said Rhul. "I do not know how many generations that required nor how many failures they must have had. But they found at last the invisible light that makes the stones give up their memories."

In other words they had found their needle. What wave-length or combination of wave-lengths in the electromagnetic spectrum flowed out from those crystal rods, there was no way for me to know. But where they probed the walls and the paving blocks of Shanda-kor they scanned the hidden patterns that were buried in them and brought them forth again in form and color—as the electron needle brings forth whole symphonies from a little ridged disc.

How they had achieved sequence and selectivity was another matter. Rhul said something about the 'memories' having different lengths. Perhaps he meant depth of penetration. The stones of Shan-dakor were ages old and the outer surfaces would have worn away.

The earliest impressions would be gone altogether or at least have become fragmentary and extremely shallow.

Perhaps the scanning beams could differentiate between the overlapping layers of impressions by that fraction of a micron difference in depth. Photons only penetrate so far into any given substance but if that substance is constantly growing less in thickness the photons would have the effect of going deeper. I imagine the globe was accurate in centuries or numbers of centuries, not in years.

However it was, the Shadows of a golden past walked the streets of Shandakor and the last men of the race waited quietly for death, remembering their glory.

Rhul took me below again and showed me what my tasks would be, chiefly involving a queer sort of lubricant and a careful watch over the power leads. I would have to spend most of my time there but not all of it. During the free periods, Duani might take me where she would.

The old man went away. Duani leaned herself against a girder and studied me with intense interest. "How are you called?" she asked.

"John Ross."

"JonRoss," she repeated and smiled. She began to walk around me, touching my hair, inspecting my arms and chest, taking a child's delight in discovering all the differences there were between herself and what we call a human. And that was the beginning of my captivity.

VI

THERE WERE days and nights, scant food and scanter water. There was Duani. And there was Shandakor. I lost my fear. And whether I lived to occupy the Chair or not, this was something to have seen.

Duani was my guide. I was tender of my duties because my neck depended on them but there was time to wander in the streets, to watch the crowded pageant that was not and sense the stillness and the desolation that were so cruelly real.

The Last Days of Shandakor

I began to get the feel of what this alien culture had been like and how it had dominated half a world without the need of conquest.

In a Hall of Government, built of white marble and decorated with wall friezes of austere magnificence, I watched the careful choosing and the crowning of a king. I saw the places of learning. I saw the young men trained for war as fully as they were instructed in the arts of peace. I saw the pleasure gardens, the theatres, the forums, the sporting fields—and I saw the places of work, where the men and women of Shandakor coaxed beauty from their looms and forges to trade for the things they wanted from the human world.

The human slaves were brought by their own kind to be sold, and they seemed to be well treated, as one treats a useful animal in which one has invested money. They had their work to do but it was only a small part of the work of the city.

The things that could be had nowhere else on Mars—the tools, the textiles, the fine work in metal and precious stones, the glass and porcelain—were fashioned by the people of Shandakor and they were proud of their skill. Their scientific knowledge they kept entirely to themselves, except what concerned agriculture or medicine or better ways of building drains and houses.

They were the lawgivers, the teachers. And the humans took all they would give and hated them for it. How long it had taken these people to attain such a degree of civilization Duani could not tell me. Neither could old Rhul.

"It is certain that we lived in communities, had a form of civil government, a system of numbers and written speech, before the human tribes. There are traditions of an earlier race than ours, from whom we learned these things. Whether or not this is true I do not know."

In its prime Shandakor had been a vast and flourishing city with countless thousands of inhabitants. Yet I could see no signs of poverty or crime. I couldn't even find a prison.

"Murder was punishable by death," said Rhul, "but it was most infrequent. Theft was for slaves. We did not stoop to it." He watched my face, smiling a little acid smile. "That startles you—a great city without suffering or crime or places of punishment."

I had to admit that it did. "Elder race or not, how did you manage to do it? I'm a student of cultures, both here and on my own world. I know all the usual patterns of development and I've read all the theories about them—but Shandakor doesn't fit any of them."

Rhul's smile deepened. "You are human," he said. "Do you wish the truth?"

"Of course."

"Then I will tell you. We developed the faculty of reason."

For a moment I thought he was joking. "Come," I said, "man is a reasoning being—on Earth the only reasoning being."

"I do not know of Earth," he answered courteously. "But on Mars man has always said, 'I reason, I am above the beasts because I reason.' And he has been very proud of himself because he could reason. It is the mark of his humanity. Being convinced that reason operates automatically within him he orders his life and his government upon emotion and superstition.

"He hates and fears and believes, not with reason but because he is told to by other men or by tradition. He does one thing and says another and his reason teaches him no difference between fact and falsehood. His bloodiest wars are fought for the merest whim—and that is why we did not give him weapons. His greatest follies appear to him the highest wisdom, his basest betrayals become noble acts—and that is why we could not teach him justice. We learned to reason. Man only learned to talk."

I understood then why the human tribes had hated the men of Shandakor. I said angrily, "Perhaps that is so on Mars. But only reasoning minds can develop great technologies and we humans of Earth have outstripped yours a million times. All right, you know or knew some things we haven't learned yet, in optics and some branches of electronics and perhaps in metallurgy. But..."

I went on to tell him all the things we had that Shandakor did not. "You never went beyond the beast of burden and the simple wheel. We achieved flight long ago. We have conquered space and the planets. We'll go on to conquer the stars!"

Rhul nodded. "Perhaps we were wrong. We remained here and

conquered ourselves." He looked out toward the slopes where the barbarian army waited and he sighed. "In the end it is all the same."

DAYS and nights and Duani, bringing me food, sharing her water, asking questions, taking me through the city. The only thing she would not show me was something they called the Place of Sleep. "I shall be there soon enough," she said and shivered.

"How long?" I asked. It was an ugly thing to say.

"We are not told. Rhul watches the level in the cisterns and when it's time…" She made a gesture with her hands. "Let us go up on the wall."

We went up among the ghostly soldiery and the phantom banners. Outside there were darkness and death and the coming of death. Inside there were light and beauty, the last proud blaze of Shandakor under the shadow of its doom. There was an eerie magic in it that had begun to tell on me. I watched Duani. She leaned against the parapet, looking outward. The wind ruffled her silver crest, pressed her garments close against her body. Her eyes were full of moonlight and I could not read them. Then I saw that there were tears.

I put my arm around her shoulders. She was only a child, an alien child, not of my race or breed.…

"JonRoss."

"Yes?"

"There are so many things I will never know."

It was the first time I had touched her. Those curious curls stirred under my fingers, warm and alive. The tips of her pointed ears were soft as a kitten's.

"Duani."

"What?"

"I don't know…"

I kissed her. She drew back and gave me a startled look from those black brilliant eyes and suddenly I stopped thinking that she was a child and I forgot that she was not human and—I didn't care.

"Duani, listen. You don't have to go to the Place of Sleep."

She looked at me, her cloak spread out upon the night wind, her hands against my chest.

"There's a whole world out there to live in. And if you aren't happy there I'll take you to my world, to Earth. There isn't any reason why you have to die!"

Still she looked at me and did not speak. In the streets below the silent throngs went by and the towers glowed with many colors. Duani's gaze moved slowly to the darkness beyond the wall, to the barren valley and the hostile rocks.

"No."

"Why not? Because of Rhul, because of all this talk of pride and race?"

"Because of truth. Corin learned it."

I didn't want to think about Corin. "He was alone. You're not. You'd never be alone."

She brought her hands up and laid them on my cheeks very gently. "That green star, that is your world. Suppose it were to vanish and you were the last of all the men of Earth. Suppose you lived with me in Shandakor forever—would you not be alone?"

"It wouldn't matter if I had you."

She shook her head. "It would matter. And our two races are as far apart as the stars. We would have nothing to share between us."

Remembering what Rhul had told me I flared up and said some angry things. She let me say them and then she smiled. "It is none of that, JonRoss." She turned to look out over the city. "This is my place and no other. When it is gone I must be gone too."

Quite suddenly I hated Shandakor.

I didn't sleep much after that. Every time Duani left me I was afraid she might never come back. Rhul would tell me nothing and I didn't dare to question him too much. The hours rushed by like seconds and Duani was happy and I was not. My shackles had magnetic locks. I couldn't break them and I couldn't cut the chains.

ONE evening Duani came to me with something in her face and in the way she moved that told me the truth long before I could make her put it into words. She clung to me, not wanting to talk, but at last she said, "Today there was a casting of lots and the first hundred have gone to the Place of Sleep."

"It is the beginning, then."

She nodded. "Every day there will be another hundred until all are gone."

I couldn't stand it any longer. I thrust her away and stood up. "You know where the 'keys' are. Get these chains off me!"

She shook her head. "Let us not quarrel now, JonRoss. Come. I want to walk in the city."

We had quarreled more than once, and fiercely. She would not leave Shandakor and I couldn't take her out by force as long as I was chained. And I was not to be released until everyone but Rhul had entered the Place of Sleep and the last page of that long history had been written.

I walked with her among the dancers and the slaves and the bright-cloaked princes. There were no temples in Shandakor. If they worshipped anything it was beauty and to that their whole city was a shrine. Duani's eyes were rapt and there was a remoteness on her now.

I held her hand and looked at the towers of turquoise and cinnabar, the pavings of rose quartz and marble, the walls of pink and white and deep red coral, and to me they were hideous. The ghostly crowds, the mockery of life, the phantom splendors of the past were hideous, a drug, a snare.

"The faculty of reason!" I thought and saw no reason in any of it.

I looked up to where the great globe turned and turned against the sky, keeping these mockeries alive. "Have you ever seen the city as it is—without the Shadows?"

"No. I think only Rhul, who is the oldest, remembers it that way. I think it must have been very lonely. Even then there were less than three thousand of us left."

It must indeed have been lonely. They must have wanted the Shadows as much to people the empty streets as to fend off the enemies who believed in magic.

I kept looking at the globe. We walked for a long time. And then I said, "I must go back to the tower."

She smiled at me very tenderly. "Soon you will be free of the tower—and of these." She touched the chains. "No, don't be sad,

JonRoss. You will remember me and Shandakor as one remembers a dream." She held up her face, that was so lovely and so unlike the meaty faces of human women, and her eyes were full of sombre lights. I kissed her and then I caught her up in my arms and carried her back to the tower.

In that room, where the great shaft turned, I told her, "I have to tend the things below. Go up onto the platform, Duani, where you can see all Shandakor. I'll be with you soon."

I don't know whether she had some hint of what was in my mind or whether it was only the imminence of parting that made her look at me as she did. I thought she was going to speak but she did not, climbing the ladder obediently. I watched her slender golden body vanish upward. Then I went into the chamber below.

There was a heavy metal bar there that was part of a manual control for regulating the rate of turn. I took it off its pin. Then I closed the simple switches on the power plant. I tore out all the leads and smashed the connections with the bar. I did what damage I could to the cogs and the offset shaft. I worked very fast. Then I went up into the main chamber again. The great shaft was still turning but slowly, ever more slowly.

There was a cry from above me and I saw Duani. I sprang up the ladder, thrusting her back onto the platform. The globe moved heavily of its own momentum. Soon it would stop but the white fires still flickered in the crystal rods. I climbed up onto the railing, clinging to a strut. The chains on my wrists and ankles made it hard but I could reach. Duani tried to pull me down. I think she was screaming. I hung on and smashed the crystal rods with the bar, as many as I could.

There was no more motion, no more light. I got down on the platform again and dropped the bar. Duani had forgotten me. She was looking at the city.

The lights of many colors that had burned there were burning still but they were old and dim, cold embers without radiance. The towers of jade and turquoise rose up against the little moons and they were broken and cracked with time and there was no glory in them. They were desolate and very sad. The night lay clotted around their

172

feet. The streets, the plazas and the market squares were empty, their marble paving blank and bare. The soldiers had gone from the walls of Shandakor, with their banners and their bright mail, and there was no longer any movement anywhere within the gates.

DUANI let out one small voiceless cry. And as though in answer to it, suddenly from the darkness of the valley and the slopes beyond there rose a thin fierce howling as of wolves.

"Why?" she whispered. *"Why?"* She turned to me. Her face was pitiful. I caught her to me.

"I couldn't let you die! Not for dreams and visions, nothing. Look, Duani. Look at Shandakor." I wanted to force her to understand. "Shandakor is broken and ugly and forlorn. It is a dead city—but you're alive. There are many cities but only one life for you."

Still she looked at me and it was hard to meet her eyes. She said, "We knew all that, JonRoss."

"Duani, you're a child, you've only a child's way of thought. Forget the past and think of tomorrow. We can get through the barbarians. Corin did. And after that…"

"And after that you would still be human—and I would not."

From below us in the dim and empty streets there came a sound of lamentation. I tried to hold her but she slipped out from between my hands. "And I am glad that you are human," she whispered. "You will never understand what you have done."

And she was gone before I could stop her, down into the tower.

I went after her. Down the endless winding stairs with my chains clattering between my feet, out into the streets, the dark and broken and deserted streets of Shandakor. I called her name and her golden body went before me, fleet and slender, distant and more distant. The chains dragged upon my feet and the night took her away from me.

I stopped. The whelming silence rushed smoothly over me and I was bitterly afraid of this dark dead Shandakor that I did not know. I called again to Duani and then I began to search for her in the shattered shadowed streets. I know now how long it must have been before I found her.

For when I found her, she was with the others. The last people of

Shandakor, the men and the women, the women first, were walking silently in a long line toward a low flat-roofed building that I knew without telling was the Place of Sleep.

They were going to die and there was no pride in their faces now. There was a sickness in them, a sickness and a hurt in their eyes as they moved heavily forward, not looking, not wanting to look at the sordid ancient streets that I had stripped of glory.

"Duani!" I called, and ran forward but she did not turn in her place in the line. And I saw that she was weeping.

Rhul turned toward me, and his look had a weary contempt that was bitterer than a curse. "Of what use, after all, to kill you now?"

"But I did this thing! *I* did it!"

"You are only human."

The long line shuffled on and Duani's little feet were closer to that final doorway. Rhul looked upward at the sky. "There is still time before the sunrise. The women at least will be spared the indignity of spears."

"Let me go with her!"

I tried to follow her, to take my place in line. And the weapon in Rhul's hand moved and there was the pain and I lay as Corin had lain while they went silently on into the Place of Sleep.

The barbarians found me when they came, still half doubtful, into the city after dawn. I think they were afraid of me. I think they feared me as a wizard who had somehow destroyed all the folk of Shandakor.

For they broke my chains and healed my wounds and later they even gave me out of the loot of Shandakor the only thing I wanted—a bit of porcelain, shaped like the head of a young girl.

I sit in the Chair that I craved at the University and my name is written on the roll of the discoverers. I am eminent, I am respectable—I, who murdered the glory of a race.

Why didn't I go after Duani into the Place of Sleep? I could have crawled! I could have dragged myself across those stones. And I wish to God I had. I wish that I had died with Shandakor!

SHANNACH – THE LAST

Planet Stories, November 1952

IT WAS DARK in the caves under Mercury. It was hot, and there was no sound in them but the slow plodding of Trevor's heavy boots.

Trevor had been wandering for a long time, lost in this labyrinth where no human being had ever gone before. And Trevor was an angry man. Through no fault or will of his own he was about to die, and he was not ready to die. Moreover, it seemed a wicked thing to come to his final moment here in the stifling dark, buried under alien mountains high as Everest.

He wished now that he had stayed in the valley. Hunger and thirst would have done for him just the same, but at least he would have died in the open like a man, and not like a rat trapped in a drain.

Yet there was not really much to choose between them as a decent place to die. A barren little hell-hole the valley had been, even before the quake, with nothing to draw a man there except the hope of finding sun-stones, one or two of which could transform a prospector into a plutocrat.

Trevor had found no sun-stones. The quake had brought down a whole mountain wall on his ship, leaving him with a pocket torch, a handful of food tablets, a canteen of water, and the scant clothing he stood in.

He had looked at the naked rocks, and the little river frothing green with chemical poisons, and he had gone away into the tunnels, the ancient blowholes of a cooling planet, gambling that he might find a way out of the valleys.

Mercury's Twilight Belt is cut into thousands of cliff-locked pockets, as a honeycomb is cut into cells. There is no way over the mountains, for the atmosphere is shallow, and the jagged peaks stand up into airless space. Trevor knew that only one more such pocket lay between him and the open plains. If he could get to and through that last pocket, he had thought…

But he knew now that he was not going to make it.

He was stripped to the skin already, in the terrible heat. When the weight of his miner's boots became too much to drag, he shed them, padding on over the rough rock with bare feet. He had nothing left now but the torch. When the light went, his last hope went with it.

After a while it went.

The utter blackness of the grave shut down. Trevor stood still, listening to the pulse of his own blood in the silence, looking at that which no man needs a light to see. Then he flung the torch away and stumbled on, driven to fight still by the terror which was greater than his weakness.

Twice he struck against the twisting walls, and fell, and struggled up again. The third time he remained on hands and knees, and crawled.

He crept on, a tiny creature entombed in the bowels of a planet. The bore grew smaller and smaller, tightening around him. From time to time he lost consciousness, and it became increasingly painful to struggle back to an awareness of the heat and the silence and the pressing rock.

After one of these periods of oblivion he began to hear a dull, steady thunder. He could no longer crawl. The bore had shrunk to a mere crack, barely large enough for him to pass through wormlike on his belly. He sensed now a deep, shuddering vibration in the rock. It grew stronger, terrifying in that enclosed space. Steam slipped wraithlike into the smothering air.

The roar and the vibration grew to an unendurable pitch. Trevor was near to strangling in the steam. He was afraid to go on, but there was no other way to go. Quite suddenly his hands went out into nothingness.

The rock at the lip of the bore must have been rotten with erosion. It gave under his weight and pitched him headfirst into a thundering rush of water that was blistering hot and going somewhere in a great hurry through the dark.

After that Trevor was not sure of anything. There was the scalding heat and the struggle to keep his head up and the terrible speed of the sub-Mercurian river racing on to its destiny. He struck rock several times, and once he held his breath for a whole eternity until the roof of the tunnel rose up again.

He was only dimly aware of a long sliding fall downward through a sudden brightness. It was much cooler. He splashed feebly, because his brain had not told his body to stop, and the water did not fight him.

His feet and hands struck solid bottom. He floundered on, and presently the water was gone. He made one attempt to rise. After that he lay still.

The great mountains leaned away from the Sun. Night came, and with it violent storm and rain. Trevor did not know it. He slept, and when he woke the savage dawn was making the high cliffs flame with white light.

Something was screaming above his head.

Aching and leaden still with exhaustion, he roused up and looked about him.

HE sat on a beach of pale grey sand. At his feet were the shallows of a grey-green lake that filled a stony basin some half-mile in breadth. To his left the underground river poured out of the cliff face, spreading into a wide, riffling fan of foam. Off to his right, the water spilled over the rim of the basin to become a river again somewhere below, and beyond the rim, veiled in mist and the shadow of a mountain wall, was a valley.

Behind him, crowding to the edge of the sand, were trees and ferns and flowers, alien in shape and color but triumphantly alive. And from what he could see of it, the broad valley was green and riotous with growth. The water was pure, the air had a good smell, and it came to Trevor that he had made it. He was going to live a while longer, after all.

Forgetting his weariness, he sprang up, and the thing that had hissed and screamed above him swooped down and passed the clawed tip of a leathery wing so close to his face that it nearly gashed him. He stumbled backward, crying out, and the creature rose in a soaring spiral and swooped again.

Trevor saw a sort of flying lizard, jet black except for a saffron belly. He raised his arms to ward it off, but it did not attack him, and as it swept by he saw something that woke in him amazement, greed, and a peculiarly unpleasant chill of fear.

Around its neck the lizard-thing wore a golden collar. And set into the scaly flesh of its head—into the bone itself, it seemed—was a sun-stone.

There was no mistaking that small vicious flash of radiance. Trevor had dreamed of sun-stones too long to be misled. He watched the creature rise again into the steamy sky and shivered, wondering who, or what, had set that priceless thing into the skull of a flying lizard—and why.

It was the *why* that bothered him the most. Sun-stones are not mere adornments for wealthy ladies. They are rare, radioactive crystals, having a half-life one third greater than radium, and are used exclusively in the construction of delicate electronic devices dealing with frequencies above the first octave.

Most of that relatively unexplored super-spectrum was still a mystery. And the strangely jeweled and collared creature circling above him filled Trevor with a vast unease.

It was not hunting. It did not wish to kill him. But it made no move to go away.

From far down the valley, muted by distance to a solemn bell note that rolled between the cliffs, Trevor heard the booming of a great song.

A sudden desire for concealment sent him in among the trees. He worked his way along the shore of the lake. Looking up through the branches he saw the black wings lift and turn, following him.

The lizard was watching him with its bright, sharp eyes. It noted the path of his movements through the ferns and flowers, as a hawk watches a rabbit.

He reached the lip of the basin where the water poured over in a cataract several hundred feet high. Climbing around the shoulder of a rocky bastion, Trevor had his first clear look at the valley.

Much of it was still vague with mist. But it was broad and deep, with a sweep of level plain and clumps of forest, locked tight between the barrier mountains. And as he made out other details, Trevor's astonishment grew out of all measure.

The land was under cultivation. There were clusters of thatched huts among the fields, and in the distance was a rock-built city, immense and unmistakable in the burning haze of dawn.

Trevor crouched there, staring, and the winged lizard swung in lazy circles, watching, waiting, while he tried to think.

A fertile valley such as this was rare enough in itself. But to find fields and a city was beyond belief. He had seen the aboriginal tribes that haunt some of the cliff-locked worlds of the Twilight Belt—sub-human peoples who live precariously among the bitter rocks and boiling springs, hunting the great lizards for food. None of this was ever built by them.

Unless, in this environment, they had advanced beyond the Age of Stone...

The gong sounded again its deep challenging note. Trevor saw the tiny figures of mounted men, no larger than ants at that distance, come down from the city and ride out across the plain.

Relief and joy supplanted speculation in Trevor's mind. He was battered and starving, lost on an alien world, and anything remotely approaching the human and the civilized was better luck than he could have dreamed or prayed for.

Besides, there were sun-stones in this place. He looked hungrily at the head of the circling watcher, and then began to scramble down the broken outer face of the bastion.

The black wings slipped silently after him down the sky.

ABOUT a hundred feet above the valley floor he came to an overhang. There was no way past it but to jump. He clung to a bush and let himself down as far as he could, and then dropped some four or five yards to a slope of springy turf. The fall knocked the wind out of him, and as he lay gasping a chill doubt crept into his mind.

He could see the land quite clearly now, the pattern of the fields, the far-off city. Except for the group of riders, nothing stirred. The fields, the plain were empty of life, the little villages still as death. And he saw, swinging lazily above a belt of trees by the river, a second black-winged shadow, watching.

The trees were not far away. The riders were coming toward them and him. It seemed to Trevor now that the men were perhaps a party of hunters, but there was something alarming about the utter disappearance of all other life. It was as though the gong had been a warning for all to take cover while the hunt was abroad.

The sharp-eyed lizards were the hounds that went before to find and flush the game. Glancing up at the ominous sentinel above his own head, Trevor had a great desire to see what the quarry was that hid in the belt of trees.

There was no way back to the partial security of the lake basin. The overhang cut him off from that. The futility of trying to hide was apparent, but nevertheless he wormed in among some crimson ferns. The city was at his left. To the right, the fertile plain washed out into a badland of lava and shattered rock, which narrowed and vanished around a shoulder of purple basalt. This defile was still in deep shadow.

The riders were still far away. He saw them splash across a ford, toy figures making little bursts of spray.

The watcher above the trees darted suddenly downward. The quarry was breaking cover.

Trevor's suspicions crystallized into an ugly certainty. Horror-struck, he watched the bronzed, half-naked figure of a girl emerge from the brilliant undergrowth and run like an antelope toward the badland.

The flying lizard rose, swooped, and struck.

The girl flung herself aside. She carried a length of sapling bound with great thorns, and she lashed out with it at the black brute, grazed it, and ran on.

The lizard circled and came at her again from behind.

She turned. There was a moment of vicious confusion, in which the leathery wings enveloped her in a kind of dreadful cloak, and then she was running again, but less swiftly, and Trevor could see the redness of blood on her body.

And again the flying demon came.

The thing was trying to head her, turn her back toward the huntsmen. But she would not be turned. She beat with her club at the lizard, and ran, and fell, and ran again. And Trevor knew that she was beaten. The brute would have the life out of her before she reached the rocks.

Every dictate of prudence told Trevor to stay out of this. Whatever was going on was obviously the custom of the country, and none of his business. All he wanted was to get hold of one of these sun-stones and then find a way out of this valley. That was going to be trouble enough without taking on any more.

But prudence was swept away in the fury that rose in him as he saw the hawk swoop down again, with its claws outspread and hungry for the girl's tormented flesh. He sprang up, shouting to her to fight, to hang on, and went running full speed down the slope toward her.

She turned upon him a face of such wild, fierce beauty as he had never seen, the eyes dark and startled and full of a terrible determination. Then she screamed at him, in his own tongue, *"Look out!"*

He had forgotten his own nemesis. Black wings, claws, the lash of a scaly tail striking like a whip, and Trevor went down, rolling over and staining the turf red as he rolled.

From far off he heard the voices of the huntsmen, shrill and strident, lifted in a wild halloo.

II

FOR SOME REASON the assault steadied Trevor. He got to his feet and took the club out of the girl's hands, regretting the gun that was buried under a ton of rock on the other side of the mountains.

"Keep behind me," he said. "Watch my back."

She stared at him strangely, but there was no time for questions. They began to run together toward the badland. It seemed a long way off. The lizards screamed and hissed above them. Trevor hefted the club. It was about the size and weight of a baseball bat. He had once been very good at baseball.

"They're coming," said the girl.

"Lie down flat," he told her, and went on, more slowly. She dropped behind him in the grass, her fingers closing over a fragment of stone. The wide wings whistled down.

Trevor braced himself. He could see the evil eyes, yellow and bright as the golden collars, and the brilliant flash of the sun-stones against the jetty scales of the head. They were attacking together, but at different angles, so that he could not face them both.

He chose the one that was going to reach him first, and waited. He let it get close, very close, diving swiftly with its scarlet tongue forking out of its hissing mouth and its sharp claws spread. Then he swung the club with all his might.

It connected. He felt something break. The creature screamed, and then the force of its dive carried it on into him and he lost his footing in a welter of thrashing wings and floundering body. He fell, and the second lizard was on him.

The girl rose. In three long strides she reached him and flung herself upon the back of the scaly thing that ravaged him. He saw her trying to pin it to the ground, hammering methodically at its head with the stone.

He kicked off the wounded one. He had broken its neck, but it was in no hurry to die. He caught up the club and presently the second brute was dead. Trevor found it quite easy to pick up the sun-stone.

He held it in his hand, a strange, tawny, jewel-like thing, with a scrap of bone still clinging to it. It glinted with inner fires, deep and subtle, and an answering spark of wild excitement was kindled in Trevor from the very touch and feel of it, so that he forgot where he was or what he was doing, forgot everything but the eerie crystal that gleamed against his palm.

It was more than a jewel, more even than wealth, that he held there. It was hope and success and a new life.

He had thrown years away prospecting the bitter Mercurian

wastes. This trip had been his last gamble, and it had ended with his ship gone, his quest finished, and nothing to look forward to even if he did get back safely, but to become one of the penniless, aging planet-drifters he'd always pitied.

Now all that was changed. This single stone would let him go back to Earth a winner and not a failure. It would pay off all the dreary, lonesome, hazardous years. It would…

It would do so many things if he could get out of this God-forsaken valley with it! *If!*

The girl had got her breath again. Now she said urgently, "Come! They're getting near!"

Trevor's senses, bemused by the sun-stone, registered only vaguely the external stimuli of sight and sound. The riders had come closer. The beasts they rode were taller and slighter than horses. They were not hoofed, but clawed. They had narrow, vicious-looking heads with spiny crests that stood up erect and arrogant. They came fast, carrying their riders lightly.

The men were still too far away to distinguish features, but even at that distance Trevor sensed something peculiar about their faces, something unnatural. They wore splendid harness, and their half-clad bodies were bronzed, but not nearly so deeply as the girl's.

The girl shook him furiously, stirring him out of his dream. "Do you want to be taken alive? Before, the beasts would have torn us apart, and that is quickly over. But we killed the hawks, don't you understand? Now they will take us alive!"

He did not understand in the least, but her obvious preference for a very nasty death instead of capture made him find reserves of strength he thought he had lost in the underground river. There was also the matter of the sun-stone. If they caught him with it they would want it back.

Clutching the precious thing he turned with the girl and ran.

THE lava bed was beginning to catch the sun now. The splintered rock showed through, bleak and ugly. The badland and the defile beyond seemed like an entrance into hell, but it did offer shelter of a sort if they could make it.

The drumming of padded feet behind was loud in his ears. He glanced over his shoulder, once. He could see the faces of the huntsmen now. They were not good faces, in either feature or expression, and he saw the thing about them that he had noticed before, the unnatural thing.

In the center of each forehead, above the eyes, a sun-stone was set into flesh and bone.

First the hawk-lizards, and now these...

Trevor's heart contracted with an icy pang. These men were human, as human as himself, and yet they were not. They were alien and wicked and altogether terrifying, and he began to understand why the girl did not wish to come alive into their hands.

Fleet, implacable, the crested mounts with their strange riders were sweeping in upon the two who fled. The leader took from about his saddle a curved throwing stick and held it, poised. The sun-stone set in his brow flashed like a third, and evil eye.

The lava and the fangs of rock shimmered in the light. Trevor yearned toward them. The brown girl running before him seemed to shimmer also. It hurt very much to breathe. He thought he could not go any farther. But he did, and when the girl faltered he put his arm around her and steadied her on.

He continued to keep an eye out behind him. He saw the curved stick come hurtling toward him and he managed to let it go by. The others were ready now as they came within range. It seemed to Trevor that they were watching him with a peculiar intensity, as though they had recognized him as a stranger and had almost forgotten the girl in their desire to take him.

His bare feet trod on lava already growing hot under the sun. A spur of basalt reared up and made a shield against the throwing sticks. In a minute or two Trevor and the girl were hidden in a terrain of such broken roughness as the man had seldom seen. It was as though some demoniac giant had whipped the molten lava with a pudding-spoon, cracking mountains with his free hand and tossing in the pieces. He understood now why the girl had waited for daylight to make her break. To attempt this passage in the dark would be suicidal.

He listened nervously for sounds of pursuit. He could not hear any, but he remained uneasy, and when the girl flung herself down to rest, he asked,

"Shouldn't we go farther? They might still come."

She did not answer him at once, beyond a shake of the head. He realized that she was looking at him almost as intently as the riders had. It was the first chance she had had to examine him, and she was making the most of it. She noted the cut of his hair, the stubble of beard, the color and texture of his skin, the rags of his shorts that were all he had to cover him. Very carefully she noted them, and then she said in an odd slow voice, as though she were thinking of something else,

"Mounted, the Korins are afraid of nothing. But afoot, and in here, they are afraid of ambush. It has happened before. They can die, you know, just the same as we do."

Her face, for all its youth, was not the face of a girl. It was a woman who looked at Trevor, a woman who had already learned the happy, the passionate, and the bitter things, who had lived with pain and fear and knew better than to trust anyone but herself.

"You aren't one of us," she said.

"No. I came from beyond the mountains." He could not tell whether she believed him or not. "Who, or what, are the Korins?"

"The lords of Korith," she answered, and began to tear strips from the length of white linen cloth she wore twisted about her waist. "There will be time to talk later. We still have far to go. Here, this will stop the bleeding."

In silence they bound each other's wounds and started off again. If Trevor had not been so unutterably weary, and the way so hard, he would have been angry with the girl. And yet there was nothing really to be angry about except that he sensed she was somehow suspicious of him.

Many times they had to stop and rest. Once he asked her, "Why were they—the Korins—hunting you?"

"I was running away. Why were they hunting *you?*"

"Damned if I know. Accident, perhaps. I happened to be where their hawks were flying."

The girl wore a chain of iron links around her neck, a solid chain with no clasp, too small to be pulled over the head. From it hung a round tag with a word stamped on it. Trevor took the tag in his hand.

"Galt," he read. "Is that your name?"

"My name is Jen. Galt is the Korin I belong to. He led the hunt." She gave Trevor a look of fierce and challenging pride and said, as though she were revealing a secret earldom, "I am a slave."

"How long have you been in the valley, Jen? You and I are the same stock, speaking the same language. Earth stock. How does it happen, a colony of this size that no one ever heard of?"

"It's been nearly three hundred years since the Landing," she answered. "I have been told that for generations my people kept alive the hope that a ship would come from Earth and release them from the Korins. It never came. And, except by ship, there is no way in or out of the valley."

Trevor glanced at her sharply. "I found a way in, all right, and I'm beginning to wish I hadn't. And if there's no way out, where are we going?"

"I don't know myself," said Jen, and rose. "But my man came this way, and others before him."

She went on, and Trevor went with her. There was no place else to go.

The heat was unbearable, and they crept in the shadows of the rocks wherever they could. They suffered from thirst, but there was no water. The shoulder of purple basalt loomed impossibly tall before them, and seemed never to grow nearer.

For most of the day they toiled across the lava bed, and at last, when they had almost forgotten that they had ever dreamed of doing it, they rounded the shoulder and came staggering out of the badland into a narrow canyon that seemed like the scar of some cataclysmic wound in the mountain.

Rock walls, raw and riven, rose out of sight on either side, the twisted strata showing streaks of crimson and white and sullen ochre. A little stream crawled in a stony bed, and not much grew beside it.

Jen and Trevor fell by the stream. And while they were still sprawled on the moist gravel, lapping like dogs at the bitter water, men came quietly from among the rocks and stood above them, holding weapons made of stone.

TREVOR got slowly to his feet. There were six of these armed men. Like the girl, they wore loin cloths of white cotton, much frayed, and like her they were burned almost black by a lifetime of exposure to a brutal sun. They were all young, knotted and sinewy from hard labor, their faces grim beyond their years. All bore upon their bodies the scars of talons. And they looked at Trevor with a cold, strange look.

They knew Jen, or most of them did. She called them gladly by name, and demanded, "Hugh. Where is Hugh?"

One of them nodded toward the farther wall. "Up there in the caves. He's all right. Who is this man, Jen?"

She turned to study Trevor.

"I don't know. They were hunting him, too. He came to help me. I couldn't have escaped without him. He killed the hawks. But…" She hesitated, choosing her words carefully. "He says he came from beyond the mountains. He knows of Earth and speaks our tongue. And when he killed the hawks he smashed the skull of one and took the sun-stone."

All six started at that. And the tallest of them, a young man with a face as bleak and craggy as the rocks around them, came toward Trevor.

"Why did you take the sun-stone?" he asked. His voice held an ugly edge.

Trevor stared at him. "Why the devil do you suppose? Because it's valuable."

The man held out his hand. "Give it to me."

"The hell I will!" cried Trevor furiously. He backed away, just a little, getting set.

The young man came on, and his face was dark and dangerous.

"Saul, wait!" cried Jen.

Saul didn't wait. He kept right on coming. Trevor let him get close before he swung, and he put every ounce of his strength behind the blow.

The smashing fist took Saul squarely in the belly and sent him backward, doubled up. Trevor stood with hunched shoulders, breathing hard, watching the others with feral eyes.

"What are you?" he snarled. "A bunch of thieves? All right, come on! I got that stone the hard way and I'm going to keep it!"

Big words. A big anger. And a big fear behind them. The men were around him in a ring now. There was no chance of breaking away. Even if he did he was so winded they could pull him down in minutes. The stone weighed heavy in his pocket, heavy as half a lifetime of sweat and hunger and hard work, on the rockpiles of Mercury.

Saul straightened up. His face was still gray, but he bent again and picked up a sharp-pointed implement of rock that he had dropped. Then he moved forward. And the others closed in, at the same time, quite silently.

There was a bitter taste in Trevor's mouth as he waited for them. To get his hands on a sun-stone at last, and then to lose it and probably his life too, to this crowd of savages! It was more than anybody ought to be asked to bear.

"'Saul, wait!" cried Jen again, pushing in front of him. "He saved my life! You can't just…"

"He's a Korin. A spy."

"He can't be! There's no stone in his forehead. Not even a scar."

Saul's voice was flat and relentless. "He took a sun-stone. Only a Korin would touch one of the cursed things."

"But he says he's from outside the valley! From Earth, Saul. From *Earth!* Things would be different there."

Jen's insistence on that point had at least halted the men temporarily. And Trevor, looking at Saul's face, had suddenly begun to understand something.

"You think the sun-stones are evil," he said.

Saul gave him a sombre glance. "They are. And the one you have is going to be destroyed. Now."

Trevor swallowed the bitter anguish that choked him, and did some fast thinking. If the sun-stones had a superstitious significance in this benighted pocket of Mercury—and he could imagine why they might, with those damned unnatural hawks flying around with the equally unnatural Korins – that put a different light on their attitude.

He knew just by looking at their faces that it was "give them the sun-stone or die." Dying at the hands of a bunch of wild fanatics didn't make sense. Better let them have the stone and gamble on getting it back again later. Or on getting another one. They seemed plentiful enough in the valley!

Sure, let's be sensible about it. Let's hand over a lifetime of hoping to a savage with horny palms, and not worry about it. Let's... Oh, hell.

"Here," he said. "All right. Take it."

It hurt. It hurt like giving up his own heart.

Saul took it without thanks. He turned and laid it on a flat surface of rock, and began to pound the glinting crystal with the heavy stone he had meant to use on Trevor's head. There was a look on his lined, young, craggy face as though he was killing a living thing – a thing that he feared and hated.

Trevor shivered. He knew that sun-stones were impervious to anything but atomic bombardment. But it made him a little sick, none the less, to see that priceless object being battered by a crude stone club.

"It won't break," he said. "You might as well stop."

SAUL flung down his weapon so close to Trevor's bare feet that he leaped back. Then he picked up the sun-stone and hurled it as far as he could across the ravine. Trevor heard it clicking faintly as it fell, in among the rocks and rubble at the foot of the opposite cliff. He strained to mark the spot.

"You idiot!" he said to Saul. "You've thrown away a fortune. The fortune I've spent my life trying to find. What's the matter with you? Don't you have any idea at all what those things are worth?"

Saul ignored him, speaking bleakly to the others. "No man with a sun-stone is to be trusted. I say kill him."

Jen said stubbornly, "No, Saul. I owe him my life."

"But he could be a slave, a traitor, working for the Korins."

"Look at his clothes," said Jen. "Look at his skin. This morning it was white, now it's red. Did you ever see a slave that color? Or a Korin, either. Besides, did you ever see him in the valley before? There aren't as many of us as that."

"We can't take any chances," Saul said. "Not us."

"You can always kill him later. But if he *is* from beyond the mountains, perhaps even from Earth—" She said the word hesitantly, as though she did not quite believe there was such a place. "He might know some of the things we've been made to forget. He might help us. Anyway, the others have a right to their say before you kill him."

Saul shook his head. "I don't like it. But—" He hesitated, scowling thoughtfully. "All right. We'll settle it up in the cave. Let's move." He said to Trevor, "You go in the middle of us. And if you try to signal anyone..."

"Who the devil would I signal to?" retorted Trevor angrily. "Listen, I'm sorry I ever got into your bloody valley."

But he was not sorry. Not quite.

His senses were on the alert to mark every twist and turn of the way they went, the way that would bring him back to the sun-stone. The ravine narrowed and widened and twisted, but there was only one negotiable path, and that was beside the stream bed. This went on for some distance, and then the ravine split on a tremendous cliff of bare rock that tilted up and back as though arrested in the act of falling over. The stream flowed from the left-hand fork. Saul took the other one.

They kept close watch on Trevor as he slipped and clambered and sprawled along with them. The detritus of the primeval cataclysm that had shaped this crack in the mountains lay where it had fallen, growing rougher and more dangerous with every eroding storm and cracking frost.

Above him, on both sides, the mountain tops went up and still up, beyond the shallow atmosphere. Their half-seen summits leaned and quivered like things glimpsed from under water, lit like torches by the naked blaze of the sun. There were ledges, lower down. Trevor saw men crouched upon them, among heaps of piled stones. They shouted, and Saul answered them. In this narrow throat no man could get through alive if they chose to stop him.

After a while they left the floor of the ravine and climbed a path, partly natural and partly so roughly hewn that it seemed natural. It angled steeply up the cliff face, and at its end was a narrow hole. Saul led the way through it. In single file the others followed, and Trevor heard Jen's voice echoing in some great hollow space beyond, calling Hugh.

There was a cave inside, a very large cave with dim nooks and crannies around its edges. Shafts of sunlight pierced it here and there from cracks in the cliff face high above, and far at the back of it, where the floor tipped sharply down, a flame burned. Trevor had seen flames like that before on Mercury, where volcanic gases blowing up through a fissure had ignited from some chance spark. It was impressive, a small bluish column twisting upward into rock-curtained distance and roaring evilly. He could feel the air rush past him as the burning pillar sucked it in.

There were people in the cave. Less than a hundred, Trevor thought, not counting a handful of children and striplings. Less than a third of those were women. They all bore the same unmistakable stamp. Hard as life must be for them in the cave, it had been harder before.

He felt his legs buckling under him with sheer weariness. He stood groggily with his back against the rough cave wall.

A stocky young man with knotted shoulder-muscles and sun-bleached hair was holding Jen in his arms. That would be Hugh. He, and the others, were shouting excitedly, asking and answering questions.

Then, one by one, they caught sight of Trevor. And gradually a silence grew and spread.

"All right," said Saul harshly, looking at Trevor. "Let's get this settled."

"You settle it," said Trevor. "I'm tired." He glared at Saul and the unfriendly staring crowd, and they seemed to rock in his vision. "I'm an Earthman. I didn't want to come into your damned valley, and I've been here a night and a day and haven't slept. I'm going to sleep."

Saul started to speak again but Jen's man, Hugh, came up and stood in front of him.

"He saved Jen's life," Hugh said. "Let him sleep."

He led Trevor away to a place at the side where there were heaps of dried vines and mountain creepers, prickly and full of dust but softer than the cave floor. Trevor managed a few vague words of thanks and was asleep before they were out of his mouth.

Hours, weeks, or perhaps it was only minutes later, a rough persistent shaking brought him to again. Faces bent over him. He saw them through a haze, and the questions they asked penetrated to him slowly, and without much meaning.

"Why did you want the sun-stone?"

"Why wouldn't I want it? I could take it back to Earth and sell it for a fortune."

"What do they do with sun-stones on Earth?"

"Build gadgets, super-electronic, to study things. Wave-lengths too short for anything else to pick up. Thought-waves, even. What do you care?"

"Do they wear sun-stones in their foreheads, on Earth?"

"No…" His voice trailed off, and the voices, or the dream of voices, left him.

It was still daylight when he woke, this time normally. He sat up, feeling stiff and sore but otherwise rested. Jen came to him, smiling, and thrust a chunk of what he recognized as some species of rock-lizard into his hands. He gnawed at it wolfishly while she talked, having discovered that this was not the same day, but the next one, and quite late.

"They have decided," she said, "to let you live."

"I imagine you had a lot to do with that. Thanks."

She shrugged her bare shoulders, with the raw wounds on them where the hawk-lizards had clawed her. She had that exhausted, let-down look that comes after tremendous stress, and her eyes, even while she spoke to Trevor, followed Hugh as he worked at some task around the cave.

"I couldn't have done anything if they hadn't believed your story," she told him. "They questioned you when you were too far gone to lie." He had a very dim memory of that. "They didn't understand your answers but they knew they were true ones. Also they examined your clothes. No cloth like that is woven in the valley. And the things that hold them together—" he knew she meant the zippers "—are unknown to us. So you must have come from beyond the mountains. They want to know exactly how, and if you could get back the same way."

"No," said Trevor, and explained. "Am I free to move around, then—go where I want to?"

She studied him a moment before she spoke. "You're a stranger. You don't belong with us. You could betray us to the Korins just as easily as not."

"Why would I do that? They hunted me, too."

"For sun-stones, perhaps. You're a stranger. They would take you alive. Anyway, be careful. Be very careful what you do."

From outside came a cry. "Hawks! Take cover, hawks!"

III

INSTANTLY everyone in the cave fell silent. They watched the places in the cave wall where the sunlight came in, the little cracks in the cliff-face. Trevor thought of the hawk-creatures, and how they would be wheeling and slipping along the ravine, searching.

Outside, the rough rock looked all alike. He thought that in that immensity of erosions and crevices they would have a hard time finding the few tiny chinks that led into the cave. But he watched, too, tense with a feeling of danger.

No sound at all came now from the ravine. In that utter stillness, the frightened whimper of a child came with the sudden loudness of a scream. It was instantly hushed. The shafts of sunlight crept slowly up the walls. Jen seemed not to breathe. Her eyes shone, like an animal's.

A black shadow flickered across one of the sunlight bars—flickered, and then was gone. Trevor's heart turned over. He waited for it to come back, to occlude that shaft of light, to slip in along it and become a wide-winged demon with a sun-stone in its brow. For a whole eternity he waited, but it didn't come back, and then a man crept in through the entry hole and said, "They're gone."

Jen put her head down on her knees. She had begun to tremble all over, very quietly, but with spasmodic violence. Before Trevor could reach her, Hugh had her in his arms, talking to her, soothing her. She began to sob then, and Hugh glanced at Trevor across her shoulders.

"She's had a little too much."

"Yes." Trevor looked at the shafts of sunlight. "Do the hawks come very often?"

"They send them every once in a while hoping to catch us off guard. If they could find the cave they could hunt us out of it, drive us back into the valley. So far they haven't found it."

Jen was quiet now. Hugh stroked her with big awkward hands. "She told you, I guess. About yourself, I mean. You've got to be careful."

"Yes," said Trevor. "She told me." He leaned forward. "Listen, I still don't know how you people got here or what it's all about. After we got away from the Korins, Jen said something about a landing, three hundred years ago. Three hundred Earth years?"

"About that. Some of us have remembered enough to keep track."

"The first Earth colonies were being started on Mercury about then, in two or three of the bigger valleys. Mining colonies. Was this one of them?"

Hugh shook his head. "No. The story is that there was a big ship loaded with people from Earth. That's true, of course, because the ship is still here, what's left of it. And so are we. Some of the people on the ship were settlers and some were convicts."

He pronounced the word with the same hatred and scorn that always accompanied the name "Korin." Trevor said eagerly,

"They used to do that in the early days. Use convict labor in the mines. It made so much trouble they had to stop it. Were the Korins…?"

"They were the convicts. The big ship crashed in the valley but most of the people weren't killed. After the crash the convicts killed the men who were in charge of the ship, and made the settlers obey them. That's how it all started. And that's why we're proud we're slaves—because we're descended from the settlers."

Trevor could see the picture quite clearly now, the more so because it had happened before in one way or another. The emigrant ship bound for one of the colonies, driven off its course by the tremendous magnetic disturbances that still made Mercury a spaceman's nightmare.

They couldn't even have called for help or given their position. The terrible nearness of the Sun made any form of radio communication impossible. And then the convicts had broken free and killed the officers, finding themselves unexpectedly in command of a sort of paradise, with the settlers to serve them.

A fairly safe paradise, too. Mercury has an infinite number of these Twilight valleys, all looking more or less alike from space, half hidden under their shallow blankets of air, and only the few that are both accessible and unmistakable because of their size have permanent colonies. Straight up and down, by spaceship, is the only way in or out of most of them, and unless a ship should land directly on them by sheer chance, the erstwhile prisoners would be safe from discovery.

"But the sun-stones?" asked Trevor, touching his forehead. "What about the sun-stones and the hawks? They didn't have the use of them when they landed."

"No, they came later." Hugh looked around uneasily. "Look, Trevor, its a thing we don't talk about much. You can see why, when you think what it's done to us. And it's a thing you shouldn't talk about at all."

"But how did they get them in their heads? And why? Especially, why do they waste them on the hawks?"

JEN glanced at him somberly from the circle of Hugh's arm. "We don't know, exactly. But the hawks are the eyes and ears of the Korins. And from the time they used the first sun-stone we've had no hope of getting free from them."

The thing that had been buried in Trevor's subconscious since last night's questioning came suddenly to the surface.

"Thought-waves, that's it! Sure!" He leaned forward excitedly, and Jen told him frantically to lower his voice. "I'll be damned. They've been experimenting with sun-stones for years on Earth—ever since they were discovered, but the scientists never thought of…"

"Do they have the stones on Earth, too?" asked Jen, with loathing.

"No, no, only the ones that are brought from Mercury. Something about Mercury being so close to the Sun, overdose of solar radiation and the extremes of heat, cold, and pressure while the planet was being made, that formed that particular kind of crystal here. I guess that's why they're called sun-stones."

He shook his head. "So that's how they work it—direct mental communication between the Korins and the hawks, by means of the stones. Simple, too. Set them right in the skull, almost in contact with the brain, and you don't need all the complicated machines and senders and receivers they've been monkeying with in the labs for so long." He shivered. "I'll admit I don't like the idea, though. There's something repulsive about it."

Hugh said bitterly, "When they were only men, and convicts, we might have beaten them some day, even though they had all the weapons. But when they became the Korins—" He indicated the darkling alcoves of the cave. "This is the only freedom we can ever have now."

Looking at Hugh and Jen, Trevor felt a great welling-up of pity, for them, and for all these far-removed children of Earth who were now only hunted slaves to whom this burrow in the rock meant freedom. He thought with pure hatred of the Korins who hunted them, with the uncanny hawks that were their far-ranging eyes and ears and weapons. He wished he could hit them with…

He caught himself up sharply. Letting his sympathies run away with him wasn't going to do anybody any good. The only thing that concerned him was to get hold of that sun-stone again and get out of this devil's pocket. He'd spent half a life hunting for a stone, and he wasn't going to let concern over perfect strangers sidetrack him now.

The first step would be getting away from the cave.

It would have to be at night. No watch was kept then on the ledges, for the hawks did not fly in darkness, and the Korins never moved without the hawks. Most of the people were busy in those brief hours of safety. The women searched for edible moss and lichens. Some of the men brought water from the stream at the canyon fork, and others, with stone clubs and crude spears, hunted the great rock-lizards that slept in the crevices, made sluggish by the cold.

Trevor waited until the fourth night, and then when Saul's water party left, he started casually out of the cave after them.

"I think I'll go down with them," he told Jen and Hugh. "I haven't been down that far since I got here."

There seemed to be no suspicion in them of his purpose. Jen said, "Stay close to the others. It's easy to get lost in the rocks."

He turned and went into the darkness after the water party. He followed them down to the fork, and it was quite easy then to slip aside among the tumbled rock and leave them, working his way slowly and silently downstream.

After several days in the dimness of the cave, he found that the star-shine gave him light enough to move by. It was hard going, even so, and by the time he reached the approximate place where Saul had tried to kill him he was bruised and cut and considerably shaken. But he picked his spot carefully, crossed the stream, and began to search.

The chill deepened. The rocks that had been hot under his hands turned cold, and the frost-rime settled lightly on them, and Trevor shivered and swore and scrambled, fighting the numbness out of his body, praying that none of the loose rubble would fall on him and crush him. He had prospected on Mercury for a long time. Otherwise he would not have lived.

HE FOUND it more easily than he could have done by day, without a detector. He saw the cold pale light of it gleaming, down among the dark broken rock where Saul had thrown it.

He picked it up.

He dandled the thing in his palm, touching it with loving finger tips. It had a certain cold repellent beauty, glimmering in the darkness—a freakish by-product of Mercury's birth-pangs, unique in the Solar System. Its radioactivity was a type and potency harmless to living tissue, and its wonderful sensitivity had made it possible for physicists to explore at least a little into those unknown regions above the first octave.

In a gesture motivated by pure curiosity he lifted the stone and pressed it tight against the flesh between his brows. Probably it wouldn't work this way. Probably it had to be set deep into the bone...

It worked, oh God, it worked, and something had him, something caught him by the naked brain and would not let him go.

Trevor screamed. The thin small sound was lost in the empty dark, and he tried again, but no sound would come. Something had forbidden him to scream. Something was in there, opening out the leaves of his brain like the pages of a child's book, and it wasn't a hawk, or a Korin. It wasn't anything human or animal that he had ever known before. It was something still and lonely and remote, as alien as the mountain peaks that towered upward to the stars, and as strong, and as utterly without mercy.

Trevor's body became convulsed. Every physical instinct was driving him to run, to escape, and he could not. In his throat now there was a queer wailing whimper. He tried to drop the sun-stone. He was forbidden. Rage began to come on the heels of horror, a blind protest against the indecent invasion of his most private mind. The whimpering rose to a sort of catlike squall, an eerie and quite insane sound in the narrow gorge, and he clawed with his free hand at the one that held the sun-stone, tight against his brows.

He tore it loose.

A wrench that almost cracked his brain in two. A flicker of surprise, just before the contact broke, and then a fading flash of anger, and then nothing.

Trevor fell down. He did not quite lose consciousness, but there was an ugly sickness in him and all his bones had turned to water. It seemed a long time before he could get to his feet again. Then he stood there shaking.

There was something in this accursed valley. There was something or someone who could reach out through the sun-stones and take hold of a man's mind. It did that to the Korins and the hawks, and it had done it for a moment to him, and the horror of that alien grasp upon his brain was still screaming inside him.

"But who—?" he whispered hoarsely. And then he knew that the word was wrong. *"What—?"*

For it was not human, it couldn't be human, whatever had held him there wasn't man or woman, brute or human. It was something else, but what it was he didn't want to know, he only wanted to get out—out—

Trevor found that he had begun to run, bruising his shins against rocks. He got a grip on himself, forcing himself to stand still. His breath was coming in great gasps.

He still had the sun-stone clenched in his sweating palm, and he had an almost irresistible desire to fling the thing away with all his strength. But even in the grip of alien horror a man could not throw away the goal of half a lifetime, and he held it, and hated it.

He told himself that whatever it was that reached through the sun-stones could not use them unless they were against the forehead, close to the brain. The thing couldn't harm him if he kept it away from his head.

A terrible thought renewed Trevor's horror. He thought of the Korins, the men who wore sun-stones set forever in their brows. Were they, always and always, in the icy, alien grip of that which had held him? And these were the masters of Jen's people?

He forced that thought away. He had to forget everything except how to get free of this place.

He started at once, still shaken. He couldn't go far before daylight, and he would have to lie up in the rocks through the day and try to make it to the valley wall the next night.

He was glad when daylight came, the first fires of sunrise kindling the peaks that went above the sky.

IT WAS at that moment that a shadow flickered, and Trevor looked up and saw the hawks.

Many hawks. They had not seen him, they were not heeding the rocks in which he crouched. They were flying straight up the ravine, not circling or searching now but going with a sure purposefulness, back the way he had come.

He watched them uneasily. There were more than he had ever seen together before. But they flew on up the ravine without turning, and were gone.

"They weren't looking for me," he thought. "But..."

Trevor should have felt relieved, but he didn't. His uneasiness grew and grew, stemming from an inescapable conclusion.

The hawks were going to the cave. They were heading toward it in an exact line, turning neither to right nor left, and this time they were not in any doubt. They, or whoever or whatever dominated them, knew this time exactly where to find the fugitives.

"But that's impossible," Trevor tried to tell himself. "There's no way they could suddenly learn exactly where the cave is after all this time."

No way?

A thing was forcing its way up into Trevor's anxious thoughts, a realization that he did not want to look at squarely, not at all. But it would not be put down, it would not stop tormenting him, and suddenly he cried out to it, a cry of pain and guilt,

"No, it couldn't be! It couldn't be through me they learned!"

It fronted him relentlessly, the memory of that awful moment in the canyon when whatever had gripped him through the sun-stone had seemed to be turning over the leaves of his brain like the pages of a book.

The vast and alien mind that had gripped his in that dreadful contact had read his own brain clearly, he knew. And in Trevor's brain and memories it had found the secret of the cave.

Trevor groaned in an agony of guilt.

He crawled out of his rock-heap and began to run back up the ravine, following the path the hawks had taken. There might still be time to warn them.

Stumbling, running, he passed the canyon fork. And now from above him in the canyon he heard the sounds he dreaded—the sounds of women screaming and men shouting hoarsely in fury and despair.

Farther on, over the rocks, scrambling, slipping, gasping for breath, he came to the cave-mouth and the sight he had dreaded.

The hawks had gone into the cave and driven out the slaves. They had them in the canyon now, and they were trying to herd them together and drive them down toward the lava beds. But the slaves were fighting back.

Dark wings beat and thundered in the narrow gorge between the walls of rock. Claws struck and lashing tails cut like whips. Men struggled and floundered and trampled each other. Some died. Some of the hawks died too. But the people were being forced farther down the canyon under the relentless swooping of the hawks.

Then Trevor saw Jen. She was a little way from the others. Hugh was with her. He had shoved her into a protecting hollow and was standing over her with a piece of rock in his hands, trying to beat off a hawk. Hugh was hurt badly. He was not doing well.

Trevor uttered a wild cry that voiced all the futile rage in him, and bounded over a slope toward them.

"Hugh, look out!" he yelled. The hawk had risen, and then had checked and turned, to swoop down straight at Hugh's back.

Hugh swung partly around, but not soon enough. The hawk's claws were in his body, deep. Hugh fell down.

Jen was screaming when Trevor reached them. He didn't stop to snatch up a rock. He threw himself onto the hawk that had welded itself to Hugh's back. There was a horrid slippery thrashing of wings under him, and the scaly neck of the thing was terribly strong between Trevor's hands. But not strong enough. He broke it.

It was too late. When his sight cleared, Jen was staring in a strange wild way at the man and hawk lying tangled together in the dust. When Trevor touched her she fought him a little, not as though she saw him really, not as though she saw anything but Hugh's white ribs sticking out.

"Jen, for God's sake, he's dead." Trevor tried to pull her away. "We've got to get away from here."

There might be a chance. The black hawks were driving the humans down the canyon a little below them now, and if they could make the tumbled rocks below the cliff, there was a chance.

IV

HE HAD TO DRAG Jen. Her face had gone utterly blank.

In the next minute he realized that they would never reach the rocks, and that there was no chance, none at all. Back from the winged whirl that was driving the humans, two of the hawks came darting at them.

Trevor swung Jen behind him and hoped fiercely that he could get another neck between his hands before they pulled him down.

The dark shadows flashed down. He could see the sun-stones glittering in their heads. They struck straight at him....

But at the last split second they swerved away.

Trevor waited. They came back again, very fast, but this time it was at Jen they struck, and not at him.

He got her behind him again in time. And once more the hawks checked their strike.

The truth dawned on Trevor. The hawks were deliberately refraining from hurting him.

"Whoever gives them their orders, the Korins or that *Other,* doesn't want me hurt!"

He caught up Jen in his arms and started to run again toward the rocks.

Instantly the hawks struck at Jen. He could not swing her clear in time. Blood ran from the long claw-marks they left in her smooth, tanned shoulders.

Jen cried out. Trevor hesitated. He tried again for the rocks, and Jen moaned as a swift scaly head snapped at her neck.

So that's it, Trevor thought furiously. I'm not to be hurt, but they can drive me through Jen.

And they could, too. He would never get Jen to the concealment of the rocks alive, with those two wide-winged shadows tearing at her. He had to go the way they wanted or they would leave her as they had left Hugh.

"All right!" Trevor yelled savagely at the circling demons. "Let her alone! I'll go where you want."

He turned, still carrying Jen, plodding after the other slaves who were being herded down the canyon.

All that day the black hawks drove the humans down the watercourse, around the shoulder of basalt and out onto the naked sun-seared lava bed. Some of them dropped and lay where they were, and no effort of the hawks could move them on again. Much of the time Trevor carried Jen. Part of the time he dragged her. For long vague periods he had no idea what he did.

He was in a daze in which only his hatred still was vivid, when he felt Jen pulled away from him. He struggled, and was held—and he looked up to see a ring of mounted men around him. Korins on their crested beasts, the sun-stones glittering in their brows.

They looked down at Trevor, curious, speculative, hostile, their otherwise undistinguished human faces made strangely evil and other-worldly by the winking stones.

"You come with us to the city," one of them said curtly to Trevor. "That woman goes with the other slaves."

Trevor glared up at him. "Why me, to the city?"

The Korin raised his riding whip threateningly. "Do as you're ordered! Mount!"

Trevor saw that a slave had brought a saddled beast to him and was holding it, not looking either at him or the Korins.

"All right," he said. "I'll go with you."

He mounted and sat waiting, his eyes bright with the hatred that burned in him, bright as blown coals. They formed a circle around him and the leader gave a word. They galloped off toward the distant city.

Trevor must have dozed as he rode, for suddenly it was sunset, and they were approaching the city.

Seeing it as he had before, far off and with nothing to measure it against but the overtopping titan peaks, it had seemed no more than a city built of rock. Now he was close to it. Black shadows lay on it, and on the valley, but half way up the opposite mountain wall the light still blazed, reflected downward on the shallow sky, so that everything seemed to float in some curious dimension between night and day. Trevor stared, shut his eyes, and stared again.

The size was wrong.

He looked quickly at the Korins, with the eerie feeling that he might have shrunk to child-size as he slept. But they had not changed—at least, relative to himself. He turned back to the city, trying to force it into perspective.

It rose up starkly from the level plain. There was no gradual guttering out into suburbs, no softening down to garden villas or rows of cottages. It leaped up like a cliff and began, solemn, massive, squat, and ugly. The buildings were square, set stiffly along a square front. They were not tall. Most of them were only one story high. And yet Trevor felt dwarfed by them, as he had never felt dwarfed by the mightiest of Earth's skyscrapers. It was an unnatural feeling, and one that made him curiously afraid.

There were no walls or gateways, no roads leading in. One minute the beasts padded on the grass of the open plain. The next, their claws were clicking on a stone pave and the buildings closed them in, hulking, graceless, looking sullen and forlorn in the shadowed light. There was no sound in them anywhere, no gleaming of lamps in the black embrasures of cavernous doors. The last furious glare of the hidden sun seeped down from the high peaks and stained their upper walls, and they were old—half as old, Trevor thought, as the peaks themselves.

It was the window embrasures, the doors, and the steps that led up to them that made Trevor understand suddenly what was wrong. And the latent fear that had been in him sprang to full growth. The city, and the buildings in it, the steps and the doors and the height of the windows, were perfectly in proportion, perfectly normal—if the people who lived there were twenty feet high.

He turned to the Korins. "*You* never built this place. Who built it?"

The one called Galt, who was nearest him, snarled, "Quiet, slave!"

Trevor looked at him, and at the other Korins. Something about their faces and the way they rode along the darkening empty street told him they too were afraid.

He said, "You, the Korins, the lordly demi-gods who ride about and send your hawks to hunt and slay—you're more afraid of your master than the slaves are of you!"

They turned toward him pallid faces that burned with hatred.

He remembered how that other had gripped his brain back in the canyon. He remembered how it had felt. He understood many things now.

He asked, "How does it feel to be enslaved, Korins? Not just enslaved in body, but in mind and soul?"

Galt turned like a striking snake. But the blow never fell. The upraised hand with the heavy whip suddenly checked, and then sank down again. Only the eyes of the Korin glowed with a baleful helplessness under the winking sun-stone.

TREVOR laughed without humor. "It wants me alive. I guess I'm safe, then. I guess I could tell you what I think of you. You're still convicts, aren't you? After three hundred years. No wonder you hate the slaves."

Not the same convicts, of course. The sun-stones didn't give longevity. Trevor knew how the Korins propagated, stealing women from among the slaves, keeping the male children and killing the female. He laughed again.

"It isn't such a good life after all, is it, being a Korin? Even hunting and killing can't take the taste out of your mouths. No wonder you hate the others! They're enslaved, all right, but they're not *owned.*"

They would have liked to kill him but they could not. They were forbidden. Trevor looked at them, in the last pale flicker of the afterglow. The jewels and the splendid harness, the bridles of the beasts heavy with gold, the weapons—they looked foolish now, like the paper crowns and glass beads that children deck themselves with when they pretend to be kings. These were not lords and masters. These were only little men, and slaves. And the sun-stones were a badge of shame.

The cavalcade passed on. Empty streets, empty houses with windows too high for human eyes to look through and steps too tall for human legs to climb. Full dark, and the first stunning crash of thunder, the first blaze of lightning between the cliffs. The mounts were hurrying now, almost galloping to beat the lightning and the scalding rain.

They were in a great square. Around it was a stiff rectangle of houses, and these were lighted with torchlight, and in the monstrous doorways here and there a little figure stood, a Korin, watching.

In the exact center of the square was a flat low structure of stone, having no windows and but a single door.

They reined the beasts before that lightless entrance. "Get down," said Galt to Trevor. A livid reddish flaring in the sky showed Trevor the Korin's face, and it was smiling, as a wolf smiles before the kill. Then the thunder came, the downpour of rain, and he was thrust bodily into the doorway.

He stumbled over worn flagging in the utter dark, but the Korins moved surefootedly as cats. He knew they had been here many times before, and he knew that they hated it. He could feel the hate and the fear bristling out from the bodies that were close to his, smell them in the close hot air. They didn't want to be here but they had to. They were bidden.

He would have fallen head foremost down the sudden flight of steps if someone had not caught his arm. They were huge steps. They were forced to go down them as small children do, lowering themselves bodily from tread to tread. A furnace blast of air came up the well, but in spite of the heat Trevor felt cold. He could feel how the hard stone of the stairs had been worn into deep hollows by the passing of feet. Whose feet? And going where?

A sulphurous glow began to creep up through the darkness. They went down what seemed a very long way. The glow brightened, so that Trevor could once more make out the faces of the Korins. The heat was overpowering, but still there was a coldness around Trevor's heart.

The steps ended in a long low hall, so long that the farther end of it was lost in vaporous shadow. Trevor thought that it must have been squared out of a natural cavern, for here and there in the rocky floor small fumaroles burned and bubbled, giving off the murky light and a reek of brimstone.

Along both sides of the hall were rows of statues seated in stone chairs.

Trevor stared at them, with the skin crawling up and down his back. Statues of men and women—or rather, of creatures manlike and womanlike—sitting solemn and naked, their hands folded in their laps, their eyes, fashioned of dull, reddish stone, looking straight ahead, their features even and composed, with a strange sad patience clinging to the stony furrows around mouth and cheek. Statues that would be perhaps twenty feet tall if they were standing, carved by a master's chisel out of a pale substance that looked like alabaster.

Galt caught his arm. "Oh, no, you won't run away. You were laughing, remember? Come on, I want to see you laugh some more."

They forced him along between the rows of statues. Quiet statues, with a curiously ghostly look of thoughtfulness—of thoughts and feelings long vanished but once there, different from those of humans, perhaps, but quite as strong. No two of them were alike, in face or body. Trevor noted among them things seldom seen in statues, a maimed limb, a deformity, or a completely nondescript face that would offer neither beauty nor ugliness for an artist to enlarge upon. Also, they seemed all to be old, though he could not have said why he thought so.

There were other halls opening off this main one. How far they went he had no means of guessing, but he could see that in them were other shadowy rows of seated figures.

Statues. Endless numbers of statues, down here in the darkness underneath the city...

He stopped, bracing himself against his captors, gripping the hot rock with his bare feet.

"This is a catacomb," he said. "Those aren't statues, they're bodies, dead things sitting up."

"Come on," said Galt. "Come on, and laugh!"

They took him, and there were too many to fight. And Trevor knew that it was not them he had to fight. Something was waiting for him down in that catacomb. It had had his mind once. It would—

THEY were approaching the end of the long hall. The sickly light from the fumaroles showed the last of the lines of seated figures—had they died there like that, sitting up, or had they been brought here afterward? The rows on each side ended evenly, the last chairs exactly opposite each other.

But against the blank end wall was a solitary seat of stone, facing down the full gloomy length of the hall, and on it sat a manlike shape of alabaster, very still, the stony hands folded rigidly upon the stony thighs. A figure no different from the others, except....

Except that the eyes were still alive.

The Korins dropped back a little. All but Galt. He stayed beside Trevor, his head bent, his mouth sullen and nervous, not looking up at all. And Trevor stared into the remote and somber eyes that were like two pieces of carnelian in that pale alabaster face, and yet were living, sentient, full of a deep and alien sorrow.

It was very silent in the catacomb. The dreadful eyes studied Trevor, and for just a moment his hatred was tempered by a strange pity as he thought what it must be like for the brain, the intelligence behind those eyes, already entombed, and knowing it.

"A long living and a long dying. The blessing and the curse of my people."

The words were soundless, spoken inside his brain. Trevor started violently. Almost he turned to flee, remembering the torture of that moment in the canyon, and then he found that while he had been staring, a force as gentle and stealthy as the gliding of a shadow had already invaded him. And he was forbidden.

"At this range I do not need the sun-stones," murmured the silent voice within him. "Once I did not need them at all. But I am old."

Trevor stared at the stony thing that watched him, and then he thought of Jen, of Hugh lying dead with a dead hawk in the dust, and the strangeness left him, and his bitter passion flared again.

"So you hate me as well as fear me, little human? You would destroy me?" There was a gentle laughter inside Trevor's mind. "I have watched generations of humans die so swiftly. And yet I am here, as I was before they came, waiting."

"You won't be here forever," snarled Trevor. "These others like you died. You will!"

"Yes. But it is a slow dying, little human. Your body chemistry is like that of the plants, the beasts, based upon carbon. Quick to grow. Quick to wither away. Ours was of another sort. We were like the mountains, cousin to them, our body cells built of silicon, even as theirs. And so our flesh endures until it grows slow and stiff with age. But even then we must wait long, very long, for death."

Something of the truth of that long waiting came to Trevor, and he felt a shuddering thankfulness for the frailty of human flesh.

"I am the last," whispered the silent voice. "For a while I had companionship of minds, but the others are all gone before me, long ago."

Trevor had a nightmare vision of Mercury, in some incalculable future eon, a frozen world taking its last plunge into the burned-out sun, bearing with it these endless rows of alabaster shapes, sitting in their chairs of stone, upright in the dead blackness underneath the ice.

He fought back to reality, clutching his hatred as a swimmer clings to a plank, his voice raw with passion and bitterness as he cried out.

"Yes, I'll destroy you if I can! What else could you expect after what you've done?"

"Oh, no, little human, you will not destroy me. You will help me."

Trevor glared. "Help you? Not if you kill me!"

"There will be no killing. You would be of no use to me dead. But alive you can serve me. That is why you were spared."

"Serve you—like *them?*" He swung to point to the waiting Korins, but the Korins were not waiting now, they were closing in on him, their hands reaching for him.

Trevor struck out at them. He had a fleeting thought of how weird this battle of his with the Korins must look, as they struck and staggered on the stone paving beneath the looming, watch-ing thing of stone.

But even as he had that thought, the moment of struggle ended. An imperious command hit his brain, and black oblivion closed down upon him like the sudden clenching of a fist.

V

DARKNESS. He was lost in it, and he was not himself any more. He fled through the darkness, groping, crying out for something that was gone. And a voice answered him, a voice that he did not want to hear....

Darkness. Dreams.

Dawn, high on the blazing mountains. He stood in the city, watching the light grow bright and pitiless, watching it burn on the upper walls and then slip downward into the streets, cast-ing heavy shadows in the openings of door and window, so that the houses looked like skulls with empty eyeholes and gaping mouths. The buildings no longer seemed too big. He walked be-tween them, and when he came to steps he climbed them easily, and the window ledges were no higher than his head. He knew these buildings. He looked at each one as he passed, naming it, remembering with a long, long memory.

The hawks came down to him, the faithful servants with the sun-stones in their brows. He stroked their pliant necks, and they hissed softly with pleasure, but their shallow minds were empty of everything but that vague sensation. He passed on through the familiar streets, and in them nothing stirred. All through the day from dawn to sunset, and in the darkness that came afterward, nothing stirred, and there was a silence among the stones.

He could not endure the city. His time was not yet, though the first subtle signs of age had touched him. But he went down into the catacombs and took his place with those others who were waiting and could still speak to him with their minds, so that he should not be quite alone with the silence.

The years went by, leaving no traces of themselves in the unchanging gloom of the mortuary halls.

One by one those last few minds were stilled until all were gone. And by that time age had chained him where he was, unable to rise and go again into the city where he had been young, the youngest of all... Shannach, they had named him—The Last.

So he waited, alone. And only one who was kin to the mountains could have borne that waiting in the place of the dead.

Then, in a burst of flame and thunder, new life came into the valley. Human life. Soft, frail, receptive life, intelligent, unprotected, possessed of violent and bewildering passions. Very carefully, taking its time, the mind of Shannach reached out and gathered them in.

Some of the men were more violent than the others. Shannach saw their emotions in patterns of scarlet against the dark of his inner mind. They had already made themselves masters, and a number of these frail sensitive brains had snapped out swiftly because of them. "These I will take for my own," thought Shannach. "Their mind-patterns are crude, but strong, and I am interested in death."

There had been a surgeon aboard the ship but he was dead. However, there was no need of a surgeon for what was about to be done. When Shannach had finished talking to the men he had chosen, telling them of the sun-stones, telling them the truth, but not all of it—when those men had eagerly agreed to the promise of power—Shannach took complete control. And the clumsy convict hands that moved now with such exquisite skill were as much his instruments as the scalpels of the dead surgeon that they wielded, making the round incision and the delicate cutting of the bone.

Who was the man that lay there, quiet under the knife? Who were the ones that bent above him, with the strange stones in their brows? Names. There are names and I know them. Closer, closer. I know that man who lies there with blood between his eyes...

Trevor screamed. Someone slapped him across the face, viciously and with intent. He screamed again, fighting, clawing, still blinded by the visions and the dark mists, and that voice that he dreaded so much spoke gently in his mind, "It's all over, Trevor. It is done."

The hard hand slapped him again, and a rough human voice said harshly, "Wake up. Wake up, damn it!"

He woke. He was in the middle of a vast room, crouched down in the attitude of a fighter, shivering, sweating, his hands outstretched and grasping nothing. He must have sprung there, half unconscious, from the tumbled pallet of skins against the wall. Galt was watching him.

"Welcome, Earthman. How does it feel to be one of the masters?"

Trevor stared at him. A burning flood of light fell in through the tall windows so high above his head, setting the sun-stone ablaze between the Korin's sullen brows. Trevor's gaze fixed on that single point of brilliance.

"Oh, yes," said Galt. "It's true."

It struck Trevor with an ugly shock that Galt's lips had not moved, and that he had made no audible sound.

"The stones give us a limited ability," Galt went on, still without speaking aloud. "Not like His, of course. But we can control the hawks, and exchange ideas between us when we want to if the range isn't too far. Naturally, our minds are open to Him any time he wants to pry."

"There's no pain," Trevor whispered, desperately trying to make the thing not be so. "My head doesn't ache."

"Of course not. He takes care of that."

Shannach? If it isn't so, how do I know that name? And that dream, that endless nightmare in the catacombs.

Galt winced. "We don't use that name. He doesn't like it." He looked at Trevor. "What's the matter, Earthman? Why so green? You were laughing once, remember? Where's your sense of humor now?"

He caught Trevor abruptly by the shoulders and turned him around so that he faced a great sheet of polished glassy substance set into the wall. A mirror for giants, reflecting the whole huge room, reflecting the small dwarfed figures of the men.

"Go on," said Galt, pushing Trevor ahead of him. "Take a look."

Trevor shook off the Korin's grasp. He moved forward by himself, close to the mirror. He set his hands against the chill surface and stared at what he saw there. And it was true.

Between his brows a sun-stone winked and glittered. And his face, the familiar, normal, not-too-bad face he had been used to all his life, was transformed into something monstrous and unnatural, a goblin mask with a third, and evil eye.

A coldness crept into his heart and bones. He backed away a little from the mirror, his hands moving blindly upward, slowly toward the stone that glistened between his brows. His mouth was twisted like a child's, and two tears rolled down his cheeks.

His fingers touched the stone. And then the anger came. He sank his nails into his forehead, clawing at the hard stone, not caring if he died after he had torn it out.

Galt watched him. His lips smiled but his eyes were hateful.

BLOOD ran down the sides of Trevor's nose. The sun-stone was still there. He moaned and thrust his nails in deeper, and Shannach let him go until he had produced one stab of agony that cut his head in two and nearly dropped him. Then Shannach sent in the full force of his mind. Not in anger, for he felt none, and not in cruelty, for he was no more cruel than the mountain he was kin to, but simply because it was necessary.

Trevor felt that cold and lonely power roll down on him like an avalanche. He braced himself to meet it, but it broke his defenses, crushed them, made them nothing, and moved onward against the inmost citadel of his mind.

In that reeling, darkened fortress all that was wholly Trevor crouched and clung to its armament of rage, remembering dimly that once, in a narrow canyon, it had driven back this enemy and broken free. And then some crude animal instinct far below the level of conscious thought warned him not to press the battle now, to bury his small weapon and wait, letting his last redoubt of which he was yet master go untouched and perhaps unnoticed by his captor.

Trevor let his hands drop limply and his mind go slack. The cold black tide of power paused, and then he felt it slide away, withdrawing from those threatened walls. Out of the edges of it, Shannach spoke.

"Your mind is tougher than these valley-bred Korins. They're well conditioned, but you—you remember that you defied me once. The contact was imperfect then. It is not imperfect now. Remember that, too, Trevor."

Trevor drew in a long, unsteady breath. He whispered, "What do you want of me?"

"Go and see the ship. Your mind tells me that it understands these things. See if it can be made to fly again."

That order took Trevor completely by surprise. "The ship! But why...?"

Shannach was not used to having his wishes questioned, but he answered patiently, "I have still a while to live. Several of your short generations. I have had too much of this valley, too much of these catacombs. I want to leave them."

Trevor could understand that. Having had that nightmare glimpse into Shannach's mind, he could perfectly understand. For one brief moment he was torn with pity for this trapped creature who was alone in the universe. And then he wondered, "What would you do if you could leave the valley? What would you do to another settlement of men?"

"Who knows? I have one thing left to me—curiosity."

"You'd take the Korins with you, and the hawks?"

"Some. They are my eyes and ears, my hands and feet. But you object, Trevor."

"What difference does that make?" said Trevor bitterly. "I'll go look at the ship."

"Come on," said Galt, taking up an armful of torches. "I'll show you the way."

They went out through the tall door into the streets between the huge square empty houses. The streets and houses that Trevor had known in his dream, remembering when there were lights and voices in them. Trevor noticed only that Galt was leading him out on the opposite side of the city, toward the part of the valley he had never visited. And then his mind reverted to something that not even the shock of his awakening could drive out of his consciousness.

Jen.

A sudden panic sprang up in him. How long had it been since the darkness fell on him there in the catacomb? Long enough for almost anything to happen. He envisioned Jen being torn by hawks, of her body lying dead as Hugh's had lain, and he started to reach out for Galt, who had owned them both. But abruptly Shannach spoke to him, in that eerie silent way he was getting used to.

"The woman is safe. Here, look for yourself."

His mind was taken firmly and directed into a channel completely new to him. He felt a curious small shock of contact, and suddenly he was looking down from a point somewhere in the sky at a walled paddock with a number of tiny figures in it. His own eyes would have seen them as just that, but the eyes he was using now were keen as an eagle's, though they saw no color but only black and white and the shadings in between. So he recognized one of the distant figures as Jen.

He wanted to get closer to her, much closer, and rather sulkily his point of vision began to circle down dropping lower and lower. Jen looked up. He saw the shadow of wide wings sweep across her and realized that of course he was using one of the hawks. He pulled it back so as not to frighten her, but not before he had seen her face. The frozen stoniness was gone, and in its place had come the look of a wounded tigress.

"I want her," Trevor said to Shannach.

"She belongs to Galt. I do not interfere."

Galt shrugged. "You're welcome. But keep her chained. She's too dangerous now for anything but hawk-meat."

THE ship was not far beyond the city. It lay canted over on its side, just clear of a low spur jutting out from the barrier cliff. It had hit hard, and some of the main plates were buckled, but from the outside the damage did not seem irreparable, if you had the knowledge and the tools to work with. Three hundred years ago it might have been made to fly again, only those who had the knowledge and the will were dead. And the convicts wanted to stay where they were.

The tough metal of the outer skin, alloyed to resist friction that could burn up a meteor, had stood up pretty well under three centuries of Mercurian climate. It was corroded, and where the breaks were the inner shells were eaten through with rust, but the hulk still retained the semblance of a ship.

"Will it fly?" asked Shannach eagerly.

"I don't know yet," Trevor answered.

Galt lighted a torch and gave it to him. "I'll stay out here."

Trevor laughed. "How are you ever going to fly over the mountains?"

"He'll see to that when the time comes," Galt muttered. "Take the rest of these torches. It's dark in there."

Trevor climbed in through the gaping lock, moving with great caution on the tilted, rust-red decks. Inside, the ship was a shambles. Everything had been stripped out of it that could be used, leaving only bare cubicles with the enamel peeling off the walls and a moldering litter of junk.

In a locker forward of the air lock he found a number of spacesuits. The fabric was rotted away, but a few of the helmets were still good and some half score of the oxygen bottles had survived, the gas still in them.

Shannach urged him on impatiently. "Get to the essentials, Trevor!"

The bridge room was still intact, though the multiple thickness of glassite in the big ports showed patterns of spidery cracks. Trevor examined the controls. He was strictly a planetary spacer, used to flying his small craft within spitting distance of the world he was prospecting, and there were a few gadgets here he didn't understand, but he could figure the board well enough.

"Not far, Trevor. Only over the mountains. I know from your mind—and I remember from the minds of those who died after the landing—that beyond the mountain wall there is a plain of dead rock, more than a hundred of your reckoning in miles, and then another ridge that seems solid but is not, and beyond that pass there is a fertile valley twenty times bigger than Korith, where Earthmen live."

"Only partly fertile, and the mines that brought the Earthmen are pretty well worked out. But a few ships still land there, and a few Earthmen still hang on."

"That is best. A small place, to begin…"

"To begin what?"

"Who can tell? You don't understand, Trevor. For centuries I have known exactly what I would do. There is a kind of rebirth in not knowing."

Trevor shivered and went back to studying the controls. The wiring, protected by layers of imperviplast insulation and conduit, seemed to be in fair shape. The generator room below had been knocked about, but not too badly. There were spare batteries. Corroded, yes, but if they were charged, they could hold for a while.

"Will it fly?"

"I told you I don't know yet. It would take a lot of work."

"There are many slaves to do this work."

"Yes. But without fuel it's all useless."

"See if there is fuel."

The outlines of that hidden thing in Trevor's secret mind were coming clearer now. He didn't want to see them out in the full light where Shannach could see them too. He thought hard about generators, batteries, and the hooking up of leads.

He crept among the dark bowels of the dead ship, working toward the stern. The torch made a red and smoky glare that lit up deserted wardrooms and plundered holds. One large compartment had a heavy barred and bolted door that had bent like tin in the crash. "That's where they came from," Trevor thought, "like wolves out of a trap."

In the lower holds that had taken the worst of the impact were quantities of mining equipment and farm machinery, all smashed beyond use but formidable-looking none the less, with rusty blades and teeth and queer hulking shapes. They made him think of weapons, and he let the thought grow, adorning it with pictures of men going down under whirring reapers. Shannach caught it.

"Weapons?"

"They could be used as such. But the metal in them would repair the hull."

He found the fuel bunkers. The main supply was used to the last grain of fissionable dust, but the emergency bunkers still showed some content on the mechanical gauges. Not much, but enough.

VI

A HARD excitement began to stir in Trevor, too big to be hidden in that secret corner of his mind. He didn't try. He let it loose, and Shannach murmured.

"You are pleased. The ship will fly, and you are thinking that when you reach that other valley and are among your own people again, you will find means to destroy me. Perhaps, but we shall see."

In the smoky torchlight, looking down from a sagging catwalk above the firing chambers and the rusty sealed-in tubes, Trevor smiled. A lie could be thought as well as spoken. And Shannach, in a manner of speaking, was only human.

"I'll need help. All the help there is."

"You'll have it."

"It'll take time. Don't hurry me and don't distract me. Remember, I want to get over the mountains as bad as you do."

Shannach laughed.

Trevor got more torches and went to work in the generator room. He felt that Shannach had withdrawn from him, occupied now with rounding up the Korins and the slaves. But he did not relax his caution. The open areas of his mind were filled with thoughts of vengeance to come when he reached that other valley.

Gradually the exigencies of wrestling with antiquated and partly ruined machinery drove everything else away. That day passed, and a night, and half another day before all the leads were hooked the way he wanted them, before one creaky generator was operating on one-quarter normal output, and the best of the spare batteries were charging.

He emerged from the torchlit obscurity into the bridge, blinking mole-like in the light, and found Galt sitting there.

"He trusts you," the Korin said, "but not too far."

Trevor scowled at him. Exhaustion, excitement, and a feeling of fate had combined to put him into an unreal state where his mind operated more or less independently. A hard protective shell had formed around that last little inner fortress so that it was hidden even from himself, and he had come almost to believe that he was going to fly this ship to another valley and battle Shannach there. So he was not surprised to hear Shannach say softly in his mind,

"You might try to go away alone. I wouldn't want that, Trevor."

Trevor grunted. "I thought you controlled me so well I couldn't spit if you forbade it."

"I am dealing with much here that I don't comprehend. We were never a mechanical people. Therefore some of your thoughts, while I read them clearly, have no real meaning for me. I can handle you, Trevor, but I'm taking no chances with the ship."

"Don't worry," Trevor told him. "I can't possibly take the ship up before the hull's repaired. It would fall apart on me." That was true, and he spoke it honestly.

"Nevertheless," said Shannach, "Galt will be there, as my hands and feet, an extra guard over that object which you call a control-bank, and which your mind tells me is the key to the ship. You are forbidden to touch it until it is time to go."

Trevor heard Shannach's silent laughter.

"Treachery is implicit in your mind, Trevor. But I'll have time. Impulses come swiftly and cannot be read beforehand. But there is an interval between the impulse and the realization of it. Only a fraction of a second, perhaps, but I'll have time to stop you."

Trevor did not argue. He was shaking a little with the effort of not giving up his last pitiful individuality, of fixing his thoughts firmly on the next step toward what Shannach wanted and look-ing neither to the right nor to the left of it. He ran a grimy hand over his face, shrinking from the touch of the alien disfigurement in his forehead, and said sullenly,

"The holds have to be cleared. The ship won't lift that weight any more, and we need the metal for repairs." He thought again strongly of weapons. "Send the slaves."

"No," said Shannach firmly. "The Korins will do that. We won't put any potential weapons in the hands of the slaves."

Trevor allowed a wave of disappointment to cross his mind, and then he shrugged. "All right. But get them at it."

He went and stood by the wide ports looking out over the plain toward the city. The slaves were gathered at a safe distance from the ship, waiting like a herd of cattle until they should be needed. Some mounted Korins guarded them while the hawks wheeled overhead.

Coming toward the ship, moving with a resentful slowness, was a little army of Korins. Trevor could sense the group thought quite clearly. In all their lives they had never soiled their hands with labor, and they were angry that they had now to do the work of slaves.

Digging his nails into his palms, Trevor went aft to show them what to do. He couldn't keep it hidden much longer, this thing that he had so painfully concealed under layers of half-truths and deceptions. It had to come out soon, and Shannach would know.

In the smoky glare of many torches the Korins began to struggle with the rusting masses of machinery in the after holds.

"Send more down here," Trevor said to Shannach. "These things are heavy."

"They're all there now except those that guard the slaves. They cannot leave."

"All right," said Trevor. "Make them work."

He went back up along the canting decks, along the tilted passages, moving slowly at first, then swifter, swifter, his bare feet scraping on the flakes of rust, his face, with the third uncanny eye, gone white and strangely set. His mind was throwing off muddy streams of thought, confused and meaningless, desperate camouflage to hide until the last second what was underneath.

"Trevor!"

That was Shannach, alert, alarmed.

It was coming now, the purpose, out into the light. It had to come, it could not be hidden any longer. It burst up from its secret place, one strong red flare against the darkness, and Shannach saw it, and sent the full cold power of his mind to drown it out.

Trevor came into the bridge room, running.

THE first black wave of power hit him, crushed him. The bridge room lengthened out into some weird dimension of delirium, with Galt waiting at the far end. Behind Galt the one small, little key that needed to be touched just once.

The towering might of Shannach beat him back, forbidding him to think, to move, to be. But down in that beleaguered part of Trevor's mind the walls still held, with the bright brand of determination burning in them.

This was the moment, the time to fight. And he dug up that armament of fury he had buried there. He let it free, shouting at the alien force, "I beat you once! I beat you!"

The deck swam under his feet. The peeling bulkheads wavered past like veils of mist. He didn't know whether he was moving or not, but he kept on while the enormous weight bore down on his quivering brain, a mountain tilting, falling, seeking to smother out the fury that was all he had to fight with.

Fury for himself, defiled and outraged. Fury for Jen, with the red scars on her shoulders. Fury for Hugh lying dead under an obscene killer, fury for all the generations of decent people who had lived and died in slavery so that Shannach's time of waiting might be lightened.

He saw Galt's face, curiously huge, close to his own. It was stricken and amazed. Trevor's bared teeth glistened.

"I beat him once," he said to the Korin.

Galt's hands were raised. There was a knife in his girdle, but he had been bidden not to use it, not to kill. Only Trevor could make the ship to fly. Galt reached out and took him but there was an unsureness in his grip, and his mind was crying out to Shannach, "You could not make him stop! You could not!"

Trevor, who was partly merged with Shannach now, heard that cry and laughed. Something in him had burst wide open at Galt's physical touch. He had no control now, no sane thought left, but only a wild intense desire to do two things, one of which was to destroy this monster that had hold of him.

"Kill him," said Shannach suddenly. "He's mad, and no one can control an insane human."

Galt did his best to obey. But Trevor's hands were already around the Korin's throat, the fingers sinking deep into the flesh. There was a sharp snapping of bone.

He dropped the body. He could see nothing now except one tiny point of light in a reeling darkness. That single point of light had a red key in the center of it. Trevor reached out and pushed it down. That was the other thing.

For a short second nothing happened. Trevor sagged down across Galt's body. Shannach was somewhere else, crying warnings that came too late. Trevor had time to draw one harsh triumphant breath and brace himself.

The ship leaped under him. There was a dull roar, and then another, as the last fuel bunkers let go. The whole bridge room rolled and came to rest with a jarring shock that split the ports wide open, and the world was full of the shriek and crash of metal being torn and twisted and rent apart. Then it quieted. The ground stopped shaking and the deck settled under Trevor. There was silence.

Trevor crawled up the new slope of the bridge room floor, to the shattered lock and through it, into the pitiless sunlight. He could see now exactly what he had done. And it was good. It had worked. That last small measure of fuel had been enough.

The whole after part of the hulk was gone, and with it had gone all but a few of Shannach's Korins, trapped in the lower holds.

And then, in pure surprise, Shannach spoke inside Trevor's mind. "I grow old indeed! I misjudged the toughness and the secrecy of a fresh, strong mind. I was too used to my obedient Korins."

"Do you see what's happening to the last of them?" Trevor asked savagely. "Can you see?"

The last of the Korins who had been outside with the slaves seemed to have been stunned and bewildered by the collapse of their world. And with the spontaneity of a whirlwind, the slaves had risen against this last remnant of their hated masters. They had waited for a long, long time, and now the Korins and the hawks were being done to death.

"Can you see it, Shannach?"

"I can see, Trevor. And—they're coming now for you!"

They were. They were coming, blood-mad against all who wore the sun-stone, and Jen was in the forefront of them, and Saul, whose hands were red.

Trevor knew that he had less than a half-minute to speak for his life. And he was aware that Shannach, still withdrawn, watched now with an edged amusement.

Trevor said harshly to Saul and all of them, "So I give you your freedom, and you want to kill me for it?"

Saul snarled, "You betrayed us in the cave, and now..."

"I betrayed you, but without intent. There was someone stronger than the Korins, that even you didn't know about. So how should I have known?"

Trevor talked fast, then, talking for his life, telling them about Shannach and how the Korins themselves were enslaved.

"A lie," spat Saul.

"Look for yourselves in the crypts underneath the city! But be careful."

He looked at Jen, not at Saul. After a moment Jen said slowly, "Perhaps there is a—Shannach. Perhaps that's why we were never allowed in the city, so the Korins could go on pretending that they were gods."

"It's another of his lies, I tell you!"

Jen turned to him. "Go and look, Saul. We'll watch him."

Saul hesitated. Finally, he and a half-dozen others went off toward the city.

Trevor sat down on the hot, scorched grass. He was very tired, and he didn't like at all the way the withdrawn shadow of Shannach hovered just outside his mind.

The mountains leaned away from the Sun, and the shadows crawled up the lower slopes. Then Saul and the others returned.

Trevor looked up at their faces and laughed without mirth. "It's true, isn't it?"

"Yes," said Saul, and shivered. "Yes…"

"Did he speak to you?"

"He started to. But—we ran."

And Saul suddenly cried, out of the depths of fear this time and not of hate, "We can never kill him. It's his valley. And oh God, we're trapped in here with him, we can't get out."

"We can get out," said Trevor.

VII

SAUL stared at him sickly. "There's no way over the mountains. There isn't even air up there."

"There's a way. I found it in the ship."

224

Trevor stood up, speaking with a sudden harshness. "Not a way for us all, not now, but if three or four of us go, one may live to make it. And he could bring back men with ships for the others."

He looked at Saul. "Will you try it with me?"

The gaunt man said hoarsely, "I still don't trust you, Trevor! But anything—anything, to get away from *that…*"

"I'll go too," Jen said suddenly. "I'm as strong as Saul."

That was true, and Trevor knew it. He stared at her for a long minute, but he could not read her face.

Saul shrugged. "All right."

"But it's all craziness!" murmured a voice. "You can't breathe up there on the ridges. There's no air!"

Trevor climbed painfully into what was left of the twisted wreck, and brought out the helmets and oxygen bottles that had survived for just this purpose.

"We'll breathe," he said. "These—" He tried for a word that would explain to them. "—these containers hold an essence of air. We can take them with us and breathe."

"But the cold?"

"You have tanned skins, haven't you? And gums? I can show you how to make us protective garments. Unless you'd rather stay here with Shannach."

Saul shivered a little. "No, we'll try it."

In all the hours that followed—while the women of the slaves worked with soft tanned skins and resinous gums, while Trevor labored over the clumsy helmets they must have—in all that time, Shannach was silent.

Silent, but not gone. Trevor felt that shadow on his mind, he knew that Shannach was watching. Yet the Last One made no attempt upon him.

The slaves watched him, too. He saw the fear and hatred still in their eyes as they looked at the sun-stone between his brows.

And Jen watched him, and said nothing, and he could read nothing at all in her face. Was she thinking of Hugh and how the hawks had come?

By mid-afternoon they were ready. They started climbing slowly, toward the passes that went up beyond the sky. He and Saul and Jen were three grotesque and shapeless figures, in the three-layered garments of skin that were crudely sealed with gum, and the clumsy helmets that were padded out with cloth because there was no collar-rest to hold them. Their faces were wrapped close, and they held the ends of the oxygen tubes in their mouths because no amount of ingenuity could make the helmets space-tight.

The evening shadow flowed upward from the valley floor as they climbed, and the men who had come to help them dropped back. These three went on, with Saul leading the way and Trevor last.

And still Shannach had not spoken.

The atmosphere slipped behind them. They were climbing into space now, tiny creatures clambering up an infinity of virgin rock, in the utter black between the blazing peaks above and the flaring lightnings of the evening storm below.

Up and up toward the pass, toiling forward painfully with each other's help where no man could have made it alone, through a numbing and awful cold and silence. Three clumsy, dragging figures, up here above the sky itself, walking in the awfulness of infinity, where the rocks their feet dislodged rushed away as noiseless as a dream, where there was no sound, no light, no time.

Trevor knew they must have reached the pass, for on both sides now there rose up slopes that had never been touched by wind or rain or living root. He staggered on, and presently the ground began to drop and the way was easier. They had passed the crest. And the oxygen was almost gone.

Downward now, stumbling, slipping, sliding, yearning toward the air below. And they were on the other side of the mountain, above the plain of rock that led to...

And then, at last, Shannach—laughed.

"Clever," he said. "Oh, very clever, to escape without a ship!

But you will come back, with a ship, and you will take me to the outside world. And I will reward you greatly."

"No," said Trevor, in his mind. "No, Shannach. If we make it, the sun-stone comes out, and we'll come back for the slaves, not for you!"

"No, Trevor." The gentle finality of that denial was coldly frightening. "You are mine now. You surprised and tricked me once, but I know the trick now. Your whole mind is open to me. You cannot withstand me ever again."

It was cold, cold in the darkness below the pass, and the chill went deep into Trevor's soul and froze it.

Saul and Jen were below him now, stumbling down along the rock-strewn lip of a chasm, into the thin high reaches of the air, into sound and life again. He saw them tear away their helmets. He followed them, pulling off his own, gasping the frigid breath into his starved lungs. Shannach said softly,

"We do not need them any longer. They would be a danger when you reach other men. Dispose of them, Trevor."

Trevor started a raging refusal, and then his mind was gripped as by a great hand, shaken and turned and changed. And his fury flowed away into blankness.

"But of course," he thought. *"There are many boulders, and I can topple them into the chasm so easily…"*

He started toward a jagged stone mass, one that would quite neatly brush the two clumsy figures below him into the abyss.

"That is the way, Trevor! But quickly—!"

Trevor knew that Shannach had spoken truth, and that this time he was conquered.

"No, I won't!" he cried to himself, but it was only a weak echo from a fading willpower, a dying self.

"You will, Trevor! And now! They suspect."

Saul and Jen had turned. Trevor's face, open now to the numbing cold which he could scarcely feel, must have told them everything. They started scrambling back up toward him. Only a short distance, but they would be too late.

Trevor shrieked thinly, "Look out—Shannach…!"

He had his hands on it now, on the boulder he must roll to crush them.

But there was another way! He was Shannach's while he lived, but there was a way to avoid again betraying Jen's people, and that way was to live no longer.

He used the last of his dying will to pitch himself toward the brink of the chasm. Hundreds of feet below a man could lie quiet on the rocks through all eternity.

"Trevor, no! No!"

Shannach's powerful command halted him as he swayed on the very edge. And then Jen's arms caught him from behind.

He heard Saul's voice crying, thin and harsh in that upper air, "Push him over! He's a Korin. You saw his face!"

Jen answered, "No! He tried to kill himself for us!"

"But Shannach has him!" Saul cried out.

Shannach had him, indeed, stamping down that final flicker of Trevor's revolt, fiercely commanding him.

"Slay the woman and the man!"

Trevor tried to. He was all Shannach's now. He tried earnestly and with all his strength to kill them, but both the woman and the man had hold of him now. They were too strong for him, and he could not obey the Last One as he wanted to.

"Tie his arms!" Jen was shouting. "We can take him, and he can't do us any harm!"

The anger of Shannach flooded through Trevor, and he raged and struggled, and it was useless. Strips of hide secured his arms and they were dragging him on down out of the mountains, and he could not obey. He could not!

And then he felt the anger of Shannach ebb away into a terrible hopelessness. Trevor felt his own consciousness going, and he went into the darkness bearing in his mind the echo of that last bitter cry,

"I am old—too old..."

VIII

TREVOR awakened slowly, rising above the dark sea of oblivion only to sink again, conscious in those brief intervals that he lay in a bed and that his head ached.

There came a time when he rose, not to sink again. After a while his eyes opened, and he saw a metal ceiling.

"We made it," he said.

"Yes, you made it," said a friendly voice. "This is Solar City. You've been here quite a while."

Trevor turned his head to the voice, to the white-jacketed doctor beside his bed. But he didn't see the man or the room. Not at first. He saw only, upon the bedside table in a tray, a tawny eye that winked and glittered at him.

A sun-stone.

His hand started to rise weakly to his face. The doctor forestalled him.

"Don't bother. It's out. And a delicate job getting it out, it was. You'll have a headache for a while, but anyone would take a headache for a sun-stone!"

Trevor didn't answer that. He said suddenly, "Jen — and Saul…?"

"They're here. Pretty odd folk they are, too. Won't talk to any of us. You're all a blazing mystery, you know."

He went away. When he came back, Jen and Saul were with him. They wore modern synthecloth garments now. Jen looked as incongruous in hers as a leopardess in a silk dress.

She saw the smile in his eyes and cried, "Don't laugh at me — ever!"

It occurred to Trevor that civilizing her would take a long time. He doubted if it would ever be done. And he was glad of that.

She stood looking gravely down at him and then said, "They say you can get up tomorrow."

"That's good," said Trevor.

"You'll have to be careful for a while."

"Yes. I'll be careful."

They said no more than that, but in her steady, grave gaze Trevor read that Hugh and the hawks were forgiven, not forgotten but forgiven, that they two had touched each other and would not let go again.

Saul cried anxiously, "Days we've waited! When can we go back to the valley with a ship for the others?"

Trevor turned to the curiously watching doctor. "Can I charter a ship here?"

"A man with a sun-stone can get almost anything he wants, Trevor! I'll see about it."

The chartered ship that took them back to the valley had a minimum crew, and two mining technicians Trevor had hired. They set down outside the ancient city, and the slaves came surging toward them, half in eagerness, half in awe of this embodiment of misty legend.

Trevor had told Saul what to do. Out up the valley, in the skulls of slain Korins, were sun-stones worth many fortunes. They were going out with the slaves.

"But they're evil—evil!" Saul had cried.

"Not in the outside worlds," Trevor told him. "You people are going to need a start somewhere."

When that was done, when they were all in the ship, Trevor nodded to the two mining technicians.

"Now," he said. "The entrance to the catacomb is right over there."

The two went away, carrying their bulky burden slung between them. Presently they came back again without it.

Trevor took his sun-stone from his pocket. Jen clutched his arm and cried, "No!"

"There's no danger now," he said. "He hasn't time enough left to do anything with me. And—I feel somehow that I should tell him—"

He put the sun-stone to his brow, and in his mind he cried, "Shannach!"

And into his mind came the cold, tremendous presence of the Last One. In an instant it had read Trevor's thoughts.

"So this is the end, Trevor?"

"Yes," Trevor said steadily. "The end."

He was braced for the wild reaction of alarm and passion, the attempt to seize his mind, to avert doom.

It didn't come. Instead, from the Last One, came a stunning pulse of gladness, of mounting joy.

"Why—why, you *want* me to do this?" Trevor cried.

"Yes, Trevor! Yes! I had thought that the centuries of waiting for death would be long yet, and lonely. But this, this will free me now!"

Dazed by surprise, Trevor slowly made a gesture, and their ship throbbed upward into the sky. Another gesture, and the technician beside him reached toward the key of the radio-detonator.

In that moment he felt the mind of Shannach crying out as in a vast, mingled music, a glad chorus of release against chords of cosmic sorrow for all that had been and would never be again, for the greatest and oldest of races that was ending.

The receding city below erupted flame and rock around the catacomb mouth as the key was pressed.

And the song of Shannach ebbed into silence, as the last of the children of mountains went forever into night.

Mars Minus Bisha

Planet Stories, January 1954

IT WAS close on midnight. Both moons were out of the sky, and there was only blackness below and the mighty blaze of stars above, and between them the old wind dragging its feet in the dust. The Quonset stood by itself, a half mile or so from the canal bank and the town that was on it. Fraser looked at it, thinking what an alien intrusion both it and he were in this place, and wondering if he could stick out the four and a half months still required of him.

The town slept. There was no help for him there. An official order had been given, and so he was tolerated. But he was not welcome. Except in the big trading cities, Earthmen were unwelcome almost anywhere on Mars. It was a lonesome deal.

Fraser began to walk again. He walked a lot at night. The days were ugly and depressing and he spent them inside, working. But the nights were glorious. Not even the driest desert of Earth could produce a sky like this, where the thin air hardly dimmed the lustre of the stars. It was the one thing he would miss when he went home.

He walked, dressed warmly against the bitter chill. He brooded, and he watched the stars. He thought about his diminishing whiskey supply and the one hundred and forty-six centuries of written history gone into the dust that blew and tortured his sinuses, and after a while he saw the shadow, the dark shape that moved against the wind, silent, purposeful, and swift.

Out of the northern desert someone was riding.

For the space of three heartbeats Fraser stood rigid and frozen, squinting through the darkness and the starshine at that moving shape. Then he turned and ran for the Quonset. He was not allowed

233

to possess a weapon, and if some of the fanatic northern tribesmen had decided to come and cleanse their desert of his defiling presence, there was little he could do but bar the door and pray.

He did not go inside, just yet. It was unwise to show fear until you had to. He stood by the open door, outside the stream of light that poured from it. He waited, tensed for that final leap.

There was only a single rider, mounted on one of the big scaly beasts the Martian nomads use as the Earthly desert-folk use camels. Fraser relaxed a little, but not too much. One man with a spear could be enough. The stranger came slowly into the light, wrapped and muffled against the night, curbing with a strong hand the uneasy hissings and shyings of the beast at the unfamiliar smells that came to it from the Quonset. Fraser leaned forward, and suddenly the weakness of relief came over him. The rider was a woman, and she carried before her on the saddle pad a child, almost hidden in the folds of her cloak.

Fraser gave her the courteous Martian greeting. She looked down at him, tall and fierce-eyed, hating and yet somehow desperate, and presently she said, "You are the Earthman, the doctor."

"Yes."

The child slept, its head lolled back against the woman's body. There was something unnatural in the way it slept, undisturbed by the light or the voices. Fraser said gently, "I am here only to help."

The woman's arm tightened around the child. She looked at Fraser, and then in through the open door at the unfamiliar alien things that were there. Her face, made grim and hard by hunger and long marches, and far too proud for weeping, crumpled suddenly toward tears. She lifted the bridle-chain and swung the beast around, but before he had gone his own length she curbed him again. When she had turned once more toward Fraser she was calm as stone.

"My child is—ill," she said, very quietly, hesitating over that one word.

Fraser held up his arms. "I'll see what I can do."

The child—a girl, Fraser saw now, perhaps seven years old—did not stir even when she was lifted down from the saddle pad. Fraser started to carry her inside, saying over his shoulder to the woman, "I'll need to ask some questions. You can watch while I examine—"

A wild harsh cry and a thunder of padded hooves drowned out his words. He whirled around, and then he ran a little way, shouting, with the child in his arms, but it was no use. The woman was bent low in the saddle, urging the beast on with that frantic cry, digging in the spurs, and in a minute she was gone, back into the desert and the night. Fraser stood staring after her, open-mouthed, and swearing, and looking helplessly at the girl. There was an ominous finality about the way the woman had left. Why? Even if the child was dying, wouldn't a mother wait to know? Even if the sickness was contagious, would she ride the Lord knew how many miles across the desert with her, and then run?

THERE were no answers to those questions. Fraser gave up and went into the Quonset, kicking the door shut behind him. Passing through his combination living-quarters and office, he went into the tiny infirmary which adjoined his equally small but well-equipped lab. Neither office nor infirmary had had many customers. The Martians preferred their own methods, their own healers. Fraser was not supposed anyway to be the local G.P. The Medical Foundation grant and the order of the Martian authorities permitting him to be here both stated that he was engaged in research on certain viruses. Non-cooperation of the populace had not made his work any easier.

He became suddenly hopeful about the child.

Some two hours later he put her, still sleeping, into the neat white bed and sat down in the room outside, where he could watch her through the open door. He had a drink, and then another, and lighted a cigarette with hands that had trouble putting flame and tip together.

She was sound as a dollar. Thin, a bit undersized and undernourished like most Martian youngsters, but healthy. There was nothing whatever the matter with her, except that someone had thoroughly drugged her.

Fraser rose and flung open the outer door. He went out, staring with a kind of desperation into the north, straining his ears for a sound of hooves. Dawn was not far off. The wind was rising, thickening the lower air with dust, dimming the stars. Out on the desert nothing moved, nor was there any sound.

For the rest of that night and most of the morning that came after it, Fraser sat unmoving by the child's bed, waiting for her to wake.

She did it quietly. One moment her face was as it had been, remote and secret, and in the next she had opened her eyes. Her small body stirred and stretched, she yawned, and then she looked at Fraser, very solemnly but without surprise. He smiled and said, "Hello."

She sat up, a dark and shaggy-haired young person, with eyes the color of topaz, and the customary look of premature age and wisdom that the children of Mars share with the children of the Earthly East. She asked hesitantly, "My mother—?"

"She had to go away for a while," Fraser said, and added with false assurance, "but she'll be back soon." He was comforting himself as much as the child.

She took even that shred of hope from him. "No," she said. "She will not come back." She laid her head between her knees and began to cry, not making any fuss about it. Fraser put his arm around her.

"Here," he said. "Here now, don't do that. Of course she'll come back for you, she's your mother."

"She can't."

"But why? Why did she bring you here? You're not sick, you don't need a doctor."

The child said simply, "They were going to kill me."

Fraser was silent for a long time. Then he said, *"What?"*

The thin shoulders quivered under his arm. "They said I made the sickness that was in our tribe. The Old Men came, all together, and they told my father and mother I had to be killed. The Old Men are very powerful in magic, but they said they could not make me clean." She broke off, choking over a sob. "My mother said it was her right to do the thing, and she took me way off into the desert. She cried. She never did that before. I was frightened, and then she told me she wasn't going to hurt me, she was going to take me where I would be safe. She gave me some bitter water to drink, and told me not to be afraid. She talked to me until I went to sleep."

She looked up at Fraser, a frightened and bewildered little girl, and yet with a dignity about her, too.

"My mother said our gods have cursed me, and I would never be safe with my own people any more. But she said Earthmen have different gods, who wouldn't know me. She said you wouldn't kill me. Is that true?"

Fraser said something under his breath, and then he told her, "Yes. That's true. Your mother is a wise woman. She brought you to the right place." His face had become perfectly white. He stepped back from the bed and asked, "What's your name?"

"Bisha."

"Are you hungry, Bisha?"

She hesitated, still gulping down sobs. "I don't know."

"You think about it. Your clothes are there—put them on. I'll fix some breakfast."

He went out into the next room, sick and shaking with a rage such as he had never experienced before. Superstition, ignorance, the pious cruelty of the savage. Get an epidemic going and when the magic of the Old Man fails, find a scapegoat. Call a child accursed, and send its own mother to slaughter it. Mentally, Fraser bowed to the fierce-eyed woman who had been too tough for those cowardly old men. Poor devil, only the certainty of death could have made her abandon her child to an Earthman—a creature alien and unknown, but having different gods—

"Why would they curse me?" asked Bisha, close behind him. "Our gods, I mean." Dressing was an easy proposition for her, with one thick garment to pull over her head, and sandals for her feet. Her hair hung over her face and the tears still dripped, and now her nose was running, and Fraser didn't know whether to laugh or cry. "They didn't," he said, and picked her up. "It's only superstitious nonsense—"

He stopped. That was not going to do. Seven years, a lifetime of training and belief, were not going to be wiped out by a few words from a stranger. He stood scowling, trying hard to think of a way to reach her, and then he became aware that she was looking at him with a child's intense and wondering stare, sitting quite stiffly in his arms. He asked, "Are you afraid of me?"

"I—I've never seen anyone like you before."

"Hm. And you've never seen a house like this one, either."

She glanced around, and shook her head. "No. It's—" She had no words for what it was, only a shiver of awe.

Fraser smiled. "Bisha, you told me the Old Men of your tribe were very powerful in magic."

"Oh, yes!"

He set her down and took her hand firmly in his. "I'm going to show you a few things. Come on."

He didn't know whether child psychologists and other ethical persons would approve of his method, but it was the only one he could think of. With the imposing air of one performing wonders, he introduced the child of the nomad tents to the miracles of modern gadgetry, from running water to recorded music and micro-books. As a climax, he permitted her to peer in through the door of the laboratory, at the mystic and glittering tangle of glass and chrome. And he asked her, "Are your Old Men greater in magic than I?"

"No." She had drawn away from him, her hands clutched tightly around her as though to avoid the accident of touching anything. Behind her from the living quarters Wagner's Fire Music still roared and rippled, out of a tiny spool of wire. Suddenly Bisha was down on her knees in an attitude of complete submission. "You are the greatest doctor in the world."

Her word for "doctor" meant the same as "shaman." Fraser felt contrite and ashamed. It seemed a shabby trick to impress a child. But he stuck to it, saying solemnly,

"Very well, Bisha. And now that that is understood, I tell you that curses have no power in this place, and I want no more talk of them."

She listened, not raising her head.

"You are safe here. You are not to be afraid. Look up at me, Bisha. Do you promise not to be afraid?"

She looked up. He smiled, and after a little she smiled back. "I promise."

"Good," he said, and held out his hand. "Let's eat."

238

ABOUT then it dawned on Fraser that he was saddled with a child. For the four and a half months that remained of his term here he would have to feed, look after her and keep her hidden. The people of the town would hardly shelter her—Bisha's mother hadn't trusted them, certainly—and if they did, the nomads would only find her again when they came in for the fall trading. The only other alternative was the central government at Karappa, which would surely not condone ritual murder, but that was three hundred miles away. He had a trac-car, but the work going forward in the lab would not wait for him to trundle a slow six hundred miles up and down the desert. He could not possibly leave it.

Four and a half months. He looked down at the small figure pattering beside him, and wondered what in the devil he was going to do with her all that time.

At the end of a week he would have been lost without her. The awful loneliness and isolation of the Quonset was gone. There was another voice in the place, another presence, somebody to sit across the table from him, somebody to talk to. Bisha was no trouble. She had been brought up not to be a trouble, in a hard school where survival was the supreme lesson, and that same school had impressed on her young mind the wisdom of making the best of things. She was no trouble at all. She was company, the first he had had in nearly nine months. He liked her.

Mostly she was cheerful and alert, too much engrossed in a new world of marvels to brood about the past. But she had her moods. Fraser found her one afternoon huddled in a corner, dull and spiritless, in the depths of a depression that seemed almost too deep for tears. He thought he knew what the trouble was. He took her on his lap and said, "Are you lonesome, Bisha?"

She whispered, "Yes."

He tried to talk to her. It was like talking to a blank wall. At last he said helplessly, "Try not to miss them too much, Bisha. I know I'm not the same as your own family, and this place is strange to you, but try."

"You're good," she murmured. "I like you. It isn't that. I was lonesome before, sometimes."

"Lonesome for what, Bisha?"

"I don't know. Just—lonesome."

Queer little tyke, thought Fraser, but then most kids are queer to adult eyes, full of emotions so new and untried that they don't know quite how to come out. And no wonder she's depressed. In her spot, who wouldn't be?

He put her to bed early, and then, feeling unusually tired after a long day's work, he turned in himself.

He was awakened by Bisha, shaking him, sobbing, calling his name. Leaden and half dazed, he started up in alarm, asking her what was the matter, and she whimpered, "I was afraid. You didn't wake up."

"What do you mean, I didn't wake up?" He sank back again, weighted down with the sleep he had not finished, and began to bawl her out. Then he happened to look at the clock.

He had slept a trifle over fourteen hours.

Mechanically he patted Bisha and begged her pardon. He tried to think, and his brain was wrapped in layers of cotton wool, dull, lethargic. He had had one drink before going to bed, not enough to put anyone out for one hour, let alone fourteen. He had not done anything physically exhausting. He had been tired, but nothing the usual eight hours wouldn't cure. Something was wrong, and a small pinpoint of fear began to prick him.

He asked, "How long have you been trying to wake me?"

She pointed to a chair that stood beside the window. "When I began, its shadow was there. Now it is there."

As near as he could figure, about two hours. Not sleep, then. Semi-coma. The pinprick became a knife blade.

Bisha said, so low that he could hardly hear her, "It is the sickness that was in our tribe. I have brought it to you."

"You might have, at that," Fraser muttered. He had begun to shiver, from the onset of simple panic. He was so far away from help. It would be so easy to die here, walled in by the endless miles of desert.

The child had withdrawn herself from him. "You see," she said, "the curse has followed me."

With an effort, Fraser got hold of himself. "It hasn't anything to do

240

with curses. There are people we call carriers – Listen, Bisha, you've got to help me. This sickness – did any of your tribesmen die of it?"

"No –"

Fraser trembled even more violently, this time from sheer relief. "Well, then, it's not so bad, is it? How does it –"

"The Old Men said they *would* die unless I was taken away and killed." She had retreated even farther now, to the other side of the room, to the door. Suddenly she turned and ran.

It was a minute before Fraser's numbed brain understood. Then he staggered up and followed her, out into the dust and the cold light, shouting her name. He saw her, a tiny figure running between the blue-black sky and the dull red desolation, and he ran too, fighting the weakness and the lassitude that were on him. He seemed to run for hours with the chill wind and the dust, and then he overtook her. She struggled, begging to be let go, and he smacked her. After that she was quiet. He picked her up, and she wailed, "I don't want you to die!"

Fraser looked out across the pitiless desert and held her tight. "Do you love me that much, Bisha?"

"I have eaten your bread, and your roof has sheltered me –" The old ceremonial phrases learned from her elders sounded odd in her young mouth, but perfectly sincere. "You are my family now, my mother and my father. I don't want my curse to fall on you."

For a moment Fraser found it hard to speak. Then he said gently, "Bisha, is your wisdom greater than mine?"

She shook her head.

"Is it your right to question it?"

"No."

"What is your right, Bisha, as a child?"

"To obey."

"You are never to do this again. Never, no matter what happens, are you to run away from me. Do you hear me, Bisha?"

She looked up at him. "You're not afraid of the curse, even now?"

"Not now, or any other time."

"You *want* me to stay?"

"Of course I do, you poor wretched little idiot!"

She smiled, gravely, with the queer dignity he had seen in her before. "You are a very great doctor," she said. "You will find a way to lift the curse. I'm not afraid, now."

SHE lay warm and light in the circle of his arms, and he carried her back to the Quonset, walking slowly, talking all the way. It was odd talk, in that time and place. It was about a far-off city called San Francisco, and a white house on a cliff that looked out over a great bay of blue water. It was about trees and birds and fishes and green hills, and all the things a little girl could do among them and be happy. In the past few minutes Fraser had forgotten Karappa and the authorities of Mars. In the past few minutes he had acquired a family.

Back in the lab Fraser began work. He questioned Bisha about the sickness as she had seen it in her tribe. Apparently the seizures came at irregular intervals and involved nothing more than the comatose sleep, but he gathered that the periods of unconsciousness had been much shorter, often no more than a few minutes. That could be accounted for by acquired resistance on the part of the Martians. Bisha, of course, had never had the sickness, and Fraser imagined that the accident of natural immunity had caused her to be picked for the tribal scapegoat.

His own symptoms were puzzling. No temperature, no pain, no physical derangement, only the lassitude and weakness, and by next morning they had passed off. He consulted his books on Martian pathology. There was nothing in them. He ran a series of exhaustive tests, even to a spinal tap on Bisha, which she took to be a very potent ritual of exorcism. He would rather have done one on himself, but that was impossible, and there might be evidence in the child of some latent organism.

The test was negative. All the tests were negative. He and Bisha were as healthy as horses.

Baffled but intensely relieved, Fraser began to think of other explanations for the ailment. It was not a disease, so it must be a side-effect of some physical condition, perhaps the light gravitation or pressure, or the thin atmosphere, or all three, that affected Martians as well as Earthmen, but in a lesser degree. He made a detailed report, thrusting into the back of his mind as a small worry that no such side-effect had ever been observed before.

He waited nervously for a recurrence. It didn't come, and as the work in the lab demanded more and more of his attention he began to forget about it. The time that he woke up in his chair with an untasted drink beside him and no memory of having gone to sleep he put down resolutely to weariness and overwork. Bisha had retired with another fit of the blues, so she knew nothing about that, and he didn't mention it. She seemed to be getting over the curse fixation, and he wanted to keep it that way.

More time went by. Bisha was learning English, and she could name all the trees that stood around that house in San Francisco. The confinement in the small hut was getting them both down, and she was as anxious to leave as Fraser, but apart from that everything was going well.

And then the nomads came in from the desert for the fall trading.

Fraser barred the doors and drew the blinds. For three days and nights of the trading he and Bisha hid inside, with the distant sound of the pipes and the shouting coming to them muffled but poignant, the music and the voices of Bisha's own people, her own family among the tribes. They were hard days. At the end of them Bisha retired again into the remoteness of her private grief, and Fraser let her alone. On the fourth morning the nomads were gone.

Fraser thanked whatever gods there were. Weary and dragged out, he went into the lab, hating the work now because it took so much out of him, anxious to have it finished. He started across the room to open the blind—

He was lying on the floor. The lights were on and it was night. Bisha was beside him. She seemed to have been there a long time. His arm ached. There were clumsy wrappings on it, stained with blood. Shards of glass littered the end of the lab bench and the floor. The familiar leaden numbness pervaded his whole body. It was hard to move, hard to think. Bisha crept to him and laid her head on his chest, silently, like a dog.

Very slowly Fraser's head cleared, and thoughts came into it. *I must have fallen across the bench. Good God, what if I had broken the virus cul-*

tures? Not only us, the whole town— I might have bled to death, and what would happen to Bisha? Suppose I did die, what would happen to her?

It took longer this time to return to normal. He stitched up the cuts in his arm, and the job was not neat. He was afraid. He was afraid to leave his chair, afraid to smoke, afraid to operate the stove. The hours crawled by, the rest of the night, another day, another evening. He felt better, but fear had grown into desperation. He had only Bisha's word that this illness was not fatal. He began to distrust his own tests, postulating alien organisms unrecognizable to the medical science he knew. He was afraid for himself. He was terrified for Bisha.

He said abruptly, "I am going into the town."

"Then I will come with you."

"No. You'll stay right here. I'll be all right. There is a doctor in the town, a Martian healer. He may know—"

He went out, into the bitter darkness and the blazing of the stars. It seemed a long way to the town.

He passed the irrigated land, stripped of its harvest, and came into the narrow streets. The town was not old as they go on Mars, but the mud brick of the walls had been patched and patched again, fighting a losing battle with the dry wind and the scouring dust. There were few people abroad. They looked at Fraser and passed him by, swarthy folk, hot-eyed and perpetually desperate. The canal was their god, their mother and their father, their child and their wife. Out of its dark channel they drew life, painfully, drop by drop. They did not remember who had cut it, all the long miles from the polar cap across the dead sea-bottoms, across the deserts and through the tunnels underneath the hills. They only knew that it was there, and that it was better for a man to sin the foulest sin than to neglect the duty that was on him to keep the channel clear. A cruel life, and yet they lived it, and were content.

There were no torches to light the streets, but Fraser knew the house he wanted. The door of corroded metal opened reluctantly to his knock and closed swiftly behind him. The room was small, lit by a smoky lamp and barely warmed by a fire of roots, but on the walls there were tapestries of incalculable age and incredible value.

TOR-ESH, the man of healing, did well at his trade. His robe was threadbare, but his belly protruded and his chops were plump, unusual things among his lean people. He was fetish-priest, oracle, and physician, and he was the only man of the town who had shown any interest in Fraser and his work. It was not necessarily a friendly interest. He gave Fraser the traditional greeting, and Fraser said stiffly,

"I need your help. I have contracted an illness—"

Tor-Esh listened. His eyes were shrewd and penetrating, and the smile that was habitually on his face left them untouched. As Fraser talked, even that pretense of a smile went gradually away.

When he was finished, Tor-Esh said, "Again. More slowly, please, your Martian is not always clear."

"But do you know what it is? Can you tell me—"

Tor-Esh said, "Again!"

Fraser repeated the things he had said, trying not to show the fear that was in him. Tor-Esh asked questions. Accurate questions. Fraser answered them. For a little bit Tor-Esh was silent, heavy-faced and grim in the flickering light, and Fraser waited with his heart pounding in his throat.

Tor-Esh said slowly, "You are not ill. But unless a certain thing is done, you will surely die."

Fraser spoke in anger. "Talk sense! A healthy man doesn't fall off his feet. A healthy man doesn't die, except by accident."

"In some ways," said Tor-Esh very softly, "we are an ignorant people. It is not because we have not learned. It is because we have forgotten."

"I'm sorry, I didn't mean— Look, I came to you for help. This is something I don't understand, something I can't cope with."

"Yes." Tor-Esh moved to the window, dark in the thickness of the wall. "Have you thought of the canal? Not only this one, but the many canals that bind Mars in a great net. Have you thought how they must have been built? The machines, the tremendous power that would have been needed, to make a dying world live yet a little longer. We are the children of the men who conceived and built them, and yet nothing is left to us but the end product of their work, and we must grub with our hands in the channel, digging out the blown sand."

"I know," said Fraser impatiently. "I've studied Martian history. But what—"

"Many centuries," said Tor-Esh, as though he had not heard. "Nations and empires, wars and pestilences, and kings beyond the counting. Learning. Science. Growth and splendor, and weariness, and decay. Oceans have rolled away into dust, the mountains have fallen down, and the sources of power are used up. Can you conceive, you who come from a young world, how many races have evolved on Mars?"

He turned to face the Earthman. "You have come with your thundering ships, your machines and your science, giving the lie to our gods, who we thought had created no other men but us. You look upon us as degraded and without knowledge—and yet you too are an ignorant people, not because you have forgotten, but because you have not yet learned. There are many sciences, many kinds of knowledge. There have been races on Mars who could build the canals. There were others who could see without eyes and hear without ears, who could control the elements and cause men to live or die as they willed it, who were so powerful that they were stamped out because men feared them. They are forgotten now, but their blood is still in us. Destruction of a people is never complete. We few who are left are blended into one race, but their blood is in us. And sometimes a child is born—"

Fraser stiffened.

Tor-Esh said quietly, "There was talk among the nomads about a child."

· Nerves, drawing tight in Fraser's belly. Fear-nerves, and a chill sweat. *I never mentioned Bisha. How could he know—*

"I'm not interested in folk lore. Just tell me—"

"There was a certain evil in the tribe. When the child was taken away, the evil departed. Now it is in your house. It seems that the mother lied. The child is not dead. She is with you."

"Witchcraft and sorcery," Fraser snarled. "Curses and cowardice. I thought you knew better, Tor-Esh." He started for the door. "I was a fool to come here."

Tor-Esh moved swiftly and placed his hand on the latch, that it might not be lifted until he was through.

"We are ignorant folk, but still we do not kill children because we find pleasure in it. As for witchcraft and sorcery—words are words. Only facts have meaning. If you wish to die, that is your affair. But when you are dead the child must come into the town—and that is our affair. I will send word to the nomads. The girl is theirs, and the duty belongs to them, we do not wish it. But until they come I will set a wall around your house. You are likely to die quite soon. There were twenty in her tribe to share the curse, but you are alone, and we can take no chances."

Seeing, perhaps, the absolute horror in Fraser's face, Tor-Esh added, "It will be done mercifully. We bear the child no hate."

He lifted the latch, and Fraser went into the narrow street. He turned toward the desert, and when he had crossed the plowed land he began to run. He ran fast, but a rider passed him, speeding into the desert on the track of the caravan.

Bisha was waiting for him, sleepily anxious. He said, "You know where the food is. Pack as much as you can in the trac-car. Blankets, too. Hurry up, we're leaving."

HE WENT into the laboratory. In violent haste, but with the utmost care, he destroyed the work of months, tempted as he did so to forget ethics and scatter his virus cultures broadcast into the town. Evil. Superstition. Legendary warlocks, tales of mighty wizards. He had read some of the old imaginative stories, written before space flight, in which ruthless Earthmen were pictured trampling innocent Mars under their feet. Logic and logistics both had made that impossible, when it came to the unromantic reality, and he was almost sorry. He would have liked to trample some Martians under his feet.

When the laboratory was cleansed, he threw his notes together in a steel box and took them into the dust-tight shed at the back of the Quonset where the trac-car was housed. Bisha, tear-streaked and silent, had been patiently lugging supplies. He checked them rapidly, added a few more, and swung the child up into the cab. She looked at him, and he realized then that she was frightened. "Don't worry," he told her. "We're going to be all right."

"You're not taking me back?"

He said savagely, "I'm taking you to the Terran consulate at Karappa, and after that I'm taking you to San Francisco. And nobody had better try to stop me."

He flung open the shed door and climbed in beside her. The trac-car rolled out clanking across the sand. And already there were lines of torches, streaming out from the town, flung across his way.

He said, "Crouch down on the floor, Bisha, and stay there. You won't get hurt."

He poured on the power. The trac-car lurched forward, snorting and raising a great cloud of dust. He headed it straight for the wavering line of torches, ducking his head instinctively so that he was pressed close to the wheel. The cab was metal, and the glass parts of it were theoretically unbreakable, but he could see now in the torchlight the bright metal throwing-sticks of the townsmen, the swift boomerangs that could take off a man's head as neatly as a knife blade. He ducked.

Something hit the window beside him, starring it with a million cracks. Other things whacked and rattled viciously against the car. The torches fell away from in front of him, taking with them the dark startled faces of the men who held them. He was through the line. The open desert was before him. Three hundred miles, Karappa, and civilization.

If he could beat the nomads.

He had better beat them. It was his neck as well as Bisha's. He needed care. He needed it fast, from somebody who did not believe in curses.

Dawn came, cold in a dark sky, veiled in dust. There was no canal between them and Karappa, no town, nothing but the fine dry sand that flowed like water under the wind.

"Look here," he said to Bisha. "If I should suddenly fall asleep—" He showed her how to stop the trac-car. "At once, Bisha. And stay inside the cab until I wake again." She nodded, her lips pressed tight

248

with the effort of concentration. He made her do it several times until he was sure she would not forget.

The miles flowed out before and behind, to left and to right, featureless, unbroken. How long would it take a single rider to catch a laden caravan? How long for the desert men on their fleet beasts to find a trail? The sand was soft and the clanking treads sank in it, and no matter how much you wanted to hurry you could go no faster than the desert would let you.

Bisha had been thinking hard. Suddenly she said, "They will follow us."

She was smart, too smart for her own good. Fraser said, "The nomads? We can beat them. Anyway, they'll soon give up."

"No, they'll follow. Not you, but me. And they will kill us both."

Fraser said, "We're going to Earth. The men of Mars, and the gods of Mars, can't reach there."

"They are very powerful gods— Are you sure?"

"Very sure. You'll be happy on Earth, Bisha."

She sat close to him, and after a while she slept. There was a compass on the dash, a necessity in that place of no roads and no landmarks. Fraser kept the needle centered, setting a course as though with a ship. Time and the sand rolled on, and he was tired.

Tired.

You are likely to die quite soon—there were twenty in her tribe to share the curse—

THE desert whispered. The sounds of the trac-car were accepted and forgotten by the ear, and beyond them the desert whispered, gliding, sliding, rippling under the wind. Fraser's vision blurred and wavered. He should not have pushed himself so hard at the work. Tired, no resistance to the sickness. That was why it had been light among the hardy nomads, more serious in him, an alien already worn down by months of confinement and mental strain. That was why.

—twenty in her tribe to share it—but you, alone—

Three hundred miles isn't so far. Of course you can make it. You've made it in an afternoon, on Earth.

This isn't Earth. And you didn't make it in a cold creeping desert.

You, alone—

Damn Tor-Esh!

"Bisha, wake up. We need some food. And first off, I need that bottle."

With a drink and some food inside him he felt better. "We'll keep on all night. By morning, easy, we'll be in Karappa. If the nomads are following, they'll never catch up."

Mid-afternoon, and he was driving in a daze. He lost track of the compass. When he noticed it again he was miles off his course. He sat for some minutes trying to remember the correct reading, trembling. Bisha watched him.

"Don't look so frightened," he said. His voice rose. "I'm all right. I'll get us there!"

She hung her head and looked away from him.

"And don't cry, damn it! Do you hear? I've got enough on my neck without you being doleful."

"It is because of me," she said. "You should have believed the words of the Old Men."

He struck her, the first time he had ever laid his hand on her in anger. "I don't want any more of that talk. If you haven't learned better in all this time—"

She retreated to the other side of the seat. He got the trac-car going again, in the right direction, but he did not go far. He had to rest. Just an hour's sleep would help. He stopped. He looked at Bisha, and like something that had happened years ago he remembered that he had slapped her.

"Poor little Bisha," he said, "and it isn't any of it your fault. Will you forgive me?"

She nodded, and he kissed her, and she cried a little, and then he went to sleep, telling her to wake him when the hand on the dashboard clock reached five. It was hard to rouse when the time came, and it was full dark before the trac-car was lurching and bucking its way out of the sand that had drifted around it. Fraser was not refreshed. He felt worse, if anything, sapped and drained, his brain as empty as an upturned bucket.

He drove.

He was off his course again. He must have dozed, and the car had made a circle to the south. He turned angrily to Bisha and said, "Why didn't you stop the car? I told you—"

In the faint glow from the dashboard he saw her face, turned toward the desert, and he knew the look on it, the withdrawal and the sadness. She did not answer. Fraser swore. Of all the times to pick for a fit of the blues, when he needed her so badly! She had enough to make her moody, but it was getting to be a habit, and she had no right to indulge her emotions now. She had already cost them precious hours, precious miles. He reached out and shook her.

It was like shaking a rag doll. He spoke to her sharply. She seemed not to hear. Finally he stopped the car, furious with her stubbornness, and wrenched her around to face him. For the second time he slapped her.

She did not weep. She only whispered, "I can't help it. They used to punish me too, but I can't help it."

She didn't seem to care. He couldn't touch her, couldn't penetrate. He had never tried to shake her out of these moods before. Now he found that he could not. He let her sink back into the corner, and he looked at her, and a slow corrosive terror began to creep through him because of the times before—the times that she had been like this.

The times immediately preceding the periods of blackness, the abnormal sleep.

A pattern. Every time, the same unvaried pattern.

But it made no sense. It was only coincidence.

Coincidence, three times repeated? And how had Tor-Esh known so certainly that the child was with him?

Three times, the pattern. If it happened a fourth time, it could not be coincidence. If it happened a fourth time, he would know.

Could he afford a fourth time?

Crazy. How could a child's moods affect a man?

He grabbed her again. A desperation came over him. He treated her roughly, more roughly than he could ever have dreamed of treating a child. And it did no good. She looked at him with remote eyes and bore it without protest, without interest.

Not a mood, then. Something else.

What?
Sometimes a child is born—

FRASER sent the trac-car rushing forward along the beam from its headlights, a bright gash in the immemorial dark.

He was afraid. He was afraid of Bisha. And still he would not believe.

Get to Karappa. There's help there. Whatever it is there'll be somebody to know the truth, to do something. Keep awake, don't let the curtain fall again.

Think. We know it isn't a curse, that's out. We know it isn't a disease. We know it isn't side-effects, they'd have been observed. Besides, Tor-Esh understood.

What was it he said about old races? What did they teach us about them in the colleges? Too much, and not enough. Too many races, and not enough time.

They could see without eyes and hear without ears, they could control the elements—

He tried to remember, and it was a pain and a torment. He looked at the child. Old races. Recessive genes, still cropping out. But what's the answer? ESP is known among the Martians, but this isn't ESP. What, then?

A remnant, a scrap of something twisted out of shape and incomplete?

What is she so lonesome for, that she doesn't know?

The answer came to him suddenly, clear as the ringing of a bell. A page from a forgotten text book, hoarded all these years in his subconscious, a casual mention of a people who had tried to sublimate the conditions of a dying world by establishing a kind of mental symbiosis, living in a tight community, sharing each others' minds and their potentials, and who had succeeded in acquiring by their mass effort such powers of mental control that for several centuries they had ruled this whole quadrant of Mars, leaving behind them a host of legends.

And a child.

A child normal and healthy in every way but one. Her brain was

252

incomplete, designed by a cruel trick of heredity to be one of a community of interdependent minds that no longer existed. Like a battery, it discharged its electrical energy in the normal process of thinking and living, and like a run-down battery it must be charged again from outside, because its own regenerative faculty was lacking. And so it stole from the unsuspecting minds around it, an innocent vampire draining them whenever it felt the need.

It was draining his now. There had been twenty in her tribe, and so none of them had died as yet. But he was alone. And that was why the intervals had shortened, because he could no longer satisfy her need.

And the Martians in their ignorance were right. And he in his wisdom had been wrong.

If he put her out now, and left her in the desert, he would be safe.

He stopped the car and looked at her. She was so little and helpless, and he had come to love her. It wasn't her fault. Something might still be done for her, a way might be found, and in a city she would not be so deadly.

Could he survive another plunge into the darkness?

He didn't know. But she had run away once of her own accord, for his sake. He could do no less than try.

He took her into his arms.

The curtain dropped.

Fraser woke slowly, in brazen sunshine and a great silence. As one creeping back from the edge of an abyss he woke, and the car was very still. There was no one in it with him. He called, but there was no answer.

He got out of the car. He walked, calling, and then he saw the tracks. The tracks of the nomads' beasts, coming toward the car from behind. The small tracks of Bisha's feet, going back to meet them.

He stopped calling. The sound of his voice was too loud, too terrible. He began to run, back along that trail. It ended in a little huddle of clothing that had no life in it.

She had broken her promise to him. She had disobeyed and left him, asleep and safe, to meet the riders by herself, the riders who were following her, not him.

So small a grave did not take long to dig.

Fraser drove on. There was no more danger now, but he drove fast, seeing the desert in a blur, wanting only Earth—but not a white house there that for him would be forever haunted.

Runaway

Startling Stories, Spring 1954

I

ANTHONY REID sat on his sun-deck and stared at the city. He had a splendid view of it, for the housing unit in which he lived—a charming structure of white plastibrik with solaray glass throughout and the latest in reactor heating—was built on a ledge of the low hills above Sunset Boulevard. There were others, above and below and beside it on both sides as far as he could see, so that the hills had taken on the appearance of stiffly serrated cliffs.

And to the east and west and south and north was the city, pink and white and yellow, pale blue and green and gray, squares and cubes and pylons, flowing into every crevice of the hills, inundating the crests, pouring back into the valleys and filling their flat immensity and going on, until it was stopped by two barriers it could not over-leap, the desert on one side and the Pacific on the other.

It was still a horizontal city, with few skyscrapers. Old Earthquake, as rough and primitive as ever, still lived beneath it, and the underlying shale and sandstone were no firmer than they had ever been for the bracing of deep foundations. But it was big. It used the Pacific Ocean for a reservoir, and the hydroponic tank farms that grew its food had a total area of three hundred square miles. Its name was still Los Angeles.

"It's incredible," said Anthony.

His wife glanced at him from the chaise where she was lying. "What is?"

"To think that once this was all open country. Just cattle range, from the desert to the sea."

Fern Reid finished her cocktail—a mildly stimulating synthetic with none of the deteriorating effects of the old-fashioned alcohol—and rose, stretching her soft pale arms. "It seems like an awful waste of good land," she said, yawning. "There's a program on. Will you get it while I fix the supper?"

Anthony seemed not to have heard her. He was still looking at the city.

"There used to be droughts," he said. "Years with no rain—they depended on rain, then—and all the grasses and things dried up. They had to drive whole herds of animals over the cliffs, so that the rest could have enough to eat. That must have been very hard on the ranchers to do."

"Well, fortunately, nobody has worries like that any more. For heaven's sake, Anthony, will you stop mooning and get that program? The children have to see it for their homework, and I can't do everything around here."

He got up and followed his wife into the living area. The floor was resilient under his feet, warm in winter, cool in summer. The walls were done in soft pastels. He crossed to the one that was opposite both the living and the dining areas and pushed a button. A panel slid back, revealing the large screen. He pushed two more buttons, and full automatic tuning brought the picture in clear and steady, in three dimensions and true color. Inevitably, it was the middle of a commercial.

"—ignore the warning signs of emotional disturbance," the earnest announcer was saying. "At the first symptoms of nervousness, moroseness, or any abnormal reaction, take Passif for that mild, non-habit-forming sedation prescribed by the medical profession—and see your psychiatrist *at once*. Remember, Passif is not a cure. But for the relief of—"

Anthony started, and listened with a curiously furtive interest.

PHYLLIS, aged nine, was setting the table. From behind the plastiglass screen that closed off the kitchen area came the clicking of control buttons and the low hum of the electronic rapid-heat units. In a corner of the room, at a low, broad shelf littered with games and toys, young Tony was building a complicated structure of plastic blocks. He was rising twelve. "Your program's coming on," said Anthony.

"Homework," said young Tony sourly. "I don't see why they have to load us down after school, too." He pushed the blocks petulantly aside and went over to the table.

"By the way," said Anthony, "I've been meaning to ask you. Have you learned to read yet?"

"Now stop devilling the boy!" said Fern, coming in with a tray of bright containers. "You know perfectly well what it does to a child's emotions to be forced. He just isn't adjusted to reading yet."

"Besides," said young Tony, "who reads any more?"

"I can," said Phyllis. "And spell my name, too."

"Huh," said Tony. "That doesn't prove you're so smart."

"Supper's all ready," said Fern, in her most musical voice, looking daggers at Anthony. "There, the program is on. Let's all watch it as we eat, and then we can discuss it later."

Automatically, Anthony opened his individual sterile containers and pecked at what was in them, a high-protein jelly and various processed vegetables, topped off with a synthesized sweet. Between bites he watched the program. It was in the "Earth's Proud Heritage" series, and it told the story of SC-3, the little ship that was afraid to go into space. SC-3 ran away from its launching rack and took shelter in a museum hangar, where Lieutenant Wajert's great *Luna VI* related to it in vivid flashbacks the mighty story of man's first successful flight to the Moon. Backgrounds and model work were superb, and it was intercut with some of the actual films taken by Wajert. SC-3's final release from fear and its joyous flight along the space-trail blazed *by Luna VI* was movingly done. But Anthony glowered at the screen, unsatisfied.

"They might," he said, "have mentioned the five other rockets that crashed with everyone aboard before Wajert finally made it. And I remember reading that two of Wajert's crew died on the Moon."

"Why should they mention it?" said Fern. "It's unpleasant, and it had nothing to do with the story, anyway."

"Because it isn't honest, that's why. If they're going to tell a thing, they ought to tell it."

"Oh, you're always finding fault," said Phyllis. "I thought it was lovely."

"Who cares, anyway?" said young Tony. "History. Phooey." He rose and went dourly back to his blocks.

"Honestly, Anthony, I don't know what's got into you," Fern said. "Nothing seems to suit you any more. And look there, you've hardly touched your dinner again."

"I'm just not hungry," he said, and added hastily, "Nothing about the food, it was fine." He grabbed a book and went out on the sun-deck, hearing Fern muttering behind him something about as hard as she worked to get the meals the least people could do was eat them, and Phyllis asked with shrill and ghoulish interest, "What's the matter with Daddy, is he starting to have a breakdown?"

Again Anthony started, this time quite violently. "No!" he thought. "No, of course I'm not."

He sat down and resolutely opened the book. It was a best-seller and one he had wanted to read for some time, but he could not keep his attention on the story in spite of the top-notch art-work. Captions and dialogue blurred before his eyes. His mind swirled, not producing anything in particular but a vague sense of unease and frustration. *At the first symptoms of abnormal reaction, take Passif....*

Suddenly, he was afraid.

FERN finished her task of pitching the used containers down the disposal chute and came to join him. "Your hands are shaking," she said. "Yes they are, look there! You're not eating, and you've done nothing but toss and turn all night for a week. Now, we might as well have it out, Anthony, you know as well as I do that evasions are unhealthy. What's the matter with you?"

"Nothing," said Anthony, choking down an alarming impulse to yell at her.

"Now, dear. A week, perhaps a day or two more. Yes, I remember it was Tuesday, because you quarrelled with the children over what their history teacher said about dirt-farming, and you told them their great-great-grandfather was a dirt-farmer, and Phyllis cried. Now, what happened last Tuesday? I'm trying to think—wasn't that the day Mr. Jennings was taken ill?"

"Perhaps it was. What difference does it make?" Anthony flung down the book. "There's nothing the matter with me except you won't leave me alone!"

"There!" said Fern triumphantly. "That got a reaction. It *is* Mr. Jennings!"

"Mr. Jennings, Mr. Jennings!" Anthony sprang up, and there was no possible doubt now about his nervous quivering. "What's he got to do with anything? I've worked for him for fifteen years, but I never I saw him and he never saw me. I'm still working for him, and if he spent the next century in the Recreation San it wouldn't change anything for me or any of the two-thousand-and nine other employees of the Jennings Accounting Service. No matter who lives or dies these days, it's all the same."

Fern nodded. "Exactly. That's why I can't understand why you're so upset about it."

"Oh, Lord," said Anthony. "I'm going down to the com-room and play a game of ball with George."

"All right," said Fern stiffly to his retreating back. "But if you don't straighten out pretty soon I'm going to call Dr. Eckworth."

The automatic lift took him down to the basement area where the community room was, and as usual in the evenings George Grosset was there, drinking a Peppy and waiting for someone to play with him. They solemnly tossed for ends, and then sat down at the glassed-in case. "I get first play," said George, and punched a row of buttons. The light metal ball began to dance as the magnetic impulses caught at it.

Anthony pushed his own buttons, but it was no use. George shook his head. "Off our game tonight," he said. "Really off. Try another?"

"Sure," said Anthony savagely, and scowled at the ball.

"Better relax a little first," said George. "You're all tensed up. Here, have a Sootho."

Anthony accepted the cigarette. He glanced furtively at George, seized with a desire to talk. George smiled at him. "Go ahead," he said. "I've been waiting for it all week."

"You've noticed, too?"

"No timing, no co-ordination. I could tell by your game."

Anthony leaned forward. "I did tell you about Mr. Jennings."

"Your boss? Sure. Had a breakdown—personal fulfilment trauma."

"Yes. But *why*, George? He has pots of money, a flourishing business, a nice wife and kids, and no worries. Why should a successful man like him get a fulfillment trauma?"

"The stresses and strains of modern living," said George heavily. "Fortunately, it's not too serious. He'll be right as rain in a year or two. And as for you, Tony, take my advice, as a friend. Go and get yourself pysched. It's better to nip these things in the bud." He patted his ample middle and grinned. "I've had the widgets too, Tony boy, I know all about it. But I just toddle myself right off to the doctor, and look at me. Contented as a baby."

"That's it, though," said Anthony, suddenly crystallizing the vague thought that had been tormenting him. "That's the thing. Listen, George. You and I—we both have good jobs, good pay, regular promotions, all that. We live well. We're comfortable. We don't have to worry about the future. Now why, *why*, George, you tell me, should you and I have any reason to be psyched? What are the causes?"

"The stresses," said George firmly, "and the strains of modern living. It's just a part of it, that's all. No use fighting it, boy. Just roll with the punch, and you'll get along."

He smiled, nodded wisely, and went to the dispenser for another bottle of Peppy.

That night, determined to sleep, Anthony took double his usual dose of slumber pills. It didn't do any good. For a long time he lay awake in the quiet dark, thinking of Mr. Jennings in his palatial office bursting suddenly into tears and wailing like a lost child, "Who am I? Tell me who I am and what I'm doing here!"

"If," thought Anthony into the unresponsive night, "that can happen to a man like Jennings—what hope is there for me?"

260

II

OVER breakfast, a hollow-eyed and irritable Fern said grimly, "I'm going to make an appointment for you today. Now there's no argument about it, Anthony, I simply refuse to put in any more nights like the last one, with you groaning and yelling and thrashing about. You're making a nervous wreck out of *me.* "

Anthony nodded. "I suppose you're right. Make it for next Thursday, if you can. That's my full day off."

He went down and got into his car, feeling tired and submissive. After all, getting psyched was no more awful than taking a purgative. He supposed it rather alarmed him simply because he'd always been well adjusted and had never felt the need of it before.

"I guess George was right," he thought. "Stress and strain. Oh, well. I'll get some of that Passif stuff on my lunch period."

He pushed the Engaged button on the dash, and the automatic buried-cable system picked him up and fitted him smoothly into the stream of traffic. It was a blazing hot morning, but he never noticed it. The car, like the apartment and the office building to which he was going, was perfectly air-conditioned.

Usually he watched the car video during the drive downtown, but this morning, for some reason, the songs and gay chatter of the personable young lady who starred in the "Commuter's Hour" left him sulkily unresponsive. He looked out the window instead, smoking a Sootho and trying not to fidget.

He stared at the bright storefronts and the advertising displays until he tired of them, and then gradually his attention was drawn to the cars that flowed in massed lines on either side of him. The relay systems, operating from the buried cables to control centers in the cars, kept the vehicles exactly spaced apart, moving the traffic smoothly, slowing it individually or in the mass as needed and speeding it up again, all so gently that not a shock or a jar disturbed the passengers. Most of the people in the cars were watching the "Commuter's Hour." A few were reading. A few more were talking together, and here and there one was just sitting, not doing anything.

Anthony looked at them, idly at first and then with a growing fascination, and a notion began to circle around his brain that frightened him into a conviction that he did indeed need a psychiatrist, and as soon as possible.

"They're all like one person," said the notion. "They look the same—not superficially, but really. Do I—"

Unable to resist the impulse, he peered at himself in the dashboard mirror. He looked for a long, long time in a kind of quivering horror, only rousing himself at the last minute to press the Right Turn button that took him off the freeway and into the parking area of the Jennings Accounting Service, Certified Accountants to the Solar System.

Like a man in a dream, and not a very pleasant one, Anthony left his car for the automatic parking system to take care of, and entered the building.

It was a very large building. The halls were very long, cool, polished, and softly lighted, so that the lines of people moving through them seemed almost to swim in a liquescent gloom, trailing their shadows beside them. Anthony knew only a few of them even by sight. Suddenly he was no longer sure of those. He took the escalator up to the third floor, darted around a corner, and achieved the solitude of his own calculator room. He was breathing hard. Sweat prickled on his skin, and his heart was pounding. Abnormal reactions. George was right....

Work. That was the best thing. Get to work and forget about it. He took off his jacket. Automatic relays had already activated the calculator, and the morning's work was piled under the delivery tube. He prepared to get busy.

Anglo-Martian Enterprises, semi-annual account, a vast thick spool. How many Anglo-Martians did this make for him? He counted on his fingers. Twenty-nine. Or was it thirty? Too many, anyway. He pushed a button on the calculator, and then pressed the *on* switch on the electro-scanner and started the tape feeding in. The calculator began to hum.

ANTHONY sat down and watched the metal ribbon glide slowly

in. Code dots and holes. Holes and code dots. He got up and went back to the stack again. He looked at other spools. Finally he picked one up and went out of his room and down the hall to the next door. He rapped and opened it.

Bill Stocker laid down the picture magazine he was looking at and said, "Come on in."

Anthony went in. Stocker had been here, in this same room, four years longer than Anthony. It was his boast—untrue—that he had worn out six calculators. The one beside him now was quietly devouring the data passed to it by its scanner, cerebrating with a scarcely audible hum. Stocker looked at Anthony and frowned.

"You look ragged this morning. What's on your mind?"

"This," said Anthony, pointing to the account in his hand.

"Is it wrong some way?"

"I don't know. How, when you come right down to it, would anybody know?"

"Then what—?"

"All these code dots, Bill. These long columns of little holes, with the squiggles in front of them. I've been running them into the scanner for fifteen years, and it never occurred to me to wonder before. What are they? What do they stand for, monsters? Women's underwear? Martian rubies, fire opals from Venus, six thousand vitamin-enriched candy-bars? *What?*"

"For the love," said Bill Stocker, "of the eternal Mike." And he stared.

"But don't you know? Didn't you ever wonder?"

"Look," said Stocker. "Are you crazy or something? Who knows, who cares? It comes out right on the total, and that's all that matters."

"Yes," said Anthony. "I suppose it is."

He went back to his own room and shut the door. He sat and watched the calculator. When it had eaten up all of Anglo-Martian he pushed the OFF switch on the scanner and then punched a couple more buttons. The original spool was returned to him, together with a second containing complete calculations of Anglo-Martian's debits, credits, interest, investments, and et cetera, more dots and holes that only another machine could read. He placed both spools in the OUT tube, picked up the next account, and returned to the scanner. He reached out to push the switch again, and then it happened. Something snapped.

"That," he said, staring at his extended forefinger, "is the only part of me that's really necessary. It pushes buttons. The rest is just waste material."

The account he was holding fell with a reproachful thump on the floor. "Just a great big bunch of trash," Anthony muttered, and began to shake. There was a roaring in his ears, and a suffocating tightness in his chest. The calculator leered at him, with its banks of little glowing eyes. It laughed, quite audibly, in a soft humming undertone. Its rows of buttons mocked him. They extruded themselves, became enormous, and danced horribly before his face. The wisdom of the calculator was greater than his, and it knew it. It understood the secrets of the metal tapes, and it could pass them on to others of its kind, and he was shut out. Anthony's lips pulled back, baring his teeth.

He struck at the buttons. He struck them again and again, but the circuit-breakers that guarded against the small human-fallibility quotient left in the world immediately disengaged those relays activated out of sequence. The calculator continued to laugh. He kicked it, and its shielded front repelled his foot. A small feral whine came out of Anthony's mouth. He grabbed up the account he had dropped and threw it at the thick protective glass that covered the maze of circuits. Panting, he went to the pile and gathered it all up and hurled the spools one by one after the first. He cursed them.

"Fine things for a man to spend his life at. Dots. Holes. Abstractions. Nothing. Columns of nothing, totals of nothing, and nobody even cares if there is a reality behind them, and I have trouble adding two and two myself, in my own head, because why learn, the machines can do it faster and never make a—"

THE phone rang. He turned on it and cursed it, too, but it kept on ringing and the insistence of long habit and the necessity of answering it made him calm down, at least enough to force a semblance of normality. His face ached. He rubbed it a few times with his hands, and then cast a look of guilty horror at the mess he had made. When he answered the phone he stood close to the screen so that his body would block any view of the room.

It was Fern. "I called Dr. Eckworth," she said. "You're to go at two o'clock this afternoon."

"But I told you Thursday!"

"Now don't take that tone with me, Anthony Reid. Dr. Eckworth is a very busy man, but simply because he's a personal friend he managed to work you in on a cancellation. He says it's imperative to get started on these neuroses—"

"Fern!"

"Don't interrupt me, Anthony, this is important. He—"

"Fern, how many times have you been to Dr. Eckworth?"

"You know perfectly well I go twice a year for a regular check-up. And well it would have been for you, too, but you never would listen."

"Stated in plain English," said Anthony curiously, "what reason have you got to run twice a year to a psychiatrist?"

Her voice took on that hard whining edge he knew so well. "I suppose you think that taking care of a home and two children—"

"You know something?" said Anthony, interrupting her for the fourth and last time. "That is all one big lot of bull." He was quite calm now, and his mind, or at least a part of it, was in a state of icy clarity. "You and I, and George, and the rest of us—we're not even people any more, we're just a gang of mass-produced zombies living in a dream world, and not doing one damn thing to justify our existence. And we know it. You ask Dr. Eckworth about *that,* and if he tells you different, he's a liar." Just before he cut her off he added thoughtfully, "I think young Tony is smarter than I realized. Tell him to stick to his blocks. At least they're tangible."

The screen went blank. Immediately the bell began to ring again, but he let it, standing where he was with a look of profound wonderment.

"I don't even like her. All these years, and two kids, and I don't even like her."

He turned and picked up his jacket. The calculator still watched him, unscathed and derisively humming. Anthony walked over to the steel-and-plastic chair in which he had been wont to sit out his working day. His frenzy had left him. This was something quiet, and pleasurable. He lifted the chair over his head and let it fall crashing through the glass dust shield. Then he went out, closing the door carefully behind him.

The long cool corridors were empty now. He was conscious of the hundreds of people behind those hundreds of doors, pushing their hundreds of buttons. He began to run, not making any noise on the cushioned floor. Fern would call Macklin, his supervisor, to check on him. The building was a trap. He must get out of it.

HE WAS winded and lathered when he reached his car, but even after he was on the highway again he breathed no easier. He realized now that the whole city was a trap, a vast faceless formless entity that held him and all its other millions, in a sly and subtle bondage, like a mother who lavishes every care and luxury upon her children and asks nothing in return but their individuality. No wonder that so many, even as Mr. Jennings had, sank into it without a trace. He was sinking himself. He had to escape.

"Escape," said the top one-quarter of his brain, functioning tightly over chaos. "But there are only other cities. Between them are the hydroponic and synthetics and processing plants that feed them, and the reservoirs a county broad that water them, and the atomic plants that power them, and the breeder-reactor plants that feed *them*. The cities have swallowed up the land."

"There are the deserts."

"Nothing lives there. Cattle used to live on some of them, until the water was used up and the land blew away in dust. Now there is nothing."

"All right. Then I'll go out. Listen, I want to go on being Anthony Reid and it's hard because there isn't much to be, only a name and a set of memories as flat as your hand. The only real thing I ever did was just now, and you know what that means if I stay. Dr. Eckworth, and a Recreation San, and after that—like George, contented as a baby. Only a baby grows up, but you never do. You just lie there, rolling between contentment and the Dr. Eckworths. I'm getting out."

"Money," said that top, tight bit of sanity. And Anthony stopped at the bank.

While he was there he sent a 'gram to Fern, telling her not to worry. *Take care of the kids till I get back—I'm all right, I just have to do this.* Then, with half his savings in his pocket, he headed eastward to Mojave and the spaceport.

III

THERE were always sightseers at the port. There was a feeling of expectancy and change, a quiver of thunder in the air, a vicarious thrill in the far-off flashing of a silver flank and the bursting roar of a launching. It was especially fine at night, with the rocket flames arcing against the desert stars, and Anthony had brought the family out to dine in the Pylon Room and watch. The kids had been bored with it after the second look and Fern had complained about the noise. He had not come back.

Not until now.

The interval of the drive had not been good. Things had had time to force their way up out of that submerged three-quarters of chaos into the light of his conscious mind. Doubt. Fear. Panic. Strange emotions, strange and new.

He had broken the pattern. For thirty-six years he had lived inside it, enlarging it slightly to include Fern and then the children, but never deviating from its main outlines. The city. The apartment. The schools, the amusements, the job, the amusements, life. Now he had smashed it, literally, and it dawned on him that he did not exist outside of it.

Paradox. Who are you, why are you? Break free, stand alone, find out. But when you do, where are you? You have disappeared.

He crept furtively among the sightseers, feeling ashamed and helpless. There were things he had not thought of in his first fine flush of inspiration. Passports. He didn't have one, and all the money in the world wouldn't buy you a ticket to anywhere without it. So how was he going? And what was he going to do when he got there—things like eating and sleeping went on and had to be paid for. In the glare of the desert sun, among the chattering spectators, he felt cold and very naked.

He wanted to go back. He wanted to run to Fern and the apartment, to the warm and familiar and comfortable. He wanted the pattern around him, a shelter and a guide. Maybe they were right. A good psyching, and he'd be right as rain again, contented as a baby—

No.

There we are again. Mother-image, back-to-the-womb. No. Thirty-six going on thirty-seven is too old for that, if you're not a man now you never will be. Besides—

Think of Fern. Clackety-clack, poke and pry and watch. It could never be the same again. She wouldn't leave you alone a minute, peering into your face, sniffing like a hound after symptoms, drawing the swaddling bands tighter and tighter, until—

People did have breakdowns that were permanent.

And yet—

Anthony teetered on the sharp knife edge and wished that the police would come and find him so that the decision would not be his. But they didn't, and the time was growing short, and that top one-quarter of his mind that had steered him this far jeered and said, *Making decisions is maturity. You made this one. You were passionate about it. If you can't abide by it you'd better quit.* And it added, *Coward.*

How, asked Anthony reasonably of himself, would I know whether I'm a coward or not? I've never had any occasion to find out.

Here's your chance, and you'll never do it younger. But run back if you want to. Fern will love it.

Anthony stiffened his back and began to walk. The balance swung sharply over. Now instead of wishing for capture he was frantic lest it should happen.

But what could he do—stow away? Steal a passport? Sign on as a crew member? Impossible, all of them. Anthony thought bitterly that once civilization had laid hold of you it was mighty hard to get loose from it.

He had reached the stage of desperation where he would have tried anything when his eye fell upon a sign over a doorway. EMIGRATION. He went in.

SOME ninety or a hundred people, counting children, were inside in a big bare room, grouped around their separate islands of luggage, waiting. They glanced at him, or the nearest ones did, incuriously, and then forgot him again, sunk in their own thoughts. Anthony looked at them. Family groups, couples, a few unattached men standing sour and solitary by a single bag. Bankrupts, failures, people who could not cope even with the mild complexities of push-buttons.

The Government paid their passage to the colonies, and gave them some kind of a start after they got there. Anthony didn't know much about it, but he did know you had to prove necessity before you could get emigration papers. So that way too was closed to him.

Unless –

Anthony's heart began to pound again. His nervous system was getting a workout today such as it had never had before, and at any other time he would have worried about the harmful effects of all the various secretions his glands kept pumping into him. Just now he was too excited to care. He examined the single men, discarding one by one the impossibly large or small or dark or fair. Anthony himself was on the medium side all round. He settled at last on a sulky-looking chap who fitted the same description well enough, and went up to him.

"You don't look," he said, "as though you really wanted to go out."

The sulky man glared at him. "What the hell is it to you?"

Anthony thought, "He's a bum. The video-houses, the pleasure-pools, the amusement parks – that's where he's done all his living. He doesn't want to work." His hopes began to rise. He said aloud, "I want to buy your papers."

The man stared at him for a long moment, quivering. Then he said, "Come over here, over by the window. All right, what's your proposition?" He glanced nervously at the huge clock face over the far door. "Make it fast. We're almost due to go aboard."

Anthony made it fast. But before he had finished the warning bell rang and the groups of people began to be agitated, attacking their heaps of luggage like so many ants. A babble of voices rose and filled the room. That was good. It was perfectly timed. Nobody noticed that it was Anthony who joined the stream of people moving out onto the field, carrying the sulky man's bag in his hand, and his papers in the pocket where once the wad of bills had been.

There was a line of buses drawn up. They were funneled into them and driven out across the wide field in the glaring sun toward a ship that loomed more huge and frightening with every second. Again the pendulum of Anthony's mind swung back, and he thought, Oh God, I'm going, I'm really going, and I can't, I'm scared...

The movement of people caught him up again and took him toward a gang-plank that went up and into a dark hole in the ship's side. A man in uniform, with another one beside him, stood at the foot of it and asked in a monotonous voice for papers. The dark hole fascinated Anthony with the horrid fascination he had read about snakes having for birds. He was fairly up against it now, and the inside of his head had become a blank emptiness. He fumbled automatically for the papers and never thought to worry whether or not he would be found out.

The uniformed man gave them a cursory glance and shoved them back into Anthony's hand, and the upward-moving stream carried him in through the hold. There was a corridor clangorous with the sound of boots on iron and crammed with the sound of voices. Then there was a large room odorous of disinfectants, with a table and benches bolted down in the middle and tiers of curtained bunks around the sides.

"Stow your luggage and strap in," bawled a metallic voice from a speaker overhead. "Stow your luggage and strap in. Take-off in twenty-nine minutes."

Anthony stumbled into a bunk, shoving his bag into a metal bin underneath that was labelled in red letters for the purpose. He found straps and fastened them with cold hands. After that he merely lay there and shook, very quietly.

The voice from the speaker overhead began to count. "... three... two... one... zero."

A wave of wild excitement rose in Anthony, amid the stupendous and horrifying blast of take-off. I've done it, he thought, I've really done it, and I'm free!

IV

SPACE might, or it might not be, all the things it was said to be on the TV programs, from Miss-Out-There-in-her-starry-dress to the veritable face of God. Anthony didn't know. He didn't see it. The emigrant hold was not provided with an expensive and fabric weakening viewport. And if it had been it would hardly have mattered. Like everybody else there, Anthony was spacesick, and most of the voyage passed him by in a haggard dream of misery.

The papers he had bought said that his name was Joseph Rucker, that he could operate a stamping press, and that he was bound for Venus. Anthony said that last bit over to himself quite often, but it seemed not to have any real meaning. Venus itself had never seemed very real to him, in the way that places like India and Timbuctu had not seemed very real to his middle-western ancestors. It was a long way off. He remembered a lot of talk about man's conquest of savage nature, and his engineering genius and his courage, and he knew that it was hot on Venus, and that the air was bad. He knew that Venus was important because it produced very large amounts of uranium, thorium, germanium, and a lot of other things that Earth was using up too fast. And that was all he knew, except that people had to live there under domes, and that it never rained.

"Whatever it's like," he thought, "things are moving there, growing. It's still the wilderness, the frontier, still untamed—at least a lot of it. There ought to be something there for a man to do, something real."

Among the papers was a long and detailed certificate affirming that Mr. Rucker had been examined, processed, and inoculated for and against a frightening number of things. Anthony worried about that because he wasn't, and then he passed on to worrying about being caught for his small but growing list of felonies. He knew he was going to have to go back sometime and face the music, but not until—

Well, not until.

Then the ship's thin pseudo-gravity got in its evil work again, and he ceased to worry about anything.

After the long blank interval of flight there was the roaring convulsion of a landing, and he tottered out with the others into a sealed tube that had been connected to the ship's lock, and along that into an airtight monstrosity that ran on huge grinding tracks. There were windows in it. Anthony got his first authentic look at the face of the Morning Star.

There was a reddish gloom, partly cloud and partly dust, so intermingled that it was hard to tell where one left off and the other began. It was in a state of constant turmoil, rolling and boiling in a wind that was blowing strong enough to rock the vehicle on its mighty tracks, and things moved in it, portentous shadowy shapes of carriers and mobile machinery, peering their way with glaring headlights. Here and there, made strange and enormous by the mantling clouds, were the ships, the last link with Earth and home. One by one they vanished. Dust and cloud and wind took over, and the lines of dismal faces pressed to the windows turned gradually away. Some of the women were crying, and one little girl kept demanding with monotonous insistence, "Where's the *sun?*"

The vehicle ground and grunted over a drifted road for perhaps three miles, and then Anthony saw a cluster of squatty domes in the murk ahead, transparent except for the webbing of girders. Presently the vehicle trundled in through a lock door that closed behind it, and a little while after that Anthony found himself in a long and very hot shed with a lot of signs about immigrants and procedure. He took his turn obediently at a battered table with an old, hard, weary man behind it, a man who had seen too many immigrants come and go.

"Joseph Rucker," he said, making notes off the papers Anthony handed him. "Stamping press operator—"

Anthony coughed nervously. "I—uh—I'd like some other kind of work. Something manual."

The immigration man stared at him. Then he leaned back and stared some more. Finally he asked, "Are you crazy?"

"N-no. I just—"

"Listen, mac. The government is not interested in what you'd like to do, it's only interested in what you can do. Something manual, huh?" He looked at Anthony's hands and snorted. "You better stick to the cities, you'll find 'em tough enough here." And he wrote down, "Stamping press operator."

Anthony quivered like a trapped animal. "Look, I—well, I'm afraid I lied about that." Stamping presses ran by push-button, but they were different from calculator buttons and utterly beyond his ken.

"Oh lord," said the immigration man. He picked up a damp and dirty handkerchief and wiped off the sweat that was running down his jowls, and muttered something about his sins. Then he said to Anthony, "You could go to jail for that."

"I was tired of my job," said Anthony desperately. "I wanted a change, something different—"

"Something manual. Yeah. All right, let's stop wasting time. What *was* your job?"

ANTHONY twisted from left to right, searching for some escape, but there was none. He whispered, "I ran a calculator."

"A calculator," said the immigration man, and smiled. "Now we're getting at it. What *kind* of a calculator, Mr. Rucker? Technical, astronomical, financial—? Come on, Mr. Rucker, it's an honest occupation, you don't have to be ashamed of it."

Anthony gave up. "CPA."

"Calculator operator, CPA," said the immigration man, and wrote it down. "This is how I earn my living, but sometimes I don't think it's worth it." He turned to a card index. "Associated Mines needs a man in the accounting department. Interview at ten A.M. tomorrow, and don't miss it. Here's your card, and here's your ticket to the hostel. You can stay there till you find quarters of your own, limit four weeks. If for any reason you're turned down on the job, report here to me *immediately.* We've got a check system to make sure you don't lounge on the taxpayers, so don't try it. And don't accept any kind of employment from unauthorized persons. Got it? Right through that door there for decontamination—*Next!*"

Anthony picked up his bag and crept away through the indicated door. Amid a pandemonium of shrieking children and protesting adults he allowed himself to be rayed, dusted and gassed, to kill what external bacteria he might be carrying. Then there was an ultimate door and he was through it, standing half dazed in a street so narrow and so full of people and trucks and heat under the low dome that the simple act of breathing became a conscious labor.

He stepped to one side, out of the way of the other immigrants coming through. The hostel, marked by a huge sign, was just across the street, but he made no move to go there. His face was red and his eyes were unnaturally bright. He looked at the card he still held in his hand. Calculator operator, CPA. Couldn't you get away from it, wouldn't they let go of you? Suddenly he tore the card in pieces and threw it away. Then he walked swiftly down the street.

In half a block he was drenched with sweat and ready to fall. Man's conquest of savage nature had not been as complete as he had been led to believe. The outside temperature stood around the boiling point of water, and the dome was refrigerated, all right—to a point where existence was possible, but not much more. The people on the streets wore so little clothing that Anthony felt conspicuous. The air was stale, like spaceship air, re-used and stagnant in spite of manufactured oxygen, in spite of blowers and conditioners, in spite of the masses of huge coarse broad-leaved plants that grew in every crevice, in islands in the streets, in holes and alleys. A use had at last been found for the terrestrial burdock.

It was a nightmarish kind of a city. The flimsy buildings huddled and crowded and overlapped one another, and the dome pressed down on top of them, a thin and claustrophobic barrier against death. The ocherous half-light was depressing and hard on the eyes. Most of the buildings were white or bright metal, but they only looked dull and dingy. Anthony walked slower and slower.

He came to a corner. Traffic, wild and jerky, filled the streets before him. He guessed at electric motors—exhaust fumes would be an impossibility here—and after he had stared for a minute or two he realized that the vehicles were manually operated. A lifetime of mental conditioning aroused in him a terror of these ill-controlled juggernauts that had slaughtered over two million people in the United States alone before they were finally tamed by the cable systems. He looked for a pedestrian underpass, but there didn't seem to be any. How did you get across?

Then a wave of furious shame at his own helplessness came over him. He gritted his teeth and stepped off the curb. In the next second a hand closed on his collar and wrenched him back, and a truck went by so close that he felt it brush him. Shaking, Anthony turned around. "Let go," he said, "I'm going to do it myself."

The man who had hold of him nodded. "Sure, sure. But you'll live longer if you watch the lights. See there? Primitive, but we can't afford a cable system here yet, or at least everybody says we can't. All right, it's green our way. Make sure everything's stopped, watch that slob sneaking around the corner—okay, now run like hell!"

They made it.

"Don't feel that way about it," said the man, grinning. "We're all like that when we first get here." He was, short and barrel-shaped, dressed in rumpled shorts. His pale body gleamed with sweat, and there was more of it on his cheeks and the bald top of his head. He had an affable face, with eyes in it like two little blue marbles.

"My name's Crider," he said. "Listen, I saw you tear up your card back there—"

Anthony began to walk again, fast. Crider's short thick legs carried him right alongside.

"Easy, boy. Easy does it, you don't run any foot-races in this climate. You want a job?"

Anthony slowed down.

"Right around the corner here," said Crider. "There's a place we can talk."

THERE was a narrow six-story shack squeezed in between a string of video-houses and a place that sold mining equipment. The ground floor was a bar, and the upper windows were painted with the signs of assay offices, mining company agents, and small outfitters.

"Everything's mining here," said Crider. "People only come out for two reasons, because they want to or because they have to, and money's at the back of both of 'em, and there's money in mining. This stinking planet's made of money. All you have to do is dig it out."

The bar was small and badly lighted. There were as many women in it as men, drinking the synthetic stimulants that gave them the illusion of liquor without the effects. Crider motioned Anthony into a private cubbyhole at the back.

"If," he said, "anybody could manage to make some honest old-fashioned whisky like I've read about, he'd have his fortune made without digging a spoonful of ore. Notice all the video houses and pleasure halls? More to the square foot here than any city on Earth. Know why?"

Anthony shook his head. He was looking hard at Crider, trying to figure him, trying to understand why he felt uneasy.

"Because," said Crider, "people need the relief, the relaxation. They go psycho here a lot." Drinks had appeared on the table, and he pushed one toward Anthony. "Really psycho, not just fancy neurotic. I'm a little that way. Got a fire phobia. I saw fire in a dome once, and now a lighter flame can send me screaming. Why'd you tear up your card?"

Anthony shook his head.

"Okay, so it's none of my business. But you do want a job?"

"Depends on what it is."

"Oh," said Crider. "Picky. Don't exactly trust me, do you?"

"It's not that," said Anthony, lying. "It's just—"

"I know. They warned you at Immigration not to accept employment from 'unauthorized persons.'" Crider swore. "Sure, they've got a tie-up with the big companies, and us little guys never get a chance. Listen, how do you suppose I happened to be there just when you came out? How do you suppose I happened to follow you?"

"I suppose," said Anthony slowly, "you wait there to look over the new bunch as they come through." *I want a job, a real job,* he thought, *but do I want it from him? Am I being wise to hesitate, or only cowardly?*

"I have to do it," Crider said, pounding the table, "or I'd never get anybody. And I'm not the only one. Labor's at a premium here, and the big boys have got it all sewed up. Now look, fella. Just hear me out, that's all I ask, and then you can make up your own mind. I represent a small outfit. We don't have maybe the last word in equipment and so on, but we're taking out uranium, more than I've ever seen before, and I've been around here a long time. We're growing. We have something to offer for the future, where these big companies just want a gang of little wage slaves. We—say, you're feeling the heat, aren't you? Have another drink, it's as cold as you'll ever get here. Good for you. Like I was saying—"

It was hot in the cubbyhole. Crider's voice droned on. Anthony's lungs lifted and labored against the close air. Crider got farther and farther away until he was just a voice with two bright hard little eyes. A pulse of alarm began to beat in Anthony, a presentiment that this strange withdrawal was not due to the heat, or the suffocating air, or the after-effects of space-sickness. He got up, pushing the table over. And suddenly Mr. Crider's smiling face was close to his, and a great pale fist came floating toward him with a terrible deliberation that he could not by any means evade.

V

SOMEBODY was screaming.

Anthony heard it from a long way off, a fleck of sound in a thick blank nothingness. It didn't have anything to do with him. It wasn't Fern, or one of the kids. Somebody in the next building, maybe.

Deep. Down deep. How many slumber pills had he taken? Too deep.

It was a man's voice screaming. George? It was coming closer. George running down the hall screaming. Out, got to get out, for God's sake let me out. Nightmare? Fire? Earthquake?

Earthquake.

Everything shaking, the bed lurching, the long ominous sliding rumble of the thing rolling down the fault, sounds of the building falling, got to get out, get Fern and the kids. Fern… *Fern*… FERN—

"—isn't one of 'em enough? Listen. Listen, you! Shut up!"

Anthony choked on his voice, staring into a dizzy vortex where vague Ferns and Georges and apartments spun round and round on top of another image, a little iron box with men in it. The Ferns and the Georges and the apartments went away, but the iron box stayed, and the men. One of them was trying to butt his way head-first through a wall. The sounds stayed too, the rumbling and clattering and screaming. It was not George who was screaming. It was the butting man.

Crider was looking into the box through a square hole covered with wire mesh. "Quiet him down, can't you?" he was saying. "He'll have us all yammering, if that keeps up."

There were six men beside Anthony. Some were still stuporous, but two of them were struggling with the butting man. They kept dragging him back from the wall and he kept springing at it again, shrieking to be let out.

"A claustro," said Crider disgustedly. "Who brought *him* in?"

Anthony could see the shoulder of a man who was sitting next to Crider. It was bare and glistening with sweat. "I did," said the owner of the shoulder in a you-want-to-make-something-out-of-it tone. "How the hell was I to know? Anyway, he'll be okay when he's out of the truck."

"Sure," said Crider gloomily, "for a while. And then the dome gets too small for him." He spoke again to the two who were trying to keep the claustrophobe from battering his own head in. "Quiet him down! What's the matter, can't you think of a simple thing like knocking him out?"

One of them, a tall lean man with a face like white leather, seamed and creased, glanced at Crider and called him a name. The other one, shorter and thicker but with that same washed leathery look, muttered, "Yeah, but I guess we better do it." He was the one who had told Anthony to shut up.

"I guess so," said the tall man. "Hold him." He doubled up his fist and swung. He swung again. The screaming stopped, and the butting. Reminded of something, Anthony put his hand to his own jaw.

The shorter man laid his burden on the iron floor. "He's better that way," he said. "He'd only drive himself nuts."

"And us," said Crider, mopping his face. "Whew! That's a relief."

The tall man flung himself at the wire-mesh screen. He tried to pull it loose to get at Crider. Crider watched him, and the man who was driving the truck turned and watched too, and they both laughed. After a while the tall man gave up.

"Crimpers," he said, to everybody. "Dirty lousy crimpers. They don't run mines, they run death-traps. They have to drag men in doped and hog-tied to work for 'em." He turned on Crider again and cursed him until the tears ran out of his eyes. "I had a good job. In a year or two I could have gone back to Earth. Why couldn't you let me alone?"

"Ah, cool down," said Crider, not unkindly. "Things are tough for everybody around here, and I got to live too."

"Why?" asked Anthony.

Crider looked at him. "I don't know," he said quite seriously. "It's just a habit you get into."

The sealed truck rumbled and jolted along, pitching up and down over the drift dunes. The furnace wind outside gnawed at it, whining, as though it wanted to get at the men inside and drown them in the waste products of their own lungs. Anthony's fingers touched again and again the painful lump on his jaw. He watched Crider, safe behind the wire-mesh screen.

AFTER a time the truck slowed, lurched on again, and then stopped. The wind-sound ceased. Crider and the driver struggled with the door and got out, and then a heavy flanged hatch was opened in the back of the truck. "All right," said Crider. "Everybody out."

They clambered down. The claustrophobe had not come to yet. Anthony helped to lift him through the hatch, recoiling inwardly from the sodden weight of him, the limpness and the lolling head.

There was light outside, the smoky furnace glow of the long day that broke men's hearts with a hunger for the night—until the night came, too long and too black, and they yearned for day again. Anthony was conscious of a very small, very low dome, intensely hot and filled with the racket of machinery, but his attention was all on Crider. A knot of men had collected to see the new arrivals, and Crider had stepped aside to speak with two of them. Anthony went up to him and hit him as hard as he could in the face.

Crider's eyes popped open in anguished surprise. A small trickle of blood came out of his right nostril. A strange fever burned suddenly in Anthony. He lifted his hand again, but it was caught and held and wrenched around, and he was thrown to his knees in the native dust that was all the paving the dome had. He whimpered a little from the pain and looked hungrily at Crider.

"Well, I'll be—" said Crider between his teeth, and then hastily to the hard-looking men who held Anthony, "No, don't ruin him! Men are too hard to get." He kicked Anthony gently to his feet. "Just don't try that again, see? Now get over with the others."

They stood in a hang-dog little group, resentful, frightened, furious, but not knowing what to do about it. Crider spoke to them briskly.

"Let's face it, you're here, and you can't get away unless I take you. But I'm going to be fair with you. I'm going to give you regular working contracts with guaranteed wages and a specified term of employment. When it's up you'll be taken back—"

"Feet first," said the tall man. "Wages!" He pointed at the machinery, at the mine head, at the four or five ancient collapsible shacks. "Who's gonna get paid with what? Junk, that's all you got here. Junk machinery, junk buildings, and all you're mining is copper."

"Copper," said Anthony, and glared at Crider. "But you told me—"

"So I lied," said Crider.

The claustrophobe, who had managed to get on his feet again, whispered, "I can't go down in a mine. Not any more." He looked at the low dome over his head, and the narrow circle of it around him, and licked his lips.

Anthony said, "He only wants us to sign up so it'll look legal."

"Sign 'em or not," said Crider, "just as you please. I'm not forcing you."

One of the other men said suspiciously, "What's the catch?"

"Starvation," said the tall man. "He's got all the food."

Crider shook his head. "Not me. You can have all the grub you want, I wouldn't see a dog starve." He looked around at them, spreading his hands. "It's just a matter of necessity. We've got a well here, but it isn't the best on Venus. It doesn't make all the water in the world, and if a man isn't working for me I can't afford to supply him, that's all." He turned around and walked toward the shack that had a sign on it, CRIDER MINING COMPANY, OFFICE. "When you make up your minds, let me know."

Anthony thrust his hands in his pockets. "I won't sign."

The tall man cursed Crider and came and stood beside Anthony. "If we hang together he can't make us. What's he going to do with seven bodies? That's too many to take chances with. If we hang together—"

"He'll have to take us back," said Anthony.

The five other men stood irresolute in the dust, talking to each other, glancing around, moving their hands emphatically. Mechanics and miners passed by them, men impregnated with the rufous soil, leached with sweating and boiled stringy with the heat, looking at the newcomers, some with a vague sympathy, some with a savage pleasure that somebody else was going to suffer too, some with no emotion at all. One of them said, "I'll give the hold-outs three work-periods." And another answered sadly, "Two."

"Well?" said Anthony.

The claustrophobe shook his head. "I know when I'm licked. It'll be bad enough without making more trouble."

He started away toward the office shack. Another one said disgustedly, "Oh, what's the use, Crider holds all the cards." He went along with the claustrophobe. The three that were left hesitated, and then two of them went, leaving the shorter man who had yelled at Anthony in the truck. He came and joined the hold-outs.

"My name's Linson," he said. "I'm with you."

"Holfern," said the tall man. He cursed Crider again, repeating himself with undiminished emphasis. "Two years. Only two little Venusian years, and I could have gone home again."

"Reid," said Anthony, without thinking. He walked over and sat down by the curve of the dome wall, beside a clump of the inevitable burdocks. The others sat with him. Their attitude said they were going to stay there till Venus froze over.

For a while they talked, angrily and excitedly, passing from the personal to the general and back again. Gradually their voices got lower and their speech slower, until at last they pinched out and were gone. Holfern brooded, and Linson seemed to sleep.

OUTSIDE the dome Anthony could see a narrow strip of desert and then a wall of red rock. The killing wind and the scouring dust had taken out geologic ages of their spite on the helpless stone, torturing and tearing it into shapes of static agony. It seemed to Anthony that the whole cliff was one great frozen shriek. He shivered and turned his back on it.

It was hot. He had thought that only hell could be hotter than the city, but this was. He opened his shirt. After a while he took it off. Next to him, the sleeping Linson had his head bent forward. Sweat dripped off the end of his nose, monotonously, like a leaking faucet.

Suddenly Anthony said, "It's crazy. It's absolutely insane."

Holfern started. "What is?"

"This. The city. Venus. Domes and refrigeration and canned air—" He fumbled for words, his head reeling a bit in the heat. Artificiality, that was it. Artificiality carried to its *n*th power. "Isn't anything real any more? What is the human race trying to do to itself?"

Holfern stared at him. "You nuts, or something? How could we live here if it wasn't for those things, and how would Earth get along without us?" He grunted. "You sound like my old lady. She was always honing for the good old times she couldn't remember either, when people did their own cooking and kept their own little houses. Real!" He passed his hands over his face. "What's realer than this heat?"

The machinery clanked deafeningly, crushing ore and feeding it through hatches into giant bins outside the dome. Men drooped at huge control panels, or went up and down in the creaky mine lift.

One rusty crusher was inoperative, and three mechanics peered and poked in it, banging it now and again with pneumo-hammers.

"It's the same on Mars," said Holfern dreamily. "Domes and all, only there it's the cold and the thin air instead of heat and carbon dioxide. I was there once. Wish I was there now. Seemed like you never got warm."

"I'm thirsty," said Linson, out of his stupor.

"Shut up," Holfern told him.

Anthony swallowed, and his mouth and throat were as parched as the ground he sat on.

Silence again, and time. Time intolerable under an unchanging sky. He could feel the dome quiver in the wind. He dozed, and started awake, and dozed again. Thirst became a private fire, an internal holocaust. A whistle shrilled. Men came from the mine head and the machines. They sat down beside the shacks and ate and drank while others took their places. Linson had waked. He watched them and groaned, and Holfern cursed. Anthony sat, and thought with a vague surprise, "This is torture."

"Look," said Holfern, and began to laugh. "We've beaten him. See? Look at him come."

Crider was walking toward them. He carried a sack in one hand and a bucket in the other. Drops of water slopped over the sides of it, leaving a little moist trail in the dust. His partners, or foremen, or whatever they were, walked behind him. The men at the table watched covertly.

"Beat him," said Holfern exultantly, and got up. He started for the bucket.

The foremen pushed him away. Crider tossed the sack down in front of Anthony and Linson. Squares of food concentrates fell out of it. "Dinner," said Crider, and smiled. "How you feeling?"

Linson made a grab for the bucket.

Crider sidestepped. He shook his head and poured the water carefully around the roots of the burdocks. "Sorry," he said. "I really am. But we have so many needs for water. Take these docks. We breathe out carbon dioxide and they take it in and give us back oxygen. We can't let them die. You see how it is."

Anthony's eyes were fixed on the wet spot soaking into the ground. He didn't see what happened. He heard a scuffle and a thud, and when he turned around Holfern was lying flat. Linson beat his hands together. "All right," he moaned. "I'll sign your bloody contract." He avoided meeting Anthony's gaze. "It's no use, you can see it isn't."

Anthony crossed his arms stubbornly. The dome was beginning to waver in front of his eyes, and Crider looked like something painted on water. Presently he and Linson and the others were gone, leaving only Holfern lying on the ground. After a while Anthony lost track of Holfern.

He dreamed of water. He dreamed of the reservoirs, the enormous man-made lakes that drowned the land between the cities. Billions of gallons of water rushing out of them along the mighty aqueducts, through the pumping stations, into the pipes, into the apartments. Millions of people turning taps, drinking, taking showers, running washers, flushing tanks at five gallons a flush. Millions upon millions of people, wallowing in water and never thinking about it. He woke up in a kind of weak hysteria.

Holfern was gone.

Anthony sat a while longer, alone, light-headed and suffering. Two or three times he started to get up, and each time he stopped, muttering, "I won't."

NOBODY came near him. Once he saw Linson and Holfern pass by at a distance. They seemed not to want to look at him. There was a bad taste in Anthony's mouth, along with the burning and the swollen dryness. After a time he understood that it was the taste of defeat.

He began to drag himself toward the office.

Crider was coming toward him. Crider and a foreman. They picked him up. "I'll sign," he told them, and added, "Water."

Crider was hauling him along. "Water. Yeah, give him water, put a couple of cans in the truck. Round up those other birds, fast, and tell Jim to have another truck ready—"

His voice had a strange sound. It was the voice of a man upon whom disaster has fallen so suddenly and swiftly that the inevitable effects of it are still obscure to him.

The foreman said, "There's Everett, too. He was driving."

"Sure, Everett. Oh God, what a mess. Here, damn you, into the truck. Get him some water. Oh damn you, damn you –!"

Out of the awful lethargy of heat and thirst, Anthony asked, "What is it?"

"What is it? *You, you* –" Crider's anguish was so great as to be beyond any further profanity. "And I was sore at Everett about that claustro! Will he get a laugh!"

Water came. Water, life heaven. Anthony sucked it down. "What did *I* do?"

"You came in illegally, that's what you did. They've got the guy you bought your papers from. It's on a general broadcast, all over Venus. You didn't have your shots, you didn't have anything. You're a walking menace. And I've got to take you back alive and in one piece so they can find out what you're carrying and keep the rest of us from getting it."

"But I'm healthy," said Anthony, laving himself with water. "I haven't even had a cold for years."

Crider groaned. "Do you know how much UV we get through the cloud blanket? Almost exactly none. Most places have UV equipment, but mine is busted, and anyway, it isn't enough. Do you have any idea how germs can breed under these domes, in this heat, with everybody packed in together and using the same air over and over again? Do you know –" His voice cracked. "Do you know you've probably ruined me?"

"Is that so?" said Anthony, and a light flickered briefly in his red-rimmed eyes. Over Crider's shoulder he saw Holfern and Linson and the others being loaded into another truck.

Crider leaned forward. With a plaintive earnestness that bordered on the tragic, he asked, "Why did you do it?"

Anthony told him, still looking over Crider's shoulder, at the dome and all that was under it.

"You mean you didn't have to come? You weren't broke, or in trouble with the law? Nobody made you?"

"No."

"My God," said Crider. And again, "My God!"

"And it wasn't any use," said Anthony. "This isn't any escape, it's the same thing only more so, pressed down and running over, *reductio ad absurdum*. Not even on the other planets—" He wanted to cry, but he had no moisture left in him to make tears. "Isn't there any place?" he asked desperately of Crider. "Isn't there any place a man can go?"

Crider told him.

VI

THE room was high up in the Justice building. The windows were discreetly barred, and the door had a magnetic lock on the outside but none inside. Anthony sat in the corner. He had a stubbornly closed-off look. Beyond the windows and far below he could hear the city, purring softly. It had got him back and it was pleased.

"Just a few more questions," said Dr. Eckworth persuasively. "We're almost through."

Anthony inspected his shoes.

"Really, Anthony!" said Fern, from across the room. "There isn't any reason to be rude." She looked expressively at Dr. Eckworth, and from him to the state alienist, Dr. Hinojosa, and then to Mr. Horst, the special officer from Immigration. "You see what I've had to put up with."

"Well," said Dr. Hinojosa, "we've made a pretty thorough examination, and I don't think there's any disagreement in our conclusions, Dr. Eckworth. If Mr. Horst is satisfied...."

"My department," said Horst, "is willing to be guided by your opinion as to the degree of responsibility involved. Fortunately there were no serious consequences of the violation—matter of fact, the local authorities were able to get hold of Crider because of it. So if you say Mr. Reid was—"

Anthony sprang up. His face was red and his voice was loud. "I *was* responsible, I *am* responsible. I knew exactly what I was doing, and why, and I'm perfectly willing to pay the penalty."

"Anthony!" cried Fern. "I know you don't care about me, but think of the children. Think what it would do to them, to have their father in prison!"

"A nuthouse is considerably more respectable," said Anthony savagely, "and I suppose it doesn't matter what that does to me." He glowered at Fern and Dr. Eckworth. "A conspiracy, that's what it is. That's one reason I went away, because you were trying to make me think I was crazy."

"Now, now, we don't use that word any more," said Eckworth kindly. "We simply say emotionally disturbed. Let me ask you one final question. Do you feel that you are willing and able, at this moment, to return to that place in organized society from which you felt it so necessary to escape?"

"No," said Anthony. "No, I won't, and you can't make me!"

Dr. Eckworth turned to Dr. Hinojosa and smiled. Dr. Hinojosa nodded and looked at Mr. Horst. Mr. Horst said that whatever they said was good enough for him. And Fern remarked with a certain tragic satisfaction, "If you had listened to me in the first place, Anthony, none of this would have happened."

"I'm glad it did," said Anthony. "In one way, it was worth it, well worth it." He looked at them all with a proud and tremendous satisfaction. "There were seven of us at Crider's. And I held out the longest."

"Ah," said Dr. Eckworth, and made a notation. He turned to Dr. Hinojosa. "What would you say to Rustic Rest?"

"Perfect. I'll make the arrangements today."

"Good. And now, Mr. Reid, please try to understand that we're—"

"You can skip the speech," said Anthony wearily. "I'm not going to make any trouble. It doesn't really matter where I go."

He had learned something else at Crider's. He knew when he was licked.

They took him to Rustic Rest that afternoon. It was a pleasant madhouse, and not at all what Anthony had expected. It was located on the extreme northern rim of the city, just before it touched the great central reservoir. There were many acres of wooded land there, carefully preserved, and once you were inside the high wire fence that enclosed them you could almost imagine that the city was not there at all.

The main building was a rambling unfunctional old structure that did not look at all like an institution. The resident psychiatrist was a pleasant bronzed young man in a sport shirt who did not look at all like a psychiatrist. Everybody talked a little while, and then Fern and the kids went away, and Anthony was surprised to find himself not wanting them to go, and asking them to be sure and come every visiting day. Then Eckworth and the resident, Dr. Buerhle, walked with him down a gravel path that wandered away among the trees.

"I think," said Dr. Buerhle, "you'll find the accommodations quite pleasant here."

SCATTERED here and there, with no attempt at order, each with its individual plot of ground and its individual picket fence around it, were innumerable tiny cottages. They were painted every color under the sun, and decorated in every possible way. The little gardens flourished, and men worked in some of them, or tinkered with old-fashioned hand tools, or simply sat in the sun.

"The reality-image is so often bound up in men's minds with things like this," said Buerhle quietly. "We give it to them here."

Oh lord, thought Anthony, oh no! Maybe this was what I was looking for, but not like this, not like this!

"We may have come away a little too fast from the old tradition of the soil," said Eckworth. "After all, we were peasants and husbandmen a long while before we were urbanites. Dig in the ground, Anthony. Paint your house. Work with your hands. It does wonders for cases like yours."

Anthony did not answer. He was filled with a terrible regret for—for what? For everything. For the past, the future, himself. His feet dragged in the gravel.

"Your time is your own here," said Buerhle, "outside of what you spend with your doctor, or with me. Occupational Therapy will supply you with any tools or materials you want. Books, music, scientific apparatus, anything within reason, we will be happy to get for you."

"Thanks," said Anthony bitterly. "It ought to be fun."

"I think you'll like your neighbors," said Eckworth blandly, ignoring his tone. "I have some other patients here, and I've got to know the boys pretty well. By the way, your ex-employer is one of them—better caution him about Jennings, Buerhle."

"Jennings," said Anthony, and laughed. "Well, why not?"

"He grows vegetables," said Buerhle, pointing to the nearby garden patches. "You may have noticed that tall plant with the tassels on it?"

Anthony had not. He didn't care.

"It's corn," said Buerhle. "He's got them all doing it now. Jennings grows all kinds of things, even potatoes. The—ah—point is, Mr. Reid, he eats them."

Anthony looked up with a faint flicker of interest. "Right out of the ground?"

"It does seem too much of a return to the primitive, I'll admit—but he was so insistent about it. Anyway, please, no adverse comment. It upsets him."

They rounded a turn in the gravel path. There was an unoccupied cottage ahead, and a little group had gathered by the open gate. "Welcoming committee," said Buerhle. They joined the group. "Mr. Reid, Mr. Haggerty, Mr. Perez, Mr. Jennings—"

Mr. Haggerty, a small bright-eyed man, rushed forward and caught Buerhle's sleeve. "Don't you think I could go home now, Doctor? My circuits are working perfectly, they don't hum any more, not at all. I mean, I'm not conscious of them, so that's the same as being sure I haven't any, isn't it? Oh, bother!" he added suddenly, as Mr. Perez reached out and tried gently to detach him from Buerhle. "Now look, you've shut off the switch." Mr. Haggerty stood stiff as a plank.

"I'm sorry," said Perez, and punched him on the other shoulder.

Mr. Haggerty moved again. He looked sheepishly at Buerhle, and Buerhle laughed. "Relax," he said. "I recommended you for another year this morning. Well, Reid, I'll leave you to get settled. If you want anything, there's a phone in your cottage. Coming, Eckworth?"

"No, I'll stay a while."

Buerhle went away. Haggerty looked at Eckworth. "I guess I laid that on a little thick."

"A little."

"What's the difference?" said Jennings. "You got your year." He held out his hand to Anthony. "Glad you're here. Throw your bag inside and come on over to my place. We'll give you a real Rustic Rest welcome."

Anthony glowered at Eckworth. "I don't know what goes on here, or who's crazy—I think you all are. But I—"

"You'll figure it out," said Perez. "Come on. You too, Doc."

"Thanks," said Eckworth. "Jennings is inviting you to dinner, Anthony. Don't you want to taste some real, unprocessed, unsynthesized food?"

"All right," said Anthony defiantly, "yes, I do."

Perez made a wry face. "You won't like it."

"Matter of fact," said Jennings, "I found I didn't like it myself. But I'm stuck with it now."

THEY took Anthony away down a narrow path that ended at a white cottage. Inside, the place was not too neat, but comfortable, fitted with an antique electric range and crammed with books—the old-fashioned thick hard-bound books that were all type and no pictures to speak of. Jennings moved a big chair and began to pry at the floorboards. From a hole underneath he lifted up a lopsided ceramic contrivance with a stopper in it.

"Made it myself," he said, "in Occupational Therapy."

"What is it?" asked Anthony. "A jug?"

"A jug," said Jennings. "And it's full of whisky. Real old honest-to-God whisky. Made it myself, out of my own corn." He chuckled. "I've got everybody growing the stuff now. That's why I'm stuck with the potatoes and the rest of the junk. Cover-up."

Haggerty had brought out glasses. Jennings began to pour. "You won't like this, either, at first gulp. But stay with it. It has its points."

Anthony stayed with it. And it did have its points, but he wasn't sure they were good ones. He could feel the hot raw stuff creeping through his brain, burning away barriers, doing queer things to his emotions. The others talked, but after a while he lost track of what they were saying. He only heard their voices, vigorous and cheerful, full of hope. The voices began to grate on him. It seemed unthinkable that these men could accept the shame that had been put upon them, and not only accept it but apparently thrive on it. Sane men, making a deliberate pretense of insanity so that they could cling to this ridiculous, this pathetic and unutterably sad imitation of a way and a world that were vanished and could never come again, a world they wouldn't even want to live in if it did come again. It was—

He told them what it was. Or at least he thought he was telling them. His tongue didn't work properly, and his thought-processes were confused. And then all the tension of disappointment and frustration that had been growing in him since—when? All his life, maybe. Or did it just seem that way? Anyway, it all clapped down on him at once in a wave of utter futility.

"No place to go," he muttered. "I've hit bottom."

"Good," said Eckworth. "At least you've stopped running away."

Anthony lifted his head. He must have leaned it on the table, because he had to lift it quite high. He snarled at Eckworth.

"You put me here. But I won't—I won't—" He had no real idea what he wouldn't. His voice trailed off, and Eckworth looked accusingly at Jennings.

"You didn't have to drown him in the stuff. If you're not more careful somebody is going to find out and take your still away."

"Made it myself," said Jennings. "Occupational Therapy is a wonderful thing." He chuckled, and then a doubt seemed to strike him. "You wouldn't, would you, Doc?"

"I'm here unofficially," Eckworth said. "Just as a friend. Pass the jug, will you?"

"Friend," said Anthony, sobering a bit as he got madder. "Fine friend you are. Sending me here to play with old toys instead of new ones. Give me a saw and a hammer instead of a television set, and you think I'll be happy."

"That's what you wanted, isn't it? Something manual."

"But not make-believe!" shouted Anthony. "I want to do something real."

"This boy," said Mr. Perez, "has a head start."

Eckworth nodded. "High I.Q. No genius, you understand, but intelligent. Too intelligent for the job he was doing, which of course is why he blew up. And a strong personality, extremely well integrated—which is why he didn't blow up sooner. Stability can be a handicap at times." He said to Anthony, "If you'd come to me when I wanted you to, I could have saved you a lot of trouble."

"I didn't want to be saved a lot of trouble. It taught me things."

"Um. Yes. About yourself. You found out that you have determination, and a normal amount of courage, and sense enough to know how far to push it. That's good. But you didn't find the other thing you were looking for—the important thing."

"Reality," said Anthony, and shook his head. He reached for the jug, feeling very sad.

"Of course, you didn't," said Eckworth, and grinned. "You weren't looking for it at all. You were running away from it."

Anthony stared at him. There was a brief, hard silence, and then Eckworth said, "Shut up and listen. I'm not going to give you a lot of psychiatric double-talk, and I'm not speaking right now as your doctor. Just as one reasonably intelligent man to another. Jennings, if he squawks, sit on him. I want to get this through his head."

"All right," said Anthony, between his teeth. "Go on."

"Before you can find reality, you have to define it—to your own satisfaction if not to anyone else's. How you define it is what makes the difference between the 'normal' social neurotic, which covers nearly everybody, including me, and the true psychopath. When your reality-concept equates more or less with the accepted norm, you're allowed to run loose. When it doesn't, you have to be locked up, and not in a place like this, either. So you want to be extremely careful."

"But—" said Anthony furiously.

ECKWORTH drowned him out. "The most important thing is to be able to recognize a reality when you see it. That's what you refused to do. You ran all the way out to Venus to get away from having to recognize a few. But I think you're beginning to realize now that there isn't any escape."

Anthony got up. He started to say something, or to shout it, rather, and Jennings pushed him down again.

"The calculator was a reality," said Eckworth. "You rejected it. Your job, the city, civilization, even your wife—you rejected them all. You said they were all artificial, and you wouldn't have anything more to do with them." He leaned forward, getting warmed up to his subject. "Look, Reid. Reality isn't something that happened a generation ago, or a thousand years ago. Reality is now, the contemporary matrix, the frame of reference you were born into. You may not like it. You may even think others would have been better. But it's real. You can't evade it, except by dying or retreating into genuine insanity."

Anthony took a vicious pull at the jug. "You're just playing with words. You can't tell me I haven't been living in a completely artificial environment."

"It is. It has to be, to feed, house, clothe, and employ the biggest population Earth has ever had. But how far back do you want to go? The first splay-footed human who made fire himself instead of waiting for the lightning to do it was exercising an artificial control over his natural environment. Clothes are artificial. So are houses. So were domesticated herds and agriculture. I guess if you really want to live in a cave we can fix one up for you, but it seems rather silly."

"Sit quiet there," said Jennings. "Listen to the doc. We can't have you punching his nose. We like him."

"I never wanted to go back," Anthony panted. "That's a lie." He glared at Perez and Haggerty and Jennings. "You all seem willing to do it, though."

"There's nothing wrong with going back a little—far enough to get a new perspective and then start forward again on a different path." Perez nodded. "Dig in the dirt. Use a hoe and shovel. Get it out of your system. After you've done enough of it you'll think gratefully of those lazy but brilliant men who invented the well-sweep and the wheel, and started us on our long ascent toward the push-button. The future belongs to the mind, not to the back."

"So," said Anthony, "what's the good of the future? It'll just be more of the same. More push-buttons, more fairy tales on bigger and better TV sets, more gadgets to make human beings unnecessary."

"I used to think so," said Perez slowly. "But it isn't really so. We're awfully new in this universe as creation goes, but we're growing up pretty fast, all things considered. Infancy went on a long time, but our childhood was considerably shorter, say only about six thousand years, give or take a few centuries. Isn't that so, Doc?"

"We exhibited all the child traits. Impatience, megalomania, tantrums, a very imperfect grasp of realities and a tendency to reject all the ones we didn't like. In other words, wars, aggressive nationalism, segregation, trouble."

"But now," said Perez, "no—damn it, Reid, let me talk. This is my one ewe lamb of wisdom, and I want to walk it around. Now we don't do those things any more. Maybe we've got softer, but we have sort of learned to live with ourselves. And that's a symptom of on-coming maturity."

"We *had* to learn that," murmured Haggerty, "way back in the Twentieth Century. Or else. I guess the doc would call that a survival mechanism."

"We licked a few other 'natural' things," said Perez, as though he hadn't heard, "things like famines and disease. That's why we've got so many people nowadays. Where *are* we going to put them all eventually, Doc? I haven't figured that yet. Will somebody finally crack that problem of the ultra-speed drive and let us get out even farther? Anyway, Reid, we haven't reached dead end, not yet. We've just got into our adolescence. We're lazy, gadget-happy, easily distracted by every outside stimulus, trying on one fad and attitude after another—worthless, if you like, but only apparently, not potentially. We'll be dragged up just as we always have been, step by step, toward adulthood. Only I'm not going to wait to be dragged. I'm going to help do it."

A THOUGHT was beginning to percolate through the fumes that filled Anthony's head, but he was not ready to accept it yet, any more than he was ready to accept Dr. Eckworth as a friend.

"How?" he said. "In this place, with you all gibbering at doctors so you'll be let to stay?"

"Sure," said Haggerty. "I'm working on a technical problem, and it'll take me another year to finish it. I blew my fuses, you know, because as a technician I was only taught to understand the function of one particular circuit on one particular type of machine. The other forty million technicians had to eat, too. But I wanted to do more, and finally the frustration got me. I developed circuits on the brain, quite literally."

"Same with me," said Perez, "only it was pushing buttons in a factory. Same operation over and over."

"I know," said Anthony.

"With me," said Jennings, "I was living in a mental vacuum and never knew it till I fell in."

"There you are," said Anthony triumphantly to Eckworth. "That proves it. I still say what we've all been doing is piffling and—and unworthy."

"Which is quite a different thing from saying it isn't real. If you feel that way, do something about it, don't run away from it. Here's your chance. There isn't much room for individualists any more, there can't be, in an overcrowded society where everything has to be organized right down to the last decimal point. We try—we psychiatrists, Reid, in spite of what you think of us—to keep the mediocre minds feeling important and happy, and weed out the exceptional ones so they can do some good. But there are so many that we can't do anything about until they show themselves by rebelling against the norm of mediocrity that social organization has forced upon them."

He waved his hand to indicate the acres outside, the trees darkening in the late twilight, the little separate houses with the lights burning in them.

"We try to give them a chance to dissociate themselves from the conditioned mass-consciousness and discover their individuality. We provide places like this, an oasis away from all the pressures and stimuli and distractions that keep people from thinking for themselves. We give them aptitude tests. We let them read, and putter, and play with anything they want—and finally something emerges. Something new, something real."

"Creative," said Jennings. "That's us. Breeding ground of the future." He patted his lopsided jug. "So far this is all I've created, but it's a start."

There was another silence. Anthony stared into his glass, and drank, and stared again. Finally he said, "All right, I'll go along with the gag. I still think it's crazy, but I'll go along." He looked at Eckworth. "I guess what you've been trying to put over to me is that the only true reality is right here, inside your own head."

"Something like that. Externals, above a certain basic level of necessity, aren't important. It's what you think, and how you implement the thinking, that matters."

Anthony put his head between his hands. "That doesn't sound nearly as exciting as running away to Venus."

"It isn't," said Jennings. "Not at first. But it's real." He laughed, and filled Anthony's glass again. "Just as real as the old-fashioned hangover you're going to have tomorrow!"

THE TWEENER

The Magazine of Fantasy & Science Fiction, February 1955

A TAXICAB turned the corner and came slowly down the street.

"Here he is!" shrieked the children, tearing open the white gate. "Mother! Dad! He's here, Uncle Fred's here!"

Matt Winslow came out onto the porch, and in a minute Lucille came too, flushed from the purgatory of a kitchen on a July day. The cab stopped in front of the house. Josh and Barbie pounced on it like two small tigers, howling, and from up and down the street the neighbors' young came drifting, not making any noise, recognizing that this was the Winslows' moment and not intruding on it, but wanting to be close to it, to breathe and see and hear the magic.

"Look at them," said Matt, half laughing. "You'd think Fred was Tarzan, Santa Claus, and Superman, all rolled into one."

"Well," said Lucille proudly, "not many people have been where he has."

She went running down the path. Matt followed her. Inside, he was jealous. It was nothing personal, he liked Lucille's brother and respected him. It was only that Josh and Barbie had never had that look in their eyes for him. This was a secret jealousy, that Matt hid carefully, frighteningly, even from himself.

Fred got out of the cab, trim and soldierly in his uniform with the caduceus on the collar tabs, but forgetting all about dignity as he tried to hug the kids and kiss his sister and shake Matt's hand all at once. "I'll get your bags," said Matt, and the neighbors' children stared with enormous eyes and sent the name of Mars whispering back and forth between them.

"Be careful," Fred said. "That one there, with the handle on it—let me." He lifted it out, a smallish box made from pieces of packing case that still showed Army serial numbers. It had little round holes bored in its top and sides. Fred waved the children back. "Don't joggle it, it's a rare Martian vase I brought back for your mother, and I don't want it broken. Presents for you? Now what do you think of that—I clean forgot! Oh well, there wasn't much out there you'd have wanted, anyway."

"Not even a *rock?*" cried Josh, and Fred shook his head solemnly. "Not a pebble." Barbie was staring at the holes in the box. Matt picked up Fred's suitcase. "He hasn't changed," he thought. "Lost some weight, and got some new lines in his face, but with the kids he hasn't changed. He still acts like one himself." He, too, looked at the holes in the box, but with apprehension. "This is going to be good," he thought. "Something special."

"God, it's hot," said Fred, screwing up his eyes as though the sunlight hurt them. "Ten months on Mars is no way to train up for an eastern summer. Barbie, don't hang on your old uncle, he's having trouble enough." He glanced at Matt and Lucille, grinning ruefully, and made a pantomime of giving at the knees. "I feel as though I'm wading in glue."

"Sit down on the porch," Lucille said. "There's a little breeze—"

"In a minute," Fred said. "But first, don't you want to see your present?" He set the box down, in a shady spot under the big maple at the corner of the house.

"Now Fred, what are you up to?" she demanded suspiciously. "Martian vases, indeed!"

"Well, it's not exactly a vase. it's more of a—*I'll* open it, Josh, you just stand back. This doesn't concern you."

"Oh, Uncle Fred!" wailed Barbie, dancing up and down like a doll on strings. "Open it up, *please* open it up."

Matt had put the suitcase inside the door. Now he came and joined the others under the tree.

Fred opened the lid of the box. Then he sat back on his heels, watching the children's faces, and Matt thought, "He's been waiting for this for nearly a year, dreaming it up… he should have married and had kids of his own."

298

Josh and Barbie let out one mingled cry, and then were still. For a moment.

"Is it really alive?"

"Can we touch it?"

"Will it bite?"

"Oh, Uncle Fred—oh, *look*—it does belong to us, doesn't it?"

Along the fence small boys and girls impaled their meager bellies on the pickets in an effort to see. Matt and Lucille peered down into the box. On a mat of red sand and dry lichens a thing was crouching, a neat furry thing about the size of a big rabbit and not unlike one in outline, except that its ears were cup-shaped, and except that its coat was mottled in the exact rust red and greenish gray of the native sand and lichens. It looked up at the unfamiliar faces with a sort of mild incuriosity, its eyes half shut against the glare, but otherwise it did not move.

"What on earth is it?" asked Lucille.

"Nothing," said Fred, "on Earth. On Mars, he's the dominant form of life—or was, until we came. In fact, he's the sole surviving mammal, and almost the sole surviving vertebrate. He doesn't have an official name yet. It'll be years before the zoologists can decide on their classifications. But the boys out there call him tweener."

"What?" said Lucille.

"Tweener. Because he's sort of between things. You know—if anyone asked you what he was like, you'd say he was something between a rabbit and a ground-hog, or maybe between a monkey and a squirrel. Go ahead, Barbie, pick him up."

"Now wait a minute," said Matt. He pushed Barbie back. "Wait just a minute. Fred, are you sure about this thing? Is he safe? I don't want the kids bitten, or catching anything."

"Beside him," said Fred, "a rabbit is dangerous. The tweeners have had no enemies for so long they've forgotten how to fight, and they haven't yet acquired any fear of man. I've pulled 'em out of their burrows with my bare hands."

He reached into the box and lifted the creature gently, clucking to it. "Anyway, this one has been a pet all his life. I picked him especially because of that. He's acclimated to warmer temperatures and approximately Earth-normal atmosphere, from living in a Base hut, and I thought he'd stand the shock of transplanting better." He held the tweener out. "Here, you take him, Matt. You and Lucille. Set your minds at rest."

Matt hesitated, and then received the tweener into his hands. It felt like—well, like an animal. Like any small animal you might pick up. Warm, very thick-furred, perhaps more slight in the bone and light in the muscle than he had expected. It had no tail. Its hind legs were not at all rabbit-like, and its forelegs were longer than he had thought. It placed a paw on his arm, a curious paw with three strong fingers and a thumb, and lifted its head, sniffing. The sunlight was brighter here, falling in a shaft between the branches, and the tweener's eyes were almost shut, giving it a look of sleepy imbecility. Matt stroked it awkwardly, once or twice, and it rubbed its head against his arm. Matt shivered. "That soft fur," he said. "It tickles, sort of. Want him, Lucille?"

She looked sternly at Fred. "No germs?"

"No germs."

"All right." She took the tweener the way she would have taken a cat, holding him up under the forelegs and looking him over while he dangled, limp and patient. Finally she smiled. "He's cute. I think I'm going to like him." She set him carefully on his feet in the green grass. "All right, you kids. And be careful you don't hurt him."

Once more Josh and Barbie were speechless, if not silent. They lay on the ground and touched and patted and peered and took turns holding, and the ragged fringe of small bodies on the fence dripped and flowed inward until the yard was full of children and the stranger from Mars was hidden out of sight.

"Kids," said Fred, and laughed. "It's nice to see them again. And normal people."

"What do you mean, normal?"

Fred said wryly, "I had to be doctor *and* psychiatrist. I've had xenophobes crawling all over me for ten long months."

"Xeno—what?" asked Lucille.

"A two-dollar word for men who fear the unknown. When chaps got to worrying too much about what was over the horizon, they were dumped on me. But the heck with that. Take me somewhere cool and drown me in beer."

It was a long hot afternoon, and a long hot evening, and they belonged mostly to Fred. To the children he seemed ten feet high and shining with the hero-light. To the neighbors who dropped in to say hello, he was a man who had actually visited a place they still did not quite believe in.

The children, the whole gaggle of them, hunkered in a circle around the chairs that had been dragged to the coolest spot in the yard.

"Is it like in the books, Uncle Fred? Is it?"

Fred groaned, and pointed to the tweener in Barbie's arms. "Get him to tell you. He knows better than I do."

"Of course he does," said Barbie; "John Carter knows everything. But—"

"Who?" asked Fred.

"John Carter. John Carter of Mars."

Fred laughed. "Good. That's a good name. You get it, don't you, Matt? Remember all those wonderful Edgar Rice Burroughs stories about the Warlord of Mars, and the Swordsman of Mars, and the Gods of Mars?"

"Sure," said Matt, rather sourly. "The kids read 'em all the time. John Carter is the hero, the kind with a capital H." He turned to the children. "But John Carter was an Earthman, who went to Mars."

"Well," said Josh, scornfully impatient of adult illogic, *"he's* a Martian who came to Earth. It's the same thing. Isn't it, Uncle Fred?"

"You might say that, like the other John Carter, he's a citizen of two worlds."

"Yes," said Barbie. "But anyway, we can't understand his language yet, so you'll have to tell us about Mars."

"Oh, all right," said Fred, and he told them about Mars, about the dark canals and the ruined cities, about the ancient towers standing white and lonely under the twin moons, about beautiful princesses and wicked kings and mighty swordsmen. And after they had gone away again to play with John Carter, Matt shook his head and said, "You ought to be ashamed, filling their heads up with that stuff."

Fred grinned. "Time enough for reality when they grow up."

It got later, and the night closed in. Neighbors came and went. The extra children disappeared. It grew quiet, and finally there was no one left but the Winslows and Fred. Matt went inside to the kitchen for more beer.

From somewhere in the remote darkness beyond the open windows, Barbie screamed.

The can he was opening fell out of Matt's hand, making a geyser of foam where it hit the floor. "If that little—" he said, and did not stop to finish the sentence. He ran out the kitchen door.

Fred and Lucille had jumped up. Barbie's shrieks were coming from the foot of the lot, where the garage was, and now Matt could hear Josh yelling. He ran across the lawn and onto the drive. Lucille was behind him, calling, "Barbie! Josh! What is it?"

In the dim reflection of light from the house, Matt could make out the small figure of Josh bent over and tugging frantically at the handle of the overhead door, which was closed tight. "Help!" he panted. "It's stuck, or something."

Matt brushed him aside. Beyond the door, in the dark garage, Barbie was still screaming. Matt took hold of the handle and heaved.

It was jammed, but not so badly that his greater strength could not force it up. It slid, clicking and grumbling, into place, and Matt rushed into the opening.

Barbie was standing just inside, her mouth stretched over another scream, her cheeks running streams of tears. John Carter was beside her. He was standing on his hind legs, almost erect, and the fingers of one forepaw were gripped tightly around Barbie's thumb. His eyes were wide open. In the kindly night there was no hot glare to bother them, and they looked out, green-gold and very, very bright. Something rose up into Matt's throat and closed it. He reached out, and Barbie shook off John Carter's grip and flung herself into Matt's arms.

"Oh, Daddy, it was so dark and Josh couldn't get the door open—"

Josh came in and picked up John Carter. "Aw, girls," he said, quite scornful now that the emergency was over. "Just because she gets stuck in the garage for a few minutes, she has to have hysterics."

"What in the world were you doing?" Lucille demanded weakly, feeling Barbie all over.

"Just playing," said Josh, sulking. "How should I know the old door wouldn't work?"

"She's okay," Fred said. "Just scared."

Lucille groaned deeply. "And they wonder why mothers turn gray at an early age. All right, you two, off to bed. Scoot!"

Josh started toward the house with Barbie, still clutching John Carter.

"Oh, no," said Matt. "You're not taking that thing to bed with you." He caught John Carter by the loose skin of his shoulders and pulled him out of the boy's arms. Josh spun around, all ready to make trouble about it, and Fred said smoothly, "I'll take him."

He did, holding him more gently than Matt. "Your father's right, Josh. No pets in the bedroom. And anyway, John Carter wouldn't be comfortable there. He likes a nice cool place where he can dig his own house and make the rooms just to suit him."

"Like a catacomb?" asked Barbie, in a voice still damp and tremulous.

"Or a cave?" asked Josh.

"Exactly. Now you run along, and your father and I will fix him up."

"Well," said Josh. "Okay." He held out a finger and John Carter wrapped a paw around it. Josh shook hands solemnly. "Good night." Then he looked up. "Uncle Fred, if he digs like a woodchuck, how come his front feet are like a monkey's?"

"Because," said Fred, "he didn't start out to be a digger. And he is much more like an ape than a woodchuck. But there haven't been any trees in his country for a long time, and he had to take to the ground anyway to keep warm. That's what we call adaptation." He turned to Matt. "How about the old root cellar? It'd be ideal for him, if you're still not using it for anything."

"No," said Matt slowly. "I'm not using it." He looked at John Carter in the dim light from the house, and John Carter looked back at him with those bright unearthly eyes.

Matt put a hand up to his head, aware that it had begun to ache.

"My sinus is kicking up—probably going to rain tomorrow. I think I'll turn in myself, if you don't mind."

"Go ahead, honey," Lucille said. "I'll help Fred with the tweener."

Matt took two aspirin on top of his beer, which made him feel no better, and retired into a heavy sleep, through which stalked dark and unfamiliar dreams that would not show their faces.

The next day was Sunday. It did not rain, but Matt's head went on aching.

"Are you sure it's your sinus?" Lucille asked.

"Oh, yes. All in the right side, frontal and maxillary. Even my teeth hurt."

"Hm," said Fred. "Don't ever go to Mars. Sinusitis is an occupational hazard there, in spite of oxygen masks. Something about the difference in pressure that raises hob with terrestrial insides. Why, do you know—"

"No," said Matt sourly, "and I don't want to know. Save your gruesome stories for your medical conference."

Fred winced. "I wish you hadn't mentioned that. I hate the thought of New York in this kind of weather. Damn it, it's cruelty to animals. And speaking of which—" he turned to Josh and Barbie—"keep John Carter in the cellar until this heat wave breaks. At least it's fairly cool down there. Remember he wasn't built for this climate, nor for this world. Give him a break."

"Oh, we will," said Barbie earnestly. "Besides, he's busy, building his castle. You ought to see the wall he's making around it."

Working slowly, resting often, John Carter had begun the construction of an elaborate burrow in the soft floor of the old root cellar. They went down and watched him from time to time, bringing up earth and then patting and shaping it with his clever paws into a neat rampart to protect his front door. "To deflect wind and sand," Fred said, and Barbie, watching with fascinated eyes, murmured, "I'll bet he could build anything he wanted to, if he was big enough."

"Maybe. Matter of fact, he probably was a good bit bigger once, a long time ago when things weren't so tough. But—"

"As big as me?" asked Josh.

"Possibly. But if he built anything then we haven't been able to find it. Or anything at all that *anybody* built. Except, of course," he added hastily, "those cities I was telling you about."

The heat wave broke that night in a burst of savage line-squalls. "That's what my head was complaining about," thought Matt, rousing up to blink at the lightning. And then he slept again, and dreamed, dim sad dreams of loss and yearning. In the morning his head still ached.

Fred went down to New York for his conference. Matt went to the office and stewed, finding it hard to keep his mind on his work with the nagging pain in the side of his skull. He began to worry. He had never had a bout go on this long. He fidgeted more and more as the day wore on, and then hurried home oppressed by a vague unease that he could find no foundation for.

"All right?" Lucille echoed. "Of course everything's all right. Why?"

"I don't know. Nothing. The kids—?"

"They've been playing Martian all day. Matt, I've never seen them so tickled with anything in their lives as they are with that little beastie. And he's so cute and patient with them. Come here a minute."

She led him to the door of the children's room, and pointed in. Josh and Barbie arrayed in striped beach towels and some of Lucille's junkier costume jewelry, were engaged in a complicated ritual that involved much posturing and waving of wooden swords. In the center of the room enthroned on a chair, John Carter sat. He had a length of bright cloth wrapped around him and a gold bracelet on his neck. He sat perfectly still, watching the children with his usual half-lidded stare, and Matt said harshly, "It isn't right."

"What isn't?"

"Any ordinary animal wouldn't stand for it. Look at him, just squatting there like a—" He hunted for a word and couldn't find it.

"The gravity," Lucille reminded him. "He hardly moves at all, poor little thing. And it seems quite hard for him to breathe."

Josh and Barbie knelt side by side in front of the throne, holding their swords high in the air. *"Kaor!"* they cried to John Carter, and then Josh stood up again and began to talk in gibberish, but respectfully, as though addressing a king.

"That's Martian," said Lucille, and winked at Matt. "Sometimes you'd swear they were actually speaking a language. Come on and stretch out on the couch a while, honey, why don't you? You look tired."

"I am tired," he said. "And I—" He stopped.

"What?"

"Nothing." No, nothing at all. He lay down on the couch. Lucille went into the kitchen. He could hear her moving about, making the usual noises. Faintly, far off, he heard the children's voices. Sometimes you'd swear they were actually speaking a language. Sometimes you'd swear—

No. No you wouldn't. You know what is, and what isn't. Even the kids know.

He dozed, and the children's voices crept into his dream. They spoke in the thin and icy wind and murmured in the dust that blew beneath it, and there was no doubt at all now that they were speaking a tongue they knew and understood. He called to them, but they did not answer, and he knew that they did not want to answer, that they were hiding from him somewhere among the ridges of red sand that flowed and shifted so that there was never a trail or a landmark. He ran among the dunes, shouting their names, and then there was a tumble of ancient rock where a mountain had died, and a hollow place below it with a tinge of green around a meager pool. He knew that they were there in that hollow place. He raced toward it, racing the night that deepened out of a sky already dark and flecked with stars, and in the dusk a shape rose up and blocked his way. It bore in its right hand a blade of grass—no, a sword. A sword, and its face was shadowed, but its eyes looked out at him, green-gold and bright and not of the Earth—

"For heaven's sake, Matt—wake up!" Lucille was shaking him. He sprang up, still in the grip of his dream, and saw Josh and Barbie standing on the other side of the room. They had their ordinary clothes on, and they were grinning, and Barbie said, "How can you have a nightmare when it's still daytime?"

"I don't know," said Lucille, "but it must have been a dandy. Come on Matt, and get your dinner, before the neighbors decide I'm beating you."

"Other people's nightmares," Matt snarled, "are always so funny. Where's John Carter?"

"Oh, we put him back down cellar," Josh said, quite unconcerned. "Mom, will you get him some more lettuce tomorrow? He sure goes for it."

Feeling shamefaced and a little sick, Matt sat down and ate his dinner. He did not enjoy it. Nor did he sleep well that night, starting up more than once from the verge of an ugly dream. Next day Gulf Tropical had come in again worse than before, and his head had not stopped aching.

He went to his doctor, who could find no sign of infection but gave him a shot on general principles. He went to his office, but it was only a gesture. He returned home at noon on a two-day sick leave. The temperature had crept up to ninety and the humidity dripped out of the air in sharp crashing showers.

"I'll bet Fred's suffering in New York," Lucille said. "And poor John Carter! I haven't let the kids take him out of the cellar at all."

"Do you know what he did, Daddy?" Barbie said. "Josh found it this morning after you left."

"What?" asked Matt, with an edge in his voice.

"A hole," said Josh. "He must've tunneled right under the foundation. It was in the lawn, just outside where the root cellar is. I guess he's used to having a back door to his castle, but I filled it in. I filled it real good and put a great big stone on top."

Matt relaxed. "He'll only dig another."

Barbie shook her head. "He better not. I told him what would happen if he did, how a big dog might kill him, or he might get lost and never find his way home again."

"Poor little tyke," Lucille said. "He'll never find *his* home again."

"Oh, the hell with him," Matt said angrily. "Couldn't you waste a little sympathy on me? I feel lousy."

He went upstairs away from them and tried to lie down, but the room was a sweat-box. He tossed and groaned and came down again, and Lucille fixed him iced lemonade. He sat in the shade on the back porch and drank it. It hit his stomach cold and sour-sweet and it tied him in knots, and he got up to pace the lawn. The heat weighed and dragged at him. His head throbbed and his knees felt weak. He passed the place where Josh had filled in the new tunnel, and from the cellar window he heard the children's voices. He turned around and stamped back into the house.

"What are you doing down there?" he shouted, through the open cellar door.

Barbie's answer came muffled and hollow from the gloom below. "We brought John Carter some ice to lick on, but he won't come out." She began to talk in a different tone, softly, crooning, calling. Matt said, "Come up out of there before you catch cold!"

"In a minute," Josh said.

Matt went down the steps, his shoes thumping on the wooden treads. They had not turned on the lights, and what came through the small dusty windows was only enough to show the dim outlines of things. He banged his head on a heating duct and swore, and Barbie said rather impatiently, "We said we'd be up in a minute."

"What's the matter?" Matt demanded, blundering around the furnace. "Am I not supposed to come down here any more?"

"Sh-h!" Josh told him. "There, he's just coming out. Don't scare him back in again!"

The door of the root cellar was open. The children were crouched inside it, by the earthen rampart John Carter had constructed with such labor. In the circle of the rampart was a dark hole, and from it John Carter was emerging, very slowly, his eyes luminescent in the gloom. Barbie put two ice cubes on the ground before him, and he set his muzzle against them and lay panting, his flanks pulsing in a shallow, uneven rhythm.

"You'll be all right," Josh told him, and stroked his head. To Matt he said, "You don't understand how important he is. There isn't another kid anywhere around who has a real genuine Martian for a pet."

"Come on," said Matt harshly. "Upstairs." The clammy air was making him shiver. Reluctantly the children rose and went past him. John Carter did not stir. He looked at Matt, and Matt drew back, slamming the door shut. He followed the children out of the cellar, but in his mind's eye he could still see John Carter crouched behind his wall in the dark, tortured by a world that was not his, a world too big, too hot, too heavy.

Crouched behind his wall in the dark, and thinking.

No. Animals do not think. They feel. They can be lost, or frightened, or suffering, or a lot of things, but they're all feelings, not thoughts. Only humans think.

On Earth.

Matt went out in the yard again. He went clear to the back of it where the fence ran along the alley, and took hold of the pickets in his two hands. He stood there staring at the neighbors' back fences, at their garages and garbage cans, not seeing them, feeling the vague conviction that had been in the back of his mind grow and take shape and advance to a point where he could no longer pretend he didn't see it.

"No," he said to himself. "Fred would have known. The scientists would know. It couldn't be, and not be known."

Or couldn't it? How did you measure possibility on another world?

The only mammal, Fred had said, and almost the only vertebrate. Why should one sole species survive when all the others were gone, unless it had an edge to begin with, an advantage?

Suppose a race. Suppose intelligence. Intelligence, perhaps, of a sort that human men, Earthly men, would not understand.

Suppose a race and a world. A dying world. Suppose that race being forced to change with its dying, to dwindle and adapt, to lose its cities and its writings and inventions, or whatever had taken the place of them, but not its mind. Never its mind, because mind would be the only barrier against destruction.

Suppose that race, physically altered, environmentally destitute, driven inward on its own thoughts. Wouldn't it evolve all kinds of mental compensations, powers no Earthman would suspect or look for because he would be thinking in terms of what he knew, of

Earthly life-forms? And wouldn't such a race go to any lengths to hide its intelligence, its one last weapon, from the strangers who had come trampling in to take its world away?

Matt trembled. He looked up at the sky, and he knew what was different about it. It was no longer a solid shell that covered him. It was wide open, ripped and torn by the greedy ships, carrying the greedy men who had not been content with what they had. And through those rents the Outside had slipped in, and it would never be the same again. Never more the safe familiar Earth containing only what belonged to it, only what men could understand.

He stood there while a shower of rain crashed down and drenched him, and he did not feel it.

Then again, fiercely, Matt said, "No. I won't believe that, it's too—it's like the kids believing their games while they play them."

But were they only games?

He started at the sound of Lucille's voice calling him in. He knew by the sound of it she was worried. He went back toward the house. She came part way to meet him, demanding to know what he was doing out in the rain. He let her chivvy him into the house and into dry clothes, and he kept telling her there was nothing wrong, but she was alarmed now and would not listen. "You lie down," she said and covered him with a quilt, and then he heard her go downstairs and get on the telephone. He lay quiet for a few minutes, trying to get himself in hand, frightened and half ashamed of the state of his nerves. Sweat began to roll off him. He kicked the quilt away. The air inside the room was thick with moisture, heavy, stale. He found himself panting like—

Hell, it was no different from any summer heat wave, the bedroom was always hot and suffocating. It was always hard to breathe.

He left it and went downstairs.

Lucille was just getting up from the phone. "Who were you calling?" he asked.

"Fred," she said, giving him that no-nonsense look she got when she decided that something had to be done. "He said he'd be here in the morning. I'm going to find out what's the matter with you."

Matt said irritably, "But my doctor—"

"Your doctor doesn't know you like Fred does, and he doesn't care as much about you, either."

Matt grumbled, but it was too late to do anything about it now. Then he began to think that maybe Fred was the answer. Maybe if he told him —

What?

All right, drag it out, put it into words. I think John Carter is more than a harmless little beast. I think he's intelligent. I think that he hates me, that he hates this Earth where he's been brought so casually as a pet. I think he's doing something to my children.

Could he say that to Fred?

Lucille was calling the children for supper. "Oh lord, they're down in that damp cellar again. Josh, Barbie, come up here this minute!"

Matt put his head between his hands. It hurt.

He slept downstairs that night, on the living room couch. He had done that before during heatwaves. It gave the illusion of being cooler. He dosed himself heavily with aspirin, and for a time he lapsed into a drugged slumber full of dark shapes that pursued him over a landscape he could not quite see but which he knew was alien and hateful. Then in the silent hours between midnight and dawn he started up in panic. He could not breathe. The air was as thick as water, and a weight as of mountain ranges lay along his chest, his thighs, his shoulders.

He turned on a lamp and began to move up and down, his chest heaving, his hands never still, a glassy terror spreading over him, sheathing him as a sleet storm sheathes a tree.

The living room looked strange, the familiar things overlaid with a gloss of fear, traces everywhere of Josh and Barbie, of Lucille and himself, suddenly significant, suddenly sharp and poignantly symbolic as items in a Dali painting. Lucille's lending-library novel with the brown paper cover, Lucille's stiff Staffordshire figures on the mantel staring with their stiff white faces. An empty pop bottle, no, two empty pop bottles shoved guiltily behind the couch. Small blue jacket with the pocket torn, a drift of comic books under the lamp, his own chair with the cushion worn hollow by his own sitting. Patterns.

Wall-paper, slipcovers, rug. Colors, harsh and queer. He was aware of the floor beneath his feet. It was thin. It was a skim of ice over a black pool, ready to crack and let him fall, into the place where the stranger lay, and thought, and waited.

All over Mars they lie and wait, he thought, in their places under the ground. Thinking back and forth in the bitter nights, hating the men, human men who pull them out of their burrows and kill them and dissect them and pry at their brains and bones and nerves and organs. The men who tie little strings around their necks and put them in cages, and never think to look behind their eyes and see what lurks there.

Hating, and wanting their world back. Hating, and quietly driving men insane.

Just as this one is doing to me, he thought. He's suffering. He's crushed in this gravity, and strangling in this air, and he's going to make me suffer too. He knows he can never go home. He knows he's dying. How far can he push it? Can he only make me feel what he's feeling, or can he…?

Suppose he can. Suppose he knows I'm going to tell Fred. Suppose he stops me.

After that, what? Josh? Barbie? Lucille?

Matt stood still in the middle of the floor. "He's killing me," he thought. "He knows."

He began to shake. The room turned dark in front of him. He wanted to vomit, but there was a strange paralysis creeping over him, tightening his muscles, knotting them into ropes to bind him. He felt cold, as though he were already dead.

He turned. He did not run, he was past running, but he walked faster with every step, stiffly, like a mechanical thing wound up and accelerating toward a magnetic goal. He opened the cellar door, and the steps took him down. He remembered to switch on the light.

It was only a short distance to the north corner, and the half-open door.

John Carter made a sound, the only one Matt had ever heard him make. A small thin shriek, purely animal and quite, quite brainless.

It was the next morning, and Fred had come on the early train. They were standing, all of them, grouped together on the lawn near the back fence, looking down. The children were crying.

"A dog must have got him," Matt said. He had said that before, but his voice still lacked the solid conviction of a statement known and believed. He wanted to look up and away from what lay on the ground by his feet, but he did not. Fred was facing him.

"Poor little thing," said Lucille. "I suppose it must have been a dog. Can you tell, Fred?"

Fred bent over. Matt stared at his own shoes. Inside his pockets, his hands were curled tightly into fists. He wanted to talk. The temptation, the longing, the lust to talk was almost more than he could endure. He put the edges of his tongue between his teeth and bit it.

After a minute Fred said, "It was a dog."

Matt glanced at him, and now it was Fred who scowled at his shoes.

"I hope it didn't hurt him," Lucille said.

Fred said, "I don't think it did."

Miserably, between his sobs, Josh wailed, "I used the biggest stone I could find. I never thought he could have moved it."

"There, now," said Lucille, putting her arms around the children. She led them away toward the house, talking briskly, the usual mixture of nonsense and sound truth that parents administer at such times. Matt wanted to go away too, but Fred made no move, and somehow he knew that it was no use going. He stood with his head down, feeling the sun beat on the back of it like a hammer on a flinching anvil.

He wished Fred would say something. Fred remained silent.

Finally Matt said, "Thanks."

"I didn't see any reason to tell them. They'd find it hard to understand."

"Do *you* understand?" Matt cried out. "I don't. Why did I do such a thing? How could I have done such a thing?"

"Fear. I think I mentioned that once. Xenophobia."

"But that's not—I mean, I don't see how it applies."

"It's not just a fear of unknown places, but of unknown *things*.

Anything at all that's strange and unfamiliar." He shook his head. "I'll admit I didn't expect to find that at home, but I should have thought of the possibility. It's something to remember."

"I was so sure," Matt said. "It all fitted together, everything."

"The human imagination is a wonderful thing. I know, I've just put in ten months nursing it. I suppose you had symptoms?"

"God, yes." Matt enumerated them. "Last night it got so bad I thought—" He glanced at the small body by his feet. "As soon as I did that it all went away. Even the headache. What's the word? Psycho-something?"

"Psychosomatic. Yes. The guys out there developed everything from corns to angina, scared of where they were and wanting to leave it."

"I'm ashamed," Matt said. "I feel..." He moved his hands.

"Well," said Fred, "it was only an animal. Probably it wouldn't have lived long anyway. I shouldn't have brought it."

"Oh for Chrissake," Matt said, and turned away. Josh and Barbie were coming out of the house again. Josh carried a box, and Barbie had a bunch of flowers and a spade. They passed by the place on the lawn where the big stone had been moved and the hole opened up again—only part way, and from the outside, but Matt hoped they would not know that. He hoped they would not ever know that.

He went to meet them.

He kneeled down and put an arm around each of them. "Don't feel bad," he said desperately. "Look I'll tell you what we'll do. We'll go and find the best place in the country to buy a pup. Wouldn't you like that, a fine new puppy, all your own?"

LAST CALL FROM SECTOR 9G

Planet Stories, Summer 1955

ARTIE SAID MONOTONOUSLY, "There is someone at the door sir shall I answer? There is someone at the door sir shall I—"

Durham grunted. What he wanted to say was go away and let me alone. But he would only grunt, and Artie kept repeating the stupid question. Artie was a cheap off-brand make, and bought used, and he lacked some cogs. Any first class servall would have seen that the master had passed out in his chair and was in no condition to receive guests. But Artie did not, and presently Durham got one eye open and then he began to hear the persistent knocking, the annunciator being naturally out of order. And he said quite clearly,

"If it's a creditor, I'm not in."

"—shall I answer?"

Durham made a series of noises. Artie took them for an affirmative and trundled off. Durham put his face in his hands and struggled with the pangs of returning consciousness, He could hear a mutter of voices in the hall. He thought suddenly that he recognized them, and he sprang, or rather stumbled up in alarm, hastily combing his hair with his fingers and trying to pull the wrinkles out of his tunic. Through a thick haze he saw the bottle on the table and he picked it up and hid it under a chair, ashamed not of its emptiness but of its label. A gentleman should not be drunk on stuff like that.

Paulsen and Burke came in.

Durham stood stiffly beside the table, hanging on. He looked at the two men. "Well," he said. "It's been quite a long time." He turned to Artie. "The gentlemen are leaving."

Burke stepped quickly behind the servall and pushed the main toggle to OFF. Artie stopped, with a sound ridiculously like a tired sigh. Paulsen went past him and locked the door. Then both of them turned in to face Durham.

Durham scowled. "What the devil do you think you're doing?"

Burke and Paulsen glanced at each other as though resolve had carried them this far but had now run out, leaving them irresolute in the face of some distasteful task. Both men wore black dominos, with the cowls thrown back.

"Were you afraid you'd be recognized coming here?" Durham said. A small pulse of fright began to beat in him, and this was idiotic. It made him angry. "What do you want?"

Paulsen said in a reluctant voice, not looking at him, "I don't want anything Durham, believe me." Durham had once been engaged to Paulsen's sister, a thing both of them preferred not to remember but couldn't quite forget. He went on, "We were sent here."

Durham tried to think who might have sent them. Certainly not any of the girls; certainly not any one of the people he owed money to. Two members of the Terran World Embassy corps, even young and still obscure members in the lower echelons, were above either of those missions.

"Who sent you?"

Burke said, "Hawtree."

"No," said Durham. "Oh no, you got the name wrong. Hawtree wouldn't send for me if I was the last man in the galaxy. Hawtree, indeed."

"Hawtree," said Paulsen. He drew a deep breath and threw aside his domino. "Come on, Burke."

Burke took off his domino. They came on together.

Durham drew back. His shoulders dropped and his fists came up. "Look out," he said. "What you going to do? Look out!"

"All right," said Burke, and they both jumped together and caught his arms, not because Durham was so big or so powerful that he frightened them, but because they disliked the idea of brawling with a drunken man. Paulsen said,

"Hawtree wants you tonight, and he wants you sober, and that, damn it, is the way he's going to get you."

AN HOUR and seven minutes later Durham sat beside Paulsen in a 'copter with no insigne and watched the roof of his apartment tower fall away beneath him. Burke had stayed behind, and Durham wore the Irishman's domino with the cowl up over his head. Under the domino was his good suit, the one he had not sent to the pawnbroker because he could not, as yet, quite endure being without one good suit. He was scrubbed and shaved and perfectly sober. Outside he did not look too bad. Inside he was a shambles.

The 'copter fitted itself into a north-south lane. Paulsen, muffled in his cowl, sat silent. Durham felt a similar reluctance to speak. He looked out over The Hub, and tried to keep from thinking. Don't run to meet it, don't get your hopes up. Whatever it is, let it happen, quietly.

The city was beautiful. Its official name was Galactic Center, but it was called The Hub because that is what it was, the hub and focus of a galaxy. It was the biggest city in the Milky Way. It covered almost the entire land area of the third planet of a Type G star that someone with a sense of humor had christened Pax. The planet was chosen originally because it was centrally located and had no inhabitants, and because it was within the limits of tolerance for the humanoid races. The others mostly needed special accommodations anyway.

And so from a sweet green airy world with nothing on it but trees and grass and a few mild-natured animals The Hub had grown to have a population of something like ten billion people, spread horizontally and stacked up vertically and dug in underneath, and every one of them was engaged in some governmental function, or in espionage, or in both. Intrigue was as much a part of life in The Hub as corpuscles are a part of blood. The Hub boasted that it was the only inhabited world in space where no single grain of wheat or saddle of mutton was grown, where nothing was manufactured and nobody worked at a manual job.

Durham loved it passionately.

Both moons were in the sky now. One was small and low, like a white pearl hung just out of reach. The other was enormous. It had an atmosphere, and it served as warehouse and supply base for the planet city, handling the billions of tons of shipping that kept it going. The two of them made a glorious spectacle overhead, but Durham did not bother to see them. The vast glow of the city paled them, made them unimportant. He was remembering how he had seen it when he was fresh from Earth, for the first time—the supreme capital, beside which the world capitals were only toy cities, the heart and center of the galaxy where the decisions were made and the great men came and went. He was remembering how he had felt, how he had been so sure of the future that he never gave it a second thought.

But something happened.

What?

Liquor, they said.

No, not liquor, the hell with them. I could always carry my drinks.

Liquor, they said, and the accident.

The accident. Well, what of it? Didn't other people have accidents? And anyway, nobody really got hurt out of it. He didn't, and the girl didn't—what if she wasn't his fiancee?—and the confidential file he had in the 'copter hadn't fallen into anybody's hands. So there wasn't anything to that.

No. Not liquor and not the accident, no matter what they said. It was Hawtree, and a personal grudge because he, Durham, had had Hawtree's daughter out with him in the 'copter that night. And so what? He was only engaged to Willa Paulsen, not married to her, and anyway Susan Hawtree knew what she was doing. She knew darn well.

Hawtree, a grudge, and a little bad luck. That's what happened. And that's all.

The 'copter swerved and dropped onto a private landing stage attached to a penthouse. Durham knew it well, though he hadn't seen it for over a year. He got out, aware of palpitations and a gone feeling in the knees. He needed a drink, but he knew that he would have to go inside first and he forced himself to stand up and walk beside Paulsen as though nothing had ever happened. The head high, the face proud and calm, just a touch of bitterness but not too much.

Hawtree was alone in the living room. He glanced at Durham as

he came in through the long glass doors. There was a servall standing in the corner and Hawtree said to it, "A drink for the gentleman,
straight and stiff."

A small anger stirred in Durham. Hawtree might at least have giv-
en him the choice. He said sharply, "No thanks."

Hawtree said, "Don't be a fool." He looked tired, but then he always had. Tired and keyed up, full of the drive and the brittle excitement of one who has juggled peoples and nations, expressed as black
marks on sheets of varicolored paper, for so long that it has become a
habit as necessary and destructive as hashish. To Paulsen he said, "I'll
ring when I need you."

Paulsen went out. The servall placed the drink in Durham's hand.
He did not refuse it.

"Sit down," said Hawtree, and Durham sat. Hawtree dismissed the
servall. Durham drank part of his drink and felt better. "Well," he
said, "I'm listening."

"You were a great disappointment to me, Durham."

"What am I supposed to say to that?"

"Nothing. Go ahead, finish your drink, I want to talk to a man,
not a zombie."

Durham finished it angrily. "If you brought me all the way here
to shake your finger at me, I'm going home again." That was what
he said aloud. Inside, he wanted to get down and embrace Hawtree's
knees and beg him for another chance.

"I brought you here," said Hawtree, "to offer you a job. If you do
it, it might mean that certain doors could be opened for you again."

Durham sat perfectly still. For a moment he did not trust himself
to speak. Then he said, "I'll take it."

Certain doors. That's what I've waited for, living like a bum, dodging creditors, hocking my shoes, waiting for those doors to open
again.

HE TRIED not to show how he felt, sitting stiffly at ease in the chair,
but a red flush began to burn in his cheeks and his hands moved.
About time. About time, damn you, Hawtree, that you remembered
me.

Damn you, oh damn you for making me sweat so long!

Hawtree said, "Did you ever hear of Nanta Dik?"

"No. What is it?"

"A planet. It belongs to a green star system, chart designation KL421, Sub-sector 9G, Sector 80, Quadrant 7. It's a very isolated system, the only inhabited one in 9G, as a matter of fact. 9G is a Terran quota sector, and since Nanta Dik is humanoid, it's become headquarters for our nationals who are engaged in business in that sub-sector."

Durham nodded. Unassimilated territory lying outside the Federation was divided among Federation members, allowing them to engage in trade only in their allotted sectors and subject to local law and license. This eliminated competitive friction between Federation worlds, threw open new areas to development, and eventually—usually under the sponsorship of the federated world—brought the quota sectors into the vast family of suns that had already spread over more than half the galaxy. There were abuses now and again, but on the whole, as a system, it worked pretty well.

"I take it that Nanta Dik is where I'm going."

"Yes. Now listen. First thing in the morning, go and book a third-class passage to Earth on the *Sylvania Merchant,* leaving on the day following. Let your friends know you're going home. They won't be surprised."

"Don't rub it in."

"Sorry. When you reach the spaceport, walk across the main rotunda near the newsstand. Drop your ticket and your passport, folded together, go on to the newsstand and wait. They will be returned to you by a uniformed attendant, only your passport will be in a different name and your ticket will now be on a freighter outbound for Nanta Dik. You will then embark at once. Is that all clear?"

"Everything but the reason."

"I'll come to that. How good is your memory?"

"As good as it ever was."

"All right. When you reach Nanta Dik a man will meet you as you leave the ship. He will ask if you are the ornithologist. You will say yes. Then – pay close attention to this – you will say, *The darkbirds will soon fly.* Got that?"

"The darkbirds will soon fly. Simple enough. What's it mean?"

"9G is a rich sector, isolated, improperly policed, underpopulated. There has been a certain amount of trouble, poaching, claim jumping, outright piracy. The 'darkbirds' are a couple of suspected ships. We want to set a trap for them, and you know how things are on The Hub. If a man buys a pair of socks, the news is all across the galaxy in a week. That's the reason for all the secrecy."

"Is that all?"

"No." Hawtree got up, turning his back on Durham. He said harshly, "Listen, Lloyd." It was the first time he had used Durham's Christian name. "This is an important job. It may not seem like one, but it is. Do it. There's somebody else who wanted you to have another chance."

Durham did not say anything. He waited for Hawtree to turn around and face him and say the name. But he didn't, and finally Durham said,

"Susan?"

"I don't know what she sees in you," said Hawtree, and pushed a button. Paulsen came in. Hawtree jerked a thumb at Durham. "Take him back. And tell Burke to give him the money."

Durham went out and got into the 'copter. He felt dizzy, and this time it was not from drinks or the lack of them. He sat, and Paulsen took the 'copter off.

Hawtree watched it from inside the glass doors until it was out of sight above the roof. And another man came from behind a door that led into Hawtree's private study, and watched it with him.

"Are you sure about him?" asked the man.

"I know him," Hawtree said. "He's a slob."

"But are you sure?"

"Don't worry, Morrison," Hawtree said. "I know him. He'll talk. Bet you a hundred he never even makes the spaceport."

"Blessed are the fools," said Morrison, "for they shall inherit nothing."

II

BAYA sat on the bed and watched him pack. She was from one of the worlds of Mintaka, and as humanoid as they came, not very tall but very well shaped, and colored one beautiful shade of old bronze from the crown of her head to the soles of her feet, except for her mouth, which was a vivid red.

"It seems funny," she said, "to think of you not being here tomorrow."

"Will you die of missing me?"

"Probably, for a day or two. I was comfortable. I hate upheavals."

Durham reached across her for his small stack of underwear. She was wearing the yellow silk thing that made her skin glow by contrast. He saw that it was dubiously clean about the neck, and when he paused to kiss her he noticed the tiny lines around her mouth and eyes, the indefinable look of wear and hardness that was more destructive to beauty than the mere passing of years. Yesterday they had been two of a kind, part of the vast backwash left behind by other people's successes. Today he was far above her. And he was glad.

"The least you could do," she said, "would be to make this a really big evening. But I suppose you couldn't run to that."

"I've got money." Burke had given him some, but that was for expenses and he would neither mention it nor touch it. "Artie brought a pretty good price, so did the furniture." There was nothing left in the apartment but the bed, and even that was sold. He had bought back a few of his better belongings, and he still had a wad of credits. He felt good. He felt joyous and expansive. He felt like a man again.

He poured two drinks and handed one to Baya.

"All right," he said, "here's to a big last evening. The biggest."

They had cocktails in a bar called The Moonraker because it was the highest point in that hemisphere of the city. It was the hour between sunset and moonrise, when the towers stood sharply defined against a sky of incredible dark blueness, with the brighter stars pricked out in it, and the dim canyons at the feet of the towers were lost in the new night, spectral, soft and lovely. And the night deepened, and the lights came on.

They wandered for a while among the high flung walkways that spanned the upper levels of the towers so that people need not spend half their lives in elevators. They skirted the vast green concourse from which the halls of government rose up white and unadorned and splendid. They only skirted one corner of it, because this galactic Capitol Hill ran for miles, dominating the whole official complex, and one enormous building of it was fitted up so that the non-humanoid Members of Universal Parliament could "attend" the sessions in comfort, never leaving their especially pressurized and congenially poisonous suites. Between humanoid and non-humanoid there were many scientific gradations of form. But for governmental purposes it boiled down simply to oxygen-breather or non-oxygen-breather.

"Human or not," said Durham, standing on an upper span, with the good liquor burning bright inside him, "human or not, they're only men like me. What they've done, I can do."

"This is dull," said Baya.

"Dull," said Durham. He shook his head in wonderment, staring at her. She was beautiful. Tonight she wore white, and her hair curled softly on her neck, and her mouth was languorous, and her eyes—her eyes were hard. They were always hard, always making a liar out of that pliant, generous mouth. "Dull," he said. "No wonder you never got anywhere."

She flared up at that, and said a few things about him. He knew they were no longer true, so he could afford to be amused by them. He smiled and said,

"Let's not quarrel, Baya. This is goodbye, remember. Come on, we'll have a drink at the Miran."

They floated down on the bright spider web levels of the walkways, drifting east, stopping at the Miran and then going on to another drinking place, and then to another. The walks were thronged with other people, people from hundreds of stars, thousands of worlds. People of an infinite variety of sizes, shapes and colors, dressed in every imaginable and unimaginable fashion. Ambassadors, MP's, wives and mistresses, couriers, calculator jockeys, topologists and graph men, office girls, hairdressers, janitors, pimps, you-name-it. Durham saw them through a golden haze, and loved them, because they were the city and he was a part of them again.

He was out of the backwash of not-being. Hawtree had had to give in, and this footling errand to some dust speck nobody ever heard of was simply a necessary device to save his own face. All right, Hawtree, fine. We will go along with the gag. And you may inform the haughty Miss Hawtree, who can, believe us, be also the naughty Miss Hawtree, that we don't know if we want her back or not. We'll see.

"–take me with you," Baya was saying.

Durham shook his head. "Lone trip, honey. Can't possibly."

"Are you ashamed of me, Lloyd? That's it, you're ashamed to take me to Earth."

"No. No. Now, Baya–"

He looked at her. His vision was a bit blurred by now, he could see just enough background to wonder how the devil they'd got to this closed-in-looking drinking place. But Baya's face was clear enough. She was crying.

"Now, Baya, honey, it's not that–it's not that at all."

"Then why can't I go with you to Earth?"

"Because–listen, Baya, can you keep a secret?" He laughed, and his own laughter sounded blurred too. "Promise?"

"Promise."

"I–"

DEAD stop. The words rattled on his tongue, but remained unspoken. Why? Was it because of Baya's eyes, that wept tears but had no sorrow in them? He could see them quite clearly, and they were not sorrowful at all, but avid.

"I promised, Lloyd. You can tell me."

There was a table under his hands, with an exotically patterned cloth on it. He had no memory of having sat down at it. There was a wall of plasticoid cement covered with a crude mural in bright primaries. There was a low, vaulted ceiling, also painted. There were no windows.

"How did we get here?" Durham asked stupidly. "It's underground."

"It's just a place," Baya said impatiently. And then she said sharply, "What's the matter with you?"

Blood and fumes hammered together in his bulging temples, and his back felt cold. "Where's the men's room, Baya?"

Her mouth set in anger and disgust. She called, "Varnik!"

A tall powerful man with a very long neck and skin the color of a ripe plum came up to the table. He wore an apron.

Baya said, "Better take him there, Varnik."

The plum colored man took him and ran him to a door and put him through it. From there a servall took over. It was very efficient.

"Are you through, sir?"

"God, no. Not nearly."

One more word and you would have been through. Forever. Drunken blabbermouth Durham, smart aleck Durham, would-be big shot Durham, ready to babble out his secret and blow his last chance of a comeback. But why did Baya have to be so insistently curious?

Why, indeed?

He began to feel both sick and scared. After a time he made it to the row of basins and splashed cold water on his face and head. There was a mirror above the basin. He looked into it. "Hello, bum," he said.

Face it, Durham. You're a drunken bum. You are exactly what Willa Paulsen said you were, what Susan Hawtree said you were, what they all said you were. You get a second chance, and you go right out and get drunk and blow it. Or, almost. Another minute and you'd have blabbed everything you know to Baya.

Baya, who cried because he wouldn't tell her; who had brought him to this rathole.

He took a clearer look at it when he went shakily out of the men's room. The place was almost empty, and it had a close, smothery feeling. Durham had never liked these underground streets, this vaguely unsavory demi-world that wound itself around the foundations of the city. It was considered smart to go slumming here, but this place was somehow wrong.

There were a man and woman at a table across the room, a young, pale green couple who pretended too carefully not to see him. There was Varnik, the plum colored proprietor, at a tall desk beside the main door. And there was Baya at their table.

She handed him a glass when he came over. "Feel better? I ordered you a sedative."

Without sitting down he put the glass to his lips. It did not taste like any sedative he could remember, and he thought he had tried them all.

"I don't want it."

"Don't be a fool, Lloyd. Take it." Her eyes were cold now, and he was suddenly quite sure why he had been brought here.

Durham said softly, "Good night, tramp. Good night and goodbye." He ran around the table and made a rush for the entrance.

Varnik stepped from the tall desk to bar his way, holding out a piece of paper.

"Sir," he said. "Your check."

Durham heard three chairs scrape behind him. He did not pause. He bent and drove the point of his shoulder as hard as he could at a spot just above Varnik's wide belt. Varnik let go a gasping sigh and wheeled away. Durham went out the door.

The underground street was brightly lighted. It ran straight to right and left, under a low roof, and disappeared on either hand around a right angle turn. Durham went to the left for no particular reason. There were people on the street. He dodged among them, running. They stopped and stared at him, and there was an echo of other feet behind him, also running. He sped around the corner, and it occurred to him that he was completely lost, that he did not even know what part of the city lay above him, or how far. There were different levels to this under-city, following down the foundations, the conduits and tubes and sewers and pumping stations. For the first time he began to feel genuinely trapped, and genuinely afraid.

The street ran straight ahead until it ended against a buttressed foundation wall. There were doors and windows on either side of it. People lived here. There were joints, some fancy-exotic for the carriage trade, others just joints. A couple of smaller streets opened off it,

darker and more winding. Durham plunged into one, pausing briefly
to look back. Fleeting like deer around the corner were the young
pale green couple who had sat at the other table in Varnik's. There
was something about the purposeful way they ran that sent a quiver
of pure terror through Durham's insides.

He ran again, as hard as he could, wondering who the devil they
were and what they wanted with him.

What did anyone want with him, and the small bit of a secret he
carried?

THE narrow street wound and twined. Clearly echoing along the
vault of the roof he could hear footsteps. One. Two. Coming fast. He
saw an opening no wider than a crack in the wall. He turned into
it. It was quite dark in there and he knew he could not go much
farther, and that fact added to his burden of shame. There had been
a time when this much of a sprint would hardly have breathed him.
He tottered on, looking for a place to hide in, and there wasn't any,
and his heart banged and floundered against his ribs, and the muscles
of his thighs were like wet strings.

There was a square opening with blank walls all around it and a
great big manhole cover in the middle. There was the way he had
come in, and there was another narrow way he might have come
out, but Varnik was coming through it, running a little crooked and
breathing hard. He stopped when he saw Durham. Baya, panting up
behind, almost ran into him. Varnik grunted and sprang.

With feeble fierceness, Durham resisted. It got him nowhere. The
plum colored man struck him several times out of pure pique, cursing Durham for making trouble, for bruising his gut, for making him
run like this. Baya stood by and watched.

"Will you behave now?" Varnik demanded. He whacked Durham
again, and Durham glared at him out of dazed eyes and felt the world
tilt and slide away from him.

Suddenly there were new voices, footsteps, confusion. He fell,
what seemed a long way but was really only to his hands and knees.

The young couple had come into the square space. They were
small lithe people, muscled like ocelots, and their skin color was a

pale green, very pretty, and characteristic of several different races, but no good for identification here. The girl's tunic had slipped aside over the breast, and the skin there was a clear gold, like new country butter. They both had guns in their strong little fists, and they were speaking over Durham to Varnik and Baya.

"We will question this man alone."

"Oh, no," said Varnik angrily. "You don't get away with that." Baya bent over Durham. "Come on, lover," she said. "Get up." Her voice was cooing. To the strangers she said, "That wasn't our deal at all."

"You failed," said the girl with the two-colored skin, and she fired a beam with frightening accuracy, exactly between them. A piece of the wall behind them fused and flared. Varnik's eyes came wide open.

"Well," he said. "Well, if that's the way you feel about it."

He turned. Baya hesitated, and the muzzle of the gun began to move her way. She snarled something in her own language and decided to go after Varnik.

Durham got his hands and feet bunched under him. He didn't know what he was going to do, but he knew that once he was left alone with the two small fleet strangers he would eventually talk, and after that it would not matter much what happened to him.

He said to them, hopefully, "You have the wrong man. I don't know—"

There were the five of them in the small space. There were the two couples facing each other, and Durham on his knees between them. And then there was something else.

There was a spiky shadow, perfectly black, of undetermined size and nameless shape, except that it was spiky.

Baya did not quite scream. She pressed against Varnik, and they both recoiled into the alley mouth. The young couple paled under their greenness, and they, too, drew back. Durham crouched on the ground.

The shadow bounded and rolled and leaped through the air and hung cloudlike over Durham's head. Suddenly it shrieked out, in a high, toneless voice like that of a deaf child, a clatter of gibberish in which one syllable stood clear, repeated several times.

328

"Jubb!" said the shadow. "Jubb! Jubb! Jubb!"

III

JUBB.

It might have been a name, a curse, or a battle cry. Whatever it was, the young couple did not like it. Their faces twisted into slim masks of hate. They raised their guns at the shadow, and the shadow laughed. Abruptly it bunched up small and shot at them.

Durham heard them yell, in pain or fright or both, and he heard their running feet, but he did not see what happened to them. He was going away himself, down the narrow alley that Varnik and Baya were no longer interested in blocking. When he reached the end of the alley he came out onto a well lighted street with lots of people on it, but he still did not feel safe.

Varnik and Baya were not far away. Baya was leaning against a wall, with her mouth wide open. She was not used to running. Varnik was standing beside her looking sulky. He scowled at Durham when he came out of the alley. Durham stopped, bracing himself and ready to yell for help. But Varnik shook his head. "Nyuh!" he said.

Baya panted. "What's the matter, you afraid?"

"Yes," said Varnik. "Those two little green ones, they are not playing for fun. And that black one—" He quivered all over. "I'm afraid. I see you again, Baya."

He went away. Baya was close onto tears, partly from her own fright, partly from sheer fury and frustration. But she did not cry. She turned and looked at Durham.

"What got into you?" she said. "It was all set, and then you had to louse it up." She cursed him. "It's just like you, Lloyd, to cost me a nice chunk of money."

"Who are those people, Baya?"

"They didn't tell me. I didn't ask."

"Total strangers, eh?"

"Turned up this afternoon at my apartment. I should think you could tell. They're not the type *I* run with."

"No." He frowned, still breathing hard and wiping sweat from his face. "How did they know about us?"

She shrugged, and said maliciously, "Somebody must have told them. Well, so long, Lloyd. I wish you all the luck you deserve."

She walked off slowly, patting her hair into place, straightening the line of her white dress. She did not look back. Durham watched her for a second. Then he began to walk as fast as he could in the opposite direction, keeping in the brightest lights. After a bit he found a stairwalk. He rode up on it through two levels, and all the while the roots of his hair were prickling and he was darting nervous glances over his shoulder and into the air over his head.

Jubb. Jubb. Jubb.

He envied Varnik who could go away and forget the whole thing.

It was still night when he reached the surface. The shadow did not seem to have followed him, but how could you tell? Even a city as brilliantly lighted as The Hub always has shadowy corners by night. He kept listening for that high, flat, hooting voice. It did not speak to him, and he hailed a skycab, appalled by how little time he had left to catch the pre-dawn ferry.

He made it with no minutes to spare. He found a place on the dark side and settled himself for the four-hour run, and then everything caught up to him at once and he began to shake. He sat there in the grip of a violent reaction, living over again Hawtree's instructions and the evening with Baya and the nightmare run through the underground streets, and the coming of the shadow. *The dark birds will soon fly.* Was that enough for people to kill for? It might be if they had an interest in those ships, but the young couple did not look the type. And the shadow?

He shivered and looked out the port. The long thin shadow of the ship extended itself indefinitely into space, but all around it there was light, and the curve of the planet below was a blaze of gold. Down there was Hawtree and a big part of his life. Above and ahead was the huge cool face of the moon, and that was the future, all unexplored. Durham clenched his cold hands together between his knees and thought, I've got to do this, stay sober and do it, a little for Hawtree but mostly for myself. A man can't look at himself twice the way I did tonight. Once is all he can stand. And once ought to be enough.

The brightness blurred and swam. Presently he slept, and his dreams were thronged with shadows hooting "Jubb! Jubb! Jubb!"

Four hours later Durham walked across the vast main rotunda of the lunar spaceport, dropping his little bundle of passport and ticket as casually as he could. He continued on to the newsstand and made a pretense of looking over the half credit microbooks, waiting.

While he waited he wondered. He wondered how the young couple had known about Baya. He wondered what the shadow was and where it came from, and why it had defended him from the young couple, and what was the meaning of the rather ridiculous word "Jubb." He wondered if he wasn't crazy not to pick up his ticket to Earth and use it.

He wanted a drink very badly.

A uniformed attendant came and said, "I think you dropped this, sir."

He held out a passport with a ticket folded in it. Durham examined them, put them in his pocket, and tipped the attendant, who went away. Durham bought three microbooks and moved on. He could not see anybody watching him, and he told himself it was only nerves that made the skin creep on his back as though eyes were boring into it.

The switch had been made all right on his papers. His name was now John Mills Watson and he had a passage to Nanta Dik aboard the freighter *Margaretta K.* He still wanted a drink. He was determined that he would not go and get it, and he headed grimly for a stairwalk that led down to the port cab system. He had almost stepped onto it, and then from the loudspeakers all over the huge rotunda a voice boomed out, saying,

"Mr. Lloyd Durham, please come to the Information Desk."

Durham flinched as though somebody had struck him. He thought, Hawtree's sent word to recall me. Perhaps it was a trap.

HE APPROACHED the desk cautiously, while his name continued to blare forth from the loudspeakers. Somebody was standing there.

A woman, with her back to him. He had not seen that back for over a year, not since the night of the accident, but he had not forgotten it.

"Hello, Susan," he said.

She turned around, and he added bitterly, "He needn't have sent *you.*" He was convinced now that she had come to call him back.

She seemed surprised. "Who?"

"Your father."

"Dad? Good heavens, Lloyd, you don't suppose he knows I'm here!" She was tall, as he remembered her, and handsome, and beautifully dressed, and very self-assured. She smiled, one of those brittle things with no humor in it, and then she asked, "How long have you before take-off?"

Durham said slowly, "Time enough."

"We can't talk here."

"No. Come on, I'll buy you a drink."

They walked in silence to the crowded, noisy spaceport bar. They found a place and sat down. Durham ordered. Susan Hawtree sat opening and closing her handbag as though the operation was of the most absorbing interest.

He asked, "Why did you come here?"

"It seemed as though somebody ought to say good-bye."

"Who told you I was leaving?"

"I have a friend in the travel office. She tells me if anybody I know books passage home."

"Convenient."

"Yes."

The drinks came. There was a clatter of voices, speaking in a thousand tongues, laughing, crying, saying hello and good-bye and till we meet again. Susan turned her glass round and round in her fingers, and Durham watched her.

"I'm sorry, Lloyd. Sorry everything could not have turned out better."

"Yes. So am I."

"I hope you'll have better luck at home."

"Thanks."

Another silence in which Durham tried hard to figure her angle.

He said, "I heard you tried to talk your father into giving me another chance. Thanks for that."

She stared at him blankly and shook her head. "You know how Dad feels about you. I've never dared mention your name." A cold feeling settled in the pit of Durham's stomach. *There's somebody else, Lloyd, who wanted you to have another chance.* Fatherly intuition?

Or a big fat lie?

Let's face it, Durham, why would Hawtree send you on a mission to the dog pound? There are ten billion people on The Hub. He could have found somebody else.

The whole business smells. It reeks.

But wait. Suppose he sent Susan here to test me; to see if I'd talk? Not too believable, but a pleasanter belief than the alternative. Let's see.

"Susan. Look, I can say this now because I'm going home and that's the end of it. We won't see each other any more. I should never have got engaged to Willa, I didn't love her. It was you all the time."

He caught the quick glint of tears in her eyes and was appalled. Tears for him? From Susan Hawtree?

"That's why I went with you that night," she whispered. "I thought I could take you from her. I thought I could make you be what you ought to be—oh, damn you, Lloyd, I should never have come here!"

She jumped up and walked rapidly away from the table. He followed her, with his eyes and his mouth both wide open and something very strange happening inside him.

One thing sure. She was no plant.

"Susan."

"Don't you have to get aboard or something?"

"Yes, but—Susan, ride down with me, I want to talk to you."

"There's nothing to talk about."

But she went to the stairwalk with him, and rode down, her face turned away and her head held so high she seemed to tower over him.

"Susan," he said. "Do you think—could you give me—"

No, that's not the gambit. But what do you say—Susan, I'm a changed man. Susan, wait for me?

The stairwalk slid them gently off onto a very long platform. There was a crowd on it, sorting itself into the endless lines of purple monorail taxis that moved along both sides.

"Susan."

"Good-bye, Lloyd."

"No, wait a minute. Please. I don't know quite how—"

Suddenly they were not alone. A young couple had joined them. The color of their skin had changed from pale green to a warm burnt orange, and their clothing was different, but Durham recognized them without difficulty. A hard object prodded him in the side, and the young man, smiling, said to him, "Get into that cab." The woman, also smiling, said to Susan Hawtree, "Don't scream. Keep perfectly quiet."

Susan's face went white. She looked at Durham, and Durham said to the young man, "Let her go, she has nothing to do with this!"

"Get in the cab," said the young man. "Both of you."

"I think," said Susan, "we'd better do it."

They got in. The doors closed automatically behind them. The young man, with his free hand, took out a ticket and laid it in the scanner slot, with the code number of the ship's docking area uppermost. The taxi clicked, hummed, and took off smoothly.

Durham saw the ticket as the young man removed it from the scanner. It was a passage to Nanta Dik aboard the freighter *Margaretta K.*

IV

THE MONORAILS came out onto the surface in bunches like very massive cables and then began to branch out, the separate "wires" of the cables eventually spreading into a network that covered the entire moon. The taxi picked up speed, clicking over points as it swerved and swung, feeling its way onto the one clear track that led where its scanner had told it to go. Durham was aware obliquely of other monorail taxis in uncountable numbers going like the devil in all directions, and of other types of machines moving below on the surface, and of mobile cranes that walked like buildings, and of an horizon filled with the upthrust noses of great ships like the towers of some fantastic city. Beside him Susan Hawtree sat, rigid and quivering, and before him on the opposite seat were the two young people with the guns.

Durham said, in a voice thick with anger and fright, "Why did you have to drag her into it?"

The man shrugged. "She is perhaps part of the conspiracy. In any case, she would have made an alarm."

"What do you mean, conspiracy? I'm going home to Earth. She came to say good-bye—" Durham leaned forward. "You're the same two bastards from last night. What do you—"

"Please," said the man, contemptuously. He gestured with the gun. "You will both sit still with your hands behind your heads. So. Wanbecq-ai will search you. If either one should attempt to interfere, the other will suffer for it."

The wiry young woman did her work swiftly and efficiently. "No weapons," she said. "Hai! Wanbecq, look here!" She began to gabble in a strange tongue, pointing to Durham's passport and ticket, and then to Susan's ID card. Wanbecq's narrow eyes narrowed still further.

"So," he said to Durham. "Your name has changed since yesterday, Mr. Watson. And for one who returns to Sol III, you choose a long way around."

Susan stared hard at Durham. "What's he talking about?"

"Never mind. Listen, you—Wanbecq, is that your name? Miss Hawtree has nothing to do with any of this. Her father—"

"Is a part of the embassy which sent you out," said Wanbecq, flicking Susan's ID card with his finger. "Do not expect me to believe foolishness, Mr. Watson-Durham." He spoke rapidly to Wanbecq-ai. She nodded, and they both turned to Susan.

"Obviously you were sent with instructions for Mr. Durham. Will you tell us now what they were?"

Susan's face was such a blank of amazement that Durham would have laughed if the situation had not been so extremely unfunny.

"Nobody sent me with anything. Nobody even knows I came. Lloyd, are these people crazy? Are you crazy? What's going on here?"

He said, "I'm not sure myself. But I think there are only two possibilities. One, your father is a scoundrel. Two, he's a fool being used by scoundrels. Take your pick. In either case, I'm the goat."

Her white cheeks turned absolutely crimson. She tried twice to say something to Durham. Then she turned and said to the Wanbecqs, "I've had enough of this. Let me out."

They merely glanced at her and went on talking.

"You might as well relax," said Durham to her, in colloquial English, hoping the Wanbecqs could not understand it. "I'm sorry you got into this, and I'll try to get you out, but don't do anything silly."

She called him a name she had never learned in the Embassy drawing rooms. There was a manual switch recessed in the body of the taxi, high up and sealed in with a special plastic. It said EMERGENCY on it. Susan took off her shoe and swung.

The plastic shattered. Susan dropped the shoe and grabbed for the switch. Wanbecq yelled. Wanbecq-ai leaped headlong for Susan and bore her back onto the seat. She was using her gun flatwise in her hand, solely as a club. Susan let out one furious wail.

And Durham, moving more by instinct than by conscious thought, grabbed Wanbecq-ai's uplifted arm and pulled her over squalling onto his lap.

Wanbecq started forward from the opposite seat.

"Don't," said Durham. He had Wanbecq-ai's wrist in one hand and her neck in the other, and he was not being gentle. Wanbecq-ai covered him, and the two of them together covered Susan. Wanbecq stood with his knees bent for a spring, his gun flicking back and forth uncertainly. Wanbecq-ai had stopped squalling. Her face was turning dark. Susan huddled where she was, half stunned. Durham shifted his grip on Wanbecq-ai's arm and got the gun into his own hand.

"Now," he said to Wanbecq. "Drop it."

Wanbecq dropped it. Durham scrabbled it in with his heel until it was between his own feet. Then he heaved Wanbecq-ai forcibly at her husband. It was like heaving a rag doll, and while Wanbecq was dealing with her Durham managed to pick up the other gun.

Susan lifted her head. She looked around with glassy eyes and then, with single-minded persistence, she got up.

Durham said sharply, "Sit down!"

Susan reached up for the emergency.

Durham smacked her across the stomach with the back of his left hand, not daring to take his eyes off the Wanbecqs. She doubled over it and sat down again. Durham said, "All right now, damn it, all of you—sit still!"

THE taxi sped on its humming rail, farther and farther into the reaches of the spaceport. Below there were the wide clear spaces of the landing aprons, and great ships standing in them, their tails down and their noses high in the air, high above the monorail, towering over the freight belts and the multitude of machines that served them.

Ahead there was the onracing edge of twilight, and beyond it, coming swiftly, was the lunar night.

Durham said to Wanbecq, "What's this all about?"

Wanbecq sneered.

"You know," said Durham, "there's a law against changing the color of your skin for the purpose of committing criminal acts. That's so the wrong people won't get blamed. There's a law against carrying lethal weapons. There is even, humorously enough, a law against espionage on The Hub. You know I'm going to turn you over to the authorities?"

Again Wanbecq sneered. He was a hateful little man, but he looked so young and so proudly martyred that Durham almost felt sorry for him.

Almost. Not quite.

"On second thought," he said, "I guess I'll save you both for Jubb."

That was a random shot, prompted by the memory of how their faces looked when the shadow-thing had squealed that word at them.

It hit. Wanbecq's face became distorted with a fanatic hatred, and Wanbecq-ai, rubbing her throat, croaked, "Then you *are* in league with The Beast."

She pronounced that name with unmistakable capitals.

"Who said I was?" asked Durham.

"The darkbird came to help you. It told us Jubb had claimed you."

"It did," said Durham softly, "did it?" The dark birds will soon fly. The dark birds merely refer to a couple of ships engaged in poaching. That's what you say, Mr. Hawtree.

"What is a darkbird? You mean that shadow thing?"

"They are the servants, the familiars of The Beast," said Wanbecq. "The instruments by which he hopes to enslave all humanity. Do not pretend, Mr. Durham."

"I'm not. This Jubb—what is he beside The Beast?"

Wanbecq stared at him, and Durham made a menacing gesture. "Come on, I want to know."

"Jubb is the ruler of Senya Dik."

"And Senya Dik?"

"Our sister planet. A dark and evil sister, plotting our destruction. A demon sister, Mr. Durham. Have you ever heard of the Bitter Star?"

"I never heard of any of it but I find it interesting. Go on."

"Whoever controls the darkbirds controls the Star, and whoever controls the Star can do anything he wishes. This is Jubb." Wanbecq thrust out his hands. "You're human, Mr. Durham. If you have sold your soul, take it back again. Fight with us, not against us."

"I assume," said Durham, "that Jubb is not human."

Wanbecq-ai made an abrupt sound of disgust. "This is silly, Mr. Durham. If you know so little why are you going to Nanta Dik at all?"

Durham did not answer. He did not have any answer to that one. Wondered if ever he would have it.

"If you are so ignorant," continued Wanbecq-ai viciously, "of course you don't know that the Terran consul Karlovic is over his head in intrigue, conniving with Jubb in order to make this treaty of Federation."

Durham sat up straight. "A treaty of *what?*"

"The sector," said Wanbecq slowly, "will belong either to the human race or to the beast, but it cannot belong to both."

"Federation," said Durham, answering his own question. And suddenly many formless things began to fit together into a shape that was still cloudy but had a sinister solidity. In order for a solar system to become a member of the Federation its member planets were required to have achieved unity among themselves, with common citizenship, a common council, common laws. And in order for a sub-sector to become federated, all its solar systems must have reached a like accord.

In this case, since the system of the two Diks was the only inhabited one in the sub-sector, the two things were the same. The fate of 9G rested solely on the behavior of two planets.

If 9G remained unfederated, the company or companies engaged in mining or other business under local license could continue to operate in almost any way they chose as long as they kept the local officials happy. They could strip the whole area of its mineral resources, pile up incredible fortunes, and leave the native worlds with nothing. But if 9G became a member of the Federation, Federation law would immediately step in, and Federation enforcement of same, and if there were any abuses of native rights, the people responsible would suffer for it.

Postulate a company. Postulate a connection between it and Hawtree. Postulate and postulate.

At around three hundred miles an hour the taxi plunged into the twilight zone. Light sprang on automatically. Outside it became dark very swiftly, and the darkness roared, and glittered with a million lamps.

"Who," asked Durham, "is principally against your two worlds uniting so that the treaty can go through?"

"All of us," said Wanbecq fiercely. "Shall we give up our rights, our independence, our human institutions, everything our race has stood for—"

339

Wanbecq-ai cried out, "We will never unite, never! No one can force us to betray our species!"

Susan began to cry.

"Please," said Durham. "Baby. You're all right."

"You hit me."

"I had to. I'll apologize later. Be quiet now, Susan, please." He turned back to the Wanbecqs. "Everybody on Nanta Dik feels that way?"

"There are traitors everywhere," said Wanbecq darkly. "Some of them, unfortunately, are in positions of power."

"They won't be for long," said Wanbecq-ai. "Look here, Mr. Durham, you're going to Nanta Dik with a message. We aren't the only ones who want to know what it is. Jubb has sent a darkbird for you. Take my advice. Tell us your message and go back to The Hub."

Susan said in a nasty muffled voice, "You're insane. Nobody would trust him with a message to the milkman. He lost his job because he couldn't be trusted."

Without rancor, Durham said, "You're absolutely right, darling. And wouldn't it be strangely fitting if that's why I got my job back again?" He said to the Wanbecqs, "Somebody tipped you off about me. Who?"

"We know him only as a friend of humanity."

"Somebody must have sent you here from Nanta Dik."

"On our world there are many friends of humanity. Think of them, Mr. Durham, when you kiss the Bitter Star."

THE taxi slowed, strongly, smoothly. The blurred panorama of lights and ships became separable into individual shapes. Durham stared out ahead. There was the form of a freighter, ugly and immensely powerful, on a landing apron only partially lighted. The *Margaretta K.*

Durham asked, "Who owns her?"

"Universal Minerals."

"And who owns Universal Minerals?"

"Several people, I think, all Earthmen."

"Who speaks for Universal Minerals on Nanta Dik?"

A little reluctantly, Wanbecq said, "There is a man named Morrison."

The name rang no bell in Durham's mind. It brought no visible reaction to Susan's face either, though he was watching it closely.

"And how," he asked, "does Morrison feel about humanity?"

"Ask the Bitter Star," said Wanbecq, and the taxi slid to a halt beside the platform on which Durham now saw that several men were standing. Wanbecq and Wanbecq-ai hunched forward expectantly.

"No," said Durham. "I'm getting out, but you're not." He nudged Susan. "Get ready."

The doors slid open automatically. Susan scrambled out. Durham went right behind her, twisted like a cat in the opening, and splashed a brief warning blast off the floor at the feet of the Wanbecqs, who had raised a frantic cry and were trying to follow.

Susan said breathlessly, "Oh!"

The men who had been standing on the platform were now rushing forward. Three were lean and butter-colored. One was a burly Earthman, who said in a tone of amazement, "What the hell—"

"Hold it!" Durham shouted. He swept Susan behind him and tried to cover all fronts at once, not knowing whether the men were there to capture him or were only there by chance and responding to the Wanbecqs' cry for help. "These people attacked us. I have passage on your ship—"

From out of the night there came a shrill, flat, hooting cry of "Jubb! Jubb! Jubb!"

The butter-colored men yelled. They scattered away and out, their feet scrabbling on the platform. The Earthman was slower and more belligerent. He turned around and the spiky little blob of darkness came leaping at him. He put up his hands and struck at it, and the darkbird hooted as the fists passed through it, crackling. The Earthman opened his mouth in a round shocked O and went rigid, rising up on the tips of his toes. The darkbird seemed to merge with his skull for the fraction of a second, and he crumpled down with his mouth still open and his chest rising and falling heavily. The darkbird swooped toward Durham.

Durham fired at it.

It soaked up part of the beam and left the rest, like a well-fed cat rejecting an overplus of milk. It darted past Durham and into the taxi, where it bounced agilely, once and twice. Wanbecq and Wanbecq-ai fell down on the floor. The doors closed softly and the taxi mechanism whirred and the rail hummed as it took off, heading back to the main terminal. The darkbird returned to Durham.

Susan said in a strange voice, "What is that?"

"Never mind now. Come on."

He started to drag her toward the ramp that led down from the platform. She fought him. She was getting hysterical, and he didn't blame her. The darkbird followed along behind. When they readied the level, Susan planted her feet mulishly and refused to go any farther.

"I don't dare leave you alone out here," he said desperately. "Come along to the ship and the captain will see that you get back safely—"

The darkbird circled and dived at Susan. She bolted. It dived at Durham. He bolted too, off to the right, to the edge of the apron, where he caught up with Susan again. They ran between the storage sheds, onto a spur of the freight-belt system. It was still now, not carrying any freight. They tried to run across it to the other side, but the darkbird drove them back. It was immediately apparent, of course, that the thing was herding them. He shouted at it to let Susan alone, but it did not listen to him. And he thought, it wants us to go somewhere, so it won't knock us out. Maybe? It's worth a try.

He took Susan and jumped off the belt and ran.

The darkbird touched him, ever so gently. He tried to yell, gave up, and tottered back where it wanted him to go, with every nerve in him pulled taut and twangling in a horrible half-pleasurable fashion that made his legs and arms move unnaturally, as though he were dancing. The darkbird followed, once again placid and unconcerned.

They went along the belt for some distance. It was limber, sagging a bit between the giant rollers, and it boomed under their feet with a sharp slapping sound. Susan stumbled so often he picked her up and carried her. There was nobody to call to, nobody to ask for help. The towering ships were far away.

The darkbird nudged him again at last, out across a landing apron where a very strange looking ship stood in the solitary majesty of impending take-off. The flood lights were blinking at twenty-second intervals, visual warning to stand clear, and Durham ran staggering through a stroboscopic nightmare, with the white-faced girl in his arms.

Dark, light. Black, bright. A haze of exhaustion swam before his eyes. Things moved in it, jerky shapes in an old film, in an antique penny peep show. Day, night. Dark, bright. The things moved closer, unhuman things clad in fantastic pressure suits. Durham screamed.

He tried to run again, and the darkbird touched him. Once more there was the unbearable twitching of the nerves and he danced in the black, bright, day, night. He danced into a large box that was waiting for him, and he kept going until he struck the end wall of hard metal. He turned then, and saw the very thick door go sighing shut and the dogs go slipping into place snick-snick one after the other, and it was too late even to try to get out again.

He set Susan down as gently as he could and sank down beside her. The floor moved up under him sharply. There was a bonging and clattering of tackle overhead, and then a sickening sidewise lurch. The on-off pattern of the light changed outside the two round windows that were in the box. It became a steady green, in which his hands showed like two sickly-white butterflies on his knees. There were more noises, hollow and far away, and then a second lurch, a lift, a drop, and after that a larger motion encompassing the box and the entire locus in which it stood.

Durham put his face in his hands and gave up.

V

SUSAN was screaming. Let me out, let me out. She was pounding on something. Durham started up. He must have slept or passed out. The box was perfectly still now. There was no sense of motion. But he could tell by the change in gravity that the ship was in space.

Susan was by one of the windows. She was pounding on it with her favorite implement, the heel of her shoe. Durham went to her and glanced out. Cold sweat broke out on him, and he grabbed her hand.

"Stop it! Are you crazy?" He wrenched the shoe from her and threw it across the small space of the box. Then he felt of the glass, peering at it, frantic lest she should have cracked it.

"I'm going to get out," said Susan grimly, and groped around for something heavier.

"Look." He shook her and turned her face to the window. "Do you see that air out there?"

The box now stood in a large empty hold. He could see the curve of the ship's hull, ribbed with tremendous struts of steel, and a deck of metal plates, glistening in the green light. *Green* light? Earth should have a yellow-white type light, the kind that the sun gives off. Well, yes—but suppose that the sun was green?

Nanta Dik circles a green star.

So does Senya Dik. Those creatures outside the ship were anything but humanoid. Jubb's darkbird herded us in here. Easy. Now we know.

"What about the air?" asked Susan. "Let go of me."

"It's poisonous. Can't you tell by looking at it?" It rolled and roiled and sluggishly shifted in vapors of thick chartreuse and vivid green. "And don't you remember, they were wearing pressure suits? They couldn't live in our atmosphere. We surely couldn't live in theirs."

There was no answer.

"Susan. Susan?"

"I want to go home," she said, and began to cry.

"There now, Susie. Take it—"

"Don't call me Susie!"

"All right, but take it easy. I'll find out what the situation is and then I'll—"

"You'll what? You'll make a mess of things just like you always have. You'll get me into more trouble, just like you got me into this. You're no good, Lloyd, and I wish I'd never seen you. I wish I'd never come to say good-bye!" She rushed to the window and began to pound on it again, this time with her fists.

Durham hauled her away and shook her until her jaw rattled together. "I'm sorry you came too," he said savagely. "You're the last person in the galaxy I'd pick to be in trouble with. A damned spoiled female with no honesty, no courage, no nothing but your father's position to trade on." He wrapped his arms tight around her. "Hell, this is no time to be quarrelling. Let's both keep our mouths shut. Come on, honey, we're not dead yet."

She choked a little, and stood trembling against him. Then she said,

"I think I fell over a chair a while ago. Maybe there's a lamp. Let's look."

The green light was dim, but their eyes were used to it. They found a lamp and turned it on. The box was flooded with a clear white glare, very grateful to Earthly senses. Durham looked around and said slowly, "I'll be damned."

The box was about the size of a small room. It had in it an armchair, a bunk, compact cupboards and lockers, a sink and hotplate, and a curtained-off corner with a sanitary device. Durham turned on one of the sink taps. Water came out. He turned it off and went and sat down in the armchair.

"I'm damned," he said again.

"Freezer," said Susan, looking into things. "Food concentrates. Pots and pans. Blanket. Change of clothes—all men's. Booze, two bottles of it. Rack of microbooks. Somebody went to a lot of trouble."

"Yes."

"Pretty comfortable. Everything you need, all self-contained."

"Uh."

"But Lloyd—it's only for one."

He said dismally, "We'll take turns on the bunk." But it wasn't the bunk that worried him. He went and looked out of the other window. By craning his head he could see an assembly of storage tanks, pressure tanks, pumps, purifiers, blower units, all tightly sealed against any admixture of Senyan air. That, too, was only for one. A most ghastly claustrophobia came over Durham, and for a moment he saw Susan, not as a spoiled and pretty girl, but as his rival for the oxygen that was life.

Susan said, "Lloyd. Something is coming in."

For an instant he thought she meant into the box, and then he realized that the reverberating clang he heard must be the hatch door of the hold. He joined her at the opposite window.

There were two—no, three dark shapes coming toward the box, moving swiftly through the green and chartreuse vapors. They undulated on two pairs of stubby legs set fore and aft under a flexible lower body. Their upper bodies, carried erect, were rather bulbous and tall, with well-defined heads and two sets of specialized arms, the lower ones thick and powerful for heavy work, the upper ones as delicate as an engraver's fine tools. Their skin was a glossy black, almost like patent leather. They wore neat harnesses of what looked like metal webbing in the way of dress, and on the breast strap each one carried an insigne.

"Ship's officers," Durham guessed. "Probably one of them's the captain."

"They're horrible," said Susan. She backed away from window until the end of the bunk caught her behind the knees and she sat down.

Durham laughed. "Fine pair of cosmopolites we are. We're used to the idea of non-humanoids. There are a lot of them on The Hub, but they're mostly segregated by necessity, so we practically never really see any. But now we're the ones who have to be segregated. And the reality is quite another thing from the idea, isn't it?"

HE BACKED away himself, a step or two, until shame made him stop. The three non-humanoids came and looked with large iridescent eyes, through the window. Their oddly shaped mouths moved rapidly, so he knew that they were talking, and their slender upper arms were as mobile and expressive as the hands of so many girls at a sorority tea. Then one of them turned and did something to the wall of the box, and suddenly Durham could hear them clearly. There was a speaker device beside the window. Durham sprang at it.

"Can you hear me? Can you hear me out there? Listen, you have no right to do this, you've got to take us back! Miss Hawtree is the daughter of—"

"Mr. Durham." The voice was unhuman but strong, and the esperanto it spoke was perfectly understandable. "Please calm yourself and listen to what I have to say. I appreciate your feelings—"

"Hah!"

"—but there is nothing I can do about it. I have my orders, and I can assure you—"

"From Jubb?"

"You'll be fully informed when you reach Senya Dik. Meanwhile, I can assure you that no harm will come to you, now or later. So please put your fears at rest. A little patience—"

Susan had leaped up. Now she flung herself upon the speaker mike. "What about me?"

"Your presence was unexpected, and I fear it's going to be rather difficult for you both. But you must make the best of it. In regard to air and water, I must caution you that the supply will hardly be adequate for you both unless you are extremely careful."

This had not occurred to Susan before.

"You mean—"

"I mean that you must use no more water than is absolutely necessary for drinking and preparing your food. The food you must share between you, on half rations. As for the air—"

"Yes," said Durham. "What about the air?"

"I believe that activity has the effect of increasing your metabolism, thereby consuming more oxygen. So I would advise you both to move and speak as little as possible. Remain calm. Remain quiet. In that way you should be able to survive. It is not that we are grudging. It is simply that we cannot share any of our supplies with you, because you are alien life forms and totally incompatible. If we had known there would be two, we would have prepared. As it is, you must work together to conserve."

"But," said Susan, "but this isn't fair, it isn't right! You'll take me back or my father will see to it—"

"Keep this speaker open," said the Senyan, "so that you will be sure to hear the audio signal, a sustained note repeated at intervals of forty seconds. Prepare to enter overdrive."

He did not say good-bye. He merely went away with his two officers. Susan screamed after them. Durham clapped his hand over her mouth, and took her forcibly and put her on the bunk.

"Lie there," he said. "Quiet. Didn't you hear him? Don't move, don't talk."

He sat down in the chair, consciously trying not to breathe deeply.

"But—"

"Shut up."

"Don't you say shut up to me, Lloyd. This is all your fault."

"My fault? Mine? Because you had to shove yourself in—"

"Shove myself? Father was right about you. And it is your fault. If you hadn't asked me to ride down with you—"

"Oh, shut up, damn it, that's just like a woman! If you knew your next breath was your last one you'd still have to use it for talk. You want to asphyxiate us both with your gabbling?"

She was quiet for a long while. Then he realized that she was crying.

"Lloyd, I'm scared."

"So am I." He began to laugh. "When I come to think of it, it was your father that got us both into this. I hope he sweats blood in great gory streams."

"You're a drunken ungrateful swine! If dad really did give you another chance—"

"Ah ah! Remember the oxygen! He did. And I was such a fatheaded idiot I thought it was on the level. I even reformed." He laughed again, briefly. "Overcome with gratitude, I did exactly what I was supposed not to do. I sobered up and held my tongue."

"I don't understand at all."

"I was supposed to talk, Susan. I was given a message, and I was supposed to babble it all over The Hub. I don't know exactly what that message was intended to trigger off when it got into circulation. Probably a war. But I'll bet I know what I triggered off by not talking. Trouble for your old man."

"I don't believe a word of it."

Durham shrugged. It was very little effort to reach out and lift a bottle from a nearby cupboard. He opened it and took a long pull.

Then he looked at the bottle, shook his head, and passed it to Susan.

She made a derisive noise, and he shrugged again.

"That's right. Funny thing. First I was stricken with remorse and determined to be worthy. Now I'm just mad. Before I get through, I'm going to hang your father higher than Haman."

The audio signal, shrill and insistent and sounding somehow as unhuman as the voices of the Senyans, came piercingly through the speaker.

Susan gasped. "Wherever they're taking us – they're not going to kill us, are they?"

"I think they want to question us. I think some dirty work is going on, one of those million-credit-swindle things you hear about once in a while, and I think your father is right up to his neck in it. If I'm right, that's the chief reason you were brought along."

"I think you're a dirty low down liar," she said, in a voice he could hardly hear.

The signal continued to squeal. Durham moved to the bunk. "Slide over."

"No."

But she did not fight him when he pushed himself in beside her and took her in his arms.

"The haughty Miss Hawtree," he said, and smiled. "You're a mess. Hair in your eyes. Make-up all smeared. Tears dripping off the end of your nose."

The light dimmed, became strange and eerie.

"They could have made this damned bunk a little wider."

"It doesn't matter. After a trip like this, I won't have any reputation left, anyway. Nobody would believe me on oath."

The fabric of the ship shifted, strained, slipped, moved. The fabric of Durham's body did likewise. He set his teeth and said,

"Don't worry, dear. I can always ask the captain to marry us."

By the time the audio-signal shrilled again, heralding a return to solar system speeds and space, it seemed that ages had passed.

THEY did not talk about marriage now, even in jest. They hated each other. "Cabin fever," they had said politely for a while, making excuses. But they did not bother with excuses any more. They just had simply and quietly loathed each other, as the long, timeless time went by.

Pity, too, thought Durham, looking at Susan where she lay in the bunk. She's really a handsome wench, even without all the makeup and the hairdo and those incredible undergarments that women use, as though they were semi-liquescent. Just lying there in her slip now, she looks younger, gentler, nice and soft, as though she'd be pleasant to hold in your arms again if you had the strength and the oxygen and if you didn't hate her so.

"Lloyd?"

"Huh?"

"How long before we land?"

"How should I know?"

"Well, you could find out."

"You find out. You can yell as loud as I can. Louder."

"I'll yell," said Susan ominously. "The second I get out of here, I'll yell so loud the whole galaxy will hear me."

"I should think they've already heard you clear out to Andromeda."

The lights dimmed. The peculiar noises and wrenchings that went with coming out of overdrive began. Durham braced himself.

"It's too bad you reformed," said Susan. "You used to be amusing company, at least. Now you're sour and bad tempered. You're also—"

What he was also Durham never heard. There was a crashing, roaring, rending impact. The chair went out from under him so that he fell face up into the ceiling. The lights went out entirely. He heard a thin faint sound that might have been Susan screaming. Then the ceiling slid away from him and spilled him down a wall. As he went scrabbling past the window he looked out and saw that there were now long vertical rents in the outer hull through which the stars were shining.

The pumps had stopped.

A long settling groan and then silence. The antigrav field was dead. Durham floated, along with everything else that was not bolted down.

"Susan," he said. "Susan?"

"Here."

They met and clung together in mid air while the hull began a slow axial rotation around them.

"What happened?"

"We hit something."

"The Senyans—"

"They must all be done for. The hull is split open. Head-on ram, I think, just as we came out of overdrive. They wouldn't have had time to get space armor."

"Then are we—"

"Hush. Don't talk. Just wait and see."

They clung together, silent. The hull turned without sound, and the stars shone in through the long slits, into the empty vacuum of the hold.

"Lloyd, I can't breathe."

"Yes you can. We still have as much air as ever. It just isn't circulating now."

"I don't know if I can stand this, Lloyd. It's such an awful way."

"There isn't any way that's good. It won't be so bad, really. You'll just go off to sleep."

"Hold onto me?"

"Sure."

"Lloyd."

"What?"

"I'm sorry."

"So am I."

The hull turned and the stars glittered. The vitiated air grew foul, grew thick and leaden. The man and woman floated in the closed space, their arms tight around each other, their faces close together.

Something jarred against the hull.

"Lloyd! I see a light!"

"It's only a star."

"No. Look through the window. Moving—"

Men, humans, wearing pressure suits, had come into the hull. Two of them were dragging oxygen bottles. They came up to the box and flashed their lights in through the windows. They knocked and made reassuring signs. After a minute or two fresh oxygen hissed in under pressure through the air duct. Susan laughed a little and then fainted. Durham still held her in his arms. Everything got pleasantly dark and far away, lost in the single simple joy of breathing.

There were sounds and motions but he did not pay much attention to them, and he was mildly surprised when he happened to float past a window and noticed that now there was only space outside, very large and full of hot and splendid lights. When he passed the other window he saw part of a ship, and he understood that the box was being hoisted across the interval between it and the wreck. It seemed a remarkably kind dispensation of fortune to have provided a ship at exactly the right time and place, and not just any ship but one equipped with the specialized tackle required for moving heavy loads in space.

A mighty cargo hatch swallowed the box. Susan came to, and they waited, weakly hysterical, Durham not even noticing that a spiky shadow had slipped in with the box. Suddenly again there was man-made light, and then the sound of heavy air pumps reached them. The pumps stopped, and, quite simply, men came in and opened the door of the box.

There was a considerable noise and confusion, everybody talking at once. Durham lost track of Susan. He was only partly conscious of what he was doing, but he felt that everybody was in a hurry to get something done. Then there was a cabin with a port in it, and beyond the port there was space, and in that space a great light flared blindingly and was gone.

VI

MORRISON said, "Murder is a harsh word, Durham. After all, they weren't human."

"There's no such difference under Federation law."

"We're not under Federation law here."

"No. And you're engaged in a life-or-death struggle to make sure you don't come under it. This happened to be one of the death parts."

Morrison looked at him in mild surprise. "You figured that out, Durham?" He was a lean gray, kindly looking man, the conventional father type. Susan was staring at him in blank horror, as though she could not believe what she was hearing. "I wasn't told you were that bright. Well, you're right. Universal Minerals and its various dummy corporations in this sub-sector are making such profits as you wouldn't believe if I told you, and we have no intention of giving it up."

"Even if you have to slaughter a whole ship's crew. What did you do, tow an asteroid into position?"

Morrison shrugged. "Spacial debris is not uncommon."

"You could have killed us, too, you know," Durham said angrily. "You could have killed her. Hawtree wouldn't have liked that."

"It was a risk we had to take. It was a reasonably small one." He looked Durham up and down. "You made us one whale of a mess of trouble. If my yacht wasn't a good bit faster than Jubb's ship, we'd have been whipped. What happened to you? Why didn't you talk like you were supposed to?"

"You'd die laughing."

"I can control my emotions. Go ahead."

Durham told him. "Virtue," he finished sourly, "is sure enough its own reward. I should have stayed drunk. I was happier that way. What happened to the Wanbecqs?"

Morrison was still laughing. "They had not come to when their taxi reached the terminus. The port police picked them up."

He took a bottle out of a locker and pushed it and a glass across the cabin table to Durham. "Here. You've earned it. Wait till I tell Hawtree. And he was so sure of you. Just goes to show you can't trust anybody."

Susan said, "But *why?*" Shock was making her mind move slowly. It was a minute before they realized she was referring to the Senyan ship.

She added, very slowly, "It's true about my father?"

"I'm afraid it is," said Morrison. "But I wouldn't worry about it too much. He's a very rich man. He's also a shrewd one, and it looks now as though he's going to be all right. Give her a drink, Durham, she needs it. Would you like to lie down, Miss Hawtree? All right, then, I'll tell you why."

He leaned over her with no look of kindness at all. "Get this all clearly in mind, Miss Hawtree, so you'll understand that if at any time you try to hang me, you'll hang your father too. We're partners, equally guilty. You understand that."

"Yes." She looked so white that Durham was frightened. But she sat quietly and listened.

"For years now," Morrison said, "I have managed the company here, and Hawtree has used his position with the Embassy to see that I have a free hand. He sees that no complaints get to ears higher up. He sees that any annoying red tape is taken care of. Most important of all, he sees that any official communication from either of the Diks that might be unfavorable to us is permanently lost in the files—including all requests for aid in achieving Federation status. Our connection, naturally, is one of the best kept secrets in the galaxy.

"We had very easy sailing until Jubb rose to power on Senya Dik. Jubb is an able leader. He knows what's happening to the resources of the sector, and he knows the only way to put a stop to it. Unfortunately for us, all the leaders on Nanta Dik aren't fools either, and there is a growing movement toward unification. Jubb has pushed it and pushed it, so that we've been forced to take more and more vigorous steps. The human supremacy groups, made up of such people as the Wanbecqs, have been very useful. And of course Senya Dik has its lunatic fringe too, in reverse but equally useful. But Jubb started a campaign of petitioning the Embassy. He poured it on so hard that Hawtree knew he wasn't going to be able to pigeonhole all the petitions forever. Furthermore, it was obvious that Jubb knew there must be collusion somewhere and was hammering away to find it. So Hawtree sent for me."

"And," said Durham, "you said, 'Let's start a war between the two planets. Then unification can't possibly take place, and Jubb will have too much on his hands to bother us.' Maybe he'll even be eliminated. And you went looking for a goat."

"Exactly. You were given a message about dark birds that would have significance only to a Nantan. The Wanbecqs were put on your trail. All you had to do was talk."

"What if I had talked too much?"

"How could you? You didn't know anything. And Hawtree's story would be that he had simply given you passage home, which you had bought."

"And anyway," said Durham thoughtfully, "I would have been either dead in an alley somewhere, or aboard a ship going to Nanta Dik—which I would not have reached."

"It was a flexible situation."

Susan said, "Then you admit that you—" She could not finish.

MORRISON turned on her irritably. "You very nearly wrecked us, Miss Hawtree. Durham's disappearance wouldn't have raised a ripple, but the daughter of a highly placed diplomat vanishing was quite another thing. Your father had to think fast and talk faster, or public curiosity would have forced an investigation right then. Fortunately the Wanbecqs helped. They painted a pretty dark picture of Jubb, and Hawtree was able to smooth things over since everybody knew you'd been sweet on Durham and had obviously gone to say good-bye. Hawtree did such a good job, in fact, that he had the whole Hub seething with indignation against Jubb even before I left. So it turned out well, in spite of you."

"But why did you have to wreck the ship?"

"Well, we had to get you back. We couldn't let Jubb have Mr. Durham to use as a witness against us, and we certainly couldn't let him have Hawtree's daughter to use as a club over Hawtree. Now, you see, the situation is this."

He nodded to the cabin port beyond which the bright flare had come and gone, leaving nothing but emptiness.

"There's nothing left of the ship but atoms, and no one can say what happened to it. Jubb does not have you two, but he can't prove it as long as you're kept out of sight. So we keep you out of sight, and at the same time press demands to Jubb for your return. It looks as though he's hiding you, or has killed you, in fear of the storm he has raised. The more he doesn't give you up the more human opinion turns against him, and the more his own people figure he's made them nothing but trouble. Meanwhile, the Wanbecqs are on their way home with a big story. We can still have our war if we want it. And Jubb's days are numbered."

Durham said slowly, "What if he decides to use the Bitter Star?"

Morrison stared at him, and then laughed. "Don't try to frighten me with my own bogeyman. I took a story a thousand years old and resurrected it and talked it up until it caught. But that's all it is, a story."

"Are you sure? And what about the darkbirds? They seem to get around. Won't they tell Jubb where we are?"

"He'd have a hard time proving it on the word of a shadow. Besides, there are defenses against them. They won't interfere."

"I suppose," said Durham, taking the bottle into his hand as though to pour again, "that it wouldn't bother you to know that one of them is in here now."

Morrison did not take his eyes from Durham's face. "Hawtree made a stinking choice in you. Put down that bottle."

Durham grinned. He raised the bottle higher and chanted, "Jubb, Jubb, Jubb!"

Morrison said between his teeth, "This would have had to be done anyway." Still watching Durham, he reached one swift hand

356

into the belt of his tunic. Susan made a muffled cry and started to get up. None of the motions were finished. A shadow came out from the darkness of a corner behind Morrison's chair. It flicked against him and he fell across the table, quite still. The darkbird came and hung in the air in front of Durham.

"Jubb," it said.

Durham put down the bottle and wiped the sweat off his forehead. He looked at the darkbird, feeling cold and hollow.

"I want to go to him. You understand? To Jubb."

Up and down it bounced, like the nodding of a head.

Susan said, "What are you going to do?"

"Try and steal a lifeboat."

"I'm going with you."

"No. Morrison doesn't want to kill you, but don't push him too far. You stay. Then if I don't make it you'll still be—" He broke off. "That's taking a lot for granted, isn't it? After all, Hawtree is your father."

She whispered, "I don't care."

"It's the biggest decision you'll ever make. Don't make it too fast." He kissed her. "Besides, if you wait, you may not have to make it at all."

He took Morrison's gun and went out, and the darkbird went with him, bunched small and darting so swiftly that the two men it struck down never saw it. Durham turned aside into the communications room, and the darkbird saw to it that there was no alarm. He damaged radio and radar so that it would take some time to fix them. Then he went on down the corridor to the plainly marked hatch that led to Lifeboat No. 1. He got into it, with the darkbird. As soon as the boat hatch itself was shut, automatic relays blew him free of the pod on a blast of air.

"Jubb," said the darkbird. It touched him, and to his amazement there was no shock, only a chilly tingling that was not unpleasant. Then it simply oozed out through the solid hull, the way smoke oozes through a filter, and was gone.

Durham had no time for any more astonishments. The controls of the lifeboat were designedly very simple and plainly marked. Durham got himself going and away from Morrison's ship as fast as he could. But he knew that it was not going to be anything like fast enough if the darkbird didn't hurry.

It hurried. And Durham was closer to Senya Dik than he realized. In less than three hours he was in touch with a planetary patrol ship, following it in toward the green blaze of KL421, and a dim cool planet that circled it, farther out than the orbit of Earth around Sol, but not quite so far as Mars.

VII

THE spaceport was in a vast flat plain. Far across the plain Durham could see the dark outline of a city. He stood at the edge of the landing area, between two Senyan officers from the ship. He wore a pressure suit from the lifeboat's equipment, and the wind blew hard, beating and picking and pushing at the suit and the bubble helmet. It was difficult for Durham to stand up, but the Senyans, braced on their four sturdy legs, stood easily and swayed their upper bodies back and forth like trees.

They were big. He had not really understood how big they were until he stood beside them. He gathered that they were waiting for a ground conveyance, and he was not surprised. Light air cabs were hardly suited to their build.

He had talked briefly to Karlovic by radio, and he was impatient to get to the consulate where Karlovic was waiting for him. The minute or two in which they waited for the truck seemed interminable. But it came, a great powerful thing like a moving van, and one of the Senyans said,

"Permit me?"

With his two lower arms he lifted Durham onto the platform. The two Senyans spoke to the driver and then got on themselves. The truck took off, going very fast in spite of its size. The Senyans held Durham between them, because there was nothing for a human to hang to, and nowhere to sit down.

They left the spaceport. Huge storage buildings lined the road, and then smaller buildings, and then patches of open country, inexpressibly dreary to Durham's eyes. High overhead the sun burned green and small in a sky of cloudy vapor from which fell showers of glinting rain. Poison rain from a poison sky. Durham shivered, and a deep depression settled on him. Nothing hopeful would be done in this place. Not by humans.

The truck roared on. Durham watched the city grow on the murky horizon, rising up into huge ugly towers and blocky structures like old prisons greatly magnified. It was a big city. It was a frightening city. He wished he had never seen it. He wished he was back in The Hub, standing on a high walk with the good hot sun pouring on him and no barriers between him and the good clean air. He wanted to weep with mingled weariness and claustrophobia. Then he noticed that little crowds had collected along the way into the city. They shouted at the truck going by, and waved their arms, and some of them threw stones that rattled off the sides.

"What's the matter?" Durham asked.

"They are members of the anti-human party. Prejudice cuts both ways, a thing our neighbors of Nanta Dik do not seem to understand. Human and non-human are intellectual concepts. On the emotional level it is simply us or not-us. You are not-us, and as such quite distasteful to some. What I do not understand is how they knew you were coming."

"Morrison must have got his radio working. He's been using the extremists here just like the ones on Nanta Dik, to make trouble."

"There are times—" said the Senyan grimly. "But then I make myself remember that there are scoundrels among us, too."

The truck rumbled through the traffic of wide boulevards, between rows of massive buildings that had obviously never been designed with anything so small and frail as human beings in mind. There were Senyans on the streets, apparently going about whatever business they did, and Durham wondered what their home life was like, what games the children played, what they ate and how they thought, what things they worried about in the dark hours of the night. He felt absolutely alien. It was not a nice feeling.

Presently the truck turned into an open circle surrounded by mighty walls of stone. In one place bright light shone cheerfully from the windows, and the Senyan said, "That is the consulate."

They set him off and showed him where the airlock was. Durham performed the ritual of the lock chamber, frantic to get out of the confining suit. When the inner door swung open he began to tear at the helmet, and a man came in saying, "Let me help."

When Durham was free of the suit, the man looked at him with very tired, very angry eyes. "I'm Karlovic. Jubb's waiting. Come on."

He led Durham down an echoing corridor that dwarfed them by its size. The colors of the polished wood and stone were not keyed to the glaring yellow light, and the rooms that Durham could see into as he passed were not keyed to the small incongruous furnishings that had been forced upon them. Somewhere below there was a throbbing of pumps, and the air smelled of refresher chemicals.

Durham said, "You knew I was being brought here, didn't you?"

Karlovic nodded. "You, yes. The girl, no. She was an overzealous mistake on the part of the darkbird. Yes, I was in on it. I hoped that finally we could get proof, a witness against whoever in the Embassy was working with Morrison. Hawtree, is it? I'm glad to know his name."

He pushed open a door. The room beyond it was only half a room, cut in the middle by a partition of heavy glass. On the other side of the glass wall was the thick green native air, and three Senyans, one of whom came forward when Durham and Karlovic came in. A darkbird hovered close above him. He said to Durham,

"I am Jubb."

There were communicator discs set in the glass. Jubb motioned Durham to a chair beside one. "First let me offer the apology that is due you. You were carrying a message which was not true, which would have made the people of Nanta Dik believe that we were about to come against them with the Bitter Star. The darkbirds warned me, and I felt that I had no choice. I could not let that message be delivered."

Durham said, "No one could blame you for that."

"You understand, I had another motive, too."

"Yes. I don't think you could be blamed for that, either."

JUBB looked at him with his large inscrutable eyes, totally alien, unmistakably intelligent. "I didn't know what you would be like, Mr. Durham, whether you would be in sympathy with your employers or not. Now of course it is evident that you can't be."

Durham said quietly, "I've been to a lot of trouble already to put a rope around their necks. I'm ready to go to a lot more. They've used me like—" He could not think of the right word. Jubb nodded.

"Contempt is not an easy thing to take. I know. Then you will help?"

"In any way I can."

"I want you to go back with me to The Hub, Mr. Durham. Before, I was helpless without proof. Now, as head of a planetary government, I can insist on seeing the ranking Ambassador himself, and I can bypass Hawtree now that I know who he is. I want you to be my witness."

"Nothing," said Durham, "would please me more."

"Good," said Jubb. "Good. Karlovic, it looks as though the end of our long fight may be in sight at last. Take good care of Mr. Durham. He is more precious than gold.

"Meanwhile, Morrison had made us a problem on transportation. We provided that particular ship for the consul's comfort, when there was reason for him to travel in our territory, and we had planned to refit it so that it would accommodate two on the return journey. Now I must ask a ship from our friends on Nanta Dik, and that may take a little time. So rest well, Mr. Durham."

He went out, and Karlovic led Durham back into the hall and from there into a tall gloomy chamber that had a shiny little kitchen lost in one corner of it. There was a table and chairs. Durham sat down and watched Karlovic busy himself with packages of food.

"You don't look very happy about all this," he said.

"I'm not unhappy. I'm worried."

"About what? Morrison can't do anything now."

"No? Listen, Mr. Durham, the emperors of Rome only ruled part of one little world, but they didn't give it up easily. Morrison won't, either. Remember, things are so bad for him now they can't possibly get any worse, only better."

Durham looked out the window. It was a double one, with a vacuum between the panes and protective mesh on the outside. The green air pressed thick against it. The sun had wheeled far over, and the shadows of the buildings were long and black.

"Do you stay here much?" he asked.

"I have lately," said Karlovic. "I had to. My life wasn't safe on Nanta Dik. You've no idea how high their feelings run there, thanks to Morrison." He began to set the table. Durham made no move to help. He was tired. He watched the shadows lengthen and fill the circle of lofty walls with their darkness.

"Couldn't the government there protect you?"

"Only part of the government wants to. And Morrison is working hard to frighten them with all this propaganda about the Bitter Star."

"Propaganda. That's what he said. Is it?"

"Absolutely—as far as the Senyans using it is concerned. But the thing itself is real. It's in the city here. I've seen it."

Karlovic put the heated containers on the table and sat down. He began methodically to eat.

"It's kind of a weird story. Probably it could only have happened on a world like this, with a totally non-human, biochemical set-up. Senyan science started early and advanced fast, a good deal faster than it did on Nanta Dik, for some reason. They did a lot of experimenting with solar energy and atomics and the forces that lie just on the borderline of life—or maybe intelligence would be a better word."

"Aren't the two more or less synonymous?"

"A hunk of platinum sponge or a mess of colloids can be intelligent, but never alive. The Star is. The darkbirds are. They're not matter, they're merely a nexus of interacting particles. But they live and think."

"What about the Star?"

"The scientists were trying for an energy matrix that would absorb solar power and store it like a battery. Something slipped, and the result was the Bitter Star. It absorbs solar power, all right, but in the form of heat, and it will take heat from anything. And it doesn't give it up. It merely absorbs more and more until every living thing near it is frozen and there's no more heat to be had. The Senyan scientists didn't know quite what to do with this thing they had created, but they didn't want to destroy it, either. It had too many angles they wanted to study. So they made the darkbirds, on the same pattern but without the heat-hunger, and with a readier intelligence, to be a bridge between themselves and the Star, to control it. They studied the thing until it proved too dangerous, and they prisoned it by simply starving it at a temperature of absolute zero. So it has stayed ever since, but the darkbirds still guard it in case anything should happen to free it again. They almost seem to love it, in some odd un-fleshly way."

Durham frowned. "Then it *could* be used against Nanta Dik."

"Oh yes," said Karlovic sombrely. "In fact it was, once. The Star shone in their sky in midsummer, and the crops blackened and the rivers froze, and men died where they stood in the fields. The Senyans won the war. That was a thousand years ago, but the Nantans never quite forgot it."

He got up and went morosely to the sink, carrying dishes. "I keep telling Jubb he ought to get rid of the thing. It's a sore point. But—"

Somewhere below there was a very loud noise. The floor rose up and then settled again. Almost at once the air was full of dust, and an alarm bell began a strident ringing. Karlovic's mouth opened and closed twice, as though he was trying to say something. He let the dishes fall clattering around his feet, and then he ran with all his might out of the room and along the hall.

Durham followed him. There was now no sound at all from below. The pumps had stopped.

Karlovic found his tongue. "Cover your face. Don't breathe."

DURHAM saw a thin lazy whorl of greenish mist moving into the hall. He pressed his handkerchief over his mouth and nose and made his legs go, hard and fast. He was right on top of Karlovic when they stumbled into the airlock. It was still clear.

They helped each other into their suits, panting in the stagnant air. Then, through the helmet audio, Durham could hear sounds from outside, muffled shouts and tramplings. Karlovic went back into the consulate where the green mist was already clinging around his knees, and looked out a window into the circle. Over his shoulder Durham could see Senyans milling around and he thought they were rioters, but Karlovic said, "It's all right, they're Jubb's guards."

They went back to the airlock, and from there into the open circle. Senyans escorted them hastily into the adjoining building, and Durham saw that guard posts were being set up. There was a gaping hole in the side of the consulate and the pavement was shattered, and there were pieces of machinery and stuff lying around. Durham figured rapidly in his head how much oxygen he had in his suit pack, and how long it would take to repair the consulate and get the air conditioning working again, and how long it would be before a ship could get here from Nanta Dik. He looked at Karlovic, whose face was white as chalk inside his helmet.

"The lifeboat," he said.

Karlovic nodded. Some color came back into his face. "Yes, the lifeboat. We can live in it until the ship comes." He ran his tongue over his lips as though they were very dry. "Didn't I tell you Morrison wouldn't give up easy? Oh lord, the lifeboat!" He began to jabber urgently at the Senyans in their own tongue, and again his expression was agonized. Durham didn't need to be told what he was thinking. If anything happened to that lifeboat, they were two dead men on a world where humans had no biological right to be.

They were brought into a room where Jubb was busy with a bank of communicators and a batch of harried aides. The room was enormous, but it did not dwarf the Senyans, and the sombre colors did not seem depressing in their own light. Jubb said, as they came in the door,

"I've had a heavy guard set on your lifeboat. I don't think anyone can repeat that hit-and-run bombing—" He cursed in a remarkably human fashion, naming Morrison and the Senyan fools who let themselves be used. "You are all right, Karlovic—Mr. Durham? Quite safe? I've ordered a motor convoy. There are signs of unrest all over the city—apparently word has gone out that you, Durham, are carrying the unification agreement for my signature, and that the terms are a complete surrender on our part to human rule. Does it cheer you two to know that the human race is not alone in producing fools and madmen? Once on the spaceport you will be safe, my naval units will see to that, and my troops are already in the streets. They have orders to look out for you. Go with fortune."

They were taken out another way, where three heavy trucks and several smaller vehicles were drawn up. The Senyans in them wore a distinctive harness and were armed, and the vehicles all had armor plated bodies. Durham and Karlovic were lifted into one of the trucks, which was already filled with Senyan soldiers. The convoy moved off.

Durham braced himself in a corner and looked at Karlovic. "Happened fast, didn't it? Awfully fast."

"Violent things always do. You're not much used to violence, are you? Neither am I. Neither are most people. They get it shoved at them."

"I don't think we're through with it yet," said Durham.

Karlovic said, "I told you."

For some time there was only the rushing and jolting of the truck, the roar of motors and a kind of dim uneasy background of sound as though the whole city stirred and seethed. Durham was frightened. The food he had eaten had turned against him, he was stifling in his own sweat, and he thought of Morrison cruising comfortably somewhere out in space, smoking cigarettes and drinking good whiskey and sending down a message now and then, the way a man pokes with a stick at a brace of beetles, stirring them casually toward death. He ground his jaws together in an agony of hate and fear, and the taste of them was sour in his mouth.

Somebody said to them, "We're on the spaceport highway now. It won't be long."

A minute later somebody shouted and Karlovic caught the Senyan word and echoed it. "Barricade!" The truck rocked and whirled about and there were great crashes in the night that had fallen. Durham was thrown to his knees. The truck raced at full speed. There were sounds of fighting that now rose and now grew faint, and the truck lurched and swerved, and then there were more roars and crashes and it came violently to a halt. The Senyans began firing out of the loopholes in the armored sides. Some of them leaped out of the truck, beckoning Durham and Karlovic to come after them. A large force of rioters was attacking what remained of the convoy, which had been forced back into the city. Four of the Senyan soldiers ran with the two men into a side street, but a small body of rioters caught up with them. The soldiers turned to fight, and Karlovic said in a voice that was now curiously calm,

"If we're quick enough they may lose sight of us in the darkness."

He turned into an areaway between two buildings, and then into another, and Durham ran beside him through the cold green mist and the dim glow of lamps that glimmered on the alien walls. The sound of the fighting died away. They turned more corners, hunting always for the darkest shadows, hoping to meet a patrol. But the streets were deserted and all the doors barred tight. Finally Durham stopped. "How much oxygen you got left?"

Karlovic peered at the illuminated indicator on the wrist of his suit. "Hour. Maybe less."

Both men were breathing hard, panting, burning up the precious stuff of life. Durham said,

"I won't last that long. Listen, Karlovic. Where is the Bitter Star?"

Karlovic's face was a pale blur inside his helmet. "You crazy? You can't—"

Durham put his two hands on the shoulders of Karlovic's suit and leaned his helmet close so that it clicked on Karlovic's.

"Maybe I'm crazy. In thirty, forty minutes I'll be dead, so what will it matter then? Listen, Karlovic, I want to live." He pointed back the way they had come. "You think we can walk through that to the spaceport in time?"

"No."

"We got anyplace else to go?"

"No."

"All right then. Let's give 'em hell."

"But they're not all our enemies. Jubb, my friends—"

"Friend or enemy, they'll clear the way. We might just make it, Karlovic. You said the darkbirds control it, and you can talk to them." He shook Karlovic viciously. "Where is it? Don't you understand? If we use it we can hound Morrison out of space!"

Karlovic turned and began to walk fast, sobbing as he went. "The darkbirds will never let us. You don't know what you're doing."

"I know one thing. I'm sick of being pushed, pushed, pushed, into corners, into holes, where I can't breathe. I'm going to—" He shut his teeth tight together and walked fast beside Karlovic, starting at every sound and shadow.

By twining alleys and streets where nothing moved for fear of the violence that was abroad that night, Karlovic led Durham to an open space like a park with vast locked gates that could keep a Senyan out but not a little agile human who could climb like a monkey with the fear of death upon him. Beyond the gates great wrinkled lichens as tall as trees grew in orderly rows, and a walk led inward. The lichens bent and rustled in the wind, and Durham's suit was wet with a poisonous dew.

The walk ended in a portico, and the portico was part of a building, round and squat as though a portion of its mass was underground. They passed through a narrow door into a place of utter silence, and a darkbird hung there, barring their way.

"Jubb," said Durham. "Tell it Jubb has sent us. Tell it the Bitter Star must be freed again to destroy Jubb's enemies."

Karlovic spoke to the shadow. Others came to join it. There was a flurry of hooting and chittering, and then the one Karlovic had been speaking to disappeared in the uncanny fashion of its kind. The others stayed, a barrier between the two men and a ramp that led steeply down.

Karlovic sat down wearily on the chill stone. "It isn't any use," he said. "I knew it wouldn't be. The darkbird has gone to ask Jubb if what we say is true."

Durham sat down, too. He did not even bother to look at the indicator on his wrist. No use. The end. Finish. He shut his eyes.

There was a stir and a hooting in the air. Karlovic gasped. Then he began to shake Durham, laughing like a woman who has heard a risque story. "Didn't you hear? The bird came back, and Jubb said—Jubb said Morrison has been preaching the war of the Bitter Star, so let him have it."

He grasped Durham's suit by the shoulders and pulled him to his feet, and they ran with the cloud of shadows, down into the dimness below.

VIII

THERE was a small sealed chamber with a thick window, and beyond it was a circular space, not too large, walled with triple walls of glass with a vacuum between. The air was full of dark-birds, moving without hindrance through the walls or hovering where they chose, above the thing that slept inside.

Durham blinked and turned his head away, and then looked

back again. And Karlovic said softly, "Beautiful, isn't it? But sad, too, somehow, I don't know why."

Durham felt it, a subliminal feeling without any reason to it, like the sadness of a summer night or of birth and laughter or of gull's wings white and swift against the sky. The Star shone, palely, gently. He tried to see if it was round or any other shape, if it was solid or vaporous, but he could not see anything but that soft shining, like mist around a winter moon.

Durham shook himself and wondered why, when he was already so sure of death, he should be so afraid. "All right," he said. "How is it freed?"

"The darkbirds do that. Watch."

He spoke to them, one word, and in the glass-walled prison there was a stirring and a swirling of shadows around the soft shining of the Star. Durham saw a disc set in the metal overhead. One of the darkbirds touched it. There was an intense blue flare of light, and Durham felt the throbbing of hidden dynamos, a secret surge of power. The glass walls darkened and grew dim, the low roof turned and opened to the sky. And through the barrier window, Durham watched the waking of a star.

He saw the frosty shining brighten and spread out in slow unfurling veils. There was a moment when the whole building seemed filled with moonfire as cold as the breath of outer space and as beautiful as the face of a dream, and then it was gone, and the darkbirds were gone with it.

"Come on," said Karlovic, a harsh incongruous voice in the stunned darkness that was left behind, and Durham came, up the ramp and out into the parklike space beyond, and all the tall lichens were standing dead and sheathed in ice.

High above, burning cold over the city, a new star shone.

They followed it, through a silence as deep as the end of the world. Everything had taken cover at the rising of that star, and only the two men moved, the thermal units of their suits turned on high, through streets all glazed with ice and cluttered here and there with the wreckage and the dead of the rioting. The darkbirds were forcing the Star to stay high, but even so nothing could live long without protection in that sudden, terrible winter.

The road to the port lay blank and bare. They found one of the smaller vehicles, its driver dead beside it. Karlovic got it going, moving the great levers with Durham's help. After that they rushed faster through the empty night. Durham shut his eyes, thinking.

He opened them, and the spaceport of Senya Dik lay black and deserted around him, and Karlovic was gasping to him for help. Together they pulled down the lever that stopped their conveyance. They scrambled down and ran out toward the small lifeboat, slipping and stumbling, dying inside their suits. They fell into the airlock, and Durham slammed the door and spun the wheel, waiting out the agonizing seconds while the tiny chamber cleared and then refilled, and they could tear off their helmets and breathe again. They looked at each other and laughed, and hugged each other, and laughed again, and then went in to the cabin.

The communicator was flashing its light and burring stridently.

Durham switched it on. Jubb's face appeared in the tiny screen. "You are safe? Good, good. For a moment I thought—! Listen. I have word from my patrol that Morrison has other ships with him now, spread out to catch you if by chance you get through. That is what decided me to use the Bitter Star. I am angry, Karlovic. I am tired of mockery and lies and secret violence. I am tired of peace which is only a cloak for another man's aggression."

A darkbird came into the cabin and hung over Durham's shoulder. "It will carry your messages," said Jubb. "I am leaving now for the port, and my own flagship. We go together. Good luck."

The screen went dead. Durham said, "Strap in, we're taking off."

THE Star, with its herding pack of shadows, set a course that took them steeply up out of Senya Dik's shadow, into the full flood of the green sun's light. The dark-bird spoke by Durham's shoulder, and Karlovic said, "The Star must feed—or recharge itself, as you would say, with solar heat. Watch it, Durham. Watch it grow."

He watched. The Star spread out its misty substance, spreading it wide to the sun, and the soft shining of it brightened to an angry glare that grew and widened and became like a burning cloud, not green like the sunlight but white as pearl.

Far off to one side of it Durham saw the glinting of a ship's hull. He pointed to it.

Karlovic worked with the communicator. In a minute the screen lit up, and Morrison's face was in it.

"Hello, Morrison," he said. "Hello, thief."

Morrison's face was as hard and white as something carved from bone.

"It wasn't just an old wives' tale, Morrison," he said. "It was true, and here it is. The Bitter Star, Morrison."

Karlovic reached over and shook him, pointing out the viewport. Coming swiftly in toward them was a small ship, curiously shaped before.

"Space-sweep," Karlovic said. "Those funny bulges are torpedo tubes, and the torpedoes carry heavy scatter charges to clear away debris so the ore ships can come in."

Durham said to the image in the screen, "Call him off."

Morrison showed the edges of his teeth, and asked, "Why should I?"

Durham nodded to Karlovic, who spoke to the darkbird. It disappeared. Within a few seconds the Star had begun to move. It moved fast, the angry gleaming of its body making a streak like a white comet across the green-lit void. It wrapped itself around the space-sweep, and then it lifted and the ship continued on its way unchanged. Morrison laughed.

The sweep rushed on toward the lifeboat. Its tubes were open, but nothing came out of them. Durham shifted course to clear it, and it blundered on by. In the screen, Morrison's image turned and spoke to someone, and the someone answered, "I can't, they just aren't there."

Morrison turned again to Durham, or rather to the image of him that was on his own screen. "I know what I'm supposed to say now, but I'm not going to say it. I've got Miss Hawtree with me, had you forgotten that? I don't think you've suddenly acquired that kind of guts."

Durham shook his head. "I don't need them. I want you alive, Morrison. But I don't give a tinker's damn what happens to anybody else in this whole backside of nowhere you call 9G. Nobody and nothing. And I have the Bitter Star to back me up. I am wondering how many loyal employees of Universal Minerals and how many stupid Wanbecqs are going to sacrifice their lives just to keep me from getting my hands on you. Call them up, Morrison, and count them out, and we'll send the Star to see them."

The Star glowed and glimmered and grew to a great shining, and a look of worry deepened on Karlovic's face. Morrison did not answer, and Durham could see the thoughts going round and round in his mind, the possibilities being weighed and evaluated. Then the someone who was behind Morrison and out of scanner range said in a queer flat voice,

"The tug *Varney* calling in, sir. They boarded the sweep."

"Well?"

"All dead, sir. Frozen. Even the air was frozen. They said to tell you they're going home."

"All right," said Morrison softly. "Durham, I'm going home too, to Nanta Dik. Let's see if you can follow me there."

He broke contact. In the distance Durham saw the bright speck that was Morrison's ship make a wheeling curve and speed away. Durham said grimly to Karlovic,

"Tell the darkbirds to follow with the Star. And then get hold of somebody on Nanta Dik, somebody with authority. Tell them everything that's happened. Tell them Morrison is all we want. We'll see how close they let him get to home."

"I don't know," said Karlovic, and got busy with the communicator. Half an hour later he sighed and blanked the screen.

"They're sending up a squadron to intercept Morrison. But they're scared. They're scared of the Star. I've promised them—and nothing had better happen, Durham."

Durham said, "We'd better send word to Jubb."

For what seemed an eternity they fled through the green blaze of the sun, after the ship Durham could no longer see. And ahead of the lifeboat, a light and a portent in the void, went the Bitter Star with its attendant shadows. And Durham, too, began to worry, he was not sure why. Jubb's flagship closed up to them, a vast dark whale beside a minnow. And after a while a tiny bright ball that was a planet came spinning toward them. Karlovic pointed.

Hung like a net across space, between them and the planet, was a series of glittering metallic flecks.

"The squadron."

The communicator buzzed. Karlovic snapped it on, and the face of a Nantan officer appeared on the screen.

"We have Morrison," he said. "Come no closer with the Star."

Karlovic spoke to the darkbird. Durham's hands, heavy with weariness, slowed the lifeboat until it hung almost motionless. Jubb's great dark cruiser slowed also. Above and between them burned the Bitter Star. It had ceased to move.

Durham said, "The Star will come no closer."

"Mr Karlovic," said the Nantan. "Bring your lifeboat in slowly, and alone."

The lifeboat came in among the ships of the squadron.

"Now," said the Nantan officer, "withdraw the Star."

Karlovic said, "Jubb will do so—"

"No," said Durham suddenly, "Jubb will not. Look there!"

SHINING with a furious light, the Star had torn itself away from the clustering shadows that hung around it.

Durham's heart congealed with a foretaste of icy death. The face of the Nantan officer paled, and Karlovic said in a voice that was not like his voice at all. "I must talk to Jubb."

He reached out to shift their single screen, and the Nantan officer said, "Wait, he is speaking on our alternate. I can adjust the scanner—"

The picture flopped, blurred, and cleared again, showing now in addition to the officer a part of the Nantan's alternate-channel screen. Jubb was speaking, and it seemed to Durham that the Senyan's strange face was clearly, humanly alarmed.

He said, "I cannot withdraw the Star. No, this is not a lie, a trick—hold your fire, you idiots! I'm the only hope you have now. The Star has profited by the lesson of its docility a thousand years ago, when it let itself be led back into captivity. Now it has grown too much. It cannot be brought back to any world."

Durham looked out at the beautiful deadly thing blazing so splendidly in the void. "Can it be destroyed?"

"The darkbirds can destroy it," said Jubb. "If they will."

The Nantan officer, speaking from lips the color of ashes, said to the image of Jubb on the screen, "You have one minute to get it out of here before I fire."

Jubb turned his face away and spoke to something they could not see.

Durham turned to Karlovic. "He said, 'If they will.' Does that mean—"

"I told you," said Karlovic, looking out the port, "that the darkbirds were created to guard the Star. And that, in a way, they love it. Who can say how much?"

They watched.

Out in space the little cloud of darkbirds moved toward the Star. Then, hesitantly, they stopped.

"They won't," said Karlovic, in a whisper. "Not even for Jubb."

Again Jubb spoke to the unseen messenger, as quietly as though it was a casual order. And presently a troubled movement rippled the swirling darkbirds.

Suddenly they moved, again herding the Star. Slowly at first, then more and more swiftly until it was only a streak of brilliant light, the darkbirds drove the Star straight toward the sun. And it was less a driving than an urging, a tempting, a promise of glory, a sweet betraying call from the mouth of the eternal Judas. The darkbirds led it, and it followed them.

In a moment, in that greater blaze, the star was lost to view.

Karlovic's breath came out of him in a long sigh. "The only way it could be destroyed. Even its appetite for thermal energy could not swallow a sun."

"The darkbirds are coming back," Durham said. Then, wonderingly, "But they're not—"

The darkbirds were coming back from the green sun, but not toward Jubb's ship. And not toward any planet. They were flying like blurring shadows toward outer space, and if they heard Jubb's calling voice they paid no heed at all.

"They're gone," Karlovic said unbelievingly.

"Yes," said Jubb, very slowly. "They obeyed that order, but it was the last." He looked at the humans facing him, the men of Earth and the men of Nanta Dik. He said, "Do you see now that there is no difference between us, that we of Senya Dik can teach betrayal just like men?"

Durham looked out into the shining void but there was no sign now of the fleet and flying shadows. Intelligences, minds, beyond the understanding of heavy creatures like himself and Jubb. He wondered how far they would go, how long they would live, what things they would see.

Darkbirds, darkbirds, will you come back some day when we of flesh are ghosts and shadows, to frolic on our lonely worlds?

The Queer Ones

Venture Science Fiction, March 1957

I RAN DOWN Buckhorn Mountain in the cloud and rain, carrying the boy in my arms. The green lightning flashed among the trees. Buckhorn is no stranger to lightning, but this was different. It did not come from the clouds, and there was no thunder with it. It ran low, searching the thickets, the brush-choked gullies, the wet hollows full of brambles and poison ivy. Thick green hungry snakes looking for something. Looking for me.

Looking for the boy who had started it all.

He peered up at me, clinging like a lemur to my coat as I went headlong down the slope. His eyes were copper-colored. They had seen a lot for all the two-and-a-half years they had been open on this world. They were frightened now, not just vaguely as you might expect from a child his age, but intelligently. And in his curiously sweet shrill voice he asked:

"Why mus' they kill us?"

"Never mind," I said, and ran and ran, and the green lightning hunted us down the mountainside.

It was Doc Callendar, the County Health Officer, who got me in on the whole thing. I am Hank Temple, owner, editor, feature writer, legman, and general roustabout of the *Newhale News,* serving Newhale and the rural and mountain areas around it. Doc Callendar, Sheriff Ed Betts and I are old friends, and we work together, helping out where we can. So one hot morning in July my phone rang and it was Doc, sounding kind of dazed.

"Hank?" he said. "I'm at the hospital. Would you want to take a run up here for a minute?"

"Who's hurt?"

"Nobody. Just thought something might interest you."

Doc was being cagey because anything you say over the phone in Newhale is public property. But even so the tone of his voice put prickles between my shoulder blades. It didn't sound like Doc at all.

"Sure," I said. "Right away."

Newhale is the county seat, a small town, and a high town. It lies in an upland hollow of the Appalachians, a little clutter of old red brick buildings with porches on thin wooden pillars, and frame houses ranging from new white to weathered silver-gray, centered around the dumpy courthouse. A very noisy stream bisects the town. The tannery and the feed-mill are its chief industries, with some mining nearby. The high-line comes down a neat cut on Tunkhannock Ridge to the east and goes away up a neat cut on Goat Hill to the west. Over all towers the rough impressive hump of Buckhorn Mountain, green on the ridges, shadowed blue in the folds, wrapped more often than not in a mist of cloud.

There is not much money nor any great fame to be made in Newhale, but there are other reasons for living here. The girl I wanted to marry couldn't quite see them, and it's hard to explain to a woman why you would rather have six pages of small-town newspaper that belong to you than the whole of the *New York Times* if you only work for it. I gave up trying, and she went off to marry a gray flannel suit, and every time I unlimber my fishing-rod or my deer rifle I'm happy for her.

The hospital is larger than you might expect, since it serves a big part of the county. Sitting on a spur of Goat Hill well away from the tannery, it's an old building with a couple of new wings tacked on. I found Doc Callendar in his office, with Bossert. Bossert is the resident doctor, a young guy who knows more, in the old phrase, than a jackass could haul downhill. This morning he looked as though he wasn't sure of his own name.

"Yesterday," Doc said, "one of the Tate girls brought her kid in, a little boy. I wasn't here, I was out testing those wells up by Pinecrest.

But I've seen him before. He's a stand-out, a real handsome young-ster."

"Precocious," said Jim Bossert nervously. "Very precocious for his age. Physically, too. Coordination and musculature well developed. And his coloring—"

"What about it?" I asked.

"Odd. I don't know. I noticed it, and then forgot it. The kid looked as though he'd been through a meat-grinder. His mother said the other kids had ganged up and beaten him, and he hadn't been right for several days, so she reckoned she'd better bring him in. She's not much more than nineteen herself. I took some X-rays—"

Bossert picked up a couple of pictures from the desk and shoved them at me. His hands shook, making the stiff films rattle together.

"I didn't want to trust myself on these. I waited until Callendar could check them, too."

I held the pictures up and looked at them. They showed a small, frail bony structure and the usual shadowy outline of internal organs. It wasn't until I had looked at them for several minutes that I began to realize there was something peculiar about them. There seemed to be too few ribs, the articulation of the joints looked queer even to my layman's eyes, and the organs themselves were a hopeless jumble.

"Some of the innards," said Doc, "we can't figure out at all. There are organs we've never seen nor heard of before."

"Yet the child seems normal and perfectly healthy," said Bossert. "Remarkably so. From the beating he'd taken he should have had serious injuries. He was just sore. His body must be as flexible and tough as spring steel."

I put the X-rays back on the desk. "Isn't there quite a large litera-ture on medical anomalies?"

"Oh, yes," said Doc. "Double hearts, upside-down stomachs, extra arms, legs, heads—almost any distortion or variation you can think of. But not like this." He leaned over and tapped his finger emphati-cally on the films. "This isn't a distortion of anything. This is *different*. And that's not all."

He pushed a microscope slide toward me.

379

"That's the capper, Hank. Blood sample. Jim tried to type it. I tried to type it. We couldn't. There isn't any such type."

I stared at them. Their faces were flushed, their eyes were bright, they quivered with excitement, and suddenly it got to me too.

"Wait a minute," I said. "Are you trying to tell me—"

"We've got something here," said Doc Callendar. "Something—" He shook his head. I could see the dreams in it. I could see Callendar standing ten feet tall on a pedestal of medical journals. I could see him on podiums addressing audiences of breathless men, and the same dreams were in Bossert's eyes.

I had my own. The *Newhale News* suddenly a famous name on the wire-services, and one Henry Temple bowing with modest dignity as he accepted the Pulitzer Prize for journalism.

"Big," said Bossert softly. "The boy is more than a freak. He's something new. A mutation. Almost a new species. The blood-type alone—"

Something occurred to me, and I cut him short. "Listen," I said. "Listen, are you sure you didnt make a mistake or something? How could the boy's blood be so different from his mother's?" I hunted for the word. "Incompatibility. He'd never have been born."

"Nevertheless," said Doc Callendar mildly, "he was born. And nevertheless, there is no such blood-type. We've run tests backward and forward, together and independently. Kindly allow us to know what we're talking about, Hank. The boy's blood obviously must have been compatible with his mother's. Possibly it's a more advanced Type O, universally compatible. This is only one of the many things we have to study and evaluate."

He picked up the X-ray films again and looked at them, with an expression of holy ecstasy in his eyes.

I lighted another cigarette. My hands were shaking now, like theirs. I leaned forward.

"Okay," I said. "What's the first thing we do?"

Doc's station wagon, with COUNTY HEALTH SERVICE painted on its side, slewed and snorted around the turns of the steep dirt road. Jim Bossert had had to stay at the hospital, but I was sitting beside Doc, hunched forward in a sweat of impatience. The road ran up around the shoulder of Tunkhannock Ridge. We had thick dark woods on our right going up, and thick dark woods on our left going down. Buckhorn hung in the north like a curtain across the sky.

"We'll have to be careful," Doc was saying. "I know these people pretty well. If they get the idea we're trying to pull something, we'll never get another look at the kid."

"You handle it," I said. "And by the way, nobody's mentioned the boy's father. Doesn't he have one?"

"Do you know the Tate girls?"

"No. I've been through Possum Creek all right, but through it is all."

"You must have gone fast," said Doc, grinning. "The answer is physiologically yes, legally are you kidding?" He shifted into second, taking it easy over a place where the road was washed and gullied. "They're not a bad bunch of girls at that, though," he added reflectively. "I kind of like them. Couple of them are downright married."

We bucketed on through the hot green shadows, the great centers of civilization like Newhale forgotten in the distance behind us, and finally in a remote pocket just under Tunkhannock's crest we came upon a few lean spry cattle, and then the settlement of Possum Creek.

There were four ancient houses straggled out along the side of the stream. One of them said GENERAL STORE and had a gas pump in front of it. Two old men sat on the step.

Doc kept on going. "The Tates," he said, straight-faced, "live out a little from the center of town."

Two more turns of the road, which was now only a double-rutted track, brought us to a rural mailbox which said TATE. The house behind it was pretty well run down, but there was glass in most of the windows and only half the bricks were gone from the chimney. The clapboards were sort of a rusty brown, patched up with odds and ends of tarpaper. A woman was washing clothes in an old galvanized tub set on a stand in the side yard. There was a television aerial tied on cockeyed to the gable of the house. There was a sow with a litter in a pen right handy to the door, and a little way at the back was a barn with the ridge-pole swayed like an old horse. A tarpaper shack and a battered house-trailer were visible among the trees—probably the homes of the married daughters. An ancient man sat in an ancient rocking-chair on the porch and peered at us, and an ancient dog beside him rose up heavily and barked.

I've known quite a lot of families like the Tates. They scratch out enough corn for their pigs and their still-houses, and enough garden for themselves. The young men make most of their money as guides during hunting season, and the old men make theirs selling moonshine. They have electricity now, and they can afford radios and even television sets. City folks call them lazy and shiftless. Actually, they find the simple life so pleasant that they hate to let hard work spoil their enjoyment of it.

Doc drove his station wagon into the yard and stopped. Instantly there was an explosion of dogs and children and people.

"There he is," Doc said to me, under cover of the whooping and woofing and the banging of screen doors. "The skinny little chap with the red hair. There, just coming down the steps."

I looked over and saw the boy.

He was an odd one, all right. The rest of the Tate tribe all had straight hair ranging from light brown to honey-blond. His was close and curly to his head and I saw what Jim Bossert had meant about his coloring. The red had undertones of something else in it. One would almost, in that glare of sunlight, have said silver. The Tates had blue eyes. His were copper-colored. The Tates were fair and sunburned, and so was he, but there was a different quality of fairness to his skin, a different shading to the tan.

He was a little boy. The Tate children were rangy and big boned. He moved among them lightly, a gazelle among young goats, with a totally unchildlike grace and sureness. His head was narrow, with a very high arch to the skull. His eyes were grave, precociously wise. Only in the mouth was there genuine childishness, soft and shy.

We got out of the car. The kids—a dozen of them, give or take a couple—all stopped as though on a signal and began to study their bare feet. The woman came from the washtub, wiping her hands on her skirt. Several others came out of the house.

The little boy remained at the foot of the steps. His hand was now in the hand of a buxom girl. Judging by Bossert's description, this would be his mother. Not much over nineteen, handsome, big-breasted, full-hipped. She was dressed in tight jeans and a boys shirt, her bare feet stuck into sandals, and a hank of yellow hair hung down her back.

Doc spoke to them all, introducing me as a friend from town. They were courteous, but reserved. "I want to talk to Sally," he said, and we moved closer to the steps. I tried not to look at the boy lest the glitter in my eye give me away. Doc was being so casual and hearty it hurt. I could feel a curious little prickle run over my skin as I got close to the child. It was partly excitement, partly the feeling that here was a being different from myself, another species. There was a dark bruise on the child's forehead, and I remembered that the others had beaten him. Was this *otherness* at the bottom of their resentment? Did they sense it without the need for blood samples and X-rays?

Mutant. A strange word. A stranger thing to come upon here in these friendly familiar hills. The child stared at me, and the July sun turned cold on my back.

Doc spoke to Sally, and she smiled. She had an honest, friendly smile. Her mouth was wide and full, frankly sensuous but without coquetry. She had big blue eyes, and her sunburned cheeks were flushed with health, and she looked as uncomplicated and warmly attractive as a summer meadow. I wondered what strange freak of genetics had made her the fountainhead of a totally new race.

Doc said, "Is this the little boy you brought in to the hospital?"

"Yes," she said. "But he's better now."

Doc bent over and spoke to the boy. "Well," he said. "And what's your name, young man?"

"Name's Billy," he answered, in a grave sweet treble that had a sound in it of bells being rung far off. "Billy Tate."

The woman who had come from the washtub said with unconcealed dislike, "He ain't no Tate, whatever he might be."

She had been introduced as Mrs. Tate, and was obviously the mother and grandmother of this numerous brood. She had lost most of her teeth and her gray-blonde hair stood out around her head in an untidy brush. Doc ignored her.

"How do you do, Billy Tate," he said. "And where did you get that pretty red hair?"

"From his daddy," said Mrs. Tate sharply. "Same place he got his sneaky-footed ways and them yellow eyes like a bad hound. I tell you, Doctor, if you see a man looks just like that child, you tell him to come back and get what belongs to him!"

A corny but perfectly fitting counterpoint to her words, thunder crashed on Buckhorn's cloudy crest, like the ominous laughter of a god.

Sally reached down suddenly and caught up the boy into her arms....

The thunder quivered and died on the hot air. I stared at Doc and he stared at me, and Sally Tate screamed at her mother.

"You keep your dirty mouth off my baby!"

"That ain't no way to talk to Maw," said one of the older girls. "And anyway, she's right."

"Oh," said Sally. "You think so, do you?" She turned to Doc, her cheeks all white now and her eyes blazing. "They set their young ones on my baby, Doctor, and you know why? They're jealous. They're just sick to their stomachs with it, because they all got big hunkety kids that can't do nothin' but eat, and big hunkety men that treat them like they was no better'n brood sows."

She had reached her peak of fury so quickly that it was obvious this row had been going on for a long while, probably ever since the child was born.

Possibly even before, judging by what she said then.

"Jealous," she said to her sisters, showing her teeth. "Every last one of you was dancing up and down to catch his eye, but it was me he took to the hayloft. *Me.* And if he ever comes back he can have me again, for as often and as long as he wants me. And I won't hear no ill of him nor the baby!"

I heard all this. I understood it. But not with all, or even most of my mind. That was busy with another thing, a thing it didn't want to grapple with at all and kept shying away from, only to be driven back shivering.

Doc put it into words.

"You mean," he said, to no one in particular, "the boy looks just like his father?"

"Spit an' image," said Sally fondly, kissing the red curls that had that queer glint of silver in them. "Sure would like to see that man again, I don't care what they say. Doctor, I tell you, he was beautiful."

"Handsome is as handsome does," said Mrs. Tate. "He was no good, and I knew it the minute I saw—"

"Why, Maw," said Mr. Tate, "he had you eating out of his hand, with them nicey ways of his." He turned to Doc Callendar, laughing. "She'd a' gone off to the hayloft with him herself if he'd asked her, and that's a fact. Ain't it, Harry?"

Harry said it was, and they all laughed.

Mrs. Tate said furiously, "It'd become you men better to do something about getting some support for that brat from its father, instead of making fool jokes in front of strangers."

"Seems like, when you bring it up," said Mr. Tate, "it would become us all not to wash our dirty linen for people who aren't rightly concerned." He said courteously to Doc, "Reckon you had a reason for coming here. Is there something I can do?"

"Well—," said Doc uncertainly, and looked at the boy. "Just like his father, you say."

And if that is so, I thought, *how can he be a mutant? A mutant is something new, something different, alien from the parent stem. If he is the spit an' image outside, then build and coloring bred true. And if build and coloring bred true, probably blood-type and internal organs—*

Thunder boomed again on Buckhorn Mountain. And I thought, *Well, and so his father is a mutant, too.*

But Doc said, "Who was this man, Sally? I know just about everybody in these hills, but I never saw anyone to answer that description."

"His name was Bill," she said, "just like the boy's. His other name was Jones. Or he said it was."

"He lied," said Mrs. Tate. "Wasn't Jones no more than mine is. We found that out."

"How did he happen to come here?" asked Doc. "Where did he say he was from?"

"He come here," Mrs. Tate said, "driving a truck for some appliance store, Grover's I think it was, in Newhale. Said the place was just new and was making a survey of teevees around here, and offering free service on them up to five dollars, just for goodwill. So I let him look at ours, and he fussed with it for almost an hour, and didn't charge me a cent. Worked real good afterward, too. That would 'a been the end of it, I guess, only Sally was under his feet all the time and he took a shine to her. Kept coming back, and coming back, and you see what happened."

I said, "There isn't any Grover's store in Newhale. There never has been."

"We found that out," said Mrs. Tate. "When we knew the baby was coming we tried to find Mr. Jones, but it seems he'd told us a big pack of lies."

"He told me," Sally said dreamily, "where he come from."

Doc said eagerly, "Where?"

Twisting her mouth to shape the unfamiliar sounds, Sally said, "Hrylliannu."

Doc's eyes opened wide. "Where the hell is that?"

"Ain't no place," said Mrs. Tate. "Even the schoolteacher couldn't find it in the atlas. It's only another of his lies."

But Sally murmured again, "Hrylliannu. Way he said it, it sounded like the most beautiful place in the world."

The stormcloud over Buckhorn was spreading out. Its edges dimmed the sun. Lightning flicked and flared and the thunder rolled. I said, "Could I take a look at your television?"

"Why," said Mrs. Tate, "I guess so. But don't you disturb it, now. Whatever else he done, he fixed that teevee good."

"I won't disturb it," I said. I went up the sagging steps past the old man and the fat old dog. I went into the cluttered living room, where the springs were coming out of the sofa and there was no rug on the floor, and six kids apparently slept in the old brass bed in the corner. The television set was maybe four years old, but it was the best and biggest made that year. It formed a sort of shrine at one end of the room, with a piece of red cloth laid over its top.

I took the back off and looked in. I don't know what I expected to see. It just seemed odd to me that a man would go to all the trouble of faking up a truck and tinkering with television sets for nothing. And apparently he hadn't. What I did see I didn't understand, but even to my inexpert eye it was obvious that Mr. Jones had done something quite peculiar to the wiring inside.

A totally unfamiliar component roosted on the side of the case, a little gadget not much bigger than my two thumbnails.

I replaced the back and turned the set on. As Mrs. Tate said, it worked real good. Better than it had any business to. I got a peculiar hunch that Mr. Jones had planned it that way, so that no other serviceman would have to be called. I got the hunch that that component was important somehow to Mr. Jones.

I wondered how many other such components he had put in television sets in this area, and what they were for.

I turned off the set and went outside. Doc was still talking to Sally.

"… some further tests he wants to make," I heard him say. "I can take you and Billy back right now…"

Sally looked doubtful and was about to speak. But the decision was made for her. The boy cried out wildly, "No! No!" With the frantic strength of a young animal he twisted out of his mother's arms, dropped to the ground, and sped away into the brush so swiftly that nobody had a chance even to grab for him.

Sally smiled. "All them shiny machines and the funny smells frightened him," she said. "He don't want to go back. Isn't anything wrong with him, is there? The other doctor said he was all right."

"No," said Doc reluctantly. "Just something about the X-rays he wanted to check on. It could be important for the future. Tell you what, Sally. You talk to the boy, and I'll come back in a day or two."

"Well," she said. "All right."

Doc hesitated, and then said, "Would you want me to speak to the sheriff about finding this man? If that's his child he should pay something for its support."

A wistful look came into her eyes. "I always thought maybe if he knew about the baby—"

Mrs. Tate didn't give her time to finish. "Yes, indeed," she said. "You speak to the sheriff. Time somebody did something about this, 'fore that brat's a man grown himself."

"Well," said Doc, "we can try."

He gave a last baffled glance at the woods where the boy had disappeared, and then we said goodbye and got into the station wagon and drove away. The sky was dark overhead now, and the air was heavy with the smell of rain.

"What do you think?" I said finally.

Doc shook his head. "I'm damned if I know. Apparently the external characteristics bred true. If the others did—"

"Then the father must be a mutant too. We just push it back one generation."

"That's the simplest explanation," Doc said.

"Is there any other?"

Doc didn't answer that. We passed through Possum Creek, and it began to rain.

"What about the television set?" he asked.

I told him. "But you'd have to have Jud or one of the boys from Newhale Appliance look at it, to say what it was."

"It smells," said Doc. "It stinks, right out loud."

The bolt of lightning came so quickly and hit so close that I wasn't conscious of anything but a great flare of livid green. Doc yelled. The station wagon slewed on the road that now had a thin film of mud over it, and I saw trees rushing at us, their tops bent by a sudden wind so that they seemed to be literally leaping forward. There was no thunder. I remembered that, I don't know why. The station wagon tipped over and hit the trees. There was a crash. The door flew open and I fell out through a wet whipping tangle of branches and on down to the steep-tilted ground below. I kept on falling, right down the slope, until a gully pocket caught and held me. I lay there dazed, staring up at the station wagon that now hung over my head.

I saw Doc's legs come out of it, out the open door. He was all right. He was letting himself down to the ground. And then the lightning came again.

It swallowed the station wagon and the trees and Doc in a ball of green fire, and when it went away the trees were scorched and the paint was blistered on the wrecked car, and Doc was rolling over and over down the slope, very slowly, as if he was tired and did not want to hurry. He came to rest not three feet away from me. His hair and his clothes were smoldering, but he wasn't worrying about it. He wasn't worrying about anything, any more. And for the second time there had not been any thunder, close at hand where the lightning was.

The rain came down on Doc in heavy sheets, and put the smoldering fire out.

Jim Bossert had just come from posting Doc Callendar's body. For the first time I found myself almost liking him, he looked so sick and beat-out. I pushed the bottle toward him, and he drank out of it and then lighted a cigarette and just sat there shaking.

"It was lightning," he said. "No doubt at all."

Ed Betts, the sheriff, said, "Hank still insists there was something screwy about it."

Bossert shook his head at me. "Lightning."

"Or a heavy electric charge," I said. "That comes to the same thing, doesn't it?"

"But you saw it hit, Hank."

"Twice," I said. "Twice."

We were in Bossert's office at the hospital. It was late in the afternoon, getting on for supper time. I reached for the bottle again, and Ed said quietly,

"Lightning does do that, you know. In spite of the old saying."

"The first time, it missed," I said. "Just. Second time it didn't. If I hadn't been thrown clear I'd be dead too. And there wasn't any thunder."

"You were dazed," Bossert said. "The first shock stunned you."

"It was green," I said.

"Fireballs often are."

"But not lightning."

"Atmospheric freak." Ed turned to Jim Bossert. "Give him something and send him home."

Bossert nodded and got up, but I said, "No. I've got to write up a piece on Doc for tomorrow's paper. See you."

I didn't want to talk any more. I went out and got my car and drove back to town. I felt funny. Hollow, cold, with a veil over my brain so I couldn't see anything clearly or think about anything clearly. I stopped at the store and bought another bottle to see me through the night, and a feeling of cold evil was in me, and I thought of green, silent lightning, and little gimcracks that didn't belong in a television set, and the grave wise face of a child who was not quite human. The face wavered and became the face of a man. A man from Hrylliannu.

I drove home, to the old house where nobody lives now but me. I wrote my story about Doc, and when I was through it was dark and the bottle was nearly empty. I went to bed.

I dreamed Doc Callendar called me on the phone and said, "I've found him but you'll have to hurry." And I said, "But you're dead. Don't call me, Doc, please don't." But the phone kept ringing and ringing, and after a while I woke part way up and it really was ringing. It was two-forty-nine A.M.

It was Ed Betts. "Fire up at the hospital, Hank. I thought you'd want to know. The south wing. Gotta go now."

He hung up and I began to put clothes on the leaden dummy that was me. The south wing, I thought, and sirens went whooping up Goat Hill. The south wing. That's where X-ray is. That's where the pictures of the boy's insides are on file.

What a curious coincidence, I thought.

I drove after the sirens up Goat Hill, through the clear cool night with half a moon shining silver on the ridges, and Buckhorn standing calm and serene against the stars, thinking the lofty thoughts that seem to be reserved for mountains.

The south wing of the hospital burned brightly, a very pretty orange color against the night.

I pulled off the road and parked well below the center of activity and started to walk the rest of the way. Patients were being evacuated from the main building. People ran with things in their hands. Firemen yelled and wrestled with hoses and streams of water arced over the flames. I didn't think they were going to save the south wing. I thought they would be doing well to save the hospital.

Another unit of the fire department came hooting and clanging up the road behind me. I stepped off the shoulder and as I did so I looked down to be sure of my footing. A flicker of movement on the slope about ten feet below caught my eye. Dimly, in the reflected glow of the fire, I saw the girl.

She was slim and light as a gazelle, treading her furtive way among the trees. Her hair was short and curled close to her head. In that light it was merely dark, but I knew it would be red in the sunshine, with glints of silver in it. She saw me or heard me, and she stopped for a second or two, startled, looking up. Her eyes shone like two coppery sparks, as the eyes of an animal shine, weird in the pale oval of her face. Then she turned and ran.

I went after her. She ran fast, and I was in lousy shape. But I was thinking about Doc.

I caught her.

It was dark all around us under the trees, but the firelight and the moonlight shone together into the clearing where we were. She didn't struggle or fight me. She turned around kind of light and stiff to face me, holding herself away from me as much as she could with my hands gripping her arms.

"What do you want with me?" she said, in a breathless little voice. It was accented, and sweet as a bird's. "Let me go."

I said, "What relation are you to the boy?"

That startled her. I saw her eyes widen, and then she turned her head and looked toward the darkness under the trees. "Please let me go," she said, and I thought that some new fear had come to her.

I shook her, feeling her small arms under my hands, wanting to break them, wanting to torture her because of Doc. "How was Doc killed?" I asked her. "Tell me. Who did it, and how?"

She stared at me. "Doc?" she repeated. "I do not understand." Now she began to struggle. "Let me go! You hurt me."

"The green lightning," I said. "A man was killed by it this morning. My friend. I want to know about it."

"Killed?" she whispered. "Oh, no. No one has been killed."

"And you set that fire in the hospital, didn't you? Why? Why were those films such a threat to you? Who are you? Where—"

"Hush," she said. "Listen."

I listened. There were sounds, soft and stealthy, moving up the slope toward us.

"They're looking for me," she whispered. "Please let me go. I don't know about your friend, and the fire was—necessary. I don't want anyone hurt, and if they find you like this—"

I dragged her back into the shadows underneath the trees. There was a huge old maple there with a gnarly trunk. We stood behind it, and now I had my arm around her waist and her head pressed back against my shoulder, and my right hand over her mouth.

"Where do you come from?" I asked her, with my mouth close to her ear. "Where is Hrylliannu?"

Her body stiffened. It was a nice body, very much like the boy's in some ways, delicately made but strong, and with superb coordination. In other ways it was not like the boy's at all. I was thinking of her as an enemy, but it was impossible not to think of her as a woman, too.

She said, her voice muffled under my hand, "Where did you hear that name?"

"Never mind," I said. "Just answer me."

She wouldn't.

"Where do you live now? Somewhere near here?"

She only strained to get away.

"All right," I said. "We'll go now. Back up to the hospital. The sheriff wants to see you."

I started to drag her away up the hill, and then two men came into the light of the clearing.

One was slender and curly-headed in that particular way I was beginning to know. He looked pleasantly excited, pleasantly stimulated, as though by a game in which he found enjoyment. His eyes picked up the fitful glow of the fire and shone eerily, as the girl's had.

The other man was a perfectly ordinary type. He was dark and heavy-set and tall, and his khaki pants sagged under his belly. His face was neither excited nor pleasant. It was obvious that to him this was no game. He carried a heavy automatic, and I thought he was perfectly prepared to use it.

I was afraid of him.

"… to send a dame, anyway," he was saying.

"That's your prejudice speaking," said the curly-haired man. "She was the only one to send." He gestured toward the flames. "How can you doubt it?"

"She's been caught."

"Not Vadi." He began to call softly. "Vadi? Vadi!"

The girl's lips moved under my hand. I bent to hear, and she said in the faint ghost of a whisper:

"If you want to live, let me go to them."

The big dark man said grimly, "She's been caught. We'd better do something about it, and do it quick."

He started across the clearing.

The girl's lips shaped one word. "Please!"

The dark man came with his big gun, and the curly-headed one came a little behind him, walking as a stalking cat walks, soft and springy on its toes. If I dragged the girl away they would hear me. If I stayed where I was, they would walk right onto me. Either way, I thought, I would pretty surely go to join Doc on the cold marble.

I let the girl go.

She ran out toward them. I stood stark and frozen behind the maple tree, waiting for her to turn and say the word that would betray me.

She didn't turn, and she didn't say the word. The curly-headed man put his arms around her and they talked rapidly for perhaps half a minute, and I heard her tell the dark man that she had only waited to be sure they would not be able to put the fire out too soon. Then all three turned and went quickly away among the dark trees.

I stayed where I was for a minute, breathing hard, trying to think. Then I went hunting for the sheriff.

By the time I found Ed Betts, of course, it was already too late. But he sent a car out anyway. They didn't find a trace of anyone on the road who answered the descriptions I gave.

Ed looked at me closely in the light of the dying fire, which they had finally succeeded in bringing under control. "Don't get sore at me now, Hank," he said. "But are you real sure you saw these people?"

"I'm sure," I said. I could still, if I shut my eyes and thought about it, *feel* the girl's body in my arms. "Her name was Vadi. Now I want to talk to Croft."

Croft was the Fire Marshal. I watched the boys pouring water on what was left of the south wing, which was nothing more than a pile of hot embers with some pieces of wall standing near it. Jim Bossert joined us, looking exhausted and grimy. He was too tired even to curse. He just wailed a little about the loss of all his fine X-ray equipment, and all his records.

"I met the girl who did it," I said. "Ed doesn't believe me."

"Girl?" said Bossert, staring.

"Girl. Apparently an expert at this sort of thing." I wondered what the curly-haired man was to her. "Was anybody hurt?"

"By the grace of God," said Bossert, "no."

"How did it start?"

"I don't know. All of a sudden I woke up and every window in the south wing was spouting flame like a volcano."

I glanced at Ed, who shrugged. "Could have been a short in that high-voltage equipment."

Bossert said, "What kind of a girl? A lunatic?"

"Another one like the boy. There was a man with her, maybe the boy's father, I don't know. The third one was just a man. Mean looking bastard with a gun. She said the fire was necessary."

"All this, just to get rid of some films?"

"It must be important to them," I said. "They already killed Doc. They tried to kill me. What's a fire?"

394

Ed Betts swore, his face twisted between unbelief and worry. Then Croft came up. Ed asked him, "What started the fire?"

Croft shook his head. "Too early to tell yet. Have to wait till things cool down. But I'll lay you any odds you like it was started by chemicals."

"Deliberately?"

"Could be," said Croft, and went away again.

I looked at the sky. It was almost dawn, that beautiful bleak time when the sky is neither dark nor light and the mountains are cut from black cardboard, without perspective. I said, "I'm going up to the Tates'. I'm worried about the boy."

"All right," said Ed quickly, "I'll go with you. In my car. We'll stop in town and pick up Jud. I want him to see that teevee."

"The hell with Jud," I said. "I'm in a hurry." And suddenly I was. Suddenly I was terribly afraid for that grave-faced child who was obviously the unwitting key to some secret that was important enough to justify arson and murder to those who wanted to keep it.

Ed hung right behind me. He practically shoved me into his car. It had COUNTY SHERRIFF painted on its door, and I thought of Doc's station wagon with its COUNTY HEALTH SERVICE, and it seemed like a poor omen but there was nothing I could do about it.

There was nothing I could do about stopping for Jud Spofford, either. Ed went in and routed him out of bed, taking the car keys with him. I sat smoking and looking up at Tunkhannock Ridge, watching it brighten to gold at the crest as the sun came up. Finally Jud came out grumbling and climbed in the back seat, a tall lanky young fellow in a blue coverall with *Newhale Electric Appliance Co.* embroidered in red on the pocket. His little wife watched from the doorway, holding her pink wrapper together.

We went away up Tunkhannock Ridge. There was still a black smudge of smoke above the hospital on Goat Hill. The sky over Buckhorn Mountain was clear and bright.

Sally Tate and her boy were already gone.

Mrs. Tate told us about it, while we sat on the lumpy sofa in the living room and the fat old dog watched us through the screen door, growling. Sally's sisters, or some of them at least, were in the kitchen listening.

"Never was so surprised at anything in my life," said Mrs. Tate. "Pa had just gone out to the barn with Harry and J. P.—them's the two oldest girls' husbands, you know. I and the girls was washing up after breakfast, and I heard this car drive in. Sure enough it was him. I went out on the stoop—"

"What kind of a car?" asked Ed.

"Same panel truck he was driving before, only the name was painted out. Kind of a dirty blue all over. 'Well,' I says, 'I never expected to see *your* face around here again!', I says, and he says—"

Boiled down to reasonable length, the man had said that he had always intended to come back for Sally, and that if he had known about the boy he would have come much sooner. He had been away, he said, on business, and had only just got back and heard about Sally bringing the child in to the hospital, and knew that it must be his. He had gone up to the house, and Sally had come running out into his arms, her face all shining. Then they went in together to see the boy, and Bill Jones had fondled him and called him Son, and the boy had watched him sleepily and without affection.

"They talked together for a while, private," said Mrs. Tate, "and then Sally come and said he was going to take her away and marry her and make the boy legal, and would I help her pack. And I did, and they went away together, the three of 'em. Sally didn't know when she'd be back."

She shook her head, smoothing her hair with knotted fingers. "I just don't know," she said. "I just don't know."

"What?" I asked her. "Was there something wrong?" I knew there was, but I wanted to hear what she had to say.

"Nothing you could lay your hand to," she said. "And Sally was so happy. She was just fit to burst. And he *was* real pleasant, real polite to me and Pa. We asked him about all them lies he told, and he said they wasn't lies at all. He said the man he was working for did plan to open a store in Newhale, but then he got sick and the plan fell through. He said his name was Bill Jones, and showed us some cards and things to prove it. And he said Sally just misunderstood the name of the place he come from because he give it the old Spanish pronunciation."

"What did he say it was really?" Ed asked, and she looked surprised.

"Now I think of it, I guess he didn't say."

"Well, where's he going to live, with Sally?"

"He isn't settled yet. He's got two or three prospects, different places. She was so happy," said Mrs. Tate, "and I ought to be too, 'cause Lord knows I've wished often enough he would come back and get that pesky brat of his, and Sally too if she was minded. But I ain't. I ain't happy at all, and I don't know why."

"Natural reaction," said Ed Betts heartily. "You miss your daughter, and probably the boy too, more than you know."

"I've had daughters married before. It was something about this man. Something—" Mrs. Tate hesitated a long time, searching for a word. "Queer," she said at last. "Wrong. I couldn't tell you what. Like the boy, only more so. The boy has Sally in him. This one—" She made a gesture with her hands. "Oh, well, I expect I'm just looking for trouble."

"I expect so, Mrs. Tate," said Ed, "but you be sure and get in touch with me if you don't hear from Sally in a reasonable time. And now I'd like this young man to look at your teevee."

Jud, who had been sitting stiff and uncomfortable during the talking, jumped up and practically ran to the set. Mrs. Tate started to protest, but Ed said firmly, "This may be important, Mrs. Tate. Jud's a good serviceman, he won't upset anything."

"I hope not," she said. "It does run real good."

Jud turned it on and watched it for a minute. "It sure does," he said. "And in this location, too."

He took the back off and looked inside. After a minute he let go a long low whistle.

"What is it?" said Ed, going closer.

"Damnedest thing," said Jud. "Look at that wiring. He's loused up the circuits, all right—and there's a couple tubes in there like I never saw before." He was getting excited. "I'd have to tear the whole thing down to see what he's really done, but somehow he's boosted the power and the sensitivity way up. The guy must be a wizard."

Mrs. Tate said loudly, "You ain't tearing anything down, young man. You just leave it like it is."

I said, "What about that dingus on the side?"

"Frankly," said Jud, "that stops me. It's got a wire to it, but it don't seem to hitch up anywhere in the set." He turned the set off and began to poke gently around. "See here, this little hairline wire that comes down and bypasses the whole chassis? It cuts in here on the live line, so it draws power whether the set's on or not. But I don't see how it can have anything to do with the set operating."

"Well, take it out," said Ed. "We'll take it down to the shop and see whether we can make anything of it."

"Okay," said Jud, ignoring Mrs. Tate's cry of protest. He reached in and for the first time actually touched the enigmatic little unit, feeling for what held it to the side of the case.

There was a sharp pop and a small bright flare, and Jud leaped back with a howl. He put his scorched fingers in his mouth and his eyes watered. Mrs. Tate cried, "Now, you've done it, you've ruined my teevee!" There was a smell of burning on the air. The girls came running out of the kitchen and the old dog barked and clawed the screen.

One of the girls said, "What happened?"

"I don't know," Jud said. "The goddamned thing just popped like a bomb when I touched it."

There was a drift of something gray—ash or dust—and that was all. Even the hairline wire was consumed.

"It looks," I said, "as though Mr. Jones didn't want anybody else to look over his technological achievements."

Ed grunted. He looked puzzled and irresolute. "Hurt the set any?" he asked.

"Dunno," said Jud, and turned it on.

It ran as perfectly as before.

"Well," said Mrs. Tate, "thank goodness."

"Yeah," said Ed. "I guess that's all, then. What do you say, Hank? We might as well go."

I said we might as well. We climbed back into Ed's car and started—the second time for me—back down Tunkhannock Ridge.

Jud was still sucking his fingers. He wondered out loud if the funny-looking tubes in the set would explode the same way if you touched them, and I said probably. Ed didn't say anything. He was frowning deeply. I asked him what he thought about it.

"I'm trying to figure the angle," he said. "This Bill Jones. What does he get out of it? What does he *make*? On the television gag, I mean. People usually want to get paid for work like that."

Jud offered the opinion that the man was a nut. "One of these crazy guys like in the movies, always inventing things that make trouble. But I sure would like to know what he done to that set.

"Well," said Ed, "I can't see what more we can do. He did come back for the girl, and apart from that he hasn't broken any laws."

"Hasn't he?" I said, looking out the window. We were coming to the place where Doc had died. There was no sign of a storm today. Everything was bright, serene, peaceful. But I could feel the cold feeling of being watched. Someone, somewhere, knew me. He watched where I went and what I did, and decided whether or not to send the green lightning to slay me. It was a revelation, like the moments you have as a young child when you become acutely conscious of God. I began to shake. I wanted to crawl down in the back seat and hide. Instead I sat where I was and tried to keep the naked terror from showing too much. And I watched the sky. And nothing happened.

Ed Betts didn't mention it, but he began to drive faster and faster until I thought we weren't going to need any green lightning. He didn't slow down until we hit the valley. I think he would have been glad to get rid of me, but he had to haul me all the way back up Goat Hill to get my car. When he did let me off, he said gruffly,

"I'm not going to listen to you again till you've had a good twelve hours' sleep. And I need some myself. So long."

I went home, but I didn't sleep. Not right away. I told my assistant and right-hand man, Joe Streckfoos, that the paper was all his today, and then I got on the phone. I drove the local exchange crazy, but by about five o'clock that afternoon I had the information I wanted.

I had started with a map of the area on my desk. Not just Ne-whale, but the whole area, with Buckhorn Mountain roughly at the center and showing the hills and valleys around its northern periphery. By five o'clock the map showed a series of red pencil dots. If you connected them together with a line they formed a sprawling, irregular, but unbroken circle drawn around Buckhorn, never exceeding a certain number of miles in distance from the peak.

Every pencil dot represented a television set that had within the last three years been serviced by a red-haired man—for free.

I looked at the map for a long time, and then I went out in the yard and looked up at Buckhorn. It seemed to me to stand very high, higher than I remembered. From flank to crest the green unbroken forest covered it. In the winter time men hunted there for bear and deer, and I knew there were a few hunting lodges, hardly more than shacks, on its lower slopes. These were not used in summer, and apart from the hunters no one ever bothered to climb those almost perpendicular sides, hanging onto the trees as onto a ladder, up to the fog and storm that plagued the summit.

There were clouds there now. It almost seemed that Buckhorn pulled them down over his head like a cowl, until the gray trailing edges hid him almost to his feet. I shivered and went inside and shut the door. I cleaned my automatic and put in a full clip. I made a sandwich and drank the last couple of drinks in last night's bottle. I laid out my boots and my rough-country pants and a khaki shirt. I set the alarm. It was still broad daylight. I went to bed.

The alarm woke me at eleven-thirty. I did not turn on any lamps. I don't know why, except that I still had that naked feeling of being watched. Light enough came to me anyhow from the intermittent sulfurous flares in the sky. There was a low mutter of thunder in the west. I put the automatic in a shoulder holster under my shirt, not to hide it but because it was out of the way there. When I was dressed I went downstairs and out the back door, heading for the garage.

It was quiet, the way a little town can be quiet at night. I could hear the stream going over the stones, and the million little songs of the crickets, the peepers, and the frogs were almost stridently loud.

400

Then they began to stop. The frogs first, in the marshy places beside the creek. Then the crickets and the peepers. I stopped too, in the black dark beside a clump of rhododendrons my mother used to be almost tiresomely proud of. My skin turned cold and the hair bristled on the back of my neck and I heard soft padding footsteps and softer breathing on the heavy air.

Two people had waded the creek and come up into my yard.

There was a flare and a grumble in the sky and I saw them close by, standing on the grass, looking up at the unlighted house.

One of them was the girl Vadi, and she carried something in her hands. The other was the heavy-set dark man with the gun.

"It's okay," he told her. "He's sleeping. Get busy."

I slid the automatic into my palm and opened my mouth to speak, and then I heard her say:

"You won't give him a chance to get out?"

Her tone said she knew the answer to that one before she asked it. But he said with furious sarcasm:

"Why certainly, and then you can call the sheriff and explain why you burned the house down. And the hospital. Christ. I told Arnek you weren't to be trusted." He gave her a rough shove. "Get with it."

Vadi walked five careful paces away from him. Then very swiftly she threw away, in two different directions, whatever it was she carried. I heard the two things fall, rustling among grass and branches where it might take hours to find them even by daylight. She spun around. "Now," she said in a harsh defiant voice, "what are you going to do?"

There was a moment of absolute silence, so full of murder that the far-off lightning seemed feeble by comparison. Then he said:

"All right, let's get out of here."

She moved to join him, and he waited until she was quite close to him. Then he hit her. She made a small bleating sound and fell down. He started to kick her, and then I jumped out and hit him over the ear with the flat of the automatic. It was his turn to fall down.

Vadi got up on her hands and knees. She stared at me, sobbing a little with rage and pain. Blood was running from the corner of her mouth. I took the man's gun and threw it far off and it splashed in the creek. Then I got down beside the girl.

"Here," I said. "Have my handkerchief."

She took it and held it to her mouth. "You were outside here all the time," she said. She sounded almost angry.

"It just happened that way. I still owe you thanks for my life. And my house. Though you weren't so tender about the hospital."

"There was no one to be killed there. I made sure. A building one can always rebuild, but a life is different."

She looked at the unconscious man. Her eyes burned with that catlike brilliance in the lightning flares.

"I could kill him," she said, "with pleasure."

"Who is he?"

"My brother's partner." She glanced toward Buckhorn and the light went out of her eyes. Her head became bowed.

"Your brother sent you to kill me?"

"He didn't say—"

"But you knew."

"When Marlin came with me I knew."

She had begun to tremble.

"Do you make a career of arson?"

"Arson? Oh. The setting of fires. No. I am a chemist. And I wish I—"

She caught herself fiercely and would not finish.

I said, "Those things are listening devices, then."

She had to ask me what I meant. Her mind was busy with some thorny darkness of its own.

"The little gadgets your brother put in the television sets," I said. "I figured that's what they were when I saw how they were placed. A string of sentry posts all around the center of operations, little ears to catch every word of gossip, because if any of the local people get suspicious they're bound to talk about it and so give warning. He heard my calls this afternoon, didn't he? That's why he sent you. And he heard Doc and me at the Tates'. That's why—"

Moving with that uncanny swiftness of hers, she rose and ran away from me. It was like before. She ran fast, and I ran after her. She went splashing through the shallow stream and the water flew back against me, wetting my face, spattering my clothes. On the far bank I caught her, as I had before. But this time she fought me.

"Let me go," she said, and beat her hands against me. "Do you know what I've done for you? I've asked for the knife for myself. Let me go, you clumsy fool—"

I held her tighter. Her soft curls pressed against my cheek. Her body strove against me, and it was not soft but excitingly strong.

"—before I regret it," she said, and I kissed her.

It was strange, what happened then.

I've kissed girls who didn't want to be kissed, and I've kissed girls who didn't like me particularly. I've kissed a couple of the touch-me-not kind who shrink from any sort of physical contact. I've had my face slapped. But I never had a girl *withdraw* from me the way she did. It was like something closing, folding up, shutting every avenue of contact, and yet she never moved. In fact she had stopped moving entirely. She just stood with my arms around her and my lips on hers, and kind of a coldness came out of her, a rejection so total I couldn't even get mad. I was shocked, and very much puzzled, but you can't get mad at a thing that isn't personal. This was too deep for that. And suddenly I thought of the boy.

"A different breed," I said. "Worlds apart. Is that it?"

"Yes," she said quietly. "Worlds apart."

And the coldness spread through me. I stood on the bank of the stream in the warm night, the bank where I had stood ten thousand times before, boy and man, and saw the strange shining of her eyes, and I was more than cold, I was afraid. I stepped back away from her, still holding her but in a different way.

"It wasn't like this," I said, "between your brother and Sally Tate."

The girl-thing said, "My brother Arnek is a corrupt man."

"Vadi," I said. "Where is Hrylliannu?"

The girl-thing looked past my shoulder and said, "Marlin is running away."

I looked too, and it was so. The big man's head was harder than I had thought. He had got up, and I saw him blundering rapidly away along the side of my house, heading for the street.

"Well," I said, "he's gone now. You must have come in a car, didn't you?"

She nodded.

"Good," I said. "It won't be challenged as soon as mine. We'll take it."

"Where are you going?" she asked, catching her breath sharply.

"Where I was going when you stopped me. Up Buckhorn."

"Oh no," she said. "No, you can't, you mustn't." She was human again, and afraid. "I saved your life, isn't that enough for you? You'll never live to climb Buckhorn and neither will I if—"

"Did Sally and the boy live to climb it?" I asked her, and she hung her head and nodded. "Then you'll see to it that we do."

"But tonight!" she said in a panic. "Not tonight!"

"What's so special about tonight?" She didn't answer, and I shook her. "What's going on up there?"

She didn't answer that, either. She said with sudden fierceness, "All right, then, come on. Climb Buckhorn and see. And when you're dying, remember that I tried to stop you."

She didn't speak again. She led me without protest to the car parked on the dirt road. It was a panel truck. By day it would have been a dirty blue.

"He's going to kill them, isn't he?" I said. "He killed Doc. You admit he wants to kill me. What's going to save Sally and the child?"

"You torture me," she said. "This is a world of torture. Go on. Go on, and get it done."

I started the panel truck. Like the television set, it worked better than it had any business to. It fled with uncanny strength and swiftness over the dirt roads toward Buckhorn, soft-sprung as a cloud, silent as a dream.

"It's a pity," I said. "Your brother has considerable genius."

She laughed. A bitter laugh. "He couldn't pass his second year of technical training. That's why he's here."

She looked at Buckhorn as though she hated the mountain, and Buckhorn, invisible behind a curtain of storm, answered her look with a sullen curse, spoken in thunder.

I stopped at the last gas station on the road and honked the owner out of bed and told him to call Sheriff Betts and tell him where I'd gone. I didn't dare do it myself for fear Vadi would get away from me. The man was very resentful about being waked up. I hoped he would not take out his resentment by forgetting to call.

"You're pretty close to Buckhorn," I told him. "The neck you save may be your own."

I left him to ponder that, racing on toward the dark mountain in that damned queer car that made me feel like a character in one of my own bad dreams, with the girl beside me—the damned queer girl who was not quite human.

The road dropped behind us. We began to climb the knees of the mountain. Vadi told me where to turn, and the road became a track, and the track ended in the thick woods beside a rickety little lodge the size of a piano-box, with a garage behind it. The garage only looked rickety. The headlights showed up new and sturdy timbers on the inside.

I cut the motor and the lights and reached for the handbrake. Vadi must have been set on a hair-trigger waiting for that moment. I heard her move and there was a snap as though she had pulled something from a clip underneath the dashboard. The door on her side banged open.

I shouted to her to stop and sprang out of the truck to catch her. But she was already out of the garage, and she was waiting for me. Just as I came through the door there was a bolt of lightning, bright green, small and close at hand. I saw it coming. I saw her dimly in the backflash and knew that in some way she had made the lightning with a thing she held in her hand. Then it hit me and that was all.

When I came to I was all alone and the rain was falling on me just the way it had on Doc....

But I wasn't dead.

I crawled around and finally managed to get up, feeling heavy and disjointed. My legs and arms flopped around as though the coordinating controls had been burned out. I stood inside the garage out of the rain, rubbing my numb joints and thinking.

All the steam had gone out of me. I didn't want to climb Buck-born Mountain any more. It looked awfully black up there, and awfully lonesome, and God alone knew what was going on under the veil of cloud and storm that hid it. The lightning flashes—real sky-made lightning—showed me the dripping trees going right up into nothing, with the wind thrashing them, and then the following thunder cracked my eardrums. The rain hissed, and I thought, it's crazy for one man to go up there alone.

Then I thought about Sally Tate and the little red-headed kid, and I thought how Ed Betts might already be up there somewhere, plowing his way through the woods looking for me. I didn't know how long I'd been out.

I made sure I still had my gun, and I did have. I wished I had a drink, but that was hopeless. So I started out. I didn't go straight up the mountain. I figured the girl would have had time to find her brother and give him warning, and that he might be looking for me to come that way. I angled off to the east, where I remembered a ravine that might give me some cover. I'd been up Buckhorn before, but only by daylight, with snow on the ground and a couple of friends with me, and not looking for anything more sinister than a bear.

I climbed the steep flank of the mountain, leaning almost into it, worming and floundering and pulling my way between the trees. The rain fell and soaked me. The thunder was a monstrous presence, and the lightning was a great torch that somebody kept tossing back and forth so that sometimes you could see every vein of every leaf on the tree you were fighting with, and sometimes it was so dark that you knew the sun and stars hadn't been invented yet. I lost the ravine. I only knew I was still going up. There wasn't any doubt about that. After a while the rain slacked off and almost stopped.

In an interval between crashes of thunder I heard voices.

They were thin and far away. I tried to place them, and when I thought I had them pegged I started toward them. The steep pitch of the ground fell away into a dizzying downslope and I was almost running into a sort of long shallow trough, thickly wooded, its bottom hidden from any view at all except one directly overhead. And there were lights in it, or at least a light.

I slowed down and went more carefully, hoping the storm would cover any noise I made.

The voices went on, and now I could hear another sound, the scrinch and screek of metal rubbing on metal.

I was on the clearing before I knew it. And it wasn't a clearing at all really, just one of those natural open places where the soil is too thin to support trees and runs to brush instead. It wasn't much more than ten feet across. Almost beside me were a couple of tents so cleverly hidden among the trees that you practically had to fall on them, as I did, to find them at all.

From one of them came the sleepy sobbing of a child.

In the small clearing Vadi and Arnek were watching a jointed metal mast build itself up out of a pit in the ground. The top of it was already out of sight in the cloud but it was obviously taller than the trees. The lamp was on the ground beside the pit.

The faces of Vadi and her brother were both angry, both set and obstinate. Perhaps it was their mutual fury that made them seem less human, or more unhuman, than ever, the odd bone-structure of cheek and jaw accentuated, the whole head elongated, the silver-red hair fairly bristling, the copper-colored eyes glinting with that unpleasantly catlike brilliance in the light. They had been quarreling, and they still were, but not in English. Arnek had a look like a rattlesnake.

Vadi, I thought, was frightened. She kept glancing at the tents, and in a minute the big man, Marlin, came out of one of them. He was pressing a small bandage on the side of his head, over his ear. He looked tired and wet and foul-tempered, as though he had not had an easy time getting back to base.

He started right in on Vadi, cursing her because of what she had done.

Arnek said in English, "I didn't ask her to come here, and I'm sending her home tonight."

"That's great," Marlin said. "That's a big help. We'll have to move our base anyway now."

"Maybe not," said Arnek defiantly. He watched the slim mast stretching up and up with a soft screeking of its joints.

"You're a fool," said Marlin, in a tone of cold and bitter contempt. "You started this mess, Arnek. You had to play around with that girl and make a kid to give the show away. Then you pull that half-cocked trick with those guys in the station wagon and you can't even do that right. You kill the one but not the other. And then *she* louses up the only chance we got left. You know how much money we're going to lose? You know how long it'll take us to find a location half as good as this? You know what I ought to do?"

Arnek's voice was sharp, but a shade uncertain. "Oh, stop bitching and get onto those scanners. All we need is another hour and then they can whistle. And there are plenty of mountains."

"Are there," said Marlin, and looked again at Vadi. "And how long do you think she'll keep her mouth shut at *your* end?"

He turned and walked back into the tent. Arnek looked uncertainly at Vadi and then fixed his attention on the mast again. Vadi's face was the color of chalk. She started once toward the tent and Arnek caught her roughly and spoke to her in whatever language they used, and she stopped.

I slid around the back of the tents to the one Marlin was in. There was a humming and whining inside. I got down on my hands and knees and crawled carefully over the wet grass between the tents, toward the front. The mast apparently made its last joint because it stopped and Arnek said something to Vadi and they bent over what seemed to be a sunken control box in the ground. I took my chance and whipped in through the tent flap.

I didn't have long to look around. The space inside was crammed with what seemed to be electronic equipment. Marlin was sitting hunched up on a stool in front of a big panel with a dozen or so little screens on it like miniature television monitors. The screens, I just had time to see, showed an assortment of views of Buckhorn and the surrounding areas, and Marlin was apparently, by remote control, rotating one by one the distant receivers that sent the images to the screens. They must have been remarkably tight-beamed, because they were not much disturbed by static. I knew now how the eye of God had watched Doc and me on Tunkhannock Ridge.

I didn't know yet how the lightning-bolts were hurled, but I was pretty sure Ed Betts would get one if his car showed up on a scanner screen, and who would be the wiser? Poor Ed hit by lightning just like old Doc, and weren't the storms something fierce this summer?

Marlin turned around and saw it wasn't Arnek. He moved faster than I would have thought possible. He scooped up the light stool he was sitting on and threw it at me, leaping sideways himself in a continuation of the same movement. In the second in which I was getting my head out of the way of the stool he pulled a gun. He had had a spare, just as he must have had a car stashed somewhere in or near the town.

He did not quite have time to fire. I shot him twice through the body. He dropped but I didn't know if he was dead. I kicked the gun out of his hand and jumped to stand flat against the canvas wall beside the front flap, not pressing against it. The canvas was light-proof, and the small lamps over the control panels did not throw shadows.

Arnek did not come in.

After a second or two I got nervous. I could hear him shouting "Marlin! Marlin!" I ran into the narrow space behind the banks of equipment, being extremely careful how I touched anything. I did not see any power leads. It dawned on me that all this stuff had come up out of a pit in the ground like the mast and that the generator must be down there below. The floor wasn't canvas at all, but some dark gray material to which the equipment was bolted.

I got my knife out and started to slit the canvas at the back. And suddenly the inside of the tent was full of green fire. It sparked off every metal thing and jarred the gun out of my hand. It nearly knocked me out again. But I was shielded by the equipment from the full force of the shock. It flicked off again almost at once. I got the canvas cut and squirmed through it and then I put three or four shots at random into the back of the equipment just for luck.

Then I raced around the front and caught Arnek just as he was deciding not to enter the tent after all.

He had a weapon in his hand like the one Vadi had used on me. I said, "Drop it," and he hesitated, looking evil and upset. "Drop it!" I told him again, and he dropped it. "Now stand away," I said. "Walk out toward your sister, real slow, one step at a time."

He walked, and I picked up the weapon.

"Good," I said. "Now we can all relax." And I called Sally Tate, telling her it was safe to come out now.

All this time since I was where I could see her Vadi had stood with one hand over her mouth, looking up into the mist.

Sally Tate came out of the other tent. She was carrying the boy, and both their faces were pale and puffy-eyed and streaked with tears.

"It's all right now," I said. "You can go—" I was going to say "home," and then there was a sound in the sky that was not wind or thunder, that was hardly a sound at all, but more of a great sigh. The air pressed down on me and the grass was flattened as by a down-driven wind and all the branches of the trees bowed. The mist rolled, boiled, was rent, torn apart, scattered.

Something had come to rest against the top of the mast.

Arnek turned and ran to Vadi and I did not stop him. I moved closer to Sally Tate, standing with her mouth open and her eyes big and staring.

The mast began to contract downward, bringing the thing with it.

I suppose I knew then what the thing was. I just didn't want to admit it. It was cylindrical and slender, about fifty feet long, with neither wings nor jets. I watched it come slowly and gracefully down, attached by its needle-sharp nose to the magnetic grapple on top of the mast. The mast acted as automatic guide and stabilizer, dropping the ship into a slot between the trees as neatly as you would drop a slice of bread into the slot of a toaster.

And all the time the bitter breath of fear was blowing on me and little things were falling into place in my mind and I realized that I had known the answer for some time and had simply refused to see it.

A port opened in the side of the ship. And as though that was the final symbolic trigger I needed, I got the full impact of what I was seeing. Suddenly the friendly protecting sky seemed to have been torn open above me as the veiling cloud was torn, and through the rent the whole Outside poured in upon me, the black freezing spaces of the galaxy, the blaze and strangeness of a billion billion suns. I shrank beneath that vastness. I was nothing, nobody, an infinitesimal fleck in a cosmos too huge to be borne. The stars had come too close. I wanted to get down and howl and grovel like a dog.

No wonder Arnek and Vadi and the boy were queer. They were not mutants—they were not even that Earthly. They came from another world.

A little ladder had extended itself downward from the port. A man came briskly to the ground and spoke to Arnek. He resembled Arnek except that he was dressed in a single close-fitting garment of some dark stuff. Arnek pointed to me, speaking rapidly. The man turned and looked at me, his body expressing alarm. I felt childish and silly standing there with my little gun. Lone man of Earth at an incredible Thermopylae, saying, "You shall not land."

All the time Arnek and the stranger had been talking there had been other activities around the ship. A hatch in the stern had opened and now from both hatches people began to come out helter-skelter as though haste was the chief necessity. There were men and women both. They all looked human. Slightly odd, a little queer perhaps, but human. They were different types, different colors, sizes, and builds, but they all fitted in somewhere pretty close to Earthly types. They all looked a little excited, a little scared, considerably bewildered by the place in which they found themselves. Some of the women were crying. There were maybe twenty people in all.

I understood then exactly what Arnek and Marlin had been up to and it seemed so grotesquely familiar and prosaic that I began to laugh.

"Wetbacks," I said aloud. "That's what you're doing, smuggling aliens."

Aliens. Yes indeed.

It did not seem so funny when I thought about it.

The stranger turned around and shouted an order. The men and women stopped, some of them still on the ladders. More voices shouted. Then those on the ladders were shoved aside and eight men in uniform jumped out, with weapons in their hands.

Sally Tate let go one wild wavering shriek. The child fell out of her arms. He sat on the wet ground with the wind knocked out of him so he couldn't cry, blinking in shocked dismay. Sally tottered. Her big strong healthy body was sunken and collapsed, every muscle slack. She turned and made a staggering lunge for the tent and fell partly in through the doorway, crawled the rest of the way like a hurt dog going under a porch, and lay there with the flap pulled over her head.

I didn't blame her. I don't even know what obscure force kept me from joining her.

Of the eight men, five were not human. Two of them not even remotely.

I can't describe them. I can't remember what they looked like, not clearly.

Let's be honest. I don't *want* to remember.

I suppose if you were used to things like that all your life it would be different. You wouldn't think anything about it.

I was not used to things like that. I knew that I never would be, not if we ourselves achieved space-flight tomorrow. I'm too old, too set in the familiar pattern of existence that has never been broken for man since the beginning. Perhaps others are more resilient. They're welcome to it.

I picked up the boy and ran.

It came on again to rain. I ran down Buckhorn Mountain, carrying the boy in my arms. And the green lightning came after us, hunting us along the precipitous slope.

The boy had got his breath back. He asked me why we had to die. I said never mind, and kept on running.

I fell with him and rolled to the bottom of a deep gully. We were shaken. We lay in the dripping brush looking up at the lightning lancing across the night above us. After a while it stopped. I picked him up again and crept silently along the gully and onto the slope below.

And nearly got shot by Ed Betts and a scratch posse, picking their cautious way up the mountainside.

One of the men took the child out of my arms. I hung onto Ed and said inanely, "They're landing a load of wetbacks."

"Up there?"

"They've got a ship," I told him. "They're aliens, Ed. Real aliens."

I began to laugh again. I didn't want to. It just seemed such a hellishly clever play on words that I couldn't help it.

Fire bloomed suddenly in the night above us. A second later the noise of the explosion reached us.

I stopped laughing. "They must be destroying their installations. Pulling out. Marlin said they'd have to. Christ. And Sally is still up there."

I ran back up the mountain, clambering bearlike through the trees. The others followed.

There was one more explosion. Then I came back to the edge of the clearing. Ed was close behind me. I don't think any of the others were really close enough to see. There was a lot of smoke. The tents were gone. Smoking trees were slowly toppling in around the edges of a big raw crater in the ground. There was no trace of the instruments that had been in the tents.

The ship was still there. The crew, human and unhuman, were shoving the last of the passengers back into the ship. There was an altercation going on beside the forward port.

Vadi had her arm around Sally Tate. She was obviously trying to get her aboard. I thought I understood then why Sally and the boy were still alive. Probably Vadi had been insisting that her brother send them along where they wouldn't be any danger to him, and he hadn't quite had the nerve to cross her. He was looking uncertain now, and it was the officer who was making the refusal. Sally herself seemed to be in a stupor.

Vadi thrust past the officer and led Sally toward the ladder. And Sally went, willingly. I like to remember that, now, when she's gone.

I think—I hope—that Sally's all right out there. She was younger and simpler than I, she could adapt. I think she loved Bill Jones—Arnek—enough to leave her child, leave her family, leave her world, and still be happy near him.

Ed and I started to run across the clearing. Ed had not said a word. But his face was something to look at.

They saw us coming but they didn't bother to shoot at us. They seemed in a tremendous hurry. Vadi screamed something, and I was sure it was in English and a warning to me, but I couldn't understand it. Then she was gone inside the ship and so were Arnek and Sally and the officer and crewmen, and the ladders went up and the ports shut.

The mooring mast began to rise and so did the ship, and the trees were bent with the force of its rising.

I knew then what the warning was.

I grabbed Ed bodily and hauled him back. The ship didn't have to be very high. Only above the trees. I hauled him as far as blind in-stinct told me I could go and then I yelled, "Get down! Get down!" to everybody within earshot and made frantic motions. It all took possibly thirty seconds. Ed understood and we flopped and hugged the ground.

The mast blew.

Dirt, rocks, pieces of tree rained down around us. The shock wave pounded our ears. A few moments later, derisive and powerful, a long thin whistling scream tore upward across the sky, and faded, and was gone.

We got up after a while and collected the muddy and startled posse and went to look at what was left of the clearing. There was nothing. Sally Tate was gone as though she had never existed. There was no shred of anything left to prove that what Ed and I had seen was real.

We made up a story, about a big helicopter and an alien racket. It wasn't too good a story, but it was better than the truth. Afterward, when we were calmer, Ed and I tried to figure it out for ourselves. How it was done, I mean, and why.

The "how" was easy enough, given the necessary technology. Pick a remote but not too inconveniently isolated spot, like the top of Buckhorn Mountain. Set up your secret installation—a simple one, so compact and carefully hidden that hunters could walk right over it and never guess it was there when it was not in use. On nights when conditions are right—that is to say, when the possibility of being observed is nearest to zero—run your cargo in and land it. We figured that the ship we saw wasn't big enough to transport that many people very far. We figured it was a landing-craft, ferrying the passengers down from a much bigger mothership way beyond the sky.

A star-ship. It sounded ridiculous when you said it. But we had seen the members of the crew. It is generally acknowledged by nearly everybody now that there is no intelligent life of any terrestrial sort on the other planets of our own system. So they had to come from farther out.

Why? That was a tougher one to solve. We could only guess at it.

"There must be a hell of a big civilization out there," said Ed, "to build the ships and travel in them. They obviously know we're here."

Uneasy thought.

"Why haven't they spoken to us?" he wondered. "Let us in on it too."

"I suppose," I said, "they're waiting for us to develop space-flight on our own. Maybe it's a kind of test you have to pass to get in on their civilization. Or maybe they figure we're so backward they don't want to have anything to do with us, all our wars and all. Or both. Pick your own reason."

"Okay," said Ed. "But why dump their people on us like that? And how come Marlin, one of our own people, was in on it?"

"There *are* Earthmen who'll do anything for money," I said. "Like Marlin. It'd not be too hard to contact men like him, use them as local agents.

"As for why they dump their people on us," I went on, "it probably isn't legal, where they came from. Remember what Marlin said about Vadi? *How long will she keep her mouth shut at your end?* My guess is her brother was a failure at home and got into a dirty racket, and she was trying to get him out of it. There must be other worlds like Earth, too, or the racket wouldn't be financially sound. Not enough volume."

"But the wetbacks," Ed said. "Were they failures, too? People who couldn't compete in the kind of a society they must have? And how the hell many do you suppose they've run in on us already?"

I've wondered about that myself. How many aliens have Marlin, and probably others like him, taken off the star-boats and dressed and instructed and furnished with false papers, in return doubtless for all the valuables the poor devils had? How many of the people you see around you every day, the anonymous people that just look a little odd somehow, the people about whom you think briefly that they don't even look human—the queer ones you notice and then forget—how many of them *aren't* human at all in the sense that we understand that word?

Like the boy.

Sally Tate's family obviously didn't want him back. So I had myself appointed his legal guardian, and we get on fine together. He's a bright kid. His father may have been a failure in his own world, but on ours the half-bred child has an I.Q. that would frighten you. He's also a good youngster. I think he takes after his aunt.

I've thought of getting married since then, just to make a better home for the boy, and to fill up a void in my own life I'm beginning to feel. But I haven't quite done it yet. I keep thinking maybe Vadi will come back some day, walking with swift grace down the side of Buckhorn Mountain. I do not think it is likely, but I can't quite put it out of my mind. I remember the cold revulsion that there was between us, and then I wonder if that feeling would go on, or whether you couldn't get used to that idea of differentness in time.

The trouble is, I guess, that Vadi kind of spoiled me for the general run of women.

I wonder what her life is like in Hrylliannu, and where it is. Sometimes on the bitter frosty nights when the sky is diamond-clear and the Milky Way glitters like the mouth of hell across it, I look up at the stars and wonder which one is hers. And old Buckhorn sits black and silent in the north, and the deep wounds on his shoulder are healing into grassy scars. He says nothing. Even the thunder now has a hollow sound. It is merely thunder.

But, as Arnek said, there are plenty of mountains.

416

ALL THE COLORS
OF THE RAINBOW

Venture Science Fiction, November 1957

It had rained in the valley, steadily and hard, for thirty-six hours. The ground was saturated. Every fold in the rough flanks of the hills spouted a muddy torrent and the torrents flowed in sheets over the flat country below and poured through raw self-gouged channels into the river. And the river, roused from its normal meek placidity, roared and rolled like a new Mississippi, tearing away its banks, spreading wide and yellow across the fields, into the orchards and over the roads, into the streets of Grand Falls where the people had left their houses and fled to the safety of higher land. Uprooted trees and broken timbers knocked at the walls of the old brick buildings on the main street. In the lobby of the Grand Falls Hotel the brass spittoons floated ever higher, clanging mournfully when they struck their sides together.

High on the ridges that enclosed the valley to the northeast and the southwest, hidden by a careful hand, two small mechanisms hummed quietly, ceaselessly. They were called miniseeders and they were not part of Earth's native technology. Their charges would run out in a matter of days, but in the meantime they were extremely efficient, hurling a steady stream of charged particles into the sky to seed the clouds moving over the ridges.

In the valley, it continued to rain....

IT WAS HIS first big job on his own responsibility, with no superior closer than Galactic Center, which was a long way off. He was not at all sure he was going to be able to do it.

He said so to Ruvi, slowing down the cumbersome ground car so she could see what he meant.

"Look at it. How can this mess ever be made into a civilized continent?"

She turned her head in the quick way she had and said, "Scared, Flin?"

"I guess I am."

He was ashamed to say it, particularly since it was not really the difficulty and importance of the job that daunted him but the planet itself.

He had studied weather-control engineering on his home-world at Mintaka, which was one of the science's earliest triumphs, and he had done research and field work on five other worlds, at least two of which were in fairly early stages of control. But he had never been anywhere before that was so totally untouched by galactic civilization.

Peripheral Survey had made contact with these fringe systems only in the last couple of decades and that was far too short a time to make much of an impress on them. Even in the big urban centers an alien like himself could hardly walk down the street yet without attracting an unwelcome amount of attention, not all of it polite. Coming from the Federation worlds with their cosmopolitan populations, Flin found this hard to take.

But Galactic Center was enthusiastic about these fringe worlds because quite a few of them had an amazingly high, if highly uneven, degree of civilization which they had developed literally in their several vacuums. Center was in a rush to send them teachers and technicians and that was why he, far ahead of his due time, had been pitchforked into the position of leading a four-man planning-and-instruction team of weather-control experts.

It was a splendid opportunity with splendid possibilities for the future, and the raise in pay had enabled him to take on Ruvi as a permanent mate much sooner than he had hoped. But he hadn't bargained for the loneliness, the constant uncertainty in relationships, the lack of all the vast solid background he was used to on the Federation worlds.

Ruvi said, "All right then, I'll admit I'm scared too. And hot. Let's stop this clumsy thing and get a breath of air. Right over there looks like a good place."

He eased the car off the narrow road, onto a point of land with a few big stones around the edge to mark the drop-off. Ruvi got out and went to stand by them, looking out over the valley. The breeze pressed her thin yellow tunic against her body and ruffled the soft short silvery mass of curls around her head. Her skin glistened even under this alien sun with the dark lovely green of youth and health. Flin's heart still turned over in him every time he looked at her. He did not suppose this would last forever but as long as it did it was a beautiful sort of pain.

He made sure he had done the required things to keep the car from bolting away over the cliff and then joined her. The breeze was hot and moisture-laden, full of strange smells. The valley wound away in a series of curves with a glint of water at the bottom. On either side of it the rough ridges rolled and humped, blue in the distance where the heat haze covered them, rank green closer at hand with the shaggy woods that grew wild on them, the trees pushing and crowding for space, choked with undergrowth and strangling vines, absolutely neglected.

"I suppose," said Ruvi, "they're full of wild animals, too."

"Nothing very dangerous, I believe."

Ruvi shivered slightly. "Whenever I get just a little way out of the cities I begin to feel that I'm on a truly savage world. And every-thing's wrong. The trees, the flowers, even the grass-blades are the wrong shape, and the colors are all wrong, and the sky isn't at all the way it ought to be."

She laughed. "Anyone would know this was my first trip away from home."

Two huge birds came into sight over one of the ridges. They hung in the sky, wheeling in slow circles on still gray-brown wings. In-stinctively Flin put his arm around Ruvi, uncertain whether the birds would attack. They did not, drifting on down over the valley where the air currents took them. There was no sign of human habitation and except for the narrow road they might have been in a complete wilderness.

"It is rather beautiful, though," Ruvi said, "in its own way."

"Yes."

"I guess that's the only standard you really should use to judge things, isn't it? Their own."

Flin said sourly, "That's easier to do when you know what 'their own' standard is. They seem to have thousands of them here. That's why Sherbondy keeps telling us to get out and see the country, to learn what his people are really like." Sherbondy was their contact with the local Government, a big hearty man with an enormous enthusiasm for all the things that were going to be done. "The only trouble with that is that it would take a lifetime to—"

There was a noise like an avalanche behind them. Flin jumped and turned around, but it was only a huge red vehicle roaring by, spouting smoke from a pipe behind the driver's compartment. The driver noticed them just before the truck passed out of sight and Flin thought the man was going to drive it right into the woods while he was staring.

He sighed. "Let's go."

They got back into the car and Flin managed to get it back onto the road and headed in the direction he wanted to go without mishap—always, he felt, a minor triumph. The primitive vehicles that were subject to everybody's individual whim of operation on these equally primitive road systems still frightened the wits out of him after nearly six months.

It was just as hot as ever. As a gesture of courtesy, and to avoid attracting any more attention than was necessary, he had adopted the local variety of shirt and pants. Most of the men in the various instruction groups did this soon after landing. It didn't seem to matter what the women of the groups wore as long as certain puritanical tabus were observed, but the men found it less embarrassing to conform. Flin thought the garments abominably uncomfortable and envied Ruvi her relatively cool tunic.

She seemed wilted and subdued, leaning back in the corner of the wide overstuffed seat, her eyes half closed, the graceful tilted contours of her face accentuated by the gleaming of sweat on the delicate ridges.

"I think of home," she said, "and then I think of the money."

"It's something to think of."

The woods rolled by, clotted underneath with deep shadow, full of rustlings and rank dusty smells. Sometimes they passed a kind of food-raising station that had not been seen in the Federation for centuries, where part of the land was in several kinds of crops and part of it in pasture and the whole thing was operated by one man and his family. Sometimes they passed through little towns or villages with very strange names, where the people stared at them and the children pointed and yelled, *Green niggers, lookit the green niggers!*

Flin studied the houses. They were different from each other, and quite different from the ones he had grown used to in the cities, but they were all built on the same hut-based principle. He tried to imagine what life would be like in one of these towns, in one of these wooden or stone or brick houses with the queer decorations and the pointed roofs. Probably Sherbondy was right. Probably all the Federation people should try to get closer to the everyday life of the planet, familiarize themselves with what the people thought and felt, how they coped with their environment. The next few decades would see changes so radical and complete that this present life would soon begin to be forgotten....

The change had already begun. This planet—the native name for it was Earth, a rather pretty one, Flin thought—had been making its first wobbling steps into space on its own when the Survey ships arrived. With Federation technicians and techniques that process had been enormously accelerated. The first manned ships built on Earth and operated by Federation-trained but native-born personnel had been licensed for limited service within the last seven or eight years. Planning surveys were under way, guided by groups like his own, not only in weather-control but in global unification, production, education, and above all pacification—the countless things that would have to be accomplished to make Earth a suitable member of the Federation.

But these things had not yet made themselves felt on the population as a whole. Most of Earth was going along just as it always had, and Flin knew from experience that many of the natives even on the administrative level were extremely touchy and proud, not inclined to accept any sudden alterations in their thinking; probably the more provincial masses were even more so. It would be necessary to win them over, to make them feel that they were equals in the task and not merely the recipients of gifts from an older and wider culture.

It would be a long, interesting business. An energetic young man who stuck with it could make a career out of it, a satisfying and very profitable one.

The only trouble was—

Ruvi's thoughts seemed to have paralleled his own, because she said, "Are we going to stay on here?"

"We have to stay until we've finished our immediate job."

"But after that? I know some of the men have already decided to."

"The offers these people make are very good," Flin said slowly. "They'll need technicians and educators for a long time yet, and Center is in favor of it because it'll speed up integration." He reached out and patted her. "We could be rich and famous."

She smiled, very fleetingly. "All right," she said in a quiet voice, "I'll start making myself like it."

She began to stare grimly at the queerly shaped and colored trees, the peculiar houses that looked so dreadfully unfunctional, the crowds of chattering natives in the towns. Finally she shook her head and gave up, lying back with her eyes closed.

"I'll try it again sometime when it isn't so hot."

"Weather-control will fix that."

"But not for years."

They drove in silence. Flin felt vaguely ill at ease and unhappy, but he kept thinking of Sherbondy's offer and the things it might lead to for them, and he did not say anything. He did not want to commit himself with Ruvi yet, one way or the other.

About mid-afternoon there was a violent downpour of rain accompanied by thunder and lightning. As a weather expert Flin knew perfectly well what caused the disturbance, but the knowledge did nothing to decrease the effect of it on himself. Ruvi simply hid her head in the corner and shook. Flin kept on driving. If you let the natives know that you were afraid of their weather, they would never believe that you would be able to control it. He made it a practice in

Washington to walk out in storms that had even the natives cowering. He could barely see the road well enough to stay on it and he was nervous about floods, but he trundled resolutely ahead.

Eventually he ran out of the storm, or it passed over. The sun came out again, boiling and steaming the saturated air. It was difficult to breathe. Great black clouds still bulked in the sky, presaging more trouble later. In the strange light the countryside took on a look completely alien and somehow ominous, the little scattered houses crouching among their weird trees like suspicious gnomes with hostile eyes, the empty fields and dripping woods suggestive of infinite loneliness.

"I'm tired and hungry," Ruvi said. "Let's stop."

"The next town that has accommodations." Flin was tired himself. He found driving a strain and yearned for the fleet little air-cars that darted so easily and safely through the peaceful skies of the Federation worlds. They would not be practical here until global weather-control was an actuality.

The next town was a long way off. The road lifted and wound through low rough mountains and over brawling stream beds. The villages they passed through were very tiny, sometimes with only two or three dwellings.

The shadows grew heavy in the valleys. Ruvi began to fret a bit. Flin knew that it was only because the shadows and the wild country made her nervous, but it irritated him. He was having trouble enough of his own. An animal of some sort scuttered across the road and he nearly went into the ditch avoiding it. The light was bad. He was worried about the fuel gauge, which was low. And the road seemed to go on forever through a steadily darkening tunnel of trees.

They passed a tiny wooden temple next to one of the absolutely barbaric native burying grounds that always horrified them, the ritual stones gleaming pallid among uncut grass and briar roses. It all flashed by so quickly that Flin realized he had pushed the speed of the big car beyond the limit of safety. So he was already slowing down when he swung around a curve and came right onto a farm vehicle moving very slowly in the road. He managed to go around it without hitting anything but it gave him a sharp fright. The man driving the thing shouted after them. Flin could not hear exactly what he said but there was no doubt he was angry. After that Flin went carefully.

There began to be painted signs along the edge of the road.

Ruvi read them off. "Restaurant. Hotel. Garage. There *is* a town ahead. Grand Falls, I think."

The road passed suddenly over a crest and there was a wide irregular valley below them, full of light from the low sun which shone through a gap in the west. Perhaps Flin was in an exceptionally receptive mood but it struck him as one of the loveliest places he had seen. There was a river flashing with curious dull glints from the setting sun, rolling smoothly over a pretty little falls that burst into bright foam at the bottom. The white houses of the town were bowered in trees and blooming vines, slumbrous and peaceful in the hot evening, with one tall white spire standing over them.

"Look, I see the hotel," said Ruvi, pointing. "Oh glorious, how I will love a cool bath before dinner!"

She ran her fingers through her silvery curls and sat up straight beside him, smiling as he drove down the hill into Grand Falls.

It had rained here recently. The pavements still glistened and the air steamed with it. There was a fragrance of nameless flowers, very sweet and heavy. On the shadowy porches of the houses along the way there was a sound of voices and hidden laughter, and the small scurrying shapes of children moved under the dripping trees.

The road became the main street splashed with the crude colors of neon signs, the lighted windows showing yellow in the dusk. On both sides now there were curious low buildings, apparently quite old, built tight together so that each row looked like one building except its front was broken up into narrow vertical sections with different cornices and different patterns of wood or brickwork around the windows. They were mostly of red brick, which seemed to be a common building material, and not above two stories high.

The shops and offices were closed. The eating and drinking places were open and busy, and somewhere inside there was music playing, a strong simple beat with a high-pitched male voice wailing over it. The smell of flowers was drowned out by the pungence of hot wet brick and hotter, wetter asphalt. A few couples walked toward the gaudily lighted entrance of a theatre farther along the street, the women wearing bright-colored dresses, their long hair done in elaborate coiffures, their thick sturdy legs and arms bare. Knots of young men lounged against the walls near the drinking places. They were smoking the universal cigarettes and talking, looking after the women.

Seen close up now the town was less beautiful than it had looked from the crest. The white paint was dirty and peeling, the old buildings poorly kept up.

"Well," Flin muttered, "Sherbondy said to get off the beaten track and see the real native life undiluted."

"The hotel looks charming," Ruvi said determinedly. "I am not going to quarrel with anything."

Even in the dusk they were beginning to draw attention. First the little knots of idlers were attracted by the long gleaming car with the Government plates, and then by Flin and Ruvi themselves. There were other cars in the street, both moving and parked along the curb, but the one Flin was driving seemed to be newer and fancier than most. He could see people pointing and looking at them. He swore silently and wondered if they could have dinner sent up to their room.

The hotel was on the corner of the main intersection. It was three stories high, built of the red brick, with a crudely ornate cornice and long narrow windows. A balcony ran around its two exposed sides at the second floor level, extending over the street and supported on slender metal pillars which had once been painted white. A second tier of pillars on the balcony itself supported a roof. There were five or six oldish men sitting in chairs on the balcony, and several more below on the covered portion of the street.

Flin looked at it doubtfully. "I wonder if it *has* a bath."

Her own enthusiasm somewhat cooled, Ruvi said, "It'll do for one night. It might be a long way to the next one and I don't suppose it would be any better."

Flin grunted and pulled the car in to the curb and stopped.

There was a scraping of chair legs as the men sat forward or rose

425

to come closer. Flin got out and walked around the car. He smiled at the men but they only stared, blowing strong smoke and squinting through it at him and the car and the license plates and then at Ruvi.

Flin turned and opened the door for her. He noticed over the low roof of the car that men were beginning to come from across the street, and already a number of boys had sprung from nowhere and were clustering like insects, their eyes bright and excited.

He helped Ruvi out, slim in her yellow tunic, her silver curls picking up the light from the tall front door of the hotel.

One of the men said in a high shrill voice, "Green as grass, by God!" There was laughter and somebody whistled.

Flin's face tightened but he did not say anything nor look at the men. He took Ruvi's arm and they went into the hotel.

They walked on a faded carpet, between islands of heavy furniture in worn leather and dusty plush. Fans turned slowly against the ceiling, barely disturbing either the hot air or the moths that had come in to flutter around the lights. There was a smell that Flin could not fully identify. Dust, the stale stink of dead tobacco, and something else—age, perhaps, and decay. Behind the large wooden desk a gray-haired man had risen from a chair and stood with his hands spread out on the desk top, watching them come.

The men from the street followed, crowding quickly through the doors. One particular man seemed to lead them, a red-faced fellow wearing an amulet on a gold chain across his broad paunch.

Flin and Ruvi stood in front of the desk. Once more Flin smiled. He said, "Good evening."

The gray-haired man glanced past them at the men who had come in, bringing with them a many-faceted odor of sweat to add to what was already inside. They had stopped talking, as though they were waiting to hear what the gray-haired man would say. The fans in the ceiling creaked gently as they turned.

The gray-haired man cleared his throat. He, too, smiled, but there was no friendliness in it.

"If you're wanting a room," he said, with unnecessary loudness as

426

though he were speaking not to Flin but to the others in the lobby, "I'm sorry, but we're filled up."

"Filled up?" Flin repeated.

"Filled up." The gray-haired man took hold of a large book which lay open in front of him and closed it in a kind of ceremonial gesture. "You understand now, I'm not refusing you accommodations. I just don't have any available."

He glanced again at the men by the door and there was a little undertone of laughter.

"But—" said Ruvi, on a note of protest.

Flin pressed her arm and she stopped. His own face was suddenly hot. He knew the man was lying, and that his lie had been expected and was approved by the others, and that he and Ruvi were the only two people there who did not understand why. He also knew that it would do them no good to get into an argument. So he spoke, as pleasantly as he could.

"I see. Perhaps then you could tell us of another place in town—"

"Don't know of any," said the gray-haired man, shaking his head. "Don't know of a single place."

"Thank you," said Flin and turned around and walked back across the lobby, still holding Ruvi's arm.

The crowd had grown. Half the people in Grand Falls, Flin thought, must be gathered now on that one corner. The original group of men, reinforced to twice its size, blocked the doorway. They parted to let Flin and Ruvi through but they did it with a certain veiled insolence, staring hard at Ruvi who bent her head and did not look at them.

Flin walked slowly, refusing to notice them or be hurried. But their nearness, the heat and smell of them, the sense of something menacing about them that he did not understand, twisted his nerves to a painful tightness.

He passed through the door, almost brushing against a young girl who squealed and jumped back out of his way with a great show of being afraid of him. There was a bunch of young people with her, both boys and girls, and they began a great cackling and shoving. The crowd had become more vocal as it grew. There were a lot of women

427

in it now. Flin waited politely for them to separate, moving a step at a time toward the car, and the voices flew back and forth over his head, at him, around him.

—ain't even human!

Hey, greenie, can't you afford to feed your women where you come from? Lookit how skinny—

Are they kidding with that crazy hair?

—just like I seen on the teevee, and I says to Jack then, Jack Spivey I says, if you ever see anything like them coming down the road—

Hey, greenie, is it true your women lay eggs?

Laughter. Derision. And something deeper. Something evil. Something he did not understand.

He reached the car and got Ruvi into it. As he bent close to her he whispered in her ear, in their own language, "Just take it easy. We're getting out."

Mama, how come them funny niggers got a bigger car'n we got?

Because the Government's payin' them big money to come and kindly teach us what we didn't know before.

"Please hurry," whispered Ruvi.

He started around the car to get in and found his way blocked by the red-faced man with the gold chain, and beyond him a solid mass in the street in front of the car. He sensed that they were not going to let him through, so he stopped as though he had intended to do so and spoke to the man with the chain.

"I beg your pardon—could you tell me how far it is to the next city?"

The girls were giggling loudly over Ruvi's tunic and the way she looked generally. They were all the fat-hipped, heavy-breasted local type, with thick legs and thick faces. Flin thought they had very little to criticize. Just beyond the man with the gold chain were four or five younger men standing together. They had very obviously come out of one of the taverns. They were lean rangy young men with their hair slicked down and their hips thrust forward in a curiously insolent slouch. They had eyes, Flin thought, like animals. They had been by the door when he came out. They were still looking at Ruvi.

428

"The next city?" said the man with the gold chain. He accented the word *city* as Flin had. He had a deep, ringing voice, apparently well used to addressing crowds. "A hundred and twenty-four miles."

A long way at night through strange country. A great anger boiled up in Flin but he kept it carefully inside.

"Thank you. I wonder where we might get something to eat before we start?"

"Well now, it's pretty late," the man said. "Our restaurants have just about now stopped serving. Am I right, Mr. Nellis?"

"You are, Judge Shaw," said a man in the crowd.

This too was a lie, but Flin accepted it. He nodded and said, "I must have fuel. Where—"

"Garage is closed," Shaw said. "If you got enough to get you down the road apiece there's a pump at Patch's roadhouse. He's open late enough."

"Thank you," said Flin. "We will go now."

He started again, but Shaw did not move out of Flin's way. Instead he put up his hand and said, "Now just a minute there, before you go. We've been reading about you people in the papers and seeing you on the teevee but we don't get much chance to talk to celebrities here. There's some questions we'd like to ask."

The rangy young men with the animal eyes began to sidle past Shaw and behind Flin toward the car, leaving a heavy breath of liquor where they moved.

"A damn lot of questions," somebody shouted from the back, "like why the hell don't you stay home?"

"Now, now," said Shaw, waving his hand, "let's keep this friendly. Reverend, did you have something to say?"

"I certainly do," said a fat man in a soiled dark suit, shouldering his way through the crowd to stand peering at Flin. "I bet I've preached a sermon on this subject three Sundays out of five and it's the most important question facing this world today. If we don't face it, if we don't answer this question in a way that's acceptable to the Almighty, we might just as well throw away all these centuries of doing battle with Satan and admit we're licked."

"Amen," cried a woman's voice. "Amen to that, Reverend Tibbs!"

429

Reverend Tibbs thrust his face close to Flin's and said, "Do you consider yourselves human?"

Flin knew that he was on dangerous ground here. This was a religious man and religion was strictly a local affair, not to be discussed or meddled with in any way.

So he said cautiously, "On our own worlds we consider ourselves so. However, I am not prepared to argue it from your viewpoint, sir."

He moved toward the car, but the crowd only pulled in and held him tighter.

"Well now," said the Reverend Tibbs, "what I want to know is how you *can* call yourselves human when it says right in Scriptures that God created this good Earth here under my feet and then created man—*human* man—right out of that self-same earth. Now if you—"

"Oh, hell, save that stuff for the pulpit," said another man, pushing his way in front of Tibbs. This one was sunburned and leathery, with a lantern jaw and keen hard eyes. "I ain't worried about their souls and I don't care if they're all pups to the Beast of the Apocalypse." Now he spoke directly to Flin. "I been seeing faces on my teevee for years. Green faces like yours. Red ones, blue ones, purple ones, yellow ones—all the colors of the rainbow, and what I want to know is, ain't you got any white folks out there?"

"Yeah!" said the crowd and nodded its collective heads.

The man they called Judge Shaw nodded too and said, "I reckon you put the question for all of us, Sam."

"What I mean is," said the lantern-jawed Sam, "this here is a white town. In most other places nowadays, I understand, you'll find blacks and whites all run together like they were out of the same still, but we got kind of a different situation here, and we ain't the only ones, either. There's little pockets of us here and there, kind of holding out, you might say. And we ain't broken any laws. We didn't refuse to integrate, see. It was just that for one reason or another what colored folks there was around—"

Here the crowd snickered knowingly.

"—decided they could do better somewheres else and went there.

So we didn't need to integrate. We don't have any color problem. We ain't had any for twenty years. And what's more, we don't want any."

A shout from the crowed.

Shaw said in his big booming voice, "The point we'd like to make clear to you, so you can pass it on to whoever's interested, is that some of us like to run our lives and our towns to suit ourselves. Now, this old Earth is a pretty good place just as she stands, and we never felt any need for outsiders to come and tell us what we ought to do. So we ain't any too friendly to begin with, you see? But we're not unreasonable, we're willing to listen to things so as to form our own judgments on them. Only you people had better understand right now that no matter what goes on in the big cities and other places like that, *we* aren't going to be told anything by a bunch of colored folks and it doesn't matter one damn bit what color they are. If—"

Ruvi gave a sudden cry.

Flin spun around. The young men who smelled of liquor were beside the car, all crowded together and leaning in over the door. They were laughing now and one of them said, "Aw now, what's the matter? I was just—"

"Flin, *please!*"

He could see her over their bent backs and bobbing heads, as far away from them as she could get on the seat. Other faces peered in from the opposite side, grinning, hemming her in.

Somebody said in a tone of mock reproach, "You got her scared now, Jed, ain't you ashamed?"

Flin took two steps toward the car, pushing somebody out of the way. He did not see who it was. He did not see anything but Ruvi's frightened face and the backs of the young men.

"Get away from there," he said.

The laughter stopped. The young men straightened slowly. One of them said, "Did I hear somebody say something?"

"You heard me," said Flin. "Get away from the car."

They turned around, and now the crowd was all quiet and watching. The young men were tall. They had big coarse hands, strong for any task. Their mouths hung open a little to show their teeth, and they breathed and smiled, and their eyes were cruel.

431

"I don't think," said the one they called Jed, "I liked the tone of your voice when you said that."

"I don't give a damn whether you liked it or not."

"You gonna take that, Jed?" somebody yelled. "From a nigger, even if he is a green one?"

There was a burst of laughter. Jed smiled and tilted his weight forward over his bent knees.

"I was just trying to talk friendly with your woman," he said. "You shouldn't object to that."

He reached out and pushed with his stiffened fingers hard against Flin's chest.

Flin turned his body and let the force of the thrust slide off his shoulder. Everything seemed to be moving very slowly, in a curiously icy vacuum which for the moment contained only himself and Jed. He was conscious of a new and terrible feeling within him, something he had never felt before. He stepped forward, lightly, strongly, not hurrying. His feet and hands performed four motions. He had done them countless times before in the gymnasium against a friendly opponent. He had never done them like this before, full force, with hate, with a dark evil brute lust to do injury. He watched the blood spurt from Jed's nose, watched him fall slowly, slowly to the pavement with his hands clutching his belly and his eyes wide open and his mouth gasping in astonishment and pain.

Outside this center of subjective time and hate in which he stood Flin sensed other movement and noise. Gradually, then with urgent swiftness, they came clear. Judge Shaw had thrust himself in front of Flin. Others were holding Jed, who was getting up. A swag-bellied man with a badge on his shirt was waving his arms, clearing people away from around the car, Jed's friends among them. There was a confused and frightening clamor of voices and over it all Shaw's big authoritative voice was shouting.

"Calm down now, everybody, we don't want any trouble here."

He turned his head and said to Flin, "I advise you to be on your way just as fast as you can go."

Flin walked around the car where the policeman had cleared the way. He got in and started the motor. The crowd surged forward as

432

though it was going to try and stop him in spite of Shaw and the policeman.

Suddenly he cried out at them.

"Yes, we have white folks out there, about one in every ten thousand, and they don't think anything of it and neither do we. You can't hide from the universe. You're going to be tramped under with color—all the colors of the rainbow!"

And he understood then that that was exactly what they feared.

He let in the drive and sent the big car lurching forward. The people in the street scattered out of his way. There were noises as thrown objects struck the top and sides of the car and then the street was long and straight and clear ahead of him and he pushed the throttle lever all the way down.

Lights flashed by. Then there was darkness and the town was gone.

Flin eased back on the throttle. Ruvi was bent over in the seat beside him, her hands covering her face. She was not crying. He reached out and touched her shoulder. She was trembling, and so was he. He felt physically sick, but he made his voice quiet and reassuring.

"It's all right now. They're gone."

She made a sound—a whimper, an answer, he was not sure. Presently she sat erect, her hands clenched in her lap. They did not speak again. The air was cooler here but still oppressive with moisture, almost as clammy as fog against the skin. No stars showed. Off to the right there were intermittent flashes of lightning and a low growling of thunder.

A clot of red light appeared on the night ahead, resolving itself into a neon sign. Patch's. The roadhouse with the pump.

Ruvi whispered, "Don't stop. Please don't stop."

"I have to," he said gently, and pulled off the road onto a wide gravelled space beside a ramshackle frame building with dimly lighted windows. Strongly rhythmic music played inside. There was a smaller building, a dwelling-house, beside the tavern, and midway between them was a single fuel pump.

Flin stopped beside it. Hardly realizing what he was doing, he turned and fumbled in the back seat for his hat and jacket and put them on, pulling the hatbrim down to hide his face as much as possible. Ruvi had a yellow shawl that matched her tunic. She drew it over her head and shoulders and made herself small in the corner of the seat. Flin switched off the dashboard lights.

A raw-boned lanky woman came out of the dwelling. Probably the man ran the tavern, leaving her to tend to smaller matters. Trying to keep his voice steady, Flin asked her to fill the tank. She hardly glanced at him and went surlily to the pump. He got out his wallet and felt with shaking hands among the bills.

On the dark road beyond the circle of light from the tavern, a car went slowly past.

The pump mechanism clicked and rang its solemn bells and finally was still. The woman hung up the hose with a clash and came forward. Flin took a deep breath. He thrust a bill at her. "That'll be eight-eighty-seven," she said and took the bill and saw the color of the hand she took it from. She started to speak or yell, stepping back and bending suddenly in the same movement. He saw her eyes shining in the light, peering into the car. Flin had already started the motor. He roared away in a spurt of gravel, leaving the woman standing with her arm out, pointing after them.

"We won't have to stop again until we reach the city. It'll be all right there."

He threw his hat into the back seat. Ruvi let the shawl fall away from her head.

"I've never wanted to hide my face before," she said. "It's a strange feeling."

Flin muttered savagely, "I've got a lot to say but I can't say it now, not if I'm going to drive."

The road was narrow and black beneath the thunderous sky, between the empty fields and dark woods.

There was another car in the road ahead, moving slowly.

Flin overtook it.

It was well out in the middle. He waited a moment for the driver to see that he wanted to pass and make room for him. The car continued to block the road. He sounded his horn, politely at first and

434

then loudly. The car stayed where it was, moving slower and slower so that he had to brake to keep from hitting it.

"What are they doing?" whispered Ruvi. "Why won't they let us by?"

Flin shook his head. "I don't know."

He began to be afraid.

He pulled as far as he could to the left, riding on the rough berm. He sounded the horn and tramped on the throttle.

The other car swerved too. Its rear fender struck his front one. Ruvi screamed. Flin steadied the wildly lurching car. Sweat prickled like hot needles all over his skin. He stamped his foot hard on the brake.

The other car skidded on ahead. Flin swung the wheel sharp right and pushed the throttle down, whipping the big car across the road and onto the berm on the other side.

For one brief moment he thought he was going to make it. But the other car swayed over with ruthless speed and punched and rebounded and punched again with its clattering fenders like a man pushing another with his shoulder. Holes and stones threw Flin's car back and forth. He fought to control it, hearing the voices of men shouting close by...

Hit the sonofabitch, knock his goddam ass off the road, That's the way—

There was a tree ahead. His headlights picked it up, brought it starkly into view, the rough-textured bark, the knots and gnarls, the uneven branches and dark leaves. Flin spun the wheel frantically. The lights made a wide slicing turn across meadow grass and weeds. The car bounded, leaped, sprang over uneven ground and fell with a jarring crash into the ditch of a little stream and died.

Silence, dazed and desperate.

Flin looked back. The other car had stopped at the side of the road. Men were getting out of it. He counted five. He thought he knew what men they were.

He reached across Ruvi and opened the door and pushed her ahead of him. "We're going to run now," he said, surprised at the flat banality of his voice, as though he were speaking to a child about some unimportant game. The car tilted that way and Ruvi slid out easily. Flin came behind her into mud and cold water that lapped around his ankles. He half helped, half threw her up the low steep bank and followed, grabbing her hand then and pulling her along.

He did not look back again. He did not have to. The men called as they ran, laughing, hooting, baying like great hounds.

Crooked fire lighted a curtain of black cloud. Flin saw trees, a clump of woods. The fire died and was followed by a hollow booming. The woods vanished. He continued to run toward them. The grass and weeds tangled around his legs. Ruvi lagged, pulling harder and harder against his grip, sobbing as she ran.

They were among the trees.

He let go of her. "Go on. Hide yourself somewhere. Don't make a sound no matter what happens."

"No. I won't leave—"

He pushed her fiercely, trying not to scream at her aloud. "Go on!"

The young men came loping through the long grass, into the trees. They had a light. Its long white beam probed and poked.

See anything?

Not yet.

Who's got the bottle? I'm dry from runnin'.

See anything?

They're in here somewhere.

Breath rasping in big hard throats, legs ripping the undergrowth, feet trampling the ground.

I'm gonna find out, by God. After I take care of that sonofabitch I'm gonna find out.

Whatcha gonna find out, Jed?

If it's true they lay eggs or not.

Laughter.

Who's got the goddam bottle?

Wait a minute, hey, right there, swing that light back, I hear the bastards moving—

Hey!

Flin turned, straightening his shoulders, standing between them and Ruvi.

436

One of them held the light in his face. He could not see them clearly. But he heard the voice of the one called Jed speaking to him.

"All right, greenie, you're so anxious to teach us things—it ain't fair for us to take and not give, so we got a lesson for you."

"Let my wife go," said Flin steadily. "You have no quarrel with her."

"Your wife, huh?" said Jed. "Well now, how do we know she's your wife? Was you married here under the laws of this land?"

"We were married under our own laws—"

"You hear that, boys? Well, your laws don't cut any ice with us, greenie, so it don't seem that you are man and wife as we would say. Anyway, she stays. That's part of the lesson."

Jed laughed. They all laughed.

In their own language Flin said to Ruvi, "Run now."

He sprang forward at the man holding the light.

Another man moved quickly from the side and struck him across the shoulders and neck with something more than the naked hand. A tree branch, perhaps, or a metal bar. Flin went down, stunned with pain. He heard Ruvi cry out. He tried to tell her again to run but his voice had left him. There were scuffling sounds and more cries. He tried to get up and hard-shod feet kicked him and stamped him down. Iron knuckles battered his face. Jed bent over him and shook him.

"Hold him up there, Mike, I want to be sure he hears this. You hear me, greenie? Lesson One. Niggers always keep to their own side of the road."

Crash. Blood in the mouth, and pain.

Ruvi?

"Hold him, Mike, goddam it. Lesson Two. When a white man takes a mind to a female nigger, she ain't supposed to get uppity about it. It's an honor, see? She's supposed to be real nice and happy and flattered. See?"

More blood, more pain.

Ruvi, Ruvi!

"Lesson Three. And this one you better remember and write out and hang up where all the other red, blue, green, and purple niggers can see it. *You never lay a hand on a white man.* Never. No matter what."

Ruvi was quiet. He could not hear her voice.

"You understand that? No matter what!"

Hya-hoo!

Give it to him, Jed. Tell him so he don't forget.

Dark, night, thunder, red fire, red blood, silence, distance, one long fading echoing voice.

—just like a real human woman by God what do you know—

Laughter.

Ruvi—

Gone.

There was a great deal of public indignation about it. Newspapers all over the world had editorials. The President made a statement. The Governor made a formal apology for his state and a sincere promise to find and punish the handful of men responsible for the outrage.

Grand Falls protected its own.

No witnesses could be found to identify the men involved in the incident that had occurred in town. Judge Shaw was sure he had never seen them before. So was the policeman. The attack itself had taken place out in the country, of course, and in the dark. Flin did not remember the license number of the car nor had he seen the faces of the men clearly. Neither had Ruvi. They could have been anyone from anywhere.

The name "Jed" by itself meant nothing. There were a number of Jeds in the neighborhood but they were the wrong ones. The right Jed never turned up, and if he had Flin could only have identified him definitely as the man he himself had struck in front of the Grand Falls Hotel. ("Mighty hot tempered, he seemed," Judge Shaw said. "Took offense where I'm sure none was meant. Like he just didn't understand our ways.")

So there was no finding and no punishment.

As soon as the doctors told him he was fit to travel, Flin informed his group that he was returning home. He had already been in contact with Galactic Center. Someone else would be sent to take his place. They were very angry about the whole thing at home and various steps were being considered. But since Earth was not a member planet she was not subject to galactic law, and since the future of a world was considerably more important than the actions of a few individuals or the feelings of their victims, probably nothing very drastic would be done. And Flin recognized that this was right.

Sherbondy came to see him.

"I feel responsible for all this," he said. "If I hadn't advised that trip—"

"It would have happened sooner or later," Flin said. "To us or to somebody else. Your world's got a long way to go yet."

"I wish you'd stay," said Sherbondy miserably. "I'd like to prove to you that we're not all brutes."

"You don't have to prove that. It's obvious. The trouble now is with us—with Ruvi and me."

Sherbondy looked at him, puzzled.

Flin said, "*We* are not civilized any more. Perhaps we will be again some day. I hope so. That's one reason we're going home, for psychiatric treatment of a kind we can't get here. Ruvi especially…"

He shook his head and began to stride up and down the room, his body taut with an anger he could only by great effort control.

"An act like that—people like that—they foul and degrade everything they touch. They pass on some of themselves. I'm full of irrational feelings now. I'm afraid of darkness and trees and quiet places. Worse than that, I'm afraid of your people. I can't go out of my rooms now without feeling as though I walk among wild beasts."

Sherbondy sighed heavily. "I can't blame you. It's a pity. You could have had a good life here, done a lot—"

"Yes," said Flin.

"Well," said Sherbondy, getting up, "I'll say good bye." He held out his hand. "I hope you don't mind shaking my hand—"

Flin hesitated, then took Sherbondy's hand briefly. "Even you," he said, with real sorrow. "You see why we must go."

Sherbondy said, "I see." He turned to the door. "God damn those

bastards," he said with sudden fury. "You'd think in this day and age—
Oh, hell… Goodbye, Flin. And the best of luck."

He went away.

Flin helped Ruvi with the last of the packing. He checked over
the mass of equipment the weather-control group had brought with
them for demonstration purposes, which he would be leaving behind for his successor.

Then he said quietly, "There is one more thing I have to do before we go. Don't worry about me. I'll be back in plenty of time for
the take-off."

She looked at him, startled, but she did not ask any questions.

He got into his car and drove away alone.

He spoke as he drove, grimly and bitterly, to someone who was
not there.

"You wanted to teach me a lesson," he said. "You did. Now I will
show you how well you taught me, and how well I learned."

And that was the real evil that had been done to him and Ruvi.

The physical outrage and the pain were soon over, but the other
things were harder to eradicate—the sense of injustice, the rankling
fury, the blind hatred of all men whose faces were white.

Especially the hatred.

Some day, he hoped and prayed, he could be rid of that feeling,
clean and whole again as he had been before it happened. But it was
too soon. Far too soon now.

With two fully charged miniseeders in his pockets he drove steadily toward Grand Falls.…

440

THE ROAD TO SINHARAT

Amazing Science Fiction, May 1963

THE DOOR was low, deep-sunk into the thickness of the wall. Carey knocked and then he waited, stooped a bit under the lintel-stone, fitting his body to the meagre shadow as though he could really hide it there. A few yards away, beyond cracked and tilted paving-blocks, the Jekkara Low-Canal showed its still black water to the still black sky, and both were full of stars.

Nothing moved along the canal-site. The town was closed tight, and this in itself was so unnatural that it made Carey shiver. He had been here before and he knew how it ought to be. The chief industry of the Low-Canal towns is sinning of one sort of another, and they work at it right around the clock. One might have thought that all the people had gone away, but Carey knew they hadn't. He knew that he had not taken a single step unwatched. He had not really believed that they would let him come this far, and he wondered why they had not killed him. Perhaps they remembered him.

There was a sound on the other side of the door.

Carey said in the antique High Martian, "Here is one who claims the guest-right." In Low Martian, the vernacular that fitted more easily on his tongue, he said, "Let me in, Derech. You owe me blood."

The door opened narrowly and Carey slid through it, into lamplight and relative warmth. Derech closed the door and barred it, saying,

"Damn you, Carey. I knew you were going to turn up here babbling about blood-debts. I swore I wouldn't let you in."

He was a Low-Canaller, lean and small and dark and predatory. He wore a red jewel in his left ear-lobe and a totally incongruous but comfortable suit of Terran synthetics, insulated against heat and cold. Carey smiled.

"Sixteen years ago," he said, "you'd have perished before you'd have worn that."

"Corruption. Nothing corrupts like comfort, unless it's kindness." Derech sighed. "I knew it was a mistake to let you save my neck that time. Sooner or later you'd claim payment. Well, now that I have let you in, you might as well sit down." He poured wine into a cup of alabaster worn thin as an eggshell and handed it to Carey. They drank, sombrely, in silence. The flickering lamp-light showed the shadows and the deep lines in Carey's face.

Derech said, "How long since you've slept?"

"I can sleep on the way," said Carey, and Derech looked at him with amber eyes as coldly speculative as a cat's.

CAREY did not press him. The room was large, richly furnished with the bare, spare, faded richness of a world that had very little left to give in the way of luxury. Some of the things were fairly new, made in the traditional manner by Martian craftsmen. They were almost indistinguishable from the things that had been old when the Reed Kings and the Bee Kings were little boys along the Nile-bank.

"What will happen," Derech asked, "if they catch you?"

"Oh," said Carey, "they'll deport me first. Then the United Worlds Court will try me, and they can't do anything but find me guilty. They'll hand me over to Earth for punishment, and there will be further investigations and penalties and fines and I'll be a thoroughly broken man when they've finished, and sorry enough for it. Though I think they'll be sorrier in the long run."

"That won't help matters any," said Derech.

"No."

"Why," asked Derech, "why is it that they will not listen?"

"Because they know that they are right."

Derech said an evil word.

"But they do. I've sabotaged the Rehabilitation Project as much as I possibly could. I've rechanneled funds and misdirected orders so they're almost two years behind schedule. These are the things they'll try me for. But my real crime is that I have questioned Goodness and the works thereof. Murder they might forgive me, but not that."

He added wearily, "You'll have to decide quickly. The UW boys are working closely with the Council of City-States, and Jekkara is no longer untouchable. It's also the first place they'll look for me."

"I wondered if that had occurred to you." Derech frowned. "That doesn't bother me. What does bother me is that I know where you want to go. We tried it once, remember? We ran for our lives across that damned desert. Four solid days and nights." He shivered.

"Send me as far as Barrakesh. I can disappear there, join a southbound caravan. I intend to go alone."

"If you intend to kill yourself, why not do it here in comfort and among friends? Let me think," Derech said. "Let me count my years and my treasure and weigh them against a probable yard of sand."

Flames hissed softly around the coals in the brazier. Outside, the wind got up and started its ancient work, rubbing the house walls with tiny grains of dust, rounding off the corners, hollowing the window places. All over Mars the wind did this, to huts and palaces, to mountains and the small burrow-heaps of animals, laboring patiently toward a city when the whole face of the planet should be one smooth level sea of dust. Only lately new structures of metal and plastic had appeared beside some of the old stone cities. They resisted the wearing sand. They seemed prepared to stay forever. And Carey fancied that he could hear the old wind laughing as it went.

THERE was a scratching against the closed shutter in the back wall, followed by a rapid drumming of fingertips. Derech rose, his face suddenly alert. He rapped twice on the shutter to say that he understood and then turned to Carey. "Finish your wine."

He took the cup and went into another room with it. Carey stood up. Mingling with the sound of the wind outside, the gentle throb of motors became audible, low in the sky and very near.

Derech returned and gave Carey a shove toward an inner wall. Carey remembered the pivoted stone that was there, and the space behind it. He crawled through the opening. "Don't sneeze or thrash about," said Derech. "The stonework is loose, and they'd hear you."

He swung the stone shut. Carey huddled as comfortably as possible in the uneven hole, worn smooth with the hiding of illegal things for countless generations. Air and a few faint gleams of light seeped through between the stone blocks, which were set without mortar as in most Martian construction. He could even see a thin vertical segment of the room.

When the sharp knock came at the door, he discovered that he could hear quite clearly.

Derech moved across his field of vision. The door opened. A man's voice demanded entrance in the name of the United Worlds and the Council of Martian City-States.

"Please enter," said Derech.

Carey saw, more or less fragmentarily, four men. Three were Martians in the undistinguished cosmopolitan garb of the City-States. They were the equivalent of the FBI. The fourth was an Earthman, and Carey smiled to see the measure of his own importance. The spare, blond, good-looking man with the sunburn and the friendly blue eyes might have been an actor, a tennis player, or a junior executive on holiday. He was Howard Wales, Earth's best man in Interpol.

Wales let the Martians do the talking, and while they did it he drifted unobtrusively about, peering through doorways, listening, touching, *feeling*. Carey became fascinated by him, in an unpleasant sort of way. Once he came and stood directly in front of Carey's crevice in the wall. Carey was afraid to breathe, and he had a dreadful notion that Wales would suddenly turn about and look straight in at him through the crack.

The senior Martian, a middle-aged man with an able look about him, was giving Derech a briefing on the penalties that awaited him if he harbored a fugitive or withheld information. Carey thought that he was being too heavy about it. Even five years ago he would not have dared to show his face in Jekkara. He could picture Derech listening amiably, lounging against something and playing with the jewel in his ear. Finally Derech got bored with it and said without heat,

"Because of our geographical position, we have been exposed to the New Culture." The capitals were his. "We have made adjustments

444

to it. But this is still Jekkara and you're here on sufferance, no more. Please don't forget it."

Wales spoke, deftly forestalling any comment from the City-Stater. "You've been Carey's friend for many years, haven't you?"

"We robbed tombs together in the old days."

" 'Archeological research' is a nicer term, I should think."

"My very ancient and perfectly honorable guild never used it. But I'm an honest trader now, and Carey doesn't come here."

He might have added a qualifying "often," but he did not.

The City-Stater said derisively, "He has or will come here now."

"Why?" asked Derech.

"He needs help. Where else could he go for it?"

"Anywhere. He has many friends. And he knows Mars better than most Martians, probably a damn sight better than you do."

"But," said Wales quietly, "outside of the City-States all Earthmen are being hunted down like rabbits, if they're foolish enough to stay. For Carey's sake, if you know where he is, tell us. Otherwise he is almost certain to die."

"He's a grown man," Derech said. "He must carry his own load."

"HE'S carrying too much…" Wales said, and then broke off. There was a sudden gabble of talk, both in the room and outside. Everybody moved toward the door, out of Cary's vision, except Derech who moved into it, relaxed and languid and infuriatingly self-assured. Carey could not hear the sound that had drawn the others but he judged that another flier was landing. In a few minutes Wales and the others came back, and now there were some new people with them. Carey squirmed and craned, getting closer to the crack, and he saw Alan Woodthorpe, his superior, Administrator of the Rehabilitation Project for Mars, and probably the most influential man on the planet. Carey knew that he must have rushed across a thousand miles of desert from his headquarters at Kahora, just to be here at this moment.

Carey was flattered and deeply moved.

Woodthorpe introduced himself to Derech. He was disarmingly simple and friendly in his approach, a man driven and wearied by many vital matters but never forgetting to be warm, gracious, and human. And the devil of it was that he was exactly what he appeared to be. That was what made dealing with him so impossibly difficult.

Derech said, smiling a little, "Don't stray away from your guards."

"Why is it?" Woodthorpe asked. "Why this hostility? If only your people would understand that we're trying to help them."

"They understand that perfectly," Derech said. "What they can't understand is why, when they have thanked you politely and explained that they neither need nor want your help, you still refuse to leave them alone."

"Because we know what we can do for them! They're destitute now. We can make them rich, in water, in arable land, in power—we can change their whole way of life. Primitive people are notoriously resistant to change, but in time they'll realize…"

"Primitive?" said Derech.

"Oh, not the Low-Canallers," said Woodthorpe quickly. "Your civilization was flourishing, I know, when Proconsul was still wondering whether or not to climb down out of his tree. For that very reason I cannot understand why you side with the Drylanders."

Derech said, "Mars is an old, cranky, dried-up world, but we understand her. We've made a bargain with her. We don't ask too much of her, and she gives us sufficient for our needs. We can depend on her. We do not want to be made dependent on other men."

"But this is a new age," said Woodthorpe. "Advanced technology makes anything possible. The old prejudices, the parochial viewpoints, are no longer…"

"You were saying something about primitives."

"I was thinking of the Dryland tribes. We had counted on Dr. Carey, because of his unique knowledge, to help them understand us. Instead, he seems bent on stirring them up to war. Our survey parties have been set upon with the most shocking violence. If Carey succeeds in reaching the Drylands there's no telling what he may do. Surely you don't want…"

"Primitive," Derech said, with a ring of cruel impatience in his voice. "Parochial. The gods send me a wicked man before a well-meaning fool. Mr. Woodthorpe, the Drylanders do not need Dr. Carey to stir them up to war. Neither do we. We do not want our wells and our water-courses rearranged. We do not want to be resettled. We do not want our population expanded. We do not want the resources that will last us for thousands of years yet, if they're not tampered with, pumped out and used up in a few centuries. We are in balance with our environment, we want to stay that way. And we will fight, Mr. Woodthorpe. You're not dealing with theories now. You're dealing with our lives. We are not going to place them in your hands."

He turned to Wales and the Martians. "Search the house. If you want to search the town, that's up to you. But I wouldn't be too long about any of it."

LOOKING pained and hurt, Woodthorpe stood for a moment and then went out, shaking his head. The Martians began to go through the house. Carey heard Derech's voice say, "Why don't you join them, Mr. Wales?"

Wales answered pleasantly, "I don't like wasting my time." He bade Derech good night and left, and Carey was thankful.

After a while the Martians left too. Derech bolted the door and sat down again to drink his interrupted glass of wine. He made no move to let Carey out, and Carey conquered a very strong desire to yell at him. He was getting just a touch claustrophobic now. Derech sipped his wine slowly, emptied the cup and filled it again. When it was half empty for the second time a girl came in from the back.

She wore the traditional dress of the Low-Canals, which Carey was glad to see because some of the women were changing it for the cosmopolitan and featureless styles that made all women look alike, and he thought the old style was charming. Her skirt was a length of heavy orange silk caught at the waist with a broad girdle. Above that she wore nothing but a necklace and her body was slim and graceful as a bending reed. Twisted around her ankles and braided in her dark hair were strings of tiny bells, so that she chimed as she walked with a faint elfin music, very sweet and wicked.

"They're all gone now," she told Derech, and Derech rose and came quickly toward Carey's hiding place.

"Someone was watching through the chinks in the shutters,"

he said as he helped Carey out. "Hoping I'd betray myself when I thought they were gone." He asked the girl, "It wasn't the Earthman, was it?"

"No." She had poured herself some wine and curled up with it in the silks and warm furs that covered the guest-bench on the west wall. Carey saw that her eyes were green as emerald, slightly tilted, bright, curious and without mercy. He became suddenly very conscious of his unshaven chin and the gray that was beginning to be noticeable at his temples, and his general soiled and weary condition.

"I don't like that man Wales," Derech was saying. "He's almost as good as I am. We'll have him to reckon with yet."

"We," said Carey. "You've weighed your yard of sand?"

Derech shrugged ruefully. "You must have heard me talking myself into it. Well, I've been getting a little bored with the peaceful life." He smiled, the smile Carey remembered from the times they had gone robbing tombs together in places where murder would have been a safer occupation. "And it's always irked me that we were stopped that time. I'd like to try again. By the way, this is Arrin. She'll be going with us as far as Barrakesh."

"Oh." Carey bowed, and she smiled at him from her nest in the soft furs. Then she looked at Derech. "What is there beyond Barrakesh?"

"Kesh," said Derech. "And Shun."

"But you don't trade in the Drylands," she said impatiently. "And if you did, why should I be left behind?"

"We're going to Sinharat," Derech said. "The Ever-living."

"Sinharat?" Arrin whispered. There was a long silence, and then she turned her gaze on Carey. "If I had known that, I would have told them where you were. I would have let them take you." She shivered and bent her head.

"That would have been foolish," Derech said, fondling her. "You'd have thrown away your chance to be the lady of one of the two saviors of Mars."

"If you live," she said.

"But my dear child," said Derech, "can you, sitting there, guarantee to me that you will be alive tomorrow?"

"You will have to admit," said Carey slowly, "that her odds are somewhat better than ours."

II

THE barge was long and narrow, buoyed on pontoon–like floats so that it rode high even with a full cargo. Pontoons, hull, and deck were metal. There had not been any trees for shipbuilding for a very long time. In the center of the deck was a low cabin where several people might sleep, and forward toward the blunt bow was a fire-pit where the cooking was done. The motive power was animal, four of the scaly-hided, bad-tempered, hissing beasts of Martian burden plodding along the canal bank with a tow-cable.

The pace was slow. Carey had wanted to go across country direct to Barrakesh, but Derech had forbidden it.

"I can't take a caravan. All my business goes by the canal, and everyone knows it. So you and I would have to go alone, riding by night and hiding by day, and saving no time at all." He jabbed his thumb at the sky. "Wales will come when you least expect him and least want him. On the barge you'll have a place to hide, and I'll have enough men to discourage him if he should be rash enough to interfere with a trader going about his normal and lawful business."

"He wouldn't be above it," Carey said gloomily.

"But only when he's desperate. That will be later."

So the barge went gliding gently on its way southward along the thread of dark water that was the last open artery of what had once been an ocean. It ran snow-water now, melt from the polar cap. There were villages beside the canal, and areas of cultivation where long fields showed a startling green against the reddish-yellow desolation. Again there were places where the sand had moved like an army, overwhelming the fields and occupying the houses, so that only mounded heaps would show where a village had been. There were bridges, some of them sound and serving the living, others springing out of nowhere and standing like broken rainbows against the sky. By day there was the stinging sunlight that hid nothing, and by night the two moons laid a shifting loveliness on the land. And if Carey had not been goaded by a terrible impatience he would have been happy.

But all this, if Woodthorpe and the Rehabilitation Project had their way, would go. The waters of the canals would be impounded behind great dams far to the north, and the sparse populations would be moved and settled on new land. Deep-pumping operations, tapping the underground sources that fed the wells, would make up the winter deficit when the cap was frozen. The desert would be transformed, for a space anyway, into a flowering garden. Who would not prefer it to this bitter marginal existence? Who could deny that this was Bad and the Rehabilitation Project Good? No one but the people and Dr. Matthew Carey. And no one would listen to them.

At Sinharat lay the only possible hope of making them listen.

THE sky remained empty. Arrin spent most of her time on deck, sitting among the heaped-up bales. Carey knew that she watched him a great deal but he was not flattered. He thought that she hated him because he was putting Derech in danger of his life. He wished that Derech had left her behind.

On the fourth day at dawn the wind dropped to a flat calm. The sun burned hot, setting sand and rock to shimmering. The water of the canal showed a surface like polished glass, and in the east the sharp line of the horizon thickened and blurred and was lost in a yellow haze. Derech stood sniffing like a hound at the still air, and around noon he gave the order to tie up. The crew, ten of them, ceased to lounge on the bales and got to work, driving steel anchor pins for the cables, rigging a shelter for the beasts, checking the lashings of the deck cargo. Carey and Derech worked beside them, and when he looked up briefly from his labors Carey saw Arrin crouched over the fire-pit in the midst of a great smoke, cooking furiously. The eastern sky became a wall, a wave curling toward the zenith, sooty ochre below, a blazing brass-color at its crest. It rushed across the land, roared, and broke upon them.

450

They helped each other to the cabin and crouched knee to knee in the tight space, the twelve men and Arrin, while the barge kicked and rolled, sank down deep and shot upward, struggling like a live thing under the blows of the wind. Dust and sand sifted through every vent-hole, tainting the air with a bitter taste. There was a sulphurous darkness, and the ear was deafened. Carey had been through sand-storms before, and he wished that he was out in the open where he was used to it, and where he did not have to worry about the barge turning turtle and drowning him idiotically on the dryest world in the System. And while all this was going on, Arrin was grimly guarding her pot.

The wind stopped its wild gusting and settled to a steady gale. When it appeared that the barge was going to remain upright after all, the men ate from Arrin's pot and were glad of the food. After that most of them went down into the hold to sleep because there was more room there. Arrin put the lid back on the pot and weighted it to keep the sand out, and then she said quietly to Derech,

"Why is it that you have to go—where you're going?"

"Because Dr. Carey believes that there are records there that may convince the Rehabilitation people that our 'primitives' know what they are talking about."

Carey could not see her face clearly in the gloom, but he thought she was frowning, thinking hard.

"You believe," she said to Carey. "Do you know?"

"I know that there were records, once. They're referred to in other records. Whether they still exist or not is another matter. But because of the peculiar nature of the place, and of the people who made them, I think it is possible."

He could feel her shiver. "But the Ramas were so long ago."

SHE barely whispered the name. It meant Immortal, and it had been a word of terror for so long that no amount of time could erase the memory. The Ramas had achieved their immortality by a system of induction that might have been liked to the pouring of old wine into new bottles, and though the principle behind the transplanting of a consciousness from one host to another was purely scientific, the reactions of the people from among whom they requisitioned their supply of hosts was one of simple emotional horror. The Ramas were regarded as vampires. Their ancient island city of Sinharat lay far and forgotten now in the remotest desolation of Shun, and the Drylanders held it holy, and forbidden. They had broken their own tabu just once, when Kynon of Shun raised his banner, claiming to have rediscovered the lost secret of the Ramas and promising the tribesmen and the Low-Canallers both eternal life and all the plunder they could carry. He had given them only death and since then the tabu was more fanatically enforced than ever.

"Their city has not been looted," Carey said. "That is why I have hope."

"But," said Arrin, "they weren't human. They were only evil."

"On the contrary. They were completely human. And at one time they made a very great effort to atone."

She turned again to Derech. "The Shunni will kill you."

"That is perfectly possible."

"But you must go." She added shrewdly, "If only to see whether you can."

Derech laughed. "Yes."

"Then I'll go with you. I'd rather see what happens to you than wait and wait and never know." As though that settled it, she curled up in her bunk and went to sleep.

Carey slept too, uneasily, dreaming shadowed dreams of Sinharat and waking from them in the dusty claustrophobic dark to feel hopelessly that he would never see it.

By mid-morning the storm had blown itself out, but now there was a sandbar forty feet long blocking the channel. The beasts were hitched to scoops brought up from the hold and put to dredging, and every man aboard stripped and went in with a shovel.

Carey dug in the wet sand, his taller stature and lighter skin perfectly separating him from the smaller, darker Low-Canallers. He felt obvious and naked, and he kept a wary eye cocked toward the heavens. Once he got among the Drylanders, Wales would have to look very hard indeed to spot him. At Valkis, where there was some trade with the desert men, Derech would be able to get him the proper clothing and Carey would arrive at the Gateway, Barrakesh, already in the guise of a wandering tribesman. Until then he would have to be careful, both of Wales and the local canal-dwellers, who had very little to choose between Earthmen and the Drylanders who occasionally raided this far north, stripping their fields and stealing their women.

In spite of Carey's watchfulness, it was Derech who gave the alarm. About the middle of the afternoon he suddenly shouted Carey's name. Carey, laboring now in a haze of sweat and weariness, looked up and saw Derech pointing at the sky. Carey dropped his shovel and dived for the water.

THE barge was close by, but the flier came so fast that by the time he had reached the ladder he knew he could not possibly climb aboard without being seen. Arrin's voice said calmly from overhead,

"Dive under. There's room."

Carey caught a breath and dived. The water was cold, and the sunlight slanting through it showed it thick and roiled from the storm. The shadow of the barge made a total darkness into which Carey plunged. When he thought he was clear of the broad pontoons he surfaced, hoping Arrin had told the truth. She had. There was space to breathe, and between the pontoons he could watch the flier come in low and hover on its rotors above the canal, watching. Then it landed. There were several men in it, but only Howard Wales got out.

Derech went to talk to him. The rest of the men kept on working, and Carey saw that the extra shovel had vanished into the water. Wales kept looking at the barge. Derech was playing with him, and Carey cursed. The icy chill of the water was biting him to the bone. Finally, to Wales' evident surprise, Derech invited him aboard. Carey swam carefully back and forth in the dark space under the hull, trying to keep his blood moving. After a long long time, a year or two, he saw Wales walking back to the flier. It seemed another year before the flier took off. Carey fought his way out from under the barge and into the sunlight again, but he was too stiff and numb to climb the ladder. Arrin and Derech had to pull him up.

453

"Anyone else," said Derech, "would be convinced. But this one—he gives his opponent credit for all the brains and deceitfulness he needs."

He poured liquor between Carey's chattering teeth and wrapped him in thick blankets and put him in a bunk. Then he said, "Could Wales have any way of guessing where we're going?"

Carey frowned. "I suppose he could, if he bothered to go through all my monographs and papers."

"I'm sure he's bothered."

"It's all there," Carey said dismally. "How we tried it once and failed—and what I hoped to find, though the Rehabilitation Act hadn't come along then, and it was pure archaeological interest. And I have, I know, mentioned the Ramas to Woodthorpe when I was arguing with him about the advisability of all these earth-shatter-ing—mars-shattering—changes. Why? Did Wales say something?"

"He said, 'Barrakesh will tell the story.'"

"He did, did he?" said Carey viciously. "Give me the bottle." He took a long pull and the liquor went into him like fire into glacial ice. "I wish to heaven I'd been able to steal a flier."

Derech shook his head. "You're lucky you didn't. They'd have had you out of the sky in an hour."

"Of course you're right. It's just that I'm in a hurry." He drank again and then he smiled, a very unscholarly smile. "If the gods are good to me, someday I'll have Mr. Wales between my hands."

THE local men came along that evening, about a hundred of them with teams and implements. They had already worked all day clear-ing other blocks, but they worked without question all that night and into the next day, each man choosing his own time to fall out and sleep when he could no longer stand up. The canal was their life, and their law said that the canal came first, before wife, child, brother, parent, or self, and it was a hanging matter. Carey stayed out of sight in the cabin, feeling guilty about not helping but not too guilty. It was backbreaking work. They had the channel clear by the middle of the morning, and the barge moved on southward.

Three days later a line of cliffs appeared in the east, far away at first but closing gradually until they marched beside the canal. They were high and steep, colored softly in shades of red and gold. The faces of the rock were fantastically eroded by a million years of water and ten millennia of wind. These were the rim of the sea-basin, and presently Carey saw in the distance ahead a shimmering line of mist on the desert where another canal cut through it. They were approaching Valkis.

It was sunset when they reached it. The low light struck in level shafts against the cliffs. Where the angle was right, it shone through the empty doors and window holes of the five cities that sprawled downward over the ledges of red-gold rock. It seemed as though hearthfires burned there, and warm lamplight to welcome home men weary from the sea. But in the streets and squares and on the long flights of rock-cut steps only slow shadows moved with the sinking sun. The ancient quays stood stark as tombstones, marking the levels where new harbors had been built and then abandoned as the water left them, and the high towers that had flown the banners of the Sea-Kings were bare and broken.

Only the lowest city lived, and only a part of that, but it lived fiercely, defiant of the cold centuries towering over it. From the barge deck Carey watched the torches flare out like yellow stars in the twilight, and he heard voices, and the wild and lovely music of the double-banked harps. The dry wind had a smell in it of dusty spices and strange exotic things. The New Culture had not penetrated here, and Carey was glad, though he did think that Valkis could stand being cleaned up just a little without hurting it any. They had two or three vices for sale there that were quite unbelievable.

"Stay out of sight," Derech told him, "till I get back."

It was full dark when they reached their mooring, at an ancient stone dock beside a broad square with worn old buildings on three sides of it. Derech went into the town and so did the crew, but for different reasons. Arrin stayed on deck, lying on the bales with her chin on her wrists, staring at the lights and listening to the noises like a sulky child forbidden to play some dangerous but fascinating game. Derech did not allow her in the streets alone.

Out of sheer boredom, Carey went to sleep.

He did not know how long he had slept, a few minutes or a few hours, when he was wakened sharply by Arrin's wildcat scream.

III

THERE were men on the deck outside. Carey could hear them scrambling around and cursing the woman, and someone was saying something about an Earthman. He rolled out of his bunk. He was still wearing the Earth-made coverall that was all the clothing he had until Derech came back. He stripped it off in a wild panic and shoved it far down under the tumbled furs. Arrin did not scream again but he thought he could hear muffled sounds as though she was trying to. He shivered, naked in the chill dark.

Footsteps came light and swift across the deck. Carey reached out and lifted from its place on the cabin wall a long-handled axe that was used to cut loose the deck cargo lashings in case of emergency. And as though the axe had spoken to him, Carey knew what he was going to do.

The shapes of men appeared in the doorway, dark and huddled against the glow of the deck lights.

Carey gave a Dryland war-cry that split the night. He leaped forward, swinging the axe.

The men disappeared out of the doorway as though they had been jerked on strings. Carey emerged from the cabin onto the deck, where the torchlight showed him clearly, and he whirled the axe around his head as he had learned to do years ago when he first understood both the possibility and the immense value of being able to go Martian. Inevitably he had got himself embroiled in unscholarly, unarcheological matters like tribal wars and raiding, and he had acquired some odd skills. Now he drove the dark, small, startled men ahead of the axe-blade. Yelling, he drove them over the low rail and onto the dock, and he stood above them in the torchlight while they stared at him, five astonished men with silver rings in their ears and very sharp knives in their belts.

Carey quoted some Dryland sayings about Low-Canallers that

brought the blood flushing into their cheeks. Then he asked them what their business was.

One of them, who wore a kilt of vivid yellow, said, "We were told there was an Earthman hiding."

And who told you? Carey wondered. Mr. Wales, through some Martian spy? Of course Mr. Wales—who else? He was beginning to hate Mr. Wales. But he laughed and said, "Do I look like an Earthman?"

He made the axe-blade flicker in the light. He had let his hair grow long and ragged, and it was a good desert color, tawny brown. His naked body was lean and long-muscled like a desert man's, and he had kept it hard. Arrin came up to him rubbing her bruised mouth and staring at him as surprised as the Valkisians.

The man in the yellow kilt said again, "We were told..."

Other people had begun to gather in the dockside square, both men and women, idle, curious, and cruel.

"My name is Marah," Carey said. "I left the Wells of Tamboina with a price on my head for murder." The Wells were far enough away that he need not fear a fellow-tribesman rising to dispute his story. "Does anybody here want to collect it?"

THE people watched him. The torch-flames blew in the dry wind, scattering the light across their upturned faces. Carey began to be afraid.

Close beside him Arrin whispered, "Will you be recognized?"

"No." He had been here three times with Dryland bands but it was hardly likely that anyone would remember one specific tribesman out of the numbers that floated through.

"Then stand steady," Arrin said.

He stood. The people watched him, whispering and smiling among themselves. Then the man in the yellow kilt said,

"Earthman or Drylander, I don't like your face."

The crowd laughed, and a forward movement began. Carey could hear the sweet small chiming of the bells the women wore. He gripped the axe and told Arrin to get away from him. "If you know where Derech's gone, go after him. I'll hold them as long as I can."

He did not know whether she left him or not. He was watching the crowd, seeing the sharp blades flash. It seemed ridiculous, in this age of space flight and atomic power, to be fighting with axe and knife. But Mars had had nothing better for a long time, and the UW Peace and Disarmament people hoped to take even those away from them some day. On Earth, Carey remembered, there were still peoples who hardened their wooden spears in the fire and ate their enemies. The knives, in any case, could kill efficiently enough. He stepped back a little from the rail to give the axe free play, and he was not cold any longer, but warm with a heat that stung his nerve-ends.

Derech's voice shouted across the square.

The crowd paused. Carey could see over their heads to where Derech, with about half his crew around him, was forcing his way through. He looked and sounded furious.

"I'll kill the first man that touches him!" he yelled.

The man in the yellow kilt asked politely, "What is he to you?"

"He's money, you fool! Passage money that I won't collect till I reach Barrakesh, and not then unless he's alive and able to get it for me. And if he doesn't, I'll see to him myself." Derech sprang up onto the barge deck. "Now clear off. Or you'll have more killing to do than you'll take pleasure in."

His men were lined up with him now along the rail, and the rest of the crew were coming. Twelve tough armed men did not look like much fun. The crowd began to drift away, and the original five went reluctantly with them. Derech posted a watch and took Carey into the cabin.

"Get into these," he said, throwing down a bundle he had taken from one of the men. Carey laid aside his axe. He was shaking now with relief and his fingers stumbled over the knots. The outer wrapping was a thick desert cloak. Inside was a leather kilt, well worn and adorned with clanking bronze bosses, a wide bronze collar for the neck and a leather harness for weapons that was black with use.

"They came off a dead man," Derech said. "There are sandals underneath." He took a long desert knife from his girdle and tossed it to Carey. "And this. And now, my friend, we are in trouble."

"I thought I did rather well," Carey said, buckling kilt and harness.

458

They felt good. Perhaps someday, if he lived, he would settle down to being the good gray Dr. Carey, archeologist emeritus, but the day was not yet. "Someone told them there was an Earthman here."

DERECH nodded. "I have friends here, men who trust me, men I trust. They warned me. That's why I routed my crew out of the brothels, and unhappy they were about it, too."

Carey laughed. "I'm grateful to them." Arrin had come in and was sitting on the edge of her bunk, watching Carey. He swung the cloak around him and hooked the bronze catch at the throat. The rough warmth of the cloth was welcome. "Wales will know now that I'm with you. This was his way of finding out for sure."

"You might have been killed," Arrin said.

Carey shrugged. "It wouldn't be a calamity. They'd rather have me dead than lose me, though of course none of them would dream of saying so. Point is, he won't be fooled by the masquerade, and he won't wait for Barrakesh. He'll be on board as soon as you're well clear of Valkis and he'll have enough force with him to make it good."

"All true," said Derech. "So. Let him have the barge." He turned to Arrin. "If you're still hell-bent to come with us, get ready. And remember, you'll be riding for a long time."

To Carey he said, "Better keep clear of the town. I'll have mounts and supplies by the time Phobos rises. Where shall we meet?"

"By the lighthouse," Carey said. Derech nodded and went out. Carey went out too and waited on the deck while Arrin changed her clothes. A few minutes later she joined him, wrapped in a long cloak. She had taken the bells from her hair and around her ankles, and she moved quietly now, light and lithe as a boy. She grinned at him. "Come, desert man. What did you say your name was?"

"Marah."

"Don't forget your axe."

They left the barge. Only one torch burned now on the deck. Some of the lights had died around the square. This was deserted, but there was still sound and movement in plenty along the streets that led into it. Carey guided Arrin to the left along the canal bank. He did not see anyone watching them, or following them. The sounds and the lights grew fainter. The buildings they passed now were empty, their doors and windows open to the wind. Deimos was in the sky, and some of the roofs showed moonlight through them, shafts of pale silver touching the drifted dust that covered the floors. Carey stopped several times to listen, but he heard nothing except the wind. He began to feel better. He hurried Arrin with long strides, and now they moved away from the canal and up a broken street that led toward the cliffs.

THE street became a flight of steps cut in the rock. There were roofless stone houses on either side, clinging to the cliffs row on ragged row like the abandoned nests of sea-birds. Carey's imagination, as always, peopled them, hung them with nets and gear, livened them with lights and voices and appropriate smells. At the top of the steps he paused to let Arrin get her breath, and he looked down across the centuries at the torches of Valkis burning by the canal.

"What are you thinking?" Arrin asked.

"I'm thinking that nothing, not people nor oceans, should ever die."

"The Ramas lived forever."

"Too long, anyway. And that wasn't good, I know. But still it makes me sad to think of men building these houses and working and raising their families, looking forward to the future."

"You're an odd one," Arrin said. "When I first met you I couldn't understand what it was that made Derech love you. You were so—quiet. Tonight I could see. But now you've gone all broody and soft again. Why do you care so much about dust and old bones?"

"Curiosity. I'll never know the end of the story, but I can at least know the beginning."

They moved on again, and now they were walking across the basin of a harbor, with the great stone quays towering above them, gnawed and rounded by the wind. Ahead on a crumbling promontory the shaft of a broken tower pointed skyward. They came beneath it, where ships had used to come, and presently Carey heard the jingling and padding of animals coming toward them. Before the rise of Phobos they were mounted and on their way.

"This is your territory," said Derech. "I will merely ride."

"Then you and Arrin can handle the pack animals." Carey took the lead. They left the city behind, climbing to the top of the cliffs. The canal showed like a ribbon of steel in the moonlight far below, and then was gone. A range of mountains had come down here to the sea, forming a long curving peninsula. Only their bare bones were left, and through that skeletal mass of rock Carey took his little band by a trail he had followed once and hoped that he remembered.

They travelled all that way by night, lying in the shelter of the rocks by day, and three times a flier passed over them like a wheeling hawk, searching. Carey thought more than once that he had lost the way, though he never said so, and he was pleasantly surprised when they found the sea-bottom again just where it should be on the other side of the range, with the ford he remembered across the canal. They crossed it by moonlight, stopping only to fill up their water bags. At dawn they were on a ridge above Barrakesh.

They looked down, and Derech said, "I think we can forget our southbound caravan."

Trade was for times of peace, and now the men of Kesh and Shun were gathering for war, even as Derech had said, without need of any Dr. Carey to stir them to it.

They filled the streets. They filled the *serais*. They camped in masses by the gates and along the banks of the canal and around the swampy lake that was its terminus. The vast herds of animals broke down the dikes, trampled the irrigation ditches and devoured the fields. And across the desert more riders were coming, long files of them with pennons waving and lances glinting in the morning light. Wild and far away, Carey heard the skirling of the desert pipes.

"The minute we go down there," he said, "we are part of the army. Any man that turns his back on Barrakesh now will get a spear through it for cowardice."

HIS face became hard and cruel with a great rage. Presently this horde would roll northward, sweeping up more men from the Low-Canal towns as it passed, joining ultimately with other hordes pouring in through the easterly gates of the Drylands. The people of the City-States would fall like butchered sheep, and perhaps even the dome of Kahora would come shattering down. But sooner or later the guns would be brought up, and then the Drylanders would do the falling, all because of good men like Woodthorpe who only wanted to help.

Carey said, "I am going to Sinharat. But you know how much chance a small party has, away from the caravan track and the wells."

"I know," said Derech.

"You know how much chance we have of evading Wales, without the protection of a caravan."

"You tell me how I can go quietly home, and I'll do it."

"You can wait for your barge and go back to Valkis."

"I couldn't do that," Derech said seriously. "My men would laugh at me. I suggest we stop wasting time. Here in the desert, time is water."

"Speaking of water," Arrin said, "how about when we get there? And how about getting back?"

Derech said, "Dr. Carey has heard that there is a splendid well at Sinharat."

"He's heard," said Arrin, "but he doesn't know. Same as the records." She gave Carey a look, only half scornful.

Carey smiled briefly. "The well I have on pretty good authority. It's in the coral deep under the city, so it can be used without actually breaking the tabu. The Shunni don't go near it unless they're desperate, but I talked to a man who had."

He led them down off the ridge and away from Barrakesh. And Derech cast an uneasy glance at the sky.

"I hope Wales did set a trap for us there. And I hope he'll sit a while waiting for us to spring it."

There was a strict law against the use of fliers over tribal lands without special permission, which would be unprocurable now. But they both knew that Wales would not let that stop him.

"The time could come," Carey said grimly, "that we'd be glad to see him."

He led them a long circle northward to avoid the war parties coming in to Barrakesh. Then he struck out across the deadly waste of the sea-bottom, straight for Sinharat.

HE lost track of time very quickly. The days blurred together into one endless hell wherein they three and the staggering animals toiled across vast slopes of rock up-tilted to the sun, or crept under reefs of rotten coral with sand around them as smooth and bright as a burning-glass. At night there was moonlight and bitter cold, but the cold did nothing to alleviate their thirst. There was only one good thing about the journey, and that was the thing that worried Carey the most. In all that cruel and empty sky, no flier ever appeared.

"The desert is a big place," Arrin said, looking at it with loathing. "Perhaps he couldn't find us. Perhaps he's given up."

"Not him," said Carey.

Derech said, "Maybe he thinks we're dead anyway, and why bother."

Maybe, Carey thought. Maybe. But sometimes as he rode or walked he would curse at Wales out loud and glare at the sky, demanding to know what he was up to. There was never any answer.

The last carefully-hoarded drop of water went. And Carey forgot about Wales and thought only of the well of Sinharat, cold and clear in the coral.

He was thinking of it as he plodded along, leading the beast that was now almost as weak as he. The vision of the well so occupied him that it was some little time before the message from his bleared and sun-struck eyes got through it and registered on his brain. Then he halted in sudden wild alarm.

He was walking, not on smooth sand, but in the trampled marks of many riders.

IV

THE others came out of their stupor as he pointed, warning them to silence. The broad track curved ahead and vanished out of sight beyond a great reef of white coral. The wind had not had time to do more than blur the edges of the individual prints.

Mounting and whipping their beasts unmercifully, Carey and the others fled the track. The reef stood high above them like a wall. Along its base were cavernous holes, and they found one big enough to hold them all. Carey went on alone and on foot to the shoulder of the reef, where the riders had turned it, and the wind went with him, piping and crying in the vast honeycomb of the coral.

He crept around the shoulder and then he saw where he was.

On the other side of the reef was a dry lagoon, stretching perhaps half a mile to a coral island that stood up tall in the hard clear sunlight, its naked cliffs beautifully striated with deep rose and white and delicate pink. A noble stairway went up from the desert to a city of walls and towers so perfectly built from many-shaded marble and so softly sculptured by time that it was difficult to tell where the work of men began and ended. Carey saw it through a shimmering haze of exhaustion and wonder, and knew that he looked at Sinharat, the Ever-Living.

The trampled track of the Shunni warriors went out across the lagoon. It swept furiously around what had been a parked flier, and then passed on, leaving behind it battered wreckage and two dark sprawled shapes. It ended at the foot of the cliffs, where Carey could see a sort of orderly turmoil of men and animals. There were between twenty-five and thirty warriors, as nearly as he could guess. They were making camp.

Carey knew what that meant. There was someone in the city.

Carey did not move for some time. He stared at the beautiful marble city shimmering on its lovely pedestal of coral. He wanted to weep, but there was not enough moisture left in him to make tears, and his despair was gradually replaced by a feeble anger. All right, you bastards, he thought. All right!

464

He went back to Derech and Arrin and told them what he had seen.

"Wales just came ahead of us and waited. Why bother to search a whole desert when he knew where we were going? This time he'd have us for sure. Water. We couldn't run away." Carey grinned horribly with his cracked lips and swollen tongue. "Only the Shunni found him first. War party. They must have seen the flier go over—came to check if it landed here. Caught two men in it. But the rest are in Sinharat."

"How do you know?" asked Derech.

"The Shunni won't go into the city except as a last resort. If they catch a trespasser there they just hold the well and wait. Sooner or later he comes down."

Arrin said, "How long can we wait? We've had no water for two days."

"Wait, hell," said Carey. "We can't wait. I'm going in."

Now, while they still had a shred of strength. Another day would be too late.

Derech said, "I suppose a quick spear is easier than thirst."

"We may escape both," said Carey, "If we're very careful. And very lucky."

He told them what to do.

AN hour or so later Carey followed the warriors' track out across the dry lagoon. He walked, or rather staggered, leading the animals. Arrin rode on one, her cloak pulled over her head and her face covered in sign of mourning. Between two of the beasts, on an improvised litter made of blankets and pack lashings, Derech lay wrapped from head to foot in his cloak, a too-convincing imitation of a corpse. Carey heard the shouts and saw the distant riders start toward them, and he was frightened. The smallest slip, the most minor mistake, could give them away, and then he did not think that anything on Mars could save them. But thirst was more imperative than fear.

There was something more. Carey passed the two bodies in the sand beside the wrecked flier. He saw that they were both dark-haired Martians, and he looked at the towers of Sinharat with wolfish eyes.

Wales was up there, still alive, still between him and what he wanted. Carey's hand tightened on the axe. He was no longer entirely sane on the subject of Howard Wales and the records of the Ramas.

When the riders were within spear-range he halted and rested the axe-head in the sand, as a token. He waited, saying softly, "For God's sake now, be careful."

The riders reined in, sending the sand flying. Carey said to them, "I claim the death right."

He stood swaying over his axe while they looked at him, and at the muffled woman, and at the dusty corpse. They were six, tall hard fierce-eyed men with their long spears held ready. Finally one of them said, "How did you come here?"

"My sister's husband," said Carey, indicating Derech, "died on the march to Barrakesh. Our tribal law says he must rest in his own place. But there are no caravans now. We had to come alone, and in a great sandstorm we lost the track. We wandered for many days until we crossed your trail."

"Do you know where you are?" asked the Drylander.

Carey averted his eyes from the city. "I know now. But if a man is dying it is permitted to use the well. We are dying."

"Use it, then," said the Drylander. "But keep your ill-omen away from our camp. We are going to the war as soon as we finish our business here. We want no corpse-shadow on us."

"Outlanders?" Carey asked, a rhetorical question in view of the flier and the un-Dryland bodies.

"Outlanders. Who else is foolish enough to wake the ghosts in the Forbidden City?"

Carey shook his head. "Not I. I do not wish even to see it."

The riders left them, returning to the camp. Carey moved on slowly toward the cliffs. It became apparent where the well must be. A great arching cave-mouth showed in the rose-pink coral and men were coming and going there, watering their animals. Carey approached it and began the monotonous chant that etiquette required, asking that way be made for the dead, so that warriors and pregnant women and persons undergoing ritual purifications would be warned to go aside. The warriors made way. Carey passed out of the cruel sunlight into the shadow of an irregular vaulted passage, quite high and wide, with a floor that sloped upward, at first gently and then steeply, until suddenly the passage ended in an echoing cathedral room dim-lit by torches that picked out here and there the shape of a fantastic flying buttress of coral. In the center of the room, in a kind of broad basin, was the well.

NOW for the first time Arrin broke her silence with a soft anguished cry. There were seven or eight warriors guarding the well, as Carey had known there would be, but they drew away and let Carey's party severely alone. Several men were in the act of watering their mounts, and as though in deference to tabu Carey circled around to get as far away from them as possible. In the gloom he made out the foot of an age-worn stairway leading upward through the coral. Here he stopped.

He helped Arrin down and made her sit, and then dragged Derech from the litter and laid him on the hard coral. The animals bolted for the well and he made no effort to hold them. He filled one of the bags for Arrin and then he flung himself alongside the beasts and drank and soaked himself in the beautiful cold clear water. After that he crouched still for a few moments, in a kind of daze, until he remembered that Derech too needed water.

He filled two more bags and took them to Arrin, kneeling beside her as though in tender concern as she sat beside her dead. His spread cloak covered what she was doing, holding the water-bag to Derech's mouth so that he could drink. Carey spoke softly and quickly. Then he went back to the animals. He began to fight them away from the water, so that they should not founder themselves. The activity covered what was going on in the shadows behind them. Carey led them, hissing and stamping, to where Arrin and Derech had been, still using them as a shield in case the guards were watching. He snatched up his axe and the remaining water-bag and let the animals go and ran as fast as he could up the stairway. It spiralled, and he was stumbling in pitch darkness around the second curve before the guards below let out a great angry cry.

He did not know whether they would follow or not. Somebody

fumbled for him in the blackness and Derech's voice muttered something urgent. He could hear Arrin panting like a spent hound. His own knees shook with weakness and he thought what a fine militant crew they were to be taking on Wales and his men and thirty angry Shunni. Torchlight flickered against the turn of the wall below and there was a confusion of voices. They fled upward, pulling each other along, and it seemed that the Shunni reached a point beyond which they did not care to go. The torchlight and the voices vanished. Carey and the others climbed a little farther and then dropped exhausted on the worn treads.

Arrin asked, "Why didn't they follow us?"

"Why should they? Our water won't last long. They can wait."

"Yes," said Arrin. And then, "How *are* we going to get away?"

Carey answered, "That depends on Wales."

"I don't understand."

"On whether, and how soon, somebody sends a flier out here to see what happened to him." He patted the water-bags. "That's why these are so important. They give us time."

They started up the stair again, treading in the worn hollows made by other feet. The Ramas must have come this way for water for a very long time. Presently a weak daylight filtered down to them. And then a man's voice, tight with panic, cried out somewhere above them, "I hear them! They're coming..."

The voice of Howard Wales answered sharply. "Wait!" Then in English it called down, "Carey. Dr. Carey. Is that you?"

"It is," Carey shouted back.

"Thank Heaven," said Wales. "I saw you, but I wasn't sure... Come up, man, come up, and welcome. We're all in the same trap now."

V

SINHARAT was a city without people, but it was not dead. It had a memory and a voice. The wind gave it breath, and it sang, from the countless tiny organ-pipes of the coral, from the hollow mouths of marble doorways and the narrow throats of streets. The slender towers were like tall flutes, and the wind was never still. Sometimes the voice of Sinharat was soft and gentle, murmuring about everlasting youth and the pleasures thereof. Again it was strong and fierce with pride, crying *You die, but I do not!* Sometimes it was mad, laughing and hateful. But always the song was evil.

Carey could understand now why Sinharat was tabu. It was not only because of an ancient dread. It was the city itself, now, in the sharp sunlight or under the gliding moons. It was a small city. There had never been more than perhaps three thousand Ramas, and this remote little island had given them safety and room enough. But they had built close, and high. The streets ran like topless tunnels between the walls and the towers reached impossibly thin and tall into the sky. Some of them had lost their upper storeys and some had fallen entirely, but in the main they were still beautiful. The colors of the marble were still lovely. Many of the buildings were perfect and sound, except that wind and time had erased the carvings on their walls so that only in certain angles of light did a shadowy face leap suddenly into being, prideful and mocking with smiling lips, or a procession pass solemnly toward some obliterated worship.

Perhaps it was only the wind and the half-seen watchers that gave Sinharat its feeling of eerie wickedness. Carey did not think so. The Ramas had built something of themselves into their city, and it was rather, he imagined, as one of the Rama women might have been had one met her, graceful and lovely but with something wrong about the eyes. Even the matter-of-fact Howard Wales was uncomfortable in the city, and the three surviving City-State men who were with him went about like dogs with their tails tight to their bellies. Even Derech lost some of his cheerful arrogance, and Arrin never left his side.

The feeling was worse inside the buildings. Here were the halls and chambers where the Ramas had lived. Here were the possessions they had handled, the carvings and faded frescoes they had looked at. The ever-young, the Ever-living immortals, the stealers of others' lives, had walked these corridors and seen themselves reflected in the surfaces of polished marble, and Carey's nerves quivered with the nearness of them after all this long time.

There were traces of a day when Sinharat had had an advanced technology equal to, if not greater, than any Carey had yet seen on Mars. The inevitable reversion to the primitive had come with the exhaustion of resources. There was one rather small room where much wrecked equipment lay in crystal shards and dust, and Carey knew that this was the place where the Ramas had exchanged their old bodies for new. From some of the frescoes, done with brilliantly sadistic humor, he knew that the victims were generally killed soon, but not too soon, after the exchange was completed.

STILL he could not find the place where the archives had been kept. Outside, Wales and his men, generally with Derech's help and Arrin as a lookout, were sweating to clear away rubble from the one square that was barely large enough for a flier to land in. Wales had been in contact with Kahora before the unexpected attack. They knew where he was, and when there had been too long a time without a report from him they would certainly come looking. If they had a landing place cleared by then, and the scanty water supply, severely rationed, kept them alive, and the Shunni did not become impatient, they would be all right.

"Only," Carey told them, "if that flier does come, be ready to jump quick. Because the Shunni will attack then."

He had not had any trouble with Howard Wales. He had expected it. He had come up the last of the stairway with his axe ready. Wales shook his head. "I have a heavy-duty shocker," he said. "Even so, I wouldn't care to take you on. You can put down the axe, Dr. Carey."

The Martians were armed too. Carey knew they could have taken him easily. Perhaps they were saving their charges against the Shunni, who played the game of war for keeps.

Carey said, "I will do what I came here to do."

Wales shrugged. "My assignment was to bring you in. I take it there won't be any more trouble about that now—if any of us get out of here. Incidentally, I saw what was happening at Barrakesh, and I can testify that you could not possibly have had any part in it. I'm positive that some of my superiors are thundering asses, but that's nothing new, either. So go ahead. I won't hinder you."

Carey had gone ahead, on a minimum of water, sleep, and the dry desert rations he had in his belt-pouch. Two and a half days were gone, and the taste of defeat was getting stronger in his mouth by the hour. Time was getting short, no one could say how short. And then almost casually he crawled over a great fallen block of marble into a long room with rows of vault doors on either side, and a hot wave of excitement burned away his weariness. The bars of beautiful rust-less alloy slid easily under his hands. And he was dazed at the treasure of knowledge that he had found, tortured by the realization that he could only take a fraction of it with him and might well never see the rest of it again.

THE Ramas had arranged their massive archives according to a simple and orderly dating system. It did not take him long to find the records he wanted, but even that little time was almost too much.

Derech came shouting after him. Carey closed the vault he was in and scrambled back over the fallen block, clutching the precious spools. "Flier!" Derech kept saying. "Hurry!" Carey could hear the distant cries of the Shunni.

He ran with Derech and the cries came closer. The warriors had seen the flier too and now they knew that they must come into the city. Carey raced through the narrow twisting street that led to the square. When he came into it he could see the flier hanging on its rotors about thirty feet overhead, very ginger about coming down in that cramped space. Wales and the Martians were frantically waving. The Shunni came in two waves, one from the well-stair and one up the cliffs. Carey picked up his axe. The shockers began to crackle.

He hoped they would hold the Drylanders off because he did not want to have to kill anyone, and he particularly did not want to get killed, not right now. "Get to the flier!" Wales yelled at him, and he saw that it was just settling down, making a great wind and dust. The warriors in the forefront of the attack were dropping or staggering as the stunning charges hit them, sparking off their metal ornaments and the tips of their spears. The first charge was broken up, but no one wanted to stay for the second. Derech had Arrin and was lifting her bodily into the flier. Hands reached out and voices shouted unnecessary pleas for haste. Carey threw away his axe and jumped for the hatch. The Martians crowded in on top of him and then Wales, and the pilot took off so abruptly that Wales' legs were left dangling outside. Carey caught him and pulled him in. Wales laughed, in an odd wild way, and the flier, rose up among the towers of Sinharat in a rattle of flung spears.

★ ★ ★

The technicians had had trouble regearing their equipment to the Rama microtapes. The results were still far from perfect, but the United Worlds Planetary Assistance Committee, hastily assembled at Kahora, were not interested in perfection. They were Alan Woodthorpe's superiors, and they had a decision to make, and little time in which to make it. The great tide was beginning to roll north out of the Drylands, moving at the steady marching pace of the desert beasts. And Woodthorpe could no longer blame this all on Carey.

Looking subdued and rather frightened, Woodthorpe sat beside Carey in the chamber where the hearing was being held. Derech was there, and Wales, and some high brass from the City-States who were getting afraid for their borders, and two Dryland chiefs who knew Carey as Carey, not as a tribesman, and trusted him enough to come in. Carey thought bitterly that this hearing should have been held long ago. Only the Committee had not understood the potential seriousness of the situation. They had been told, plainly and often. But they had preferred to believe experts like Woodthorpe rather than men like Carey, who had some specialized knowledge but were not trained to evaluate the undertaking as a whole.

Now in a more chastened mood they watched as Carey's tapes went whispering through the projectors.

They saw an island city in a blue sea. People moved in its streets. There were ships in its harbors and the sounds of life. Only the sea had shrunk down from the tops of the coral cliffs. The lagoon was a shallow lake wide-rimmed with beaches, and the outer reef stood bare above a feeble surf. A man's voice spoke in the ancient High Martian, somewhat distorted by the reproduction and blurred by the

voice of a translator speaking Esperanto. Carey shut his ears to everything but the voice, the man, who spoke across the years.

"Nature grins at us these days, reminding us that even planets die.
We who have loved life so much that we have taken the lives of
countless others in order to retain it, can now see the beginning of
our own inevitable end. Even though this may yet be thousands of
years in the future, the thought of it has had strange effects. For the
first time some of our people are voluntarily choosing death. Others demand younger and younger hosts, and change them constantly.
Most of us have come to have some feeling of remorse, not for our
immortality but for the method by which we achieved it.

"One murder can be remembered and regretted. Ten thousand
murders become as meaningless as ten thousand love affairs or ten
thousand games of chess. Time and repetition grind them all to the
same dust. Yet now we do regret, and a naive passion has come to us,
a passion to be forgiven, if not by our victims then perhaps by ourselves.

"Thus our great project is undertaken. The people of Kharif, because their coasts are accessible and their young people exceptionally
handsome and sturdy, have suffered more from us than any other
single nation. We will try now to make some restitution."

THE scene shifted from Sinharat to a desolate stretch of desert
coastline beside the shrunken sea. The land had once been populous. There were the remains of cities and town, connected by paved
roads. There had been factories and power stations, all the appurtenances of an advanced technology. These were now rusting away, and
the wind blew ochre dust to bury them.

"For a hundred years," said the Rama voice, "it has not rained."

There was an oasis, with wells of good water. Tall brown-haired
men and women worked the well-sweeps, irrigating fields of considerable extent. There was a village of neat huts, housing perhaps a
thousand people.

"Mother Mars has killed far more of her children than we. The
fortunate survivors live in 'cities' like these. The less fortunate…"

A long line of beasts and hooded human shapes moved across a bitter wasteland. And the Dryland chiefs cried out, "Our people!"

"We will give them water again," said the Rama voice.

The spool ended. In the brief interval before the next one began, Woodthorpe coughed uneasily and muttered, "This was all long ago, Carey. The winds of change…"

"Are blowing up a real storm, Woodthorpe. You'll see why."

The tapes began again. A huge plant now stood at the edge of the sea, distilling fresh water from the salt. A settlement had sprung up beside it, with fields and plantations of young trees.

"It has gone well," said the Rama voice. "It will go better with time, for their short generations move quickly."

The settlement became a city. The population grew, spread, built more cities, planted more crops. The land flourished.

"Many thousands live," the Rama said, "who would otherwise not have been born. We have repaid our murders."

The spool ended.

Woodthorpe said, "But we're not trying to atone for anything. We…"

"If my house burns down," said Carey, "I do not greatly care whether it was by a stroke of lightning, deliberate arson, or a child playing with matches. The end result is the same."

The third spool began.

A different voice spoke now. Carey wondered if the owner of the first had chosen death himself, or simply lacked the heart to go on with the record. The distilling plant was wearing out and metals for repair were poor and difficult to find. The solar batteries could not be replaced. The stream of water dwindled. Crops died. There was famine and panic, and then the pumps stopped altogether and the cities were stranded like the hulks of ships in dry harbors.

THE Rama voice said, "These are the consequences of the one kind act we have ever done. Now these thousands that we called into life must die as their forebears did. The cruel laws of survival that we caused them to forget are all to be learned again. They had suffered once, and mastered it, and were content. Now there is nothing we can do to help. We can only stand and watch."

"Shut it off," said Woodthorpe.

"No," said Carey, "see it out."

They saw it out.

"Now," said Carey, "I will remind you that Kharif was the homeland from which most of the Drylands were settled." He was speaking to the Committee more than to Woodthorpe. "These so-called primitives have been through all this before, and they have long memories. Their tribal legends are explicit about what happened to them the last time they put their trust in the transitory works of men. Now can you understand why they're so determined to fight?"

Woodthorpe looked at the disturbed and frowning faces of the Committee. "But," he said, "it wouldn't be like that now. Our resources..."

"Are millions of miles away on other planets. How long can you guarantee to keep *your* pumps working? And the Ramas at least had left the natural water sources for the survivors to go back to. You want to destroy those so they would have nothing." Carey glanced at the men from the City-States. "The City-States would pay the price for that. They have the best of what there is, and with a large population about to die of famine and thirst..." He shrugged, and then went on,

"There are other ways to help. Food and medicines. Education, to enable the young people to look for greener pastures in other places, if they wish to. In the meantime, there is an army on the move. You have the power to stop it. You've heard all there is to be said. Now the chiefs are waiting to hear what you will say."

The Chairman of the Committee conferred with the members. The conference was quite brief.

"Tell the chiefs," the Chairman said, "that it is not our intent to create wars. Tell them to go in peace. Tell them the Rehabilitation Project for Mars is cancelled."

★   ★   ★

The great tide rolled slowly back into the Drylands and dispersed. Carey went through a perfunctory hearing on his activities, took his reprimand and dismissal with a light heart, shook hands with Howard Wales, and went back to Jekkara, to drink with Derech and walk beside the Low-Canal that would be there now for whatever ages were left to it in the slow course of a planet's dying.

And this was good. But at the end of the canal was Barrakesh, and the southward-moving caravans, and the long road to Sinharat. Carey thought of the vaults beyond the fallen block of marble, and he knew that someday he would walk that road again.

PURPLE PRIESTESS
OF THE MAD MOON

The Magazine of Fantasy & Science Fiction, October 1964

IN THE OBSERVATION bubble of the TSS *Goddard* Harvey Selden watched the tawny face of the planet grow. He could make out rose-red deserts where tiny sandstorms blew, and dark areas of vegetation like textured silk. Once or twice he caught the bright flash of water from one of the canals. He sat motionless, rapt and delighted. He had been afraid that this confrontation would offer very little to his emotions; he had since childhood witnessed innumerable identical approaches on the tri-di screen, which was almost the same as being there one's self. But the actuality had a flavor and imminence that he found immensely thrilling.

After all, an alien planet…

After all, *Mars*…

He was almost angry when he realized that Bentham had come into the bubble. Bentham was Third Officer and at his age this was an admission of failure. The reason for it, Selden thought, was stamped quite clearly on his face, and he felt sorry for Bentham as he felt sorry for anyone afflicted with alcoholism. Still, the man was friendly and he had seemed much impressed by Selden's knowledge of Mars. So Selden smiled and nodded.

"Quite a thrill," he said.

Bentham glanced at the onrushing planet. "It always is. You know anybody down there?"

"No. But after I check in with the Bureau…"

"When will you do that?"

"Tomorrow. I mean, counting from after we land, of course…a little confusing, isn't it, this time thing?" He knew they did three or four complete orbits on a descending spiral, which meant three or four days and nights.

Bentham said, "But in the meantime, you don't know anybody."

Selden shook his head.

"Well," said Bentham, "I'm having dinner with some Martian friends. Why don't you come along? You might find it interesting."

"Oh," said Selden eagerly, "that would be… But are you sure your friends won't mind? I mean, an unexpected guest dragged in at the last minute…"

"They won't mind," Bentham said. "I'll give them plenty of warning. Where are you staying?"

"The Kahora-Hilton."

"Of course," said Bentham. "I'll pick you up around seven." He smiled. "Kahora time."

He went out, leaving Selden with some lingering qualms of doubt. Bentham was perhaps not quite the person he would have chosen to introduce him to Martian society. Still, he was an officer and could be presumed to be a gentleman. And he had been on the Mars run for a long time. Of course he would have friends, and what an unlooked-for and wonderful chance this was to go actually into a Martian home and visit with a Martian family. He was ashamed of his momentary uneasiness, and was able to analyze it quite quickly as being based in his own sense of insecurity, which of course arose from being faced with a totally unfamiliar environment. Once he had brought this negative attitude into the open it was easy to correct it. After a quarter of an hour of positive therapy he found himself hardly able to wait for the evening.

Kahora had grown in half a century. Originally, Selden knew, it had been founded as a Trade City under the infamous old Umbrella Treaty, so-called because it could be manipulated to cover anything, which had been concluded between the then World Government of Terra and the impoverished Martian Federation of City-States. At that time the city was housed under a single dome, climate-conditioned for the comfort of the outworld traders and politicians who frequented it and who were unused to the rigors of cold and thin-aired Mars. In addition to the climate, various other luxuries were installed in the Trade Cities, so that they had been compared with certain Biblical locales, and crimes of many different sorts, even murder, had been known to occur in them.

But all of that, or nearly all of that, was in the bad old days of *laissez-faire,* and now Kahora was the administrative capital of Mars, sheltered under a complex of eight shining domes. From the spaceport fifteen miles away, Selden saw the city as a pale shimmer of gossamer bubbles touched by the low sun. As the spaceport skimmer flew him across the intervening miles of red sand and dark green moss-grass, he saw the lights come on in the quick dusk and the buildings underneath the domes rose and took shape, clean and graceful and clothed in radiance. He thought that he had never seen anything so beautiful. From the landing stage inside one of the domes a silent battery-powered cab took him to his hotel along gracious streets, where the lights glowed and people of many races walked leisurely. The whole trip, from debarkation to hotel lobby, was accomplished in completely air-conditioned comfort, and Selden was not sorry. The landscape looked awfully bleak, and one needed only to glance at it to know that it was damnably cold. Just before the skimmer entered the airlock it crossed the Kahora canal, and the water looked like black ice. He knew that he might have to cope with all this presently, but he was not in any hurry.

Selden's room was pleasantly homelike and the view of the city was superb. He showered and shaved, dressed in his best dark silk, and then sat for a while on his small balcony overlooking the Triangle with the Three Worlds represented at its apices. The air he breathed was warm and faintly scented. The city sounds that rose to him were pleasantly subdued. He began to run over in his mind the rules he had learned for proper behavior in a Martian house, the ceremonial phrases and gestures. He wondered whether Bentham's friends would speak High or Low Martian. Low, probably, since that was most commonly in use with outsiders. He hoped his accent was not too barbarous. On the whole he felt adequate. He leaned back in his comfortable chair and found himself looking at the sky.

There were two moons in it, racing high above the glow and dis-

tortion of the dome. And for some reason, although he knew perfectly well that Mars had two moons, this bit of alienage had a powerful
effect on him. For the first time he realized, not merely with his in-
tellect but with his heart and bowels, that he was on a strange world
a long, long way from home.

He went down to the bar to wait for Bentham.

The man arrived in good time, freshly turned out in civilian silks
and, Selden was glad to see, perfectly sober. He bought him a drink
and then followed him into a cab, which bore them quietly from the
central dome into one of the outer ones.

"The original one," Bentham said. "It's chiefly residential now.
The buildings are older, but very comfortable." They were halted at
a concourse waiting for a flow of cross traffic to pass and Bentham
pointed at the dome roof. "Have you seen the moons? They're both
in the sky now. That's the thing people seem to notice the most when
they first land."

"Yes," Selden said. "I've seen them. It is…uh…striking."

"The one we call Deimos…that one there…the Martian name is
Vashna, of course…that's the one that in certain phases was called the
Mad Moon."

"Oh no," Selden said. "That was Phobos. Denderon."

Bentham gave him a look and he reddened a bit. "I mean, I think
it was." He knew damn well it was, but after all… "Of course you've
been here many times, and I could be mistaken…"

Bentham shrugged. "Easy enough to settle it. We'll ask Mak."

"Who?"

"Firsa Mak. Our host."

"Oh," said Selden, "I wouldn't…"

But the cab sped on then and Bentham was pointing out some
other thing of interest and the subject passed.

Almost against the outer curve of the dome there was a building
of pale gold and the cab stopped there. A few minutes later Selden
was being introduced to Firsa Mak.

He had met Martians before, but only rarely and never *in situ*. He
saw a dark, small, lean, catlike man with the most astonishing yellow
eyes. The man wore the traditional white tunic of the Trade Cities,

exotic and very graceful. A gold earring that Selden recognized as a priceless antique hung from his left earlobe. He was not at all like the rather round and soft Martians Selden had met on Terra. He flinched before those eyes, and the carefully mustered words of greeting stuck in his throat. Then there was no need for them as Firsa Mak shook his hand and said, "Hello. Welcome to Mars. Come on in."

A wiry brown hand propelled him in the most friendly fashion into a large low room with a glass wall that looked out through the dome at the moon-washed desert. The furniture was simple modern stuff and very comfortable, with here and there a bit of sculpture or a wall-plaque as fine as, but no better than, the Martian handcrafts obtainable at the good specialty shops in New York. On one of the couches a very long-legged, gaunt and white-haired Earthman sat drinking in a cloud of smoke. He was introduced as Altman. He had a face like old leather left too long in the sun, and he looked at Selden as from a great height and a far distance. Curled up beside him was a dark girl, or woman…Selden could not decide which because of the smoothness of her face and the too-great wisdom of her eyes, which were as yellow and unwinking as Firsa Mak's.

"My sister," Firsa Mak said. "Mrs. Altman. And this is Lella."

He did not say exactly who Lella was, and Selden did not at the moment care. She had just come in from the kitchen bearing a tray of something or other, and she wore a costume that Selden had read about but never seen. A length of brilliant silk, something between red and burnt orange, was wrapped about her hips and caught at the waist by a broad girdle. Below the skirt her slim brown ankles showed, with anklets of tiny golden bells that chimed faintly as she walked. Above the skirt her body was bare and splendidly made. A necklace of gold plaques intricately pierced and hammered circled her throat, and more of the tiny bells hung from her ears. Her hair was long and deeply black and her eyes were green, with the most enchanting tilt. She smiled at Selden, and moved away with her elfin music, and he stood stupidly staring after her, hardly aware that he had taken a glass of dark liquor from her proffered tray.

Presently Selden was sitting on some cushions between the Altmans and Firsa Mak, with Bentham opposite. Lella kept moving distractingly in and out, keeping their glasses filled with the peculiar smoky-tasting hellfire.

"Bentham tells me you're with the Bureau of Interworld Cultural Relations," Firsa Mak said.

"Yes," said Selden. Altman was looking at him with that strange remote glare, making him feel acutely uncomfortable.

"Ah. And what is your particular field?"

"Handcrafts. Metalwork. Uh...the ancient type of thing, like that..." He indicated Lella's necklace, and she smiled.

"It is old," she said, and her voice was sweet as the chiming bells. "I would not even guess how old."

"The pierced pattern," Selden said, "is characteristic of the Seventeenth Dynasty of the Khalide Kings of Jekkara, which lasted for approximately two thousand years at the period when Jekkara was declining from her position as a maritime power. The sea was receding significantly then, say between fourteen and sixteen thousand years ago."

"So old?" Lella said, and fingered the necklace wonderingly.

"That depends," said Bentham. "Is it genuine, Lella, or is it a copy?"

Lella dropped to her knees beside Selden. "You will say."

They all waited. Selden began to sweat. He had studied hundreds of necklaces, but never *in situ*. Suddenly he was not sure at all whether the damned thing was genuine, and he was just as suddenly positive that they did know and were needling him. The plaques rose and fell gently to the lift of Lella's breathing. A faint dry spicy fragrance reached his nostrils. He touched the gold, lifted one of the plaques and felt of it, warm from her flesh, and yearned for a nice uncomplicated textbook that had diagrams and illustrations and nothing more to take your mind off your subject. He was tempted to tell them to go to hell. They were just waiting for him to make a mistake. Then he got madder and bolder and he put his whole hand under the collar, lifting it away from her neck and testing the weight of it. It was worn thin and light as tissue paper and the under surface was still pocked by the ancient hammer strokes in the particular fashion of the Khalide artificers.

482

It was a terribly crude test, but his blood was up. He looked into the tilted green eyes and said authoritatively, "It's genuine."

"How wonderful that you know!" She caught his hand between hers and pressed it and laughed aloud with pleasure. "You have studied very long?"

"Very long." He felt good now. He hadn't let them get him down. The hellfire had worked its way up into his head, where it was buzzing gently, and Lella's attention was even more pleasantly intoxicating.

"What will you do now with this knowledge?" she asked.

"Well," he said, "as you know, so many of the ancient skills have been lost, and your people are looking for ways to expand their economy, so the Bureau is hoping to start a program to reeducate metal-workers in places like Jekkara and Valkis…"

Altman said in a remote and very quiet voice, "Oh good God Albloodymighty."

Selden said, "I beg your pardon?"

"Nothing," Altman said. "Nothing."

Bentham turned to Firsa Mak. "By the way, Selden and I had a difference of opinion on the way here. He's probably right, but I said I'd ask you…"

Selden said hastily, "Oh, let's forget it, Bentham." But Bentham was obtuse and insistent.

"The Mad Moon, Firsa Mak. I say Vashna, he says Denderon."

"Denderon, of course," said Firsa Mak, and looked at Selden. "So you know all about that, too."

"Oh," said Selden, embarrassed and annoyed with Bentham for bringing it up, "please, we thoroughly understand that that was all a mistake."

Altman leaned forward. "Mistake?"

"Certainly. The early accounts…" He looked at Firsa Mak and his sister and Lella and they all seemed to be waiting for him to go on, so he did, uncomfortably. "I mean, they resulted from distortions of folklore, misinterpretation of local customs, pure ignorance…in some cases, they were downright lies." He waved his hand deprecatingly. "We don't believe in the Rites of the Purple Priestess and all that nonsense. That is to say, we don't believe they ever *occurred,* really."

He hoped that would close the subject, but Bentham was determined to hang to it. "I've read eye-witness accounts, Selden."

"Fabrications. Traveller's tales. After all, the Earthmen who first came to Mars were strictly the piratical exploiter type and were hardly either qualified or reliable observers…"

"They don't need us any more," said Altman softly, staring at Selden but not seeming to see him. "They don't need us at all." And he muttered something about winged pigs and the gods of the marketplace. Selden had a sudden horrid certainty that Altman was himself one of those early piratical exploiters and that he had irreparably insulted him. And then Firsa Mak said with honest curiosity,

"Why is it that all you young Earthmen are so ready to cry down the things your own people have done?"

Selden felt Altman's eyes upon him, but he was into this now and there was no backing down. He said with quiet dignity, "Because we feel that if our people have made mistakes we should be honest enough to admit them."

"A truly noble attitude," said Firsa Mak. "But about the Purple Priestess…"

"I assure you," said Selden hastily, "that old canard is long forgotten. The men who did the serious research, the anthropologists and sociologists who came after the…uh…the adventurers, were far better qualified to evaluate the data. They completely demolished the idea that the rites involved human sacrifice, and of course the monstrous Dark Lord the priestess was supposed to serve was merely the memory of an extremely ancient earth-god…mars-god, I should say, but you know what I mean, a primitive nature thing, like the sky or the wind."

Firsa Mak said gently, "But there was a rite…"

"Well, yes," said Selden, "undoubtedly. But the experts proved that it was purely vestigial, like…well, like our own children dancing around the Maypole."

"The Low-Canallers," said Altman, "never danced around any

Maypoles." He rose slowly and Selden watched him stretch higher and higher above him. He must have stood a good six inches over six feet, and even from that height his eyes pierced Selden. "How many of your qualified observers went into the hills above Jekkara?"

Selden began to bristle a bit. The feeling that for some reason he was being baited grew stronger. "You must know that until very recently the Low-Canal towns were closed to Earthman..."

"Except for a few adventurers."

"Who left highly dubious memoirs! And even yet you have to have a diplomatic passport involving miles of red tape, and you're allowed very little freedom of movement when you get there. But it *is* a beginning, and we hope, we hope very greatly, that we can persuade the Low-Canallers to accept our friendship and assistance. It's a pity that their own secretiveness fostered such a bad image. For decades the only ideas we had of the Low-Canal towns came from the lurid accounts of the early travellers, and the extremely biased...as we learned later...attitude of the City-States. We used to think of Jekkara and Valkis as, well, perfect sinks of iniquity..."

Altman was smiling at him. "But my dear boy," he said. "They are. They are."

Selden tried to disengage his hand from Lella's. He found that he could not, and it was about then that he began to be just the least little bit frightened.

"I don't understand," he said plaintively. "Did you get me here just to bait me? If you did, I don't think it's very...Bentham?"

Bentham was at the door. The door now seemed to be much farther away than Selden remembered and there was a kind of mist between him and it so that Bentham's figure was indistinct. Nevertheless he saw it raise a hand and heard it say, "Good by." Then it was gone, and Selden, feeling infinitely forlorn, turned to look into Lella's eyes. "I don't understand," he said. "I don't understand." Her eyes were green and enormous and deep without limit. He felt himself topple and fall giddily into the abyss, and then of course it was far too late to be afraid.

Hearing returned to him first, with the steady roar of jets, and then there was the bodily sensation of being borne through air that was shaken occasionally by large turbulences. He opened his eyes, in wild alarm. It was several minutes before he could see anything but a thick fog. The fog cleared gradually and he found himself staring at Lella's gold necklace and remembering with great clarity the information concerning it that he had rattled off so glibly and with such modest pride. A simple and obvious truth came to him.

"You're from Jekkara," he said, and only then did he realize that there was a gag in his mouth. Lella started and looked down at him.

"He's awake."

Firsa Mak rose and bent over Selden, examining the gag and a set of antique manacles that bound his wrists. Again Selden flinched from those fierce and brilliant eyes. Firsa Mak seemed to hesitate, on the verge of removing the gag, and Selden mustered his voice and courage to demand explanations. A buzzer sounded in the cabin, apparently a signal from the pilot, and at the same time the motion of the copter altered. Firsa Mak shook his head.

"Later, Selden. I have to leave you this way because I can't trust you, and all our lives are in danger, not just yours…though yours most of all." He leaned forward. "This is necessary, Selden. Believe me."

"Not necessary," Altman said, appearing stooped under the cabin ceiling. "Vital. You'll understand that, later."

Lella said harshly, "I wonder if he will."

"If he doesn't," Altman said, "God help them all, because no one else can."

Mrs. Altman came with a load of heavy cloaks. They had all changed their clothes since Selden had last seen them, except Lella, who had merely added an upper garment of native wool. Mrs. Altman now wore the Low-Canal garb, and Firsa Mak had a crimson tunic held with a wide belt around his hips. Altman looked somehow incredibly right in the leather of a desert tribesman; he was too tall, Selden guessed, to pass for a Jekkaran. He wore the desert harness easily, as though he had worn it many times. They made Selden stand while they wrapped a cloak around him, and he saw that he had been stripped of his own clothing and dressed in a tunic of ochre-yellow,

486

and where his limbs showed they had been stained dark. Then they strapped him into his seat again and waited while the copter slowed and dropped toward a landing.

Selden sat rigid, numb with fear and shock, going over and over in his mind the steps by which he had come here and trying to make sense out of them. He could not. One thing was certain, Bentham had deliberately led him into a trap. But why? *Why?* Where were they taking him, what did they mean to do with him? He tried to do positive therapy but it was difficult to remember all the wisdom that had sounded so infinitely wise when he had heard it, and his eyes kept straying to the faces of Altman and Firsa Mak.

There was a quality about them both, something strange that he had never seen before. He tried to analyze what it was. Their flesh appeared to be harder and drier and tougher than normal, their muscles more fibrous and prominent, and there was something about the way they used and carried themselves that reminded him of the large carnivores he had seen in the zoo parks. There was, even more striking, an expression about the eyes and mouth, and Selden realized that these were violent men, men who could strike and tear and perhaps even kill. He was afraid of them. And at the same time he felt superior. He at least was above all that.

The sky had paled. Selden could see desert racing past below. They settled onto it with a great spuming of dust and sand. Altman and Firsa Mak between them half carried him out of the copter. Their strength was appalling. They moved away from the copter and the backwash of the rotors beat them as it took off. Selden was stricken by the thin air and bitter cold. His bones felt brittle and his lungs were full of knives. The others did not seem to mind. He pulled his cloak tight around him as well as he could with his bound hands, and felt his teeth chattering into the gag. Abruptly Lella reached out and pulled the hood completely down over his face. It had two eyeholes so that it could be used as a mask during sandstorms, but it stifled him and it smelled strangely. He had never felt so utterly miserable.

Dawn was turning the desert to a rusty red. A chain of time-eaten mountains, barren as the fossil vertebrae of some forgotten monster, curved across the northern horizon. Close at hand was a tumbled mass of rocky outcrops, carved to fantastic shapes by wind and sand. From among these rocks there came a caravan.

Selden heard the bells and the padding of broad splayed hoofs. The beasts were familiar to him from pictures. Seen in their actual scaly reality, moving across the red sand in that wild daybreak with their burdens and their hooded riders, they were apparitions from some older and uglier time. They came close and stopped, hissing and stamping and rolling their cold bright eyes at Selden, not liking the smell of him in spite of the Martian clothing he wore. They did not seem to mind Altman. Perhaps he had lived with the Martians so long that there was no difference now.

Firsa Mak spoke briefly with the leader of the caravan. The meeting had obviously been arranged, for led animals were brought. The women mounted easily. Selden's stomach turned over at the idea of actually riding one of these creatures. Still, at the moment, he was even more afraid of being left behind, so he made no protest when Firsa Mak and Altman heaved him up onto the saddle pad. One of them rode on each side of him, holding a lead rein. The caravan moved on again, northward toward the mountains.

Within an hour Selden was suffering acutely from cold, thirst, and the unaccustomed exercise. By noon, when they halted to rest, he was almost unconscious. Altman and Firsa Mak helped him down and then carried him around into some rocks where they took the gag out and gave him water. The sun was high now, piercing the thin atmosphere like a burning lance. It scalded Selden's cheeks but at least he was warm, or almost warm. He wanted to stay where he was and die. Altman was quite brutal about it.

"You wanted to go to Jekkara," he said. "Well, you're going...just a little bit earlier than you planned, that's all. What the hell, boy, did you think it was all like Kahora?"

And he heaved Selden onto his mount again and they went on.

In midafternoon the wind got up. It never really seemed to stop blowing, but in a tired sort of way, wandering across the sand, picking up a bit of dust and dropping it again, chafing the upthrust rocks a little deeper, stroking the ripple-patterns into a different design. Now it seemed impatient with everything it had done and determined to wipe it out and start fresh. It gathered itself and rushed screaming across the land, and it seemed to Selden that the whole desert took up and went flying in a red and strangling cloud. The sun went out. He lost sight of Altman and Firsa Mak at either end of his reins. He hung in abject terror to his saddle pad, watching for the small segment of rein he could see to go slack, when he would know that he was irretrievably lost. Then as abruptly as it had risen the wind dropped and the sand resumed its quiet, eternal rolling.

A little while after that, in the long red light from the west, they dipped down to a line of dark water strung glittering through the desolation, banded with strips of green along its sides. There was a smell of wetness and growing things, and an ancient bridge, and beyond the canal was a city, with the barren hills behind it.

Selden knew that he was looking at Jekkara. And he was struck with awe. Even at this late day few Earthmen had seen it. He stared through the eyeholes of his hood, seeing at first only the larger masses of rose-red rock, and then as the sun sank lower and the shadows shifted, making out the individual shapes of buildings that melted more and more gently into the parent rock the higher they were on the sloping cliffs. At one place he saw the ruins of a great walled castle that he knew had once housed those self-same Khalide Kings and lord knew how many dynasties before them in the days when this desert was the bottom of a blue sea, and there was a lighthouse still standing above the basin of a dry harbor half way up the cliffs. He shivered, feeling the enormous weight of a history in which he and his had had no part whatever, and it came to him that he had perhaps been just the tiniest bit presumptuous in his desire to teach these people.

That feeling lasted him half way across the bridge. By that time the western light had gone and the torches were flaring in the streets of Jekkara, shaken by the dry wind from the desert. His focus of interest shifted from the then to the now, and once more he shivered, but for a different reason. The upper town was dead. The lower town was not, and there was a quality to the sight and sound and smell of it that petrified him. Because it was exactly as the early adventurers in their dubious memoirs had described it.

The caravan reached the broad square that fronted the canal, the beasts picking their way protestingly over the sunken, tilted paving stones. People came to meet them. Without his noticing it, Altman and Firsa Mak had maneuvered Selden to the end of the line, and now he found himself being detached and quietly led away up a narrow street between low stone buildings with deep doorways and small window-places, all their corners worn round and smooth as stream-bed rocks by time and the rubbing of countless hands and shoulders. There was something going on in the town, he thought, because he could hear the voices of many people from somewhere beyond, as though they were gathering in a central place. The air smelled of cold and dust, and unfamiliar spices, and less identifiable things.

Altman and Firsa Mak lifted Selden down and held him until his legs regained some feeling. Firsa Mak kept glancing at the sky. Altman leaned close to Selden and whispered, "Do exactly as we tell you, or you won't last the night."

"Nor will we," muttered Firsa Mak, and he tested Selden's gag and made sure his cowl was pulled down to hide his face. "It's almost time."

They led Selden quickly along another winding street. This one was busy and populous. There were sounds and sweet pungent odors and strange-colored lights, and there were glimpses into wickednesses of such fantastic array and imaginative genius that Selden's eyes bulged behind his cowl and he remembered his Seminars in Martian Culture with a species of hysteria. Then they came out into a broad square.

It was full of people, cloaked against the night wind and standing quietly, their dark faces still in the shaking light of the torches. They seemed to be watching the sky. Altman and Firsa Mak, with Selden held firmly between them, melted into the edges of the crowd. They waited. From time to time more people came from the surrounding streets, making no sound except for the soft slurring of sandalled feet and the faint elfin chiming of tiny bells beneath the cloaks of the women. Selden found himself watching the sky, though he did not understand why. The crowd seemed to grow more silent, to hold all breath and stirring, and then suddenly over the eastern roofs came the swift moon Denderon, low and red.

The crowd said, "Ah-h-h!", a long musical cry of pure despair that shook Selden's heart, and in the same moment harpers who had been concealed in the shadow of a time-worn portico struck their double-banked harps and the cry became a chant, half a lament and half a proud statement of undying hate. The crowd began to move, with the harpers leading and other men carrying torches to light the way. And Selden went with them, up into the hills behind Jekkara.

It was a long cold way under the fleeting light of Denderon. Selden felt the dust of millennia grate and crunch beneath his sandals and the ghosts of cities passed him to the right and left, ruined walls and empty marketplaces and the broken quays where the ships of the Sea-Kings docked. The wild fierce music of the harps sustained and finally dazed him. The long chanting line of people strung out, moving steadily, and there was something odd about the measured rhythm of their pace. It was like a march to the gallows.

The remnants of the works of man were left behind. The barren hills bulked against the stars, splashed with the feeble moonlight that now seemed to Selden to be inexpressibly evil. He wondered why he was no longer frightened. He thought perhaps he had reached the point of complete emotional exhaustion. At any rate he saw things clearly but with no personal involvement.

Even when he saw that the harpers and the torch-bearers were passing into the mouth of a cavern he was not afraid.

The cavern was broad enough for the people to continue marching ten abreast. The harps were muffled now and the chanting took on a deep and hollow tone. Selden felt that he was going downward. A strange and rather terrible eagerness began to stir in him, and this he could not explain at all. The marchers seemed to feel it too, for the pace quickened just a little to the underlying of the harpstrings. And suddenly the rock walls vanished out of sight and they were in a vast cold space that was completely black beyond the pinprick glaring of the torches.

The chanting ceased. The people filed on both sides into a semicircle and stood still, with the harpers at the center and a little group of people in front of them, somehow alone and separate.

One of these people took off the concealing cloak and Selden saw that it was a woman dressed all in purple. For some obscure reason he was sure it was Lella, though the woman's face in the torchlight showed only the smooth gleaming of a silver mask, a very ancient thing with a subtle look of cruel compassion. She took in her hands a pale globed lamp and raised it, and the harpers struck their strings once. The other persons, six in number, laid aside their cloaks. They were three men and three women, all naked and smiling, and now the harps began a tune that was almost merry and the woman in purple swayed her body in time to it. The naked people began to dance, their eyes blank and joyous with some powerful drug, and she led them dancing into the darkness, and as she led them she sang, a long sweet fluting call.

The harps fell silent. Only the woman's voice sounded, and her lamp shone like a dim star, far away.

Beyond the lamp, an eye opened and looked and was aware.

Selden saw the people, the priestess and the six dancing ones, limned momentarily against that orb as seven people might be limned against a risen moon. Then something in him gave way and he fell, clutching oblivion to him like a saving armor.

They spent the remainder of that night and the following day in Firsa Mak's house by the dark canal, and there were sounds of terrible revelry in the streets. Selden sat staring straight ahead, his body shaken by small periodic tremors.

"It isn't true," he said, again and again. "It isn't true."

"It may not be true," Altman said, "but it's a fact. And it's the facts that kill you. Do you understand now why we brought you?"

"You want me to tell the Bureau about...about *that*."

"The Bureau and anyone that will listen."

"But why me? Why not somebody really important, like one of the diplomats?"

"We tried that. Remember Loughlin Herbert?"

"But he died of a heart... Oh."

"When Bentham told us about you," Firsa Mak said, "you seemed young and strong enough to stand the shock. We've done all we can now, Selden. For years Altman and I have been trying…"

"They won't listen to us," Altman said. "They will not listen. And if they keep sending people in, nice well-meaning children and their meddling nannies, not knowing… I simply will not be responsible for the consequences." He looked down at Selden from his gaunt and weathered height.

Firsa Mak said softly, "This is a burden. We have borne it, Selden. We even take pride in bearing it." He nodded toward the unseen hills. *"That* has the power of destruction. Jekkara certainly, and Valkis probably, and Barrakesh, and all the people who depend on this canal for their existence. It can destroy. We know. This is a Martian affair and most of us do not wish to have outsiders brought into it. But Altman is my brother and I must have some care for his people, and I tell you that the Priestess prefers to choose her offerings from among strangers…"

Selden whispered, "How often?"

"Twice a year, when the Mad Moon rises. In between, it sleeps."

"It sleeps," said Altman. "But if it should be roused, and frightened, or made angry… For God's sake, Selden, tell them, so that at least they'll *know* what they're getting into."

Selden said wildly, "How can you live here, with that…"

Firsa Mak looked at him, surprised that he should ask. "Why," he said, "because we always have."

Selden stared, and thought, and did not sleep, and once he screamed when Lella came softly into the room.

On the second night they slipped out of Jekkara and went back across the desert to the place of rocks, where the copter was waiting. Only Altman returned with Selden. They sat silently in the cabin, and Selden thought, and from time to time he saw Altman watching him, and already in his eyes there was the understanding of defeat.

The glowing domes of Kahora swam out of the dusk, and Denderon was in the sky.

"You're not going to tell them," Altman said.

"I don't know," whispered Selden. "I don't know."

Altman left him at the landing stage. Selden did not see him again. He took a cab to his hotel and went directly to his room and locked himself in.

The familiar, normal surroundings aided a return to sanity. He was able to marshall his thoughts more calmly.

If he believed that what he had seen was real, he would have to tell about it, even if no one would listen to him. Even if his superiors, his teachers, his sponsors, the men he venerated and whose approval he yearned for, should be shocked, and look at him with scorn, and shake their heads, and forever close their doors to him. Even if he should be condemned to the outer darkness inhabited by people like Altman and Firsa Mak. Even if.

But if he did not believe that it was real, if he believed instead that it was illusion, hallucination induced by drugs and heaven knew what antique Martian chicanery... He had been drugged, that was certain. And Lella *had* practised some sort of hypnotic technique upon him...

If he did *not* believe...

Oh God, how wonderful not to believe, to be free again, to be secure in the body of truth!

He thought, in the quiet and comforting confines of his room, and the longer he thought the more positive his thinking became, the more free of subjectivity, the deeper and calmer in understanding. By the morning he was wan and haggard but healed.

He went to the Bureau and told them that he had been taken ill immediately upon landing, which was why he had not reported. He also told them that he had had urgent word from home and would have to return there at once. They were very sorry to lose him, but most sympathetic, and they booked him onto the first available flight.

A few scars remained on Selden's psyche. He could not bear the sound of a harp nor the sight of a woman wearing purple. These phobias he could have put up with, but the nightmares were just too much. Back on Earth, he went at once to his analyst. He was quite honest with him, and the analyst was able to show him exactly what had happened. The whole affair had been a sex fantasy induced by drugs, with the Priestess a mother-image. The Eye which had looked at him then and which still peered unwinking out of his recurring dreams was symbolic of the female generative principle, and the feeling of horror it aroused in him was due to the guilt-complex he had because he was a latent homosexual. Selden was enormously comforted.

The analyst assured him that now that things were healthily out in the open, the secondary effects would fade away. And they might have done so except for the letter.

It arrived just six Martian months after his unfortunate dinner date with Bentham. It was not signed. It said, *"Lella waits for you at moonrise."* And it bore the sketch, very accurately and quite unmistakably done, of a single monstrous eye.

COME SING THE
MOONS OF MORAVENN

The Other Side of Tomorrow, 1973

THE VANGUARD FOUNDATION people told us that Moravenn was a young person's world, and they were right.

I'm eighteen. My name is Art Farrell.

I was seventeen when we landed. *Vanguard Beautiful* stood off-planet in a stationary orbit while the shuttles brought us down – two hundred of us, with an age limit of twenty-two, sponsored by the Foundation. And we stood looking at this world where we hoped to spend the rest of our lives building a new civilization, fresh and clean and untainted by the sins of our fathers on Earth. We would start anew, with respect for each other and the land.

Moravenn's primary is a topaz-colored star way out in the Vela Spur. There are four other planets, either too close to the sun or not close enough to be habitable. Nature is very wasteful. The site chosen by the Vanguard survey for the colony was a wide alluvial plain between two rocky mountain ranges. The soil was rich, the climate dry and healthful, with enough seasonal change to keep us alert. The water in the small river ran clear as glass, humming over glistening stones, the day we landed.

Marta took my hand and we stood close together, breathing in the alien air, feeling the alien ground beneath our feet. Our hearts were pounding, and I could see the tears of joy and excitement in her eyes.

"It's wonderful," she whispered. "So empty, so… innocent."

That night, rolled in our sleeping bags on the sweet-smelling turf, we saw for the first time the moons of Moravenn.

There are three of them. One is almost as large as our own Luna.

The other two are smaller and closer to the planet. They rose one after the other and spanned the sky like three great dusky pearls, drowning the starshine. I think we were all awed by the beauty of them, because out of the two hundred voices raised, none was much more than a whisper.

Then I heard someone say that we ought to name the moons, and Jamie Hunter said, "They may already have names, you know. The survey party said there might be people here. Of some sort."

We looked at the mountains, eerie and still in the moonlight, and listened to the silence, and wondered whether there was somebody out there and how it would be if we met. We were not frightened, only curious. We had no prejudices and no warlike impulses, and we were certain that we could get along with anybody. But we were all Earth children and we had never met any extraterrestrials, though we had seen plenty of them on the Tri-D.

Marta reached over and took my hand again, comfort for both of us against the strangeness. I know it was very late before I fell asleep.

The shuttles brought down our tools and supplies: the field hospital, the microlibrary, the seeds that would be our crops, the animals that would be our companions, enough food to keep us until harvest time. There were no weapons, and no power sources to pour out their poisons into the air. We would use animals and our own unpolluting muscles. *Vanguard Beautiful* went away with six hundred more colonists to plant among the star-worlds. For the next two years we would be on our own.

We set up camp on higher ground midway between the east bank of the river and the abrupt red-gold scarp of the mountains. We would live in pre-cut shelters provided for us until we could build permanent houses. With all hands working, it didn't take long to survey the campsite, lay out the streets—which followed the contours of the land so as to be pleasing to the eye as well as functional—and set up the metal frames of the shelters. The plastic panels slipped easily into place, and we had our first town, all our own. There was no single shelter large enough to hold all of us, so our community meetings were in the open. I can still remember the first one, the immense feeling of strength and pride and dedication we had.

We were all specialists, of course, trained by the Foundation. My own field is agriculture, and so I was glad when the next phase of our settlement began, the laying out of the fields. Then it was my turn, to test the soil and say which areas were best for root crops, legumes, leaf crops, and the all-important grains. A large area had been set aside for grazing, and our animals seemed to be thriving.

Those were hard days. This alien spring was already well along and it was important to get the crops in the ground as rapidly as possible. Everybody worked. Those who were trained in irrigation methods showed us how to prepare the fields, and then they went up into the mountains with the carpenters, to cut timber for well sweeps and water wheels.

We broke the sod, and we broke our backs. We were city-bred, and found that our gymnasium courses hadn't fitted us for plain, hard manual labor. By the end of the day we were too tired for meetings or cultural events. We ate our rations, fell into our cots, and slept.

I had a lot of responsibility here. Jamie Hunter was agricultural coordinator and I consulted with him, but the decisions were mine.

We got the planting done, then rested our aching muscles. Every day I walked among the fields, searching impatiently for the first signs of green. I had never grown anything before except in the Foundation's training plots, and the sheer size and importance of this operation scared me.

We got two good rains. That and the warm sun brought everything leaping up. We watched our growing crops and loved them, and reckoned we could start thinking about building our houses. We had a big meeting on that, to decide whether to bring down timber from the mountains or to make bricks. We decided against the timber because we would have had to cut too many trees, and that was against our beliefs. We hunted around for a good deposit of clay instead.

We found one, and the construction experts got busy. The weather turned hot, which was good for drying the adobe bricks, but the river began to shrink and I had to call for extra help to keep water coming into the irrigation ditches.

One afternoon, looking northward where the lines of the mountain ranges converged, we saw enormous clouds pile up. They were purple-black and we could see the distant flicker of lightning. The thunder came muffled, like a distant growl, rumbling on the threshold of hearing. Jamie Hunter looked at the beasts walking their patient circles around the creaking water wheels, and at the people working the well sweeps.

"It's got to be raining up there," Jamie said. "Maybe that'll help us."

We went to bed hoping that the river would rise.

In the middle of the night all two hundred of us tumbled out. By the glorious moonlight of Moravenn we watched a foaming wall of water come down our valley, carrying uprooted trees and great booming boulders. The river had risen, all right. We ran from it, and in the morning we saw that half of our fields had been torn away and half of what was left was flooded, and one shelter house was gone.

Marta cried, and she wasn't the only one.

All that work!

All that time and loving care.

All that irreplaceable food. Our supplies wouldn't last us to another harvest.

This wasn't fair. We felt betrayed. Outraged. And frightened.

"It's your fault!" somebody screamed. "You, Jamie Hunter! And you, Art Farrell!"

Jamie bristled. "What do you mean, it's our fault? Our job was to get the crops in and growing. We did it. Who can help a flood?"

"You ought to have done your planting somewhere else," shouted another voice, and a lot more chimed in. I looked at all those faces, black, white, brown, yellow, Indian bronze, every one hostile and accusing, glaring at Jamie and me. And we were all brothers and sisters! I took a step forward, my fists doubled. I felt hot all over.

"We had to have water, didn't we?" I yelled. "Where the hell else could we have done our planting?"

"Hold it, hold it," said Tom Chen. He was the elected president of our Council, twenty-one years old. He climbed up on a rock. "Listen, all of you! We've taken a hard blow, we're in trouble, and it isn't going to do any good to start fighting among ourselves." He turned to Jamie and me. "We must salvage as much as we can. Get to it. The rest of you, start cleaning up the camp."

One truculent girl cried out, "Are you giving us orders, Tom Chen?" But somebody silenced her and we all went grumbling off to see what had to be done and where to start it.

Marta spoke to me, worried. "You were ready to hit somebody, Art."

"Yes, I was," I said, ashamed. "But they made me angry, blaming Jamie and me. They ought to blame the river."

"It's only a river," Marta said. "It doesn't know what it's doing."

I couldn't find much charity in my heart for the great slop of muddy water that was drowning my young crops.

"Rivers," I said, "can be tamed."

The water went down, leaving big raw gouges and piles of debris behind. For days we worked in the mud, digging and hoeing, desperate to save what we could. But when, in our first full meeting after the flood, Tom Chen asked me how much we had saved, I had to admit I didn't know. "I've done everything I could think of, but this is all new to me. We'll have to wait and see."

"A great ag expert you are!" somebody said.

"Let it be," said Tom Chen wearily. "None of us has any real experience. We've read the books, and that's it, and there aren't any books for Moravenn. We'll have to write those ourselves." He was beginning to get lines and shadows in his face that had not been there before. "Anyway, what are you crying about? They told us at the Foundation that this would be hard."

Sure, they did. But how could we have imagined an existence bordering on nightmare?

Tom Chen went on. "We've inventoried the food stocks. It must be obvious to all of you that we'll have to go on reduced rations in order to stretch our supply as far as we can. And I warn you right now, we may have to start killing things."

"You mean, eat meat?" a horrified voice said.

"Start getting used to the idea."

The animal husbandry team jumped up and began making a lot of noise.

"Of course not your animals!" said Tom Chen. "We need them for other things. I'm suggesting hunters and wild game." We had seen animals from time to time, but they were shy and stayed away from us. Perhaps they didn't like our alien smell. "I won't put it to the vote now. But consider it."

"That's silly," Marta said. "We couldn't kill game if we wanted to. We haven't got any weapons."

"We can learn to make some. Art Farrell?"

I was standing up, asking for the floor. I said, "We've got to dam that river. Control it. Otherwise, every dry season we'll hurt for water, and every time there's a storm in the mountains we'll get washed away."

"That's interfering with the environment," said Antelope Woman, the head of our ecology team.

"We've already interfered with it, haven't we? We ploughed up the land. We planted seeds, we introduced animals that don't belong here, including ourselves. Where do we stop? And there are the fall crops to think about."

Everybody started talking at once. Finally, when he could make himself heard, Tom Chen said he wouldn't put that to a vote either, but he would appoint a committee of engineers to make a feasibility study.

Some more of the young wheat yellowed and died. Then we had another flood. It wasn't as big as the first one, but it got people thinking. At the next meeting the engineers said they could build a dam, and when it came to a vote the ayes had it.

There was a place where the river came through a canyon. The canyon narrowed at one point, and there was a natural basin there to form a big reservoir. The engineers, with all the labor that could be spared from other duties, started work on the dam.

In all this time we had never seen any native humans, or humanoids.

Now, suddenly, they came.

I don't know who saw them first. I was carrying a basketful of stones, coolie-fashion, and I heard the silence kind of close in around me. People were stopping whatever they were doing, putting down their loads and just standing there. I stopped, too, and set my basket on the ground.

And I was scared. Gut-scared. These were *aliens*.

They weren't doing anything frightening. They were just watching us. They were stockily built and very agile, about the same size as ourselves, taking a median height. They were naked except for a few strings at the neck and waist for carrying necessities, so we could see that they were all males. Their skin was a ruddy bronze-pink. They had arms and legs, feet and hands—the hands held weapons—and heads.

The heads were what curdled me. They were perfectly human—two eyes set frontward, a small nose, a largish mouth—but the bone structure was so oblong and blocky, the jaw so enormously squared and elongated, that they looked like horses' heads. The resemblance was carried even further, in spite of little close-set ears, by the tight white curls that grew on the tops of their heads and continued on down the back of the neck to the shoulders.

About thirty of them, looking like so many ponies with their hides off.

Tom Chen, who had been toting stones with the rest of us, said, "Everybody stand easy." He beckoned to the two other council members who were there. The three of them joined up and stepped forward, their right hands raised in the universal gesture of peace.

Universal?

We hoped so.

One of the aliens courteously laid his weapons aside and came to meet them. I judged he was an old man. He was weathered and wrinkled, and his eyes had an expression of patient wisdom. In spite of their nakedness, these people did not strike me as being savages.

Our spokesman and theirs stood face to face, gabbling and making gestures. The gabble was useless so they dropped that. The old man did a series of things with his hands, pointing to the river and then to the dam, and then making a motion of *going*. He repeated this several times, and finally Tom Chen said, "I think he's telling us that water must be free to run."

He imitated the old man. The old man's face brightened and he wagged his huge chin. I noticed they seemed to talk a lot with their chins. The ones in the background were having a busy discussion about us.

The old man trotted over to our embryonic dam. He picked up a stone and threw it away. He looked at Tom Chen to see if he understood.

He did. "He wants us to tear it down," Tom said, and stared at the old man in baffled annoyance. "How do you explain to him?"

"Why not invite them to our camp?" I said. "Let them see why we want to dam the river. Let Sammy have a crack at them." That was Sam Agatelli, our extraterrestrial anthropologist. "Maybe he can communicate with them." Sammy had been filling in on everybody else's work; it was time he had his chance to show off.

And for all our sakes, we hoped he knew his business.

It was no struggle to get them to come with us. They were curious, and I guess they felt strong enough to take us on, if it should come to that. We all marched back to the camp together.

On the way, I found myself walking next to a young native about my own age, as near as I could guess. His skin was still fresh and glossy, and his blue eyes had a bright sparkle to them. He seemed to want to strike up an acquaintance, so I smiled and said my name, pointing to myself. He bared a set of big white teeth in his equine face and made a noise that sounded like *Hrrng*.

"Hrung?" I said, pointing to him.

He wagged his chin and laughed. He shifted spear and throwing stick to his left hand, reached out his right hand, and touched me three times on the chest, over the heart. I couldn't help flinching a bit, but I guessed it was a ritual gesture indicating friendship so I reached out and touched him the same way. This time we both laughed, and some of the feeling of strangeness began to ebb.

There was big excitement in the camp when we showed up. Tom Chen had sent a runner ahead to warn them. Sam Agatelli was out to meet us, quivering like a puppy. People were setting out food at the meeting ground. They were falling over themselves to make our guests feel welcome, and at the same time trying to hide their own nervousness.

Come Sing the Moons of Moravenn

We did the hospitality bit. The natives—they called themselves the R'Lann, as nearly as Sammy could make it out—were grave and courteous. They examined all our off-planet things with less amazement than we expected. Then we took them down to the fields and showed them what the river had done.

Very carefully, Sammy drew pictographs in the dust. He drew the immature crop, then the mature grain, then a picture of a man eating it. The old man rubbed them out impatiently with his foot.

"I guess they know about agriculture," Sammy said, and drew a picture of the river. He set two stones to be the cliffs and he built a little earthen dam between them. He drew a lake behind the dam. He indicated how the water would flow through a floodgate, nice and tame and well-behaved. He indicated the fields. He smiled and made gestures meaning "good."

The old man shook his head. He took Sammy's stick and began to draw pictures of his own. First he drew a big circle, and stamped on the ground; the circle was Moravenn. Our name, not his. Then he drew a moon. He drew two more moons, in the positions where we now saw them. He erased the two smaller moons and redrew them, in different positions. He did this rapidly three or four times, until the smaller moons were superimposed on the big one. He said something sonorous and very emphatic, and kicked over Sammy's little dam. He threw the stick down and called his people together and they marched away. Hrung looked back and wagged his jaw at me, and I waved.

Then we stared at the old man's drawing.

"What's it mean?" asked Tom Chen.

Sammy shook his head. "When the three moons are in line, the dam goes out? I don't know. Maybe. Or maybe it's a symbol of some kind, something to do with their worship. Everybody's got moon myths."

"When the three moons are in line," said Tom Chen, frowning. "Gravitational pull? If it's strong enough, it could make trouble. But how often does that happen—if ever?"

Nobody could answer that. And we had no computer to do the enormously complicated math that might have told us.

Thoughtfully, Tom Chen erased the old man's picture. "We'll build the dam anyway."

"Maybe we ought to think about that, Tom," said Sammy. "This is their world. They might know something we don't."

"Bunch of bare-backed savages," somebody said. "What would they know?"

"Besides," said Antelope Woman, "if it is something to do with their worship, and we break a taboo, they might get angry enough to attack us, and they're armed. We're not."

"And we don't know how many more of them there may be," somebody said. "We ought to do something—"

"Make some clubs!"

"Pile up stones!"

"Build a wall around the camp!"

In a minute everybody was quarreling about what we ought to do. Tom Chen waved his arms and shouted.

"You want to eat, don't you? Then we've got to build that dam!"

Through the clamor of voices I said to Tom, "Looks to me as though there's only one way to find out for sure what they mean. I'll go and stay with them for a while, learn the language."

"Do you think they'll let you?"

"I can try."

Tom nodded and turned again to the crowd. I said good-by to Marta. She wasn't at all happy. Neither was Sammy, but he didn't make any offers to go himself. I picked up my bedroll and hurried after the R'Lann.

I had a time catching up with them. They really traveled. But I finally did. They stopped when they saw me. I didn't know what they might do, but I held up my hands and smiled, and prayed. Hrung said something to the old man. The old man nodded, and Hrung came, wagging his chin and grinning, and led me into the group.

We all went on at a loping trot, up over some cliffs and along a ridge, with the sun hot on my back and my legs aching, and then down some more cliffs into a red rock valley with its own stream and its patches of green and gold where things were growing. The patches were irregular and looked natural, and there were no houses.

That was why the survey people had not been sure, on their flyover, whether anybody actually did live here.

I learned later that the different bands of the R'Lann—this was only one of them—moved from place to place according to the seasons, and they were somewhere else when the survey crew had a look at their valley. Otherwise they might have seen the women and children tending the garden patches or dressing game.

The R'Lann live in caves, neat rooms cut into the soft rock and walled up in front with stones. I found out that a cave is pretty nice—cool in summer, warm in winter, and if you want to heat it a tiny little blaze will do, hardly more than a lamp flame. If you keep the front wall in repair, a cave is impervious to weather. There's no better place to be at night when a thunderstorm is trying to pound the world apart. The R'Lann decorate their dwellings with carvings outside and bright wall paintings in the rooms.

It was a strange new life I settled into. Hrung seemed to have adopted me as his special property. He spent hours teaching me the language, and I felt the old man was anxious to have him do this as quickly as possible.

So the dry hot days were spent in learning, and at night we watched the moons.

I mean, *watched*. There was a special place high on the cliff, where a very elaborate diagram was incised into the rock. There were three stone counters on the diagram, and someone had to sit up there all night long moving the counters as the moons moved. Normally, Hrung told me, this was done only once a month. But now something was about to happen. I could feel the undercurrent of excitement, and the fear. You could smell the fear in the air of the valley. Something was coming.

When it was Hrung's turn to watch, he let me sit up with him. The floor of the watching place was worn smooth and hollow, and it was strange to touch it. It was as though I touched time.

The moons seemed to be lower and brighter and more beautiful than ever. But as they drew closer together in their orbits, the cool moonfire seemed to change and grow baleful. The valley was unreal in that wicked light, the cliffs flaring with queer shifting colors. A wind rose and ruffled my hair, and my back went cold. I wanted to crouch and howl like a dog.

"They will build the Ladder of Souls," Hrung said, "so the spirits of our dead may climb to the holy sky. It is a time of judgment." His voice was very quiet, as if he feared the moons might hear him. He didn't look real, either, sitting like a statue with his massive head bent forward and the shadows on his long face. "I am unlucky."

"Why is that?"

"Unless I die very soon, which I don't want to do, my soul will have to wait many years for its turn at the Ladder. My father has not seen it before. The oldest of the old men has not seen it."

"How long is it between these—these happenings?"

Hrung shrugged. "The old men say words, but I don't know what they mean. A long time." He swung his head around and the moonlight burned on his white curls. "There are no old men in your band."

"No."

"But the old men keep wisdom alive."

"Old men keep war alive, and lies, and greed," I said. "We do not trust old men."

"Well," said Hrung, "perhaps it is so on your world."

The moonfire died in the west. The old R'Lann—his name was Kladth and he was chief of the band—came and looked at the markers. Then he motioned with his chin, and we followed him down to the floor of the valley and far along to a desolate and lonely place I hadn't seen before. There was a cave opening and we went to it. The path was worn hollow like the watching place.

It was a natural cave. The walls had been smoothed for the paintings that covered them. Thin strips of limber bone were set into cracks in the floor. They stood up like white wands. Kladth led me around to study the paintings. Hrung stayed by the opening. I think he didn't like this place. There was a coldness in it.

I couldn't believe what I saw there. I wasn't even certain that I understood. R'Lann art is very stylized and full of symbols.

Kladth pointed to the floor. "Down," he said. "Look. Feel."

He made me lie down on the rock with my nose almost touching one of the bone wands. I wondered what I was supposed to feel.

Deep down beneath me there came a groaning and stirring, as though Moravenn moved in her sleep. The bone wand bent from side to side.

"It begins," Kladth said.

We left the cave, with all those white wands quivering.

"Your band is still building," Kladth said to me.

"The dam?"

"And houses. This world does not consent to buildings. Go and tell them. Tell them to stop or they will die."

Hrung led me back over the ridges to where my people still sweated on the dam. It was higher than I had thought possible. Water had already backed up behind it, a blue lake shimmering in the sun.

Hrung said, "I will stop here." I went on alone.

Tom Chen and some others met me. The others went on working. They looked thin and sullen; the short rations were telling on them.

"You look fat enough," said Sam Agatelli.

"I've been eating meat," I said. "It was that or starve."

"Savage," somebody said, and spat.

Tom Chen told her to shut up. "What did you find out, Art?"

"They say you must stop building or die."

"Tear down the dam?"

"And the houses."

"Or they'll kill us, is that it?"

"Kladth said, 'This world does not consent to buildings.' I think he meant the planet will kill you. Tom, they have a cave, with strips of bone set in the floor. Sort of primitive seismographs. Something is happening, deep down in the rock. I felt it. And there are paintings. Pictures of cities, and how they were destroyed. Quakes and tidal waves. It's the moons, I think. They watch. They have a diagram—"

"How can you be sure of all this?" asked Sammy. "You're not a trained anthropologist." He was sulky because he knew he ought to have gone instead of me.

"According to anthropologists," I said, "their name ought to mean

something like The People, or The Real Men. Right?" Sammy nodded. "Well, R'Lann means The Survivors. They believe they were
colonists themselves, long ago. Their legends say they came from the
stars, and there was a picture of a great ship in the cave. At least—"

"At least what?" asked Tom Chen.

"That's what Kladth said it was."

Word had spread now that I wanted them to pull down the dam.
More people came. Some carried stones, or clubs.

"We've worked too hard on this to destroy it because of a legend,"
Tom said, and the crowd growled. "Our winter crops depend on it,
our lives depend on it. Have you any better evidence?"

"The moons," I said. "When the three moons are in line, that's
when everything breaks loose. It doesn't happen very often. There's
time enough between for men to forget, and build again. That's why
they have the paintings, and the diagram at the watching place."

"Is that all they told you?"

I thought I had to be honest and tell them everything. Maybe if I
hadn't.... But I told them what Hrung had said about the Ladder of
Souls.

"Moon myth," said Sammy contemptuously. "Just myth."

"And I can tell you this," somebody shouted. "If your hammer-
headed friends come here looking for trouble, they'll get it. We
haven't sweated our hearts out for nothing."

Hands waved sticks and stones. Tom Chen sighed and sent them
back to work. "We have to go on what we know and believe," he
said. "Don't hold it against them, Art. We're tired and hungry. What's
worse, we found that somebody's been stealing from the food supplies. I've had to post guards." He shook his head. "Where did it go,
Art? Everything we started with—love, brotherhood, faith…"

"I guess," I said, "things just aren't as simple as we thought."

"Simple!" Tom said bitterly. "No. Art, will you go back to the
R'Lann and find out for certain about the moons? They make me
uneasy, too."

I went back to the red valley with Hrung. And that night the
Singing began.

In every cave the sacred bundles were taken from the niches and opened, and the sacred garments taken out. Only the stars know how old they were. They were woven of a silvery thread that looked like finely drawn metal, and they weighed a lot. I don't know what the cloth had been used for originally. Shelter tents, perhaps, for the colony. I knew now that that legend was true. The R'Lann reverently clothed their nakedness and marched in solemn procession up the cliff path, past the watching place, to the highest point, where there was an altar cut from the living rock.

Those of us who had no garments came behind, and sat down modestly at the back of the space below the altar. The robed men gathered around it. Kladth mounted the low step and laid a wrapped object on the altar. He undid the wrappings, and I saw without too much surprise that the object was a small telescope. The robed men chanted. Kladth stepped down. The chant continued, with halts for our responses.

I whispered to Hrung, "What are we doing?"

"Singing the moons," he said. "Telling them how to make the Ladder of Souls, reminding them to spare the living who obey their laws. The Singing is very important. You see, in so much time, the moons may have forgotten."

So we sang. Night after night we sang, and the moons came closer together, and the trouble of the world increased. The small river in the valley began to behave strangely. It rose and fell, overflowing its banks and washing back again. The women and children hurried to harvest the last of the crops, and there was no joy about it, only a furtive haste. People hardly spoke during those days. The oppression of fear and holiness was stifling. I wanted to leave it, but Tom Chen had told me to find out for certain.

Then came a night when the innermost moon took a large bite out of her middle sister, who was almost touching the outermost moon. I looked down from our rocky platform and saw the river stand straight up out of its bed, shining in the wild light, and I knew for certain. I touched Hrung and said good-by, very softly so as not to disturb the Singing. I went down the path with the mountain shaking under me, and the standing river fell suddenly apart in lashing coils of water. Some of it wetted me, and I was cold enough already.

I knew the way back now, and the beautiful, gliding, deadly moons gave me light enough. The sound of the Singing followed me for a long while. When it faded I could listen to the stones knocking together whenever the world shook.

I found Tom Chen sitting above the dam, watching the lake. I sat down beside him. The water had a life of its own. We could hear it moving, talking to itself, searching for a way to freedom. The moons were calling it, and it wanted to go.

"How long do we have?" asked Tom Chen.

"I don't know," I said, and told him about the standing-up river.

"Not long, then," he said, and rose. "We'll do what we can."

Day was breaking as we came into the town. I don't think anybody had slept much, tired as they were. People who had moved into permanent houses were out looking at them to see what damage the night's quakes had done. Tom called them all to the meeting place.

Marta came to me, but she treated me like a stranger. Her face was hollow and her hands were scarred with work.

Tom Chen spoke. "I think now the R'Lann were right. I think we made a mistake. The pull of the moons has been getting stronger and stronger—you can feel that. When they come into line, everything on this side of the planet that isn't nailed down will be obeying that pull. That includes our lake. And I think we had better get the hell out."

"Just leave all this? Everything we've worked for?" The pinched, tired faces squinted at him in the morning light.

"You're only guessing," said Antelope Woman. "You don't *know.*"

"Of course I don't know," said Tom irritably. "We have no past on this world. But the R'Lann—"

"You've been listening to Art Farrell," said Sammy. "He's been swallowing everything those people fed him. Legend, superstition..."

"The quakes aren't superstition," I said. "The river came up out of its bed. I saw that. The lake will do the same thing."

"Let the water out!" somebody shouted.

Gust Clausen, our chief engineer, said, "We can't. The floodgate's not finished. All we could do is blow the dam, and the whole lake would come down on us anyway. We weren't counting on anything like this."

The voices rose, blaming Tom, me, the engineers, the Foundation, and the survey for getting them into this mess. Tom finally quieted them.

"Those of you who want to gamble that things won't really get that bad are free to stay, though I don't advise it. Those of you who want to come with me, get busy. Take the animals up into the hills, except for the draught teams. Food, supplies, tools, hospital, library, anything we have time to move, we'll move." Somebody protested, and Tom snarled, "If nothing happens, we can bring them all down again, can't we?"

So we took refuge, such as it was, among the hills. Eighteen people elected to stay behind.

On the night of the Ladder of Souls, when the two inner moons eclipsed the outer one and the sky turned dark and coppery, and the stars blazed bright, we lay hugging the ground that rumbled and shook and sent the loose rock crashing down. And we saw a great pillar of water rise up above the dam and then slowly, slowly lean over, with tatters of itself shredding away around it. It fell into the valley with a roar like the end of the world, and when the night cleared we couldn't see anything at all below but a glistening wetness.

So here we are, one hundred and eighty-two of us. The R'Lann have been good friends. They helped to feed us until we learned how to make spears and hunt, and they're helping us cut caves in the cliffs. They helped us to bury our dead, the eleven we could find, and I'm listening to Kladth about agricultural methods. We'll make it.

But it's strange. Nothing worked out the way we expected, not even ourselves. Tom Chen and I haven't got many friends now. People seem to blame Tom for bad leadership, even though we all voted on everything. And the dam was my idea. I *thought* I was right, I was doing the best I knew how at the time, and I did try to warn them. It's not my fault they wouldn't listen. But they thought they were right. As for the eighteen who died, they made their own decision, and I'm finding out that if you make a wrong one, nothing can protect you from the consequences.

Some of our people are determined to go home when *Vanguard Beautiful* comes again. This wasn't what they bargained for, and they've had it. Most of them, though, seem to be taking up the challenge. They're beginning to think of Moravenn as their world. We have a past here now, and a burying ground, and the beginning of a legend, and I think the colony will stay. Perhaps we'll even get recruits in time to come.

And I will stay, of course. Someone has to teach our children how to sing the moons of Moravenn.

How Bright the Stars

Flame Tree Planet, 1973

IT WAS A hellish world to be wandering on, this second planet of Barnard's Star. In fact it looked almost exactly as Jerry Baird had always pictured hell. The sun was red and angry, capable of intense heat. There were volcanoes and fumaroles, pits of bubbling mud, geysers, and great plumes of steam that smelled of sulphur. It was a restless, bad-tempered world, at least in these parts, and Jerry had no good feeling about it.

The PPS (Preliminary Planetary Study) team had spent more than a year encamped on this sparsely populated world, by a Grllan village called Beautiful Water because of the incredibly clear, cool lake that was there, with fern-trees leaning over it and green hills all around. The Grllan lived partly in brush shelters and partly in dens hollowed out beneath the twisty roots of the trees. They were almost, or not quite, human, depending on how you looked at it, but they were friendly, and the team had learned a lot from them about life on Barnard II.

They learned some more on that subject when a fiercer and more predatory clan came down from the hills. Trouble began almost at once and ended with the team camp and almost all of its equipment in ashes. The folk of Beautiful Water had hidden the Earthmen in the deep bush until their wild cousins went away. After that, with the ever-present danger of the predators' return, with no radio and no means of getting help, and with no prospect of continuing their work, the team had decided to trek out.

The decision was not taken lightly. Earth Base was 500 miles away.

They had been able to save only one thing of value from the camp, and that was the small case of microtapes which contained all the records of their research. The case was assigned to Dr. Felter, the vulcanologist, to be carried as part of his load.

On the morning of departure, with the red sun just glaring up over the hilltops, turning the mists to fire and the lake to blood, the Earthmen took up their makeshift packs and the clumsy water bottles made from sections of a giant joint grass. The Grllan, grunting and clicking mournfully, were still bringing parting gifts of roots and seeds and squirming things from the lake. Nobody was very cheerful, but nobody was crying.

Suddenly Dr. Felter threw down his pack, plucked out the case of microtapes and shoved it into the hands of Wainwright, the xenobiologist. "You take it," Felter said. He went over to a fern-tree log and sat down.

Dr. Baird, team coordinator and physician, turned to him and said, "What's wrong, James? Not well?"

Felter shook his head. "Just lazy. I don't have to walk that far to die."

Jerry saw his father's jaw tighten. But Baird spoke quietly.

"It's too soon to lose heart. We'll make it."

"If you do," said Felter, "send a flier back to get me."

"We need you," Baird said, with a note of cold iron in his voice. "We need every one of us."

Felter rose and walked away into the fiery morning among the trees.

Baird looked around to see if any of the others were like minded. Nobody moved. "Share out his load," said Baird. They did, and a few minutes later they marched out of the village. The Grllan went with them to the edge of their green domain, howled once, and were gone.

The PPS team settled down to the longest walk of their lives.

Strange planets were nothing new to young Jerry Baird. He had been with his father on the worlds of Alpha and Proxima Centauri before coming here to Barnard II. Man had finally made the Big Jump outward, with the Wenz-Boroda FTL (faster-than-light) drive, and the exploration of the galaxy had begun. Lying at night in wild places, looking up at the sky, Jerry was both crushed and exalted by the immensity of the adventure. The great wheeling star-swarms of the Milky Way, rivers of light across the black deep, called to him to come and see their wonders. Men were just on the threshold now, visiting their nearest neighbors, but Jerry was only 16, and the future burned bright, lit by the suns of outer space.

Those suns continued to burn in the sky of Barnard II, but now it was required of Jerry to crawl across the planet's surface like a stubborn fly. It was required of him to survive.

Looking at his father, Jerry had no doubt that he would. Dr. Baird had begun his career as a medical missionary among the last of the stone-age peoples who continued obstinately to exist side by side with atomic energy and spaceships. He had been among the first to go starward, and he was now the foremost authority on interstellar medicine. A superb coordinator in the field, Baird was also an expert on survival techniques. Jerry watched the tall, rangy figure striding in the lead, and felt a great surge of love and pride.

Wainwright walked behind Dr. Baird, a bearded young giant, always cheerful and confident. In no set order followed Harding the anthropologist, a dark man with his face pulled down in a perpetual scowl of disapproval, Thompson the chemist, Soderman the geologist, Souter the botanist. Jerry, chief cook and bottlewasher, brought up the rear. It had never occurred to him to feel downtrodden. He was part of the team, and it didn't matter what part as long as it was a Baird team.

The slope of the land lay downward, with the humped volcanic cones thrusting up out of the flat. The men had frequently to make long detours around places where the ground heaved and trembled and spat up steam. The heat became unbearable at midday, and they rested, trying to forget how thirsty they were, watching the lacy plumes of geysers spouting up and praying that none of the sullen little cones would let go while they were near them. When it was cooler they moved on again, across tumbled lava beds that cut their boots to ribbons.

For days they stumbled and staggered through this landscape

of hell, and Jerry felt that he was drying up like old leather, turning black and hard all the way through. At night the furnace winds blew, and there were red gleamings around the horizon. They tried to replenish their water supply from the hot pools, but each time Thompson the chemist would shake his head, and they would leave the bitter-smelling stuff untouched.

"I'm beginning to think," said Harding, "that Felter was right. We must have been out of our minds."

Secretly Jerry was almost inclined to agree with him, remembering the sweet coolness of Beautiful Water. Then he remembered the spears of the hill folk and was not so sure.

Baird unfolded a small plastic satellite map. "The river is ahead. One more day."

The calm, strong voice made Jerry ashamed.

One more day. They said you could always get through one more day. Maybe they were right. He hoped so.

Camp that night was less a camp than a potential graveyard. No one could eat; mouths and throats were too dry. Even breathing was painful. They lay where they dropped. Some time later Jerry awoke with someone shaking him. He thought at first it was his father, and then he realised that the whole world was shaking. There were rumblings and roarings and a fountain of fire in the sky, and a reek of brimstone in the scorching wind. Jerry got up. He could see the others around him as dim shapes in the fire-glow.

"Stay together," Baird said. "Let's go."

They went, finding strength where they had not believed there was any left.

A great cloud of smoke and ash swallowed up the sky and drowned the glare of the volcano. The night became utterly black. They could no longer see each other. At Baird's order they grouped together and took each other's hands.

The slope of the land was still downward, and they followed it blindly in the blind night. Jerry had never been so close to death before, and he was afraid—not so much of dying, though the prospect wasn't pleasant, but of what was happening to *him,* his inner, personal self. He was weak from thirst, hunger, and exhaustion; and his body, always healthy and strong, would not obey him. His senses, always keen, were baffled and useless. He was losing himself in blackness and noise and choking stench. He had always accepted his youthful vitality without question, and it shook him to his foundations to find himself as feeble as an old woman. He wanted very much to lie down and cover his face and let the night roll over him. But nobody else was doing that, and he wouldn't be the first.

They stopped at last, in an evil dawn, behind a ridge that would deflect the lava flow that crept behind them. And as the light grew stronger they could see the river, far ahead, with a streak of blessed green along its bank.

When they had rested they went to the river. It took them the best part of the day. And the streak of blessed green turned out to be a marsh.

They could not cross it. They looked up and down and could not see the end of it. They scooped holes in the mud and drank the black foul-tasting liquid that collected in them, and watched the clear water flowing by out of reach.

"We must go downstream," Baird said. "The marsh will end somewhere."

"Ten miles?" asked Souter. "Forty miles? A hundred? I can't do it." He lay back on the ground.

Harding said bitterly, "Felter was right. We ought to have stayed where we were." He seemed to blame Baird for the whole trek, though all of them had agreed on the necessity for it.

Soderman and Thompson said nothing. They were like scarecrows—with blank faces.

Baird knelt down and examined Souter. "Come on, man," he said gently. "Just a little farther."

Souter rolled his head. "Can't." He seemed to slip into unconsciousness.

Wainwright said, "I'll carry him." He dropped his load and lifted Souter onto his back. He started walking, slowly, one step at a time. Souter was a small man and Wainwright carried him like a grain sack. Baird took the microtape case from Wainwright's pack and added it to his own. He nodded to Jerry and they started after Wainwright.

Soderman and Thompson got up and followed. Harding remained where he was.

Jerry kept looking back. "Are we just going to leave him?"

"He'll come," Baird said.

After a while, he did.

They walked beside the unattainable river, with the sight and sound and smell of the water torturing them. For a while Jerry forgot where he was. When he came to, he realized that he had been asleep on his feet—out but still moving. What had roused him were the voices. It was night, and they had come to the end of the marsh.

They splashed into the shallows. Jerry lay soaking up the life that flowed over him.

"We made it," he said.

"So far, thank God." Baird roused himself. "I must look at Souter."

But Souter wasn't there. Neither was Wainwright.

Baird filled a water container and started back. Jerry didn't feel like it, but he dragged himself out of the river and went with him. The night was clear, with the usual small red flickerings in the distance and the bright stars overhead. There was light enough to see by, and in any case they had not far to go. Wainwright was sitting no more than a hundred feet from the bank. Souter lay beside him, very still.

"I couldn't make it," Wainwright whispered. "Only a few steps, and I couldn't make it."

Baird handed him the water bottle. He waved it away as though a creature so contemptible as he had no right to water. "Give it to Souter."

"Don't be a fool," said Baird harshly. "There's enough for both." He shoved the container into Wainwright's hands and bent over Souter.

"Besides," he said, in a different voice, "Souter doesn't need it. He's dead."

Wainwright began to weep. How long, Jerry wondered, had he been staggering along carrying a dead man?

He helped his father straighten Souter's body, and he laid his wet shirt to cover him as decently as possible. Then they returned to Wainwright, who was making deep dry noises, his mouth open and his chest heaving as though he couldn't get his breath. He did not seem to hear when they spoke to him. They took hold of him. He allowed himself to be raised up and taken to the river, where he lay in the water and would not speak to anyone.

"What's happened to him?" Jerry asked.

"He's always had enormous strength," Baird said. "He just never knew there was an end to it."

Jerry, who had come very close to the end of his, was comforted to know that even giants like Wainwright had their human limits. And suddenly he remembered something.

"A little while back," he said, "when I was wandering along… you were holding me up, weren't you?"

"I was giving you a hand," Baird said, and smiled. "Why not? You're my son."

They slept on the bank that night. In the morning they buried Souter, in the cool shade of a grove of feathery things that resembled tamarisks, farther along the bank. Baird brought out the little worn Book that had been with him since his college days and read the service. The familiar words sounded strange in this strange place, under this alien sun. Jerry said so, and Baird shook his head.

"Are you forgetting that He made the stars also? It's all one to God."

They made a camp at the other end of the grove and stayed there until they were fit to move on again. They had left the volcanic lands now, at least for the time being, and there was vegetation here, different kinds of grasses and flowers, and queer small life that twittered and scurried through the trees. They built weirs and took food from the river, and they dragged together deadfall trees and vines to make a raft. When they felt strong enough they launched the raft and went wallowing away downstream.

After what they had been through, this was silken luxury. The river flowed wide and unhurried, with a steady current. They watched the changing banks glide by and fished and cooled themselves in the water. It seemed that their troubles were over. Earth Base was no more than 20 miles from where the river emptied into the Western Sea. All they had to do was drift along.

But the mapping satellites could only show the major features of a planet's surface. They had passed over small details such as cataracts.

It was a hot morning, with the red sun glaring down. The landscape had become more tropical, with forests of gigantic trees, larger than any Jerry had ever seen before, and there were many more life-forms. Great curious heads broke the surface to stare at the raft. Bright eyes peered from the banks. There were flying creatures, some large and ugly like the archaeopteryx, some bright-colored, small and darting. None of these forms seemed inimical, and if some were carnivorous the men saw no sign of it. There was a kind of steaming lazy peacefulness over the land. And then they heard the river sounds ahead of them.

They grabbed the steering poles and clawed for the bank, but the current was strong now, and it held them fast. If Wainwright had helped they might have made it, but since that night when he failed to reach the river Wainwright had done nothing, as though he lacked the courage to try and perhaps fail again. He had simply withdrawn into himself. Now, as they were swept into the rapids, he barely lifted his head to look.

The raft shot down a long swift slide, picking up speed. It hit white water, flew into the air, and broke apart. Jerry went on by himself, tossing over and over. He was a strong swimmer, but that wasn't doing him much good now. Dizzy, deafened, and battered, he dropped over a cliff, and the whole river fell on his back. Then it was deep and quiet, and he was far down and too tired to worry about coming up again.

Something took hold of him. Something lifted him, brought him bursting up into light and air.

He saw a face close by him, laughing. Bright drops shook out of silvery hair. Green eyes sparkled, tilted above slanting cheekbones. The mouth, small and delicate, spoke words he did not understand, except that they were reassuring. He thought that he had never seen such a joyous face. He smiled back, and let himself be towed to the warm shallows of a sandbar. He scrambled out and sat trying to replace the water inside him with air, while the silver-haired folk, a dozen of them, brought his father and the other men in from the wide pool below the cataract. After that they began diving like otters after the scattered packs that had come down with the wreckage.

They were beautiful to watch. "What... who are they?" he asked.

Baird shook his head. "I don't know. I hope they're hospitable." He was prodding at his left ankle, which was beginning to swell. "Not broken, I think, but I've torn the ligaments. Thompson's got a concussion. We won't be travelling for a while."

Jerry hugged his own bruises and felt very grateful to the strangers. "I wonder where they came from," he said, and turned around. There was no sign of a village, but he saw that there were 20 or 30 of the silver-haired ones standing along the bank and looking at them.

They were slender and graceful, man-shaped and man-high, with smooth greenish skin decorated here and there in patterns of gold and russet and black lines. Jerry could not tell whether the patterns were natural or not, but they were oddly attractive. Men and women alike wore garments made of leaves and flowers, and they carried no weapons. They seemed as free and happy as the wind.

Some of the packs were smashed beyond redemption, but the precious microtape case had been saved, and the rest didn't matter. The swimmers came out of the water. Baird thanked them and they smiled, standing like sprites in the red sunlight, all wet and shining.

Baird pointed to Thompson, who lay with his head in Soderman's lap, and then to his own injured leg. The silver tops all nodded. Lilting voices sang back and forth from sandbar to bank. As though it were the greatest game in the world, the folk on the bank came running out and picked up Baird and Thompson and the packs.

And now Jerry learned where the village was.

A grove of the huge trees they had been seeing for the past few days grew above the pool. The trunks were 40 to 50 feet through. Great thick branches sprang out from them, bearing sprays of coppery foliage. Swaying ladders made of vines led up to the branches, at a fairly appalling height; and there was a whole complex of aerial walkways connecting reed-and-sapling houses with other dwellings that were hollowed out of the trees themselves. These people lived like bowerbirds under the sky.

They went skipping up agilely enough with their burdens. Jerry climbed a lot more slowly, as did the others, except Wainwright. He sat down at the foot of a tree and stayed there. At the top of a ladder was a tree-branch street, and a slender green-eyed girl all garlanded with flowers was beckoning Jerry. He followed her, thankful for the vines that were rigged on either side like lifelines. They at least gave him the illusion that he couldn't fall.

The girl led them to a large room in the heart of a giant tree. Care had been taken to leave the vital sap-bearing outer layers intact so that the tree did not die. The floor was covered with a soft mat of dried moss and ferns. Two round window-holes pierced the walls, letting in the warm breeze. Baird and Thompson were already there.

Jerry went to one of the windows and looked out at the leafy world beyond. There was something heady about it—being so high up between earth and air. He could feel the room moving as the wind stirred the tree. The branches rustled. He thought suddenly that it beat living in a dead house, a mere artificial lump on the land-scape.

In a little while their hosts brought baskets and woven trays of food, and before Jerry knew it, there was a feast going on, to the music of reed pipes and queer long-necked viols with only one string, and little flat drums played with the fingers. The crowd became too large for the room and moved outside to a broad platform built between the trees. The sun went down. The stars came out, seeming closer than they had ever been before. In the center of the platform young girls danced—sweetly as spring leaves floating on the wind.

Jerry was young and adaptable. In a few days it seemed the most natural thing in the world to live in a tree and scamper up and down hanging ladders. There was a curious timelessness about the place. The people themselves seemed to live with the slow swing of the seasons—like the trees and the flowers. Nature was bountiful here. Food plants grew for the gathering; and the pool was always full of fish which the people caught with their bare hands, flashing and darting and laughing through the water. When it was too hot, the upper breezes cooled them in their airy nests, and when it rained, the showers washed everything clean and made the breezes fragrant. Jerry had no doubt that these were the happiest people he had ever known. Happy, innocent, untroubled, forgetting yesterday and not looking for tomorrow, because all the days were sweet and there was no telling one from another.

Harding had begun the first night to learn the language. The people called themselves *Hwyl*. The sky was their father, the trees their mother, the river was a kind of sacred brother, and they all lived together in a close family group. The Hwyl were much interested in the Earthmen. The river brought them strange cattle once in a while, but seldom living. They tried politely to understand about Earth and starships and exploration. Jerry didn't think that much got through to them. There were no words in their language for most of the functions of a vastly more complicated culture, and there was no way to express the concepts that underlie these functions. At last the Hwyl would shake their silver heads and laugh, and somebody would bring fruit and somebody else would start playing the pipes, and that would be the end of the lecture.

While he waited for Thompson and his father to heal of their hurts, Jerry went with the Hwyl to gather food, and he swam with them and tried to learn some of their birdlike songs. He slept on the moss and listened to the tree house talking with the wind at night. He lay along cool branches and let soft rain touch him, and at other times he sat in the sunlight, plaiting reeds to make things the way the Hwyl showed him. Imperceptibly he ceased to be anxious for the sick to mend. There was no hurry. He felt rested and at peace. He didn't want to think about the harsh cruelty of the outside world. He didn't want to go and face it again.

Soderman put the feeling into words. The Hwyl had helped him to weave a little house for himself, and he had moved into it. He was sitting now in the round door-hole, his bare feet dangling, while the house rocked gently back and forth.

"I'm getting old and tired," he said. "I don't want to fight any more. This is heaven."

Harding had joined them. There had been a great change in the man. He looked 10 years younger, and all the sour lines had left his face. He could smile; he could even laugh. "I'm with you," he said. "No more of man's inhumanity to man. I'm going to stay right here and make the Hwyl my life's work."

Jerry didn't take him seriously. He only sighed and said, "I'm going to hate leaving."

Harding looked at him and then at Soderman; but they said nothing.

Soderman pointed downward through the leafy boughs. There was a glimpse of the pool. Thompson was making lazy circles in the water, rolling over to float from time to time. There was something about the relaxed posture of his body that expressed perfect contentment.

"He doesn't seem too anxious to get well, does he?"

Thompson was still complaining of dizzy spells and lack of strength. "You think he's pretending?" asked Jerry, surprised.

"He might be," said Harding. "One thing I know; your old man isn't."

"Yes," said Soderman. "He'll be fit enough in a few days."

That night there was a feast. No particular reason. The Hwyl did not need reasons. They held it on the platform, and there was much laughter, and presently the girls scudded out to dance with the wind and the starlight. Jerry left early. He went to the tree house and found his father alone, standing by one of the windows and looking out at the night.

"Why do you never join the others, Dad?" he asked. "Why are you always here by yourself?"

"Because," said Baird, "I'm afraid."

Jerry was astonished. "You've never been afraid of anything." He came closer. It was dark in the room; the Hwyl made fire but only in the cooking pits by the river, and there were no lamps in the village. He tried to see his father's face by the faint light from the window. "What is there here to be afraid of?"

"Losing myself," said Baird.

"I don't understand."

"Don't you?" asked Baird gently. He looked at Jerry. Then he said, "We'll leave here in the morning."

It was like a blow. Jerry cried, "Tomorrow? But Dad, you're not well yet, and Thompson..."

Baird said, "We've waited too long as it is."

"The boy's right," said Harding from the doorway. "You'd better not go."

He came in. Soderman and Thompson followed him. Something else entered with them, a tension, an antagonism that set Jerry's nerves prickling. His father stirred and turned to face the men, three dark shapes in the warm sweet-smelling gloom.

"You've made your decision, then."

"Yes," said Harding. "We're staying. All of us."

"What's there to go back to?" Soderman said. "What do we need that we haven't got here?"

"Your work," said Baird.

Harding made a derisive sound. "What did my work ever bring me? Fame? Fortune? Niggardly little men tucked it away in pigeonholes and forgot it."

"I'm not well," said Thompson. "I need rest."

"It's different with you, Baird," Soderman said. "You're a preacher—Lutheran, isn't it? You have an outlook; we don't. And we know what we want."

Baird sighed. "It doesn't matter what I am. Listen, I won't talk to you about your souls because you don't believe in them, but what about your minds? They make you what you are. Do you want to throw them away? You're not Hwyl, neither am I. Perhaps I wish we were, but we lost our innocence too long ago. If we try to go back, we die."

He picked up something and held it out. Jerry saw that it was the box of microtapes.

"A year's work," Baird said. "Seven men, one of them dead now. Do you want to throw this away?"

Harding said, "I used to think that knowledge was everything; now I think I don't need it."

"Very well, then." Baird set the box down. "The boy and I will go on alone."

"No," said Harding. "I know your zealous soul. You'd send people back to rescue us. You stay right here, Doctor."

In the heavy silence Jerry could hear the leaves rustling outside. The tree creaked softly as it moved.

Baird said, "You'll prevent me?"

"We will," said Harding, "so don't make us." He laughed. "Relax that puritan spirit, Baird. You may even find you like it."

They left, but they didn't go far.

Baird leaned on the smooth bark of the window opening. His head was bowed, and his voice sounded very tired.

"And you, Jerry. Whose side are you on?"

Jerry had never been able to lie to his father even when he wanted to. "I don't know," he said. "I'm happy here. Is that so wrong?"

"You'll have to answer that question yourself," said Baird. He brought Jerry to the window and pointed upward. Through the high branches Jerry could see the stars, glowing like lamps in the sky.

"You always wanted to go out there," Baird said. "If you stay here, you never will."

He turned abruptly. "Get out now, Jerry. Find some other place to sleep."

Jerry went without saying a word. He knew how deeply his father was hurt. He also knew that now he was on his own. Whatever decision he made would be made as an adult, and whatever the consequences, they would be his alone to deal with.

Harding and the others glanced at him curiously as he passed. They didn't speak, and they didn't try to stop him. Probably they reckoned he was no threat. He slid down the ladder and walked out past the cooking pits to the sandbar. He sat there alone in the night, trying to think. But the stars watched him with brilliant implacable eyes. He didn't want them watching him. He got up and went back under the trees.

Sounds of music and laughter floated down to him. He thought of returning to the feast. He even started up the ladder. Then he came down again. He was not in the mood, not tonight. This was the special night, his night, the rite of passage. He didn't know what he was going to make of it.

Wainwright still sat at the base of the tree. The Hwyl had made a shelter for him and they brought him food. His hair and beard had grown long. He was gaunt and not very clean. Jerry could hear him breathing, and the shelter was uncannily like a shrine.

"Wainwright," he said, "I need help."

"There is no help," said Wainwright. "Man is weak. The universe is too large for him. He can only wait for death."

Jerry said angrily, "That's just you talking, because you couldn't stand one single kick under the jaw." He shouted. "You're a coward, Wainwright. You make me sick."

He strode away. The river sang to him, and he followed it down below the sandbar, where there was slack water. The remains of the raft were here. In the first days, he and the others had begun to patch together what was left and to add to it from the fallen branches of the great trees. They had become less and less vigorous about it and finally, by tacit consent, the work had stopped altogether. There was half a raft tied up there, soggy and forgotten. It could take one boy down the river to within walking distance of Earth Base. All he had to do was cut the moorings.

He didn't. He continued to wander about until he was too tired to wander any more. Then he curled up and went to sleep.

The morning was like any other morning, except that it was not.

The Hwyl dived and splashed in the pool, fishing. Jerry watched them. He could see his whole life stretching ahead of him in a beautiful red-gold haze—all without pain or problems or the threat of failure.

Wasn't that what everybody wanted? Hadn't he been blessed with extraordinary good fortune: to find what most people looked for all their lives and never found?

He thought of his father, and then he thought, No, this is not my father's life, it's mine, and I must decide for myself how I want to live it. Without fear, without favor.

He made his decision.

He stayed away from his father. For three days he swam with the

Hwyl, gathered food, joined in the feasting, and laughed and sang. And every night the stars came out and looked at him. They hounded him. He couldn't get away from them.

On the third night he understood that he had not made his decision at all. He had only been putting off making it.

When the village was asleep, he filled a basket with food from the cooking pits and went below the sandbar and cut away the vines that held the raft. The river took him—broad and peaceful now that the travail of the cataract was over.

A week later, hungry and footsore, he limped into Earth Base. Next day he was in a helicopter, heading upriver to get his father. He knew that he could see the Hwyl again without regret. As for Harding and the others, they could do as they wished. Jerry knew what he wanted.

He wanted the stars.

MOMMIES AND DADDIES

Crisis, 1974

THE WARD was never entirely quiet. Some of the kids talked in their sleep, or cried or groaned or tossed around. This night, the night Deke had been waiting for, thunder drowned out the smaller sounds. He slid out of bed, pulled on shirt and shorts, and fished underneath for his sandals. Holding them in his hand, he crept barefoot between the flashes of lightning, past the cubicle where Matron slept, down the stairs and out the door, into the wind and the hissing rain. Then he put on his sandals and ran.

The tree was thrashing its branches angrily, but Deke didn't let that stop him. He only hung tighter to the wet bark as he climbed. The big limb took him over the top of the wall like a bridge.

He dropped unhurt into the soggy weeds on the other side. There was an area all around the Institute, which had been cleared by the demolition crews. He had to cross that, and he did so crouched over, with his heart beating up into his throat. There were no lights or voices from the wall, calling him back. It was common talk around the Institute that they were glad to have you go if you could make it. They always needed room. Nevertheless, when he got into the tangle of ragged streets with no alarm being raised, he felt like yelling for sheer joy.

He didn't. He kept very quiet, loitering in the shadows. And now he began to be afraid. For the first time in his short life he was alone, out of the Institute, away from Matron, the doctors, Mr. Timmins the teacher; away from neat lawns and playgrounds, the rows of clean white beds and the smell of yellow soap. He had never seen the city before. It was one thing to talk and dream about it. It was another thing entirely to be in it.

He shivered, cold in the beating rain. The thunder shook him. When the lightning flashed he could see broken pavement, shining with wet, and black buildings leaning up into the sky. Things creaked and banged, lonely noises in the wind. He would have liked to get inside somewhere, into shelter, but the doorless holes in the walls did not invite him. They were like mouths to catch him and chew him up.

He moved on, stepping furtively, with the water running over his feet.

He wished he had a pill. But it wasn't time for that yet.

All his senses seemed to be painfully alert. Underneath the rain-smell he could distinguish an old sour mustiness, unpleasant and sad. And underneath the thunder and the wind-born creakings he could hear the silence. The black buildings were dead. Life had gone away from them. They were corpses with empty hearts.

He began to go more quickly, a small denim-clad figure scuttering through the summer storm. Every so often one of the kids who had made it out was forced to come back to the Institute for treatment, and they talked a lot. All the real information about the city came from them. So Deke knew where he had to go. He just didn't know how to get there.

The storm passed over. The rain stopped. The water stayed in the low places because the old drains were choked up. Sometimes Deke was over his knees in it. The damp air began to thicken into a clammy mist. He came into an area of wider streets. The buildings here were very tall and wide, but a lot of them had been burned out. There was an open space ahead that had once been a park. And all of a sudden Deke stopped, then darted aside into a tumble of ruins. He hunkered down and stared.

There were fires in the park. They made big flickery patches of red in the mist. Shadows moved around them. There were voices, and dim sounds that he could not identify. The hairs at the back of his neck lifted, and something happened inside his middle that almost made him be sick.

Mommies and Daddies

There they were, the Free People. In the living flesh.

"They'll roast you in one of those fires if they catch you," said a quiet voice behind him.

Deke whirled around. The children had come up on him without a sound. There were four or five of them, he thought, and mostly taller than he.

"Don't try to run," said the voice. "And don't make any noise. Come on."

He did as he was told. They led him through the dark streets, keeping close together, moving at a trot. Deke noticed that there was a very big fire burning now over on the east side of the city. Lightning must have struck somewhere. His companions paid no attention, and he supposed there was nothing unusual about it, so he didn't mention it either. From time to time penned dogs barked and voices hailed them, and the leader answered with some sort of password.

It seemed to Deke that they did a lot of unnecessary jinking and jogging, turning aside from the direction in which they were going only to return to it again a few blocks farther on. The leader, speaking from great heights, enlightened him.

"Some streets are neutral. Anybody can use them. But if you tread on somebody else's turf without permission, you get clobbered. Remember that."

"I will."

"Unless you're hunting," the leader added. "If you're wearing the green cockade, you can pass anywhere, as long as you don't stop."

A horrid, delicious thrill contracted Deke's innards.

Hunting.

Yes.

That's what he was here for.

The buildings along the way, those that were left, were as dark as all the others from the outside, but Deke began to sense a difference. They weren't dead. Things lived and moved and breathed in them.

There was another open space, another park. "This one belongs to us," said the leader. "It's safe, as much as anything is in the city, but don't trust it. The Freebies raid us sometimes."

They pattered around the perimeter of the misty open, which seemed quite empty, with no fires showing, yet Deke was certain there were watchers there. The air smelled a little of barnyard. He knew that one. The Institute was self-supporting. It had to be, because you never knew when the supply trucks were going to be held up. Drugs, of course, were another thing, and sometimes that got pretty hairy, but they tried to keep an oversupply on hand at all times.

There was a big tall building with a lot of balconies sticking out. There was a bricked-up, boarded-up entrance with stuff piled in front so you had to come in one at a time, and Deke could see wicked-pointed sticks poking at him from loopholes. But the words were right and the sticks didn't do anything. They went inside, with what seemed like a thousand dogs yammering at them.

It was like being in a huge dark cave. In the middle of a concrete floor a fire burned on a round hearth of stones. The smoke went up and got lost in whatever space was up there. Deke couldn't see, but it felt high. There were lots of echoes.

His captors pushed him over to the hearth. He stood shivering, sucking in the heat through every pore. Now in the firelight he could see that the leader of the group was a girl, a tall girl almost at the age when she was going to have to stop being a hunter and go away into the country. He felt sorry for her. She had a short-cropped mane of reddish-brown hair as rough as a terrier's coat, and a lean face with sharp cheekbones. Her nondescript rags left her muscular legs and arms free for running and throwing things. She had an assortment of weapons stuck in around her waist. The other four graded down in size, two boys and two girls, all thin and bright-eyed.

Kids began to come out of the shadows beyond the firelight. They stood in a ring and looked at Deke in his blue denims.

"Another one fresh from the Institute," said the tall girl. "They grow 'em smaller every year."

"That's because they're junkies," somebody said. They all began to shout, "Junky! Junky!" leaping up and down and jeering at him.

"It's not my fault I'm a junky," Deke said equably. "Any more than it's your fault you're all bastards."

534

"Aren't you a bastard too?" asked the tall girl.

Deke shrugged. "Who isn't?"

She leaned over him. "Where were you found?"

"In a garbage dump," said Deke. Actually he had been taken away from his mother at a perfectly ordinary mobile clinic where her friends had brought her, suffering from an overdose of heroin, and where she just incidentally happened to have a baby, which started screaming with withdrawal symptoms shortly after birth and so was sent at once to the Institute for Congenital Addiction. But he wasn't going to admit that. "Where were you found?"

"In a ditch. In the snow. I was almost dead."

"I was found in the river!" a little voice shrilled.

"...in a junkyard."

"...an abandoned bus."

"...a doorway."

"...wrapped in a brown paper bag."

"...a shoe box."

"...a lavatory."

They chanted their brags at him. After a while he said, "I know who you are. You're all from the Foundling Home. You're not the real Wild Ones." Those were the little healthies who had never been institutionalized at all. A lot of loose kids had stayed behind, gradually inheriting the city as the people left it in search of a more decent life. They ran a kind of foundling service of their own, and it was generally accepted that because of this they had begun the practice of hunting.

"Yah," said the tall girl scornfully. "They don't *know* anything. They've never been taught." She turned abruptly and called out, "Somebody throw him a scrap to lie on." With a certain rough kindliness she said to Deke, "You can sleep by the fire, it's warmer. In the morning I'll show you where to go." A boy came with a piece of old red carpet and flung it down. "You hungry?"

Deke shook his head. He was tired, with all the excitement and exertion, and he was beginning to feel rotten. He wanted to curl up and be alone.

When they had all gone away, back to their pads, and he thought nobody was looking, he dug the stoppered vial out of his pocket and took one of his pills. After that he slept.

It was still dark in the big room when the girl shook him awake, but it was daylight outside. From somewhere else in the building, kids were driving animals into the park, which was getting quite busy now under the warm sun. There were a lot of garden plots. Deke and the others at the Institute had been taught to help with the farm work, and he supposed the Foundlings had been taught as well.

The girl—her name was Stella—led him into the park, between the gardens where everything was fresh and green from the night's rain. And he asked her a question.

"When can I go hunting?"

"You have to learn all the rules first. You have to learn how to survive yourself, and how not to get your mates in trouble, and you have to earn your place here. That means work. We don't have any dropouts."

"I'll work," Deke said. "I'll learn."

"Good." Stella caught him and whirled him around to face her. She towered over him with a dreadful ferocity. "And never you forget," she said, "we're the lucky ones. Even you. We hunt for all of them—the murdered, the diseased, the LSD babies. You remember that."

"I'll remember."

They went on again, past little flocks of goats and grazing cows, taking a shortcut across the top of the park. There was a building there, with an entrance much like the other one, boarded and heaped against intruders. Some kids were cooking over a fire out in front. Deke recognized Tell and John and Sara and a couple of others who had left the Institute before him.

"This is Junkyville," said Stella. "So long."

She left him. Tell walked over and said, "Hello, Deke. Come and eat."

It was good seeing his friends again. He was ravenously hungry. The sun burned pleasantly on his back. They shared the stories of their escape around the fire. He felt great. The thing was done now, the big move made, and he was here and safe, with a new life ahead of him. Then Tell stood up. He put a digging-stick into Deke's hands and led him to a garden plot where the potato plants were beginning to blossom.

"No weeds," said Tell, "and no potato bugs. For every one you leave behind, you get a belting from me."

"Okay," said Deke and grinned, and got to work.

There was a lot to learn. The social scale, for one thing. The Junkies were right at the bottom. The Foundling gangs were in the middle, and the Wild Ones at the top. Only it was more complicated than that. The Junkies and the Foundlings felt superior to the Wild Ones because they had some learning and some technical skills. The Wild Ones felt superior because they didn't have any learning, and because they were first.

"They are the best hunters," Tell said. "You have to give them that. If you can get one of their gangs to let you hunt with them, you've got it made."

Deke did not suppose that that would ever happen to him.

In the meantime he weeded and hoed, and acted as herd boy, and did his share of policing the common room in the building. That was another law. Only the Free People lived in filth. The children were clean and shorn, and it was the ultimate shame to be found lousy. The condition of the common room would no doubt have given Matron fits, but it was swept and the sleeping pallets were neat. The stable quarters were kept mucked out, and fly-catching was a perpetual sport.

Nobody knew exactly what the building had been originally. Everything portable had been stripped, either by its departing tenants or the looters and scroungers who came after them. Bare concrete floors and boarded windows made for spartan living, but they only used the place at night, really, and it wasn't bad at all around the fire, when you had the animals penned in the next room and the barricades were up and you felt safe against the dark.

Up the many stairs there were the many rooms, all empty and quiet, and if you wanted you could have a lair to yourself in one of them. Deke fixed himself up a pad in one that had a balcony overlooking the park, where he could sleep on hot nights and take his turn at sentry duty. Often he sat there alone, looking out from his high perch at the black sprawl of the city, with no sound in it except the occasional bark of a dog or a cat-yowl or the call of a night bird, and he would try to imagine what it must have been like in the days before he was born, crammed with people and machines and lights and noise.

Mr. Timmins had taught them about Hellerism and what had come of it. Somebody named Heller a long time back had preached the doctrine that small towns had become useless anachronisms and must go, and everybody must live in the cities, where people could be better managed. Apparently nearly everybody had tried to do that, and after a while the cities died of their own weight and foulness and the madness of people overcrowded into a faceless limbo where everything was hard and loud and artificial. There were lots of old films left, showing how it had been, and Deke had seen them as part of his education; but somehow the reality wouldn't come away from the remembered screen, and the film image was superimposed on the actual streets below him.

Daytimes you could hear the demolition crews working, gnawing away at the edges of the city, freeing the land of its stifling burden so that it could live and breathe again. Some day, Deke knew, they would reach the inner city and this would all be gone. But that was too far ahead to worry him. He'd be gone, too, by then, out among the old villages and the new road towns where the scattered-site industrial plazas were. He thought he would probably work on a farm, but there was no need to worry about that yet, either. This was the good time, the young time.

The hunting time.

The reason the Junkies were at the bottom of the social heap was because they dealt with the pushers for meth pills. They had to, and everybody knew that. It wasn't held against them in itself. But the pushers, who came and went usually in armed convoys and by night, did their main business with the Freebies, and it was almost like consorting with the enemy. The Junkies were forbidden to barter away any food, which was communal property, so they were always on the lookout for treasures among the ruins. It had been impossible, even for determined thieves, to clean out an entire city. The Free People kept themselves going by scrounging in between hijacking the supply trucks meant for the Institutes. It didn't bother them that they were robbing their own children. Why should it?

When Deke had memorized all the free streets and the different turfs, Tell allowed him to go out on patrol. Deke liked that. It was scary and exciting. Sometimes by day, sometimes by night, they would slip through the derelict streets and spy on that other park across town, lurking like small rats among the abandoned buildings. On clinic days you could see the big semis roll up, built like armored cars and accompanied by guards with guns. Permanent clinics were impossible, the Freebies knocked them over too often looking for drugs. In one of these mobile clinics, perhaps the very one he was looking at, Deke had been born.

He finally got so that the smell from the park no longer turned his stomach. It only made him more eager, and whenever he saw a girl with a big belly he had to hold himself very hard.

Sometimes they would find a live baby. The law was that you turned babies over to the Wild Ones, who kept them to raise if they were healthy, or passed them on to the appropriate Institute if they were not. There were other, and worse, Institutes for congenital affliction than the one Deke had come from. The child population of the city was growing. The park population stayed about the same. The number of dropouts who couldn't hack it in Squaresville and came looking for a different life-style just about balanced the number of Freebies who cashed out.

The thing Deke liked best of all was the games.

Each gang had a different time assigned so they didn't step on each other, and you could range the whole park, learning to go cat-foot through rank grasses, holding the killing-stick just so to stop its catching in brambles and hanging vines. When the weather was hot and dry, the grass smelled wonderful of warm dusty sweetness, and there was a jungle of honeysuckle run wild where the bees made droning music all day long. At night, by moonlight or starlight, you learned to drift between the trees, letting your bare feet sense for themselves where to come down. You learned not to cry out if you trod on something painful. You learned to breathe quietly, to keep track of where you were…not just the single spot where you happened to be, but that spot in relation to the whole city and its escape routes…and you learned to stay with your gang, always. Because you were too little to hunt alone, and if you got separated you could only run.

You learned the killing-chant, which was simple enough, but you never used it. Like the green cockade, that was only for the real thing.

It was during game time that Deke met the chief of the Wild Ones. His name was Chad, and he was tough and undersized like most of them, with a small, fierce face and muscles that showed like knotted strings under his sun-blackened skin. His hair was bleached almost as white as one of Matron's sheets, cut short and ragged, and it grew down the back of his neck and right down between his shoulder blades. He used to join the game now and then, letting the other kids know what ham-footed blunderers they were, pouncing and mock-stabbing and vanishing again before they hardly saw him. He would laugh then, and give them a lesson in weaponry. He had a real knife. A lot of the Wild Ones did, and some of the others. But most had to make out with sticks, and he would take one and show them the best way to use it, the sharp end for cutting, the heavy end for clubbing.

He began to watch Deke, who was small and neatly made and could move well.

"It isn't only that, though," Chad said to him one day. "A lot of you can do as much. But you're a real good hater, aren't you?"

Deke nodded. Something in Chad's little tough face matched something he felt within himself. A great shining, burning, glorious hate.

"Would you like to hunt with me?"

Deke was speechless. Finally he managed to say, "When?"

"Learn," said Chad. "I'll let you know."

Deke learned.

And one evening a hard brown girl-child trotted up and stood by the cooking fire. "Chad says come."

Deke got his stick. He put on the headband for the first time, and pulled green leaves to thrust into it. His hands trembled, and the others watched him with silent envy, and respect. He went away with the girl-child.

Chad's hunters with their green cockades were ready. Chad nodded to Deke. There was no need for any talk. They set off through the streets, passing where they would, and no one stopped them, and the darkness came down on them and hid them. Deke felt light and strong, and inside him there was a lovely fire.

Chad took them a long curve around and into the park through a dense thicket of brambles. There was a run like a rabbit run cut through the thicket. Deke went on his hands and knees with the others, and at the end of the run there was a ledge of rock where you could crouch in the night and look down.

"Quiet," Chad whispered. "Something going on."

There was a fire in a hollow not too far away below, with a dozen or so of the Free People around it. Much farther away there was a sound of howling, and a thumping and a twanging, all coming closer. The Freebies around the fire got to their feet, except for three or four who were already out of the world, and went straggling off toward the noise. Presently Deke saw a crowd of people, moving slowly, carrying something.

"Funeral," said Chad. "Good. We wait."

You could smell the mourners. You couldn't see any faces. The corpse was male and naked. Its bones stuck out, and Deke thought it wouldn't look much different a year from now. Its mouth hung open, making a slack hole in the middle of its beard, and its skinny ulcerated arms dangled. And, Deke thought, for all I know, that could be my father.

The mourners banged and twanged, and sang in their high-pitched nasal voices a lament for the sadness of dead youth.

He's left us, our brother the world couldn't keep,
The world made him suffer, the world made him weep.
He was young, he was lost, he was searchin' for love,

Reachin' out, reachin' out, searchin' for love....

The procession passed on out of sight behind a grove of trees. Somewhere beyond it the body would be shoveled under in a shallow grave, shrouded in its own hair.

Deke's thigh muscles were jumping and he put his hands on them to steady them down.

The Freebies came back to the fire. They were excited and restless, upset by the presence of death. They talked and moved about. Some kind of a vial passed from hand to hand. Their voices rose, becoming shrill and loud. They began to make music, working themselves up, jerking and stamping and shouting. Finally, when they had done all the preliminary things, the men and women began tumbling each other on the ground.

"Now," said Chad, and the hunters went down off the ledge.

They went cat-foot on their small bare feet, through the long grass and the weeds, toward the hollow where the men and women were. And Deke thought, This is how I...how all of us were made.

Chad started the hunting chant and Deke joined in, speaking the words for the first time in his life.

"Mommy! Daddy! Mommy! Daddy!"

The children rushed in among the couples and the killing-sticks flashed in the firelight, up and down.

SCIENCE FICTION WRITING
EXPERIENCES AS A WRITER

Interview with Leigh Brackett Hamilton by
Juanita Roderick and Hugh G. Earnhart
Youngstown State University Oral History Program
October 7, 1975

JUANITA RODERICK: Mrs. Hamilton, I wonder if you can tell us something about your family and childhood?

LEIGH BRACKETT HAMILTON: Well, my father came from Portsmouth, New Hamphshire and he died when I was a baby, in a flu epidemic after World War I. My mother and her family came from St. Louis, Missouri and I was a first generation Californian, which in those days was quite unusual, but which is not anymore.

I had a very happy childhood, I grew up at the beach. My grandfather was a father to me and we had a very close relationship, I had a very happy time of it as a youngster, and a rather haphazard education because we moved around quite a bit. That is, my grandfather didn't but my mother vibrated between him and her aunt and uncle, so part of the time I was living in San Francisco. They had a good bit of money and we traveled with them. I think my mother was more or less a companion to my great aunt, so I was fortunate enough to see a good bit of the country, or rather more than most children do. We took a trip through the Panama Canal and went to New England and Virginia and did quite a bit of travelling in the West.

At the age of eight I was a great reader. I learned to read when I was about five, I think, and I haven't stopped since. I got hold of a copy of Edgar Rice Burroughs' *The Gods of Mars* and I was never the same after that. Suddenly, I became

543

aware of other worlds out there and then, from that time on, I was destined to be a science fiction writer. Nothing, apart from that, very fascinating happened. I had just a more or less normal childhood.

R: Did you have any brothers or sisters?

H: No, I was an only child. My mother never remarried for some reason. She was a beautiful woman. I don't know why, but she never remarried.

R: Can you tell us something about your school days?

H: I went to a little private school in Santa Monica. My mother was a segregationist; she didn't want me to be with boys, so I went to an all girl school. Then she was quite ill for several years and she took me out of school. By the time I got to being of college age, I was offered a scholarship, but I couldn't go because I had to get work for we were a little short on money.

I had started to write quite seriously when I was thirteen. I had decided right then that I would be a writer, because obviously, it was a very easy way to make a living; all you had to do was sit down and write stories. Ten years later, at the end of 1939, I sold the first one. It was published in 1940. I tried writing almost everything. I finally decided that I would stick to science fiction because that is what I wanted to do, even though there wasn't that much money in it. Everybody warned me, "You'll starve to death. It's not a very respectable field, you know, I mean, only nut cases write for it and only nut cases read it." Things have changed since then. My aunt used to say, "Why don't you write nice stories for the *Ladies' Home Journal?*" I used to say, "I wish I could, because they pay well, but I can't read the *Ladies' Home Journal* and I'm sure I couldn't write for it." So there we were.

I did have a knack for science fiction which I dearly loved, so for quite a while I wrote nothing but science fiction. I was never a quantity producer and it was a very small field. Inasmuch as I had some financial responsibilities, I had to broaden out so I took to writing detective stories. I wrote quite a few of them for the pulp magazines. Then at long last I wrote a novel, which was perfectly frightful, and I couldn't say that it set any worlds on fire, but I loved it. It was my child, my first born, full-length novel.

It was published and Howard Hawks read it. I had a friend in Martindale's bookstore. Hawks came in every couple of weeks and bought an armload of thrillers and my friend saw to it that mine got in the pile. A few days later my agent rang me up and said, "Howard Hawks wants to see you." I fell on the floor. I went to Warner Brothers for an interview and started to work on "The Big Sleep" and we got a contract for two and one half years then.

R: This was unusual for a woman at that time, or didn't you feel that?

H: Well, I never felt it. See, I don't know, I guess I was liberated on the day I was born, because my mother was a feminine, helpless little person and all of the women in my family were professional ladies with a capital "L." A lady never did anything for herself; somebody always did it for her. They looked down on me a great deal because I was big and husky and active, running up and down the beach, playing with the boys and doing things. Oh, goodness, I got so many lectures. I think I was just the opposite type, that's all, and possibly became even more opposite because I so despised their attitude. I thought it was so ridiculous.

I didn't believe that you were supposed to sit around waiting for a man to come along and want you and provide you with this, that, and the other. I don't need anybody to provide for me. I'll provide for myself. My father and mother dearly loved each other and they were wonderful people and they got married and he died. So where was she? I always prefer to have a little something in my own hands that I have control of.

Everybody says, "How does it feel to be the first woman to crack the science fiction field, which was almost exclusively masculine?" Well, my answer is: I am not the first woman. There was Francis Stevens, who was writing science fiction for *Argosy* long before and then there was Catherine Moore—C.L. Moore—who was writing science fiction for *Weird Tales* before I did. There was never the slightest opposition.

Everybody in the field welcomed me with open arms. All the other writers and editors and everybody were just great because we were such a small clubby group in those days that if you found another nut case that you could talk to, it was great. We were so busy talking about *Worm Ouroboros* and the "Lensman" series and all these things. Everybody on the outside was saying, "Why do you waste your time on that childish drivel and space ships? How would they fly? What would they push against?" We just fell on each other's necks and I was just another one of the club.

There was never any feeling of discrimination at all, except one writer whose works I began to displace in one particular magazine. He kept writing very gentlemanly letters stating that ladies were delicate little flowers and should be taken out and given wine and champagne and roses and so on, but they shouldn't write science fiction. I realized there was a sort of personal motive there. I didn't find out until later that he had been writing the letters because he wrote under a different name. Then somebody told me and I thought it was very funny.

When I started to write these hard boiled detective stories for *Popular Detective, Flynn's Detective Weekly,* et cetera, which were also masculine markets, there was no problem. They bought them and made no secret of my sex, because I was writing what they wanted to buy.

R: When you became a veteran writer did it come naturally to you, would you say?

H: No, it did not. It did not at all. I had to really fight and struggle. Like most new writers, I think I overwrote dreadfully. I never used one adjective when ten would do. Something I had to learn was to blue pencil. The editors were very patient with me and told me what to do and I did it. Ed, my husband, was always big on construction. His style in his early years was very cranky, but he was good on construction. He always knew the last word in the story before he wrote the first one.

Plot was always a great mystery to me and if I tried to do an outline I killed the story dead. I had to feel it. It was like Byron's words, "If I miss my pounce I go grumbling back into the thickets like an old tiger." I had more half stories because I had written myself into a box and couldn't get myself out of it. I had no idea where I was going. Learning how to construct a story was a long and painful process. It was hit or miss at the beginning, which was one reason that I didn't sell more. I could have sold more if I would have known what I was doing. It took me a long time to learn. The characters and the background and the color and everything were more important to me than the bones of the thing and it took a long time before I could see the bones without killing the flesh.

R: Did you write on a regularly structured or scheduled basis or as the spirit moved you?

H: I wrote every bloody morning, as many words as I could write and I also wrote in the evenings while I was working on my novel. I wrote pulp in the morning for the money, for one or two cents a word, two cents if I was lucky, and then in the evening I worked on my novel. Of course, when I got to work in the studio, it was a day's work. You know, you check in at nine thirty and out at five thirty and that was it.

R: Would you care to tell us something about the association with the studios in Hollywood in terms of writing and things that you recall?

H: I was very fortunate, I think, because I was never under contract to the studio. I was under contract personally to Howard Hawks and Charles Feldman of H-F Productions, which dissolved about two and one half years later and I got dissolved along with it. I never had to go through the business of checking out and all that. I came in through the side gate. Hawks had his own bungalow, whereas so many of the people who were under contract to the studio were working in sort of a barracks and they were checked in and out. Of course, that's all changed now. You walked by the gate and they checked you in at nine thirty and you had better not be late and you had better not be caught leaving before five-thirty in the afternoon. Of course, this is absolutely ridiculous, because nobody writes that many hours of the day.

HUGH G. EARNHART: What was a typical day like when you were writing for the studio?

H: Well, a typical day simply meant that you got to the office and sat down and started to write. You wrote as many pages as you could get out. You took a fairly long break for lunch. I met an awful lot of people at the Warner commissary in what they call the Green Room, which is where us intermediates, us middle class people went. The executives had their own dining room, we had the Green Room, and the lesser folk had a much larger place on the other side with long trestle tables. Hank and Catherine Kuttner were working there at the same time I was, when I went back out many years later. They said they felt people were eating from trenchers, over where the peasants were. Warner Brothers was one of the few studios that did that. Anyway, we had the writer's table, so this was beautiful. I was so green and I was very much in awe; this was my first time out in the big world. I met Christopher Isherwood, John Collier, Steven Longstreet, and William Faulkner. Of course, I worked with William Faulkner on *The Big Sleep*. That is to say, we worked in adjoining offices; we didn't work together at all. I met very fascinating people at Warner Brothers.

Hawks would sit you down for a couple of days and give you his ideas. Then, he'd go away and you wouldn't see him for weeks or months until he decided that there was a start date and he was going to go with the picture. Then you worked your tail off. That's always been a fact with him. It was not really typical of most studio jobs.

The one small job I had before then was over at Republic. I worked a week and a half on the treatment. Because this was my first job, I was teamed up with a writer who knew what he was doing, Johnny Butler, who was one of the old *Black Mask* crowd. We did the script in three days, they shot the picture in ten days and that was two days over schedule.

Of course, those were the days when there was plenty of money. Howard Hawks was always his own boss. He was an independent who would make a deal with the studio. He would use their facilities, there would be financing and so on, but he was actually the complete boss. He never had to answer to anybody else and this was very helpful.

E: You know, many of the stars of that era complained very bitterly about the tremendous pressure and the way they were used. Of course, those of us who were Judy Garland fans have a sour taste if those things really happened; we sort of resent it. Did writers feel the same kind of pressure and feel that they were being used?

H: They either felt that or they felt that they were being neglected, depending on the situation. There was a script that had been kicking around Warner Brothers for a number of years. When a contract writer would find this script on his desk as the next assignment, he knew that the pink slip was coming in about one week. Nobody could solve this script so it gave them a chance to boot out the contract writers.

They were kind of an unhappy crew, really. They were making tremendous pots of money and most of them were not pressured too hard on the work. There was the usual feeling of frustration; you know, you start out with a beautiful idea and it gets lost. There are so many other elements that enter into it. I really couldn't say because I was not in the writers' building. I didn't have too much conversation with them on that score. I know both Isherwood and Collier were working on Wilkie Collins' *The Woman in White* and *The Moonstone*. I forget which one was working on which. I don't think either picture was produced.

I know my friends the Kuttners were there. They adored their producer, who was a nice man, but they were pressured to do *Rappucini's Daughter*. There were considerable problems with that. They were just working away like little beavers, then the whole project was cancelled. There's a feeling of not being very sure.

This is one reason I never gave up fiction writing. When you write fiction, you don't have to wait for somebody to do it and pay you to do it; you just sit down and do it, If you're any reasonable amount of a professional, you're pretty darn sure you'll sell it somewhere. There isn't as much money, by any manner of means, but you make a living at it. You are your own man. In the studios, you're always between heaven and earth. Of course, you can sit down and write an original screenplay on your own time and hope to sell it. I did that I don't know how many years ago, six, seven, eight years ago, and I'm still hoping to sell it. We were right at the top with it and all we had to do was sign the contracts, then in the last minute, boom.

R: Did you ever have the experience where someone stole your ideas and took credit for some of them?

H: I'm sure it's done, but I've never had it done to me. Ed's had it done many times and the older science fiction writers have had it done many times, because they would originate so many things. For example, Ed originated the space suit. He was the first one to write a story about people who put on space suits and go outside of the ship in space. He also originated many other concepts in science fiction like that. Now, the younger ones come in and they take this all as public domain. I've had stories of mine lifted practically whole; they hardly even bothered to change the names in science fiction. I suppose that this is the sincerest form of flattery, but you do get a little annoyed. In the films or in television I don't think I have ever had that happen.

E: You mentioned earlier that you had an agent. What was the role of an agent when you were beginning a career in writing? Did you lean on him for many things; was he a necessary tool which one cannot do without?

H: In the field of fiction, one can do without, but it's much better to have an agent. I lived on the West Coast, and I was selling stories in New York. My then agent, Julius Schwartz, was an agent to both of us and still is a very dear friend. He has been out of the agency business for a long time. Now he's one of the top men at National Comics. They're right on the spot. They know who has a need for a story. In those days, they could take it around, submit it, and send you back the editorial comments. Very often, Julie would send back a story saying, "just isn't good enough," "try again," or "do thus and such to it." He was very useful to me, very useful.

Later on, I worked without an agent for a while because Julie quit and got a job. By this time, I was sufficiently established in the science fiction field. Also, you can sell novels, you don't need an agent for that. But there are so many things you can't do for yourself now, much more than then. There are all the foreign markets, which often pay as much or more than your domestic markets, because it's a continuing thing. I've just signed contracts for three books in Japan to a Japanese publisher. Well, I don't know Gengen Sha from a hole in the ground; I only know the name. But an agent who has connections all over the world can make many sales for you that you would not make yourself. So, I had, and have, a literary agent in New York.

In Hollywood, it's different. You don't work without an agent because unless you have an agent, you don't get interviews. They don't come to you, they come to the agent, unless you're all personal friends. Then, they'll ring you up and say, "Would you like to do so and so?" and you get in touch with your agent. In the studios, they would never accept for a very long time, any unsolicited manuscripts or scenarios for screenplays. The reason for this is that they got sued too many times and they won't even open them. You have to have an agent present; you can't go in and fight for yourself on money. You'd be working for base the rest of your life if it was left up to the producers.

E: How has the fee for agents changed through the years?

H: In my time it hasn't changed at all. They passed a state law in California and it has been a Guild regulation that an agent gets a flat ten percent. There is some jockeying back and forth now on packaging and stuff that is out of my ken. An agent cannot take more than ten percent. In the very early days, some of the agents were unscrupulous and they were taking fifty and sixty and seventy percent. This also goes for agents for actors and producers, not only for writers. It's always been ten percent, even for literary agents in New York.

R: Would you reflect on, shall I use the word, the "quality" of science fiction? I don't know from the writer's viewpoint if that is the correct word. How has the field changed since the early days?

H: Well, it's become more literary. This is probably heresy, but I think in the earlier days stories were better. I'm sure that if I were eight years old now and reading Harlan Ellison, for instance, I wouldn't get the thrill and the charge that I got out of Edgar Rice Burroughs. The people who wrote science fiction in the early days wrote it not for money, because there wasn't any, practically speaking, but for love.

    They absolutely adored the field and they had these tremendous bursts of imagination. The stories had so much more vigor and excitement than they have now. Of course, there was some terrible stuff done, admittedly. There were some great stories, some great ideas. Now, it's a much broader field and it's respectable now and they teach it in the universities. The people coming to it are, on the whole, better writers in the sense that they have a smoother style, from a literary standpoint. It was always a great thrill to me to read about strange worlds and shooting the nebula and getting lost in the Horsehead, or the Coalsack, and the drowned suns, burning like candles in the dark nebulae, and all this. This is what just sent me skyrocketing.

    Now they do all this inner world stuff, Freudian psychology, and sort of grotty sex. I'm not saying that it ought not to be done; I'm saying that it doesn't have the same excitement for me that the older stuff did.

R: Do you think that that spark of creativity and imagination can be imparted to a child or cultivated, or do you think some of it is inherited? Some children seem to be more imaginative than others.

H: I don't really know. My father was a frustrated writer and he made his living as a CPA. Long, long after his death, I came across some of his papers. This was long after I had become a writer myself. I knew that he had written things, because my mother told me. He was trying very hard to sell stories to films in those days. I found quite a batch of his short stories and ideas and so on. I was working on a story called "The Dancing Girl of Ganymede" and I picked up a story of his called "The Dancing Girl of Gades." I thought, the more it changes, the more it's the same thing. He had a good pulp writer's mind, I can tell you. The thoughts were good, the ideas were good.

Perhaps I got that from him, I don't know. He died so young, and of course, he was married and had a wife and child, so he didn't have time to write. I don't think we're particularly noted for literary people in the family. Way back in the fifteenth century there was a Gavin Douglass—I'm a Douglass on my mother's side—who translated Virgil's *Aeneid* into English. But as far as I know, that's the only literary light there has been on either side.

R: That whole question of imagination and train of thought intrigues me.

H: Well, it's a delicate little spark and It could so easily be crushed out if conditions aren't right. It's like any little seed that's dropped into the ground, it's got to have a place to grow. I was fortunate, my grandfather subsidized me until I had begun to sell. Otherwise I might have had to get a job and I might never have had enough energy left over to develop as a writer. I think this may happen with quite a few people. On the other hand, if the urge is strong enough, writers will overcome that one way or another, because many writers have. Many have had to work as dishwashers and you name it, to make a living. It's really been that they had this tremendous urge to write.

In music, usually if a musician hasn't shown talent by the time that he is five or six years old, he isn't going to have it. But writing seems to develop later. Costain was fifty when he began to write; Edgar Rice Burroughs was fifty or older when he began. Everybody's different; it's difficult to pin down.

R: I keep thinking about the possibility of canned entertainment, television, or the packaged form of entertainment compared to my childhood when you had to think of ways to entertain yourself.

H: When we were youngsters, the last thing we wanted was to be supervised and have older people telling us what to do. We just wanted to get off by our little selves and do what we wanted to do, providing that it wasn't vandalism or something we ought not to do. Not that we were little angels. Of course, in those days, we were taught a little more respect for other people's property, I think, than kids are now. It never occurred to me to break somebody's window. I would have gotten punished too harshly. I wouldn't have enjoyed it. Anyway, this has been instilled into me, taboo, you don't touch. We thought up our own games. I think they should be encouraged to speak for themselves and imagine for themselves.

R: If somebody were to ask you, "What advice would you give to a young writer?" what kind of advice would you give that writer?

H: Well, the only possible advice is: If you want to write, write. Write whatever you want to write and keep at it. As I say, it took me ten years. Of course, I started at thirteen, and at thirteen you don't know a blooming thing. I wasn't a genius like Daisy Ashford or Margery Fleming. It took me a little longer. One of the things you have got to learn is to take criticism. I have met people in the writing field and people in the acting field where it's even worse. They simply cannot take the least little criticism or blow to their egos. They can not accept the fact that something that they've done isn't good. You must be able to do that, and it hurts. You don't like it. It is not pleasant, but you've got to be able to do it, or otherwise, you never become a professional and you never grow into the profession.

I've seen girls go into absolute hysterics because the director said, "Look, you're not doing the scene right." Well, they weren't. They were nineteen or twenty and obviously they didn't know their business. You've simply got to learn. So many writers wouldn't dream of revising a story. It would be like chopping their heads off trying to get them to do it. You can't do this.

There's the talented amateur and there's the professional. You never make that jump until you learn to accept the kicks in the teeth, the discouragement, and the fact that the market has fallen in on you. You know, we wrote pulp for so many years and we knew everybody, we had no problem, then pulp magazines were gone. Presently, the slick magazines were gone as well. I know some pretty unhappy and disoriented people out there in Hollywood who made a fat living writing for the *Saturday Evening Post*. Now they're trying to do films. It's a whole new world and they are lost. You are going to get lumps and bumps all the way along the road. You have to be able to ride with them. Some people get horribly discouraged and they want to cut their throats or quit writing. They get terribly upset about people who are working or who are able to get over these bumps. They have negative attitudes, which is fatal.

R: Do you still write frequently now?

H: I'm writing frequently and like mad. You catch me at a bad moment. I'm writing a television pilot script for a new series. I was ill this summer and I wasn't able to go back out there, so I'm doing it here. I just got two acts done and I think, "Ah, isn't that nice. I'm going to be on schedule." They want the thing in three weeks and I just got the first treatment okayed by the network. Last night my little producer called me and I said, "If you don't stop making me revise act one, you're never going to get this thing."

R: We broke right into her act, didn't we?

H: Now, I'm trying to compress two very long acts into one, because the cliffhanger has got to come at the end of act one and not at the end of act two. This is something you run into. You don't write it the way it ought to be written, but the way it has to be written, trying to make the two things come together.

E: Speaking of television, there's been a sudden flurry of interest awakened in science fiction, obviously with the space program and so on, How do you see such weekly features as *Star Trek* and the specials they did on "Did man from outer space come to the earth and leave his mementoes behind in various places in South America?" and so forth. How do you react to this?

H: Well, I'm all for it. I think science fiction right through the years has been very valuable in providing the general reading public with the idea that these things are possible. Many of the people in NASA and many of the astronauts were science fiction readers in their youth. This gives the idea that these things might be or can be. There's the possibility if the concept is there. We had to wait for the engineer to come along and do it.

Of course, when Sputnik went up, that was the cutoff right there. Then everybody had to admit that it was possible. I remember there was a good bit of panic among non-science fiction readers who kept looking up there and saying, "But what could be looking down at us that's making a hole in the sky? Something might be looking in." The question was brought up at a seminar out in California in the spring, "Why have so many women entered the science fiction field?" Kate Wilhelm said, "Well, after Sputnik went up, it all became real. We realized that so many things were happening in the world, and we just had to get in." Well, that's fine. I was in a long time before it was real because just the idea of the thing fascinated me.

There's no longer any need to tell them that space flight is possible. I think what they need to be told now is that it's necessary. You keep hearing this crud about all the money that's going into the space program just to put a man on the moon, as if that were all of it and the end of it. Any scientist, any

557

technician, any physician, any surgeon will tell you that the knowledge that has come out of the space program already, the fallout from it—miniaturization of circuitry and so on, and things they have found out medically—will more than pay for it in benefits to the general public. But the general public, of course, and some of our more myopic politicians don't choose to see that. As far as I'm concerned, the more science fiction they put on the television and the more they do to keep the idea in front of the public, the better.

E: No doubt, you followed all the NASA ascensions?

H: Oh, yes. We were down there for the Apollo 12 shot. Through Esther, we were accredited from the *Youngstown Vindicator* and we were in the pressbox. Oh my, that was a thrill!

E: That was my question. You watched things you may have thought about or written about or hinted at in your stories, and now, suddenly, there it happens.

H: I think this has been the biggest thrill for both of us, because we labored in these vineyards when it took many a sneer and so on.

E: The old Buck Rogers days.

H: Right. Then, everybody said, "Ha, ha, ha, how stupid." I re-member having a terrible fight with my grandfather when I was about eight years old and I said, "I want to be on the first rocket ship that goes to Mars." He said, "There never will be a ship that goes to Mars." I said, "But why?" He said, "There's nothing out there but space. What would it push against? It's impossible. At age eight, I didn't know what it would push against either, but I remember stamping my foot and saying, "But it will, it will, I know it will."
        I think this has been the greatest thrill for both of us, to see

this actually happen in our lifetimes. I don't think either one of us thought it would occur really, in our lifetimes. We were positive it would occur sometime, but we were both delighted that we were around when it did happen.

R: I'm going to ask you a strange question about a strange phenomenon. What is your opinion of UFOs?

H: We have an open mind on that. You can dismiss ninety percent or ninety-five percent of it as delusion or crackpot, publicity seeking, nut cases. We actually met a flying saucer nut, a perfectly charming, well educated gentleman, just as crazy as a hatter. There is small percentage of these sightings that just won't go away. We're just waiting. Of course, we have to fight against the idea that maybe they're going to land right in our meadow and we'll be the first ones to welcome the Martians or whoever, because we want to be. Therefore, we have to push it off. I think it's not at all unlikely that people are sending probes and having a look at us.

E: Do you subscribe, then, to the theory that there is a window out there in space that is a corridor to provide an avenue to travel around?

H: You mean to alternate universes? This is beyond me. We have enough in this universe right now. When the astronauts speak of a window or a corridor for a launch, they're talking about a physical thing, when the other planet is in the proper position in its orbit. Of course, we're way out on one of the spiral arms. We're a very small little pebble, we're a few little dust spots spinning around it. Who knows, maybe further in toward the center of the galaxy where there are so many more suns, there could be a tremendous star-traveling civilization. Perhaps they don't want to make contact; perhaps they aren't interested. Heaven knows. I don't know. We've speculated and written stories from all angles. I don't think it's the least bit impossible.

R: Mrs. Hamilton, since I'm interested in telling children about you, hopefully, what could you tell me to tell them about letting them dream their dreams and that sort of thing? In other words, you said you had playmates and you weren't necessarily a loner. It isn't necessarily the loner that spins daydreams to become a writer.

H: I was both. I think Ed and I were very much alike in that because we had our little friends and we played with them, then we had a life that was apart from that. Most of these kids were not great readers and they couldn't follow me where I went in books. I was fortunate, I grew up at the beach, which in those days was a very lonely place. There were other houses, I don't mean it was isolated; we were only a mile or so from the town. But there was an awful lot of empty beach. I remember that one of the happiest things I used to do as a child was to walk out to the empty jetty and sit on the stringer with my feet in the ocean and just listen to the breathing of the sea and look out at the horizon and just feel and think. I loved being alone.

R: How long did you sit there?

H: Until I got cold. I don't think any of the other kids ever did that. I don't know if they did it or not, but I never encountered any of them doing it. I think there is something in being a loner. I think you have to be enough of an individual yourself, or otherwise nothing that is individual is going to come out of you.

   A lot of people that I have known who are extremely bright, intelligent people who have made a success of their lives are not oriented toward books. They can get something from technical books, but they hardly ever read fiction. They don't go to movies much; they didn't even know if the movies were any good. This was just not part of their makeup. There's no reason why it should be. But these people are never going to be writers. If you have the instinct and you're drawn to painting or music or any of these things, you should be allowed, encouraged to go that way. Some people I know don't think it's a good living or they don't want their kid to get into that particular kind of life. They try to stifle it and sometimes they do. I don't think it's a good thing. This isn't saying that everybody has to be a loner, but if you're just a community thing, then you're like a jellyfish; you're a collection of cells.

R: It seems that people are afraid to be alone.

H: Solitude is one of the most difficult things to find these days and it's one of the most valuable, but as you say, people do seem to be frightened to be alone with themselves.

E: It's part of our culture that people want to be in crowds. They want to be in the big city and yet they move out and create a Boardman and an Austintown and Liberty, which are just as crowded. They're not like Daniel Boone, who thought anybody who lived within ten miles was ten miles too close and he wanted to move.

R: It's the pressure to conform. You've got to conform, and it starts with the children in the schools. You've got to be like twenty five others in the class. You don't dare to be different. There was a book written once by I'm sure not a very famous author, entitled, *Where Are You Going? Out. What Are You Doing? Nothing.* It was written by someone of my vintage. If you saw a kid lying out there in the meadow, looking up at the sky, most times he was taken to the nearest child guidance center to be analyzed. They're just not allowed to do that anymore. That's considered strange and weird.

H: I think that hardly anybody has enough time to really think now; they're bombarded by so many external stimuli that it's much easier to sit down and look at television.

R: And have it given to you. In the ten years that I've been here at the College, students seem to have the attitude that "the teacher should entertain me. It's not going to be for me to do it." I don't know. That sense of resourcefulness seems not to be cultivated anymore.

H: Well, most of the science fiction writers were or are scientists. I mean, they got their master's in science or worked in some related field. They know a whale of a lot more science than I do because what I know you could put in a teaspoon. Ed was going to be an electrical engineer, and majored in physics, chemistry, and whatnot. I took physics and chemistry in high school, like everybody else. I can't write hard science stories; I never could. This is one reason I sold three stories to *Astounding,* the first two I ever sold, and then one later on, and then I gave up because John Campbell liked a different kind of story. Really, I don't know why he bought those three to begin with; they weren't good and they weren't his kind of story. I don't know enough about ram jets and all these things to write that kind of story, whereas Ed does and Larry Niven does. Isaac Asimov and all these other people have their Ph.D's or are scientists of one sort or another themselves and they have the background. That's fine.

       When I was, I think, in the seventh or eighth grade, they gave us Breasted's *The Ancient World.* I became an ancient history buff right then. Anything about prehistoric man or Babylonia, Assyria, and Egypt was all fascinating. I read a fair bit of astronomical material. I bone up pretty well before I write anything so that I won't sound absolutely stupid. Then I try to fake it so that it looks good, but we don't get right into the heart of a computer and tell exactly how those little relays work. We just assume that the reader knows what a computer is and go on from there.

       Ray Bradbury knows, I think, even less science than I do. He once wrote a story called *Golden Apples of the Sun* where the cold got colder and colder, thousands of degrees below zero and thus and such. Somebody wrote, "Ray, did you ever hear about absolute zero? There's a point below which it don't go." No, he never had. It hasn't hurt his career particularly. It just depends on what type of thing you're oriented toward and what you like to write. I have exposure to what you call the "soft sciences" like anthropology. I delight in creating worlds and building civilizations. I always want to know how the people eat, what crops they grow, what kind of houses they live in, where they get the building material, do they build with mud, brick, stone, or wood or what? All these things working together fascinate me.

R: Is there anything else that you would like to share about your career?

H: Well, I will say one thing about science fiction: It is unique in that we are a very friendly and clubby group. Anywhere you go in the world, there are science fiction clubs and if the science fiction people know that you are coming, they will roll out the red carpet for you. We landed in Sidney, Australia, and they carried us around in their hands for a week. We had a simply marvelous time. There are friends wherever you go. You go to England and you're invited here and taken there; you get to meet all these lovely people. This is a very rewarding thing. Of course, I met my husband and most of our friends that we've had all our lives in the science fiction field.

R: Is that unusual?

H: I think it is. In the other writing fields there isn't that fan group. The glue that holds it together is the fans. There isn't a fan group in any other field. Millions of people read westerns, millions of people read detective stories. I belong to the Western Writers of America and they gave me a very handsome prize once for a novel. I used to belong to Mystery Writers of America and I went to the meetings. You meet a lot of fabulous people there. It's fascinating and a lot of fun, but they don't have conventions every year. The fan groups put on conventions, a world convention, every year, and there are little regional gatherings. It's like a big family.

R: Is there a group or a club in this area at all?

H: I don't think there's one. There's one in Cincinnati that is tremendously influential. In fact, we're going to a little gathering in Sandusky a week from Friday. They have what they call the Midwest Conference, which is in June. It was a small affair, but it's been getting big in the last few years because so many people have been attending. It used to be kind of a small family group, a grand bunch of people. You go and you have parties and you chum around and talk. They never have a formal program.

Some of the others put on more elaborate ones. There are programs, panels, seminars, and all that stuff. There's the big Worldcon, and the last one I went to was in Washington. This year it was in Australia and it wasn't possible for us to go and enjoy it. Next year, it's going to be in Kansas City, I think.

Now the "Trekkies" have come along and that's a totally separate group. The trekkies are the fans of *Star Trek*. This is a phenomenon, because the program went off the air several years ago, but it has formed a tremendous group of fans. Some of them seem to be borderline cases. They come out by the thousands and they wear their little Spock ears and antennae.

E: You know, they're replaying it again on television.

H: I know. It's in syndication and they're doing a Saturday morning cartoon version of it. There's some talk that they're going to do a feature film. Even the people who did *Star Trek* have been absolutely astounded. They put on these *Star Trek* conventions and the people who attend them are a whole different group. However, we do have *Star Trek* material, and certain number of

Trekkies come to the regular conventions. They come out in hordes and they have to be turned away because the fire department says you can't have any more people in this hotel.

E: It's no worse than the Mickey Mouse Club. Everyone ran around in big ears in California. There were people who jammed the Aragon Ballroom every Saturday night to hopefully dance with Lawrence Welk. The world's big enough for us all.

R: Hugh, can you think of anything we overlooked?

E: Not right now. I'll probably think about something two hours after this interview is over. I might ask one question: Where do you see science fiction writing going to in the twenty-first century?

H: Well, that's very fascinating. Science has been breathing down the backs of our necks, of course. You have to keep one jump ahead of them. I don't know. I don't know what is going to happen to the world in that time. I don't know what the economic situation will be at that time. I don't know if there is even going to be a world. As far as science fiction is concerned, I think it's going to go on the way it has gone. There will be innovators and there will be people who follow along. It's such a multiple field. This is one reason it does attract so many brilliant and talented people. It never hardened into any particular form; it's never fossilized. New ideas are always coming up and there are new directions.

I really couldn't make any prediction, except that I'm sure whatever it does, it will be good. The new wave has kind of faded out now. More people are getting back to just writing stories. We had a tremendous new wave phase where everyone was left hanging in mid-air and it was all frightfully esoteric. People would write and say, "So and so's story was absolutely great. I couldn't understand a word of it." They could not understand it, so they knew it was magnificent. Any idiot could write a story that you could understand, but it takes a genius to write one that you can't figure out.

E: Would you say that the current interest in astrology and the stars helped encourage the interest in science fiction?

H: I don't think astrology has too much to do with it, really. I think that the main thing that has encouraged interest in science fiction is simply the fact that so much of it has come true. Most of the people in the science fiction field are pretty hard-headed scientists and pragmatists and I don't think many of them go in much for that sort of mysticism. One of Ed's oldest friends, and a very, very dear friend of mine, is a professional astrologer. He believes in it implicitly. He says, "No, I can't explain it, but if the bloody thing works, then it works." That's another thing I have an open mind on. I've stayed away from it myself.

I don't think, simply for that reason, that it's had too much effect on science fiction. I'm sure that it's had an effect on all the occult material that has been coming out. That has had a tremendous resurgence in the last few years with *The Exorcist* and possession by the devil and all this stuff. I read Van Daniken's book and it was fascinating, but I want a little more proof before I accept some of these things. I would like to know what some of these strange constructions are, what they actually meant, and what the people thought they were doing when they built them.

It's no new thought that people came to Earth to teach. There's a legend of Oahnnes that's much older than Babylon. It has always fascinated us. So many people believed in Kukulcan who came from somewhere and taught the Maya everything they knew. This goes on through a lot of ancient history. It's perfectly simple to believe that a few people dropped in with their spaceships. Also, there are so many gaps in pre-historic man. Cro-Magnon man appeared suddenly, practically full blown, but from where? There's nothing leading up to him; he's just there all of a sudden. Of course, they just probably haven't found the links, or they've been destroyed, or something. But, it's an interesting speculation.

E: Do you remember the two, probably not well educated police officers, I think it was in Mississippi, or Alabama, who claimed that they were captured and taken aboard a spaceship? Their story has been put to the test so many times in a variety of ways. As a science fiction writer, how do you see the story? did you in your own mind try to put any of these things they said to the test because you thought there was the possibility of them being true?

H: I'm not familiar with that particular case. I read about the one that occurred in Exeter, Massachusetts, which was extremely fascinating. There have been so many of these things where apparently you can't really doubt the people, because they don't seem to be the type to lie about sightings. When Clyde Tombaugh tells me he saw something, I believe him. I might not believe that I myself saw something, but I believe him, because he knows what he's looking at. Airline pilots and ground observers caught something on a theodolite once; they caught it on their instruments. I'm pretty sure there's something out there.

    Now actually, whether these people were taken into a spaceship and were interviewed, I don't know. I have no way of proving it one way or another. It's easy enough to pull a hoax like that because there isn't really any way it can be disproved, unless you have witnesses who knew you weren't there, or unless you have negative evidence of some kind which is very difficult to find.

E: Do those types of things which are reported occasionally provide any kind of inspiration to hit the typewriter again?

H: We've both written stories about people who got involved with spaceships. One of mine is being reprinted in January. A fellow had a feeling that he just wasn't happy or comfortable. He kept going back and trying to find the origins of his birth and so on. He tracked it back to Brittany. Way out in the Laudes the spaceship came down. The book thoroughly explained why nobody knew about it. He was taken aboard and passed his test as one of the star travelling race, the only one. There we were, off galloping away on our plot.

Ed wrote one about a fellow who was sprung out of jail in a small midwestern town ruled by a mysterious individual and discovered that he was ruler of a farflung space empire. He had been thoroughly brainwashed, had his memory removed, and been tucked away on this remote little planet. There are all kinds of beautiful ways you can use it.

E: You know, we always talk about writing. A favorite phrase in the historical field is "we brought Thomas Jefferson to the dinner table with us for four years while we labored over a biography." Do you ever have the feeling that you're sitting in the room or you're sitting down to lunch with these people whom you have been talking about, describing, and thinking about? To write and make it come alive requires almost jumping on that page and rolling around with the typewriter. It's rare the person that can close the door, walk into other surroundings and forget that. You just don't pull window shades. Do you have these people come to dinner with you and sit around here in the meadow?

H: Oh, yes. The mind is obviously compartmented that way. One part of it is always working on the story that you're working on and the people are always there. Then, there's the other department that says, "Gee, I've got to get eggs," and "What am I going to have for dinner?" It all seems to be separate tanks. I have found that oftentimes, if I get stumped on a story and a plot, something that isn't working, I just forget it for a couple of days. Then, all of a sudden, the subconscious will start popping it up to you.

R: Then, when it comes to the forefront, do you stick to that typewriter?

H: That's true. You carry these things around with you all the time. Very often, I get this far-away look and Ed will say, "You're thinking, aren't you?"

R: Do you try on your thoughts with each other?

H: Yes, a good bit. Our marriage almost broke up shortly after it began because I had an order for a novel from *Startling Stories*. It was a whole $800 and boy did we need it.

E: What year was this?

H: This was in 1947; we were married at the end of 1946. I sat down at my typewriter and wrote the opening chapters. I handed them to Ed, he read it and said, "This is great. Where do you go from here?" I said, "I haven't the foggiest idea." He said, "That is a so and so way to write a story." Right there, we discovered we couldn't collaborate too well. So, I went on with it. Then I said, "I think I'm getting into a little bit of trouble here." He said, "Let me read it." So he read it and he said, "Back of chapter two, put in a Dhuvian—a Dhuvian being a strange alien character—on the ship." I could have killed him. The trouble was, he was right. So I had to throw away four chapters and start over again.

R: Thank you for this interview. We really feel it's been a privilege. We've enjoyed it so much.

H: You're so welcome. I hope I have been helpful to you. I'm flattered that you came all this way.

Acknowledgments

"The Truants," Copyright © 1950 Better Publications, Inc., for *Startling Stories*, July 1950.

"The Citadel of Lost Ages," Copyright © 1950 Standard Magazines, Inc., for *Thrilling Wonder Stories*, December 1950.

"The Woman from Altair," Copyright © 1951 Better Publications, Inc., for *Startling Stories*, July 1951.

"The Shadows" Copyright © 1952 Better Publications, Inc., for *Startling Stories*, February 1952.

"The Last Days of Shandakor," Copyright © 1952 Better Publications, Inc., for *Startling Stories*, April 1952.

"Shannach–The Last," Copyright © 1952 Love Romances Publishing Company, Inc., for *Planet Stories*, November 1952.

"Mars Minus Bisha," Copyright © 1954 Love Romances Publishing Company, Inc, for *Planet Stories*, January 1954.

"Runaway," Copyright © 1954 Better Publications, Inc., for *Startling Stories*, Spring 1954.

"The Tweener," Copyright © 1955 Fantasy House, Inc., for *The Magazine of Fantasy & Science Fiction*, February 1955.

"Last Call from Sector 9G," Copyright © 1955 Love Romances Publishing Company, Inc., for *Planet Stories*, Summer 1955.

"The Queer Ones," Copyright © 1957 Fantasy House, Inc., for *Venture Science Fiction*, March 1957.

"All the Colors of the Rainbow," Copyright © 1957 Fantasy House, Inc., for *Venture Science Fiction*, November 1957.

"The Road to Sinharat," Copyright © 1963 Ziff-Davis Publishing Company, for *Amazing Stories*, May 1963.

"Purple Priestess of the Mad Moon," Copyright © 1964 Mercury Press, Inc., for *The Magazine of Fantasy & Science Fiction*, October 1964.

"Come Sing the Moons of Moravenn," Copyright © 1973 Random House, Inc., from *The Other Side of Tomorrow*.

571

FIRST EDITION

2011

SHANNACH–THE LAST: FAREWELL TO MARS
by Leigh Brackett, was published by Haffner Press, 5005
Crooks Road, Suite 35, Royal Oak, Michigan 48073-
1239.

One thousand trade copies, and a limited edition of one
hundred numbered and slipcased copies signed by Anne
McCaffrey, the author of the introduction, have been
printed on 55# Booktext Natural from Adobe Bembo.
The printing was done by Edwards Brothers of Ann Arbor,
Michigan. The binding cloth is Holliston Roxite B.